Seasons
OF THE
Heart

ONCE UPON A SUMMER

THE WINDS OF AUTUMN

WINTER IS NOT FOREVER

SPRING'S GENTLE PROMISE

JANETTE OKE

Seasons
OF THE
Heart

BETHANYHOUSE
Minneapolis, Minnesota

Seasons of the Heart
Copyright © 1981, 1987, 1988, 1989
Janette Oke

Previously published in four separate volumes:
    Once Upon a Summer © 1981
    The Winds of Autumn © 1987
    Winter Is Not Forever © 1988
    Spring's Gentle Promise © 1989

Cover design by Jennifer Parker

Scripture quotations are from the King James Version of the Bible.

Published by Bethany House Publishers
11400 Hampshire Avenue South
Bloomington, Minnesota 55438

Bethany House Publishers is a division of
Baker Publishing Group, Grand Rapids, Michigan.

Printed in the United States of America

Library of Congress Cataloging-in-Publication Data

Oke, Janette, 1935–
    Seasons of the heart / Janette Oke.
        p.   cm.
    ISBN 978-0-7642-0653-5 (alk. paper)
    1. Bildungsromans, American. 2. Christian fiction, American. I. Title.

PR9199.3.O38A6   20008
813'.54—dc22

                                       2008028778

JANETTE OKE was born in Champion, Alberta, during the depression years, to a Canadian prairie farmer and his wife. She is a graduate of Mountain View Bible College in Didsbury, Alberta, where she met her husband, Edward. They were married in May of 1957 and went on to pastor churches in Indiana as well as Calgary and Edmonton, Canada.

The Okes have three sons and one daughter and are enjoying the addition of grandchildren to the family. Edward and Janette have both been active in their local church, serving in various capacities as Sunday school teachers and board members. They make their home near Calgary, Alberta.

Books by Janette Oke

CANADIAN WEST

When Calls the Heart • *When Comes the Spring*
When Breaks the Dawn • *When Hope Springs New*
Beyond the Gathering Storm
When Tomorrow Comes

LOVE COMES SOFTLY

Love Comes Softly • *Love's Enduring Promise*
Love's Long Journey • *Love's Abiding Joy*
Love's Unending Legacy • *Love's Unfolding Dream*
Love Takes Wing • *Love Finds a Home*

A PRAIRIE LEGACY

The Tender Years • *A Searching Heart*
A Quiet Strength • *Like Gold Refined*

SEASONS OF THE HEART

Once Upon a Summer • *The Winds of Autumn*
Winter Is Not Forever • *Spring's Gentle Promise*

SONG OF ACADIA*

The Meeting Place • *The Sacred Shore*
The Birthright • *The Distant Beacon*
The Beloved Land

WOMEN OF THE WEST

The Calling of Emily Evans • *Julia's Last Hope*
Roses for Mama • *A Woman Named Damaris*
They Called Her Mrs. Doc • *The Measure of a Heart*
A Bride for Donnigan • *Heart of the Wilderness*
Too Long a Stranger • *The Bluebird and the Sparrow*
A Gown of Spanish Lace • *Drums of Change*

www.janetteoke.com

*with T. Davis Bunn

Once Upon a Summer

Dedicated with love to
Fred and Amy (Ruggles) Steeves,
my dear parents,
who have given me
unmeasured love and support.

CONTENTS

CHAPTER 1

Josh

I could hardly wait to finish my chores that mornin'. I needed to sneak off to my favorite log along the crik bank and find myself some thinkin' time. Too many things had been happening too fast; I was worried that my whole world was about to change. I didn't want it changed. I liked things jest the way they were, but if I was to keep 'em that way, it was going to take some figurin' out.

I toted the pail of milk to the house and ran back to the barn to let Bossie back out to pasture to run with the range cows. She just mosied along, so I tried to hurry her along a bit, but she didn't pay much notice. Finally she went through the gate; I slapped her brown-and-white rump and hurried to lift the bars in place. Bossie jest stood there, seeming undecided as to where to go now that the choice was hers.

Me, I knew where I was headin'. I took off down the south trail, between the summer's green leafy things, like a rabbit with a hawk at its back.

The crik was still high, it being the middle of summer, but the spot that I called mine was a quiet place. Funny how one *feels* it quiet, even though there isn't a still moment down by the crik. One bird song followed another, and all sorts of bugs buzzed continually. Occasionally a frog would croak from the shallows or a fish would jump in the deeper waters. That kind of noise didn't bother me, though. I still found the spot restful, mostly 'cause there weren't any human voices biddin' ya to do this or git that.

I sorta regarded this spot as my own private fish hole; I hadn't even shared it with my best friend, Avery Garrett. Avery wasn't much for fishin' anyway, so he didn't miss the information. Today I never even thought to stop to grab my pole—I was that keen on gettin' off alone.

Even before I finally sat down on my log, I had rolled my overall legs up to near my knees and let my feet slip into the cool crik water. I pushed my feet down deep, stretchin' my toes through the thin layer of coarse sand so I could wiggle them around in the mud beneath. Too late I saw that my overalls hadn't been rolled up high enough and were soaking up crik water. I pulled at them, but being wet they didn't slide up too well. I'd get spoken to about that unless the sun got the dryin' job done before I got home. I sat there, wigglin' my toes and trying to decide jest what angle to come at my problems from.

Seemed to me that everything had gone along jest great until yesterday. Yesterday had started out okay, too. Grandpa needed to go to town, and he called to me right after I'd finished my chores.

"Boy." He most always called me Boy rather than Joshua, or even Josh, like other folks did. "Boy, ya be carin' fer a trip to town with me?"

I didn't even answer—jest grinned—'cause I knew that Grandpa already knew the answer anyway. I went to town every chance I got.

"Be ready in ten minutes," Grandpa said and went out for the team.

Wasn't much work to get ready. I washed my face and hands again, slicked down my hair and checked my overalls for dirt. They looked all right to me, so I scampered for the barn, hoping to get in on the hitchin' up of the horses.

The trip to town was quiet. Grandpa and I both enjoyed silence. Besides, there really wasn't that much that needed sayin'—and why talk jest to make a sound? Grandpa broke the quiet spell.

"Gettin' a little dry."

I looked at the ditches and could see brown spots where shortly before everything had been green and growin'. I nodded.

We went on into town and Grandpa stopped the team at the front of Kirk's General Store. I hopped down and hitched the team to the rail while Grandpa sort of gathered himself together for what needed to be done.

Soon we were inside the store and after exchangin' "howdys" and small-town talk with Mr. Kirk and some customers, Grandpa and I set about our business. Grandpa's was easy enough. He was to purchase the supplies needed back at the farm. I had a tougher job. Before I'd left, Uncle Charlie had, as usual, slipped me a nickel on the sly; now I had to decide how to spend it. I moved along the counter to get a better look at what Mr. Kirk had to offer. Mrs. Kirk was toward the back talkin' to someone over the telephone. Only a few folks in town had telephones; I never could get used to watching someone talkin' into a box. She finally quit and walked over to me.

"Mornin', Daniel. Nice day again, isn't it? Fear it's gonna be a bit hot afore it's over, though."

Without even waiting for a reply, she said to Grandpa, "Wanted to be sure that ya got this letter that came fer ya."

Mrs. Kirk ran our local post office from a back corner of the general store. She was a pleasant woman, and her concern for people was jest that—concern rather than idle curiosity.

Grandpa took the letter, his face lighting up as he did so. We didn't get much mail out our way.

"From my pa," he volunteered, giving Mrs. Kirk his rather lopsided grin. "Thank ya, ma'am." He stuffed the letter into his shirt pocket.

I forgot about the letter and went back to the business of spending my nickel. It seemed it was next-to-no-time when Grandpa was gathering his purchases and askin' me if I was about ready to go. I still hadn't made up my mind.

I finally settled on a chocolate ice-cream cone, then went to help Grandpa with the packages. I wasn't much good to him, havin' one hand occupied, but I did the best I could.

He backed the team out and we headed for home, me makin' every lick count—that ice cream plum disappears in summer weather. When we were clear of the town, Grandpa handed the reins to me.

"I'm kinda anxious to see what my pa be sayin'," he explained as he pulled the letter from his shirt pocket. He read in silence and I stole a glance at him now and then. I wanted to find out how a letter written jest to you would make a body feel. This one didn't seem to be pleasin' my grandpa much. Finally he folded it slowly and tucked it into the envelope, then turned to me.

"Yer great-granny jest passed away, Boy."

Funny that at that moment he connected her with me instead of himself. He reached for the reins again in an absent-minded way. If he'd really been thinkin', he would have let me keep drivin'—he most often did on the way back from town.

I watched him out of the corner of my eye. I was sorry to hear about Great-granny, but I couldn't claim to sorrow. I had never met her and had heard very little about her. Suddenly it hit me that it was different for Grandpa. That faraway old lady who had jest died was his ma. I felt a lump come up in my throat then—a kind of feelin' fer Grandpa—but I didn't know how to tell him how I felt.

Grandpa was deep in thought. He didn't even seem to be aware of the reins that lay slack in his hands. I was sure that I could have reached over and taken them back and he never would have noticed. I didn't though. I jest sat there quiet-like and let the thoughts go through his mind. I could imagine right then that Grandpa was rememberin' Great-granny as he had seen her last. Many times he'd told me that when he was fifteen, he'd decided that he wanted to get away from the city. So he had packed up the few things that were rightly his, bid good-bye to his folks and struck out for the West. Great-granny had cried as she watched him go, but she hadn't tried to stop him. Grandpa had been west for many years, had a farm, a wife and a family, when he invited Uncle Charlie, his older and only brother, to join him. Uncle Charlie was a bachelor and Grandpa needed the extra hands fer the crops and hayin'. Uncle Charlie had been only too glad to leave his job as a hardware-store clerk and travel west to join Grandpa.

Every year or so the two of them would sit and talk about hopping a train and payin' a visit "back home," but they never did git around to doin' it. Now Great-granny was gone and Great-grandpa was left on his own—an old man.

I wondered what other thoughts were scurryin' through my grandpa's mind. A movement beside me made me lift my head. Grandpa reached over and placed his hand on my knee. I was surprised to see tears in his eyes. His voice was a bit husky as he spoke.

"Boy," he said, "you and me have another thing in common now—the hurt of havin' no ma."

He gave my knee a squeeze. As the words that he'd jest said sank in, I swallowed hard.

He started talkin' then. I had rarely heard my Grandpa talk so much at one time—unless it was a neighbor-visit or a discussion with Uncle Charlie.

"Funny how many memories come stealin' back fresh as if they'd jest happened. Haven't thought on them fer years, but they're still there fer jest sech a time."

He was silent a moment, deep in thought.

"Yer great-granny weren't much of a woman far as size goes, but what she lacked in stature she made up for in spunk." He chuckled. It seemed strange to hear him laugh and see tears layin' on his tanned and weathered cheeks.

"I was 'bout five at the time. There was an old tree in a vacant lot near our house, and it was my favorite climbin' tree. I was up there livin' in my own world of make-believe when the neighborhood dogs came around and started playin' around the tree. I didn't pay 'em any mind until I was hot and thirsty and decided I'd had enough play. I started to crawl down, but a big black mutt I'd never seen before spotted me and wouldn't let me out of that tree.

"I yelled and bawled until I was hoarse, but I was too far away to be heard at the house. Mama—" when that one word slipped out so easily I knew that Grandpa was truly back relivin' the boyhood experience again—"she waited my dinner fer me and fussed that I was late again. But as time went on and I still didn't come, her worry drove her out lookin' fer me.

"When she caught sight of the tree, she spied the mutt standin' guard at that tree and figured out jest what was goin' on. She grabbed a baseball bat lyin' in a neighbor's yard and came a-marchin' down. I can see her yet—that little bit of a woman with her club fairly blazin', she was so mad! Well, that mutt soon learned that he was no match fer my mama. Never did see that dog again."

Grandpa chuckled again.

"Funny how a woman can be bold as an army when there's a need fer it, and yet so gentle. Yer great-granny was one of the kindest, gentlest people I ever knew. Jest the touch of her hand brushed the fever from ya. And when she gathered ya into her arms in her old rockin' chair after she had washed ya all up fer bed, and held ya close against her, and rocked back and forth hummin' an old hymn and kissin' yer hair . . ."

Grandpa stopped and swallowed and another tear slid down his cheek.

"Shucks," he said, "I knew that I was too old fer that, but as long as the neighbor kids didn't catch me at it . . . Funny how loved I felt."

"Then one day I knew that I was jest too big to be hugged and rocked anymore—but I missed it, and I think Mama did, too. I often caught that longin' look in her eye. She'd reach fer me, and I thought that she was goin' to pull me into her lap again. Then instead, her hand would scoot to my head and she'd tousle my hair and scold me fer my dirty feet or torn overalls."

Grandpa had forgotten all about the team that he was supposed to be drivin', and the horses were takin' every advantage given them. No horse could have gone any slower and still have been puttin' one foot in front of the other. Old Bell, who always insisted on havin' her own way, drew as far to her side of the road—which happened to be the wrong side—as she dared. Every now and then she would reach down and steal a mouthful of grass without really stoppin' to graze. Nellie didn't particularly seem to mind goin' slowly either.

I watched the horses and glanced back at Grandpa, wondering jest how long he was going to put up with the situation. I think he had even forgotten *me*.

He stopped talkin' but I could tell by the different expressions on his face that his mind was still mullin' over old memories. Many of them had been happy memories, but they brought sadness now that they were never to be again.

Suddenly Grandpa roused himself and turned to me.

"Memories are beautiful things, Boy. When the person that ya loved is gone, when the happy time is over, then ya've still got yer memories. Thank God fer this special gift of His that lets ya sorta live yer experiences again and again. S'pose there ain't no price one would settle on fer the worth of memories."

A new thought washed over me, makin' me feel all at once cheated, frustrated, and angry. I was sure that Grandpa was right. I had never thought about memories much before; but deep down inside me there would sometimes awaken a somethin' that seemed groping, looking, reaching out for feelings or answers that were beyond me. It seemed to me now that Grandpa had somehow put his finger on it for me. He had said when he read his letter that he and I shared the loss of our mothers. That was true. But even as he said it I knew somehow there was a difference. As I heard him talk, it suddenly hit me what the difference was; it was the memories—or for me, the lack of them. Grandpa could go on and on about things he recalled from his childhood: his mother's face, her smile, her smell, her touch. Me, all I had was a great big blank spot—only a name—"You had a mother, Boy, her name was Agatha. Pretty name, Agatha."

Sometimes I laid awake at night tryin' to put a face to that name, but I never could. When I was younger I'd watch the faces of ladies, and when I found one that I liked, I'd pretend that was the way my mother's face had looked. One time I went for almost two years pretendin' about the banker's wife in town; then I realized how foolish I was and made myself stop playin' the silly game. And now Grandpa sat there thankin' God for memories.

A sick feelin' began to knot up my stomach and I felt a little angry with God. Why did He think it fair to take my parents when I was only a baby and not even leave me with memories like other folks? Wasn't it bad enough to be a kid without a ma to hug him or a pa to go fishin' with him?

I didn't dare look at Grandpa. I was afraid that he'd look right through me and see the ugly feelings inside. I looked instead at the horses. Old Bell grabbed another mouthful of grass, but this time she made the mistake of stoppin' to snatch a second bite from the same clump. Nellie sort of jerked the harness because she was still movin'—if you could call it that. Anyway, the whole thing brought Grandpa out of his remembering, and his attention swung back to the horses. He could hardly believe his eyes. He'd never allowed a team such liberties. His hands yanked the slack from the reins, and Bell felt a smack on her round gray rump which startled her so that she dropped her last mouthful of grass. Soon the team was back on its proper side of the road and hustling along at a trot.

Grandpa turned to me with a foolish-lookin' grin.

"If we don't hurry some, we'll be late fer dinner and Lou will have both of our heads."

I grinned back rather weakly, for I was still feelin' sort of mad that I'd been badly cheated in life. Besides, we both knew that what he'd said wasn't true. Auntie Lou didn't make much fuss at all when we were late for a meal. Maybe that's why all three of us—Grandpa, Uncle Charlie, and me—always tried not to keep her waitin'. I guess we all counted Auntie Lou as someone pretty special. And without really thinkin' about it, we each tried hard to keep things from being any tougher for her than they needed to be.

CHAPTER 2

Changes

As was often his habit after our evening meal, Grandpa had me fetch his Bible so's we could have what he called "family worship time." I generally found it sort of borin', listenin' to all that stuff about "The Lord is my shepherd," and other things that people wrote way back in ancient times.

Grandpa's mood seemed to be a little different that night while he read. I guess it was because of the letter from his pa. Anyway, it made me feel a bit strange, too, to see him feelin' that way.

The letter that Grandpa received was jest the first of the things to start causin' me to feel a little uneasiness about life—the life of one Joshua Chadwick Jones in particular. The next upsetting thing happened that night after I had been sent to bed.

Now I knew that my bedtime was s'posed to be at nine, but I never did go up when the clock said the time had arrived. I'd wait first to hear Grandpa say, "Bedtime, Boy," then I'd wash myself in the basin by the door and slowly climb the stairs to my room.

I always kinda figured that maybe some night Grandpa would become occupied with something and forget to watch the clock, but it never happened.

Tonight Grandpa's mind was busy elsewhere, I could tell that. He had read the letter to Auntie Lou and Uncle Charlie. Auntie Lou had put her arms around each of them and given them a warm hug as the tears formed in her eyes. Uncle Charlie hadn't said much, but I was sure that he was busy sortin' memories jest as Grandpa had done, and I felt a tug at my stomach again.

As the hands of the clock crawled toward nine, I waited. If ever Grandpa was goin' to miss his cue, tonight would be the night. But he didn't. Promptly at nine he said, "Boy, it's yer bedtime." I let out a long sigh. I had been prepared to steal a little extra time like Bell had stolen the extra mouthfuls of summer grass—but it hadn't worked.

I went through my usual routine. As I headed for the stairs I heard Auntie Lou say, "I think I'll go up now, too, Pa." She leaned over and kissed Grandpa on the cheek. "Good-night, Uncle Charlie." He nodded at her and Lou and I climbed the stairs together. As we climbed she let her hand rest on my shoulder.

"Won't be long," she said, "until I'll have to reach *up* to put my hand on yer shoulder. Yer really growin', Josh. Look at those overalls—short again!"

Auntie Lou made it sound like a real accomplishment to outgrow overalls, and I jest grinned.

" 'Night Josh."

" 'Night."

I settled into bed but I couldn't get to sleep. I lay there twistin' and turnin', and inside I seemed to be twistin' and turnin', too. Finally I decided that a drink of water might help. Grandpa didn't take too kindly to a boy using the drink excuse too often, but I reckoned that jest this once I oughta be able to get away with it.

My room was the first one at the top of the stairs that came up from the kitchen. I knew that Grandpa and Uncle Charlie would be sitting at the kitchen table having a last cup of coffee before bed and talking over anything that needed talking over, or jest sitting there in companionable silence. I put on my most innocent little-boy expression and started down the stairs. A voice from below stopped me short.

" . . . it's the only thing that can be done as fer as I can see." It was Grandpa talkin'.

I heard a sucking noise. I knew what it was. Folks 'round about said that Uncle Charlie could down a cup of coffee hotter and quicker than any other man they knew. Not too much distinction for a man, but at least it was something, and I often took to watchin' Uncle Charlie empty his cup, mentally figurin' if he might have broken his own record. Before Uncle

Charlie would take a swallow of the scalding liquid, he would sorta suck in air with a funny whistlin' sound. I s'pose the mouthful of air served to cool the coffee some on its way down, I don't know.

I heard that sound now and I could almost see the steaming cup leaning against Uncle Charlie's lips. He'd be sittin' there with his chair tilted back slightly, restin' on only the back two legs. This was hard on chairs, I was told when I tried to copy Uncle Charlie, but nobody ever scolded Uncle Charlie for it.

There came the sound of the cup being replaced on the table and then the gentle thump of the two front legs of the chair joinin' the back two on the hardwood kitchen floor.

"Do ya think he'll agree to it?"

"I don't know. He's so stubborn 'n' independent. You remember that as well as I do. But now, maybe he'd welcome the change. He's gonna be powerful lonely. Ya know what she was to him."

By now I had changed my mind about the drink of water and settled myself quietly on the step. I could feel a shiver go through my whole body. Things were changin'. I didn't know why and I didn't know how it was going to affect me, but I wasn't welcomin' it.

"Well, we've at least gotta try. We can't jest let him stay there alone. I'll go to town tomorrow and call him on Kirk's tellyphone. It'll take him awhile to sort things out, but I really would like him to come and stay. Lots of room here. No reason at all that he can't move right in."

"S'pose."

I knew that they must be talking about Great-grandpa. Why, he was an old man. I had watched the old men in town shufflin' their way down the street, lookin' weak-kneed and watery-eyed. Sometimes three or four of them gathered on the bench outside the livery stable and jest sat and talked and chewed tobacco that dribbled down their old quivery chins and stained their shirt fronts. I don't suppose I could have put it into words, but I didn't like the idea of an old man coming here—even if he was my great-grandpa. I didn't want to hear anymore, but I couldn't pull myself away.

"Something seems to bother ya," Grandpa said to Uncle Charlie. "Don't ya agree that Pa should come?"

Uncle Charlie stirred himself.

"Well, he's got to be looked after, that's fer sure, and I'm—well, I'd be right happy to see him. It's been a long time, but I was wonderin'—maybe—maybe I should go on back East and sorta care fer him there."

Grandpa seemed surprised at Uncle Charlie's suggestion; I knew that I was. I jest couldn't imagine life without Uncle Charlie.

"You wantin' to go back East?" Grandpa exclaimed.

"Lan' sakes no." Uncle Charlie's reply was rather loud, as though Grandpa was kinda dull to even think that such a thing could be possible.

"Ya thinkin' Pa couldn't make the trip?"

"By the way his letter reads he's still sound enough."

"Then what—"

"Lou."

"Lou?"

"Yeah, Lou."

"Lou wouldn't object."

"No, she wouldn't. That's jest the point—she should."

"I'm afraid I don't follow."

"Daniel, how many other seventeen-year-old girls do ya know who care fer a big house, a garden, chickens, two old men, and a boy?"

There was silence for a while and then Uncle Charlie spoke again.

"And now we want to saddle her with another old man. Ain't fair—jest ain't fair. She should be out partyin' and—"

Grandpa cut in. "Lou ain't much fer partyin'."

" 'Course she ain't. She's never had a chance. We've kept her bakin' bread and scrubbin' floors ever since she laid her dolls aside."

Silence again. Grandpa broke it.

"Ya think Lou's unhappy?"

" 'Course she's happy!" snorted Uncle Charlie. "She's too unselfish *not* to be happy. She knows if she wasn't happy we'd all be miser'ble. Lou wouldn't do that to anyone."

Grandpa sighed deeply, like an old wound was suddenly painin' him. He roused and I could hear him rattlin' around with the coffeepot. Now I knew that he was agitated. Grandpa never, never drank more than one cup of coffee before bed, but I heard him pour them each another cup now.

"Yer right," he finally said, "it's been tough fer Lou."

"What'll happen is, she'll go right from keepin' this house to keepin' someone else's." A slight pause. "And that might happen 'fore we know it, too."

"Lou? Why she's jest a kid!"

"Kid nothin'! She's reachin' fer eighteen. Her ma was married at that age iffen you'll remember, and so was her grandma."

"Never thought of Lou—"

"Other people been thinkin'. Everytime we go to town, be it fer business or church, I see those young whipper-snappers eyin' her and tryin' to tease a smile or a nod from her. One of these days she's gonna notice it, too."

Grandpa stirred uneasily in his chair.

"She's pretty."

" 'Course she's pretty—those big blue eyes and that smile. Why iffen I was a young fella, I'd never be a hangin' back like I see those fellas doin'."

Uncle Charlie had barely finished his sentence when Grandpa's fist came down hard on the table.

"Confound it, Charlie, we been sleepin'. Here's Lou sneakin' right up there to marryin' age, and we ain't even been workin' on it."

"And what ya figurin' *we* git to do 'bout it?"

"Like ya say, it's gonna happen, and it could be soon. We gotta git busy lookin' fer someone fittin' fer Lou. I ain't gonna give my little girl away to jest any starry-eyed young joe who happens to come along."

"Don't ya trust Lou?"

"Look! Ya know and I know that she can't see evil in a skunk! Now iffen the wrong guy should start payin' calls, how is a young innocent girl like Lou gonna know what's really under that fancy shirt? You and I, Charlie, we've been around some. We know the kind a fella that would be good fer Lou. We've jest gotta step in there and see to it that Lou meets the right one."

"How we gonna manage that?"

"I don't know 'xactly; we gotta find a way. Git a piece of paper, Charlie, and I'll find a pencil."

"Fer what?"

"We gotta do some thinkin' and make a list. We don't wanna be caught off-guard."

Uncle Charlie grumbled but I heard him tear a spent month from the calendar on the kitchen wall and return to the table.

"Let's be systematic 'bout this," said Grandpa. "We'll work to the south first, then west, then north, then to the east, includin' town."

"First there's Wilkins—no grown boys there. The Petersons—all girls. Turleys—s'pose that oldest one must be gittin' nigh to twenty, but he's so shy."

"Lazy too—never lifts a hand if he doesn't have to."

"Put him on the re-ject side."

The pencil scratched on the paper, and I could picture Jake Turley's name bein' entered on the back side of the calendar sheet under "rejected."

"Crawfords—there's two there: Eb and Sandy."

"Eb's got a girl."

Again the pencil scratched and another candidate was eliminated.

"Sandy?"

"He's 'bout as bullheaded as—"

"Scratch 'im."

"Haydon?"

"There's Milt."

"What do ya think 'bout Milt?"

"He's a good worker."

"Not too good lookin'."

"Looks ain't everything."

"Hope Lou knows that."

"He wouldn't be so bad if it wasn't fer his crooked teeth."

"Lou's teeth are so nice and even."

"S'pose all their kids would have crooked teeth like their pa."

I heard the pencil at work again and I didn't even have to wonder what side Milt's name was bein' written on. By now I'd had enough. Jest as I pulled my achin' self up from the step and was about to turn back up to bed, I heard Uncle Charlie speak again.

"We still haven't settled 'bout Pa."

"No problem now," said Grandpa. "It'll take him awhile to git here and with Lou married and settled on her own, she won't need to be carin' fer three old men. We can batch. We've done it before."

Uncle Charlie grunted, "Yeah, guess so." They went on to the next neighbor and I went back up the stairs.

A sick feelin' in my stomach was spreadin' all through me. We were an unusual family, I knew that, but we belonged together. We fit somehow, and I guess I was foolish enough to somehow believe that things would always stay that way. Suddenly, with no warnin', everything was now about to change. Jest like that, I was to trade Auntie Lou for an old tottery great-grandfather that I had never seen. It sure didn't seem like much of a trade.

I started going to my room and then changed my mind. I couldn't resist going on down the hall to the end room where Auntie Lou slept. I paused at her door which was open just a crack. I could hear her soft breathin'. I pushed the door gently and eased myself into the room. The moon cast enough light through the window so that I could see clearly Auntie Lou's face. She *was* pretty! I had never thought about it before. I had never stopped to ask the question nor to look for the answer. She was Auntie Lou. She was jest always there. I'd never had to decide what she was to me. Now that I might be losing her I realized that she was *everything*—the mother I'd never known, a big sister, a playmate, my best friend. Auntie Lou was all of these and more, wrapped up in one neat little five-foot-three package.

I swallowed the lump in my throat, but I couldn't keep the tears from runnin' down my cheeks. I brushed them away feelin' angry with myself.

There she slept, so peaceful-like, while downstairs two old men were deciding who she would spend the rest of her life with; and Lou was so easy-goin' that they'd likely get away with it. Unless . . .

I backed slowly out of the door and tip-toed to my room, makin' sure I missed the spot that always squeaked. Down below the voices droned on. I shut my door tight against them and crawled back under the covers. I realized suddenly jest how tired I was. I pulled the blankets right up to my chin.

Somehow there had to be a way I could stop this. Somehow! It wasn't gonna be easy; it was gonna take a lot of thinkin', but surely if I worked it over in my mind enough I'd find some way.

My thoughts began to get foggy as I fought sleep. I'd have to figure it all out later. Then a new idea flashed through my mind—prayer. I'd already said my evenin' prayers as Auntie Lou had taught me, but this one was extra. I'm not sure jest what I asked from God in my sleepy state, but I think that it went something like this:

"Dear God. You know what they're plannin' fer Auntie Lou, but I want to keep her. You didn't let me keep my ma—or my pa. You didn't even give me any memories. Now you gotta help me to find a way to stop this.

"And about Great-grandpa—maybe you could find him a new wife, even if he is old, so that he won't need to come here. Or maybe he could die on the train comin' out or somethin'. Anyway, please do what you can, God. You sorta owe me a favor after all you've taken from me. Amen."

Satisfied that I had done what I could for the time bein', I crawled back into bed. I wasn't sure that God would pay too much attention to my prayer, but anyway, I'd tried. Tomorrow I'd work on a plan so that I'd be ready on my own if God decided not to do anything for me.

I went to sleep with the voices from the kitchen risin' and fallin' as the two men sorted through their lists. I wondered if they had come up with anyone for the accepted side of the page yet. Then I rolled over and went to sleep.

CHAPTER 3

About Lou

That had all taken place yesterday. Somehow as I sat on my log it seemed long ago and hardly even real, yet at the same time, present and frightenin'. I had to worry it through and find a solution.

Again, as I had in times past, I wished that I had a dog. Somehow it seemed that jest the presence of *something* with me would make the whole thing easier to handle. Well, I *didn't* have a dog, so I'd jest have to find an answer on my own.

Before, I had always been able to go to Auntie Lou with the things that bothered me, but I knew this was one problem that I couldn't discuss with her. On the one hand, I found myself achin' to tell her so that she would be warned; on the other hand, I knew that I would do all that I could to hide the ugly facts from her—to protect her from knowin'.

Guess I should explain a bit about Auntie Lou and why she is only five years older than me. Grandpa had met and fallen in love with my grandma, a bubbly wisp of a girl. They married young and went farmin'. A year later they had a baby boy whom everyone said was a combination of the two of them. He had the colorin' and the size of my grandpa who was a big man, but the disposition and looks of my grandma.

When my pa, who they named Chadwick, was three years old, Grandma was stricken with some awful illness. I never did hear a name put to it, but she was dreadfully sick and the baby that she was expectin' was born only to die two days later. Grandpa and the doctor were so busy fightin' to save my grandma that the loss of the baby didn't really hit them until Grandma came 'round enough to start askin' for her. She had wanted that baby girl so much and she cried buckets over losin' her. For days she grieved and cried for her baby. The doctor feared that she would jest sorrow herself right into her grave, so he had a talk with Grandpa.

The next day Grandpa washed and combed my pa and dressed him in his fanciest clothes. Then he lifted the little fella up in his arms and they paid a call to Grandma's bedside. Grandpa never did say what words were spoken as he and the boy stood there by the bed, but Grandma got the message and from then on she laid aside her sorrow and determined to get well again.

It was a long uphill pull, but she made it—by sheer will-power many said. But never again was she strong enough to be the bouncy young woman that my grandpa had married. He accepted her as she was and gradually talked and loved her into accepting herself as well. She finally agreed that rest periods must now be a part of her daily schedule, but it took awhile to adjust to her new way of life.

The years slipped quickly by. My pa grew to be a lanky kid, then a young man. But all the while, though her eyes glowed with pride over her son, deep down in her heart Grandma still yearned for a baby girl. Finally she admitted, "If the Lord wills, I still wish to be blessed with a daughter before I leave this old world." My pa was twenty when his baby sister arrived. Grandma was beside herself with joy. She named the wee baby Louisa Jennifer, the Jennifer bein' her own name.

Even though her prayer had been answered—her dream fulfilled— Grandma never regained her strength. Most of the fussin' over her new baby had to be done upon her own bed, she bein' only strong enough to be up for short periods of time. She smothered love on my Auntie Lou. Grandpa often said that Auntie Lou had no choice but to be lovin' when she had love piled on her in such big batches.

Lou was only two when Grandma's condition worsened. Chad, my pa, was about to go farmin' on his own, havin' met and married a certain sweet young gal by the name of Agatha Creycroft—my ma. That's when Uncle Charlie was sent for. He came gladly and has been with us ever since.

The next winter Grandma passed away and the two men, a father, more up in years than most fathers, and a bachelor uncle, were left to raise a little girl not yet turned three.

She was a bright, happy little sprite. Grandma always declared that God sure knew what He was doin' when He saw fit to answer my grandma's prayer. Lou was their sunshine, their joy, the center of their attention. Odd, with all of the love and attention she got that she didn't spoil, but she didn't. She grew up jest as ready to love and accept others.

Then I came along. My folks were farmin' only four miles away from my grandpa's home place. I was jest big enough to smile and coo when both my folks were killed in an accident on their farm. Again the two men had a child to raise, but this time they had help. The five-year-old Lou sorta claimed me right from the start. I can't remember any further back than to Lou—this strange woman-child whose pixie face leaned over my crib or hushed me when I fussed. We grew up together. She was both parent and playmate to me. The parents that I never knew really weren't missed—except when I would purposely set my mind to wonderin'. Usually, as my childhood days ticked by I was happy and content. When Lou needed to go to school, I stayed with Grandpa or Uncle Charlie, chafin' for her return in the afternoon. She would run most of the way home and then she would scoop me into her arms. "Oh, Joshie sweetheart," or, "My little darlin'," she'd say, then ask, "Did ya miss me, honey? Come on, let's go play"; and we would, while Grandpa got the evenin' meal and Uncle Charlie did the chores.

At last the day arrived when I placed my hand in Auntie Lou's, and sharin' a pail filled with our lunch, we went off to school together. Those were good years. The two men home on the farm enjoyed a freedom that they hadn't had for years, and I never had to be separated from Lou.

Grandpa held fast to the rules of proper respect, so at home I always addressed her as Auntie Lou. But at school we conspired to make it jest Lou, in order not to be teased by the other kids.

The school years went well. I was a fair student and anytime that I did hit a snag, I had special coachin' from Lou who was always near the head of her class.

As we grew up, Grandpa assigned us responsibilities; Lou took on more and more of the housework, and I began to help with outside chores. Still we used all of the minutes that we could find to play together. I would, with some convincing, pick flowers with Lou in exchange for her carryin' the pail while we hunted frogs. Often she didn' jest carry—she caught as many frogs as I did. She could shinny up a tree as fast as any boy, too, tuckin' her skirt in around her elastic bloomer legs in order to get it out of her way. She could also skip rocks and throw a ball.

She would take a dare to walk the skinniest rail on the fence and outdo any fella at school. Yet somehow when she hopped to the ground and assumed her role as "girl," she could be as proper and appealin' as could be, and could give you that look of pure innocence fittin' for a princess or an angel.

Lou completed the grades in the local school, and then it was me who went off alone each mornin'. She stayed behind, responsible now for managin' the house and feedin' two hungry men and a growing boy.

It was my turn to run home at day's end, knowing that if I hurried there would still be a few minutes of fun before chore time. We still knew how to make the most of the minutes that we had. We took quick trips to the crik where we laid on our stomachs and startled minnows or worried turtles. We visited the pond where we skipped rocks or turned over stones to see who could win by findin' the highest number of insects underneath. We hunted bird nests, being careful not to disturb the inhabitants. We played on the haystacks, makin' ourselves a slide that was a bit hard on the clothes, but great fun regardless. On colder days we'd tell a story or play a game—or jest talk.

All of the time that I was growin' up with Auntie Lou, I had never stopped to consider what kind of a human being she was. She was jest there; she was necessary, she was mine, and now, now all of a sudden, I was forced to realize that she was a girl—a girl almost a woman, a girl who might marry and move away to live with some man. Again anger swept through me. I hated him—this other man whoever he would be; I hated him. Somehow I planned to stop this awful thing from happenin' if I could. I still hadn't figured out how I'd do it, but I'd take 'em as they came, one by one, and I'd git rid of 'em. They'd all be on the reject list.

I pushed my toes down deeper into the mud. The water gurgled about my legs. A small turtle poked his head above the water's surface beside the log, and I reached down angrily and pushed him under again. I hadn't hurt him, I knew that, but somehow I felt a tiny bit better gettin' a chance to spend some of the meanness I was feelin'.

I heard a soft step on the trail behind me and knew without havin' to look that it was Auntie Lou. Only she walked like that—gently and quickly. I didn't even turn my head but busied myself tryin' to get my face back to what she was used to seeing so that she wouldn't start askin' questions. I heard her slip her shoes off and then she stepped to the log. Her hand rested on my shoulder for balance as she carefully sat down beside me and stretched her feet into the water.

We said nothin'—jest sat there swishin' our feet back and forth. She tucked her skirts up so that the hems wouldn't reach the water. She seemed to settle in for a long stay.

"Hungry?"

All of a sudden it hit me. Boy, was I hungry! I glanced up at the sky and was shocked at where the sun hung. It must've been past time for lunch. I should have been to table ages ago. I supposed she'd waited and waited. I started to stammer an apology or an excuse; I wasn't sure which it was going to be, but Auntie Lou interrupted me.

"Brought some lunch."

Then I spied our old lunch pail in her hand.

"Pa and Uncle Charlie went to town. They want to git in touch with Grandpa right away. They're gonna try to telephone him. Doesn't it seem funny to be able to talk with someone hundreds of miles away? If they can't git him by phone, they'll send a telegram."

As Auntie Lou talked she removed the lid and passed the pail to me to help myself to the sandwiches. I fairly drooled.

"Boy," I said, avoiding the Great-grandpa issue, "never realized how hungry I was. Good thing that ya came along or I might've starved right here and slipped into the crik, stone dead."

Auntie Lou giggled softly as though what I had said was really clever.

"Good thing that I saved the turtles and the fish from the disaster."

We ate in silence for a while. Finally Lou broke it.

"Did ya know that Pa is goin' to ask Grandpa to come out here to live, now that Grandma is gone?"

I nodded my head, hopin' that she wouldn't ask me where I'd gathered the knowledge. She didn't.

"What do *you* think?" I finally asked.

"About Grandpa comin'?"

"Yeah."

I pulled out another sandwich.

"I hope he does. What do *you* think?" Lou returned the question.

I hunched my shoulders carelessly.

"Don't know. Doesn't matter to me much I guess. It's you that'll have to wash his clothes and get his meals and care fer 'im iffen he's too old to care fer himself."

"He'll care fer himself."

I turned toward her. My voice sounded sharp and impatient. "He's an old man, Lou—an old man. He's *my great-grandpa*. He could be yer great-grandpa, too, as far as years go. We don't know; he could be drooly or half-blind or all crippled up with arthritis or anything!"

Lou's answer was typically Lou.

"If he is—then he needs us even more."

I turned back to the water and kicked my feet harder. Lou wasn't going to see it. She didn't want to see it. She was going to let them bring him out here—that old man. Then the only way she would be freed from the burden of carin' for him would be to marry some young fella and move away. I kicked again.

"Yer pant legs are all wet, Josh." She said it softly, matter-of-factly, but I knew that what she really meant was that my pant legs had no business being wet.

"Sorry," I mumbled and squirmed back farther onto the log so that my legs didn't reach as deeply into the water.

She didn't comment further but jest passed me the cookies and an apple.

"Are ya worried, Josh?"

"Worried?"

"Yeah, that Grandpa might not fit in or like us or something?"

The last thing that I was worried about was whether Great-grandpa would like us or not, but I didn't say that to Auntie Lou. I shrugged.

Auntie Lou took a delicate bite from her apple.

"Don't think that ya need to worry none. Pa has told me some things about him. I think that we'll git along jest fine."

"Maybe," I said, not committing myself.

Lou put the lid back on the pail.

"Well, I'd best git back to the house. Still haven't finished the washin'— jest the socks left. Ugh! I hate scrubbin' socks."

She screwed up her face, then laughed at her own teasin'. *Sure,* I thought, *you hate scrubbing socks and here ya are askin' for some more.* But I didn't say it.

"Pa said that you should hoe another row or two of potatoes this afternoon."

I started up from the log, knowin' that if those potatoes were going to get done, I'd better get at them. Lou put on her shoes and we started off toward the house together, her shoes and my bare feet leaving side-by-side prints in the dust of the path. She hummed as she walked and swung the pail playfully in large sweeps.

"Lou?"

"Yeah."

I hesitated. "Oh, skip it," I finally said.

She looked at me, her big blue eyes looking serious and even bluer.

"Go ahead," she said. "If ya have something to say, say it."

"Are you plannin' on gittin' married?" She stopped short and looked sharply at me like I'd lost my senses.

"Me?" She pointed a finger at herself.

"Yeah."

"Whatever made ya ask somethin' like that? Why I—I ain't even got a beau." She blushed slightly.

"Well, I don't mean tomorrow or nothin' like that—but someday?"

"Someday?" She thought a bit and chuckled then. "Oh, Josh, ya dumbhead." She ruffled my mop of hair. "Yeah, I s'pose. Maybe someday I'll git married."

Fear grabbed at my throat. She seemed to like the idea by the light in her eyes. Then she hurried on.

"Someday, maybe, but not fer a long, long time."

I could feel the air comin' back into my lungs.

"Ya sure?"

"I'm sure. Why, I haven't even given it any serious thought. And I sure am not ready to take on another man and another house jest now."

"Yet you'd take on Great-grandpa?"

"That's different," said Lou. She sounded so certain that I was prepared to believe her. "Grandpa is *ours* and he will be in the same house. It scarce will make any difference at all."

I wanted to believe her. With all of my heart I wanted to believe her. If it was like she said and Great-grandpa fit into the house and the family, and everything worked out well, maybe Grandpa and Uncle Charlie would soon realize that they wouldn't have to marry Auntie Lou off after all. Maybe it *could* work out. I still didn't welcome the idea of the old man comin', but I no longer felt such a knot of fear tearin' at my insides.

CHAPTER 4

Correction

Feelin' a little better after my talk with Auntie Lou, I set to work on the potato patch with real determination. By the time I heard the team returning from town with Grandpa and Uncle Charlie, I was on my fourth row. Uncle Charlie took the horses on down to the barn, and Grandpa came out to the garden to see me. He was right pleased with what I had accomplished. I puffed with pride a bit.

"I think you've worked long enough in the hot sun, Boy. Best leave the rest for tomorrow. Let's go see if yer Auntie Lou has somethin' cold to drink."

Uncle Charlie fell in step beside us as we headed for the house. I didn't ask the question that I was dying to ask. I knew that it would all be laid out before us at the time of Grandpa's choosin'.

Lou had some cold milk and man-sized sugar cookies sitting on the table. We three sat down after washing our hands at the washbasin and drying them briskly on the rough towel.

I looked at Lou; I could see that she wasn't goin' to wait long for details on what happened in town. If Grandpa didn't soon volunteer the information, she'd start askin' questions.

Grandpa took a long drink of his milk. Lou had enough patience to let him swallow.

"Did you reach him?"

Lou didn't play little games of beat-around-the-bush. She was always honest and direct. So was Grandpa.

"Yeah, we did. Had to make two calls on the tellyphone. Some contraption, that. Couldn't believe my ears. Here I was a-talkin' to my own pa hundreds of miles away. A few years ago iffen someone had said that sech a thing would be possible, they'd laughed him out of town."

"Or locked him up," Uncle Charlie suggested.

"Why *two* calls?" asked Auntie Lou.

"First time he wasn't in."

Lou was gettin' real impatient by now.

"But you did get to talk to him?" She prodded.

"We sure did—both of us. He could hardly believe it. Said it made him so lonesome that he felt like jest hoppin' a west-bound train."

There was a moment's silence as Grandpa sat there lookin' down at his milk glass. Uncle Charlie was lookin' down, too, as he twisted his glass 'round and 'round in his big fingers.

"Does he plan to come?"

Both Lou and I seemed to be holdin' our breath. Grandpa looked up.

"Yeah, he'll come! He's missin' Ma something awful. He'll come! It'll take him awhile to get everything all cared for, but it shouldn't be too long; then he'll be out—by harvest time for sure."

"Did he—did he sound . . . ?" I knew that my question wasn't coming out right. I wanted to know if Great-grandpa sounded like he still had all of his senses in spite of his age, but I didn't want Grandpa and Uncle Charlie—or Auntie Lou—to figure out what I wanted to know. I wished, as I stammered around, that I had never opened my mouth. Uncle Charlie seemed to realize that I was squirmin' like a bug on a hot rock.

"Sounded good—real good. Voice still strong and steady. Talked of his garden!"

Uncle Charlie's eyes took on a twinkle.

"S'pose he out-hoed you today, Josh—and you figure that you had a pretty good day!"

I squirmed a bit more and reached for another cookie, more or less jest for something to do. In spite of my embarrassment I was glad now that I had asked the question. I had heard what I'd wanted to hear—about the old man's health, that is, not about his plans for a train-trip west. I still felt mighty uneasy about that. Still, it was only midsummer, and anything could happen between now and harvest time—well anyway, almost anything.

"Iffen you'll excuse me," I said, "I think I'll be finishin' that row before chore time."

I could feel three pairs of eyes on my back as I left the kitchen, and I knew that they must all be wonderin' iffen I'd had too much sun. I had never laid claim to enjoying hoein', and truth was, I didn't care much for it now; but it was the only excuse that I could come up with for gettin' away from the table. I knew very well that the three of them were gonna go on talkin' about Great-grandpa; and as they talked their faces and their voices showed that they were all excited about his soon comin'. The fact that I didn't share their enthusiasm made me feel kinda mean-like. Yet there was no way that I knew of to change the way I was feelin', so I chose to get me out to where there was no one to search me out.

I finished the row in record time and still had a few minutes to kill before I needed to start on the chores. I decided to take a walk to the pond to check on the ducks that had nested there.

The mother had hatched seven ducklings and already their feathers had changed. Every time I saw them they had grown some.

They didn't seem to mind me around as long as I didn't try to get too close. I would sit on the shore, my back against a big ol' tree and watch their funnin' around as long as I wanted to.

For some reason they failed to amuse me today. Guess my mind was too heavy with other things. Lou certainly hadn't seemed upset to hear that Great-grandpa was plannin' to come. In fact, she had looked pleased and excited about it. Whether she really meant it or was just tryin' to please Grand-pa and Uncle Charlie, I wasn't sure. If she really did mean it and didn't mind takin' on another family member, even if it was an old man, maybe I could relax again. I sure did feel mixed up. It wasn't until I had been threatened with losing Auntie Lou that I realized just how important she was to me.

I was headin' back toward the barn when I remembered about my prayin' the night before. Maybe God did choose to answer a kid's prayer. Jest as I started to feel kinda good about it, I remembered other parts of my prayer. If God really took me seriously, then I had the feelin' that He didn't care much for some of what I'd been askin' for. My conscience started a-prickin' at me, and I realized that if I wanted any peace, I had some correctin' to do. I stepped off the path into the trees and knelt down.

"Dear God," I said, "I wanta thank ya for spendin' yer time and energy working on my prayer.

"Please, can ya jest forget that part 'bout havin' him die on the train? It's okay if he comes—I guess.

"And don't bother 'bout a new wife. He'd jest bring her, too, and we sure don't need that. Thank ya. Amen."

I felt a little better then. I wasn't sure if it was God that I feared or my family—should they ever find out that I had brought down fire from heaven on a man they loved and wanted. Anyway, God and I had it sorted out now, so there wasn't much need to worry over it any longer.

I headed for the granary to get the feed for the pigs, pretendin', as I often did, that I had my own dog runnin' beside me.

Today he was small and black with a splash of white on his chest, and droopy ears. His coat was curly and his tail fluffed over his back. I named him Shadow because of the way he stuck with me. As I went about the chores, I'd scold him for barkin' at the pigs, then I'd sic him on the big red bull. He'd pull on my pant legs and nearly trip me by crowdin' in close to me. I'd try to quiet him down as we fed the chickens.

Grandpa might have frowned on the game had he known, but it sure helped the chorin' to be a lot more fun. I couldn't help but think how it would be if Shadow was a real live dog. I had hinted once or twice that it would sure be useful to have a good dog about the farm, but Grandpa didn't seem to catch on. He once had a dog that he thought an awful lot of. Lived to be fifteen years old, which is awfully old for a dog. Seemed like when he died, Grandpa jest never had the heart to get him another dog. Wasn't that he didn't like dogs; he jest hadn't considered fillin' the gap that his old comrade had left. I didn't want to bring sadness to Grandpa, so I didn't go beyond the hints. Still, I sure did wish that I had me my own dog.

CHAPTER 5

Uneasy Again

The summer was goin' along nice and smooth. The hayin' was all done and the crops were lookin' good. I had pushed all thoughts of impendin' doom from my mind. I was feelin' like my world would continue on as it was for jest as long as I wanted it to—which would prob'ly be forever—when Grandpa hit me with a real knock-downer.

Now if I hadn't heard the conversation that night on the kitchen stairs, I wouldn't have paid any attention to what Grandpa said now.

We were riding home from church on a hot Sunday. It would have been too hot if it hadn't been for a breeze that was blowin'. I was sitting at the back of the wagon hanging my bare feet down so that they could swing; I'd taken off my Sunday shoes and my socks as soon as we were a respectable distance from the church. Then I heard Grandpa speak to Auntie Lou.

At Grandpa's words my mind snapped to attention. I had been feelin' pretty secure thinkin' that Grandpa and Uncle Charlie had forgotten all about their fool plan concernin' Auntie Lou. What Grandpa said now made me realize that they still meant business. I twisted around so that I could hear better.

"Are you a-feelin' up to havin' some company, Lou? Been awhile since we had anyone in."

Now Grandpa knew that Lou had no objection to company. She could whip up a meal jest as tasty as any cook in the county. It was Grandpa and Uncle Charlie who usually went thumbs-down on the company idea.

Lou looked at Grandpa with interest showin' in her face—she didn't suspect a thing.

"Sure," she said. "Sounds fun! Did you have anyone particular in mind?'

Boy, does he! I could have said, but didn't. I listened hard, curious to find out who had finally passed Grandpa's and Uncle Charlie's tests.

"Well, thought maybe we could sorta start with the Rawleighs. Seem like nice folk. Kinda like to get to know them better."

Lou's blue eyes opened wide but she said nothing. I could almost see her thoughts twirlin' round.

It just so happened that Mrs. Rawleigh was a widow lady, a rather attractive one, too, as middle-aged ladies go. She only had one child, a son in his twenties. They owned a neat and prosperous farm to the east of us. Mrs. Rawleigh had used hired help on the farm for many years, but in the last few years Jedd was doing the farmin' on his own.

I thought that I could tell what Lou was thinkin', and it was on the widow—not the son—that her thoughts were centered. She tried to keep her voice very even, but I caught the tremble of excitement in it.

"Sure, that's fine—good idea. Did you have any special time in mind?"

Grandpa was feeling pleased with himself. His plan was working well.

"Kinda wondered if next Sunday dinner would be all right."

"That'll be fine. Sure, jest fine."

I felt the fear and anger risin' up in me and then I looked at Lou. She was stealin' little sideways glances at Grandpa. There was a question in her eyes, but humor, too, and I knew that she was thinkin', *You old fox you—and you never let on!*

And suddenly I wanted to snicker. This could turn out to be downright fun if I could jest keep Jedd from takin' Grandpa's bait; and that wasn't going to be an easy task with the bait as pretty as it was.

I was glad that I had been watchin' Auntie Lou. Knowin' what I did I would never have taken the turn of thought that Auntie Lou did. It wouldn't hurt none if I kinda helped those thoughts of hers to do a bit of growin' before Sunday arrived.

All week, Auntie Lou worked on the house and the meal. She must've changed her mind about what she'd be servin' at least four times. She even tried new desserts out on us. They were all good, and I was quite willing to be one of her guinea pigs.

At every opportunity I tried to drop subtle hints or ask leading questions. She didn't always follow my sneaky thinkin' and jest looked at me searchingly. Still I kept workin' away at it.

"Do you think Grandpa is lookin' happier these days? Seems he's kinda different somehow"—to which Lou replied that it was prob'ly due to anticipation about Great-grandpa's comin' to join us. After several other seemingly unsuccessful tries, I decided that I was going to have to be a bit more obvious.

"How long has Mrs. Rawleigh been a widder?" I was licking cake batter from a mixing bowl.

"Oh, about eleven years now, I guess—maybe more."

"Sure seems funny."

"Seems funny that someone's a widow?"

"No. Seems funny that no one's noticed how purty she is and married her long before now."

"I hear tell one or two have tried, but she wasn't of that mind."

"Really? Who?"

"Oh—Orvis Bixley."

"Orvis Bixley? No wonder she wasn't interested."

"Nothing so wrong with Orvis Bixley."

"He's old."

"To you maybe, but he's not so awful much older than the widow Rawleigh."

"He seems it. She still looks young—and purty, too."

"You said that."

"Oh, yeah." I licked without talkin' for a while, then set aside the bowl. "Who else?" I inquired.

"Who else what?"

"Who else tried to marry the widow Rawleigh?"

She looked at me with that questioning look of hers as if to sort out jest what I was fishin' for. I avoided her eyes.

"I don't know," she finally said. "Some hired man that she had at one time, I guess. I don't know his name."

I didn't know jest how to make my point and tie up this conversation.

"Sure wouldn't blame *any* man for takin' a likin' to her." I put lots of stress on the *any*. I left. I could feel Lou's eyes on my departin' back.

Lou took a break later in the day to sit in the shade on the back porch and do some fancy stitchin' on a pillowcase. I knew that I still had some unfinished business, but I hoped that I had given her somethin' to think on earlier. I came right to the point.

"Do you think that Grandpa would be happier married again?"

She looked up quickly.

"I don't know."

"Wonder why he never did?"

"He was too busy carin' for us I s'pose."

That was exactly what I had wanted her to say.

"Do you think we've been selfish?"

"Selfish? How?"

"Well, if it weren't for us, he could be married again and happy." I tried to make it sound like there was no way that Grandpa could have any measure of happiness while unmarried.

"There's still plenty of time," Lou said absentmindedly. "Pa is still young enough to have lots of years of happiness with another wife—if he so chooses."

"And we won't stand in his way anymore?"

"I don't know that we ever—"

"I jest mean that we're old enough now—me and you—that iffen Grandpa wanted to marry again, we could sorta look after ourselves."

"What are you driving at?" Lou eyed me suspiciously.

"Well," I said, and my words were honest, even if my meaning wasn't. "I somehow got the feelin' last Sunday when Grandpa asked about havin' the Rawleighs to dinner that there was more to it than he was lettin' on."

Now that was a mouthful. Lou took it the way I had hoped she would. Slowly she reached out to me with a quiet little smile.

"You rascal," she said. "You don't miss a thing, do you? Well, I'm glad that you're not upset. Maybe nothing will come of it anyway." She thought for a bit.

"Okay, so Pa wants to get to know the widow Rawleigh better. I don't know her well, but if Pa likes her, she has my full approval. She seems nice enough. If Pa, and I say *if* he likes her, then I, *and* you, we won't say anything.

We'll jest do our best to make everything as pleasant for Pa as we can. I'm kinda glad that you caught on to it, too. Now I know that I can count on you to help me.

"Now above all, we mustn't seem to push or fuss. That would jest make them self-conscious and uncomfortable. They have to work this out for themselves in their own way—and time. And we disappear—if we can.

"Remember, until Pa wishes to state his own case, we play ignorance. Okay?"

"Okay," I agreed.

"There's only one little thing that bothers me."

"What's that?"

"That Jedd! To think that I might end up with him for a brother!" Lou made a sour face and shuddered. "But that's our secret, okay?"

I grinned. It was sure okay with me all right.

"Not so fond of Jedd myself," I said.

"Well, let's try not to let it show if we can help it."

I nodded, feelin' sorta like takin' on something big. Lou didn't care much for Jedd. That sure helped my situation a heap!

I was jest about to draw a deep breath in relief when a funny thought went flittin' through my brain; and with it came a feelin' of uneasiness. *What if Grandpa really did go and fall for the widow Rawleigh?* I reckoned that I'd hate to lose Grandpa jest about as much as I'd hate to lose my Auntie Lou. Naw! Grandpa'd have more sense than to go and do a thing like that. Still it would bear some watchin'. Anyway, I could only handle one worry at a time, so I'd have to let that one pass for the time bein'.

I picked up the milk pails and puckered my lips into a whistle, trying to drum up confidence that I wasn't too sure I felt. Anyway, the whistlin' helped some.

CHAPTER 6

Sunday Dinner

Saturday was cloudy with a stiff wind blowin'. I saw Grandpa look out the window to check the skies several times. He seemed really worried that his well-laid plans might all come to ruin. A few times I saw him and Uncle Charlie sort of huddled together talkin' in low tones. I pretended not to notice, although I was near dyin' to know what was being said.

Lou was busy with final preparations in the house. She even toyed with the idea of opening up the front parlor, but Grandpa said that it wasn't necessary. The parlor had been closed and all of the furniture covered with sheets ever since Grandma had died. When I was little I was scared of that room; then one day Auntie Lou took me by the hand and showed me under all the sheets—nothing but furniture. There was some pretty fine furniture too—even an organ.

At first Grandpa had said, "Men don't have time to spit and polish all that fancy stuff." Later he changed it to, "No use Lou havin' to fuss with that; she's already got enough to do." But I think that the real reason for the parlor staying closed had something to do with Grandma and how Grandpa missed her. Anyway, in spite of Lou's offer, the parlor again stayed closed. The dinner table was laid as usual in our big kitchen with the family living quarters off to one side. Grandpa said that Lou kept it pretty enough for *any* company.

After the scare that the weather gave us on Saturday, Grandpa was relieved to see the clouds blown away and the sun comin' out again on Sunday mornin'.

I hadn't seen him in such good spirits for a long time, and Auntie Lou and I exchanged a wink as we watched him polishin' his shoes and brushin' his hat. Lou was convinced that he had taken a shine to the widow all right; and I might even have begun to worry myself if I hadn't overheard Grandpa whisper to Uncle Charlie, "Remember, this is jest for a get-acquainted like— no pushin' today." Uncle Charlie nodded and grinned.

The ride to church was pleasant. Even the service was okay. The singin' was really good—jest as though the folks were like birds glad to see the sun again and wanting to sing their hearts out. Old Parson White brought a sermon that even boys could understand and didn't mind listenin' to. Even Willie Corbin left off carvin' initials in the pew and paid attention; Jack Berry only pulled out his warty frog to shove it toward the girls once. I was sure that after church he'd be mad at himself for missin' so many good chances.

While folks stood around out in the sunshine after the service, Grandpa removed his hat and approached the widow Rawleigh to check that their plans to come to dinner were all in order. I saw some eyebrows go up. Mrs. T. Smith and Mrs. P. Smith were talkin' nearby. Mrs. T. stopped mid-sentence and gave the old-eyebrow trick to Mrs. P. She responded, I knew that they were thinkin' the same way as Auntie Lou was concernin' this Sunday dinner date. I snickered and ducked behind some of the boys so folks wouldn't wonder if I was up to some kind of mischief.

Grandpa, in his innocence, went right on chattin' with widow Rawleigh, and she turned coy and kinda flirty right there before all those people. Grandpa still didn't seem to notice—but others sure did. Grandpa took his leave with a lift of his hat, and Mrs. Rawleigh sorta giggled and lifted her chin. She deliberately looked around at the other ladies present to see just what kind of an impression this had made on all of them. She wasn't disappointed.

I headed for my spot at the back of the wagon and got set to remove my shoes jest as soon as the church was out of sight.

I knew that Auntie Lou was in a real hurry to get home so that she could finish the dinner preparations. The table was already laid and a fine bunch of mixed flowers stood on the small table by the window. The meal had been left in big simmerin' pots on the fire-banked kitchen stove. Things would be nigh about ready to tie into when we got home. Grandpa pushed the team a bit. He was in a hurry, too.

The wagon had hardly stopped rollin' when Auntie Lou's feet hit the ground and she was off to the kitchen almost on the run. Grandpa sort of misread her eagerness, and I saw him give Uncle Charlie an elbow and nod toward Auntie Lou. They grinned like two schoolboys who had jest put a garter snake in the teacher's desk.

We didn't have to wait too long for the Rawleighs. I guess they were kinda excited about the whole thing, too. By the time they arrived Auntie Lou had everything in order. She appeared as cool as though she had spent the day swayin' in a hammock in the shade instead of rushin' around a kitchen over a hot stove.

Grandpa made short work of the preliminaries. He was about to seat the folks at the table when Lou stepped over and did it with such grace that no one could question her right to do so. She placed Grandpa at his usual place at the far end of the table with Mrs. Rawleigh to his right. Beside Mrs. Rawleigh sat Uncle Charlie. Jedd was seated at Grandpa's left and beside Jedd, me. Lou took the hostess' chair opposite Grandpa.

We all bowed our heads while Grandpa said grace. As well as bein' thankful for the food, he thanked the Lord for "kind friends to share our table and our fellowship." I'm sure that the widow Rawleigh thought that was awfully cute of Grandpa, for she slipped him the most meaningful little smile when he raised his head.

The meal went well enough. The grown folks did most of the talkin'. Occasionally Jedd made a comment. It was usually a little off-beat, it seemed to me, and I got the impression that in spite of his prospect of becomin' a rich farmer, the guy really wasn't too bright. The widow Rawleigh didn't see it that way, and no matter what Jedd said she beamed her smile of approval. The whole thing sorta rubbed against me. There was no way that I wanted this guy for an uncle—no matter which way it might come about.

After the dinner and all the comments about how fine the food was, Lou suggested that everyone have their second cup of coffee on the back porch. That way we could all get out of the over-warm kitchen. Folks agreed and soon everyone was seated on the porch sippin' coffee—except Uncle Charlie. He gulped his.

A bit of a breeze rustled through the leaves of the honey-suckle vine. It played with Lou's hair, too—whispin' it in little curls around her flushed pink cheeks. As I looked at her I thought that her eyes seemed even bluer—maybe because of the blue dress that she was wearin'. I held my breath, hopin' that Jedd wouldn't take a good look at her. A fellow would have to have corn cobs in his brain not to see jest how pretty Auntie Lou was. I was about to blurt something out to Jedd to try to keep his attention when Auntie Lou herself saved the day.

"If you'll all jest excuse me," she said, "I think I'll put the food away."

The widow knew perfectly well that a woman couldn't properly put away another woman's leftovers, so she gave a sweet smile and remarked, "When you're ready to wash up, dear, just call."

Lou only smiled, then was gone. I followed her in. She glanced back at the porch.

"Josh," she said, "I know that it's a heap to ask, but do you s'pose you could find some way to entertain Jedd?"

I thought hard and was lucky enough to recall that I'd heard that Jedd Rawleigh liked fishin'.

"Hear he likes fishin'," I said. "I could take him to the crik."

"On Sunday?"

"Not to fish," I hurried on, "jest to look. If he likes fishin', then he must like the water, too."

This earned me a big smile and a quick hug.

"Good idea," Lou whispered.

Only for Auntie Lou would I agree to take someone down to *my* part of the crik—especially someone like Jedd Rawleigh. I was about to drag myself back out to the porch to do the invitin' when I got a bright idea. I'd take him to the part of the crik the farthest away from the house. The trail wasn't too well worn goin' that way, but I was sure that I could still follow it. I never went over that way much because the crik flowed wide and shallow there and there were no holes for fishin'. The banks were covered with marsh grass and scrub willow, and the whole area was spongy and more like swampland than anything else.

My eyes must have reflected what I was thinkin', for Auntie Lou looked at me rather closely.

"You don't mind?"

"Naw, I don't mind." I tried to sound very off-hand about it.

I slipped to the porch now with almost a bounce to my step. Grandpa was listenin' to the widder tell about her problems with hired men and how relieved she was to have dependable Jedd now doing the farmin'.

I poked Jedd. "Care to take a little walk?"

He clambered up and grinned at me, and we started off. We rounded the house and I stopped at the front porch as though I'd had a last-minute thought and pulled off my shoes and socks.

"Never did feel comfortable in Sunday shoes," I said, and I carefully rolled up the legs of my Sunday pants.

Jedd jest smiled, quite willing to accept my boyish whim. Truth was, there was no way that I wanted to be wearin' my Sunday shoes where I was intendin' to go.

"Hear ya like fishin'."

He grinned again, then quickly sobered.

"Ma won't let me fish on Sunday."

"Oh, I don't fish Sunday either; jest thought that ya might like to check out the crik for some future day."

"Sure." He was grinnin' again.

We started out toward the back cow pasture. I glanced around to check if we were being noticed. The widow Rawleigh, Grandpa, and Uncle Charlie still sat on the porch. From my own experience, added to what I was able to piece together from talking to Auntie Lou—plus usin' my imagination jest a bit—I figure that the rest of that Sunday afternoon went something like this: Uncle Charlie wasn't doin' so great at carryin' his part of the conversation, and when Lou gave him a nod from the kitchen door, he gladly hurried over to her.

"I know that Mrs. Rawleigh said for me to call her for the washing-up, but she and Pa seem to be havin' such a nice visit. Do you mind dryin', Uncle Charlie?"

Lou said it with her cutest I-know-what's-really-goin'-on smile and Uncle Charlie jest grinned and got a towel. Truth was, he much preferred being in the kitchen with Lou to sittin' miserably listenin' to that chitchat on the porch.

The dishes were done in jig time, and Uncle Charlie reluctantly eased himself toward the door again. You see with the front parlor closed off, the only way out of the house was the back door, so for Uncle Charlie it was either stay cooped up inside or else pass by the two guardin' his exit. He hesitated a moment, then stepped out onto the porch.

"Oh, my," said the widow, suddenly come to remembrance seein' Uncle Charlie materialize before her. "How the time has been flyin'! I'm sure that dear Louisa must be ready with those dishes by now."

"All done," said Uncle Charlie, and Grandpa favored him with a hard look. Uncle Charlie chose to ignore it. "Jest finished."

Uncle Charlie appeared to be going right on down the steps so Grandpa stopped him.

"Where did the young'uns git to?"

"Went fer a walk, I take it."

"That's nice," smiled Grandpa, picturin' Jedd and Lou strollin' through knee-deep meadows hand and hand, she wearin' a flower that he'd pinned in her hair.

Wasn't quite that way though. Jedd and I were sloggin' through marshy ground fightin' willow bushes. I was all right. I was barefoot and I made good and sure that my pant legs stayed rolled up to above my knees. Jedd wasn't farin' as well. His Sunday shoes were smeared with mud, and even though he lifted his pant legs some in the soggier spots, they were still splashed and spotted. He puffed as he pushed his way through the heavy growth. I kept assurin' him every few minutes that it wouldn't be long now, and we'd be there any minute, and the crik was jest beyond thet next clump.

As for Auntie Lou, she had confided to Uncle Charlie that she thought she would take a little walk. Supposin' that she had prearranged to meet "someone," he jest smiled and said, "Good idea." So after the dishes were done, Auntie Lou picked up a book and prepared to make her escape. She was more resourceful than Uncle Charlie. She climbed quietly and carefully through the kitchen window and walked down to the pond where she sat and read until she was needed to serve afternoon refreshments.

Uncle Charlie remained only a few moments on the back porch and then moved on, mumblin' something about stretchin' his legs a bit and checkin' the horses. That left Grandpa and the widow. Guess the day dragged somewhat for him. He never was much of a talker, but he wasn't a bad listener and the widow seemed to prefer it that way.

When the sun swung around to the west, Auntie Lou decided that she'd best get back to the kitchen and get the tea on. She entered the kitchen the same way that she had left, gently coaxin' her full skirts over the window ledge.

I finally did stumble upon the crik—such as it was up that way. Sure weren't much to brag about as criks go and even the slow Jedd recognized that it wasn't housing any fish. I seemed right surprised and disappointed about it all, though I did manage to keep from tellin' an outright lie. We started back, sloshin' our way through marsh and muck. Jedd's Sunday-go-meetin' clothes looked worse all the time, and I began to wonder if I'd gone a mite too far.

When we got back to the house, we were later than we should have been. Tea and strawberry shortcake were all laid out. Uncle Charlie had again put in an appearance. The widow hadn't slowed down much, though she was concerned about the lateness of her Jedd.

When she got her first good look at him, her eyebrows shot up so high that they nearly disappeared into her pompadour hair style.

Me, I looked fine. I had carefully rolled down my pant legs, easin' out the creases the best that I could, and brushed off the loose twigs and bits of dirt. I'd also cleaned my feet off with water from the rain barrel, dried them on the grass and put my socks and shoes back on. I was most as good as new. Jedd, now, was a different matter. His shoes and socks were a sight, and his pant legs didn't look so great either. He had twigs and spider webs and other clutter still clingin' to his clothes and his hair.

When the widow finally caught her breath, she gasped, "Where have you been?"

I let Jedd answer. He gave a rather weak smile, "To the crik."

Now I saw Grandpa's eyebrows go up. He knew all of the paths to the crik and every inch of the territory through which the crik flowed. I knew that it was obvious to him jest what part of the crik we had visited. He looked at Jedd, then at me, Jedd's clothes, my clothes. He frowned. Something here was strange and would bear his checkin' out later after the company left.

Mrs. Rawleigh went to work on Jedd. I thought that he looked rather like a big overgrown schoolboy as she brushed and wiped and scolded. Eventually she declared him fit to partake of the strawberry shortcake, though he still didn't look none too good.

As soon as we were finished at the table, Uncle Charlie went with Jedd to get the team, and the widow turned her attention back to Grandpa.

"This has been just delightful, Daniel."

She stretched as many syllables out of his name as her tongue could possibly manage.

"We must do it again soon."

Grandpa looked uncomfortable. I could see tiny beads of sweat standin' on his forehead, but he remained a true gentleman and a perfect host.

"Very nice," he smiled. "It's been our pleasure. Very nice."

He seemed to get a sudden inspiration.

" 'Course it's gettin' mighty close to harvest time now. 'Fraid I'm gonna have to forsake pleasure fer a while and pursue work instead."

Mrs. Rawleigh beamed. So clever this man, and such a gentleman.

"Of course, but one must rest on the Lord's Day, even in harvest. We'll expect you to return our good pleasure and join us for Sunday dinner one day soon."

"That would be most gracious of you and we'd be delighted to do so."

Grandpa was really squirmin' now. It was quite obvious, even to him, that the widow had somehow gotten entirely the wrong idea.

"Next Sunday then?"

"Next Sunday." Grandpa forced a weak smile.

The widow turned to the rest of us and nodded her good-bye.

"And again thank you for the lovely dinner, dear," she said to Auntie Lou. "You are indeed a real credit to your father." She turned those admiring eyes full on Grandpa and flashed him a most inviting smile. Grandpa's hand went up to ease his collar. I'm sure that he felt he would choke.

Eventually we got them headin' for home. Grandpa walked back to the house sheddin' his tight collar and shakin' his head. Things had somehow gone all wrong, it seemed. He decided to hold his judgment until he got Lou's report on the day. Surely she had gotten to know Jedd sometime during the long hours. Grandpa sat down at the kitchen table and mopped his brow.

"Nice folks." He was speakin' to Lou. Uncle Charlie and I both knew that, even if we were sittin' there.

"Um humm."

"Had a nice visit with Mrs. Rawleigh."

"We saw that," said Lou with a twinkle and Grandpa's face reddened. He tried to ignore it and went on.

"Did you get a chance to visit with Jedd?"

"Much as I cared to," she promptly responded.

"When?"

"At the table."

Now Grandpa knew full well how much visitin' Lou and Jedd had done at the table. I doubt that there was even so much as "Pass the butter." He gazed up at Lou. She looked back evenly, then rose and crossed over to behind his chair, and in her little girl way put her arms round his neck.

"Oh, Pa," she said as she laid her cheek against his. "It needn't spoil anything—honest. I just can't stand Jedd Rawleigh, that's all. But if you— if you enjoy the company of Mrs. Rawleigh, that's fine. I promise. I won't interfere; I'll be as agreeable and as—as—"

He jerked upright and looked at Lou like she'd lost her senses. Grandpa was gettin' the full message now.

"You think that I—that I—you think that I care in some way fer the widow?"

"Don't you?"

Grandpa's face was beet red and the cords in his neck showed up plain.

" 'Course not!" he stormed. " 'Course not."

"Then why—"

"I jest wanted you to—" Grandpa was trapped and he knew it. He couldn't let Lou know that he was out to get her married off; he couldn't lie either. He finally sputtered to a close.

"Jest—jest forgit it. Forgit it all. It was all kinda a mistake—"

"But the widow Rawleigh," cut in Auntie Lou.

"What about her?" Grandpa almost snapped, and he never snapped at Lou.

"We're invited there for Sunday dinner."

"We'll go as we said." Grandpa was definite on that.

"But she thinks—" Lou hesitated.

"Thinks what?"

"Well," said Lou rather perplexed by the whole new situation, "bein' a woman myself and seein', I'm sure she thinks that you *do* care."

"What in the world would ever give her that idea?" Grandpa huffed.

"Well, you extended the invitation, you talked—alone—for many hours."

Grandpa swung around.

"Where were the rest of you anyway? Charlie! Where did you disappear to so convenient? You could've listened to the account of her goiter operation jest as easily as me. Where'd you get to anyway? And Boy—" but I was already up the steps on the way to change my clothes and get to the woodpile. Thought that it wouldn't hurt to chop a bit of extra wood; Lou must have used an awful lot in that old kitchen stove in order to cook a meal like that.

The topic of the Rawleighs was not discussed again. We did go there for Sunday dinner as promised, but we didn't stay late, and Grandpa had given us all strict orders before we left home that no one was to desert the room. We thanked our host and hostess after a rather uneventful stay and headed for home.

Mrs. Rawleigh wasn't half the cook that Auntie Lou was. Grandpa, more with silence than words, ordered the whole case dismissed.

Mentally I crossed Jedd Rawleigh from my list—a bit smugly, I'm afraid.

CHAPTER 7

Hiram

The whole episode did manage to shake Grandpa up some, and I thought that maybe he'd drop any further efforts—but no such luck. I had gone to bed and was almost asleep when I heard the coffeepot rattlin' and the murmurin' of voices from the kitchen. I hiked myself out from under the warm covers and eased my way down the stairs. Sure enough, the two of them were at it again.

" . . . weren't either my own fault," Grandpa was sayin'. "I was deserted, that's all."

"Well, the first mistake came by pickin' on a widder. We shoulda thought how it'd look. Tongues are still waggin'."

Grandpa took a swallow of coffee that was too hot. I could hear him gulping in air to cool his tongue.

"Whole thing was ridiculous. How people could think that I'd be—I'd be—" He couldn't find words to express his feelin', so he jest ended with a "humph."

There was the sound of Uncle Charlie pursin' his lips and suckin' in air and then a long contented sigh after the hot coffee washed down his throat. His chair hit the floor to rest on all four legs again.

"So we struck out," he said matter-of-factly. "Nobody said that we were gonna git on base first time at bat. We 'xpected that it would take some time and some doin', so we don't quit now. We keep on a-lookin' before some young punk decides to do some lookin' on his own.

"You see those faces at church? Ya saw what happened last week? That there young Anthony Curtis, without a nickel to his name or a roof to put over his head, walked right up to Lou, twistin' his hat in his hands 'til he nearly wore out the brim. He asked her outright iffen he could call."

"I didn't know 'bout that," Grandpa replied with concern in his voice.

"We were lucky this time. The guy's got a face like a moose. But some-day—someday it'll be a good-looker and Lou will forgit to look past the face."

"Did you hear Lou's answer?"

" 'Course I did. She said she was awful sorry-like, but she was awful busy gettin' ready fer the arrival of her grandpa from the east, and after that it would be harvest and all."

"Good for Lou." Grandpa chuckled with relief. "She can set 'em down iffen she wants to."

"That weren't the *real* reason though."

" 'Course not. Like you say, the guy ain't exactly a good-looker."

"That weren't the reason either."

"No?"

"No." Charlie paused. "It was Nellie Halliday. Lou knows that Nellie has had a crush on that there Anthony Curtis ever since she was twelve years old. Lou didn't want to hurt her."

"Nellie Halliday?" Grandpa chuckled again. "That's sorta like a moose and a porcupine."

Uncle Charlie was in no mood to appreciate Grandpa's humor. "This ain't gettin' us nowhere. Let's get down to business."

"Who should we try for next?"

"You chose Jedd Rawleigh," said Uncle Charlie; "how 'bout me havin' a crack at it now?"

"Fair enough—long as you stick to the list we made up."

"I'll stick to the list."

Uncle Charlie pored over the list, mentally examining each candidate. Grandpa waited.

"Hiram—Hiram Woxley. He looks the most likely man to me of who we've got here. Boy, there seems to be a dry spell of first-rate men 'round here."

"Never noticed it before we started lookin' fer a proper fella fer Lou. Thought the place was crawlin' with 'em. Everywhere I go I—"

I left. I'd heard enough.

Hiram Woxley was a bachelor. No worry about a widowed mother there. For all I knew Hiram could have hatched under the sand. He had moved into the area fully grown and already on his own. Never had heard anything about any kin.

He was a decent enough fellow—about thirty, always clean-shaven and neat, quiet yet kinda forceful, attended church regularly, and stayed out of the way of girls and kids. He had a big well-kept farm to the south of town; I was sure that the farm, more than the man, had to do with his bein' on the list.

I laid in bed a long time thinkin' about Hiram Woxley. What had I heard about him? Most things ever said about him were good. In fact, I couldn't right remember any disagreeable thing that I could put my finger on.

I was gettin' sleepier and sleepier and my mind jest refused to keep workin' on it when it suddenly hit me—his money! Word had it that Hiram Woxley was tight-fisted. In fact, I'd been in the hardware store one time when Hiram was making some purchases. He tried to argue—quietly but stubbornly—the price of everything that he bought. Heard the clerk say after he'd left that he always hated to see him come through the door. Rumor had it that he would about as soon lose a finger as part with a dollar. Surely I ought to be able to use that to some advantage. I made up my mind before givin' in to sleep that come Sunday I'd see if I could find some way to sorta chat a bit with Hiram Woxley—that is, if I could get near him. As I said, he wasn't much for kids.

On Sunday mornin' I managed to somehow talk Auntie Lou into wearin' her fanciest dress. It was the one that Grandpa had sorta insisted that Lou buy for Mary Smith's weddin' last spring. Grandpa liked to have Lou look her best, and even though she bucked at the price, he finally talked her into it. Auntie Lou did look like a million bucks in that outfit.

When she came down the stairs to leave for church, I saw Grandpa and Uncle Charlie exchange worried looks. I could see that they were afraid with Lou walkin' around lookin' like that, some young fella was bound to get ideas before they had a chance to steer things in the right direction.

Lou went on out and I followed her, but I heard Grandpa whisper to Uncle Charlie, "Maybe it'll be all right. Hiram has eyes, too."

Uncle Charlie nodded. We left for church.

After the service I headed for the yard to see if I could spot old Hiram. The place was buzzin'. Everyone's mind was on the fact that old Parson White had informed the church board of his wishes to retire before too long and that they should commence the search for a new man. Every tongue was waggin'. Most people were sure that they could never properly replace the well-loved parson. Sounded as though they would have been content to work him right into his grave. Questions were flyin' back and forth—not that they expected anyone to have any worthwhile answers. Could they ever find anyone who would fit in as well as Parson and Mrs. White had done, and should they look for a man who gave inspiring addresses or one who understood and cared for the people? They all seemed to assume that you couldn't have both wrapped in the self-same package.

I shrugged my way through it all. It meant nothin' to me. Some of the older boys were beginnin' to question this whole idea of church and why any red-blooded, adventure-seekin' boy needed it anyway. It was more for old folks and kids. I thought about it sometimes, too. Anyway, it sure didn't bother me none who the old man was who stood up at the front in the black suit and read from the Book. Guess one could do it 'bout as well as another.

I found Hiram over near the fence with some of the other single fellows. It wasn't hard to figure out the game that was goin' on. It was "ogle-the-girls," or whatever you want to call it. As each of the girls made an appearance she was rated. The fellows gave their ratings with grins, elbows, nudges, and comments. Everyone there seemed to understand jest how the system worked.

I stood there quietly, knowin' that they'd feel me too young to join in if they should notice me. Their full attention was on the church entrance as they waited for another candidate to make her appearance. In the meantime I inched my way cautiously a little closer to Hiram Woxley.

One by one the girls appeared and were judged by the fellows. Finally I saw Auntie Lou's head appear above the crowd on the steps. By almost a miracle it seemed that the whole crowd cleared around her as she stopped to chat with the parson's wife.

The sun was shining right down on her, reflectin' a shimmer of light on the curls that fell to her shoulders. Her eyes were shining and even from where we stood you could see the blue of them. She was smiling—a beautiful, typically Auntie Lou smile, full of warmth and pleasure in living. Her dress was beautiful, but as I looked at her, even I could see that she would have been pretty even if she'd been wearin' a feed sack.

Every guy around me seemed to hold his breath, and then as she moved on they all let it out at once. "Toad" Hopkins threw his hat in the air and let out a whoop. Shad Davies bellowed, "Whoo-ee!" while Burt Thomas and Barkley Shaw started to punch each other in the ribs, grinning like they were plumb crazy. Things finally settled down some.

"Wow," said Joey Smith, "some looker!"

I figured that it was time to make my presence known. I took a big gulp of air.

"Well, she oughta be." I tried hard to sound real disgusted. "Coulda bought me all the fishin' gear I've a hankerin' for and a .22 rifle, too, for the money that her outfit cost my grandpa."

I didn't hang around to see what effect my words had, but pushed my way through the knot of fellows as though the thought of it all still made me mad. I figured I had at least given old Hiram something to be a-thinkin' on. Maybe it would work, maybe it wouldn't; I didn't know, but I'd keep workin' on it. Bit by bit a fella should be able to get the message across that a wife could end up costin' a man a powerful lot of money. I was bankin' on the fact that Hiram Woxley would want to be good and sure that she was worth it.

Surprises

Uncle Charlie had fulfilled his duty in gettin' the invitation to Hiram Woxley all right, but he was not able to make it for the next Sunday's dinner. It seemed that there were others in the area who saw Hiram as a good prospect for their daughters. He had agreed to grace our humble home with his presence in two Sundays. I was glad for the breathin' time.

I said nothin' at all to Lou about the stir that she caused when she left the church—saw no reason to. Lou wasn't the kind that would let it go to her head, but still I felt that it would serve no good purpose for her to be a knowin'.

Grandpa had been keepin' a sharp eye on the south field, and on Tuesday he decided that it was ready to put the binder to it.

I loved harvest time, even if I knew it meant school again soon. Our school always started a little late to give the farm boys a chance to help their pas. When we did get back to class, the teacher worked us like crazy to get us caught up to where we should be. We really didn't mind the extra work. We were glad for a chance to have the late summer and early fall days.

With Grandpa and Uncle Charlie now in the fields all of the chores fell to me. That was all right, though I was pretty tired some nights. A few times I could hardly wait for Grandpa to call, "Bedtime, Boy," but I always managed to hang on.

I felt that with Hiram Woxley expected in a week-and-a-half, Uncle Charlie and Grandpa had no other immediate plans for Auntie Lou, so I kinda relaxed and let my thoughts go to other things.

I figured that it was about time for the fish in the crik to really start bitin'. I was anxious for a chance to get a try at them. I kept my eyes open for a break in my work that would give me a little fishin' time.

Lou was busy, too. There was stuff from the garden that needed pre-servin', and hungry men to feed every day and lunches to fix for me to run to the field, plus all of her usual household chores. She didn't seem to mind it, though, but like me, she was good and ready for bed come nightfall.

Lou was working on a batch of bread and I was splittin' up some wood to get a little ahead so I could work in that fishin' trip when I heard a wagon comin'. I recognized Mr. T. Smith's team even before it turned into our lane. It was kind of unusual for a neighbor to come calling during harvest, so my head came up rather quick-like. Mr. T. pulled his horses up and flipped the reins. I went forward to say a howdy, more out of curiosity than friendliness. It was then that I spied an elderly man beside him on the high wagon seat.

He was dressed in a brown tweedy suit rather than in work clothes. His hat was a jaunty small-brimmed affair—not wide-brimmed to shed rain and sun like the locals wore. He had a clean-shaven face except for a care-fully trimmed white mustache. I sized him up pretty good in the brief time I had, then looked again to study his face. In his eyes I saw a twinkle that made me take to him right away, but I held myself back. I wished that Mr. T. would speak up and explain the presence of the stranger before I showed rudeness by asking.

"Howdy," I said, including them both. That much I felt sure was safe without bein' rude—Grandpa wouldn't tolerate "lip" from a youngster.

"Howdy," Mr. T. replied, but the older gent just gave me an amused smile. "Brought yer great-granddaddy."

My eyes jerked back to the old man, and at the same time my blood started churnin' all through me. This was him? Sure wasn't the package that I'd been expectin'. There were no baggy unkempt pants, no tobacco-stained chin, no glassed-over watery eyes. This alert, well-kept gentleman with the sparkle in his eyes was my great-grandpa?

Blood went pounding through my head, and I jest couldn't seem to think or move. I had me a lot of feelings that I couldn't put a name to—relief I guess, maybe a little leftover fear and—funny thing—jest a small amount of pride too. I suddenly realized that I was standin' there with my eyes buggin' and my mouth hangin' open.

"Howdy, Joshua." He said my name like he had said it many times before, like it was something really special to him. But the "howdy" sounded new on his tongue.

I coaxed out a rather hesitant smile and bestirred myself.

"Howdy, sir," I managed to answer.

He laughed at that—a nice, full, fun-filled laugh, and then he busied himself with gettin' down from the wagon. He took it slow and careful, but he was steady and as sure of himself as I would have been.

Mr. T. was busy setting down Great-grandpa's belongings. I reached up to give him a hand. After all was unloaded Mr. T. gathered up the reins and prepared to climb back up into the wagon.

"Wouldn't you come in, Mr. T.? Lou would be pleased to serve coffee," I asked, rememberin' some of the manners Grandpa had tried so hard to instill in me.

"No, Joshua," he answered, "I best git back to the cuttin'. Had to go in to the smithy to git some repairs done or I'd be home at it now. Seein' how I was comin' by on my way home, I was pleasured to have the company of yer great-granddaddy when I heerd he was in town and lookin' fer a way out."

"Thank you," I said. "We all most appreciate that. Grandpa will be much obliged."

"No trouble—my pleasure." He turned then to my great-grandpa. "Nice to have met you, Mr. Jones. Hope that we have the pleasure of gittin' good acquainted-like."

"And I thank you sincerely," said my great-grandpa, extendin' his hand, "for the safe and appreciated transport—and for the enjoyable company. I'm sure that we will have future opportunities to get better acquainted."

Mr. T. smiled, nodded, and turned the team in a big arc and left the yard. I came alive with excitement. I could hardly wait to show Great-grandpa to Auntie Lou—or Auntie Lou to Great-grandpa, I wasn't sure which. Something deep inside of me told me that they belonged to each other. I guess maybe it was those clear blue eyes that looked like the whole world was a fun place to be.

"Come on in, Great-grandpa." I hurried him. "I'll bring in yer things later."

He picked up one small bag, and I grabbed a couple of suitcases and we went through the gate, around to the back porch and into the kitchen.

Lou was jest lifting golden-crusted bread from the oven as we walked in. Her face was flushed and her hair curled around her forehead.

"Lou," I blurted out before she could even look up. "Great-grandpa's here."

She put down the hot pan and turned to us. For a very brief time they looked at one another, and then with a glad cry Lou rushed to him. He was ready for her, his arms held open wide. They laughed and hugged and laughed again. Anyone watchin' would never have guessed that they were seein' one another for the very first time. I saw tears on the cheeks of each of them. I wasn't sure whose tears they were. Great-grandpa squeezed Lou close.

"Louisa," he said, "little Lou. You're just like your daddy said."

"Oh, Grandpa," she pulled back now, "it's so good to have you. So good. But how did you get here?"

"A kind neighbor."

"Mr. T. Smith brought him," I offered. I wanted to be sure that they still knew that I was around.

"Sit down." Lou was still in a happy fluster. "Sit down and I'll get you some coffee. Josh, you run to the well and get some cream."

"No need for me, my dear. I drink my coffee black."

Lou nodded to Great-grandpa and turned to me again.

"Josh, do you want to whip up some grape juice for yourself?"

The grape juice was always kept on the pantry shelf. It was jest a matter of dilutin' it some with cold well water. I was even allowed the liberty of sprinklin' in a bit of sugar.

"You know," said Great-grandpa, "I think that maybe I'd prefer a bit of that grape juice, too. It was rather a warm trip sitting out there in the sun—and Lou," he added with a twinkle in his eye and a small twitch of his mustache, "just *one* slice of that delicious-smelling bread."

I fixed three glasses of the grape juice while Auntie Lou sliced some fresh bread and put out some homemade butter and crabapple jelly.

We had fun around the table. Great-grandpa told some stories about his long trip on the train—how one big lady had motion sickness, and how a little man with a funny box was discovered to have a pig in the passenger car. He also told of a mother with three small children who was havin' a very tryin' time until my great-grandpa offered to play games with the little ones. He said it made the miles go quicker for him, too. The young woman cried when she thanked him at the end of her journey.

All at once I glanced at the clock. The time had been racin' by and I had lots of chores that needed doin' before the men-folk got in from the fields. I jumped up rather suddenly and headed for the door.

"Josh," Great-grandpa called after me. I thought that he might be goin' to mention the fact that I hadn't asked to be excused, so I stood there feelin' rather sheepish.

"Josh, you are the chore-boy in harvest time I assume."

"Yes, sir."

"Do you have many chores?"

"Quite a few, sir."

He smiled.

"Let's see now." He seemed to be workin' on something as he tugged at one side of his mustache. "We should be able to come up with something better than 'sir' for you to address me by, shouldn't we?"

"Yes—Great-grandfather."

He laughed again.

"Now *that*," he said, "is really a mouthful. *That* will never do. You could drown or starve at the table before you got my attention with all of that to say."

I smiled.

"You call Daniel 'Grandpa'?"

I nodded.

"Then it can't be just grandpa or we'd never know whom you meant."

He worked on his mustache some more.

"Grandfather is *too* dignified for me." He wrinkled his nose in a humorous smile. "On the other hand, Grandpappy is not dignified enough. That leaves Gramps. What do *you* think of Gramps?"

"I rather like it, sir." I tried biting off the "sir," but it slipped out anyway. He smiled.

"Okay, Gramps it will be. Lou can call me Gramps, too, and then you'll both know whom you are talking about."

I grinned. It would be nice to share the name with Lou. I glanced again at the clock. It was gettin' late.

"Now then," said Gramps, "do you suppose an old man trailing around with you while you do the chores would slow you down too much?"

"Oh, no, sir—Gramps."

"Good! You run along and get started, and I'll get changed into the overalls that I bought in town. I'll join you as soon as I can."

I was off on a run. I knew what needed to be done and what I should tackle first to get it out of the way; I worked as quickly as I could, feeling an excitement that I couldn't put into words at the thought of Gramps comin' to join me.

Tonight my dog was a rusty brown with soft eyes and long droopy ears. But I had little time for her after explainin' the reason for my rush.

"Ginger, ya jest gonna have to stand aside so you don't git tramped on 'cause I'm in a hurry to git as much done as I can before *Gramps* comes to help me."

The pigs must have wondered what had happened, the way that I ran with the slop-pails and chop. Then I took the grain and water to the chickens. On the lope, I left for the pasture gate to let Bossie down the lane. I didn't dare to run her and I felt all agitated at her slow walk for fear Gramps would be waitin' for me. He was, though he didn't seem at all put out about it.

His new overalls looked strange on him. He had rolled up the cuffs so that they wouldn't drag in the dirt. He wore a new pair of farmer's boots, too, and an old sweater that he referred to as his "gardenin' sweater."

We walked to the house for the milk pail, then back again to the barn. He pulled up an extra stool and watched me as the white streams of milk filled the pail with foam. As I milked he talked to me. He even talked to Bossie, and I had the strangest feelin' that at any time he might turn around and begin talkin' to Ginger, too.

We took the full pail of milk to the house, and Gramps said that sometime he'd like to give it a try—it looked easy enough. Did I think that Bossie would mind? I didn't think so. She was pretty even-tempered and never really seemed to mind anything but the pesky flies that sometimes drove her runnin' with her tail flyin' high.

By the time we were back from the house, Bossie had finished her chop. I let her out of her stanchion and we drove her down the lane and back to pasture. While we walked, Gramps told me how it had been for him growin' up as a boy in a big city back east. No open pastures or acres of trees, but all tall buildings, belchin' smoke stacks, and crowded streets. I tried to see it all in my mind, but it was pretty hard to picture, me never havin' been anywhere near a big city.

We ended my chores by carryin' wood. I was glad that I had already split it. Gramps carried his share. He could take as many sticks in a load as I could. I had to admire him.

I was about to return to the house when I remembered that Grandpa and Uncle Charlie would soon be returning with thirsty and tired teams.

"You go on in," I said to Gramps. "I think that I'll jest run on down to the barn and fork down some hay for the horses, then pump the trough full of water."

"Tell you what, you do the forking and I'll do the pumping."

He could see that I wasn't sure that I should let him.

"Go ahead. If I tire, I'll rest."

I ran for the barn and pushed the hay down through the chute into the mangers, then I measured out the chop and put each horse's portion in his chop box. I ran back to the pump-house. Gramps was still pumpin'. He didn't seem too winded and the trough was almost full. I took over and finished filling it.

Mentally I checked all the chores off the list that I kept in my mind. That was it. Everything was cared for and on time, too.

We carried in Gramps' two trunks and put them in the downstairs bedroom which had been our "guest room," though we never had overnight guests. Lou had decided that would be the best place for him—before she saw that stairs really wouldn't have slowed him down that much. The room was all repapered, fresh-painted and ready. It still seemed the most appropriate place for Gramps.

Lou had supper ready and waiting on the back of the stove. We washed ourselves and prepared to wait, but while we were still sharin' the long kitchen towel, we could hear the jingling of harness and we knew that Grandpa and Uncle Charlie would soon be there to join us.

CHAPTER 9

Family

Lou got the idea that it would be fun to surprise Grandpa and Uncle Charlie, them not expectin' Gramps to show up jest out of the blue like that; Gramps went along with it whole-heartedly. He looked around the kitchen to make sure that he hadn't left anything laying around that would give him away and then slipped into his new bedroom.

Grandpa and Uncle Charlie took turns at the basin, sloshin' the warm water over their faces, necks, and arms. Then they scrubbed their hands with the strong soap and rinsed them in fresh water.

"Glad to see the mangers and the trough full, Boy," Grandpa commended me. Uncle Charlie tousled my hair but said nothin'.

They took their places at the table and Lou set on the food. Grandpa was the first to notice.

"What's the extry place?"

"Oh, my goodness," said Lou. "Can't I even count anymore?" But when she made no move to take away the plate, Grandpa became suspicious. He and Uncle Charlie were probably both afraid that Lou had stolen a march on them and was doin' a little lookin' over the field on her own. She set down the last dish of food, a heaped-up bowl of new potatoes, and gave Grandpa her innocent little girl look.

"Truth is, Pa, I invited a guest for supper."

Grandpa and Uncle Charlie really looked nervous now. Uncle Charlie recovered first.

"Well—where is he?"

We weren't in the habit in our home of sittin' down to eat before the guests arrived.

"Well—he's—he's—a—in the bedroom." Lou raised her voice as she said it and Gramps took the cue, but not before Grandpa and Uncle Charlie had nearly choked on Lou's words.

Out popped Gramps in his new, but now slightly soiled, overalls and boots, his perky mustache twitchin' humorously and his blue eyes twinklin'.

"Well, I'll be," said Grandpa as though he couldn't believe his eyes. Then a general uproar followed with handshakes and manly hugs and laughter.

"How'd you git here?" Uncle Charlie finally asked. "We thought that we'd git a letter or a telly-gram telling us when to meet yer train."

"In the midst of harvest? Even a city-slicker like me knows better than to pull a stunt like that.

"I knew that once I got to town, I'd be able to either find a way out or to send word some way for you to come and get me."

We finally got back to the table where Lou's good meal was gettin' cold. The talk continued but the food didn't suffer because of it. It seemed to disappear in the usual fashion. Gramps complimented Lou over and over.

"Now that's what I've been missing since your grandmother died. Some good cooking—and," he added more thoughtfully, "someone to share it with."

We all understood his meaning.

"Well," Grandpa put in, "we all are right glad that ya decided to come on out and be with us. It's jest real good to have ya."

I was almost surprised at how heartily I was able to agree. I already loved the old man, and he had jest been in the house a few hours.

"Gramps helped with chores," I offered.

"He did?"

"Not really helped," corrected Gramps, "just sort of tagged along to chat a bit and see what goes on on a farm. Never been on one before, you know."

"But he did help," I insisted. "He carried wood and he pumped water and—"

Gramps stopped me. "Hey, Josh, you cut that out. Your Grandpa is supposed to think of me as old and worn out. You tell him stories like that and he'll put me out hoeing or such like."

Everyone laughed together.

"Fact is," continued Gramps, "I'd a lot rather hang around the kitchen and bother the cook." He winked at me and smiled. Suddenly he grew silent and thoughtful and raised his eyes heavenward.

"You'll never know how many times on my train ride out here that I thanked the Lord for my family. Must be the most awful thing in the world not to have *anybody*. I felt at first that I had no one—when Mama died—but all that I needed to do was to make connections again. Some people now, they're not that fortunate. When their partner is gone, they are alone—really alone.

"Here I am with my family—two sons, a granddaughter, and a great-grandson. My family. I am a man mightily, mightily blessed."

He smiled on us all. Lou brushed away tears unashamedly and Grandpa cleared his throat rather noisily. I swallowed hard. I had some thanks that needed sayin', too—it was that God hadn't taken seriously my prayer when I wanted to get rid of this wonderful old man. It almost made me break out into a sweat, to discover what I had been anxious to deny myself.

Gramps had talked about his "family." Sure we were a family. You didn't have to be a ma and a pa and four kids to be a family. All you needed was people livin' together and lovin' and helpin' one another. That's what made a family—blood-ties and love-bonds.

I straightened up taller in my chair. I was right proud to be a member of this family.

CHAPTER 10

The Fishin' Hole

I still had a hankerin' to work in some time at my fishin' hole before harvest ended and I found myself back in a stuffy schoolroom. Gradually my work was caught up and even a bit ahead so that I finally freed myself for a few hours on a Friday mornin'. It was already gittin' close to the noonday meal. If I went fishin' right away I would miss my dinner, but if I waited until after dinner it would sure cut into my fishin' time. I decided that I'd sweet talk Lou into makin' me a couple of sandwiches and givin' me an apple or two.

I was on my way to the kitchen to make my request when I noticed Gramps. He had been tired after his long journey by train, and when the excitement of meetin' us all sort of quieted down he realized jest how tired he was. The dry air bothered him a bit, too, but gradually he was pickin' up steam again. He still chored with me. He was catchin' on real good as to what needed to be done. Sometimes he would even say things like, "Now I'll take the water and feed to the chickens while you run down the lane for Bossie."

Durin' the day he read a lot or even puttered in the kitchen helpin' Lou prepare fruit or vegetables for cannin'.

Right now he was sittin' on the back porch readin' a big thick book. A sudden thought hit me. Would there be any chance—any chance at all—that Gramps would care for a trip to the crik? Even if he didn't fish, he could rest on the bank and read like Auntie Lou often did.

He grinned at me and I gathered together all of my nerve.

"I got a few extry hours here," I said. "Thinkin' of goin' down to the crik to see if the fish are bitin'. Dug up some great night crawlers in the barnyard."

At once his eyes lit up.

"Mind if I tag along?"

I relaxed then and blew the breath that I'd been holdin'.

"I'd like that."

"So would I."

He gathered up his book and hurried it back to his bedroom.

Lou was busy with some yellow beans.

"Auntie Lou," I ventured, "Gramps and me are gonna take us a little time fer fishin'. Would it be okay iffen we took a couple sandwiches?"

"Great idea," responded Auntie Lou, "then I won't have to stop in the middle of this job to fix dinner for ya."

Uncle Charlie and Grandpa were workin' with a neighborhood-cuttin'-bee, for a farmer who was laid up with a broken leg, so they wouldn't be home for dinner either.

"You run on out and bring the clothes in off the line so they won't fade in the sun; I'll git your lunch ready."

By the time I deposited the clothes on the kitchen table, Lou had our old lunch pail packed and ready to go. Gramps was ready, too, but a little concerned.

"I haven't a fish pole, Josh."

"We'll cut one."

"And no line."

"I have string in my pocket."

"A hook?"

I grinned. "Yeah, I've an extry."

We started off, me leading the way because Gramps hadn't been to the crik before.

I hadn't a moment's hesitation but headed straight for my favorite spot—the one that I had never shown anyone before. I jest hoped that today the fish were bitin'.

When the path was wide enough, we walked side by side.

"You know," admitted Gramps, "you're going to find this hard to believe, but I've never been fishing before."

I did find it hard to believe. I couldn't imagine livin' without occasional fishin'.

"You're going to have to teach me, Josh."

"I'll show ya all I know," I solemnly promised. "I jest hope they're bitin'."

We got to the crik and it looked great. The dark shadows hung on the deeper water. I could hardly wait to git started, but first I got out my jackknife and cut a pole for Gramps. Then I tied the string in the notch that I made on one end. I pulled my little bottle out of my pocket, took out a hook and attached it to the other end of the string.

"This the spot?"

"This is it." Excitement filled my voice.

"You know," said Gramps, "I rather like the looks of that small island out there in the middle. Don't you think that might be a great place to sit and fish from?"

Already Gramps showed a fisherman's instincts. I liked that. That little island was the best place along the whole crik, but you had to wade to get to it, and I wasn't sure if I should suggest that to Gramps. Now I answered promptly.

"Yep! It sure is, but ya gotta wade to git there."

"Well, let's wade."

"Ya gotta go downstream a ways where the water is shallower and cross over on the sandbar, then walk upstream and come in right there at the end—slightly to the other side. That way you won't git yer clothes all soaked."

"Lead the way," prompted Gramps. "Let's go."

I led the way. When we got to the crossin' place, I set the lunch pail on the ground alongside my pole and bent down to pull up my pant legs; I was barefoot. Gramps followed suit. Then he bent over and undid his shoes and socks. When he was finished, we picked up all of our gear and started across.

The water felt cold at first, but we gradually got used to it. I tried to pick sandy places with few rocks 'cause I realized that Gramps hadn't been runnin' most of the summer with bare feet like I had and his feet wouldn't be tough like mine.

We got into a little deeper water as we made our way upstream, and I heard Gramps chucklin' behind me.

When I reached jest the right spot, I cut over and headed for the small island. It wasn't much more than room for two people to comfortably sit, but it did have some trees and bushes.

I heaved myself up the little bank, laid down my equipment and turned to give Gramps a hand. He handed me his pole and then clambered up the bank to join me. He was still chucklin'.

"Afraid I didn't do as good a job as you rolling up my pant legs, Josh. One slipped down mid-stream."

It sure had all right. A good two feet of overall leg was soakin' wet.

"Does Lou get riled about wet overalls?"

"Well, sorta," I answered honestly. "It's not the wet so much as the dirt that mixes with it. By the time one gits home, it's mud."

"I can see the problem," said Gramps, lookin' at the soggy leg.

"Well, then, we'll just have to dry it out, won't we?" And right there, on our little island, Gramps unclasped his overall straps and climbed out of his pants.

He picked up the wet leg and wrung all of the water out of it that he could, then he crossed to a nearby bush and spread the overalls out over the branches, with the wet leg layin' full in the sun.

"There now." His eyes twinkled as he chuckled again. "That should dry just fine by home time."

I looked at his wet underwear leg. He looked down, too.

"That won't matter any. It'll partly dry as I sit in the sun and fish; and the wet that remains will be covered with my overalls when I walk home on the dusty path, so it won't gather the dirt."

He had it all figured out.

"Let's get to fishing! Just hope that my white flannels don't scare the fish away."

He really did look a sight, trampin' around in his skinny-legged underwear, his plaid shirttails flappin' loose. I couldn't help it. I jest had to laugh and he joined right in.

I took off my denim shirt and spread it on the ground in what I considered a first-rate spot. I figured that we should protect that white underwear as much as possible or Auntie Lou might be askin' questions. Gramps settled down on the shirt and I handed him my pole. It was kinda special to me and had my favorite hook on it, but I knew that I wanted Gramps to have the best. He knew what I was doin'.

"Thank you, Joshua," he said softly.

I showed him where to drop the line and how to jiggle the pole, jest slightly, to give a bit of action to the hook under the water. I took the other pole, baited the hook, and threw it in.

We hadn't been there long when I felt a quick tug. I knew that I had one, and like every other time, I felt excitement shiver through my whole body.

Gramps got excited, too, and jumped to his feet cheerin' me on. I finally got the fish landed, and it flopped back and forth in the grass a safe distance from the water's edge. I tapped it with a rock so that it wouldn't suffer none.

"It's a dandy! It's a dandy!" Gramps kept yellin'. "You're a real fisherman, Josh, a real fisherman."

I had never seen anyone so excited about a fish before. It was a fair size, but I had caught bigger ones from this hole. Still, I was pleased with it and even more pleased at the fact that Gramps admired my accomplishment.

We kept right on fishin' even when we ate our sandwiches. Auntie Lou had really packed a terrific lunch. I thought when I looked in the pail that we could stay fishin' for the whole week without worryin' about runnin' out of food, but to the surprise of both of us, we emptied the pail of everything— sandwiches, pie, apples, and all.

We had jest finished the last of our lunch when I felt a tug on my line again. Gramps was a-whoopin' even before the fish jumped to try to free itself.

"It's a dandy! Hang on, Josh! Bring him in, Joshua! Easy now! That does it! It's a dandy! It's a dandy!"

I got that fish landed, too, and as the two laid there on the grass together, they were almost identical in size. Gramps' face was flushed with pleasure. He whipped off his hat and pounded the leg of his underwear.

"Boy, Josh," he said, "this beats a circus."

Now a circus was one thing that I'd always had a hankerin' to see, but none had ever come anywhere near our little town. I picked up on it.

"You seen a circus?"

Gramps slowed down a bit. He even put his hat back on. He settled back down on my shirt and picked up the fishin' pole. He tossed the line out carefully and began to jiggle it—jest a bit—like I had showed him.

"Yep. I've seen circuses."

"What are they like?"

As we continued fishin' Gramps described to me the trapeze acts, the jugglers, the sword swallowers, the fire eaters, and the animal acts. I sat there so amazed by it all that sometimes I even forgot to jiggle my hook.

"I know what I'd like best," I said slowly.

"What?"

"The animal acts."

"You like animals?"

"Love 'em."

"Then I guess it's a good thing that you live on a farm."

"That's never helped me none."

"You have all kinds of animals here," responded Gramps.

"Sure, dumb ol' chickens and pigs, barn cats and cows. I don't mean that."

"I'm sure that you must have spring calves and—"

"Who would ever train a spring calf?"

"Oh," said Gramps catchin' on. "You mean animals that you can train to do special things."

"Yeah," I sorta mumbled, but I had a lot of feelin' in what I said. "Like roll over and sit up and beg and things."

Gramps jest nodded his head. He started to say something but jest then his line jerked. Both of us were on our feet and I found myself yellin'.

"It's a dandy! Easy does it. Bring him in. That's right. Give him a little line. Bring him in again. Good work! It's a dandy!"

I don't know who was the most excited when Gramps landed that fish—him or me; but we both whooped and danced around—me in my rolled-up farm overalls, and him in his tight-legged white underwear.

When we finally stopped pattin' each other on the back, we decided that we'd better call it a day. I could tell by the sun that it would soon be chore time and besides, we could hardly wait to show Auntie Lou.

Gramps picked his overalls off the bush and tied them around his neck. He wasn't goin' to chance wet legs on the return trip. We both pulled up the legs of what we were wearin' as far as we could, then gathered our poles and the lunch pail; the fish were strung on a piece of string. We started back across the crik, me leadin' the way again.

When we reached the bank, Gramps put his overalls on again and dressed his feet. Gatherin' all of our things together, we started for home.

"We must do this again, Josh."

"I'll soon be back in school."

"Then we must try to do it at least once more before you go."

"Maybe we can—iffen I can jest keep the work caught up, maybe we can."

"I'll lend a hand," said Gramps, and I knew that he would.

CHAPTER 11

Number Two

All of the men of the house had been feelin' concern for Auntie Lou, though I guess none of us had expressed it to each other. Harvest and cannin' time was an awfully hard time of year for a farm woman—yet Auntie Lou was jest a slip of a girl and carryin' it all.

I tried to be sure that she always had lots of wood and water on hand without havin' to ask for it. Uncle Charlie most always picked up a dish towel when he got up from the supper table, and Grandpa stood guard at the door like a sentry to be sure that no one entered the kitchen with dirty boots or pant-leg cuffs. He needn't have bothered. We had all checked ourselves by the time we got there anyway.

Gramps was Lou's biggest help. He watched like a hawk and knew when there was a job that could use an extra pair of hands. Auntie Lou and he chatted and laughed as they worked together. They enjoyed one another, that was plain.

Gramps was the only person that I was willing to share Auntie Lou with without feelin' jealous. I enjoyed the pleasure that they took from one another's company—but then they always included me if I was around.

In spite of the help that we all tried to give, Auntie Lou's job was still a big one; as the Sunday drew near when we were to *entertain* Hiram Woxley,

I think Uncle Charlie felt a mite sorry that he had asked him, knowin' full well that it added to Lou's work.

Sunday came. Lou didn't fuss around for Hiram Woxley like she had for the widow Rawleigh—he was Uncle Charlie's guest. She would serve him a good Sunday dinner and that was that.

I still felt a bit uneasy about the whole thing. What if the fella should take a shine to Lou? Worse yet, what if she should take a likin' to him?

Anyway, there we were, right smack-dab in the middle of the Sunday that I had tried hard to pretend would never come.

We went to church as usual. I didn't pay much attention to the message that Parson White gave. It was all about "being prepared" and I wasn't plannin' on "going" for a good long time yet. I didn't like thinking about dying anyway, so I switched my mind over to something else.

I had a hard time at first findin' something that I cared to spend all that time on; then I thought of Gramps' circus and I settled back on the hard wooden bench to enjoy my stay. Of course it was the animal acts that I thought on.

I pictured myself as a ringmaster, with a tall black stove-pipe hat like Gramps had described, and a bright ruffly shirt and red swallow-tails. I didn't carry a whip—only a little pointin' stick, and I had dogs—lots of dogs, and all kinds, all sizes. They could all do different tricks, and the people roared and clapped and yelled to see us again and again. Before I had even taken my final bow, the service was over and the people were leavin' the church. I couldn't believe that time had gone so fast.

Soon we were all loaded in the wagon, headin' for home. I sat at the back. As soon as we turned the corner, I whipped off my Sunday shoes and my socks. I saw Gramps watchin' me.

"No use wearin' out good Sunday shoes 'fore ya need to," I explained.

Before I knew it Gramps had moved from his wagon seat and was easin' himself down beside me; then he, too, reached down and carefully removed his shoes. He put them far enough into the wagon so that they wouldn't jiggle out and swung his legs contentedly back and forth.

"Those rascals always have pinched me," he whispered in my ear.

When we turned in the lane, we both hurriedly put our socks and shoes back on. With Hiram comin' I supposed I would be stuck in them for the entire day.

Lou was unflurried as she finished the dinner preparations. Hiram drove in and was heartily welcomed by Grandpa and Uncle Charlie—and I guess two out of five ain't bad. It wasn't long until Lou summoned us for dinner. She placed Hiram down at the end with Grandpa and Uncle Charlie, and Gramps and I were on her right and left.

I could see that Hiram was mightily impressed with Lou's cooking and the knot started tightenin' up in my stomach again. I even refused a second piece of pie. I cast around in my mind for comments that I could make on jest how expensive it was to set such a good table, but anything that I could come up with I knew was in Grandpa's category of rudeness so I had to let them go unsaid.

As soon as the meal was over, Uncle Charlie took charge. He wasn't goin' to ball things up like Grandpa had.

"Now Lou," he said, "seein' as how you been a-workin' so hard on the cannin', bakin', an' all, you deserve ya a little rest. Why don't you jest go on out on the back porch and relax and visit with Hiram a bit, while yer pa and me do up these dishes."

Lou looked up, her puzzlement showin' clearly, but before she could venture a protest, Grandpa cut in quick.

"Good idee," and he almost pushed Lou toward the door. Then he went one step further. "Pa, why don't you an' Josh have ya a game of checkers. I've been tryin' to teach him, but you know that I never was the checker player that you are—an' I've forgot a lot of the good moves."

Now Grandpa was a right good checker player when he took the time to play. Fact is, he had rather made a name for himself in our community. We had played checkers a fair amount on long, quiet winter evenin's, but never before in the busy days of harvest. Even on Sundays at harvest time a man was more inclined to jest sit and relax or read, rather than to work hard on "thinkin."

Uncle Charlie was busy banging around the dishpan and filling it with hot water from the kitchen stove's reservoir, and Grandpa was scurryin' around the table gathering up the dishes.

In preference of makin' a scene, Lou, still with a bewildered look on her face, allowed herself to be shuttled out the door and onto the back porch. Hiram grinned as he followed her, and my stomach lurched again.

"Checkers are right over there, Pa. You get them, Boy—you know where they are."

So Gramps and I were herded into the far corner of the kitchen and stationed over the red and black checkerboard.

My heart wasn't in it nor my mind on it, and I played a horrible game. I began to wonder why I wasn't losing even worse than I was; then I realized that Gramps' mind definitely wasn't on the game either.

When the noise of the clatterin' dishes was at its height, Gramps whispered to me without even liftin' his eyes from the board.

"What's going on here, Joshua?"

I was a bit surprised that he had picked it up so quickly, and for a moment I wondered jest how much I should tell him. I decided to jest blurt it all out. Boy, did I need an ally, and for some reason I had the sure feelin' that Gramps would be on my side.

"Grandpa and Uncle Charlie are lookin' to marry off Auntie Lou."

He waited a few minutes; then as Uncle Charlie rattled the cutlery, he whispered again. "Does she know it?"

"Hasn't a notion!"

I thought that I heard him say "good" but I wasn't sure.

"Is she interested?"

"Nope," I replied with confidence. I would explain more later.

This time I was sure that I heard him say "good."

"Know anything about this Hiram guy?" Gramps' eyes still hadn't left the board.

I knew that Gramps meant anything that was unfavorable.

"Only that he likes money," I whispered back, pretending hard that my next move really had me puzzled.

Gramps stood up.

"You're no match for me, Joshua," he said teasingly—"unless you work on your game. Anyway, I think that that's enough checkers for today. Let's get some air."

I saw Grandpa and Uncle Charlie look at one another nervously as Gramps and I moved toward the kitchen door. I'm sure that Gramps noticed them, too, but he never let it slow him down none.

"There's a game called 'ring-knife' that we used to play when I was a kid. You use your jackknife. You draw a circle on the ground, see, and you place small stones in it—so far apart—then you stand back and toss your knife. Your knife has to stick upright in the ground—that means that you have to miss those stones. Each time that you succeed, you get to move back a pace. If your knife doesn't stand up, you have to start over. Winner is the one who can tally up the most paces back. At the end of the time limit each player uses his best score. Want to try it?"

I felt that I was pretty good with my knife and the game sounded kind of fun so I agreed.

By now we had walked together onto the back porch. Auntie Lou and Hiram were sippin' lemonade and chattin' about something. Hiram looked down-right pleased with himself, but Auntie Lou still hadn't quite been able to shake off her look of confusion.

Gramps stopped to exchange a few words.

"Joshua and I are going to have us a little game here."

We went on. Gramps drew out the circle in the dirt, and we each placed three smooth stones inside it.

It was easy for the first few paces, but it got tougher as we went along. We made the first game jest ten minutes. I had tallied up eleven paces as my best score and Gramps ten.

As I was retrievin' our knives for another go at it, Gramps did a rather funny thing. He pulled out his purse and handed me a dime. His voice was low.

"Been meaning to give you this. When you go to town next time, I'd like you to pick out a good fishhook for me—one that you think would have those fish squirming for a chance at it."

Seemed funny to me that Gramps would be thinkin' of fishhooks at such a time, but I nodded and put the dime in the pocket of my pants. I don't know jest what brought my head up at that particular time, but as my glance went to the porch I saw Hiram lookin' at us. I thought nothing about it except the usual fear and anger at seein' him there with Lou. I handed Gramps his knife. He carefully cleaned the blade of his knife and we started a new game. This one ended again as Gramps consulted his pocket watch. I bettered my score a bit that game, and Gramps ended up two paces behind me.

"Been thinking, Joshua," he said as we retrieved our knives, "maybe you'd best get two hooks so that we'll each have one."

Hadn't realized jest how "hooked" on fishin' Gramps was after only one trip to the crik. He took out his change purse and handed me another dime. He jiggled the coins as though he was having trouble locating jest the right one. I dumbly put the dime in my pocket knowin' that it was more money than I needed for two hooks. I'd git the best ones that I could find and give Gramps back his change.

Gramps raised his voice. I was only a few paces from him—but he did have his back to me, so maybe he thought I had walked away.

"Okay, Joshua, that's enough practicing. Let's get into the *real* game now."

It was then that I noticed Hiram edgin' his way off the porch and over toward us. Gramps stood there examining his knife and cleaning the dirt from the blade. Hiram came in closer.

"Interestin' game," he finally said.

"Ever play ring-knife?" Gramps asked.

"Nope."

"Know the rules?"

"I've been watchin'."

Gramps sensed his interest.

"Want to join us?"

Hiram grinned then.

"Sure would like to give it a try."

He pulled out his pocket knife and checked the tip for sharpness.

"We were just about to start the big one. Go ahead and take a few practice throws."

Gramps hauled out his watch and studied the time while Hiram threw. He looked pretty good with a knife.

Gramps let him have three throws from varyin' distances.

"Okay," he said, watching his timepiece carefully as though it had to be the exact second for startin', "Joshua, you start." A pause, then a flash of the watch in his hand—"Go."

I threw—my knife stuck upright. The game was on.

"Hiram," Gramps said with a nod.

Hiram threw. His knife held firm. Gramps took extra time as he threw, as though the game had suddenly become very important. I sensed the change and it made me feel that maybe we *had* jest been foolin' around before. Hiram seemed to sense it, too, and I could see the excitement in his face.

Gramps measured the distance, judged the position of the stones, studied his knife carefully for balance, and threw. His knife stood upright and I heard him sigh with satisfaction.

We all picked up our knives and backed up a pace. The rounds went much more slowly now. Gramps seemed to set the pace. He played so differently that it was hard to believe we were playin' the same game that he had first introduced me to. Round by round we studied, threw, took our paces backward, and retrieved our knives. Uncle Charlie and Grandpa came to watch for a while with anxious looks on their faces; but seein' our deep involvement, they finally shrugged and went away.

I'll say this for Hiram. When he takes to a game he does it with his whole heart and soul. I'd hardly seen a man so keen about playin' a game. Gramps was serious about it, too; he played slowly and carefully, but he seemed to have a calmness about him that Hiram was lackin'.

All the rest of the afternoon we played. Pace by pace we stepped back until we were so far away that we could hardly see the circle—then we'd go back to start over.

I moved backward and forward more often than the others. It was hard to believe that I had actually managed to beat Gramps in my first two games. Beginner's luck—I guess.

Hiram was in a sweat. It stood out in little drops on his forehead, and it wasn't due to the pleasant fall day.

Lou had long ago taken her leave. I had spotted her heading toward the crik with a book in her hand. Uncle Charlie and Grandpa paced back and forth on the back porch, scowlin' and upset, but the game went on.

Gramps and Hiram hung together pace by pace. Occasionally Gramps consulted his pocket watch, rattlin' its chain rather unnecessarily as he did so; then he'd shake his head to indicate that time still wasn't up and we'd go at it again.

Frankly, I was getting rather tired of the game, but Hiram didn't seem to be. Gramps was one pace behind him and Hiram seemed determined to keep it that way.

Gramps looked at his watch again.

"One minute to go. This will be our last throw."

Hiram chewed his lip. They were now both standing together at their record distance. If they both made it, it could end up a tie. Of course I was pullin' for Gramps. I was so far behind that I didn't even count anymore.

Hiram almost looked in pain as he lined up for his last toss. I thought that he was never goin' to let go of that knife, but he finally did; the blade flashed as it arced through the air. It hit the ground with a soft sound; it had cleared the stones—it quivered as it held upright. Hiram looked like he would whoop, but he didn't. He whipped out his handkerchief and wiped his brow.

It was Gramps' turn now. He took his time and aimed carefully. A calmness still showed in his face. I would have loved to put a toe to Hiram's knife. I was hopin' for at least a tie—that would take the sting out of the situation.

Hiram was almost jumpin' out of his shoes; I was afraid that his agitation would disturb Gramps' concentration. I sent him a scowl but he didn't even notice.

Gramps' knife finally left his hand and made a clean, quick flight toward the circle. It seemed that the whole of me went flyin' with that knife. No one stirred—or even breathed. I waited for the soft sound of the blade slippin' into the dirt, but instead there was a sharp "clink" and a clatter. Gramps' knife had hit the largest rock.

Hiram whooped—I wanted to kick him. Poor Gramps—after playin' so hard and so long. But Gramps was a much better loser than I was on his behalf. He turned to Hiram with a good-natured smile.

"Great game for a novice," he said, extending his hand.

I didn't know what "novice" meant, but I sure did know the meanin' I'd put to it.

Hiram was still so excited that he could hardly even shake Gramps' hand proper-like. I wondered how a supposed grown man could get so riled up about winnin' a simple little game—even if it did take all afternoon to play.

"Congratulations," I heard Gramps sayin'. "You sure are one terrific ring-knife player."

Hiram was still bouncin' around and shaking Gramps' hand vigorously.

"How much did I win?" he blurted out.

"Win?" Gramps looked dumbfounded—I knew I was. Uncle Charlie and Grandpa, who had come on over, looked a little surprised too.

"Yeah . . ." Hiram's glee began to fade from his face. "Don't ya—"

"I never played a game for money in my life." Gramps looked offended. "That's gambling. If a game can't be played for the sheer joy of the playing, then leave it alone, I always say."

"But you gave Josh—"

"I gave Josh a couple of dimes to buy fishhooks the next time he goes to town. He and I plan to do some fishing before he has to go back to school."

Hiram had added an embarrassed look to his one of disappointment. He cleared his throat and cleaned his knife with his eyes turned from everyone.

Lou, who had returned, luckily chose that moment to announce that coffee was ready, so we all trooped into the house. Her timin' couldn't have been better. The air was a mite heavy, though I still couldn't rightly understand the situation fully.

Hiram left as soon as he had swallowed the last of his cake and washed it down with coffee. He thanked Uncle Charlie rather weakly for the invitation, but he kept his eyes away from Lou's, even as he mumbled his thanks for the dinner. He also avoided Gramps. It was rather comical watchin' him scuttle around hardly knowin' which way to look.

Uncle Charlie went with Hiram to get his team and the big bays fairly thundered out of our yard. Uncle Charlie returned. Lou was busy clearin' the table; no one jumped up to protest her activity and suggest that she rest herself.

Gramps grinned at me sort of silly and gave a quick wink.

He turned to Uncle Charlie. He shook his head slowly as though he was really at a loss to understand it all.

"Your friend seemed like such a nice young man, Charles. I just can hardly believe that he would be a gambler. It's a shame, a downright shame!"

I had to run outside before I busted out laughin'.

CHAPTER 12

Fall Days

Uncle Charlie was going to town for some binder twine, and Gramps decided that he'd ride along with him. I ached to go, too, but I had too many chores that needed finishing. I still had those two dimes that Gramps had given me, and I could hardly wait to check over the fishhooks at Kirk's. I offered them back to Gramps, thinkin' that he might like to buy the hooks himself, but he said that I knew more about such things.

I worked with rather draggin' feet. It seemed strange and lonesome somehow without Gramps there to sort of spur me on.

After dinner I had some free time, so I got out my fishin' tackle and cleaned up my hooks. I nearly stuck myself with one of them; Auntie Lou got all excited and said that I'd better put them away. My handlin' fishhooks always made her nervous.

I went out to split wood. I had made quite a stack before I finally heard the wagon comin'. I slammed the axe head into the choppin' block and sauntered into the kitchen.

"They're comin'."

"Are they?"

"Yep."

There was a pause. Auntie Lou was havin' a few rare minutes with one of those mail-order catalogues. She kept right on lookin'.

"Coffee ready?"

She looked up, her fine eyebrows archin'.

"You wantin' coffee?"

"Not me—Gramps and Uncle Charlie. Jest thought that they might kinda like a cup—or juice or somethin'."

Lou smiled and laid aside the fascinating pages.

"So you're hungry, are ya, Josh?"

It wasn't what I meant, but I didn't care that Lou took me wrong. By the time the men came in from the barn, Lou had cut some molasses cake, and the coffee was about ready to boil. At my place was a tall glass of milk.

Gramps passed close to me and placed his hand on my shoulder. I sorta felt like pressin' myself against him and waggin' my tail.

"How'd chores go?"

"Fine. I got done in pretty good time. Even cleaned up my fishhooks."

"I was going to take a look at the hooks in the general store just to see what they carried, but I didn't get around to it."

I wondered what Gramps had been doin' with all of his time in town that he didn't even find time to look at fishhooks. Uncle Charlie entered.

"Saw a little notice posted in the general store that might interest you, Josh."

I looked at Uncle Charlie, wonderin' what a notice in Kirk's store would have to do with me. I didn't need to wonder long.

"Says big an' bold-like, 'School starts Monday.' "

Uncle Charlie lifted one finger as though pointin' out each one of the big black-lettered words.

My face must have dropped, because Uncle Charlie laughed, and Gramps seemed to look about as disappointed as I felt.

"So soon?" he questioned Uncle Charlie.

Uncle Charlie nodded.

"Harvest is early this year and most folks are gittin' near done. Saw Mr. T. Smith in town. He says a few hours today will finish him. Made arrangements myself for the threshing crew to come in on Thursday. Jest the little bits of greenfeed that Dan is workin' on today and all our cuttin' will be done. The other fields are stooked and dryin' real fast. They'll all be ready for sure come Thursday."

"Well, I best be gittin'."

He got up from the table and then seemed to remember something. He pulled a small brown bag from a shirt pocket and handed it to Auntie Lou. When Uncle Charlie went to town he always came home with a few gums, licorice sticks, or peppermint drops. He winked at Auntie Lou.

"Ya might even share one or two with Josh, iffen he behaves himself."

He flipped his hat onto his head and was gone.

"Next Monday . . ." Gramps repeated. "That means we have to do our fishing this week, Joshua. Think we can manage it?"

I was now doubly glad for the nice pile of firewood that I had stacked outside.

"Tomorrow," I said. "We'll count on tomorrow. I'll git out there right now and add to that woodpile before I have to start sloppin' the pigs."

As I hurried out I thought on how Uncle Charlie had brought some good news and some bad news. Wasn't hard to decide which side of the board the word about school startin' would fit. The good news was concernin' the threshin' crew. Threshin' was one of my favorite events of the year.

It usually started early in the morning. Always as I rushed about the early mornin' chores, I found myself listenin' for the chug-chug of the big threshin' rig coming up the road. Before long it would be devourin' bundles and spittin' out golden grain from one spout and blowin' high a stream of straw from another.

The first few hours were spent in settin' up the threshin' machine. After it was positioned and seemed in readiness, the giant steam tractor was started. The long flappin' belt began to whirl, and it in turn activated all manner of movin' things on the threshin' machine. At first all of the gears were in slow motion, grindin' and howlin' as they seemed to protest at bein' put to work again. The man who owned the machine never sat still for a minute. He ran back and forth, around and around, checkin' here and checkin' there. After he had looked and listened to his heart's content, he left the big machine idlin' and came to the house for breakfast.

I sat at breakfast strainin' to be the first to hear the jangle of harness and the clankin' of steel-rimmed wheels as they ground their way over the hard-packed road.

There would be at least five or six teams in all. Sometimes they stopped at the house, while other times they went right on down to the field.

When the teams arrived, the machine operator would swallow the last of his coffee and make his way back to his rig; there he'd circle and listen and open little side doors, look in and poke a bit.

Finally when the sun had been up long enough to dry the grain bundles, the lead team moved out. A couple of extra men rode along, and they would fork on the bundles as the team moved slowly down the field, stoppin' and startin' at the command of their owner who worked along beside the wagon, pitchin' bundles with the other two fellas.

They wouldn't bring in a full rack, this first load jest bein' for testin'; as soon as they had enough to test they returned to the threshin' machine. That's when things really came to life. The levers were pulled, throwin' the big machines into full motion. The steam engine roared and trembled, shootin' out gray-black smoke. The gears clashed and banged on the threshin' machine as it picked up its pace. It seemed to rock and stomp like an angry dragon. I often marveled that it didn't rock itself right on down the field. Guess the owner thought the same, because he always packed rocks up tight against the steel wheels.

At the nod of the machine operator, the team moved in close to the machine, and the bundle pitchers went into motion, too, tossin' the bundles onto the belts that carried them up and fed them into the belly of the big machine.

That was where the miracle took place. Instead of comin' out as they had gone in, or even chopped and mutilated, the grain spout soon began to let streams of clean grain pour into the box of the wagon that sat carefully teamed in beneath it. A small cloud puffed from the spout that blew away the straw; the cloud grew and grew, becoming shimmering gold and silver flashes as the sun hit the flying particles.

I always stood in awe. It never ceased to amaze me, this sudden and well-ordered change.

If the threshed sample was satisfactory—the men decided this by lookin', handlin', and even chewin' the grain—the waitin' teams were given the signal and away they went, down the field, eager to be on with the job.

There were other things that I liked about threshin' time, too—like seein' the grain grow deeper and deeper in the wagon box. It was then transported to the grain bin where it was shoveled off with rhythmic swings of scrunch—whoosh, scrunch—whoosh. It smelled good, too, though sometimes the dust made you sneeze. Then there was the fun of chasin' mice that came skitterin' out from the grain shocks.

I loved the food too. Harvest time always meant a well-loaded table, for harvesters worked hard and needed hearty meals. We always got help for Auntie Lou at harvest time. It was jest too much for one woman to handle all the work of feedin' the harvest crew alone.

As I chopped wood, I looked forward to Thursday. I could hardly wait for the sound of the teams movin' in.

Gramps and I did manage to sneak in that fishin' trip on Wednesday. My only sorrow was that I hadn't been able to get into town to pick out some new hooks. Still, my old favorites seemed to have done okay in the past, so I trusted that they would again work well.

Gramps carried his pole and the lunch pail, while I handled my pole, a can of worms and dirt, and an old coat for Gramps to sit on. We decided to try a different hole this time—one a little further upstream. There was a swell log there, made perfect for sittin'—with the help of a little padding—and a couple of sturdy trees right behind it for anyone who preferred to lean against them to rest his back.

Gramps was a quick learner. He strung his own hook and had it in the water even before I did. He jiggled it occasionally—jest enough—and we settled in to talk as we waited for a fish to strike.

"You know, Joshua," said Gramps with a bit of a chuckle, "I've been thinking that I've pretty well got it made."

I looked at him sort of puzzled.

"Meanin'?"

"You know," he explained, "I think that I've hit the best years of a man's life."

I still wasn't followin'.

He chuckled softly as though he really had a good laugh on the rest of the scurryin' world.

"Take you now," he explained. "Sure you've got your delights—your fishing, your lack of adult worries; but you work hard, too."

I was glad that Gramps had noticed.

"And then you've got your schooling, like it or not—and I hope that you do like it. But you still have to go.

"Your Grandpa and your Uncle Charlie, they have men's work and men's worries. Takes most of their time and energy to just keep up with things.

"But *me* now . . ." he sighed a contented sigh and leaned back smugly against the warm tree trunk. "Me—I don't have to go to school, privilege that it is, or even chore if I don't feel like it. No one expects me to hurry around with a pitchfork or a scoop-shovel in my hand. No one raises an eyebrow if I want to lay in a bit in the morning or crawl off to bed at a kid's bedtime at night. I don't have to make tough decisions—like which spring calves to sell and which to keep, or what crop to plant in which field, or whether to fix the old plow again, or buy a new one. No sirree, Joshua. I've got it made."

I was gettin' the point. I'd never even considered that there were advantages to being old. Gramps clearly had found some. He grinned at me with humor dancin' in his blue eyes.

"Just eat and sleep and look after the old man."

It sounded pretty good all right, but not quite accurate for Gramps. I kept gettin' pictures of him feeding the chickens, pumping water for the stock or toting wood. I also saw him with his shirt sleeves rolled up peeling vegetables, or drying dishes, or even sweeping up the kitchen floor.

Maybe he was right in a way. Maybe he didn't *have* to do those things; but knowin' Gramps, I had the feelin' that as long as he could still totter, he'd be doin' what he could to lighten someone's load. Guess he liked it that way. He was a great old guy, my Gramps.

"Yes sirree," he said again, bobbin' his line, "best part of a man's life. If I had Mama here it would be just perfect."

He started tellin' me all about Great-grandma then—how he'd met her when he was only nineteen and decided right off that she was the girl for him. He went on, through their life spent together, rememberin' little things that probably seemed insignificant when they happened. He didn't talk about what had happened after she had gone, but knowin' Great-grandma, from the tone of Gramps' voice and the descriptions he had given, it was easy for me to feel his loss. I didn't have to wonder how he felt—I'd lost family too.

We fished in silence for a while and then decided that it was time for lunch. I was beginning to worry that I had chosen the wrong fishin' hole for the day; I so much wanted to see Gramps catch another one.

We had jest lifted cold chicken drumsticks from the pail when I sensed a commotion in the water; sure enough, Gramps had one on. He jumped up, dropped his chicken, and went whoopin' and yellin' down the bank. I joined him. We were shoutin' and dancin' and callin' to one another. By the time we landed the fish and got back to the lunch pail, the ants were already havin' a picnic of the dropped chicken. I tossed it, ants and all, off to the side to try to discourage the old ants-up-the-pant-leg trick.

Gramps had jest landed one of the nicest sunnies that I'd ever seen taken from the crik, and I could hardly swallow I was so excited. I even forgot to hope that I would have equal luck; if we would have had to pack up and head for home right then and there, I would have been perfectly happy. I did catch one before we had to leave, though it wasn't as fine as Gramps'.

We went home happy.

"Glad we were able to fit this day in, Joshua," Gramps said.

"Me too."

"You're good company, Joshua."

No one had ever said anything like that to me before.

"Hope that you didn't mind an old man sharing some memories."

I looked at him. " 'Course not."

He put a hand on my hair and ruffled it the way that grown-ups have a habit of doin'.

We walked on. Shucks! Why should I mind sharin' Gramps' memories? Especially since I didn't have any of my own anyway.

That strange twistin' hurt squeezed somewhere in my insides again. I started to walk a little faster.

CHAPTER 13

Threshin'

Thursday came. We were all able to let out the breath that we'd been holdin'. There's always the threat of bad weather movin' in on a threshin' operation. It delays the plans and makes big men sweat with worry over something that they have no power to do a thing about. Used to be I'd pray for days on end before threshin', pleadin' with the Lord to favor us with fittin' weather. Last year a bad storm moved in on us in spite of my prayers, so this year I decided that I would jest leave the Lord on His own.

I rose earlier than usual. I wanted my chores out of the way so that I could catch every bit of action that I possibly could.

As I looked out on the clear autumn mornin', I did have a stirrin' of thankfulness, even if I did hold back the desire to express it.

I was bringin' Bossie in from the field when I first heard the distant chug-chuggin'. I hoped that the sound of the comin' machine didn't fill Bossie with the same wild excitement that it did me—or her milk wouldn't be worth much that mornin'.

I milked hurriedly and was jest finishing when the slow-movin' tractor, with the big black thresher in tow, turned up our lane.

Grandpa and Uncle Charlie went out to meet Mr. Wilkes, the man who operated the machine.

Mr. Wilkes had been runnin' that machine for all of the harvests that I could remember. Neither he nor the machine looked shiny-new anymore, but they did look like they belonged together. To Mr. Wilkes the machine was not only his bread and butter but his friend and companion as well. He took great pride in it. Mr. Wilkes didn't bother to plant crops of his own anymore. In fact, he share-cropped his land with Mr. T. Smith. By farmin' Mr. Wilkes' fields, Mr. T. Smith was almost certain to be the first man on the list for threshin' come fall.

Mr. Wilkes depended on the money he'd make each autumn from tourin' from farm to farm rentin' out the services of himself and his magic machine. The two things that worried him most were drought and fires. His was the only thresher available in our area and nobody seemed to think it could be any other way.

I hurried the pail of milk to the house.

Already Mrs. Corbin and her daughter, SueAnn, were there to help Auntie Lou. I don't believe that Lou shared my excitement about harvest time. She always looked as though she found the kitchen a bit crowded with other women scurryin' around. I think that she would have enjoyed spending the day with SueAnn, but Mrs. Corbin was a rather busy, take-over sort of person.

I handed Auntie Lou the milk pail and headed back for the barn on the run. By now Mr. Wilkes was movin' the black-puffin' machine into the wheat field jest beyond the house. It would take him some time to make sure that everything was set and ready to go.

I rushed through the remainder of the early mornin' chores and managed to get out to the field in time for Mr. Wilkes' final pre-breakfast inspection. Boy, did I envy him. To be able to work with all those gears and pulleys and movin' parts must be something.

I stood watchin' the trembling sides of the big thresher, trembling a little myself. Later, when she really started to roll, she wouldn't jest tremble; she'd shake and heave.

Mr. Wilkes must have been satisfied, for he put the tractor on a low idle and turned to Grandpa and Uncle Charlie, indicating that he was ready for breakfast.

That mornin' I passed up the porridge and instead enjoyed bacon, eggs, fried potatoes, pancakes and bran muffins. Only at harvest time did we have all of those things on the self-same mornin'.

The man-talk flew all around me, and from a little further away came the higher pitched, soft voices of the womenfolk as they worked over the stove, flippin' pancakes and turnin' bacon.

Gramps seemed to catch the feelin' of things. I knew that he had never been a part of threshin' time before, and I felt that life had kinda cheated him. I wouldn't have traded harvest for—well—even for a circus. I guess harvest is a kind of circus all its own, with action and excitement and noise—even trained animals. When you watched a harvest team worm its way down the field between the grain stooks without any man ever touchin' a rein, then you knew that they were well trained. I sure was looking forward to all of the action.

Before breakfast ended, I heard the jingle of harness. Without even thinkin' to excuse myself, I ran to the window.

It was Mr. T. Smith and his team of bays. Those horses were thought to be the finest team that ever turned up at a threshin' site—at least Mr. T. thought so. He was continually tellin' the fact to everyone else on the crew, much to the annoyance of some of the other farmers.

"When they're told to stand, they stand," Mr. T. would say; "never move a hair or flick an eyelash. An' when they move down the field, they always keep thet perfect five-foot distance between the side of the rack and the stooks. Never an inch more or less. Gives a man jest the right space fer workin' without costin' him a bit of extra time or energy in throwin' bundles." Mr. T. spent every lunch break and every mealtime braggin' about his team.

I should have known that Mr. T. would be first in. He always was. He never refused an invitation to sit up to a table and have a little breakfast either; but as Mr. T. was a hardworkin' man and always earned his way at harvest time, no one minded stokin' his furnace before he left for the field.

By the time Mr. T. had finished his breakfast, tellin' of his bays between each mouthful, other wagons were arriving. Six teams came in, along with three extra men who would work as field pitchers, spike pitchers, and bundle clean-up men—no one wanted even a few bundles left layin' in the field for mouse feed.

Grandpa and Uncle Charlie would man the wagons to be filled with the new grain; turn by turn they'd unload it in the grain bins.

All totaled we had twelve men out there: Mr. Wilkes, six drivers, three extra pitchers, and Grandpa and Uncle Charlie.

The sun was up and shining brightly. Mr. Wilkes made a final turn around the rumbling machine and nodded his satisfaction. He gave Mr. T. the signal, and he and Burt Thomas and Barkley Shaw moved between a long line of stooks. They jest forked on enough bundles to make a decent test batch and returned to the machine. Mr. Wilkes pulled the lever that started the long belt flappin' faster and the threshin' machine began its dusty dance. Mr. T. drove the team of bays right alongside the carrier; sure enough, they never flickered an ear at all the snortin', sneezin', stompin', and rockin' of the threshin' rig. You'd have thought that they were standin' contentedly in their own stalls.

As soon as the machine was rattlin' to Mr. Wilke's satisfaction, he waved a hand at Mr. T., and bundles were fed rhythmically unto the conveyor. Up they slowly climbed and I imagined angry clickin' teeth gnashin' at them as they disappeared behind the canvas curtain.

I ran around to the other end. I wanted to be sure to be on hand when the first trickle of grain started leavin' the spout. It soon came and Grandpa and Uncle Charlie both grabbed for handfuls. They felt it, eyed it, and then each put a few kernels in their mouth. They chewed silently for a moment, watchin' each other's eyes for the message that would be reflected there. Finally Uncle Charlie nodded and Grandpa returned the nod. Mr. Wilkes, who had been feelin' and chewin' too, took the nods as his signal and went back to wave the wagons out.

Away they rolled, each man determined to prove his brawn by bein' the first one to fill his wagon.

On this trip Burt Thomas went with Mr. P. Smith; Mr. Smith had broken his leg many years before and walked with a bad limp because of a poor settin' of the broken bone.

Barkley Shaw went with Mr. Peterson, who really was gettin' a little too old for the threshin' crew. No one would have told him so though, him seemin' to look forward to harvest each fall. They usually put a younger man on with him—sort of off-hand and matter-a-fact—and old Mr. Peterson now seemed to jest expect it.

Joey Smith walked between two wagons, throwin' bundles on one or the other, depending on which wagon the stook was closest to. Later he would take a shift as spike-pitcher, feedin' the bundles into the thresher.

I looked around from all the action and noticed that Gramps was standin' there fascinated by it all, too. It was difficult to talk—the machine made too much noise; but we grinned at one another in the commotion and the excitement.

The first teams back began to throw the bundles onto the feeder, and we watched as they were gulped up by the hungry machine. I motioned for Gramps to come with me. I led him around to the grain wagon where Uncle Charlie sat watchin' the stream of grain fall from the spout. Occasionally he'd reach out with his shovel and scrape the peak off the grain that piled in the wagon box. Gramps watched, his blue eyes sparklin'. He reached a hand into the box and let several handfuls of the wheat trickle through his fingers. He seemed to like the feel of it. Uncle Charlie grinned and nodded—I knew what he meant; this year's crop was of good quality.

I nudged Gramps and pointed a finger at the spewin' straw. Gramps lifted his eyes from the wagon box. He stood watchin' the straw sail out in a big arc, twistin' and turnin' and catchin' the sunlight.

The teams moved back and forth in the field, the men steadily working along beside them; the big machine heaved and snorted, the grain fell in a steady stream and the straw blew, light and glitterin', in the clear mornin' air.

Gramps leaned close to me.

"Better than a circus!" he yelled in my ear.

I grinned. I had wanted to hear that.

Later in the mornin' the ladies came with the mornin' lunch. The machine was idled down to give it some coolin' time, too.

The men drank pails of cold water to cool them off, followed by hot coffee to heat them up again—never could make any sense out of that. They also wolfed down large amounts of sandwiches and cookies.

The break was used for other things, too. Mr. Wilkes poked around and around his machine again, Mr. T. took the opportunity to brag about the bays, Mr. P. Smith propped up his bad leg on a couple of bundles to give it a rest, and Mr. Peterson stretched right out on the ground. He passed up an extra cup of coffee for a couple of winks.

It was quite obvious how the younger fellas preferred spendin' the few extra minutes. They seemed to be playin' a little game of seein' who could git a bit of attention from Auntie Lou. I saw Grandpa and Uncle Charlie watchin' them. Gramps watched, too, only I caught him smilin' in a secret way as though he was maybe rememberin' again.

Joey Smith drank cup after cup of coffee poured by Auntie Lou's hands. I was told later that Joey didn't even care for coffee.

Barkley Shaw was jest a little over-noisy and energetic. I think Grandpa decided about then that it was time for Barkley's shift at the feeder as spike-pitcher.

Burt Thomas was more agreeable, but not too subtle, makin' comments on how good the cookies were and "did you make them yerself," and all that.

I got kinda fed up on the whole thing and went off to see if I could find a few mice to chase.

At dinnertime Gramps and I would be eatin' with the womenfolk after the dozen men had been fed. It was all that Auntie Lou could do to squeeze twelve full-grown men around our kitchen table, even with the extension on. When the time came for the noon meal, I didn't even go in with the menfolk. I sat on a choppin' block out at the woodpile and watched and listened as they sloshed water at the outside basins and jostled one another good-naturedly.

When they had gone in I still sat there. I'd already had my fill of Mr. T.'s bays and the sheep-eyes made by love-struck dummies. In a few minutes Gramps joined me.

"Kind of fun isn't it, Joshua?"

I caught the spirit again and we sat on our blocks and talked threshin'.

After the last of the men had left the house, we waited to let the women have enough time to clear the table of the dirty dishes and make it ready for us. While we waited we watched the men rehitchin' the horses that had also had their water and feed durin' the noon break. As the last team moved out, Auntie Lou called us to come in.

I was hungry in spite of all that I had eaten at morning lunch, and I enjoyed every mouthful of the huge spread. Gramps seemed to be enjoyin' it, too. His appetite had picked up considerably since he had joined us.

Several times during our meal SueAnn giggled. I wasn't used to hearin' a girl giggle like that. Auntie Lou never did. Either she laughed softly or she gave a full-throated chuckle—never did she giggle. I finally took time out from my eatin' to look at SueAnn. Her face was flushed and she appeared right excited about something. I guessed then that she had probably gotten a big kick out of servin' the meal to the men—especially the younger ones. She giggled again and I found it to my dislikin'. I looked over at Auntie Lou.

Her face was a bit flushed, too, and her eyes danced like they had taken and given some merry teasin'. It shook me up a mite. I tried to ask myself, "Why not?" but all I could get was, "Why?" Still, Auntie Lou was young and pretty; she could get the full attention of the young men, and I guess it was kinda natural that she might sort of enjoy it some. Even so, I was glad that she wasn't silly-actin' and giggly about it. I couldn't tolerate a gigglin' girl. At least Auntie Lou carried herself with some dignity.

I forked the last of my lemon pie into my mouth in a hurry to get away from SueAnn. I could hardly manage " 'Scuse me please," through the mouthful, but before anyone could protest I slipped from the table. There were chores that needed doing and wood that needed chopping before I'd be free to go to the field for a while again. I wanted to make the most of each moment.

The wood chopping seemed to take forever. I finished jest in time to walk out to the field with the two girls who were taking out the lunch. Auntie Lou collared me to carry a couple pails of water, or I would have run on ahead.

The men had been watchin' for the women to appear and didn't take long in gatherin' for the refreshments. The cool water was the most popular item at the outset, but when the men had quenched their thirst, they turned eagerly to the sandwiches, cake, and coffee.

Things were movin' along real well. Mr. T. was horse-braggin', Mr. P. was restin' his leg, and Mr. Wilkes was inspectin' his beloved machine, a sandwich in one hand and a coffee cup in the other. Auntie Lou was doin' the pouring duties. SueAnn was passing out the sandwiches and cake.

Barkley Shaw and Joe Smith sauntered up to the girls—again. There was something about the way they approached those girls that gave me the feelin' that something was abrewin'. I wasn't wrong. All of a sudden Barkley thrust his coffee cup at Joey yellin', "Hold this! hold this!" and he started jumpin' around in a circle, clutchin' and tearin' at his pant leg, hootin' and stompin' and carryin' on something awful.

"What's wrong? What's wrong?" yelled Joey, desperately tryin' to keep both full cups from spillin'. The two girls stood there, their eyes wide with wonder, or horror, I wasn't sure which.

"Got a mouse up my pant leg!" hollered Barkley and continued to dance around and slap at his denimed leg. At the word "mouse" SueAnn turned into a wild thing. She heaved the sandwiches that she had been holdin' and with a shriek of pure terror looked frantically for some place to crawl onto. The only thing at hand was Mr. P.'s two bundles under his leg. SueAnn jumped, up the full ten inches onto the sheaves, barely missin' Mr. P.'s poor achin' leg.

She continued to squeal and screech, swishin' her skirts and stompin' 'til she had nearly threshed out those two sheaves herself.

Barkley Shaw stopped his dance and began hootin' and laughin' at SueAnn. Joey set down the coffee cups, and they leaned against one another, slappin' their thighs and poundin' each other's back as they howled with laughter.

Auntie Lou smiled a tiny smile and went over to pour coffee for the older men; she completely ignored the two young bucks who were still cacklin' away about their smart-aleck joke.

Mr. Peterson reached out and reclaimed a sandwich from the stubble. He blew away a small piece of straw or two and began to eat as calmly as though he ate off the ground every day. Gramps retrieved the rest of the dropped sandwiches.

It took SueAnn several minutes to realize that it had all been a hoax; even then she was reluctant to come down from her spot on the bundles. Mr. P. mumbled and moved his leg elsewhere. Mr. Wilkes gave a nod that meant fun and games were over and it was time for everyone to get back to work. The expression on his face had not changed so much as a flicker through the entire episode.

Slowly everyone returned to his team, Joey and Barkley still holdin' their sides and the other young fellas givin' an occasional chuckle as well. They had enjoyed it tremendously.

The girls gathered the cups and pails together. SueAnn looked red and angry. She hadn't found any part of it the least bit amusin'. She was still sputterin' a little when she and Auntie Lou headed for the house.

The rest of the day seemed rather uneventful after that. The men came in dusty and hungry for the evening meal. They first watered and fed their tired horses and then came to wash.

The threshin' machine had to be moved to our other field for the next day's work, so Mr. Wilkes didn't come for supper until he'd done jest that.

Everyone was tired, so there wasn't much talk. Every now and then one of the young fellas would look at SueAnn and grin. She pretended to be terribly upset with Barkley, but I wondered if she wasn't jest a little pleased over all of the attention. She'd lift her chin a little higher and give Barkley a poisonous glare each time that she looked at him. This would jest make the boys laugh even harder. Anyway, I figured that her dark looks and flippin' skirts sure beat her gigglin'.

About the only older man that seemed rested enough to talk was Mr. T. Smith. He was busy takin' a survey to see who had noticed how his bays had performed. Not many men had, but that jest gave Mr. T. an excuse to inform them. Most of the men looked unimpressed, but no one bothered to stop him.

They had made good progress on the first day. It looked like the weather would hold good for the next day as well. That would finish our crop. Grandpa and Uncle Charlie didn't sow as much grain now as they used to. They sowed more greenfeed and hay and fed our cattle instead. Grandpa said that that's where the money was, and even though Uncle Charlie never argued and went right along with it, I always got the feelin' that he somehow didn't quite agree.

The next day's threshin' started out pretty much the same. The teams arrived, Mr. Wilkes started his machine, and things swung into motion again.

Later in the mornin' Cullum Lewis noticed me hangin' around and asked if I'd like to go for a load with him. Cullum Lewis was a big fella for his age, and he drove a team of his own. This was already his fourth year on a threshin' crew, so I guessed he probably knew all about it.

As he forked bundles, he let me chase mice to my heart's content. When he had the rack piled high, we crawled up and settled in on the load for the return trip to the machine. Cullum even let me hold the reins. We didn't talk much. He asked me one or two questions about Auntie Lou, like, did she have a regular beau and did I think she might like one? I answered "no" to both questions and Cullum dropped the matter. He was rather a likable guy in a way, and I couldn't help but think that if ever Auntie Lou should change her mind—and I s'posed that she might—then Cullum might not be such a bad choice. He'd sure be a heap better than either Jedd Rawleigh or Hiram Woxley.

During the dinner hour Mr. Wilkes had to move the machine again. He wouldn't even stop to eat. The men took their time about dinner, knowin' that Mr. Wilkes wouldn't be ready to go for a while.

At the table Joey Smith asked Barkley Shaw if he'd had any more trouble with mice—SueAnn refused to serve them tea. That didn't bother the boys any. I got the feelin' that they preferred Auntie Lou servin' them anyway. Mrs. Corbin didn't pay any attention to the goings on. She was a simple, no-nonsense person, and I don't suppose that she ever saw humor in anything. Gramps was takin' it all in though. I could see his mustache twitch every now and then, and I knew that he was hidin' a smile.

As the men left the house, Mr. T. was busy braggin' about the bays again.

"Most dependable horses I ever had," he was saying, "an' I've had me some good ones. Nothin' would spook thet pair—not the devil hisself."

I saw Barkley exchange a quick look with Burt Thomas.

The final field was the furthest from the house. When it came time for the afternoon coffee break, the girls rode out to the field with Uncle Charlie in the empty grain wagon. They would catch a ride home with Grandpa in a full one.

The menfolk were feelin' extra good because they knew that they were near the end. They would finish the field and thus our threshin', jest in time for supper.

The older men settled themselves here and there on the ground, enjoyin' the coffee and sandwiches. They discussed the year's crops—not jest on our land, but the neighbor's as well. Everyone knew that the grain was a good quality but the yield was down. We hadn't had as much rain as we should have had, and the wheat jest didn't produce like it usually did. Still, it was a fair crop and it was nearly all in the bin, so no one at our house was complainin'.

The young fellas teased and pushed as usual. Cullum Lewis was the quiet-est one of the lot. I watched him as his eyes followed Auntie Lou. Mentally, I fought for him and against him at the same time. Auntie Lou didn't seem to notice him at all—but then maybe she did. I don't know.

I noticed Barkley and Burt wander apart from the rest, and the next time I looked for them they were gone. I paid no mind to it and went back to my ginger cake.

Mr. T.'s team had been restin' in the shade of the trees at the edge of the field, heads down, quietly and patiently standin', even though they had no rein to tie them. The rack carried a full load—Mr. T. would be the next man up to the machine.

At the signal from Mr. Wilkes the men pulled themselves up from the ground and brushed the loose stubble from their pants. Mr. P. picked up his two bundles and tossed them up on his rack so that they wouldn't be missed. He wouldn't be needin' them anymore.

Mr. T. stepped up on the tongue of his wagon and grabbed hold of the rack without even reachin' for the reins, which he would pick up on his way into the machine if he felt that he needed them. He hollered "giddup" to the bays and began to climb leisurely up into the wagon. The team took about two steps and then things really busted loose. The right bay suddenly threw up his head and neighed loudly. Then he plunged forward, smacked into the yoke, and fell back against his startled mate. By this time Mr. T. was scramblin' up the wagon rack, grabbin' for reins and wonderin' wildly if he'd gotten the wrong team.

The bay wasn't finished yet. He began to kick and to buck, strikin' out one way and then the other. By this time he had the other horse convinced that something was seriously wrong and they both decided that they'd best make a run for it. Mr. T. was still scramblin' for his reins when the horses took off on a gallop.

Uncontrolled, they nearly smashed into the wagon of Mr. Corbin but veered at the last minute, comin' very near upsettin' Mr. T.'s whole wagon. Mr. T. was flailin' his way through bundles tryin' to get hold of the elusive reins. What a ride he had! I think that the team managed to hit every chuck hole and rock in the entire field. Bundles were flyin' out from the wagon on every swerve and bounce. Every man in the field watched the crazy runaway, many of them rushin' to take the reins of their own teams so that they wouldn't get the same notion.

It was Cullum Lewis who finally got things under control. The team was circlin' the field and Cullum watched his chance. When they came near, he made a flyin' leap and grabbed the bridle. Hangin' on for dear life, his feet scrapin' the ground and raisin' a cloud of dust, he pulled on that bridle for all he was worth. To our amazement, the horses came to a stop, heavin' and puffin'. He spent a number of minutes talkin' and strokin' and finally managed to get them quieted again. He calmly handed Mr. T. the limp reins, and still talkin' and pettin' the animals, carefully checked over the harness; he wanted to be sure that in all that buckin' and rearin' nothin' had been broken. A few pieces of harness needed some readjusting to get things back in their proper place. Cullum's hands travelled along each section.

By then I was right there watchin', not wantin' to miss any of the action. Mr. T. was still up on top of what was left of his load, tryin' hard to regain his composure and somehow rationalize in his thinkin' the strange behavior of his bays. He didn't see Cullum lift out a sharp burr from under the right bay's harness, examine it briefly, and then discard it—but I did. Cullum's eyes met mine and he nodded his head jest ever so slightly in the direction of Barkley Shaw. I nodded back. It was our solemn pact to make no mention of the offendin' burr.

"Seems to be okay, Mr. Smith," Cullum called up. "No harness broken, and they seem calm enough now."

Mr. T. jest nodded, his face not seemin' to know if it should be white or red.

He didn't even say thank you, but jest moved the team off, lookin' a bit uncertain at first as to what to expect of them. He had to retrace his trip around the field and pick up the scattered bundles.

I walked along with Cullum toward his waitin' team.

"Want a lift?" he asked.

I nodded.

We climbed up onto the load together and he handed me the reins. We both sat solemnly for a while, and then as if drawn by some outside force, we both turned to each other in the same instant. As soon as our eyes met, we couldn't control ourselves any longer. We laughed all of the way back to the threshin' machine.

CHAPTER 14

Patches

Monday morning my feet seemed to drag a little; at the same time something within me said "Hurry, hurry." It was the first day back at school. I hated goin' back. The thing that bothered me the most was leaving Gramps. I wasn't sure what he'd find to fill his day with me gone. Of course there was Auntie Lou. Her work would be slowing down now and she would have time for my great-grandfather.

I suppose there were other reasons why I hated to go back. One was the shoes. I had to wear them all day for school and after bein' turned loose all summer, my feet sure did hate to be all shut in. The mornings could be rather cool at times now, and I didn't suppose that I'd fuss much about shoes from now on anyway.

Then there was Auntie Lou. I still missed her when I was away from her, and I had the feeling that with harvest over, Grandpa and Uncle Charlie would take up the "man hunt" again. I didn't like leaving Auntie Lou unguarded.

I suppose the final reason was jest the simple fact that boys are supposed to hate school. School and fancy clothes, sissy games and girls, that's what boys my age didn't go for.

Still, on the other hand, I had to admit that I kinda liked school. It was fun to be with the other boys and play ball or tag or prisoner's base. I didn't have much to play with around the farm.

I would never have admitted it for the world, but I liked the teacher, too. Her name was Martha Peterson. She was the youngest of the Petersons' houseful of girls. She was tall for a woman, but slim as a sapling, and her voice had a soft liltin' sound. I loved to hear her read. During part of each school day she would read us a chapter from a book that she had chosen. We had gone through several books together, and I could never get enough of them.

The truth was I jest plain liked my studies. I know, a boy is supposed to shy away from book learnin'. I didn't. Books held so many interesting facts and figures that I found it awful hard to hide my enthusiasm. Arithmetic was my best subject. I always led the class with no trouble at all, but I also liked spellin' and geography and jest about everything we studied. Didn't care much for the music. Miss Peterson would trill up the scale and we were supposed to follow along behind her. We never could give a decent imitation and it embarrassed and discouraged me. All in all, even though I felt like a traitor to my sex, I liked school.

I think Gramps caught on. His eyes took on a twinkle as if he'd like to scrub up good, slick down his hair, and join me.

It was good to be back. There was a lot of shovin' and yellin' and slappin' one another on the back as we met in the school yard. The bell that I'd been waiting for finally rang and we all trooped noisily in. There was Miss Peterson, smilin' softly, lookin' prettier than ever. I had to keep starin' at my feet to stop the deep red from flushin' up into my face.

The day went quickly and before we knew it we were dismissed. I hated to leave, yet I could hardly wait to get home and tell Gramps and Auntie Lou about my day.

As soon as I got over the rise and out of sight of the school, I whipped off my shoes and stuffed my socks down in the toe of one. I tied the laces together and dangled the shoes over my shoulder jest in case I needed my hands free for throwin' rocks or anything. Then I hitched up my pant legs a couple of rolls to keep them from draggin' in the dust, and set out for home. I ran most of the way. When I finally got in the door I was puffin' so hard that I had to sit down and catch my breath before I could speak. Auntie Lou laughed at my excitement and brought me a big glass of cool milk and some cookies fresh from the oven. Gramps had some too, and finally I was ready to tell about all of my adventures of that first day back at school.

When I had finished eating and talking, I went to change into my chorin'
overalls before going out to slop the pigs. Gramps was waiting for me when
I came down and we went out together.

"Joshua," he said as we walked along, "I understand that Lou has an
eighteenth birthday coming up."

I hadn't thought about it, but now that I did I realized that it was true.

"Yeah—I guess so."

"Anything that you can think of to help make it 'special'?"

I thought for a minute. "She likes parties—but she don't get to go to
very many," I finally said.

Gramps thought on it.

"I hardly see how three old men and one young one could come up
with much of a party."

"Maybe SueAnn and Nellie Halliday or some of the other girls could
help us."

Gramps chewed on his mustache as he thought about that.

"Maybe. Maybe something could be arranged. How could one get in
touch with these girls?"

"You could write a note and I'd take it to school and give it to Willie to
take home to SueAnn."

"That's good thinking, Joshua."

I beamed at the compliment from Gramps. He abruptly changed the
subject.

"Now then we'd best get those chores done."

We finished up the chores. We were even a little ahead of time. The
men weren't in from stacking greenfeed yet and supper was not quite ready
when I dropped my last load of chopped wood into the wood box. Gramps
deposited his load, too, and we stood there brushin' our clothes a bit to get
rid of wood chips, grass, and bark.

"Got something to show you, Joshua. Come with me."

Gramps led the way to the small shed that stood in the yard. It held
our rakes, hoes, wheelbarrow, and such like, so I wasn't sure that I was that
much interested in seein' anything in there, but I followed. Maybe Gramps
had found a mouse nest or something.

Gramps opened the door; as he did so a funny bit of black and white
fur came flyin' at my feet. I jumped like lightnin' had jest warmed my boots,

and stepped back a pace. Gramps was chucklin' and scoopin' up the wiggly thing, tryin' to get it under control.

"Didn't expect such an overwhelming welcome," he laughed.

I took a better look then and my breath caught in my throat. It was a pup! I reached my hands out for it, my head full of questions.

"Where'd he come from?"

"From some people in town."

"When?"

"Well, I found him awhile back, but they didn't want me to pick him up until today."

"You were in town today?"

"That's right."

"How?"

"Partly walked, partly hitched a ride."

I blinked in wonder. Gramps had walked and hitched a ride to town! He must have wanted to get there awfully bad.

"Why didn't you ask Grandpa or Uncle Charlie if you needed to get to town that bad?"

"Didn't need to—just wanted to—to pick this fellow up. They didn't get him weaned until last week."

I jerked my attention back to the pup.

"Is he yours?"

Gramps smiled real wide.

"No, Joshua—he's yours."

"Mine?"

My mind couldn't comprehend it, but my arms were already claimin' possession. I pushed my face down against the ball of fur, and had my face licked as a thank you for noticin' him. I laughed and got licked again. I put him down on the ground to get a better look at him. It was hard to do because he wouldn't hold still.

He was still plump with baby fat but looked like he would soon leave that behind and begin to really grow. His hair was mostly black and sort of curly. There were a few white spots here and there and that gave him a comical appearance.

He never was still for a moment, and I could see that he was going to be an awful lot of fun. I scooped him up into my arms again and started lovin' and pettin'.

"My dog! My very own dog!" I kept sayin' over and over to myself, hardly able to believe my good fortune.

Gramps stood by—jest smilin'.

"Hey," I said, "I didn't say 'thanks.' "

"I think you did, Joshua."

"He's beautiful, Gramps, really beautiful. I'm gonna train him to do tricks—sit up, and beg, and play dead, and roll over—and everything!"

"What are you going to call him?"

I thought for a few minutes as I looked at *my* dog. Every name that I ever heard a dog called began to pour through my mind; I rejected each one until I came to Patches. Patches seemed to fit.

"Patches," I said.

"Patches," repeated Gramps. "I think that Patches is a very fitting name."

Gramps chose himself a wood block and turned it up to sit on, so that he could sit and watch me and my dog. I rolled on the grass, he growlin' in a little dog voice and chasin' my pant leg, my sleeve, or even the top of my hair, nippin' and tusslin' and rollin' with me.

We were still playin' our crazy games when Grandpa and Uncle Charlie came home. I hadn't paid much attention until I was somehow aware that I was being looked at. There stood Grandpa and Uncle Charlie both starin' at me and the dog with puzzled looks on their faces. For one terrifyin' minute I was afraid that they wouldn't let me keep him—my arms automatically tightened on him.

"Where'd—" started Grandpa.

Gramps stood up from the wood block he'd been restin' on; it toppled over as though to take its rightful place back in the pile.

"Got him in town. *Every* boy needs a dog," said Gramps. His keen blue eyes held Grandpa's.

"Reckon so. Shoulda thought myself to get him one—sooner." Grandpa nodded. "Let's see 'im, Boy."

I brought Patches over and introduced him to Grandpa and Uncle Charlie. Grandpa rubbed his head a bit and tugged gently on his ear.

"Looks bright enough."

Then it was Uncle Charlie's turn. He patted the puppy and stroked him under the chin.

"Bet yer gonna be one small piece of nuisance," he said, "but yer bound to liven things up 'round here." His voice held teasin'.

Auntie Lou came out then and I suddenly realized that I had been so preoccupied I hadn't even shown her Patches yet.

"Look!" I cried. "Look what Gramps brought me!"

She smiled and stepped forward to rub the puppy's soft fur with the back of her finger.

"Now, who do you s'pose has been fillin' his tummy with warm milk and holdin' him when he got lonesome for most of the afternoon? But now it's suppertime. How 'bout if you put him back in the shed and come and get washed up."

I did, though it was awfully hard to do.

After supper I took some meat scraps and a saucer of milk to Patches. I begged an old jacket off Uncle Charlie and fixed Patches a comfortable bed in a box low enough for him to come and go as he wanted.

I was called for bed way too soon. It was already 9:00. Reluctantly I left Patches and went in to bed, promisin' him that I'd be down first thing in the mornin'. I went to bed, my mind boggled with plans for my dog—the doghouse that I'd build, the collar that I'd make him, the tricks that I'd teach him. There was a whole new world waitin' for me now—and all because of Gramps.

I hadn't been talkin' much to God lately. Auntie Lou would have been shocked and hurt had she known.

I was a little hesitant now about prayin' after ignorin' Him for so long, but I finally put aside my pride, crawled out of bed, and got down on my knees.

"Dear God, I wanna say thank you for a few things. I know sometimes I don't think you're doin' much special-like for me, but I do wanna thank you for bringin' Gramps here—even iffen I didn't want him at first. I really love him now, God. And thank you for Patches, too. Help me to make him a good dog so that he won't be *too* much of a nuisance. Amen."

I climbed back into bed and pulled the quilt up to my chin. I went to sleep with my mind full of pictures of me and my dog.

CHAPTER 15

Hurtin'

The next mornin' I was nearly torn in two with desire. I wanted to get to school as fast as I could to tell all of the boys about my new dog. At the same time I didn't want to leave him. If only I could have gathered him up and taken him to school with me—but even I understood that that was out of the question.

I finally tore myself away from him at the last possible minute, promising that I'd be home again jest as quickly as I could. I asked Gramps if he'd let Patches out of the shed as soon as I'd gone and he couldn't follow, so that he could get acquainted with the farm and not be locked up and bored all day.

I got to school, puffin' and pantin' because I had run so hard; before the bell rang I was only able to blurt out that I had a new dog. The boys were full of questions and I answered as many as I could while we hurried to line up for salutin' the flag and prayin' the Lord's Prayer. Avery and Willie promised to come over to see Patches the first chance that they got.

At recess and noon break we talked about my dog. I described him over and over, and some of the boys got almost as excited as I was. The news even got to the girls, and Sarah Smith and Mary Turley worked up enough nerve to come over to the boys' side to question me about him. I really felt important.

Miss Peterson had scarcely said "Class dismissed" when I was gone. I had so much to do. I didn't know whether to start on the collar and lead rope first, or work on the doghouse. Patches needed both.

I was callin' him as I ran down the lane, but I didn't notice him around anywhere.

Auntie Lou came out.

"Josh, come in the house a minute—will you?"

"Sure," I called back. "Soon's I find Patches."

"Right *now*, Josh."

I went. Maybe they had Patches with them.

A glass of milk and a piece of cake sat at my place at the table. Gramps sat there, too, but he wasn't havin' anything. Auntie Lou looked rather pale and her eyes looked suspiciously like she'd been cryin'. My mind jumped to Grandpa and Uncle Charlie, and I felt a scare hit me smack in my stomach.

"Sit down, Josh."

I sat. I jest sat like a lump and stared first at Auntie Lou and then at Gramps.

Auntie Lou swallowed hard and she bit her lip to fight back tears. Finally she was able to talk, in a soft quivery voice.

"A bad thing happened today, Josh."

I knew that much. I could tell by jest lookin'.

"Your puppy was killed."

I fought it. I fought it with all my strength. It couldn't be true, it jest couldn't. But a look at Gramps' white face and a quick glance at Auntie Lou, who was liftin' a damp handkerchief to her eyes, told me that I had to believe it.

I didn't wait to even say anything. I jest jumped up from the table, spillin' my milk, and ran for the door.

"Josh!" I heard Auntie Lou's voice.

"Let him go," said Gramps softly. His voice sounded old and tired.

I ran all the way to the crik. I wished that I could jest throw myself right into the cold water and let it wash all the feelin' from me. I threw myself on the grassy bank instead. Boys weren't supposed to cry—but I cried. I cried until my eyes ran dry, and then I jest laid and groaned.

It was gettin' dark when I finally lifted myself from the bank. It was gettin' cold, too. I hadn't noticed before, but now I realized that I was shiverin'. I knelt down by the stream and sloshed cold water over my face again and again. It nearly froze me but it sharpened things back into focus, too. Here it was dark and I hadn't done one bit of my chores. Grandpa and Uncle Charlie would be in from stackin' the greenfeed and I wouldn't have my work done. I started home at a trot.

As my mind began to clear, I found myself wonderin' how it had happened. What had gone wrong? The pup I had wanted for so long had been mine for such a short time—hardly long enough to even get the feel that he *was* mine.

When I got to the house, I found that Gramps had done all of my chores. It had taken him longer than it took me. It was a big and difficult job for an old man like Gramps. Auntie Lou had milked Bossie and helped to split the wood. It made me feel shame—but a great deal of love and gratitude, too. I wanted to start cryin' all over again, but I held myself in check.

Uncle Charlie and Grandpa had returned and supper had been served. Auntie Lou had a plateful of food saved for me in the warmin' oven. I tried to eat it but it was tough to get it past the lump in my throat.

For the first time in my life I didn't wait for Grandpa to say, "Bedtime, Boy"; I went up on my own, glad to get to my room and shut the door.

I wouldn't cry anymore. I was through with that now. I laid there quietly and let anger and disappointment seep from every pore. Why? Why? Why?

Gramps came up. He opened my door softly and hesitated at my door. "Joshua?"

I couldn't say "go away"—not to Gramps.

"Yeah."

"Do you mind?"

"It's okay."

He came forward and sat on my bed. He sat there quietly for a while and then reached out an old hand that was soft, not calloused and rough from work like Grandpa's or Uncle Charlie's, though I knew that for most of his life it had been. He touched my arm.

"I know how you hurt, Joshua."

I didn't even think, "No you don't, no you don't." Somehow I knew that he did.

"It's not easy to lose someone you love."

I gulped. If he wasn't careful I'd be cryin' again.

"I thought that you might like to know what happened."

I waited. I did want to know and I didn't.

"Patches was a busy little dog—and a smart one. But I guess he just figured that he knew a little more than he really did."

I waited.

"The range cattle were pasturing just across the fence from the garden, and I guess Patches decided that he'd be a cattle dog. Anyway, Lou and I heard the ruckus, but by the time that we got there he'd been kicked. We tried to save him but—"

He stopped there. In my mind I could see Auntie Lou with tears runnin' down her face, and my grey-haired Gramps workin' over the broken body of my little dog. Tears came again and I swallowed them away.

Gramps patted me gently, got up and moved toward the door. I was glad that he hadn't expected me to talk. I couldn't talk now.

I laid there thinkin' about my little dog, and then a lot of other bitter thoughts started comin' to me, too. I used them like a blanket, wrappin' myself up in them and findin' a queer kind of satisfaction in the thought that I had suffered more than anyone else in the world. Bitterness filled me until I could hold no more. I sniffed.

My door opened again. Auntie Lou slipped in.

"Don't cry, Josh," she pleaded, soundin' like she needed the admonition more than I did.

"I ain't cryin.'"

Now Auntie Lou could hear a sniff behind a three-foot solid rock wall, but she didn't argue with me; she jest sat beside me much as Gramps had done.

"I'm sorry, Josh—so sorry."

I knew that she was.

"There was jest no way that we could have stopped it."

"God could've."

There, it was out now—in two angry, accusin' words.

Auntie Lou sorta caught her breath, but I didn't wait for her to say anything.

"I even prayed last night, and I thanked Him for Gramps and I thanked Him for Patches, and then without even waitin' He lets my dog die. He could have stopped it! He could have! He doesn't care, that's what. He jest hurts and hurts, and iffen He thinks that I'm gonna love Him—I'm not—I won't."

I was sobbin' now and Auntie Lou sat quietly as though my words had completely stunned her.

I flipped over on my stomach.

"He doesn't even leave me memories," I almost shouted. "He takes everything."

Auntie Lou let me cry until I had completely drained myself of tears. When I finally lay quietly she took my hand and stroked it gently, feelin' each of my fingers separately.

"Josh?"

I managed to say, "Yeah."

"What did you mean about memories—about not havin' any?"

I swallowed once or twice.

"It was the same with my ma and pa," I muttered. "God took 'em, too, before I could have any memories. Grandpa has memories. Lots of them. He told me all about Grandma and Great-grandma, too. And Gramps told me all about the good years when Great-grandma was still with him. Uncle Charlie remembers, too, but *I* don't remember *nothin'—not one thing.*"

I started to whimper again.

"Josh."

"What?"

"Josh, I don't remember *my* ma either, but I have *lots* of memories."

I looked at her in the pale light, wonderin' if she'd lost her senses.

"My mama died before I was old enough to remember her. I know that she loved me—I jest feel it; but I don't remember one thing about her, not one."

"Then how—"

"My memories are different, but they're jest as real and jest as filled with love.

"I remember Pa's face above my crib, his eyes laughin' as he played with me. I remember Uncle Charlie givin' me a ride on his foot and sayin', 'This is the way the lady rides.' I remember Pa rockin' me and holdin' me before he tucked me into bed at night. I remember him leanin' over me, his hand on my cheek, a worried look in his eyes when I had the measles, and I remember them both stayin' beside my bed all night long one winter when I had the croup. They took turns for four days—day and night.

"Josh, I remember a tiny baby that was brought home wrapped in blankets, and when I asked Pa why, he swallowed away tears and said that the
baby was mine to care for now. He needed me. I remember dressin' him and
feedin' him and playin' with him—and lovin' him."

There was a pause while Auntie Lou struggled for control.

"I have lots of memories, Josh—lots of *good* memories."

It was little more than a whisper.

As I listened to Auntie Lou talk, I realized that I had some memories,
too. I'd jest been lookin' in the wrong place for them. Like families, memories
didn't come in only one kind of package.

I was fightin' an inward battle now. I was still angry and wantin' to
strike back.

"He still didn't need to take my dog."

"Josh, God *didn't* take your dog. It was jest—jest one of those things
that happens, that's all."

"But He coulda *stopped* it."

Auntie Lou hesitated a moment as she carefully thought through her
next words.

"Yes, He could have. He could let us go through all of our life, bundlin'
us and shelterin' us from anything and everything that would hurt us. I could
do that with my petunias, Josh. I could build a box around them and keep
them from the wind and the rain, the crawlers and the bees. What would
happen iffen I did that, Josh?"

I jest shrugged. The answer was too obvious.

"They'd never bear flowers," said Auntie Lou.

"Josh, I don't understand all about God, but there's one thing that I'm as
sure of as the fact that I live and breathe. He loves us. He loves us completely,
and always keeps our good in mind.

"I don't know how losin' your pup is for your good, Josh, but I *am* sure
that it can be or God wouldn't have let it happen. It's all up to you, Josh.
Whenever something comes into our life that hurts us, we do the decidin'—
do I let this work for my good, as God intended, or do I let bitterness grow
like a bothersome canker sore in my soul?

"We love you, Josh—every one of us. We don't want to see you hurt.
It's happened now. We can't change it, but don't give the hurt a chance to
grow even bigger and destroy you. God *loves* you. He can help you with

the hurt if you ask Him to; accept that even *this* can be for your good. Try, Josh. Please try."

Auntie Lou bent down and kissed me. Her cheeks were wet as they touched mine. She left the room.

I laid there thinkin' of all that she'd said. I decided that one day soon, maybe down by the crik, I'd work on some memories and see jest what I could come up with. Even as I laid there I saw a blue-eyed, laughin' pixie face bendin' over me, cooin' love words—my Auntie Lou. I pushed it aside. I didn't want to get love feelin's all mixed in with my bitter ones. The one might somehow destroy the other.

Auntie Lou loved me, of that I had no question. So did Gramps, and even, I was willin' to admit, Grandpa and Uncle Charlie. But God? Somehow that jest didn't add up.

If He did love me He sure chose some strange ways of showin' it. I knew that Auntie Lou wouldn't want me to hate God. I was even a little afraid of the consequences myself. No, I decided, I wouldn't hate Him—but I couldn't love Him either. I'd jest feel nothin'—nothin' at all. I wouldn't even think about Him. I'd jest ignore Him completely. That would give Him something to think about. Maybe He'd even feel sorry.

CHAPTER 16

Love in Action

I dreaded having to go back to school. I'd have to tell all the kids about my pup. I hated it. If ever I'd been tempted to play hooky, that was the day. I considered takin' my lunch pail and jest headin' for the crik, but I realized that I would then be cornered into tellin' lies to Auntie Lou; I jest couldn't stand the thought of that. I dragged to school, faced my friends with the facts, and dragged home again.

When I entered the kitchen, Auntie Lou was fussin' over Gramps.

"Please," she was saying, "drink up your tea. You look all done in."

My eyes turned to Gramps. He did look awfully tired. I hoped that he wasn't gettin' sick or something.

I said between clenched teeth, "If *you* take him, too . . ." My hands were at my sides tightenin' into fists.

Gramps smiled at me, rather weakly, but he showed spunk.

"Howdy, Joshua."

"Howdy."

I slipped into my chair jest as Auntie Lou set my juice down.

"Hurry with your juice, Josh. Gramps has something to show you."

After my juice was gulped down, Gramps led me to the shed again. Inside was a carefully made little box. The lid was already down. I guessed that Gramps thought it best that I not see Patches' trampled body. There was a marker there, too. It was a long sharp-pointed stick with another stick across the top of it on which were painted the words, "Patches—Joshua's first dog."

"I thought that maybe *you'd* like to—"

"Where?" I asked as I swallowed hard and nodded.

I led the way, carryin' the box. Gramps followed with a shovel. There was a bit of soft soil under the big maple tree at the end of Auntie Lou's garden. When I reached the tree I put the box down and took the shovel from Gramps.

We said nothin' until the box was lowered and covered and the marker pounded in the ground. "Patches—Joshua's first dog." I wondered at Gramps' choice of words. Auntie Lou came and put a little bouquet of late fall flowers on the tiny grave.

"In the spring," she said, "we'll plant a violet."

I looked at the two of them.

"Thanks," I said, and picked up the shovel and started off to get ready for chores.

"Joshua," called Gramps. "There's just one more thing."

Surely he wasn't askin' me to pray over that dead dog. I stopped.

"In the house," prompted Gramps.

I walked obediently into the kitchen and jest stood waitin'.

Gramps shuffled past me. He did seem tired. I'd never seen him walk like that before—without a spring to his step.

In a minute he was back from his room with something concealed beneath his sweater. When he reached in, there was a bit of motion to the lump and then a soft nose peeked out, followed by two bright, almost black eyes.

"I know that she isn't Patches," said Gramps, untanglin' her feet from his sweater, "but she could be a lot of fun."

He handed her to me. She was so little. Only a baby, really. Her hair was soft brown curls, her little ears drooped over her fine shaped head and her tail was curled and fluffy.

"She's pretty young to leave her mother," said Gramps, "so we'll have to be extra careful with her. She's going to be awfully lonesome for a while, Joshua. She'll need lots of love."

I jest held her, marvellin' that a puppy could be so tiny and so perfect. Her little tongue licked against my hand. She knew that much already.

"She'll never be a cattle dog," continued Gramps, "never be big enough for that. She won't be very big at all. I couldn't find—"

"She's fine," I cut in. I got the impression that Gramps was apologizin' about the puppy. "She's beautiful. Jest look—jest look at her face. Bet she'll learn tricks fast. Bet she might even learn how to walk on her hind legs and dance."

That *something* that had seemed dead within me was stirrin' to life again. I felt excitement creepin' through me.

I heard a sigh of relief escape Auntie Lou, and Gramps' face looked less tired.

I hugged the puppy again. She was small enough that I could hold her firmly in my two hands.

"What you gonna call her?" asked Auntie Lou.

"I don't know. I'll have to think on it while I'm chorin'. Boy—I gotta get chorin', too!"

I pulled myself away from fondlin' my puppy.

"Gramps, would you mind sorta watchin' her while I do the chores?"

Gramps grinned.

"She does look a little sleepy, doesn't she? Maybe I'll just take her in on my bed so that she can catch a little nap."

I handed the puppy to Gramps and watched as he walked to his room, talkin' softly to her.

"Thanks, Josh," whispered Auntie Lou. "He is so tired—I've been worried. I was afraid that if he went chorin' with you tonight, it would be jest too much for him."

"Is he sick?" I asked anxiously.

"No, jest tired." Auntie Lou shook her head.

"As soon as you left for school this mornin' Josh, Gramps left for town to find you another pup. I don't know how far he walked before gettin' a ride. When he got to town he walked the streets lookin' for a dog with pups. This was the only litter he found and they were really too young to wean, but Mrs. Sankey, the owner, finally let Gramps take his pick from the lot. He tried 'em, one by one, to see if he could find one that would drink from a saucer. This was the smallest one of the bunch, but she caught on quickly 'bout how to lap up milk. Gramps walked home carryin' her. She's pretty special, Josh."

I nodded. She was special all right. Seemed like she should be called "Miracle" or "Love-gift" or something like that.

I sneaked to Gramps' door. I wanted to tell him thank-you if I could get it past the lump in my throat.

He was already sleepin'—snorin' softly. The puppy was cuddled up in his arms against his chest. I swallowed again. I'd have to tell him later, and it was sure gonna be hard to put my feelings into fittin' words.

CHAPTER 17

Pixie

I called the puppy Pixie. The name suited her. She was a tiny, playful, and mischievous bit of fur, and we all took to her right away. I didn't bother to build her a doghouse. Everyone liked her so much that it was jest an accepted fact that a little mite like her couldn't sleep out of doors. Maybe it was because Grandpa and Uncle Charlie had a soft spot for raisin' babies. At any rate we fixed a box for Pixie near the kitchen stove where she could snuggle down in Gramps' old gray sweater during the day.

At night I took her up to bed with me and no one protested. I wasn't sure if it was for my comfortin' or that of the dog's, that they let me get away with it—but they did.

She was smart all right and from the start she entertained us. My whole world about turned around her, and I had to really take myself in hand to get my thoughts on other things.

Gramps reminded me again of Auntie Lou's comin' birthday, and together one night we composed a letter for SueAnn. I carefully tucked it into my pocket; I'd deliver it to Willie the next day.

SueAnn wasn't long in replying. She and some of the other girls would be more than happy to help with a party. She suggested a corn roast and said that the girls would be glad to care for the lunch. If Gramps could see that there was wood for the fire, they'd do the rest.

Gramps was pleased with the letter. He sat down right away and wrote to her again, confirming the plans and setting the date. He pulled a bill from a small box in his dresser drawer and tucked it in with the letter; the money would help the girls with their expenses for the refreshments. I took that letter to Willie, too, and he took it home to SueAnn.

Uncle Charlie and Grandpa finished the stackin' of the greenfeed and the good fall weather still held.

I had only a few chores that were my responsibility now. Uncle Charlie took over most of them again, and Auntie Lou took back the carin' for her chickens.

The last vegetables of the garden were dug and were carefully stored in the root cellar. Odd jobs for the final preparations for winter were finished. It about got to the place that it wouldn't have mattered none if a storm had decided to strike—even though we'd take all of the fair weather that we could get—but none did.

The only thing that we really were concerned about was Auntie Lou's coming party. If we could jest hold onto the good weather until after that, then we'd take whatever the season decided to send our way.

We men managed to find some talkin' time as we finished up the chores one night. Gramps had clued in Grandpa and Uncle Charlie about the plans for the party before we had written SueAnn. They were pleased about it and anxious to be a part of the action.

The party was set for a Saturday night—Lou's birthday. We decided to work in a trip to town as early as we could get away Saturday mornin'. Then we could give Auntie Lou her gifts and have our own little celebration at supper—and maybe throw her off the scent.

I gathered the coins that I had managed to collect. They didn't make much of a pile. I finally got up the nerve to ask Gramps if he'd mind if I threw in the two dimes, seein' that we wouldn't be doin' anymore fishin' before winter, anyway. He said that that would be fine and I felt a little better.

When we got to the store, we did an awful lot of lookin' before we made up our minds.

Uncle Charlie finally settled on a shawl. It was a lacy-lookin' thing. Didn't look much for warmth but it sure was pretty.

Grandpa chose a new dress. It was cream colored with pink ribbons here and there and lots of lace for trimmin'. I could jest imagine what Auntie Lou would look like in it.

I found a lace handkerchief that really drew my eye, but when I counted my money, I didn't have enough. I kept on lookin'. I never did spot anything else as pretty as the handkerchief, and I was still lookin' when the rest were ready to go.

Uncle Charlie saw me eyein' the hanky, and I guess he figured out real quick what the problem was. I felt him slip some coins into my pocket. With mine, it paid for the handkerchief and left a nickel over. I studied the candy as Mrs. Kirk wrapped up the handkerchief, but then I turned away from it, determined to give Uncle Charlie back his nickel.

We met Gramps outside at the wagon. He'd been down the street to another store and made his purchase there. On the way home he showed it to me.

"It sure is pretty all right," I agreed. "What's it for?"

"It's a box to keep jewelry in."

I didn't know whether to tell him or jest let it pass. Finally I said it.

"Looks like a first-rate jew'ry box, Gramps, but there's only one problem."

Gramps looked up at me funny-like.

"She don't got none," I whispered.

Gramps jest shook his head and smiled.

"But she *will* have," he said. "She will have."

Maybe that *was* the smart way to go, I decided. You get the box first and *then* you get the jew'ry.

We could hardly wait to finish the chores. Even Pixie took second place to Auntie Lou's birthday.

Lou knew that she was expected to have a cake ready for herself. She had been bakin' the birthday cakes in this house ever since she was big enough to use the oven. She had her cake ready and sittin' in the middle of the table. We all grinned at it and could hardly wait to get the meal over with.

We gave Auntie Lou our gifts jest before she cut the cake. They let me be first. I presented her with the handkerchief.

"Oh, Josh," she cried, "it's jest beautiful! Where'd you ever get enough money to buy such a pretty one?"

I looked at Uncle Charlie. He stared at me blankly like he didn't know a thing about it. Auntie Lou gave me a warm hug.

She opened Uncle Charlie's shawl next and that really set her eyes to sparklin'. Uncle Charlie got a hug, too, which he seemed mighty pleased about.

Grandpa handed Lou his gift. She lifted the beautiful cream and pink dress from the box and shook out the folds.

"Oh, Pa, it's beautiful. Really beautiful. I know that I don't really need it, but—but I'm glad that you bought it. It's so pretty."

That was Lou. None of this I-wish-you-hadn't-done-it stuff. She said jest what she really felt.

"I'll feel so dressed up—so special. I hope that something important happens real soon to give me a chance to wear it all."

"Go put it on," coaxed Gramps.

"Should I?" Lou's cheeks were flushed.

We all urged her to try on the finery. We were all anxious to see jest how good our purchases could look.

Lou laughed and gathered up her gifts. She was soon back whirlin' her skirts and laughin' as she pranced around the kitchen.

The dress fit her perfectly. The cream color enhanced the creaminess of her skin and the pink bows seemed about to match her cheeks.

She draped the shawl about her shoulders, waved her lace handkerchief and pretended to flirt. We all laughed.

We were enjoyin' it so that at first I didn't notice Gramps stand up. He cleared his throat and then stepped forward.

"I have something for you, too, Louisa."

Lou stopped flutterin'. Gramps handed her his package. Lou opened it carefully and gave a little gasp when she saw the embossed box.

"A jewelry box!"

I was relieved that she hadn't had to ask what the thing was.

"It's lovely, Gramps."

"Open it, Louisa."

She did, and there on the soft velvet lay the most beautiful locket that I had ever seen. It hadn't been there before when Gramps had showed me the box, I was sure of that.

Auntie Lou's big blue eyes got even bigger. She couldn't even speak. She looked down at the locket, then she gently lifted it out and let it lay in her hand.

"It was your grandmother's," Gramps said in a hushed voice. "It can be worn only by the world's most beautiful and sweetest women—your grandmother and you."

Gramps moved forward and took the locket from Auntie Lou. He stepped behind her and fastened the chain around her slim neck. Then he kissed her on the cheek.

"Happy eighteenth, Louisa."

Lou was cryin' by then, and she made the rounds again, kissin' and huggin' each one of "her men."

We probably would have kept right on laughin' and lovin' all night if Uncle Charlie hadn't suddenly noticed the clock. He drew our attention to it with a nod of his head.

Grandpa suggested the cake then. Lou made her wish and blew out the candles. Then she served us each a generous piece. She ate a small piece herself and then ran laughin' to change back into her workin' clothes.

I shared my piece with Pixie. I didn't dare give her too much for fear that it would upset her little tummy. She loved it. She licked her chops with her tiny pink tongue and then licked off my fingers to make sure that she got everything that was available to her.

We all sat talkin', the men drinkin' coffee and me washin' down my cake with milk. It had been a pretty good birthday party. We couldn't see how the next half of it could be any better. Still, we were pleased that it was still to come.

Out of the blue Grandpa sorta spoiled it for me. He turned to Uncle Charlie.

"Burt Thomas will be comin'?"

Uncle Charlie jest nodded.

So that was the next name on the list. I gathered up Pixie and started outside thinkin', *Why spoil everything? We have Auntie Lou; she's happy here. Didn't you see her laughin'? Why spoil it?*

CHAPTER 18

The Corn Roast

It was almost eight o'clock before the teams started pourin' in. Auntie Lou looked out of the window wonderin' what in the world was goin' on. It took her awhile to realize that it might have something to do with her.

I figured that everybody in the whole countryside, between the ages of seventeen and thirty, must be pullin' into our yard. There were even a few that I couldn't put a name to.

SueAnn Corbin and Rachael Morgan came in laughin' to drag Auntie Lou out. She begged time to change her dress first and it was granted. I wondered about the new cream birthday dress, but Auntie Lou had more sense than to put that on. She dressed instead in a wide-skirted cotton print with white collar and cuffs. She looked great, but then she always did.

While the girls were gettin' things set up on an outside table that Grandpa had put there for their use, the boys took care of the teams. Our barnyard was full of feedin' horses, unhitched from their wagons and tethered to the rail fences.

It was noisy out in the yard. It seemed to me that no one really talked. The boys all yelled and the girls jest giggled.

After things sorta settled down, SueAnn started some outdoor games. I found a spot beside the honeysuckle bush where I could watch the goings-on without bein' in anyone's way. I sat there, cuddlin' Pixie and wonderin' what it would be like to be part of the action. Everytime a girl squealed or giggled real loudly, I was glad that I had no part of it. The fellas didn't seem to mind though; in fact, I kind of got the idea that they deliberately did things that would make the girls squeal even louder.

The first game was one in which you needed partners. Auntie Lou was paired up with "Toad" Hopkins. He looked awfully pleased with himself. The game was a funny kind of a relay in which Lou and Toad almost won, but Burt Thomas and Nellie Halliday managed to beat them.

Several other games were played. It seemed to me that each one got a little louder and a little faster. Anyway, they sure seemed to be havin' a good time.

I noticed Cullum Lewis. He wasn't as rowdy as some of them, but he did look to be enjoyin' himself. Poor Cullum. I didn't suppose that he got to have a good time very often. His pa had been sick most of the time when Cullum was growin' up. There were seven kids in the family and five of them were girls. Cullum was the only boy for most of the time, and then the final baby turned out to be a boy, too. He was still only about four and spoiled rotten.

Cullum had to take over the farm when he was jest a kid, quittin' school early. At first the farm didn't do much; anyway, everything that Cullum was able to scrape together had to go to pay off his pa's debts. I didn't s'pose he was totally clear of the debts yet, but as hard as he worked, I hoped that the day would soon come when he would be. He still had his ma, five sisters, and a kid brother to care for. With all of that restin' on his young shoulders, no wonder he was more serious than the other young bucks his age. Now as I watched him, he joined in the games with the others but not with the same silliness. One thing I did notice though—he sure kept close track of Auntie Lou. His eyes followed her wherever she went with kind of a haunted, hungry look.

My teacher, Miss Martha Peterson, was at the party, too. Funny, I hadn't thought of her as a young person before, but I guess she was only three or four years older than Auntie Lou. Some folks said that Barkley Shaw was sweet on her, but from what I saw, Barkley Shaw was sweet on anything in a skirt. I didn't care much for Barkley.

Grandpa stood beside me for a while watchin' the action. I could see him smile every now and then as though he heartily approved.

"Lou seems to be havin' fun, don't she?"

"Guess so."

Grandpa stood a minute deep in thought.

"She oughta have fun more often."

He pulled his watch out and checked the time. I could tell by the look on his face that it must be nine o'clock. I expected him to say, "Bedtime, Boy," but he didn't. Instead he said, "Tonight's a little special"; then tucked the watch away. I knew that was my permission to stay up.

The games ended and the open fire was lit. People carried blocks from the woodpile and placed them around in a circle, side by side, with the fire in the middle. Amid much banter and teasin' the corn roastin' began. The other food was laid out, too, and it looked like they would have quite a feast.

Grandpa appeared again.

"Lou," he called, nice and loud, "yer Uncle Charlie made a big pot of hot chocolate and it's ready. Burt, would you mind givin' Lou a hand?"

So there it was, I thought. I'd wondered how and when they'd weasel him in.

Burt walked off with Lou, grinnin' rather foolishly. Barkley looked a little annoyed. He had placed his block right next to Auntie Lou's at the fire and had busied himself with explainin' to her the best way to roast a cob—or something.

Barkley was older than the other guys, but that sure didn't make him any less a kid. After Lou had left, Barkley shrugged and busied himself with smearin' butter on the block that Burt had jest been sittin' on, tellin' everyone in a loud voice to "jest you watch when the dummy gets back."

Barkley had his back turned and was loudly teasin' Nellie and SueAnn when one of the fellows switched the woodblocks. When Barkley took his seat again, he found that *he* was sittin' in the butter. I don't think that Barkley ever did know who did it, but I did. It was done jest as quietly and seriously as Cullum did everything that he did. No one else had even noticed him.

It seemed to take Auntie Lou and Burt an awful long time to get out there with that hot chocolate. I wondered jest what kind of a trick Uncle Charlie and Grandpa were usin' to detain them. Eventually they returned, and Burt seemed to assume that he now had earned his place beside Auntie Lou for the rest of the evenin'.

I was sittin' there studying all the commotion when there was a quiet voice beside me.

"Brought ya some grub, Josh."

I jumped so that I woke up Pixie who was asleep on my lap. I was so sure that no one could see me there where I was sittin'.

It was Cullum.

"Thought thet yer stomach must be fair growlin' eyein' all thet food an' not gittin' any."

"Thanks," I said, takin' it. I *was* powerful hungry.

"Got ya a dog, huh?"

Cullum reached down and picked up Pixie in his big man hands. He stroked her hair gently and chuckled to himself. I knew that he liked her. He didn't even have to say so.

"Can I git ya some more?"

"That's lots—thanks, Cullum. Me, I gotta go to bed soon anyway."

Cullum laid Pixie back on my lap and stood up.

"Good party," he said. He was lookin' at Auntie Lou.

"Yeah," I answered. I don't know why but I got the feelin' that Cullum might kinda like to talk about Lou for a while.

"We kinda had our own party before this one."

"Ya did?"

"Yeah. We gave her our presents at supper time."

"What'd *you* give her?"

"A hanky—handkerchief," I corrected, "all lace and stuff."

"Bet she liked it."

"Yeah, she did. Said it was the prettiest she'd ever seen. And Uncle Charlie gave her a new shawl. She'll prob'ly wear it to church—maybe tomorrow. Maybe you'll—"

I caught myself too late. None of the Lewises ever went to church. I hurried on.

"An' Grandpa gave her a new dress. Boy, is it pretty. Looks real nice on her, too. She tried it on already. She hopes that somebody gets married soon or somethin' so that she can wear it."

Cullum was still watchin' Auntie Lou.

"And Gramps gave her a jew'ry box and a locket on a little chain that used to be my great-grandmother's."

Burt Thomas was sayin' something to Auntie Lou and makin' her laugh. Cullum shifted his feet.

"Guess I'd better be headin' home, Josh. Got a little further to go than some of 'em."

He moved as though he was leavin'. I jumped up, almost forgettin' to rescue Pixie from bein' dumped on the ground.

"Jest wait a minute, okay?" I said hurriedly and shoved Pixie at him. "Here, hold her a minute."

It was hard to get close enough to tug on Auntie Lou's skirt. I jest waved my head and she excused herself and followed me. I could see her eyes askin' me if something was wrong, so as quickly as possible I blurted out my reason.

"Cullum has to go home early. He has a long way to drive. I jest thought that you'd like to thank him for comin', that's all."

Her face relaxed then and she put her hand on my shoulder and we walked over to Cullum. He was standin' there strokin' Pixie. He was such a big man, holdin' such a little dog, that it looked rather comical.

"Josh tells me that you need to leave," said Auntie Lou in a soft voice.

"Thet's right," answered Cullum, still fondlin' Pixie. "Takes awhile to make the drive an' I need to be up early in the mornin'. Not through with my own fall work yet, havin' worked the threshin' crew fer so long."

Auntie Lou nodded and I could guess that she was thinkin', *Tomorrow is the Lord's day*, but she didn't say so. She gave Cullum a warm smile and extended her hand. Cullum nearly dropped Pixie and I reached out to save her from impendin' disaster.

"Thank you so much for comin', Cullum. I know that you're very busy, and I do appreciate your helpin' me to celebrate my birthday."

Auntie Lou spoke the words sincerely, and I knew that she meant every one of them.

"My pleasure," replied Cullum, and I knew that he meant that, too.

Auntie Lou retrieved her hand.

"I hope that you get your harvest all cared for before a storm."

He nodded. "Thank ya."

Someone by the fire called for Auntie Lou. *If it's Burt Thomas*, I thought, *I'll wring his neck*. Auntie Lou looked around.

"I must go," she apologized. "Thank you again, Cullum."

"I was wonderin'—"

But she had turned and was leavin' and she didn't look back. I was sure that she hadn't caught the softly spoken words of Cullum. I moved forward to run after her but Cullum's hand stopped me.

"Take good care of thet pup, Josh." Then he was gone.

I went into the house then. I'd had enough. Burt Thomas was still hangin' 'round Auntie Lou like a fly around molasses, and Barkley Shaw was still teasin' all of the girls and showin' off in spite of the melted butter on the seat of his pants.

I felt a little upset with Auntie Lou. She could have been nicer to Cullum—jest given him an extra smile, or a flutter of the eyelashes, or one of those tricks that girls use—but Auntie Lou never did those things. Maybe she *did* like Cullum. I didn't know, but I sure could guess how Cullum felt about her. I felt sorry for Cullum. I would fight with every inch of me to keep Auntie Lou, but if the day ever did come when I had to lose her, I sure was cheerin' for Cullum.

I ran to shut the chicken-house door that I had forgotten in all of the excitement, and then I went into the house. It was chilly outside by now and in the kitchen I leaned close to the stove to soak up a little warmth before goin' up to bed.

Auntie Lou came in. She was alone.

"Like a piece of cake, Josh?"

I didn't answer. I was still put out with her, and I wanted to be sure that she'd get the message.

"Cake, Josh?" she said again.

When I still didn't answer she came over to me.

"Something wrong?" Her eyes checked Pixie to make sure that the dog was okay.

"Pa send ya to bed?" she tried again.

"Nope."

"Then what—"

"I jest figure that ya coulda been a little nicer, that's all. Here he comes all the way over here and all, and . . ." I really didn't know what to accuse Auntie Lou of.

"I thanked him for comin'—and I meant it, Josh."

"Yeah, but ya didn't thank him very good," I blurted. "Ya coulda—ya coulda giggled or something."

Auntie Lou looked at me sharply. I think that she understood it all then.

"Josh," she said. "I like Cullum, truly I do—as a man, as a friend; but, Josh," she searched for words, "Cullum has never—has never had time for God. I don't know that—that he even believes that there *is* a God.

"I'm happy, Josh, to have Cullum call, to be neighborly, to—uh—speak with and all. I like him. He's a nice man; but, Josh, I could never like Cullum in any other way—not as long as he chooses to leave God out of his life."

"I didn't say ya had to marry him," I snapped; "jest sort of make him—make him feel good by bein' extra nice."

"Joshua!"

Auntie Lou hardly ever called me by my full name.

"Cullum is too fine a man to play games with. I wouldn't mislead or hurt him for the world. I could never encourage him, and it wouldn't be fair to pretend that I could."

She was right, of course. I knew that. I was glad to hear that Auntie Lou thought that Cullum was a fine man. Maybe if he knew, he'd start goin' to church, and then Auntie Lou would feel different about it. But even as the thought came to me, I knew that it would take more than just his *showin'* at church. Auntie Lou would want to be good and sure that he felt about God like she did before she committed herself in any way.

Auntie Lou suddenly realized that she should be outside. They were busy cleanin' up now. They'd all soon be goin' home. She wrapped her shawl tightly about her shoulders and went out.

"Good-night, Josh."

"Good-night."

I turned to go up to bed and then decided to get a little more warmth first. I sat down on the kitchen floor, curled up tightly against the wall and close to the big old stove. I got drowsy sittin' there in the warmth. Pixie was sound asleep in my arms. I knew that I should move to my bed before I did fall asleep, but it was so warm and comfortable there. Uncle Charlie and Grandpa were both helpin' with the clean-up and Gramps had long ago taken to his bed.

I tried rousin' myself again and then I heard voices. It was Auntie Lou and dumb ol' Burt Thomas. I supposed that Grandpa and Uncle Charlie had sent them in again. Burt was sayin' something to Auntie Lou.

"Is that so?" she said, but she didn't sound very excited about it.

"I've always thought so, an' now tonight I realize it even more."

Auntie Lou didn't respond—jest started pilin' dirty dishes on the kitchen table.

"Really, Lou," Burt continued, and he sounded like he was in pain or something. "I care about ya an awful lot. You're the only girl thet I've ever felt this way about."

Lou was probably thinkin' right then about Tillie Whitecomb, who'd been Burt's girl last month, or Marjorie Anderson, who had been the one the month before.

"Oh," she said—not even a "thank ya for the compliment," or "you flatter me," or nothin'.

Burt suddenly seemed to feel that talkin' was gettin' him nowhere, and before Auntie Lou could even move he whirled her about, jerked her close and kissed her.

Everything stopped. I expected thunder and lightnin'. Auntie Lou pushed herself away from Burt and back a pace. Her eyes flashed. I was hopin' that she would hit him, but she didn't. She jest stood there with her eyes blazin', and when she spoke her voice was even and cold.

"Burt Thomas, don't you ever come near me again!" She spun on her heel, her skirts swishin' angrily, and was gone.

No one had even noticed me.

I pushed myself up after Burt had left and gathered Pixie closer.

"Scratch number three," I whispered to her and started up the stairs grinnin'.

CHAPTER 19

The Annoucement

It was a little tougher gettin' up for church the next mornin' but Grandpa saw to it that everybody did. I crawled out sleepy-eyed when I was called, dreading going out to do my chores. I was surprised to see everyone already seated at the table.

"Yer Uncle Charlie took pity on ya this mornin," Grandpa said.

Uncle Charlie grinned. "Oh, sure. I git the blame for everything 'round here. It was yer Grandpa who slopped the hogs."

"Thanks," I said to both of them.

"Was it a good party?" asked Gramps, addressin' himself to everyone, but to Auntie Lou in particular.

"Real good," she agreed.

"Everybody stay late?"

"Pretty late."

Grandpa decided that it was his turn.

"Thet there young Thomas," he said, "he sure seems like a fine young fella. I was impressed with the way thet he pitched right in and helped ya like."

Auntie Lou's expression did not change.

"You asked him to, Pa, iffen you remember."

"Well, yeah—" Grandpa hedged, "but he never tried to git out of it. Some fellas woulda begged of, hunted up excuses—"

"To get out of spending some time with the prettiest girl at the show?" asked Gramps, his eyes narrow.

"Well, I do admit," grinned Grandpa, "thet it don't take too much talkin' to git a young fella interested in givin' Lou a hand."

Things were quiet for a moment, then Grandpa tried again.

"Still in all, he does seem like a sensible, steady young fellow. They say he's a real good worker, got his own piece of land. Some young girl will be right lucky to—"

"Pa," she said and her voice was gentle yet angry. "That all may be true, but *I* won't be the girl. I *have* not, and I *do* not, and I *will never* in the future care for Burt Thomas. He is vain, borin', and—and a flirt."

Auntie Lou stood up slowly, untied her apron and draped it over her chair.

"I'm goin' to dress for church."

Gramps looked at me and his eyes were twinklin'. Somehow he seemed to know that Auntie Lou was quite capable of handlin' herself.

Nothin' of much importance happened at church. I knew that I had to go; it was one of Grandpa's unwritten laws for our household, but there wasn't much that he could do to make sure that I was really listenin'.

I turned everything off after the openin' hymn. If God wasn't on *my* side, I reasoned that He could jest stumble along without me on His.

I did pull my attention back for a few minutes when there was a stir and Mr. T. Smith stepped to the front. Everyone knew that Mr. T. Smith was the chairman of the church board. He cleared his throat and tried to look like he didn't consider the position as elevated *too* much above the rest.

"You all know," he said, "thet our good pastor and his wife have expressed a desire to retire. We will miss them deeply, but we know thet they have earned the right to some pleasant and—and . . ." He stammered around a bit. It was then that I realized that he had memorized his speech and it had slipped from him. His face started to get red. He finally gave up on the prepared speech and hurried on.

"As I was sayin', we'll miss them, but we're happy about it—for the *Whites*—we're happy that they can retire and rest after their many years of faithful service."

That last part sounded good and I figured that he may have got hold of a piece of his prepared speech again.

"Although we will miss the Whites, we are happy to announce that yer church board has been successful in findin' a replacement. The Reverend Nathaniel Crawford will come to take Reverend White's place sometime in the very near future. We trust that you will all make him welcome and give him yer support."

A general stir followed the announcement. *Nathaniel Crawford,* I thought. What a name! I had a Bible name, too, and so did my Grandpa, but it sure wasn't a mouthful like Nathaniel. I dismissed the new preacher as not worth thinkin' on and went back to my day-dreamin'. It all had very little to do with me.

Reverend White started his message. I listened for jest a minute or two to find out what I'd be missin'. It was on repentin' again. I'd heard that before. This time he was usin' poor ol' Paul as his example of a wicked man turned good. I tuned out. Ol' Paul probably never, ever had anything bothersome happen to him. Why shouldn't he be good?

After church Avery Garrett and I chased a few girls with grasshoppers that hadn't been smart enough to tuck themselves away for the cold weather ahead. Then Grandpa called that we were ready to go home.

I didn't bother takin' off my shoes. It was cool enough now that they felt kinda good on my feet.

I thought of Cullum and wondered if he'd get all his crop in before winter hit. I sure hoped so. I wished that I was big enough to give him a hand. Maybe someday I'd be able to.

The talk at the table was about the new preacher. Folks were wonderin' where he was from, and what he'd be like, and what he had for family. The only thing I wondered was if he'd still preach on "gettin' ready" and repentance and all. I didn't care much for those kinds of sermons. Something about them made me feel a queer twistin' deep on the inside of me.

I shrugged my shoulders. I really wasn't plannin' on listenin' much anyway, so I guessed it really didn't matter what he preached about. I asked to be excused and went to find Pixie.

CHAPTER 20

Something Unexpected

The men had gone to town that Saturday, and Auntie Lou and I were enjoyin' a rather leisurely day at home. I was glad to have a full day with Pixie. As little as she was she had already learned to bark on command. I still hadn't been able to teach her to be quiet though.

I worked with Pixie all that morning, tryin' to get her to roll over when she was told. Her pudgy little legs and round body couldn't manage the trick too well. Lou joined me on the kitchen floor as I worked and played with my dog. We couldn't help but laugh at Pixie's silly antics as she tried hard to twist herself over.

It wasn't until about three o'clock that I decided to chop and haul wood. I put Pixie in her box; I didn't want to take any chances on her getting in the way of the axe or flying wood chips. She needed a nap anyway.

I was busy choppin' wood, admirin' myself for my strength, when I heard a funny sound comin' from the direction of the barn. I had never heard a sound like it before, so I sank the axe head into the choppin' block and went to investigate. I found it all right. An old sow had found a pail somewhere and she had her head caught in it. She was gruntin' and squealin' and runnin' into feed troughs and fences, shakin' her tin head back and forth as she went.

I couldn't help but laugh at her; she looked and sounded so funny.

After I had seen enough of the entertainment she provided, I decided that I'd better do something about it. I climbed into the pen.

I managed to herd her into a corner and get my hands on the pail. I pulled hard but nothin' gave. After several more attempts to release her, I finally realized that I wasn't accomplishing a thing except to work up a sweat. I decided to go for Auntie Lou. Maybe she'd know what to do.

She laughed, too, when she saw the sow, but she got down to business much quicker than I had.

"We've got to pull it off."

"But how?"

"I don't know, but I'll help you. Come on."

She led the way back to the house, and when we got there she turned to me.

"Josh, bring me one of your shirts and a pair of Uncle Charlie's overalls."

I couldn't see what that had to do with gettin' the pail off that pig, but I went to do it. She took the clothes from me and hurried off to her room.

She looked pretty funny when she came down. She had plaited her loose curls into two long braids that hung down her shoulders; that was the first thing that I noticed. The rest of her I could hardly recognize. She was into the clothes that she had asked me to get. The shirt was a mite too small and the overalls way too big, and she made quite a sight. She grabbed a piece of twine from a kitchen drawer and wrapped a loop around her middle. The big baggy overalls were brought in to fit her tiny waist. They bunched up on either side of the string, givin' her a crazy clown appearance. She rolled up the cuffs. It looked like she should have rolled up the crotch, too, but there wasn't much that she could do about that. Pushin' her feet into her gardenin' boots, she took a silly curtsy and said, "Straight from Noo York."

I laughed then. I wanted to before but I didn't know if I dared. She laughed with me, slappin' her funny bulgin'-overall tummy.

"What'd you do that for?" I asked when I could talk again.

She was sober now.

"We gotta get the pail off that pig, and I've a notion that we'll have to throw her to do it. I'm not about to go wrestlin' a pig in a dress."

I could follow her reasoning but she sure did look funny. I had never seen Auntie Lou in anything so ridiculous before.

We had us a real time with that old sow. She was as dumb as she was stubborn. I couldn't figure out why she wouldn't cooperate—at least a little bit. We chased and caught her and struggled—jest to lose her again. Around and around we went. I could understand now why Auntie Lou braided her hair back. Even my short hair got full of dirt.

"We've got to throw her somehow," panted Auntie Lou.

I went for some ropes.

"Now if we can jest get these on her somehow and get her down, one of us can hold her while the other works the pail."

Away we went again. I got one rope on a front foot. It trailed around behind her as I ran after her, grabbin' and strugglin' to get another rope on her hind foot. Auntie Lou tried to help. After a lot of effort I finally got the second rope on. Lou sorta held the pig at bay while I got an end of each of the ropes. I pulled the tension up until I figured that it was jest right, and then I gave a sudden heave against those ropes with every ounce of energy that I had left. It pulled her feet right out from under her and she went down. Auntie Lou and I both pounced at once, pinnin' her to the ground.

"You get the pail," I said between clenched teeth.

She lifted herself back from the pig and grabbed the pail, eyein' the situation to determine jest how the head was stuck and which direction to pull.

"Hurry," I told her, feelin' the pig gatherin' herself together to make an effort to get free.

Auntie Lou grabbed the pail and laid back, pullin' with everything that she had. The pig squealed like we were cuttin' her throat—about that time it didn't seem like such a bad idea.

The pail all of a sudden made a funny suckin' sound, and Auntie Lou went flyin' backwards. The pig gave a big heave and left me layin' on the ground as she squealed her way around the pen draggin' the ropes behind her.

I heard a funny noise from Auntie Lou and looked up to see her sittin' in the pig trough. Potato peelin's and apple cores were splashed up her arms. She even had some of the slop on her face; she sat there blinkin' those big eyes and makin' horrible faces. One braid had broken loose and scattered hair about her face in a disorganized fashion. Uncle Charlie's overalls were an awful mess. Boy, did I want to laugh, but I didn't.

I got myself up off the ground, gave myself a quick dustin' and went over to help Auntie Lou out of her trough-straddlin' position. While I was hoistin' her up, I heard Grandpa's voice.

"Trouble?"

We didn't bother lookin' up, but kept busy dustin' ourselves off.

"That sow had her head caught."

"So I saw."

"You saw it?" I felt like sayin', *If you saw it, where were you?* but I held my tongue.

Auntie Lou stood there shakin' the messy stuff from her hands and arms. Her baggy, borrowed pants dripped peelings and slop. Grandpa cleared his throat.

"It 'pears that we came at a bad time. I brung the new parson here, out for supper."

Both Auntie Lou and I jerked as though we had been prodded; sure enough, there he stood.

He was dark. His hair looked like it would curl if he were to let the cut go for an extra week. His eyes were a dark brown, surrounded by thick lashes and heavy eyebrows. He was taller than Grandpa, but he was slimmer— except for his shoulders. They were broad. The thing that struck me was his age. He didn't look to be more than twenty-five. For some reason I had jest thought that all preachers were old.

Lou was sizin' him up, too. I wondered jest how *her* eyes saw him. No one spoke for a minute and then Lou said, very softly, "Excuse us, Parson. We weren't expectin' company."

Everyone laughed then and the tension was broken somewhat.

"This is Parson Crawford," said Grandpa, feelin' that all things were now restored to order—but he was a man. Auntie Lou didn't quite share his opinion. Her cheeks flushed a deep rose beneath her pig-slop freckles.

"How do you do, Reverend Crawford."

"How do you do, Miss Jones."

"He's come to supper," Grandpa reminded Lou.

Auntie Lou gathered together all of the dignity that she could muster. She looked straight at Grandpa's eyes. I had never seen her put her foot down so definitely and completely before and I don't think that Grandpa had either. Still she spoke in an even, sweet voice. She even managed a charmin' smile, but everyone knew that she meant *exactly* what she said.

"Supper will be ready in two hours. I would suggest that you use the time to show the Reverend the farm or to have a nice get-acquainted chat on the porch."

Loud and clear she was sayin', "Don't anyone *dare* to step into my kitchen or come near me 'til the appointed time." Grandpa got the message. He cleared his throat again.

"Come, Josh," said Auntie Lou.

On the way to the house she spoke again and her voice had a tremble.

"Josh, I want you to put the tub in my room and carry me up some bath water."

I nodded. I wondered how she planned to get out of those drippin', messy pants without draggin' them through her kitchen. I underestimated Auntie Lou. She gave me another order.

"Josh, when you go in, hand me that blanket from the kitchen couch— out the east window."

She kept right on walkin' around the house. I gathered up the blanket, hoisted up the window, and handed the blanket to her. She threw it around her shoulders and somehow under its cover, she freed herself of Uncle Charlie's awful overalls. Still clutchin' the blanket around her she climbed through the open window, shut it behind herself, and headed for her room. Uncle Charlie's pants lay where they had fallen, drawin' the flies.

I didn't hang around after I had seen to the bath water. I needed some scrubbin' up and a change of clothes myself, so I cared for that and then went back to my job of cuttin' wood.

I don't know jest where the four menfolk passed the time, but promptly when the two hours were up, they were marchin' toward the kitchen. It was cool outside in the fall evenings, and they really weren't dressed for it; I suppose that they were all right glad to get into the warmth of the kitchen.

Supper smelled good, too, and as it was later than usual, everyone was powerful hungry.

Lou hadn't really fussed about the meal. It was the usual, simple yet tasty fare that we normally enjoyed. The table was laid with the everyday dishes. It was clear to me that Auntie Lou wasn't out to impress the new preacher.

She was dressed neatly and carefully in a blue and white housedress, a clean apron tied around her waist. Her hair hung down around her shoulders. It still wasn't fully dried from its recent washin'. Her face was flushed a light pink, but whether it was from workin' over the hot stove or her memory of recent events, I wasn't sure.

She acted the perfect hostess—quiet and polite, lookin' after the needs of those at her table, but no more. The parson seemed to enjoy the cookin'—especially the hot biscuits. He ate them until he seemed embarrassed, and then ate another one anyway.

Like Auntie Lou, I didn't have too much to say during the meal. I was busy lookin' over this new preacher, tryin' to figure him out. I jest couldn't put my finger on any good reason why a young, manly fella like him would want to be a parson. There were so many other things that he could have chosen—like bein' a cowboy or a sheriff or a wrestler. (Avery Garrett had told me about wrestlers. His uncle had watched a match once.) But here he was, a preacher. I jest couldn't figure it out. It was clear that he wasn't in it for the money. Even I noticed that though his suit was neat, it was well worn and even looked to be carefully repaired in a spot or two. No, I couldn't figure it out. I finally concluded that he must be a fair amount crazy—or at least a little slow. As I listened to the conversation, that theory didn't add up either. He seemed bright enough, and pleasant, too. It was all a puzzle to me. I felt real curiosity about the man. He was certainly a strange one.

Before he left he admired Pixie. Now anyone smart enough to see what a sharp little dog Pixie was sort of had one foot in the door with me.

When he turned to go he spoke softly to Auntie Lou.

"Would you and Josh mind walking me to my horse?"

Auntie Lou looked surprised, but there wasn't really any way that she could graciously refuse; anyway he had included *me.* The rest understood that they hadn't been invited and busied themselves at putterin' with the dishes.

We walked out slowly, no one sayin' anything at first, and I was wonderin' jest what this was all about.

"I just want to thank you again for the tasty supper, Miss Jones. I—uh—" he flushed a bit, then a teasin' smile played about his lips. "I—uh—know what an unpleasant situation it was for you, and I apologize. Next time that I come for a meal, it will only be at the invitation of the *hostess.*"

Auntie Lou didn't say anything, but her blue eyes widened. She nodded and then looked down for a minute.

"Again, I say thank you," and he touched his hat briefly.

Auntie Lou looked up then. Their gaze held for a minute and then the new preacher turned to me. He held out his hand like I was a full-grown man or something.

"Take good care of Pixie, Joshua. She looks like a real winner. We'll see you both in the mornin.'"

I nodded. I'd be there. Grandpa would see to that. The next mornin' was to be Pastor White's final message and the congregation would be introduced to Reverend Crawford. There'd be a potluck dinner afterward, and then the next Sunday we'd have our new preacher. I might even listen a little—jest the one Sunday—jest to see what kind of preacher a man like him would be.

I watched him mount and start down the lane. When I turned around Auntie Lou was already back to the house.

CHAPTER 21

Parson Nathaniel Crawford

Another week passed. It was rather strange. Not the week really—but Auntie Lou; and Lou bein' the pivot for my whole world, she made everything else seem strange, too.

Gramps developed a bit of a cold, and Auntie Lou fussed and stewed about that, tryin' every remedy that she knew. Gramps tolerated it all good-naturedly, but I really think that he would have rather jest left that cold on its own. It wasn't that bad a one anyway.

Besides, I don't think that it was Gramps' cold that was really botherin' Auntie Lou. It jest gave her somethin' to do with her fidgeting.

Sunday finally rolled around. The breakfast table that mornin' was full of talk of the new preacher, wonderin' what his "delivery" would be like and if he'd be able to help the young folks and still support the old. Gramps added with a chuckle that he sure didn't expect him to have trouble gettin' the young women out. Auntie Lou, who had been lookin' down at her plate and playin' around with a piece of bacon, looked up after that remark, then quickly dropped her eyes again.

I was afraid that she was comin' down with Gramps' cold—she seemed so off-her-feed for some reason; but no one else seemed to notice anything wrong.

Lou suggested that maybe Gramps should jest stay home and nurse his cold, but Gramps would have none of it. He never missed worshippin' on the Lord's Day, he said. He had so much to be thankful for, he maintained, and he planned on bein' there to tell the Lord so. Auntie Lou seemed to think that Gramps could have had his little talk with the Lord jest as well from his own bedroom, but Gramps gently but stubbornly disagreed.

"*Not* forsaking the assembling of ourselves together," he quoted. "We weren't meant to praise Him solo, but as a great chorus."

Then he laid a hand lovingly on Lou's shinin' hair and his eyes were wet.

"Just like your granny, fussing over those you love. I'm just fine, little Lou, truly I am, but thanks for caring."

He leaned over and kissed Auntie Lou on the cheek. Lou knew that she had lost as far as Gramps goin' to church was concerned; but though she still looked worried, I think she was pleased to know that he realized jest how much she really cared about him. She turned to her dishes then, rushin' with them so that she could be ready for church.

Uncle Charlie grabbed a tea towel to give her a hand and they hurried through the mornin' chore. As always, when they were finished, Auntie Lou reached up on tiptoe and gave Uncle Charlie a light "thank-you" kiss on the cheek—Uncle Charlie's reason for helpin' her so often.

Auntie Lou ran up the stairs to her room as though she was really late— she wasn't. Fact was, she had a bit more time than she usually had on Sunday mornin's.

But she sure took a long time a gettin' ready. By the time she appeared again, we men were all standin' around in the kitchen waitin', ready to go. In fact, Grandpa was gettin' impatient. He kept pullin' out his watch and checkin' the time. He was jest ready to call—I could see it comin'—when Lou came down the stairs. At the sight of her we all sorta drew in our breath. She was wearin' her new cream-colored dress that Grandpa had given her for her birthday. The pink trim on it made her cheeks show a rosy pink. Her hair was brushed until it shone and was pinned up in a special way, with little whisps of curls teasin' around her face. She carried Uncle Charlie's shawl over one arm and the locket that Gramps gave her hung around her neck, layin' softly against the creamy bosom of her dress. I looked and sure enough, in her hand she held my lace handkerchief.

"Like it?" She stopped and turned quickly around for us to see each side of her. Her blue eyes sparkled with teasin' and pleasure.

"For my men," she said. "Nellie has been coaxin' me to wear it, and I thought, why not?"

Guess Gramps said it for all of us tongue-tied men.

"Little Lou, you look like an angel—and I'm proud to be able to escort you to church."

He offered his arm. Auntie Lou accepted it and they walked out together. The rest of us followed.

Boy, I kept thinkin', *if Cullum could see her now—bet even he wouldn't think that goin' to church was such a bad idea.*

I wasn't worried about Jedd Rawleigh or Hiram Woxley or even Burt Thomas anymore. It wasn't that I wanted her goin' off with Cullum either, but I was sure that he would take real pleasure in seein' Auntie Lou like that.

The warm Indian-summer weather was back again. It was nice to leave for church without havin' to bother to bundle up so that you could hardly move.

Grandpa pushed the team a bit. We had started later than usual, and Grandpa wasn't one to favor being late for church. We made it on time. As we walked to the door, I could feel the stir around us. Most of the young fellas were hangin' around outside yet—sorta gettin' all the air that they could before goin' in to sit a spell. At the appearance of Auntie Lou there was a great deal of head-turnin', feet-shufflin', and elbow-pokin'. She greeted them with a shy smile and a cheery good mornin' as she passed—jest as she always did, nothin' more nor less.

We took the usual pew. This morning instead of coaxing to sit with the boys, I joined my family, and planted myself between Gramps and Auntie Lou. I could feel eyes on us, and though I knew it was Auntie Lou they were lookin' at, it still made me squirm. I could hear a few girls' whispers, and I guessed that they were probably discussin' Auntie Lou's dress—girls bein' so taken up with what one another is wearin'.

The new pastor took his place and the attention shifted—especially that of the girls. *Boy oh boy!* I thought, *he looks even taller and younger up there behind the pulpit. Preacher has no business lookin' like that. He's supposed to be sorta world-worn and old lookin'.* I hadn't figured out yet what he was to do with his time while waitin' to get old, if he felt a call to preach.

He smiled at his congregation and his eyes seemed to take us all in. Auntie Lou wasn't returnin' his look. She was fidgetin' with a lace corner on her hanky.

The openin' part of the service went pretty much as usual. The songs were the ones that we were familiar with. Mrs. Cromby tramped away at the pump organ in the same fashion as always, and Mr. Shaw boomed out in a bass voice, not always quite on key. The ushers gathered the Lord's tithes and offerin's, and Deacon Brown led in prayer.

It was finally time for the sermon and even the boys my age were quiet and waitin'. I was right curious as to what kind of talkin' this new preacher would do. I didn't plan on really listenin'—jest sorta checkin' up on what he had to say.

His voice was pleasant enough, and one soon forgot how young he looked. His manner and his delivery sort of caught me up somehow, and I got to feelin' like what he had to say had greater authority than his alone.

When I summed it all up later, I felt rather tricked. Really it was the same thing that I'd been hearin' all my life—only put to us in a different way. "God's Glorious Provision" he called it, and went on to tell of man's need because of him bein' a sinful creature and what God had done to care for that need. Yea (that was *his* word)—yea, completely and forever erased the need, by supplyin' man's salvation, through the redemptive death of our Lord.

As I say, I'd heard it all before, but one thing sorta caught me and had me puzzled. This preacher looked like what he was talkin' about filled him with such happiness that he was about to bust. It seemed that he was pleased to pieces that God had gone out of His way to do all that for man. "Mercy," he called it—mercy and grace—mercy bein' the withholdin' of what you *really* deserved, like a woodshed trip if you'd been bad; and grace—the gettin' of what you really didn't deserve, like the extra dish of ice cream when there were six servin's and five people to share them.

At the end of the sermon we sang, "Amazin' Grace," and a look at the preacher's face told everyone that he truly thought it was amazin'.

Willie Corbin went up and knelt at the front cryin' and the new preacher went to pray with him. Now I knew Willie Corbin, and if ever a fella had need to be a bit concerned about some of his carryin' on, it was Willie. I jest hoped that it wouldn't take *all* the fun out of him.

I followed my family out of the pew when the pastor finally dismissed the people. Boy, was the church gettin' short of air. I couldn't wait to get outside.

Willie Corbin sat there at the front, grinnin' from ear to ear, as his ma and pa hugged him, wipin' away tears with the pastor's handkerchief.

At the door there was quite a commotion. Everyone wanted to shake the pastor's hand and say nice things about his sermon. Girls giggled a bit and flushed. Some hurried by, the others openly flirted—jest a little bit. Mothers were the worst. Anyone with an unmarried daughter seem to loiter and gush until I felt a little sick. I wanted to break rank and get out of there, but I knew that I had to wait in line or Grandpa would have something to say about it on the way home.

Finally we reached the door. Grandpa went first, shook the pastor's hand firmly and said the usual. Uncle Charlie did likewise. Gramps was next. He, too, shook the reverend's hand firmly but jest said, "God bless, young man. God bless." I kinda thought that the pastor liked that better than all those flowery speeches that he'd heard.

Auntie Lou was jest ahead of me. She stepped forward and accepted the pastor's hand—and then she proceeded to shock me half to death.

"Reverend Crawford," she said softly and controlled. "You said that you'd favor our house with a return visit when the *hostess* asked you. Could you come for dinner next Sunday?"

The pastor's face dropped.

"Mrs. Peterson has asked me for next Sunday. I'm—"

"Then the Sunday after?"

"Mrs. Corbin—"

"And then?"

"The Hallidays."

Both of them looked a bit miserable.

"I see." Auntie Lou looked about to move on, then she collected herself and smiled. "I *did* appreciate your sermon."

"Thank you." He looked directly at Auntie Lou, takin' in her creamy dress, pretty hair-do and blue eyes. It was then that I realized that he still held her hand. I guess that they realized it about then, too, for Lou flushed and quickly withdrew it; the parson sort of cleared his throat, embarrassed-like.

Lou moved to walk on by but he quickly stopped her.

"Wait," he said.

She turned.

"Does it *have* to be on a Sunday? I mean, people eat every day of the week, say Monday? Tuesday? Friday?"

Lou smiled. "Of course." She sounded almost apologetic for bein' so dumb as not to have thought of it herself.

The pastor smiled, too, seeming tremendously relieved about something.

"Friday at six?" offered Lou.

"Friday."

He beamed at her and very briefly touched her hand again. Auntie Lou returned his smile, then turned to go.

It was my turn now. I was sure that after all that, he wouldn't even notice me, but he did.

"Josh. Good to see you. How's Pixie?"

I muttered something that I hoped was at least sensible, even if not intelligent, and pulled away to follow my family.

Somethin' was brewin'. I could feel it in my bones, but I couldn't put my finger on it yet. Whatever it was, I didn't think I liked it.

CHAPTER 22

Rumors

Grandpa had to make a trip to town on Monday so he inquired if I'd like to go along. I asked if it would be okay to take Pixie, and Grandpa agreed with a smile. He said that he'd bring the dog and pick me up at school to save ourselves a little time.

As soon as class was dismissed I was off out the door, and sure enough, Grandpa was there waitin'. The kids gathered round for a look at Pixie and I showed her off a bit; then everyone who lived along the direction that we were goin' crawled in the wagon and we set off, scatterin' our passengers at the various farm sites along the way. It was a fun trip and I think that Grandpa enjoyed it almost as much as I.

There really wasn't anything much that I needed to do in town, so I asked Grandpa if I could take a run over to the Sankeys to let Pixie see her mama. He said that it would be fine, but not to be too long, so I set off.

I never did get there though. I had to pass the parsonage where the preacher lived, and it just so happened that as I was headin' by, the preacher pulled up on his horse. He seemed to think that I'd come around just to see him, and he grinned from ear to ear.

"Hi there, Josh—and you, too, Pixie," he added. "Right glad that I didn't miss you. Just let me put Big Jim away and we'll rustle up some milk and cookies."

I swallowed my reply that I was on my way to the Sankeys—it wasn't like I had to go or something—and tagged along to the barn.

I felt that I should make some kind of comment, so I looked him over— he was wearin' his preacher clothes. I said, "Been callin'?"

"Been over to see the Corbins—that's where I got the cookies."

"Pastor White jest used to call on Tuesdays and Thursdays—unless," I added quickly, "it was an emergency."

"We'll call this an emergency then. Mrs. Corbin hasn't been feeling too well. She wasn't able to be in church yesterday. But I do want to call on all my parishioners just as soon as I can; I plan to visit as many homes as possible this week and next."

He carefully looked after Big Jim, rubbin' him down and givin' him some hay.

"I'll give him water and his chop in about an hour or so," he said. We headed for the house.

"Do you mind, Josh, if I just grab my wash off the line on my way by?"

"Not at all. I'd help you iffen I didn't need to hang onto Pixie."

He asked for an up-to-date report on Pixie's training as he gathered the clothes, and I told him about all her tricks and the next one that I planned to work on. He was anxious for me to show him just how she was doin', and I guess that I was a bit eager, too.

He opened the door and let me precede him into the house. It wasn't blessed with very much furniture, but everything there was shiny clean. He laid his laundry carefully on the table and went about gettin' the milk and cookies.

I received my glass and reached for a couple of cookies from the plate. He took a drink of milk and went right on workin'. He matched his socks and rolled them up together. I noticed that most of the pairs had been mended—some of them many times. He came to a pair with a small hole in one toe and laid them aside.

"Guess I'd better take care of that one before I wear it again." He laughed. "Holes in socks are sorta like sin, Josh. If you don't tend to them right away when they're small and controllable, they grow with amazing speed."

"You mend your own socks?"

"Sure do—socks, shirts, pants, you name it."

"Don't ya hate it?"

He laughed again.

"Can't say that I rightly enjoy it, but I learned long ago that nothing gets easier or any more fun by putting it off."

"How long ago?"

"Have to think on that. I was twelve when my father died. Pa had been sick a fair while, and by the time he passed away, we had used up all of the living that he had set by. Mama wouldn't have him fretting if she could help it, so she quietly sold anything that she could slip from the house without his noticing. After Pa died, my ma had to take in wash to make enough to get by on. I did the collecting and delivering and even some of the scrubbing, as well as any other small jobs that I could find.

"Mama was a very proud and independent woman. And, my pa's cousin lived nearby—big man, big family, but not much energy. His place was unkempt and rundown, and a bit on the dirty side. Mama vowed that no matter how poor we were, our place would never look like that—not as long as she could still draw a breath. So, we both worked hard.

"It was my dream to be a preacher. I saw so many people who were hurting. God had laid His call on my heart when I was a very young boy—and I discussed it with both of my folks. Before my pa died he called both Mama and me in. 'Son,' he said, 'I know it looks a little dark right now, but if God truly wants you in His work, don't give up—there'll come a way.' I assured him that I wouldn't, and slipped out so that he and Mama could have those last minutes alone. Besides, I wanted to get away where I could cry.

"Everytime Mama could lay aside a few extra dollars from her washing, she would order another book for me to read—'to keep the vision fresh,' she would say.

"She was a great little woman, my mama. I'm proud to be her son. She used to worry that I had to become a man at twelve years of age, but looking back now I believe that it was all in God's plan. I had to grow up—to be able to make tough decisions quickly—to learn the importance of following through on one's responsibilities.

"When I was sixteen Mama died and I sold our little house in town and went away to school. I managed to find work—most of the time, and I finally made it. It took me a little longer than some of my fellow students, but God saw me through—just like Pa had said He would."

He was silent for a while; then he looked at me with a queer kind of smile.

"Did a funny thing when I finished, Josh. I took that diploma that I was given, stating me to be a preacher, and I used the last few dollars that I had, to have a weather-proof frame put on it—and then I went back to my old hometown and mounted it on a stake right there between the grave markers of my ma and pa."

As he looked at me I saw a lone tear in his eye. For some reason I felt that I wanted to cry, too.

"Does that sound crazy, Josh?"

I just shook my head and swallowed hard. "I ain't even ever thought of anything that I could do for my ma and pa."

"Your ma and pa loved the Lord, Josh?"

I nodded.

"Then the greatest thing that you could ever do for them would be to love and serve the Lord, too."

"S'pose," I said rather hesitantly, for a funny, uncomfortable gnawin' was busy workin' on my insides. I felt I had to get out of there, but right at that time the parson finished foldin' the last of the clothes and changed the subject so completely that I was soon at ease again.

"Now then, let's see what Pixie can do."

The next few minutes went very quickly, I put Pixie through her paces, and the parson rewarded her each time that she performed with a nibble of one of his cookies. He gave me a few pointers on how to work on her next trick—dancin' on her hind legs. Then I suddenly noticed the clock. I said that I had to rush or Grandpa would be waitin', scooped up Pixie and yelled back a thank-you. I left on the run.

I reached the wagon, pantin', and was pleased to see that Grandpa wasn't sittin' up top, twistin' the reins and frownin'. I crawled up and flopped down on the bit of hay that lay on the wagon bottom, hopin' to be over my puffin' by the time Grandpa showed up.

I didn't have long to wait. I heard Grandpa's voice comin' toward the wagon. He was talkin' to someone.

It turned out to be Mr. Brown, the deacon from our church. They were talkin' weather and then jest as they neared the wagon, the tone changed.

"I was thinkin' on droppin' over this evenin', Daniel."

"Got something on yer mind?" This was Grandpa.

"Don't rightly know what to think. My wife's brother from Edsell County dropped by t'other day. Seems he knows the Crawford family fairly well."

"Ya mean the parson's?"

"Well—yeah. He don't recall a Nathaniel, but he says there's so many kids that he never could git 'em straight."

"So?" Grandpa waited.

"Seems they's not too highly thought of. Shiftless, lazy, dirty—even rowdy—not much account. He couldn't believe that one of 'em ever decided to be a preacher."

"How long has he knowed 'em?"

"Five years—ever since he moved in."

"Maybe he has the wrong family."

"Only one there. Had been another but he and his wife are both buried there."

"So what ya thinkin'?"

"Seems strange to me. I don't know what to think. Henry suggested that maybe this Nathaniel was a smart rascal that figured as how the ministry was an easy way to make a livin' without workin'."

"Don't know much about the ministry then!"

Mr. Brown chuckled, then sobered and responded, "The ministry is what you make it, Daniel. Iffen you're there to help people, you're more than busy, but iffen ya want to coast, I reckon ya could do jest that."

Grandpa was silent a minute, then responded slowly. "Well, Lukus, I shore do hate to pass judgment on a man without givin' him a chance. There could be some mix-up here."

From my place in the hay I was hard put not to jump up and let him know the truth: that the parson was not from the same shiftless family; that he had worked hard and shouldered responsibility to get where he was. But I knew that to do so would be admittin' eavesdroppin' on an adult conversation right there in front of Deacon Brown, and I wasn't sure how Grandpa would respond to that. I figured there would be plenty of opportunity later to casually mention to Grandpa my unplanned visit with the parson. I could then relate the things that we had talked about. I pulled Pixie close and sorta held my breath as well as my tongue.

Mr. Brown went on. "Must admit it has upset me some."

"Now, now, Lukus. Even if he is one and the same, not all apples in the same barrel need be rotten you know. An' we ain't leavin' any room fer the work of the Lord at all. He's restored a lot of rotten apples. We both know that."

" 'Course," said Mr. Brown, " 'course. Jest thought that we should be aware and sorta keep our eyes and ears open fer signs, that's all."

Mrs. Brown yoohooed from down the street and Mr. Brown excused himself. As he turned to go, Grandpa said softly, "And Lukus, I see no need for this to pass on any further than jest to us two—at least fer the present." I could hear Grandpa gatherin' the reins and preparin' to climb up onto the wagon seat.

I got a sudden inspiration and decided to act asleep. I heard Grandpa exclaim and then chuckle when he spotted Pixie and me. He spread a couple of gunny sacks over us and then clucked to the team and we were on our way.

I peeked a look once or twice. I could see that what Mr. Brown had said truly bothered Grandpa. Sure he was willin' to give a man a fair chance, but even so, he was human, too, and some seeds of doubt had been sown.

I supposed that I was the only one around, beside the preacher himself, who knew the real truth, but it didn't seem too wise an idea for me to share my knowledge at the moment. I felt all mixed up—wantin' to defend the preacher and yet not knowin' quite how, all at the same time. I'd have to sort it out later.

I snuggled down under my gunny sack blanket and then I really did go to sleep, and slept soundly until we reached home.

CHAPTER 23

Guest Night

I had thought that Auntie Lou was strange the week before, but she was doubly so that week. One minute she laughed, the next she fell into moody silence, fussin' and frettin' over any little thing. She polished and cleaned, and polished some more. Seemed that all of a sudden the whole place was awful dirty-like.

When Friday finally came she spent the whole day in the kitchen fussin' over fried chicken, hot biscuits, and apple pie. The smells that hung in that kitchen were about enough to drive a growin' boy crazy. I could hardly wait for the supper hour to arrive. I knew better than to hang around underfoot, so I waited on the porch with Pixie until I was called for.

"Josh, come and get ready for supper."

I walked in, ready to do my usual wash-and-slick-down-the-hair job, but Lou stopped me.

"I want you to wash thoroughly, Josh, and then change to your Sunday clothes."

My mouth musta dropped open. Sunday clothes on a Friday night? I had never heard of anything so ridiculous. One look at Auntie Lou and I could see that she really meant it, so I didn't even bother to protest—outwardly. Inside I was fightin' it a bit. Silliest notion I'd ever heard.

The other men came in and somehow Lou got the same order across to them. We all went to comply—like so many dumb sheep.

I came down feelin' rather embarrassed. I'd have died if Avery or Willie had suddenly walked in. Lou rushed past me on the stairs, hurryin' to do some changin' of her own.

I walked around the kitchen sniffin' and jest checkin' to see if there might be a stray bit of something that I could sample. Didn't seem to be.

The table caught my eye. It was covered with a pure white cloth, and the dishes that were placed on it, I'd never seen before. It was a little late for decent flowers, so a bowl of apples sat in the center of the table.

I was reachin' for a polished apple when Gramps came out of his bedroom.

"I wouldn't do that, Josh," he whispered. "It would spoil your Auntie Lou's fine arrangement."

He chuckled jest slightly and gave me a wink, "Took her almost an hour to get that jest so."

Seemed really silly to me to polish and fuss like that over something that tasted jest as good without all that trouble.

We men gathered one by one. I think that each one of us felt a little foolish; we stood around self-conscious, hardly darin' to breathe lest we commit somethin' unpardonable. We were all relieved to hear Auntie Lou's step on the stairs.

She came down wearin' one of my favorite dresses. It was her special blue one and made her eyes look even bigger and bluer. She had left her hair loose and flowin' around her face and shoulders. A small blue bow secured a handful of it at the back of her head. She looked great. She also looked nervous.

She checked the meal on the stove, she checked the table, she checked us men, then she checked the clock. Five to six—and then we heard a horse clompin' down the lane. Uncle Charlie got up silently to go meet the caller and care for the horse. Grandpa cleared his throat and rearranged chairs that didn't need rearrangin'. I jest stood there wishin' that I could be cuddlin' Pixie, which I couldn't 'cause I'd get my hands dirty. Gramps spoke softly to the flustered Lou.

"Everything looks lovely, little Lou." I knew that this was to try to reassure her.

I didn't mean to help the situation any. I jest blurted out what I felt. "I'm starvin."

Somehow those two words seemed to break the spell. Everyone laughed, even Auntie Lou, and though she still hurried around with her last-minute preparations, she seemed more her old self.

Uncle Charlie brought in the preacher, who washed his hands after his ride. Uncle Charlie followed suit and then we were finally able to sit down at the table. The preacher was asked to pray; and my mouth wouldn't let me concentrate on what he was sayin'; it was waterin' so.

It didn't seem like the grown-ups were in nearly the hurry to get started that I was. They exchanged comments and fiddled around until I felt like suggestin' that it would be quite fittin' for someone to start the chicken.

There were squares of white cloth beside each plate, and I was hard put to know where to get rid of the thing so that I could properly get at my fork. The others took theirs and laid them on their laps, so I got mine out of the way by doin' that, too.

Finally the food started coming around. It was worth waitin' for, I'll tell you that. Don't suppose anybody enjoyed it anymore than me.

The preacher ate heartily, but I got the funny feelin' that he might not even be aware of what he was eatin'. Every time I looked at him he was stealin' little looks at Auntie Lou. He managed to carry on an intelligent conversation with the men-folk, includin' Lou frequently, but I wondered jest how much of his mind was really on what he was sayin'.

It was a slow, leisurely meal, filled with pleasant talk and laughter. When everyone was so full that there was no possibility of holdin' another bite of pie or sip of coffee, Grandpa told me to get his Bible. The story was halfways interesting this time—about some Gideon who sent a whole army runnin' with their tails between their legs, and he only had 300 men to do it with.

Auntie Lou set right to work on the dishes. Uncle Charlie got up slowly and picked up a towel. That preacher got a look in his eye that seemed to say that he would have gladly taken Uncle Charlie's place if he had thought that it would have been proper. Instead, he accepted Grandpa's challenge to a game of checkers.

The checker game and the dishes were finished about the same time. Auntie Lou removed her apron, gave Uncle Charlie his customary peck on the cheek, and they joined us. The evenin' went pleasantly enough.

It was nearin' my bedtime when Auntie Lou put the coffeepot on again. She had some cookies to go with the coffee.

I watched the clock hands move slowly around. It was my bedtime all right; but when Auntie Lou summoned everyone to the table, I noticed that she had a place set for me with a glass of milk; Grandpa jest moved me on over to the table with a nod of his head.

After we had enjoyed the refreshments and the conversation, the preacher said that he really had to be going. Uncle Charlie offered to get his horse, but he said not to bother—he knew where his Big Jim was. He thanked Grandpa for the fine evenin', spoke to Uncle Charlie, Gramps, and I in turn (even tickled Pixie's ear and bid her a good-night), then turned to Auntie Lou.

He took her hand and thanked her for the invitation, said that she was a most gracious hostess and a wonderful cook. Auntie Lou didn't say much— out loud. Somehow I got the impression that the two of them said a lot more to one another than what was spoken. I couldn't see Lou's face, but I did see the preacher's, and his eyes were sayin' far more than his lips.

He released Auntie Lou's hand and left. I waited for her to turn around. It took her a few minutes, but when she did her eyes were still shiny and her cheeks slightly flushed. She had a look on her face that I'd never seen there before as she busied herself clearin' away the lunch dishes.

I saw Grandpa and Uncle Charlie exchange worried frowns.

"Leave my cup, Louie," said Grandpa. He hardly ever called her Louie. "I think I'll have another cup of coffee."

"Mine too," said Uncle Charlie.

"Me, I'm off to bed." Gramps covered a yawn. "All your good cooking makes me as sleepy as a well-fed cat. Great meal, little Lou."

He kissed her on the cheek and moved toward his bedroom.

I stirred. Should have known better, but my arm was gettin' stiff from holding Pixie. As soon as I moved, Grandpa caught it.

"Bedtime, Boy."

I nodded and got up; carryin' Pixie with me I went up to bed.

It wasn't long until I heard Auntie Lou pass my door. She was hummin' softly. Normally I loved to hear her happy, but something about this bothered me. I tried to find a comfortable way to lay, but nothing felt right. Pixie finally gave up on me and crawled away to the foot of the bed where she could rest in peace.

It was then that I heard the voices from the kitchen. Worried voices—I could tell by the sound. I crept out of bed and down the stairs as far as I dared, avoidin' the squeaky third step. I sat down against the wall and listened.

"—see it as well as I do," Grandpa was sayin'.

There was the noise of Uncle Charlie sucking in air before he took a gulp of his scaldin' coffee, then his chair landed on all four legs.

" 'Course I see it."

"I've never seen Lou take to a man like thet afore."

"We knew it was bound to happen."

"Sure we knew it would happen; thet's why we been tryin' so hard to steer her in the right direction."

"Too late for any steerin' from us now."

"Not too late!" Grandpa sounded about ready to pound the table for emphasis. "It *can't* be too late," he went on a bit quieter. "This fella's jest a kid, even if he is a preacher, an' he has nothin'—nothin'. Did ya see his suit?"

"I see'd."

"All pressed an' clean, sure, but so thin ya could walk through it—the best he's got, too."

"Ya don't judge a man by his clothes—even I know thet."

"Thet ain't the point! Point is, he can't *afford* a better suit. My guess is he don't have enough change in his pocket at any one time to make a jingle. And iffen ya start with nothin', you sure ain't gonna add much to it on a preacher's salary. The man doesn't even have him a rig to drive—jest a saddle-horse. You wanna see Lou dressed in worn-out clothes, a hang-in' on, a-straddle a horse?"

"Now hold on," said Uncle Charlie, and the chair legs hit the floor again. "How'd my *wants* get into this? You know how I feel 'bout Lou. You know what I'd like to see her have. I jest don't see how you can put a stop to this here thing that's a-brewin', that's all."

"I'll have a talk with her."

"A talk?"

"Yeah, I'll have a talk."

Uncle Charlie drew in air again and swallowed some coffee. The chair protested as he tilted back on two legs again.

"Jest like that, a talk, and the girl will plumb ferget thet she ever saw the fella."

Grandpa paused. "No," he finally answered, "no, it won't be quite that simple; but Lou's a good, sensible girl. She'll respect my wishes. Iffen I ask her not to—not to—" he cleared his throat—"not to return the compliment of his favor, she'll abide by it."

"Shore she will. It may nigh break her heart, but she will."

Grandpa got up and moved to the coffeepot on the stove. A third cup? He really was upset.

"Aw c'mon, Charlie. Lou isn't thet far gone. Sure she seems to fancy the young preacher; an' truth is he appears a right fine boy, but Lou has never been one to chase after fellas and—"

"That's jest the point!"

"Ya don't believe in this business of love at first sight, do ya?"

" 'Course not. But iffen I don't miss my guess, there's gonna be some more sightin' bein' done; and she's a gonna look again and again, and then . . . Lou's never encouraged anyone before, but thet look in her eyes tonight— iffen thet weren't *encouragement,* then I've never seen it."

There was a pause.

"And ya think she'd hurt?" Grandpa said.

"Sure she'd hurt!"

"Then what do we do?"

The room was silent for an uncomfortable long spell.

"We weigh it. Is the hurt too much to ask her to pay fer her own good?"

Grandpa sloshed some more coffee into both empty cups.

"Maybe not," he mused, "maybe not."

"Lou might reckon thet love was more important than fancy things," cautioned Uncle Charlie.

"It's hard to pay the grocer with love," growled Grandpa.

"Yeah!" Uncle Charlie heaved a sigh. "But the funny thing is, love has a habit of makin' do even when the pickin's are short."

"Well I don't want thet for Lou! 'Makin' do' ain't enough fer a girl like her."

"Yeah!"

"I'll talk to her."

Uncle Charlie's chair came down on all four legs again, and I knew that they considered the matter closed. I hugged close to the wall and headed back for my bed.

I had heard all Grandpa's arguments to Uncle Charlie. Not once had he mentioned the information passed on to him by Deacon Brown. I knew that Grandpa truly did want to be fair to the parson, but I also knew that it was nigh impossible for him to completely forget what he had heard. He loved Lou and he didn't want to take any chances.

I wanted to keep Lou, too. I hoped that Grandpa's talk would work. At the same time, I felt afraid. Somehow it looked like Auntie Lou would be hurt. I didn't want that. More than anything in the world I wanted her happy.

Suddenly I wished that I was on speakin' terms with God so that I could pour the whole, miserable mess out to Him. I almost envied Willie Corbin. I turned my thoughts around with a firm hand. God probably wouldn't care anyway. He had never cared about my problems before. I pulled the sleepin' Pixie into my arms, buried my face against her and cried myself to sleep.

Of course I could, even now, call Grandpa to my room and relate the entire conversation that I had had with the preacher, but if I did that, then maybe he wouldn't bother havin' that talk with Auntie Lou after all. I felt all torn up inside. It didn't seem fair to the preacher for me to remain silent, and yet maybe my silence was all that it would take to keep Auntie Lou. Somewhere down the road, I promised myself, after everything was settled, I'd for sure tell Grandpa jest what I had learned firsthand about the preacher. Surely it wouldn't really hurt him none if I jest kept quiet for a time.

Prairie Fire

Grandpa must have had his "little talk" with Lou. I don't know what was said. Lou was attempting to be her own sweet self, but I could feel a tension or strain there. Her cheeriness now seemed put on or unnatural, and at times I saw a real wistful look on her face, like she was yearnin' for something that she couldn't have.

The next Sunday at church she smiled as she shook the pastor's hand, but when he attempted to detain her for a minute, she hurried on. He looked puzzled but was hardly in a position to run after her.

We headed into another week. Our weather still did not change.

It had been a strange fall. Everyone would look back on it and remember it for its dryness. All through the late summer and fall, we had noticed the lack of moisture. Even the farmers who were normally noted for their lateness at harvest had plenty of time to get their crops in and get all of their fall work done. Mr. Wilkes' threshin' machine had sat idle for many weeks and there were still no late rainstorms.

Now it was time for snow—in fact, it was past due. The birds had long since migrated, the animals were wearin' their heavier coats. Nights were frosty and cold, coverin' all but the swiftly movin' water with ice. Ponds were great for ice-skatin' and slidin', but already we kids were tired of that sport and were wishin' that the snow would come so that we could sled and snowball instead.

The farmers all talked about the dryness. At first it had been jest to make conversation, then it was downright concern.

The stubble fields were tinder dry, and the heaped-up dead leaves from the trees rattled like old dry bones as the winds shifted their directions. Livestock had to be watered daily, the natural waterin' holes havin' frozen over and the liquid from the snow not bein' there to slacken their thirst. People worried about the wild animals and their need for water.

It was strange—even the feelin' in the air got to be different somehow. And then it happened.

It was still afternoon, crisp but with no wind and not a cloud in the sky. We had jest been dismissed from school when Avery Garrett let out a whoop.

"Look—there in the west—clouds!"

A general holler went up.

"Snow's comin'!"

"We can sleigh ride!"

"An' snowball!"

"Yippee!"

The teacher heard the commotion and appeared behind us.

"Those aren't clouds, boys. That's smoke!"

"Smoke?"

We looked again; it *was* smoke. I could also see that it was somewhere off in the direction of our farm. Without waitin' for another word from anyone, I lit off for home.

As I got nearer I could see that the smoke was not comin' from the farm but beyond it. That relaxed me some but still I ran on. Before I even got halfway across our pasture, I could see things stirrin' in our yard. Teams and riders were millin' around and more were arrivin'. People ran back and forth between the pump and the wagons. Other wagons carryin' anything that would hold water were at the creek bridge down the road.

I thought that I'd never hold out to reach the yard, but I guess I got my second wind.

You could smell the smoke in the air now, and it appeared from the clouds that were billowin' to the sky that the stubble fire was headed directly for our place.

I stumbled into our yard, pantin' for breath, jest in time to hear Grandpa addressin' the gathered neighbor men.

"I thank ya for all comin' and offerin' to help me save the farm, but it jest won't work."

He was interrupted by protests, but he held up his hand for silence.

"Iffen we fight to save my buildin's, it will take *every* man and *every* team to win. While we're battlin' to save what we have here, the flanks of the fire will get away from us, go on to other farms and then the town. We can't 'llow that. You know it and I know it. We've got to let my farm go and concentrate on saving others—particularly the town."

It was grim business, but the men knew that what Grandpa said was true.

"I'll take a man or two," continued Grandpa, "and Charlie and me will load what we can here and try to drive the stock over across the crik before the fire gets here."

I looked around. The house with Auntie Lou's white curtains showin' at the windows, the barn that housed Bossie, the pigs in the pen, my favorite cottonwood tree, the trail to the crik—everything, everything that I knew and loved would soon be gone.

"Ya best be movin' out, men," my Grandpa said. "We don't have much time."

The men, murmurin' and shakin' their heads, turned to their teams.

I felt sick. My knees gave out and I felt myself goin' down. I managed to slide onto a wood block to make it look like I'd sorta sat down intentional like. I put my head in my hands but jerked it up again when I heard someone shout, "Wait!" Guess all heads jerked up at that one word.

It was the preacher. His horse stood there in a lather, heavin' from the run. The preacher was in his preacher-visitin' clothes so everyone knew that he had been makin' a call on someone when he spotted the fire.

"Aren't you going to try to save the farm?"

"Nope," one of the men answered flatly. "Daniel says we need to save the town instead."

"I think there's a way to save both."

The men looked at the preacher kind of dumb-like.

"Mr. Jones is right, but maybe there's a way that we can save the farm, too. We'll move toward the fire about three-quarters of a mile, where the creek cuts in the closest to the road. Since most of the fire is between the creek and the road, the flames will cover a narrower area.

"When we get there you men with the plows will make a vee between the creek and roads, pointing east, and the fire will feed itself into the vee. That way the strength of the fire will decrease as it moves east, and it won't take as many men to hold each line.

"Mr. T. Smith, you take three men and watch for fires on the south side of the road. Mr. Corbin, you take two men and follow the creek to catch any small fires from jumpers. Those on plows make that vee as fast as your teams can move. All the rest of us will be on hand with water barrels and wet gunny sacks. We'll work both sides of the vee and lick that thing before it gets this far."

In the same hurried voice the parson raised his hand and said, "Let us pray." All the men bowed their heads nervously.

"Dear Lord, you know our need and how much we depend upon your help. We're not going to give you orders about what to do, God. We are just going to thank you for being there when we need you. In the name of Jesus, your Son. Amen."

The men had looked doubtful when the preacher had first started talkin', but by the time he had finished his prayer, their faces showed new assurance and they were ready to go. Teams began to leave our yard—some of them on a reckless run. Uncle Charlie jest barely made it to the gate ahead of them and threw it wide open to give them free access through our field. There was a fence between our field and the Turley pasture, but I knew that the first man there would simply snip the wires so that the plows could pass through.

Our yard was soon boilin' with activity. Men ran for more barrels, pails, water, gunny sacks, shovels, hoes—anything that would aid in fightin' the fire.

Grandpa's partin' shout had been, "Keep an eye on thet fire, Josh, an' iffen it gets by us, you all git." Uncle Charlie had left our team hitched to the rig and tied to the rail fence for jest that purpose.

The dust finally cleared and Auntie Lou and I were standin' alone, shakin'. She was holdin' Pixie as though that little dog were her last connection with a sane world. Gramps came to stand with us.

Gramps had wanted to go, too, to do what he could as a fire fighter, but Grandpa had put his foot down.

"I jest don't want to chance it, Pa." Grandpa had said. " 'Sides, yer needed here—in case this don't work."

I took the tremblin' Pixie from Auntie Lou's arms. She stood there silent and white. Her eyes watched the departin' men and horses—one wagon in particular—where the preacher was hitchin' a ride. I didn't know what to say, so I said nothin'.

Auntie Lou suddenly came alive. I wondered for a minute what she was up to and then I realized where she was headin'. The preacher's horse stood where he had wandered after bein' left on his own. His sides still heaved with each breath he drew, and he was flecked with foam from runnin'. Auntie Lou walked up to him. He trembled and moved away a step, but she spoke softly and he let her gather the reins in her hand. Still speakin' she slipped his saddle and hung it on the rail fence; then she proceeded to rub him down with handfuls of dry grass.

The horse responded to her voice and hands, and gradually stopped shakin'. The rubbin' seemed to settle him down, and by the time he was dry his sides had stopped their jerky heaves. Lou continued rubbin' and soothin', talkin' all the while. I don't know what she was tellin' that horse, but it seemed to have a quietin' effect. By the time she had finished and had tethered him, he was ready to eat a bit.

I hadn't stirred. I felt nailed to the spot, unable to think or move. As Auntie Lou walked back toward the house, I looked again to the west. The fire had definitely drawn closer. I wondered if they'd be able to hold it, if the preacher's vee would really work. I shuddered and held Pixie so tight that she squirmed and whined.

"You'd best get on with the chores, Josh."

It was Auntie Lou speakin'. She spoke jest as though nothing out of the ordinary was happenin'.

"Do you want some milk and cookies first?"

I shook my head no, and went in to change my school clothes. Gramps and Lou followed me in. Her face was still pale, but other than that she looked composed enough,

"It could be a long fight," she said. "I'd best get on a big pot of coffee and make up sandwiches for when it's over."

Gramps spoke then for the first time.

"I was wondering, my dear, if we should pack some blankets and clothing into that wagon just in case we need to leave in a hurry—in case it doesn't work."

"It'll work."

Auntie Lou seemed so confident of the fact that I could almost believe it too.

Gramps smiled and let it go, and when Auntie Lou washed her hands and moved to her cupboards to set to work, he did likewise.

I made sure that Pixie was in a safe spot where I could find her quickly if I needed to, and set out to care for the chores.

The smoke hung heavy in the air now and at times you even could see the flicker of the flames.

I did all of the chores. Even milked Bossie. She fidgeted some, a rarity in Bossie. She usually stood still as stone for milkin'.

Instead of puttin' her back to pasture, I jest left her in the barnyard; then I went to the house with the milk.

I knew by the look to the west that the fire had reached the vee. They'd be fightin' there to hold it—all those neighborfolk and Grandpa and Uncle Charlie—and the preacher.

I had counted fifteen of them in all. Not many men to fight a runaway stubble fire, what with the fields as dry as match-sticks, but at least there was little wind blowin' to fight against them. That would give them a little extra time and make their efforts more effective.

I hurried the milk to the house. The pail wasn't as full as usual. I didn't know for sure if that was Bossie's fault or mine.

Auntie Lou and Gramps had finished fixin' and packin' sandwiches. The big black kettle filled with coffee was steamin' and fillin' the kitchen with its pleasant aroma.

"Josh," Auntie Lou said as I stepped through the door, "set the milk down and bring all of the milk cans. Fill two of them with water from the pump and bring the other one to me."

I ran.

It was a big job pumpin' those cans of water. Guess it wouldn't have been so bad if I wouldn't have been in such a hurry. I was out of breath by the time I got the job done. I couldn't carry the full cans on my own, so I put the lids on and let them sit.

Auntie Lou came out, followed by Gramps. They both were carryin' the baskets that had been packed with sandwiches and cups. I watched as they deposited them in the light wagon that had been left for our escape. They both studied the sky to the west. It was gettin' quite dark by now so the red glow showed up even brighter. The cloudy billows did seem to come from a narrower strip and we began to have real hopes that the men were holdin' the fire.

The remainin' milk can was filled with the steamin' coffee, and it was placed in the wagon with a heavy woolen quilt tucked securely around it. We loaded the cans of cold water, and after Auntie Lou did a final check to be sure that we had everything, we started off.

"We'll go around by the road," Auntie Lou advised and I knew that she was right. If we followed the road there was no danger of bein' trapped by a fresh outbreak of flames.

I tucked Pixie in a box with Uncle Charlie's old jacket inside. There was no way that I was chancin' leavin' her at home alone.

I drove, Gramps not havin' much experience with team drivin', and Lou wantin' to let me feel like a man.

It seemed to take forever to get to the fire. Now and then the smoke would almost make us choke, and we had to breathe through a sleeve or some other piece of our clothin'. The horses were skitterish, not likin' the smoke one little bit, and it took all of my attention jest to keep them under control.

It appeared that the sky was cloudin' up some, but it was awful hard to tell what was true cloud and what was smoke cover.

We pulled the team up short of the actual fire site, and Gramps walked on ahead to see how things were farin' and to pass on the word that we were there.

He came back almost on the run. They were doin' it—they were holdin' the fire! Little fires were still breakin' out all along the plowed vee, the men not havin' time to plow as many furrows as they really needed. But they were holdin' it, and already it was startin' to diminish.

The word of our bein' there passed along the ranks quickly; the men came two-by-two to take a sandwich and coffee break. Most of the men were more anxious for some cold water. I guess Auntie Lou had figured that when she set me to gettin' the two cans filled.

Two-by-two they came, hurriedly, anxious to get back to their spot in the line, their faces soot-streaked, their clothes smoke-smellin'. Some had small burns and Auntie Lou set Gramps to cleanin' them up and wrappin' the ones that needed it with strips of clean white cloth and strong smellin' ointment.

Auntie Lou poured coffee and served sandwiches and asked the news of the fire from each new pair that came. We found that the fire had given them all a real scare at one point. It had jumped the crik at a narrow spot, and the men fightin' there had had to call on others to help them get the new blaze under control. The men along the road and the vee had had to cover more area then, and it looked for a while that the fire was goin' to win. A few more men had arrived from the surroundin' farms, and that had added, jest in time, fresh strength to the firefighters. They were able to hold it and eventually beat it back.

I saw Cullum comin' for refreshments along with Joey Smith. He looked as sooty as the rest of them, even though he had been one of the late arrivers, havin' farther to come than others. He drank his coffee a little slower than some, and all the time he kept stealin' glances at Auntie Lou. She didn't seem to notice. I asked Cullum how things were goin'.

"I think we've got it," he replied. "Thet was a first-rate idea, whoever thought of it. Thanks to thet, you folk still have yer home and yer farm."

He looked at Auntie Lou again, and I knew that he was truly glad that we still had our home.

"The Turleys weren't so lucky," he went on. "They managed to save their house by concentratin' all their efforts on it, but they lost everything else— all their other buildings, their farm implements, and even most of their livestock."

I felt mighty bad about the Turleys. At the same time I couldn't help but feel relief that it looked like our place would be safe.

Cullum turned to follow Joey Smith back to the fire.

I watched Auntie Lou as she looked anxiously through the smoke at each new set of faces. I could see that she was worried. I wished that Grandpa and Uncle Charlie would hurry and come so that her mind could be put at ease. They came at last, soiled, sweaty, and tired, but overjoyed almost to the point of bein' silly. Auntie Lou was right pleased to see them and gave Grandpa a quick hug, but the worried look still didn't leave her eyes.

"It worked!" beamed Grandpa. "We're holdin' it. Still work to do stampin' and beatin' out trouble spots, but we'll hold it. It worked!"

Auntie Lou jest smiled a sweet smile, like she'd known all along that it would.

Uncle Charlie accepted his coffee, but instead of gulpin' it down, he sipped it slowly. I was glad that there was no one else watchin'. It would have spoiled his reputation.

"Got enough fire on the outside without havin' it on the inside, too," he explained.

They hurried back to take up their pails and shovels. Still Auntie Lou kept watchin' through the now lessenin' smoke.

Two fellas came carryin' Eb Crawford. He had had the misfortune of havin' a pant leg catch fire as he tramped out flames. He had rolled on the ground as quick as he could, but he still had a very painful leg. They wrapped Auntie Lou's quilt around his body and Joey Smith was sent to drive him home.

It seemed to me that all of the men must have eaten. Some had even returned for another cup of coffee or a sandwich. The fire was as good as out now. It was decided that many of the men would be free to go home. Only a few would be needed to stay to watch for any unexpected breakouts.

The smoke was still hangin' in the air but not with the same density that it formerly had.

Auntie Lou still paced agitated-like, and I was about to question her when I saw her face light up. It went from relief, to fear, to relief again, and I saw the preacher walkin' through the smoke.

Perspiration had made ugly tracks through the coatin' of soot on his face. His parson's suit was dirty and smeared from trampin' fire, sloshin' water, and shovellin' dirt. Here and there, all over his clothin', little holes had burned through the material where flyin' sparks had landed.

He walked straight to Auntie Lou who was pourin' coffee with tremblin' hands.

"It worked." His voice held intense relief.

Auntie Lou looked at him and her eyes were filled with gratitude.

"Thank you," she whispered and they looked long at one another. I wondered jest what words they would be usin' if what they were sayin' with their eyes would have been said aloud.

Mr. T. Smith came up then and Auntie Lou turned to serve him. Some of the men gathered around, laughin' and poundin' the preacher on the back, praisin' his plan and the way it worked. Everyone was talkin' and feelin' good in spite of their tiredness and the blisters on their hands and faces. Grandpa came too. He wanted a chance to thank all of his neighbors before he sent them on home. He couldn't voice what he really felt—there jest weren't words—but he tried and I think that every neighbor there understood what he wasn't able to say.

Most of them moved out, drivin' their hayracks or wagons. Through the closin'-in night they went, enjoyin', at least for a while, its welcome coolness.

"Thank ya, Lou, for thinkin' of the men," Grandpa said then. "Guess you can get on back to the house and rest yerself easy. This here fire's gonna hold now. Charlie and me will wait around jest to be sure that no live sparks are still hangin' around."

"I'll wait with you."

It was the preacher who spoke. Grandpa looked hard at him, like he was seein' the man for the first time.

"Be no need, son." He said it with feelin'. "Things are settled now, thanks to you—and the Lord—and you sure did earn yer rest at the end of this day."

"I'd still like to stay if you don't mind." He turned to me. "Josh, would you mind caring for my horse? I left him in kind of a hurry, and I'd sure like him to have some proper attention."

"Auntie Lou already did," I blurted out. "Rubbed him down and every-thing—but I'll give him a drink. Should be okay for him to have some water now. I'll put him in the barn and give him a bit of chop, too."

I would have said more, but I got the feelin' thet the preacher wasn't listenin' anyhow. He was busy lookin' at Auntie Lou.

It was cool now and as the preacher picked up his shovel and turned to go with Grandpa and Uncle Charlie, I noticed his thin suit.

"Hey wait," I hollered.

They turned.

"I got Uncle Charlie's old coat here in Pixie's box. You want it?"

Grandpa laughed as I hurried to dig out the old coat, but he did com-mend me.

"Good thinkin', Boy. It's gonna get a mite cold afore the night's over."

The preacher wasn't proud; he slipped into that old coat with real thank-fulness. It was really tight and the arms were too short, but it sure beat nothin'.

Gramps and I helped Auntie Lou gather the milk cans and cups and the empty sandwich boxes; then we headed for home.

It was quite dark now and the horses, eager to get home, had to slow their pace and pick their way carefully along the road. I didn't need to do much reinin'. When we reached home I cared for the team and the preacher's horse while Gramps and Auntie Lou unloaded the wagon and cleaned up the kitchen.

Now that the excitement and scare was drainin' out of me, I felt dog-tired. I dragged myself to the house. When I entered the kitchen, I checked to be sure that Auntie Lou had remembered to bring in Pixie. She had. Then I checked the clock and noticed with great satisfaction that it was way past my bedtime. I grinned to myself as I scooped up Pixie and started up the stairs. I didn't even bother to wash. Auntie Lou's voice stopped me.

"Thank you, Josh, for thinkin' of that jacket. It was a thoughtful thing to do and I was proud of you." She smiled at me. " 'Night now."

I grinned again and went on up the stairs. This time I was gonna get away with goin' to bed unwashed, but I was too tired to even enjoy it. I could hardly wait to fall into my bed.

CHAPTER 25

Next Mornin'

I awoke the next day to sounds comin' from the kitchen. It was more than jest the usual sounds, of Auntie Lou gettin' breakfast. There was male laughter and talkin', and the clink of cups bein' replaced on the table. I jumped out of bed and reached for my overalls. They stunk! In fact, the smell of smoke seemed to hang all about me. I pulled them on anyway and hurriedly buttoned my shirt.

At the kitchen table sat the four men waitin' for breakfast. Gramps was the only one who looked presentable. The others had washed their faces and hands, but little blisters appeared here and there, and their clothes looked just awful.

They were all in a good mood, though, and I figured that they deserved to be.

"Look outside, Boy," Grandpa said when I came down—and I did.

There was our whole farm, alive and complete—and covered with a clean, white blanket of new-fallen snow.

"Snow!"

"Yessiree—started as rain 'bout four o'clock this mornin' and now yer gettin' yer snow."

I grinned.

"Won't need to worry anymore about that fire now," Grandpa went on.

Auntie Lou was busyin' herself flippin' pancakes and fryin' eggs and bacon. Uncle Charlie crossed leisurely to the stove to give her a hand. She let him.

I took my place at the table and lifted hot pancakes onto my plate. I refrained from reachin' for the butter until after we'd prayed. I could hardly wait to introduce Pixie to the snow. I wondered jest what she would think of it.

I ate all that I could hold and the men were still eatin'. They finally indicated to Auntie Lou that they had had enough.

"I really must be going," said the preacher. "I feel badly in need of a bath and some fresh clothes."

As I looked at him I wondered what he would do for a suit come Sunday.

"I'll get yer horse," said Uncle Charlie. He put on his hat and jacket and headed for the door.

The preacher rose from the table and thanked Auntie Lou for the breakfast. He spoke a few words to Gramps and then turned to Grandpa.

"I'm thankful, Mr. Jones—truly thankful that you didn't lose your home."

Grandpa worked at swallowin'.

"And I," he said, "and I. I'll never be able to thank *you* enough for the plan that ya came up with and the way that you worked to carry it out. Seemed everywhere that I looked, there you was, diggin' and trampin' and pitchin' water and fightin' with a wet sack. I'm truly thankful. Any man that can think and fight like that ain't goin' to be stopped by the hard things in life, I reckon. Yer gonna make a great preacher—and I—ah—I jest want ya to know that yer more than welcome in my home—and at my table—anytime."

The preacher extended his hand, his face lightin' up.

"Thank you, sir. Thank you."

He hesitated a moment and then hurried on, seemin' to sense that he mustn't miss this chance of a lifetime.

"This may seem like taking advantage of the situation, Mr. Jones, but I—I would like to request your permission to call on your daughter—not as a minister, sir," he added with a smile.

Grandpa smiled, too, and extended his hand.

"And I'd be right proud to have you do that." He stole a glance at Auntie Lou, who seemed to be holdin' her breath, her hands clasped tightly in her balled-up apron. "I don't think that Lou will be objectin' to the idea either."

It seemed pretty obvious that Grandpa had made up his mind about the preacher. He'd won Grandpa's heart, and I couldn't see that anyone could convince Grandpa otherwise.

The preacher turned to Auntie Lou then. She finally breathed again and managed a smile in response. Her face was flushed and her eyes looked about to spill over. He crossed to her and took one of her small hands in his.

"Wednesday?"

She nodded. They looked at each other for a moment and then he turned and left. As soon as he was gone, Auntie Lou threw herself into Grandpa's arms.

"Oh, Pa." she cried and the brimmin' tears spilled down her cheeks.

"There now, Baby. There now." He patted her shoulder. I had never heard him call her Baby before.

"I know what I said about him and how he had nothin' and I wanted *more* for you and—and all that; but he's a man, Honey—a real man. He fought that there fire with all his might; and I reckon iffen he puts his mind to it, he'll be able to care, somehow, for a mere slip of a girl, even iffen she does jest happen to be the greatest little gal in the world."

I picked up Pixie and headed outside, stoppin' only long enough to grab my coat and hat as I left.

Sure, I liked the preacher okay, and Auntie Lou seemed to be right stuck on him, and I sure wouldn't withhold anything from Auntie Lou; but, boy, *was I gonna miss her.* I wondered if there was any way that I could be without her and still survive.

I clutched Pixie tight against my chest. I had wanted to find out her first impression of the cold, white world, but somehow it didn't seem so important now.

I arrived outside jest in time to see the preacher turn his horse from the lane to the road. He had a cold ride ahead. His thin parson suit was still partially wet and the fallin' snow wasn't gonna help his comfort none. Uncle Charlie's old, too-small coat helped some, but left a lot to be desired. Still, I kinda doubted if he'd even notice.

CHAPTER 26

The Lord's Day and the Lord's Man

Folks were still buzzin' about the fire as they gathered for the Sunday mornin' service. The new preacher had won his way into many hearts, not jest by the fast-thinkin', but also by his ability to pitch in and fight. I noticed several mothers and daughters eyein' him with added interest.

"Ya haven't got a fat chance," I said to myself, and even felt some pride in the fact that he had chosen Auntie Lou above all the rest. I felt sorrow, too, for I still wanted her to stay with us where I felt she belonged.

I was peekin' around to see where my friends were sittin'—and nearly jumped out of my shoes. Way in the back, lookin' kind of embarrassed, was Cullum! All I could figure out was that he was there as a favor to the preacher, seein' how the man was now a hero in these parts.

The preacher wore a suit. It certainly wasn't brand new, but I guess it was the best he could do. It was properly pressed, and the mended places didn't show too much. After the openin' hymn I guess most folks, like me, kinda forgot all about it.

Jest before the preacher was to bring the message, Deacon Brown asked for a chance to speak.

He expressed how thankful the people of the area and the town were to the reverend for his part in fightin' the fire that could have spelled disaster for so many. Because the parson had suffered the loss of his Sunday suit on behalf of the people, the people had taken up a collection to help him replace his loss. Deacon Brown handed an envelope to the surprised preacher, and the people all clapped as they read his unbelievin' and thankful face.

The deacon then went on to say that a fund had been set up at the General Store for any and all who wished to help the Turleys get a fresh start. If anyone had a piglet or a calf they could spare, that, too, would be appreciated.

The service then went on as usual.

As we went through the Sunday hand-shakin' line, I heard the preacher say softly to Auntie Lou, "Wednesday." She smiled and I thought that she had never looked prettier.

The preacher came Wednesday after supper as planned. He had already taken the train to town to shop for his new clothes. There wasn't a store in our small town that carried what he needed. He really did look quite grand in his new suit, though he wore a shirt, not his white collar, when he came to call on Auntie Lou.

They were still talkin' when I was sent up to bed. They didn't seem to pay too much attention to the rest of us, though Auntie Lou did think to put on the coffee for Grandpa and Uncle Charlie. Gramps had given me a knowin' wink and excused himself earlier than usual.

Uncle Charlie and Grandpa took their coffee and moved to the checkerboard in the far corner of the room.

I went up to bed draggin' my heels. I sure would have liked to hear what was bein' said, but even I knew better than to try to listen. The preacher and Auntie Lou spoke kinda soft anyway, and I didn't suppose that their voices would even carry as far as the stairs.

The next day we had more snow, and Grandpa decided that it was time to change from the wagon wheels to the sleigh runners. I went off to school wishin' that I could hang around and get in on the changin'.

Friday night the preacher came again. This time Auntie Lou had invited him for supper. It was almost more than I could do to sit at that table watchin' him watchin' Auntie Lou with that self-satisfied look in his eyes. She rested her hand ever so lightly on my shoulder as she placed a refilled plate of biscuits on the table. *It's really true,* I thought to myself. *God's gonna take away Auntie Lou, too.*

I excused myself from the table, sayin' that I didn't feel too well—which I truly didn't—and went up to my room. I laid there for a long time tryin' to sort it all out, wantin' to cry and yet not able to. Auntie Lou came up with a worried look on her face and felt my forehead.

"You're not gonna be sick, are ya, Josh?" she asked me and there was fear showin' in her voice.

"Naw," I said, "I'm fine, jest a little off-feed, that's all. I'll be fine come mornin'."

She still looked unconvinced and leaned over me fixin' my already okay pillow and brushin' back my hair. For a moment I felt a sense of victory that I still had the power to pull her away from the preacher; then the anger filled me again—not at Auntie Lou, not even at the preacher really. I mean, who could blame the guy for fallin' hard for Auntie Lou? Still, the angry feelin' gnawed at me, and I turned away from Auntie Lou.

"I'm fine," I said again, "jest need some sleep, that's all."

She rested her hand on my head again.

"I love ya, Josh," she whispered, and then she was gone.

I cried then; I couldn't help it. The tears jest started to roll down my cheeks and fall onto my pillow. I wished with all of my heart that I had remembered to bring Pixie, and then I felt her lickin' my face. She had come lookin' for me.

I drew her close and cried into her fur. At least I still had Pixie. If God would jest leave her alone—keep His hands off—at least I'd have her to love. I didn't even try to choke back the tears but jest let them run down my cheeks, where periodically Pixie's little pink tongue whisked them away.

CHAPTER 27

Another Sunday

We headed to church in the sleigh the next Sunday. I loved the crunch of the runners on the new snow.

The sun was shinin', glistenin' off the snow on the roadway and the fields. It was gettin' close to Christmas now and the feelin' was already in the air.

The preacher directed the service in his new set of clothes, sincerely thankin' the people for the opportunity of purchasin' them. He looked jest fine.

Already folks had heard that he was *callin'* on Auntie Lou; some of the girls wore disappointed looks, and their mothers weren't quite so quick to shove them forward at every opportunity.

I didn't listen much to the sermon. It was on the love of God, and I wasn't sure if I could swallow it—not with Auntie Lou sittin' there beside me, her eyes on the preacher's face. Instead, I decided to dream up a new trick to teach Pixie, somethin' really spectacular that no other dog had ever, ever learned to do. Already, Pixie could beg, roll over, play dead, sit, and walk some on her hind legs. She wasn't a puppy anymore, but she was pretty small even though she'd grown a lot. She was a smart dog, and I guess I would have jest about given an arm for her.

I had a hard time comin' up with something within a dog's reach that someone else hadn't already tried. The service ended without me gettin' the problem worked out.

As soon as I could, without bein' too pushy, I made my way past the preacher, shakin' his hand briefly. I then joined Avery and Willie in a corner of the churchyard where they were messin' around in the snow.

"Bet I could take off ol' Mr. T.'s hat," boasted Willie.

"Thought you been to the altar and prayed for God to forgive and help you," countered Avery. "Yer s'posed to be *good* now, not mean."

Willie changed his tune.

"Said *bet* I could, not thet I was gonna try."

"Does it really work?" asked Jack Berry who had joined us.

"What?"

"Goin' to the altar. I mean, do ya feel different, or anything?"

"Well, it ain't the goin' to the altar," said Willie. I had the feelin' that he was repeatin' what the preacher had said. "It's the prayin' thet makes the difference, and a fella can pray any place."

"But does it *work?*"

"Yeah," said Willie, and his eyes lit up. "Yeah, it really did. I mean—I used to be all mean and feelin' mixed up inside, and now—now, thet I told God I was sorry and thet I wanted to quit bein' thet way, I feel," he shrugged, "kinda clean and not fightin'-mad anymore."

"Ya mean—kinda—peace."

"Yeah, I guess so," Willie answered. "Jest don't feel all sad and troubled and scared. Yeah, guess that's peace, huh?"

We all stood around Willie. I suppose every one of us wished that we could feel the things he described. Mitch Turley came over and we left our discussion and went back to makin' snowballs.

I was turned facin' the church steps where the preacher stood talkin' to old Mrs. Adams. She was almost deaf and he had to lean over and raise his voice to be heard. He stopped in mid-sentence and his head jerked up; then without even excusin' himself he was off on the run toward a team hitched at the side rail fence. I looked over to see what was makin' him run so. What I saw made the back of my neck feel like a snake was movin' up my spine.

There was Pixie, my little dog! Somehow she had followed us to church, and there she was now, runnin' under 'Toad' Hopkins' team. Now Toad drove the spookiest horses around and when that small dog started dartin' among their hooves, they near went wild.

I started toward the team, too, but before I could get anywhere near them the preacher was already there. He placed a hand on the nearest horse and spoke soft words in an effort to soothe him, but he didn't wait for the horses to quiet down—not with Pixie under there, threatenin' to be tramped on at any minute. No sirree, that preacher went right under, too.

I stopped in my tracks, too scared to even holler.

The horses pitched and plunged and then out from under them—some way—the preacher rolled, and he held Pixie in his arms.

Everyone else had been too busy talkin' to even notice what had happened, and I guess the preacher was glad that they were. His new suit was snow-covered and had a patch of dirt on one pant leg where a horse's hoof had struck him.

He brushed himself off quickly. I noticed that when he walked toward me he limped, though he was tryin' hard not to.

He felt Pixie to make sure that she had no broken bones. She was tremblin' but she seemed unhurt. He handed her to me and I cuddled her close. I finally found my voice.

"Ya coulda been killed."

He didn't say anything for a minute and then, "She's okay, Josh."

"Are you?"

"Sure—I'm fine—just bumped a little. Don't bother mentioning it, all right?"

I nodded. I swallowed hard and stroked Pixie's brown curly head.

"I didn't know," I said, "that ya liked dogs so much that you'd—you'd risk yer life for 'em."

He looked at me then, and reached out and put a hand on my shoulder.

"Sure—sure, Josh, I like dogs real well. But it wasn't for Pixie that I had to get her out. It was for *you*, Josh."

My eyes must have shown my question, for he steered me away from the crowd and we walked off a few paces together, him still limpin'.

"I know how you love Pixie, Josh, and I know how a fella can feel *cheated* when he loses what he loves. You now, you've already lost your mother and your pa, and then you lost your first dog. Lou told me all about it. Pretty soon—well *pretty* soon—I hope that you'll be called on to share the most important person in your life, Josh. You might feel like you're losing her, too—but you won't be. Lou will always love you—always. She's worried about you, Josh. She's afraid that you might not understand, that you'll be hurt and grow bitter."

He stopped and turned me to face him.

"Lou is afraid that you blamed God for your first dog being killed. She's afraid that she couldn't make you understand that God loves you, that He plans for your good, not your hurt.

"It's true that things happen in life that seem wrong and are painful, but it isn't because God *likes* to see us suffer. He wants to see us *grow.* He wants us to love Him, to trust Him."

I thought back about Willie sayin' that he felt clean and not scared or mad inside anymore; I knew that that's what I wanted, too. I fought with myself for a minute, wonderin' if God could really forgive me for the selfish way that I'd been thinkin' and feelin'. The preacher said that God loved me. If He loved me, then I figured that He'd forgive me, too.

"Can we go somewhere private a minute?" I asked.

"Sure," he said. He placed an arm around my shoulder, and we went through the side door into his study in the little church.

Still clutchin' Pixie close, I poured it all out—how I'd been feelin', how I doubted God, blamed God, even tried to ignore Him if I could. I told, too, about what Deacon Brown had heard and passed on to my grandpa and how I had withheld the truth in a selfish effort to keep Auntie Lou. I cried as I told the preacher, and I think that he cried some, too. Then we prayed together. Willie Corbin was right. It did work! I felt clean and forgiven—and even better yet, *loved.*

I smiled up at the preacher, and I even thought I loved him, too. I was glad that Auntie Lou had picked him. She sure knew how to pick a man.

"Thanks, Nat," I said. That's what Auntie Lou had been callin' him, and I guessed that I'd better get used to it, too—at least until I could rightfully say *Uncle* Nat.

We hugged each other close; then I picked up Pixie and went to find my family. I had something pretty excitin' to tell them on the way home.

CHAPTER 28

Postscript

Well, I guess that jest about sums up the tellin' of how Auntie Lou did her own choosin' and ended up with the best man in the whole county—and how I did my own choosin' and made friends with God.

Auntie Lou and Nat didn't rush about gettin' married. Nat was determined to have somethin' to offer a wife, so it was the next fall, jest after Auntie Lou's nineteenth birthday, that they became man and wife.

Gramps worked out a couple of little things for them. First off, he reminded Grandpa that it was quite the accepted thing for a girl to have her mother's fine things when she married; so all of our front parlor furniture and the fancy dishes went with Auntie Lou to the parsonage.

Gramps went a step further, too. As his weddin' gift to Auntie Lou and Nat, he gave them a fine one-horse buggy.

Grandpa and Uncle Charlie caught the feelin' of excitement about the comin' event, and both managed to find ways that they could be involved in helpin' the young couple, too, without offendin' Nat any.

And Auntie Lou—she was about the prettiest and happiest bride that anyone had ever seen. Nat, standin' there beside her with his grin almost as broad as his wide shoulders, looked real good, too.

And then—bless their hearts—they had a surprise for me!

I was at the end of the schoolin' that could be had in our one-room school, so they convinced Grandpa that since I was an apt student, I should have the advantage of the extra grades that the town school had to offer. So when Auntie Lou and Uncle Nat settled into the parsonage, I moved in with them. I even got to take Pixie with me.

I would spend the week with them and go home every Friday afternoon to spend the weekend with the menfolk at the farm. Gramps and I crowded in a lot of good trips to the crik.

The three men worked out their own system for the batchin' chores, and it seemed to work out quite well. Of course Lou still fretted some about them and visited often to sort of keep things in order. She never let me leave on a Friday without sendin' home some special bakin' with me.

So my weekdays were spent with Auntie Lou and Uncle Nat, sharin' in the life and the love of the parsonage, and my weekends were crowded with activities on the farm with three men who loved me. I got the very best of two different worlds. Now how's that for a happy endin'?

The Winds
of Autumn

With love
to my Uncle Ralph Steeves,
just because
he's special.

Contents

CHARACTERS

Joshua Chadwick Jones—When Josh's parents were killed in an accident while he was still a baby, he was raised by his grandfather and his great-uncle Charlie on the family farm. Though Aunt Lou was not many years older than Josh, being a latecomer to the Jones family, she also took delight in caring for young Josh, and he saw her as a friend and a mother rather than an aunt.

Lou Jones Crawford—Josh's aunt whom he had fought to keep with the family unit in *Once Upon a Summer*. Pretty and vivacious, yet with deep concern for others, Lou was a fitting helpmate for the young minister she married.

Grandpa—the grandfather of Joshua and father of Lou.

Uncle Charlie—the quiet yet supportive brother of Grandpa. He had never married but worked along with Grandpa on his farm.

Gramps—Josh's great-grandfather who had come west to live with his two sons, his granddaughter Lou, and great-grandson Joshua after the death of his wife.

Nat Crawford—the young pastor Lou married. Josh now spends his weeks in town with Lou and Nat in order to continue his education in the town school.

Pixie—the answer to Josh's dream for a dog of his own. She was given to Josh by Gramps who went to great effort to find Josh a second puppy after his first pup was accidentally killed.

CHAPTER 1

An Autumn Surprise

I don't remember a prettier fall than the one we had the year I was fifteen. The long Indian summer days stretched on into October with only enough sprinkles of rain to keep the flowers blooming in Aunt Lou's flower beds and the lawn green enough to contrast with the yellows and golds of the autumn trees and bushes. Even the leaves seemed reluctant to "tuck in" for the winter and kept clinging to the branches week after week in all their fine, colorful array. The sun warmed up the air by noon each day, and the nights were just nippy enough to remind us that we'd best be spending our time getting ready for winter instead of loafing along beside the crik, pretending that this good weather would stay with us forever.

The farmers in the area took in all the crops, the women cleaned out their large farm gardens, we stayed loafing by the crik whenever we could, and still the good weather held. People started talking summer picnics and parties again, but I guess no one wanted to exert themselves enough to do the fixing, for the days went by and no one actually had a picnic—we all just sat around in the sun or took long, lazy walks through the colorful countryside.

As you probably have figured out by now, my favorite place was down by the crik. I took my fishing pole and headed there every chance I got. Most often Gramps, my great-grandfather, went along with me. He likes fishing—and loafing—most as much as I do. The only thing that got in the way of my fishing trips was school. Most all the area boys my age had given up on school and gone off to farm with their pa's or to work in a store or something, but I still hung in there.

Part of it was due to my aunt Lou encouraging me a lot. She was sure I had a good head and kept telling me that it would be a waste, should I not use it. Her husband, my uncle Nat, chimed right in there with her. Since he was the parson in our little town church, I felt that if anyone knew the importance of education, my uncle Nat would be the man. He had gotten his the hard way, having to work his way through school and seminary on accounta he didn't have a ma or pa to see him through, them having died when he was still quite young.

Me, I had it easy. I not only had Lou and Nat but I had Grandpa, a great-uncle Charlie and my Gramps, my great-grandpa. All of them were right keen on me getting all the education I could.

It wasn't a problem to me. In fact, I really liked book learning, even if our school wasn't a very big one and most of the students were young kids or girls. Oh, a few of the boys still attended—like my best friend, Avery Garret. He didn't care too much for school and didn't know what he wanted to do with any schooling that he did get. I figured he just continued on because I was there—and, then, there was a certain amount of fun to be had at school. I mean, with all the girls still going and all.

Then there was Jack Berry. His pa was bound and determined that Jack would be a doctor. Jack wasn't so sure. Truth was, he kinda had his heart set on being a sailor. Only there wasn't any water handy-like, any big water that is. So he didn't know just how he was going to manage to get on a boat—at least a boat any bigger than the rough-looking little two-oar one left down on the small pond near the town for anyone's use who might want to do some rowing.

Willie Corbin was still going to school, too. I wanta tell you about that Willie. He was the biggest rascal in our community when he was younger. Used to get himself in all kinds of trouble. Folks thought that he never would amount to anything but most likely end up in some jail or something. Me, I knew that Willie wasn't really bad; he just liked to have fun, that was all. But that all changed when Willie decided he'd rather spend his future in heaven than hell.

This happened way back after my uncle Nat preached his first sermon in our church. He had just been asked to be our new minister. Willie straightened himself right around and never did go back to his wild ways. I figured if God could make such a change in the likes of Willie Corbin, then He ought to be able to handle almost anyone. Anyway, Willie about had his mind made up that God wanted him to be a missionary. Willie found studying rather hard, but one had to admire him. He kept plugging away at it, determined to prepare himself for some kind of work with heathen people somewhere.

Those were the three fellows from my old country school who were still hanging in there. Then there were four older guys from town. We all hung around together, but I spent most of the time with my old buddies, mostly I guess because they were also from our small church. A couple of the town fellas were a little "wild," according to Aunt Lou, and though she didn't forbid me to see them or anything like that, still she did prefer me to make close friends with the church young folks.

I didn't complain. I liked the church kids and we had us a lot of fun with our corn roasting, sleigh riding, skating on the pond and such.

It seemed hard to believe that me and Pixie, my little dog, had already been two years with Aunt Lou and Uncle Nat in town. We didn't stay in town all the time. Whenever the weather was good—and as I said, it was good most of the time that fall—we went on out to the farm for the weekend to spend time with Grandpa, Uncle Charlie and Gramps, who batched together there.

I would have been hard put to try to say which place I liked best. While I was in town during the week I counted the days till the weekend when I could get back out on the farm again and chop some wood, or go to the pasture for Bossie, the milk cow I had milked so many times myself. I even enjoyed the squealing and grunting of the pigs as I sloshed the slop into their troughs. The chickens seemed to sort of sing their clucking when I poured out their water and grain.

Then as soon as Sunday night came around, I found myself hardly able to wait to get back to town and Aunt Lou and Uncle Nat again. I wondered what Aunt Lou had fixed for Sunday dinner and if she'd saved a piece of pie or an apple dumpling for me. I wondered if Uncle Nat had been called out on some sick call and I hadn't been there to harness Dobbin for him. I thought of all kinds of things that I wanted to ask them or tell them when I got back. You'd think I'd been gone for days the way I chomped to get back again. The truth was, I had just seen both of them at the church service that very morning.

So that was the way I spent the fall, going back and forth, back and forth, and trying to grab the best of two worlds with both hands, so to speak. I would have tired myself plumb out if it hadn't been such a long, lazy-feeling kind of fall. Even after every lick of work was done, we still had us lots of good weather for catching up on just loafing around.

Only one thing wrong with that kind of weather. It sure made it hard to concentrate on studying. I had to take myself in hand every other day, it seemed, and just make myself sit down and study. And then another strange thing happened. Miss Williams, a maiden lady who had been teaching in our school for almost forever, went and threw in a surprise that nearly rocked the whole community. She was getting married, she said, just like that!

Now, no one in his right mind ever picked Miss Williams for the marrying kind. I mean, why would you? She had lived for years and years all alone and looked like she was enjoying it, and then, real sudden-like, she says she is getting married. To a sweetheart of some thirty-seven years, she says. Now, no one in the town knew anything at all about this fella. We'd never even heard of him. But that didn't stop Miss Williams any. She was quitting, she said, and she never gave notice or anything, just packed up her books and her bags and took the train back to some eastern city to marry this man.

Well, that left us without a teacher. There weren't none of us sitting around grieving much. Not even me who liked school. Jack Berry didn't try to hide his enthusiasm—he just whooped right out. A couple of the girls gave him a real cross look, but he didn't care. He whooped again and threw his plaid cap up into the air.

"Well," demanded Jack, "what we gonna do with this here unexpected blessing?"

"What do you mean?" asked Willie. He was already having enough trouble working his way through English without losing precious time. "Blessing? Not a blessing far as I'm concerned. Miss Williams was an okay teacher. Wisht she would have stayed around and finished the job."

I figured with Miss Williams already being there for thirty-seven years that she had probably stuck with the job about as long as anyone could expect her to. But even though I felt sorry for Willie, I couldn't hide my grin. It sure did seem like a blessing. I mean with the weather beckoning one outside all the time and all. Who knew when we might have winter set in and maybe then we wouldn't see the sun again for months? We could catch up on our studying then.

"Well," Jack asked again, "what do we do with this here—a—hardship?"

Even Willie had to smile at that, and the first thing we knew we were all laughing. When we finally settled down we busied ourselves with some serious planning.

"I s'pose I'll go on out to the farm," I said. "I always do on holidays or anything."

Jack lived just on the edge of town and there weren't as many things to keep a boy busy at his place, his folks having no livestock or crops or anything.

"Iffen I go home my pa'll want me to keep my nose in a book. Might as well be back in school," complained Jack. "Fact is, I'd be better off in school. At least there we get recess."

Willie gave Jack a withering look. Jack had the brains if he just would use them, and I think it bothered Willie some that he had to work so hard for his average grade while Jack just fooled away his time and didn't even care what grade he got.

"Guess I'll have me plenty a good fishin' time," I continued, hoping to break the tension some.

"We could all get together for some football," put in Willie. He loved football and was good at it, too, in spite of the fact that none of us had any equipment to play the game and our folks were always worrying that some-one might get hurt.

Avery spoke up then. "I've been thinkin' for a long time that it sure would be fun to backpack up along the crik and spend a night or two out campin'."

"Great idea," I practically hollered. I wondered why I hadn't thought of it long ago. It surprised me some to hear Avery mention it. He had never talked about it before. I had never been on an overnight hike, and with the woods looking like they did, it sounded like a first-rate idea.

Jack and Willie were about as excited as I was.

"Do you think our folks would let us?" asked Willie.

"Why not? We're already fifteen. 'Bout time we were allowed to do some-thin' on our own."

I agreed. I suppose I would have been pressing to get the chance ages ago if I had just thought of it.

"Let's ask," said Jack. "They can't do no more'n say no."

The thought of them saying no just about made me feel sick inside now that the idea had begun to work on me. They just had to say yes! They *had* to!

"Who you gonna ask?" Avery was saying, and I suddenly realized he was speaking to me.

"Huh?" I grunted.

"You gonna ask your aunt Lou or your grandpa?"

I shrugged my shoulders. "I dunno. I'm at Aunt Lou's right now."

"Think she'll let you go?"

I thought about it. Aunt Lou was understanding enough—but she was a bit protective as well. Would she understand how much it meant to a boy to go off camping on his own? I switched my thoughts to my grandpa. He was a swell person, about as kind a fella as a boy could want to have watching over him. But I was sure he had never thought of taking off into the hills on a camping trip even if the fall work was all done. Seemed to me that he might favor me staying with the books as well.

"I dunno," I said again.

"Well, at least you've got a choice," said Avery. "Me, I've got to convince my ma. If I can sell her on the idea, she'll work it out with pa."

One thing I knew for sure, I didn't have a ma and pa to talk it over with.

"Look," said Jack Berry, "can you fellas come over to my house after your chores are done tonight? We gotta get our heads together and plan our attack."

Crazy Jack! He liked to make everything sound like we were all in a war against our folks or something, but nevertheless we all nodded our heads and agreed to try to get some time with one another over at Jack's house after we hauled the water and carried in the wood and coal.

We parted then. I think we were all sort of holding our breaths. I looked again toward the distant woods as I swung through the gate at Aunt Lou's. Boy, did they look inviting. I could visualize, from where I was, just where the crik cut through the hills and swung around to the south. I could almost hear the rustle of the gold and red leaves and feel the gentle breeze on the skin of my cheek.

A crow called, off in the distance somewhere, and I wondered why it hadn't already left for the South. Guess it just wanted to hang around and enjoy the good weather. Boy, the woods and fields really drew a body on such a day! I could hardly settle myself down to filling the woodbox and the coal scuttle.

CHAPTER 2

Pleading Our Case

I didn't say much to Aunt Lou while I wolfed down the cookies and milk she had out for me. She had already gotten the word that Miss Williams was done—had left just like that and our school was without a teacher in the middle of a term.

"It's a shame, that's what it is," remarked Aunt Lou. I guess she might have been repeating what everyone else on our block was saying, for she suddenly checked herself. She thought for a moment in silence and then continued in a lower voice, sort of confidential-like, "I think it's exciting that Miss Williams has finally made up her mind to marry the man who has been her friend for so many years. It must have taken courage. I do hope they will be happy together."

Aunt Lou's eyes wandered to the tintype of her own wedding on the mantel. I looked at it too, and even their proper-like expressions couldn't hide the light in her eyes or the triumph in Uncle Nat's. Her eyes now got a little misty, and then she sort of shook her head and spoke quietly. "It's just too bad it had to be in the middle of the school year like this, though."

Still, I knew Aunt Lou was quite ready to forgive Miss Williams for her small departure from accepted behavior for teachers.

She stood up.

"Well, it shouldn't be for too long," she said as though to comfort me. "The School Board has already called a meeting. They expect to have a new teacher here in no time." She reached out and patted my shoulder.

I tried to look properly sorrowful and downed the last of my milk.

"Better get at my chores," I said to explain why I was in such a hurry. "Some of us fellas plan to go to Jack's for a little while tonight. Sort of plan how we will handle this—this time off—without a teacher—an' all."

Lou smiled her approval. "Good for you!" she encouraged. "It's nice to see you boys are responsible enough to work it out. Even with school out for a while, I'm sure you won't suffer much with that kind of an attitude."

I nodded agreeably. I wasn't expecting to suffer much either—that is, if we could talk our folks into letting us do what we had in mind.

I hurried through my chores and opened the kitchen door wide enough to call to Aunt Lou that I was leaving but would be back in plenty of time for supper. She called back a cheerful response, the approving smile in her voice. I felt a little funny about it. I mean, here she was thinking we were planning on how we could keep up with our studies, and we were thinking on how we could get as far away from our books as possible in the short time we had.

Swishing through the leaves on the ground, I didn't let it trouble me for too long. After all, I hadn't actually told Aunt Lou that we were thinking on *studying*. She had come up with that idea herself.

I was the first one to Jack's house. He was loafing out under the apple tree in his yard, a geometry book in his hand. I knew he had been sent out there to study. When I appeared he laid aside all pretense of looking at the book and motioned me over to join him.

"Well?" he demanded.

"Aw, I ain't said nothin' yet," I told him. "Have you? I mean, I thought we were gonna meet to plan things first an'—"

"Exactly!" said Jack.

"Aunt Lou thinks I'm comin' over here to plan how I'm gonna keep up in my schoolwork," I said rather sheepishly.

"Did you tell her that?" asked Jack, his eyes narrowing to little slits.

" 'Course not!" Made me a little mad at Jack. He knew very well I didn't lie none.

"Then you can't help how she figures it," shrugged Jack.

"Guess—not," I sort of stammered. "Still, I wish she hadn't seen it that way. Might make it harder when we do ask an' all."

Jack didn't look quite so cocky. "Sure hope not," he said, and I knew he saw my point.

This time I couldn't shake my uncomfortable feeling. I had never been untruthful with Aunt Lou, and I sure didn't want to start now, even if it did cost me the planned hike.

Avery joined us, puffing from his run and his breathless question turned my thoughts back to our planned trip. "Who's gonna be the cook?"

What in the world was he talking about?

"Who's gonna cook?" he asked again, his head swiveling between us. "We gotta have someone to cook or we don't go."

Jack was the one to respond. "We'll all cook."

Avery looked doubtful. "I can't cook," he stated flatly and then added skeptically, "An' I'll bet you can't either."

"Don't be crazy!" Jack scoffed. "It don't take a cook to fix a meal over'n open fire. You just stick it over the flame and that's it."

"You ever tried it?" asked Avery, persistent.

Jack gave him a dark look. "Thought you was the fella who was so all fired rarin' to go. Why you gettin' so worked up now? Stay home if you want," he said sarcastically, and Avery quickly changed his tack.

"Guess we could take along a loaf a bread and some cheese," he stated, but he didn't sound too enthusiastic.

"I'm plannin' to eat fish," I announced on a positive note.

Avery never had been fond of fish or fishing.

"Who'll cook 'em?" he asked me.

I was getting a little tired of Avery's gloomy persistence, too.

"I'll cook 'em, that's who."

"You done it before?"

He had me there. My job was to catch them. It was Aunt Lou or Grandpa or Uncle Charlie who had done the cooking of them. I hadn't even cleaned a fish on my own. Well, I was game to give it a try. Anybody could clean and cook a fish.

Willie arrived just then and saved me the bother of convincing Avery.

The four of us settled down on the green lawn of the Berry backyard, our legs crossed in front of us Indian style. We proceeded to call to order, so to speak, our little meeting to make plans for the coming camp-out.

Since none of us had ever been on one before, we didn't know just how to approach the planning. Willie reached into his jeans pocket and came up with a stub of pencil and a sheet of folded paper. We all praised him some for his good thinking, and then we looked at one another. Jack sort of took charge.

"First of all we gotta figure what we're gonna need," he said, and that sounded sensible enough to the rest of us.

"Blankets," Jack started in, as though he had been doing more camp-out thinking than geometry studying while he was waiting for us to join him.

"Yeah," agreed Avery, "it gets pretty cold at night."

Willie scribbled "blankets" on one side of the paper.

"Food," went on Jack to Avery's energetic nod.

" 'Food' is too general. We gotta be 'pecific," said Willie, waiting with his pencil poised in the air.

None of us had ever done any meal planning before.

"Bread," ventured Avery.

Willie's pencil scratched again.

"Cheese," continued Avery.

"Bread and cheese! You crazy? I ain't living for days on bread and cheese," Jack contradicted.

"Well, you say what you want then!" snapped Avery. "Don't hear no bright ideas from you."

Willie interrupted before Jack and Avery had time to really get in a fuss. They never had been able to get along very well.

"I've got 'bread and cheese'; now what else do we want?"

"We'll need some butter 'n flour 'n salt 'n pepper for fryin' the fish," I put in rather knowledgeably. I had watched Aunt Lou mix the ingredients and put the floured fish in the sizzling butter many times, and her fried fish always tasted great.

"An' what iffen you don't catch any fish?" questioned Jack in a smart-aleck fashion.

"Then I guess you just eat bread and cheese," I threw back at him.

"We need pans for cooking—a fryin' pan and a kettle of some kind," cut in Willie to keep things from getting out of hand.

"Matches!" shouted Avery in a burst of inspiration.

We all gave him looks of appreciation. Matches at a campsite we would need all right.

Our list continued on to the back of the sheet, and before I knew it Mrs. Berry was calling Jack in for supper and the rest of us realized we'd better be getting home to our suppers, too.

Avery and I left Jack's yard on the run. Willie trotted off the other direction. It was hard to run and talk at the same time, so we didn't say a whole lot to each other.

"When you gonna ask?" Avery puffed.

"Dunno," I gasped out.

"Who you gonna ask?" went on Avery.

I shook my head. "Not sure yet," I admitted.

Truth was, I still wasn't clear on just which of my kin might make the best ally. I would sort of need to feel my way.

"Well, we can't wait," puffed Avery. "That ol' School Board is likely to go and rustle up a teacher 'fore we even get a chance to enjoy the break."

Avery was breathing hard after that long speech. I knew he was right, but I also disliked being pressured.

"I'll ask," I told him firmly; "don't you worry none about it."

We parted company at the end of Cottonwood Street, Avery heading off one direction and me the other. I looked at the sky as I ran on. I was afraid I was going to be late for supper, and though Aunt Lou might not scold, it sure wouldn't help my cause none.

I pulled into the lane that led past the parsonage and into the backyard just as Uncle Nat was dismounting Dobbin. I came to a halt beside him, struggling some to catch my breath.

"Whoa," said Nat. "Where you coming from in such a hurry?"

I waited a spell till I could talk a bit more evenly and then answered, "Been over at Jack's house—thought I might've stayed longer'n I intended. 'Fraid I was late for supper."

"Well, so am I," stated Nat, but he didn't seem worried none. "Mrs. Miranda took a bad turn again."

"Is she okay?" I asked.

"Seems to be fine again now."

I thought it must be at least once a week Uncle Nat was called to the Willises to say a prayer for "the departing Mrs. Miranda," as old Grandma Willis was called. She never had needed the final prayer yet, but then, I reckoned, someday she would and who could know just when that day might be?

I took up the reins hanging from Dobbin's bridle and waited for Uncle Nat to slip the saddle; then I led the horse toward the small barn and the stall that waited for him.

Even though Dobbin had gone about ten miles out to the Willis place and back, he still walked into the barn with a spring in his step. As always, I admired the horse. Gramps had bought him for Uncle Nat and Aunt Lou along with a sharp-looking little one-horse buggy. When Uncle Nat went alone, he usually rode the horse, though, instead of hitching up the rig. It was faster and he figured it saved the horse some too.

When we got to the barn I slipped Dobbin's bridle off and changed it for a halter. Uncle Nat reached for the currie comb and brush to give the horse a brisk rubdown. Without waiting to be asked, I crawled over the manger and forked in enough hay for the horse's supper. Then I measured out his chop. I had done this many times, so I knew just how much was needed.

"Hear you're without a teacher," commented Uncle Nat as the two of us worked side by side.

"Yeah," I responded without much emotion.

Nat smiled. "When I was your age I suppose I would've been rejoicing over having some free time—making all sorts of plans as to what I would do with it."

I didn't answer.

"This is really unusual for you," Uncle Nat went on reflectively. "No school at a time of year when there is no more farm work to be done. How do you plan to fill in those long, boring days?"

I knew he was funning me some, but I also saw it as a chance—a chance to maybe put in a word for the plans we had been making.

"Well," I said, real casual-like, "the fellas and me've been talkin'. Thought it might be a good time to try that there hike and—and camp-out we've been hopin' to work in."

I glanced from Dobbin, who was busy cleaning up his oats, to Uncle Nat. He never missed a stroke with the brush.

"Camping? Don't remember your mentioning camping."

"Well, no, we haven't," I hurried on. "Whenever the weather's been good enough, there was crops and garden still to be tended. But, just as you said, that work is all done this fall. And—and truth is," I finished in a rush, "I hadn't really thought on it before." I felt I needed to be totally honest with Uncle Nat.

Uncle Nat just nodded his head.

"We thought this might be a real good time," I pressed my point.

Then I checked myself. I didn't want to seem too eager—too pushy.

"Who's doing the planning?" asked Uncle Nat.

"Me n' Avery, n' Willie n' Jack," I blurted out.

Uncle Nat smiled a soft, teasing smile.

"When you give that list to your aunt Lou," he said, "I'd advise you to say, 'Avery, Willie, Jack and I.' "

I ducked my head. I'd been corrected on that particular grammatical error many times—especially by Aunt Lou.

"Where're you going?" asked Uncle Nat next.

My heart sort of skipped a bit. He had said, "Where're you going?" just like it had already been settled.

"Thought we'd follow the crik up into the hills where it starts at the spring," I answered, trying to make it sound like it had all been carefully figured out and approved. "Well, I just thought of it now," I continued in my efforts toward honesty, "but I think the fellas'll agree."

Uncle Nat nodded.

He turned then and put the currie comb and brush back up on the peg on the wall, gave Dobbin one more sound pat and nodded for me that we'd better get in to our supper.

I followed, just a bit hesitantly. I wasn't sure whether I'd won the round or not. Did Uncle Nat understand the need of a boy to get off on his own? Would he support me if it came to convincing the rest of the family?

We were almost to the house before he reached out a hand and let it rest on the top of my shoulder.

"Sounds like a great idea to me," he commented. "If I didn't have so many duties here at the church this week, I'd be right tempted to join you."

I let out my breath in a whoosh. Uncle Nat was on my side! That should count for something, at least. For the first time, I began to hope that I really might get to go.

CHAPTER 3

A Little Help

All the way out to the farm the next morning, Saturday, I felt my insides squirming a bit. I don't know why I was so nervous. I guess I wanted that camping trip far more than I supposed I would. I mean, I had never even thought of going camping until the day before when Avery suggested it, and now I was all het up about it. At the time I didn't even stop to wonder about Avery. He had never been one to care much for the out-of-doors that I was aware of. He didn't even like to fish, and yet here he throws out this surprise dream of his. But, as I said, I didn't think about that side of it till later.

I was busy thinking about me. More than anything in the world I wanted that camping trip. I don't know when I had ever wanted anything so much in my life except maybe when I had wanted a dog. Or when I had wanted to keep Aunt Lou instead of marrying her off to some local fella who wouldn't even fully appreciate what he was getting.

Well, I had my dog. Gramps had seen to that. I held Pixie closer to my chest and stroked the soft hair under her chin while she wiggled and strained against me. Even she, who loved to be cuddled, didn't like being held that close.

And as for Aunt Lou's marrying, when it came right down to it, I highly approved of the fella she had chosen. I felt pretty close to Uncle Nat myself.

In fact, I dared to hope he might put in a word for me if it came down to arguing my case with the three menfolk at the farm.

We turned the horse and buggy down the lane, and my stomach did another turn as well. It wouldn't be long now until I would know one way or the other.

Grandpa met us at the front gate that opened up to the old farm home. He smiled his welcome from ear to ear and reached out to hug Aunt Lou. She had her arms full of baking like she always did when she visited the farm, but she accepted the hug anyway, giving Grandpa a kiss on his weathered cheek. Then Grandpa shook Nat's hand firmly and turned to me.

"So yer without a teacher, eh, Boy?" he said.

He still called me "boy" even though I felt I had outgrown that name. Still, I didn't resent it none the way Grandpa said it.

I just nodded my head.

"We heard the news," Grandpa said to Uncle Nat. "Was plannin' to come on in an' pick Josh up this mornin'. Hope it didn't mean a special trip for ya."

Uncle Nat just smiled. "Lou was anxious to come out and check on you anyway. I had some time this morning, and we plan to stop in at the Curtises on the way back to town and see that new baby."

We were met on the porch by Gramps, who patted my shoulder and hugged Aunt Lou. I could hear Uncle Charlie clattering dishes in the kitchen and guessed it was his turn for kitchen duties. He stepped to the door, dish towel in one hand and a pot in the other.

After our hellos Lou moved to set down her baking and put on the coffeepot. It didn't matter how long it was between visits, she still took over the kitchen whenever she stepped in the door.

We all settled into comfortable spots around the room.

"So what's this we hear about your school being closed, Joshua?" asked Gramps. Him being from the city and all, he was real interested in my education. The conversation turned to the school and the need for a teacher since Miss Williams up and left to marry her longtime sweetheart.

"Any idea how long it might be before classes resume?" asked Gramps.

He was asking Uncle Nat, not me, and I was willing to let him answer.

"The School Board is already working on it," Uncle Nat assured him. "They hope they'll have another teacher in the classroom within a week."

Gramps cleared his throat.

"It's not the time factor that bothers me," he stated. "It's the quality of the replacement."

All eyes turned to Gramps.

"Meanin'?" asked Grandpa.

"Well, I don't want to be borrowing trouble—but any teacher worth his salt would already be placed for this school year, as I see it."

I hadn't thought of that, and I guess the others hadn't either, for I saw a few worried looks flicker across the faces around the room.

"We'll just have to pray," stated Aunt Lou. "If there's a fault in the teacher they find, then we'll ask the Lord to change her or him," and she moved to put another stick of wood in the firebox as though everything was now neatly cared for.

"It'll be nice to have you home for a bit, Boy," Grandpa said to me.

"Maybe we can get in some fishing," put in Gramps, his eyes twinkling at the thought.

I nodded. "I'd like that," I stated honestly.

"Josh has some big plans," Nat said slowly, his eyes on my face to read if I wanted him to bring up the subject or not.

I nodded slightly so he would know I wanted him to continue. He caught it and cleared his throat to get all the eyes in the room back on him again.

"Sounds like a good idea to me," Uncle Nat went on. He waited a moment until he was sure everyone was waiting to hear the plan.

"Josh and some of his friends thought this would be a good time for them to take a little hike up along the creek and spend a few days camping at the spring that feeds it."

Before anyone could even open their mouth to respond, Uncle Nat went on. "Sounds to me like it would be a good experience for the boys. They haven't had much chance for camping with the usual fall bringing all kinds of farm work right along with the good weather. Now this fall is different. The good weather has managed to stay right on even after the fall work is all done. Good time for a boy to take a trip on his own."

Uncle Nat stopped then and all eyes turned back to me.

Before anyone was able to make some kind of response, Aunt Lou made a dash for the stove where the coffeepot was just about to boil over. The eyes shifted off my face, and I silently thanked the boiling coffee and squirmed some on my chair.

Aunt Lou filled coffee cups for the menfolk and went about slicing some of her lemon cake.

It seemed much easier to discuss my plans over coffee and cake and my own brimming glass of Bossie's fresh, cool milk.

"Didn't realize ya had interests in campin', Boy," remarked Grandpa.

"Well, I hadn't thought much on it, there being no proper time and all, so it just didn't come to mind. It was Avery who suggested it," I stated honestly. "Like Uncle Nat said, the time's been too busy when the weather's been good enough."

Grandpa nodded.

"Who ya got to go with ya?" asked Grandpa.

"Avery, Willie and Jack," I answered.

"I mean for grown folk," explained Grandpa.

I hesitated. I didn't know just how to answer. I didn't want to sound sassy or nothing, but I wanted to let him know that boys of fifteen didn't need anyone more grown up than that.

"Well—ah—we—" I started but Gramps cut in.

"I reckon a boy who can pitch bundles like a man and shovel grain to keep up to a threshing machine might be about big enough to care for himself," he said matter-of-factly with a twinkle in his eye.

It was Aunt Lou whose face showed the most concern, though Grandpa didn't look convinced yet either.

"Where'll you eat?" Aunt Lou asked.

"Outdoors," I answered. "We'll take along the food and fix it over an open fire."

Aunt Lou started to speak again, but I saw Uncle Nat quietly reach out and press her hand. No one else noticed. Aunt Lou slowly closed her mouth again and clasped Uncle Nat's hand firmly.

"What do you think?" Grandpa surprised me by asking the question of Uncle Charlie.

Uncle Charlie took a long swallow of hot coffee, let his chair legs drop to the kitchen floor again, and answered without wavering. "S'pose it'd be all right."

I was sure then that I had won. I wanted to whoop but I didn't dare.

"I'll give you a hand with the food, Josh," Aunt Lou offered, and then she checked Uncle Nat's face again to see if he'd consider that interference.

A slight flush coloring her cheek, "That is, if you'd like me to," she finished quickly.

"I'd 'preciate it," I hastened to inform her. "Me and the boys were hard put to know what to take along, us never havin' done any campin' or much cookin' before an' all."

"The boys and I," Aunt Lou corrected me, but her smile took any sting out of the words.

It seemed to be settled. Grandpa never did really say yes—but he never said no either. After further discussion, it was decided that we could hike up to the spring on one day, spend three nights camped by the small pool at its base, and then return home on the fourth day. Before I knew what was happening all five people around that table were busy planning what I'd need to take along on that camping trip. By the way their list was growing, it sounded to me like I'd need me a wagon to be hauling it all.

Oh, well! They all meant well. I'd sorta do some sorting through the list myself after they'd had their fun. In the meantime I'd have to get word back to town to the other fellas. We needed to get ourselves going and out on that trip before the School Board announced they'd found us another teacher.

CHAPTER 4

Off Camping

I don't know who was most excited that morning two days later when the three of us hoisted packs on our backs and started off down the trail that led to the crik.

As it turned out, Jack was unable to join us. We all felt rather sorry for him. His pa had said a determined no—Jack had to stay home and stick to his studies if he was going to be ready for medical school. Jack had been just about sick over it all and, knowing how I'd felt if I'd had to stay home, I felt a little sick myself.

So it was that Avery, Willie and me packed our gear, with a lot of help and advice and instructions from our families, and started down the tree-lined path to the crik. I had only one other regret besides Jack's not getting to go—I had to leave Pixie behind. After talking it over with the three menfolk, I just didn't feel like a campsite was a fit place for a tiny little dog like her, and I knew she'd never be able to walk as far as we were planning on walk-ing. With my arms needing to be free and my back loaded down, I knew I'd never be able to carry her either.

Just before we disappeared from view of our yard, I turned for one more wave. There stood Grandpa, Uncle Charlie, Gramps, and even Uncle Nat and Aunt Lou—they came back out to the farm after the weekend because she didn't want to miss out on any of the excitement—still watching us go.

I even saw Aunt Lou blow her nose on her white hankie. You would think we were marching off to war or something. They all looked glad and sad at the same time—happy we were doing something we really wanted to do, and anxious that everything would go alright, and a bit sad that we were growing up.

We three were feeling anything but sad, though, as we stepped out briskly, hardly able to wait until we got out of sight of everyone so we'd truly feel we were on our own.

Our steps slowed down soon enough as the morning wore on. The packs on our backs were feeling a mite heavy and the sun was getting a little warm. It wasn't so good underfoot when we left the worn cow path either. The willow shrubs grew right down to the crik bank, and we sorta had to fight our way through them. We didn't want to leave the bank for fear we'd lose track of the crik among all the trees, so we just kept pushing our way through brush and briar.

I think we all breathed a sigh of relief when we began to see clearing ahead of us and realized the crik was taking us out through the brush and across Turley's cow pasture. The walking would be much easier.

We had just crawled through the fence and were ready for a better path when Avery groaned real loud, stopped and leaned against a fence post.

"I say it's time for a break," he stated. Even though Willie and me were still in a big hurry, I guess we were both getting kinda tired, too.

"We'll rest when we get across the pasture," Willie stated, but Avery didn't even budge.

"I'm resting now," Avery informed us, and we knew it was useless to argue. Avery slid the heavy pack from his shoulders and sat down with his back against it. Secretly I wondered how he'd ever make it all the way to the crik mouth if he was already played out, but I said nothing. Fact is, I didn't mind the idea of a bit of rest myself.

It hadn't been long since Aunt Lou had stuffed us with bacon, eggs and fried potatoes, but Avery seemed to have forgotten that. He reached in his pack and pulled out a handful of Aunt Lou's cookies. Willie and me didn't want to miss out, so we each took a handful, too. The rest, the cookies, and a drink from the crik seemed to refresh us and after several minutes I began to get impatient again. I knew Willie was too, so we suggested to Avery that it might be time to move on again. By my calculation, we'd come only a couple miles and we still had a good piece to go.

Rather reluctantly, Avery picked up his heavy backpack and tugged the straps on his shoulders. Willie and me both picked up ours, shrugged our way into them, and then started off again, me leading the way on account of being the most familiar with the area. It was much easier walking now. Not only were we out of the heavy brush, but the pastureland had been eaten close by the grazing cattle so even the grass was nice and short.

The herd of cattle belonging to the Turleys was feeding nearby, but we paid them no heed except to notice how nice and fat they were and how round their red sides looked.

We had almost reached the other side of the pasture when we heard the awfullest commotion! It sounded like a stampede—and heading our way, too!

I guess we all wheeled around at the sound, expecting to see that whole herd of cows headed right for us.

It wasn't the whole herd—but it might as well have been, for there, coming straight for us, his head lowered and his nostrils snorting out little puffs that blew up tiny clouds of dust, came Turleys' big red bull. Say, if you ever wanted to see three fellas move in a hurry, you would've seen it then. We forgot all about our heavy packs and how tired we were. We just lit out for the closest fence as fast as our legs could take us.

I guess I got there first. I didn't even slow down, but just dropped to the ground and rolled right under that barbed wire with one quick motion— pack and all. I heard a sickening tear-sound, and I knew I had ripped the piece of burlap that Aunt Lou had carefully wrapped my pack in. I felt bad about that, but I was powerful happy to be on the other side of the fence from that bull.

Willie whipped under the fence next and rolled right into me. I guess it was then that both of us looked back to see how Avery was faring.

Boy, were we scared! Avery was heading for the fence as fast as his legs could carry him, but he never had been too athletic or nothing, and that bull seemed to be gaining every stride.

"Drop your pack!" I hollered without even stopping to think. If I had, I might have decided that Avery would probably spend more time trying to free himself of that pack than he would save by being rid of it.

Somehow he managed to get his pack off his back and let it fall while he still kept a-running. It might have been his undoing had not that bull taken a sudden interest in that pack. He stopped chasing Avery and stood there pawing and snorting, and then he charged Avery's dumped load as it lay there on the ground. He hit it with an awful smack and wasn't content with that. He sorta ground his horns into it, then hooked it and tossed it up. When it came down he pawed at it again with a sharp hoof, then threw it back into the air, snorting and puffing and carrying on something awful.

In the meantime Avery scrambled under the fence to join Willie and me, panting and puffing and deathly white. I felt a little white myself. Especially when I saw how that bull used that pack Avery had left behind. I was sorry to see Avery's bundle being pawed and pushed right into the ground, but I was sure glad it wasn't Avery.

We lay there trying to collect our wits and quiet our breathing. First I guess we were all just happy to be alive. Then we began to worry some about our supplies.

We had divided our stuff as evenly as we could. I had my bedding, our pots and pans, dishes and cutlery and my fishing gear. Willie had his blankets, a hatchet for cutting firewood, our matches, a first-aid kit and some of our food supplies. Avery had his blankets and most of the food. So with big eyes and sick stomachs, we lay there watching that bull making a big mess of things.

"Scrambled eggs," whispered Willie, a twinkle in his eye in spite of our predicament.

"Sh-h," Avery hissed, his eye on the bull. "You might make him mad."

"Mad?" It was my turn to whisper. "He's mad now."

"Well, madder then," responded Avery.

"Don't see how he could get any madder," I insisted. "Look at him rip things up."

There was nothing we could do about it. We had to lay there and watch that bull have his fun until he decided he had done all the damage he cared to. He left off worrying the pack and came over near the fence and glared at us, still snorting and fuming. We were ready to run, but the scrubby bushes nearby would offer scant protection from this beast. I told the fellas to lay stock-still so we wouldn't rouse that bull up none, and we just held our breath and waited. We sure hoped with all our hearts that the mad bull wouldn't decide to challenge the barbed-wire fence that separated us from him.

Finally the bull wearied of standing there snorting, and he turned and went back toward the cows, bellowing and blowing as he went. He didn't go far though, and every once in a while he circled back our way and snorted at us again just to remind us that he still knew we were there.

We couldn't go on. Not without Avery's pack—or what there was left of it. We hoped at least the food Aunt Lou had packed in tins would still be okay and we would be able to salvage enough to make it through the next three days.

There was no way we could get back into the pasture with that bull still snorting around, so we just moved away from the fence a ways and sat down to wait.

Not much of a way to spend one's camping time. The sun climbed up in the sky and got even hotter and there wasn't a speck of shade. I propped my pack end-up as high as I could and tried to at least get my face out of the sun.

We were all getting awfully thirsty and hungry by the time the sun moved toward the west.

"You've got *some* food, right?" I asked Willie.

He shifted his pack around so he could get into it. It had been tied and wrapped carefully, so it wasn't easy to find the food items without disturbing everything. It had been packed to stay secure until we reached our campsite.

Willie found a loaf of bread and I dug a bread knife out of my bundle. We sliced the bread in rather thick, crooked slices and passed them around. We didn't have even the cheese we had joked about.

By late afternoon the sun was really warm. I had to shift my bit of shade several times. I think I dozed off now and then. Guess Willie and Avery did, too.

When I woke up and pulled myself into a sitting position, that bull was back at the pack again. I had hoped by now the cows might have led him clear across the pasture. They hadn't. He still sniffed and snorted but he didn't work the bundle over anymore.

"We'll never make it to the campsite by dark," grumbled Avery.

"I'm just hoping he left us something to eat," remarked Willie. "We can camp here for the night if we have to and go on in the mornin', but it sure will be a miserable night iffen we don't have somethin' more'n bread for supper."

I agreed.

We were about to give up on that bull ever leaving when the cows decided it was time to head for the barn for milking. The bull looked over at us, snorted again and started off after them.

We let him go a good distance before we even got near the fence. Even then Avery wouldn't crawl through. He had himself too big a scare.

I was the one who went for the pack. It took a bit of doing to gather everything up and bundle it together well enough so I could get the whole thing carried to the other side of the fence.

Avery's blankets had some holes in them and they had been rolled in the dirt in first-rate style, but other than that, they looked fairly usable. The food was another matter. The tins were all dented and some had popped their lids—dust and dried grass were all mixed in with the contents. There was only one egg in the whole dozen that wasn't smashed to bits, and we wondered how in the world it had escaped.

A few things were still edible, and we figured we'd at least have us enough food for our supper. We were all pretty hungry, so we busied ourselves with rustling up some kind of a meal. We blew the leaves and dirt off Aunt Lou's corn bread, covered it with butter, and chowed it all down with some beef jerky Grandpa had sent along. It was already getting dark, it being so late in the fall, and we knew we'd have to give up any idea of traveling on.

There wasn't any shelter to spread our blankets under, either, so we just did the best we could right out in the open.

"Boy, am I tired," sighed Avery. I was too, though *why* I was escaped me. We had walked only a couple of miles and spent the rest of the day dozing there in the sun.

"We'll have to get up early and get on to the campsite," said Willie. "We don't want to lose another day."

Avery pulled off his shoes and started to peel off his pants.

"Whatcha doin'?" Willie demanded. "Ya don't undress when you're campin.'"

Avery shrugged, pulled his pants back on again and crawled under his dusty blankets.

By morning I think all of us were right happy for every stitch of clothes we were wearing. In spite of the blankets, it was cold out in the open. A glaze of frost covered the grass around us and I wondered if there might be a bit of it covering my nose as well.

We didn't dare build a fire. The stubble grass around us was too flam-mable. Besides, we had no wood anyway, so we just sliced off some more bread and ate it with Aunt Lou's cold beans. It was some kind of drink we missed the most. Aunt Lou had tried to talk us into bringing milk, but we insisted that it would mean more to carry and our loads were heavy enough as it was. We'd have the cold, sweet spring water, we assured her. Well, we would've, too, if it hadn't been for that old red bull.

We wrapped up our packs the best we could, shivering while we did so, and started out for our campsite before the sun had even crawled over the eastern horizon.

CHAPTER 5

The Campsite

I guess all three of us were pretty anxious to wend our way up the crik. None of us had ever been there before, but we had all heard from folks who had seen the spot where the spring water bubbled out from the hillside on its way to the farmlands below. They all said what a swell spot it was with the water as clear and cold as ice crystals. The green trees leaned over the small pond "like they was tryin' to reach their fingers down to the water," said Grandpa.

With a long ways still to hike, we hurried as best we could—some of the hike was fairly easy, some a little harder, and some of it was downright tough. We fought our way through bush and swampy areas, always hanging close to the crik bank. There were a couple of times when we could have left the crik and taken an easier route, 'cause we knew right well which way to head and all and when we would be joining up with the crik again. But I guess we all three were pretending we were in a brand-new country, one we'd never seen before, and if we didn't hang in tight to that crik, we'd get us lost for sure.

We stopped for some bread and cheese and a couple big juicy apples (they'd been in Willie's pack) about noon. When we started off again, Willie wasn't talking much and I could see him studying everything around us with a sort of contented smile on his face. He sure was enjoying this hike all right, even though he did have the heaviest pack. He had stuffed some of Avery's broken load in his already overflowing sack. I knew he had more than his share to carry but he didn't complain.

Avery more than made up for Willie's quiet though—and all of it was complaining. I began to wish it'd been Avery 'stead of Jack who'd stayed home, even if the trip had been his idea. Willie didn't take no notice of Avery. He seemed to be totally taken with the woods, the crik, and the birds that were staying for the winter.

It was afternoon and we were all sure we must be getting near the mouth of our stream. We came around a bend in the crik right smack into a steep cliff in the hillside. We had traveled the whole time on the north side of the crik, and now it cut into the hill so there was no room to walk. We'd have to cross the crik and follow on the south side for at least the present.

The crik was not deep, nor was it wide, but there was no way we could jump across it. There were no steppingstones either, and that meant getting wet. I was preparing to take off my shoes and socks and roll up my pant legs for wading when Willie spoke up.

" 'Member that fallen log, just back a piece?"

Avery and I both looked at him. I hadn't seen any fallen log, but then I hadn't been watching as closely as Willie. I had likely been distracted by Avery's grumping. Since Willie paid him no mind, Avery had stuck with me.

"I didn't see no log," said Avery shortly.

"Just a couple hundred yards back or so," insisted Willie. "I'm sure it was put there for a crossing. It stretched right from the one bank to the other. If we go back, it'll save us gettin' our feet wet. Even though it feels hot enough, that water'll be cold, and we won't have much chance to warm up none— with night comin' so early and cool."

It made sense to me. I wasn't too anxious to have another miserable night with cold, damp feet to boot.

"Sure," I said, "iffen you saw a log to cross over on, let's go back to it. I'm not hankerin' for cold feet all night either."

"We should've crossed in the first place," groused Avery, "an' saved ourselves all this extra travelin'. This pack is heavy enough without totin' it fore and back."

I gave Avery a disgusted look. His pack, thanks to his throwing things to the bull and getting them all broke up and then palming his leavings off on Willie, was the lightest of the three. I didn't say so though, just turned and followed Willie back down the path.

Willie was right. The log was right there where he'd said it would be, from one side to the other. I daydreamed about other shoe prints on it, feet other than ours that had crossed over before us—maybe even Indians! Maybe they were the ones who'd put the log there. It was sort of like being an explorer or pioneer or something.

Willie went first. He crossed that log slick as you please. You woulda thought he'd been practicing all his life. But, then, Willie was never one to be scared of things. He'd always been the first one to take a dare—walking a high board fence, or climbing the pasture spruce trees, or most anything. I'd noticed that since he'd invited God into his life, he wasn't so apt to do crazy things that were actually dangerous just for the fun of it.

I was next over. I wasn't quite as sure of myself as Willie had been. I tried not to let it show, but every step I took I thought I'd be feeling that cold water washing over me.

Avery hollered after me, "Hey, wait for me, Josh! My shoes ain't made for scalin' slippery-barked trees. I'll never make it with this heavy pack an' all."

I couldn't turn around to look at Avery and I sure couldn't stop in the middle of that log with nothing to hang on to.

"You can make it iffen we can," I called back over my shoulder.

Avery didn't say any more and I could feel him step up onto the log and start working his way across. I still couldn't turn to look. It took all my concentration just making it myself.

I was just stepping onto the bank and heaving an inward sigh when I heard this awful screeching sound behind me. I turned around just in time to see—you've guessed right—Avery teetering back and forth, trying hard to regain his balance. But you could see he was losing out. Finally, with a shout for help he slipped off the log, still grabbing for a hold that wasn't there, and fell with a big splash right into the crik.

For a moment I thought I heard the crik giggling—but I guess it was just a gurgle as Avery slipped under and then came up again.

The water was only past his knees when he finally struggled to a standing position, but deep or not, it had thoroughly soaked Avery. He stood there with the water running off him, sputtering and wiping his face. His eyes looked scared—or angry; I couldn't tell which—and the clothes stuck close like the feathers on a rooster that has been chosen for dinner and dipped in water for plucking. Boy, did I want to laugh. I didn't dare even exchange looks with Willie. I knew what would happen if I did, and Avery already looked upset enough.

And then I noticed Avery's pack. It was still sitting there in the water, and in it was a good portion of what was left of our food supply. Boy, if we ever went camping again, Avery would be the one carrying the pots and pans, I decided right then. He probably couldn't do much harm to iron skillets and enamel pots.

Willie must've thought of that food at the same time I did, for he swished past me, throwing off his own backpack as he ran, and was in that there crik and scooping out the soaking pack. Willie hadn't stopped even to take off his shoes or socks and roll up his pant legs.

Most of the damage had already been done. Willie and I groaned as we sorted out soggy bread, cookies, and dripping bacon. The crik-washed vegetables and fruit were okay. A few things were still protected in the tins Aunt Lou had packed and the bull had dented. Still, we for sure had lost a fair amount of our provisions for the days ahead. Made me feel a little sick inside.

Avery's blankets were all wet, too, and so were his extra clothes. Wouldn't help none for him to slip behind a bush and change. What he already had on was just as dry as anything we pulled out of his pack.

Surprisingly, Avery hadn't said one word since he dragged himself out of the crik and stood shivering on the shore. Willie reached in his own pack and came up with some dry clothes.

"You'd better get outta your wet things before you catch a chill," he said, and without comment Avery took the dry clothes and headed behind a nearby scrub bush.

"What're we gonna do now?" I whispered to Willie when I thought Avery was out of earshot.

"Not many choices," Willie whispered back. "We've got to set up camp as soon as possible and try to get Avery's stuff dried out."

I nodded, but I sure did hate to stop when we must be so close to the spring.

I slowly pulled myself to my feet. "I'll get some wood for a fire," I sighed.

When I got back with the wood, Willie had spread all of Avery's clothes and blankets on the nearby bushes to dry, and he was trying to make some kind of sense out of our food supply. I could tell he was thinking of supper. He likely was as hungry as I.

I scraped away dry leaves until I reached the ground beneath. When I thought I had a safe base for the fire, I scooped handfuls of sand from the crik bank onto the spot and then went to work arranging dry leaves and grass and small chunks of wood. The fire started as soon as I put a match to it, and I think all of us greeted that cheery glow with thanks. Avery crowded in close, a mournful look on his face, almost before I had time to get myself out of the way.

As soon as the fire was going good enough, we whipped out a frying pan and put some bacon to sizzling. Boy, did it smell good. We still had some of Aunt Lou's beans, so we warmed them in a pot. We weren't sure if the crik water was pure enough to drink here, so we dipped out a can of it and put that on to boil. It was hard to get all three things to stay upright over the flame, and it took Willie and I our full time and attention to sort of keep moving things around and shoving sticks under and all. Avery just sat there and shivered.

"We'll have to plan on beddin' down here for tonight," Willie informed us. "We can put up a shelter in the trees in no time and keep a fire goin' all night iffen we have to."

I knew that meant a lot more wood, so I picked up the hatchet and went off to get some stacked up. Willie stayed near enough to the fire so he could rescue anything that started to burn; then he started piling up some tree branches against a leaned-over tree so a shelter would be formed.

Avery was the one to call us for supper. Guess he had just been sitting there near to the fire and smelling the food till he couldn't stand it anymore. We got our plates and dished up the beans and bacon, Willie making sure the portions were divided evenly. Then I stirred cocoa mixture into the bubbling water and poured out the hot liquid into our three tin cups. It sure would help to warm up our cold bodies. Willie and Avery were without shoes, them both having waded in the crik water. I had shared my extra socks with Willie, but none of us had brought extra shoes along.

The food sure tasted good. We could hardly wait till Willie had said a short grace. Then we tore into it like it was a fancy banquet or something. They say the outdoors makes things taste even better. Maybe. All I know is that supper sure did taste good. The only fault with it was that there wasn't enough. And we sure did miss bread. Guess all of us were still hungry when our plates were cleaned up.

We each had a fall pear and felt sorrowful about not having some of Aunt Lou's man-sized sugar cookies to go with it, but not one of us found the soggy mess that had been cookies too appealing.

The sun was already dipping around to the west. We knew it wasn't really late, but it was beginning to get cool. Without none of us saying so, I guess we decided the day had been long enough.

I was the only one with shoes, so I kept on hauling in the wood supply. I was sure I had far more than we would ever need, but it did seem to be important to have enough to keep us warm, so I just kept piling it higher and higher.

Willie and Avery kept putting branches up against the lean-to shelter. Then they put some more branches on the ground until they had a nice, thick mattress of sorts. Willie got out our blanket supply then. When I came in with a load of wood, he was busy making up one bed. I must have frowned or something because Willie seemed to think he owed me some kind of explanation.

"Only hope we have of stayin' warm with just two sets of blankets is to all three sleep together."

I supposed he was right, but I wasn't used to sharing a bed with anybody. I didn't think it would bother Willie much. He'd been sleeping with two brothers for about as long as he could remember.

We fed the fire, washed up our dishes and put away the remaining food supply. I wondered just how many meals it would make. I was glad I'd brought my fishing gear.

None of us undressed. I slipped off my shoes and set them under the shelter in case it should decide to rain in the night. Willie and Avery both put their shoes as close to the fire as they dared, hoping they would be dry enough to wear come morning.

Then we all crawled into the shelter and settled ourselves in our bed. It was decided that since Avery was the most chilled, he would sleep closest to the fire. And it would be his job to keep it stoked during the night.

Willie was the most used to sleeping with someone else, so he elected to sleep in the middle. I had the spot at the back—away from the fire and toward the stacked tree limbs that made our shelter.

It wasn't the best night I have ever spent, I can tell you that. The prickly little spikes of spruce needles poking up through the blankets scratched you in places where you didn't need or want to be scratched. The branches on the tree limbs, at the back of the shelter kept swiping at my face every time I moved or even breathed. Avery hogged the blankets, even if he was the closest to the fire. He seemed to roll himself in them, and I hardly had enough at the back to reach around myself.

I slept fitfully. Willie wasn't as good about sleeping in the middle as I had thought he would be. He kept twisting this way and that, and in our cramped quarters there just wasn't room for twisting. Avery slept. In fact, he slept so well he never did replenish the fire, and it was stone cold before it could do us much good. Come morning we were all shivering, the shoes were still soupy wet, and the stack of wood was just as high as it had been the night before.

We woke up grumpy and stiff before the sun was even in the sky. I fought my way out from the tree branches at the back and over Willie and Avery, pulled on my cold shoes and started to work on another fire, my fingers feeling stiff and icy as I tried to hold the matches steady.

I found the beat-up tin that Aunt Lou had filled with pancake fixings, added some crik water to the dry ingredients and poured some of the dough into the frying pan even before it was heated enough to sizzle. They didn't turn out too well—least not those first ones. They were still pale and soggy and wouldn't flip worth nothing, but we ate them anyway. They weren't too bad with maple syrup poured over them. By the time I got to the end of the batch, the pan was too hot and they were burning even before they got a chance to cook.

In spite of all that, they tasted so good I whipped up another batch and we ate them, too. That finished off our pancake fixings. What Aunt Lou had thought would feed us for three breakfasts, we had managed to polish off in one. But then, we reasoned, we hadn't eaten too well the day before.

The crik-drowned shoes were still wet, and the clothes and blankets in need of more drying time, so we knew it would be foolish to break up camp yet. We decided to stay right where we were.

"We have to stay here and get dried out," said Willie. "We only have one more night to stay. There is just no way we can get up in the mornin', walk the rest of the way to the spring and then get all the way back home again in one day."

"You mean we have to turn around from here and go on home without even seein' the spring we came all this way to see?" moaned Avery.

"Well, I'm sure not tryin' to walk on to that spring in my bare feet," said Willie. "You wantin' to?"

Now I knew Avery had never gone barefoot in the summer months like I had done for many summers. But I knew right well if it came down to seeing or missing that spring, I sure wouldn't have hesitated to go shoeless, even if it was the fall and even if there wasn't a decent path through the bush, but I didn't say anything.

"Doesn't seem fair," grumbled Avery. "Here we were tellin' all the fellas how we were gonna hike to the spring, and now we hafta go home and say we didn't see the spring at all."

I was feeling pretty low myself.

"Josh can still go—he's got shoes," Willie suddenly cut in.

Now I hadn't even thought of going on all alone. But when Willie seemed so excited and Avery's eyes lit up, I suddenly felt great relief. I would get to see the spring after all.

I knew this wasn't the way we had planned it, but it did seem better than nothing. At least one of us would be able to report to the other fellas what the spring looked like in the fall of the year.

We decided I would venture up the crik on my own while the fellas dried out their clothes at our camp. I knew Willie and Avery hated to miss the adventure and I felt real sorry for them, but there didn't seem to be much point in my just sitting with them by the fire.

I carried more wood before I left, and they snuggled back under the blankets. I knew that with nothing better to do, they would catch up on the sleep they had missed the night before. It was all I could do to keep my eyes open. I guessed I had missed more sleep than either of them.

Still I felt excitement urging me on. I was anxious to see the place where our crik was born. Was it really as pretty as folks said? Was the water as pure and cold? I decided to take a pail along with me so that when I found it, I could bring some of that famed water back to the fellas.

CHAPTER 6

The Spring

Though truly excited, as I explained before, I was also disappointed when I realized I would be going on up the crik by myself. I don't know if my disappointment was for myself or for the other fellas. I know they felt bad about having to stay at the campsite while their shoes dried out. But, too, it wouldn't be quite the same not having anyone to share the hiking experience with.

I started up the trail just a bit downcast. But I hadn't gone far when my spirits began to lift. The sun was warm and bright—who could be gloomy with all this sunshine around? A breeze rustled the leaves that stubbornly still hung on to the tree branches. Twittering birds flitted back and forth above me. In spite of the warm weather, most of the migrating birds had already left us, but I saw noisy jays and flirting chickadees, and such. I even saw a large hawk sitting on a tree stump, his preened feathers glistening in the sun.

As I said, I don't know who could have stayed feeling down on such a day. I was walking through one of the prettiest parts of the countryside I had ever seen. I had never been this far up the crik before, and I sure was enjoying the sight now.

I had no idea how far I would have to walk before coming to the spring. Maybe an hour or two? But the deeper I got into the heavy tree growth along the crik, the less I was concerned about the distance. I was just sauntering along, looking all around me at the prettiness of God's creation and thinking of how Gramps would enjoy it all if he could be there with me.

It seemed like no time until I heard a sound like falling water, and I hurried forward. I pushed my way through the trees and along the crik bank and, rounding the bend in the stream, I caught my breath with the sight before me.

There on the steep slope of a hill was a pretty little waterfall. As my eyes traveled up it to where it came out of the rocks above, I realized this was the spring—the beginning of our crik. I just stood there staring as the silvery water caught the sunlight and danced on down to the shallow pool directly beneath it, cool and clean. It was like they said—all around the pool the long, fingery tree branches seemed to stretch downward to reach toward the sparkling water. Here and there a dark spruce or pine shadowed the lighter greenery, and small shrubbery, still dressed in autumn reds and golds, looked at themselves in the mirror waters. It was a sight the like of which I'd never seen before. I just stood there, filling my eyes and my soul with it.

At last I let out my breath and moved slowly forward. I knelt at the side of the pool and eased one hand down into the water. It was so cold my fingers soon began to tingle.

I dropped down in the mossy carpet covering the bank and let my eyes travel every inch of the area and then slowly back again. I don't know just how long I sat there, drinking it all in. I finally roused myself with a sigh, then pulled myself to my feet and began exploring the ground all around the little pond.

Boy, I was sorry the other fellas weren't with me! They were really missing something, all right.

Reluctant at the thought of leaving this place, I dipped my pail in the coolness of the pond water so that I could hurry some back to the boys. Then I had another idea and let the water slip from the pail back into the pool again. I moved back around the small pool and climbed up the rocks to where the spring came out of the hillside.

This is why they call it a spring, I mused. *It does "spring" right out of that rock.*

By stretching the pail as far as I could, I managed to reach the silver stream of water that tumbled down from above. The icy water splashed over my hand as I caught the water in my bucket. I wanted to get it back to the fellas at camp as quick as I could so it would still be cold, but how I hated to leave the place.

"I'll be back," I whispered my promise; "iffen I have my way, I'll sure be back. An' when I come, I'll camp right there by that pool and listen to the song of the waterfall all night long."

I circled the little pool once more and after one last long look, I headed back the way I had come. This time I covered the ground much more quickly.

When I reached our campsite the sun had moved high in the sky and was already heading for the western horizon. I hadn't realized until I got close to the camp and smelled the lingering aroma of food how hungry I was.

When I came hurrying in, hustling that pail of spring water before it had time to become warm in the afternoon sun, both Willie and Avery looked a bit shamefaced. But I was so excited to tell them all about the pool that I didn't really notice it or pay much attention to the fact that the fire had gone out, though I sure was hungry. I went into great detail describing the waterfall, the pool, the surrounding greens and reds and golds. I shoved the pail of water toward them, insisting that they try a cold drink. At great length I told them just how cold it had been when I had started back with it and would have rattled on and on—but my stomach started to rumble. I sure was hungry.

I looked at the blackened kettle over the cold ashes of what had been the campfire, then fell to my knees and reached for the grimy pot.

Willie started to apologize but I waved it aside.

"It's okay," I assured him. "I don't mind eatin' things cold."

"Well—ah—well ah—" muttered Willie. "I'm afraid there isn't anything cold left to eat."

"Then I'll just start the fire again and cook up some more of whatever you had," I offered. "What'd you have?"

"Well—Willie baked potatoes and carrots over the coals," said Avery helpfully.

"Sounds good," I said. "Did it take long?"

But neither of them answered my question.

"We cooked all of the potatoes and carrots that we found," put in Avery after a while. "Even so we were hard put to find enough. Some animal got in our supplies last night. Seems he liked vegetables." Avery was warming to his story. "We had to scout around to find a few things left, and then we had to cut out the teeth marks before we cooked them."

"Oh," I said, then brightened at this idea. "Well, I'll just fry me up some bacon then."

Willie squirmed on the rock he was using for a stool. "Bacon's all gone, too," he said, his voice low and his eyes on the ground.

That slowed me down. I already knew we had no bread, no cheese, no more apples or pears, no cookies or no pancake fixings.

"What is there?" I finally asked the dreaded question.

"Beans," answered Willie and Avery in unison.

"I think I'll catch me a fish," I mumbled, trying hard to keep the disgust out of my voice.

"While you're gone I'll build the fire and heat up the beans," Avery quickly offered. I thanked him for that and got my fishing gear.

Willie looked worried.

"You sure you wanta wait to eat till you've caught a fish?" he inquired. "You know it can take a while to get one iffen they decide not to bite."

I didn't tell him I didn't see where I had much choice.

"I ate an apple 'n pear while I was walkin'," I said instead. "I'll be okay till I get a fish in the pan." With a show of more confidence than I felt, I started off down the trail. I thought I had spotted a likely place for the fish to hang out about a quarter mile up the crik.

It did take a bit longer than I had hoped to get a fish on the hook. I had to change my location twice before I finally caught something. When I did get a small northern I was pleased with it. My growling inwards were anxious to get it back to camp and into the pan.

As I neared the campsite I could smell something peculiar. I was expecting the rich, savory odor of baked beans to greet me, but this wasn't it.

As I stepped into the small clearing where our lean-to hugged the fallen tree, I looked about me. I could see a lump under the blankets again, and I knew someone was having another nap. It turned out that two someones were bundled in the blankets. The fire was stone cold again, though I could see it had been built up, just like Willie had promised. A blackened pot sat on three stones. I looked in. It was hard to be sure, but I guessed the charred, smelly remains in the bottom of the pot was the last of Aunt Lou's baked beans. I groaned.

It took me some time to get the fire hot enough to get the frying pan sizzling. I was glad we still had some butter and the can of flour, salt and pepper Aunt Lou had sent along for seasoning our fried fish. I cleaned the fish, washed it thoroughly in the cold creek water and then rolled it until it was completely covered with the flour mixture. Then I placed the butter in the sizzling pan and gently dropped the fish pieces into the golden fat. Boy, did it smell good.

For a fella who had only had an apple and a fall pear to tide him over since his breakfast pancakes, I certainly showed some constraint while waiting for that fish to get golden brown. I would have enjoyed some of those baked beans or a slice of bread or something else to go with it, but that sure didn't slow me down none. I lit into that fish before it was even cool enough to swallow.

The smell of the frying fish was hanging pretty thick in the air, and it wasn't long till I saw those fellas began to twitch and turn in their sleep. I heard Willie sort of groan, and I supposed they were hungry again, too. Not that I wasn't a one to share—but, after all, what was one little fish among three fellas? I ate faster.

Sure enough, before I was finished, Avery was crawling up out of the blankets, licking his lips, and Willie wasn't too far behind him.

I sorta kept my back to them and went right on finishing up my fried fish. I figured they were probably about as hungry as I had been. I didn't want to appear selfish or anything, so I half-turned toward them and said around the bite of fish in my mouth, "My pole and hook is there iffen you want to use it."

Avery had never been one for fishing, but he liked eating, so he picked up the pole and, with Willie following, set off down the trail to the crik.

"There's a fair-sized hole about a half mile or so," I called after them. "Seems to be a pretty good one."

After I had finished my supper I washed up my few dishes in the crik, put the pot to soak and went to the lean-to. It seemed it was about my turn to get a little sleep. Especially if we all had to sleep in the same small space again. I sure wasn't looking forward to that, and boy was I tired.

I took off my heavy shoes and placed them carefully under the lean-to, made sure my jacket was fastened up, crawled to the rear of the makeshift shelter and curled up in the blankets. In no time at all I was warm and drowsy. I didn't even hear the fellas come back.

CHAPTER 7

Return Home

The chill of an autumn morning stirred us from our blankets early the next day and sent us scrambling to build a fire. I had already piled wood beside the makeshift shelter and, after gathering a few dry leaves, some bark and tinder-like grass, we soon had a welcome fire going.

The sun was just pulling itself radiantly from its bed to greet the new day. I thought I could feel excitement in each ray that reached out to send delightful warm shivers along my back and across my shoulders. The sun's warmth joined the campfire in taking the last of the night's chill from our bones.

As soon as we began to thaw, we started to think about eating. We were all hungry but, like I had found out yesterday, there really wasn't much left in our packs to eat. Oh, we had a little butter, some syrup, a mixture of flour, salt and pepper, and a few little things like that. But that didn't sound like a breakfast.

"What're we gonna eat?" asked Avery, mournfully digging through the remains of our camp supplies.

"Guess we'll have to fish," responded Willie.

"We didn't have much luck last night," Avery grumped.

"Didn't you get any?" I asked, realizing then that I had fallen asleep before they had returned.

"Not a nibble," answered Avery shortly. The remembrance of it still irked him.

"Might be biting better this morning," I said as cheerfully as I could.

"Sure hope so," cut in Willie. "I'm near starved."

We picked up my pole and without speaking further headed for the crik. I led the way to the hole where I had been successful the day before, and we settled ourselves down to some serious fishing. Avery remained behind to keep the fire burning and get the frying pan hot.

We sat in silence for many minutes, not wanting to scare the fish and spoil our chances for breakfast.

Then Willie spoke in a whisper, "This trip isn't just what we'd expected, is it?"

I looked at him in silence. I knew it wasn't, but I wasn't sure just how much I was willing to admit—even to myself. Maybe camping wasn't really all it was cracked up to be, anyway.

"Not that I haven't enjoyed it," Willie hurried on, "but you must admit we've sure had our share of bad breaks."

I thought about Avery, my best friend for many years, and how he had sorta botched up a lot of things for us.

"Wasn't Avery's fault." Willie's declaration seemed to answer my thoughts. "Can't really say he's had the best time in the world either. I mean, who'd care to be chased by a bull? And then that dunkin' in the cold crik wasn't exactly fun. He's been just as hungry as the rest of us—and just as disappointed about missin' out on not seein' the spring, too."

I nodded my head in agreement. It had been a rough trip for Avery—and him not even caring too much for the out-of-doors besides.

"I've been thinkin'," Willie said thoughtfully, "maybe God sorta arranged this trip."

I looked up then, square at Willie. Now, where did he ever get an idea like that?

Willie returned my look and his eyes did not waver.

"Did you know that Avery is painin' inside?"

"Avery?"

"Yeah. He never says much—but yesterday when you were gone to the spring, well, we got to talkin' an' Avery opened up an' really said what he was feelin'. You know his mom's been awful sick an' that Avery already lost a brother. I think he wanted this trip to kinda get away and do some thinkin'. He's scared, Josh. He's really scared. He's got this silly notion that God is just out to hurt him or somethin'. He's just sure his mom is gonna die—an' for some reason he thinks it's his fault."

"Avery?" I said again, a little too loud. I checked myself. I sure didn't want to be scaring away our breakfast fish.

"Well, we had a long talk—an' then we prayed together. We gotta help him, Josh. Show him that we're his friends and we'll stick with him. Show him that God really does love *him*."

I nodded again. It sure did give one something to think about all right. If we hadn't had all of our "bad luck," Willie never would've had the chance to talk and pray with Avery like he did. We still wouldn't have known that Avery needed special friendship at this time.

We fished in silence again, but it was no use. The fish just weren't biting. We got up and moved on down the crik and tried another hole, and then another. Still nothing. I was beginning to wonder if maybe God had it in for all three of us.

"We better give up," said Willie. "Iffen we don't get packed up and on our way, we won't make it back home today."

I knew Willie was right but, boy, was my stomach complaining.

We went back to the campsite, and Avery's face, which brightened at our return, quickly fell again when he saw we had no breakfast.

We began to pack up our gear. I was about to throw out the remaining flour mixture when Avery hollered at me.

"Hey!" he yelled. "Don't throw that out. It would make a pancake."

"With pepper in it?"

"It's worth a try," Avery insisted. "I'm so hungry I could eat anything."

But he wasn't. I mean, he took that flour mixture, stirred in the one egg that we'd forgotten we had, added some crik water and fried the flat, rather distasteful-looking thing in butter in our frying pan. It didn't smell so bad as it cooked, but it didn't look too great. Avery then poured what was left of the syrup over it and sat down to have his breakfast. By then Willie and I were wishing we'd spoken up for some as well. But Avery took one bite and spit it clear across the campsite. Guess it wasn't going to be the answer after all.

We finished up our packing in silence. Inwardly I wrestled with the fact that Avery had wasted that last good egg.

Our packs were much lighter now, and we distributed the load as evenly as we could. Aunt Lou's pot still didn't clean up too good after the scorched beans. I was glad she had insisted on sending an old one. It sure was a sorry mess now.

We decided to stay on the south side of the crik rather than try to cross the fallen log again. We knew our way quite well, and we knew that if we followed the crik all the way to the Turleys', the bridge would get us across to our proper side then.

It was another beautiful fall day, and I guess that we could have really enjoyed our hike home had our stomachs not been so empty. As it was, it was a little hard to concentrate on the blue sky and the whispering fall leaves.

It was well past noon when we reached the Turleys and we had already determined to not follow the crik through their pasture. We didn't want an encounter with that bull again.

We were about to go on by their farmstead on the road when Avery stopped us.

"How about we go on in?" he suggested.

"For what?" asked Willie.

I was afraid Avery wanted to tell them about their mean old bull or something, and then they could very well say we had us no business being in their pasture anyway.

"For a drink," responded Avery. "Even a little water would help my stomach some."

We looked at one another and nodded. Maybe some water would help.

As we neared the Turley house I began to wish we hadn't stopped. Wafting out of the kitchen window and down the lane to greet us was the most wonderful smell you could imagine. Mrs. Turley was baking apple pie.

We all looked at one another and our empty stomachs began to grumble even louder. We said nothing, but the expression in our eyes was shared agony.

It was Avery who stepped up to the door and rapped gently. Fourteen-year-old Mary answered and looked rather surprised when she saw all three of us standing there. She just stared at us.

"Who is it, girl?" called Mrs. Turley, and I was sure enough relieved to hear her voice.

"Boys," answered Mary, and I was afraid she was going to close the door on us and go back to her kitchen duties.

"Well, invite them in," instructed Mrs. Turley, and she came through the kitchen and stuck her head out the door so she could see for herself.

"Come in. Come in," she invited us cheerfully, and we followed her into the kitchen. Her blue gingham sleeves were rolled up and there was flour on her hands and apron.

"What can we do for you, boys?" she asked. Mrs. Turley was known in the community as one who did not bother none with beating around the bush.

"We'd like a drink, please," responded Avery without hesitation. "We've been out on a camping trip and we're on our way home. It's powerful hot walking and we just thought that you might be kind enough to let us have a drink."

"Mary, get the boys some cold milk," said Mrs. Turley, and she went back to rolling out piecrust. Now, milk sounded a whole lot better than water.

"Never did care for milk all on its own," Mrs. Turley went on. "Mary, slice them some fresh bread and get out some of that strawberry jam." Mary hurried to carry out the instructions while Mrs. Turley deftly worked with her rolling pin, and we looked at one another like we'd been offered an expenses-paid trip to New York City. About that time I was blessing my best friend Avery for talking us into stopping.

"So you been campin'," remarked Mrs. Turley.

We managed to reply around giant bites of strawberry-jam-covered fresh bread. Mrs. Turley was a great baker.

"Where'd ya go?"

"Up to the crik mouth, ma'am."

"What fer?"

That one caught us a bit off guard. Why had we gone?

"Just to see the spring," said Willie. "We'd never been there."

"Neither've I," said Mrs. Turley, "an' I don't plan to waste no time in goin' way up there either." Then her voice softened and she even smiled. "But, then, I guess young boys with energy to spare don't quite look at things the way a tired ol' woman does."

We didn't quite know how to respond to that one. None of us were eager to refer to Mrs. Turley as a tired old woman while we sat at her kitchen table wolfing down her delicious homemade bread.

"Mary, cut them each another piece," said Mrs. Turley, watching us for a moment, "an' get them some more milk."

"That is mighty delicious, ma'am," said Avery. "We did have us some bad luck and ended up with no breakfast this morning." I held my breath for a moment, but Avery was smarter than I gave him credit for—he said nothing at all about that Turley bull.

"Then you'd best have a piece of apple pie," answered Mrs. Turley, not missing a beat with the smooth action of her rolling pin. "Mary, cut them a piece of that pie in the window. Mind you, be careful now. It's still hot."

"Oh, but—" started Willie, and I kicked him under the table.

"Sure does smell good, ma'am," I cut in quickly.

Mary was generous with her servings and I suddenly gained a new respect for the girl.

The pie was just as good as it had smelled, and we were given more milk to help cool off each bite. Boy, did it hit the spot!

"Mrs. Turley," I said as I washed down the last swallow with milk, "that was about the best apple pie I ever tasted."

"That's nice to hear," she said matter-of-factly without smiling. "The way my menfolk swallow the food around here, I'm not sure whether it be good or not. They just gulp it down and leave the table."

I supposed Mrs. Turley might not be the only woman with that complaint. I decided then and there to pay a few more compliments to the cook—whoever it might be.

We thanked Mrs. Turley again, paying her lavish compliments on her bread and pie, which eventually left her beaming, and turned back to the dusty road again.

As we left, Willie turned to Mary, who was busy cleaning up after us.

"And thank you, Mary," he said, "for feedin' us an' all."

A bit embarrassed, Avery and I quickly echoed his thanks. Mary gave us a shy smile.

Once back on the road with our stomachs full and our spirits revived, we began to pay more attention to the fall day, pointing out items of interest to one another.

We even started to reminisce about our camping trip. We first discussed all of the good things about it, like the colorful fall leaves, the fact that it hadn't rained, the clarity and freshness of the crik the closer we got to the spring. Then we started discussing the other things that had happened. We passed that old bull in the pasture, and the whole fearful experience came flooding back. But soon we were seeing the funny side of it all, and we laughed and pounded one another on the back and nearly rolled on the ground. Before we realized it we had quite convinced ourselves that our camping trip had been a tremendous success, and we could hardly wait to get home and tell everyone about it. In fact, we decided, there really wasn't one thing about it that we'd change even if we could. Well, maybe enough food for one last breakfast.

Just the same, I was looking forward to a good sleep in my own bed, with no one there to pull off the covers or breathe in my face.

CHAPTER 8

School Again

I wouldn't willingly have admitted it to anyone, but I was missing school. The local grapevine tried to keep up with the School Board's search. Rumors were always circulating about as to who they had contacted and where he or she was from and when the new teacher might be coming, but the school door stayed closed. I was getting restless, and I guess most of the other students were feeling the same way. Why, I even took to studying my textbooks—in the privacy of my own bedroom, that is.

I spent the time at the farm with the three men. Grandpa kept looking for little jobs to keep us all busy, but there really wasn't too much more that needed to be done before winter set in. Gramps laughingly suggested that we all take up knittin', but Uncle Charlie said that "mendin' was too close to a needle of any kind" for him.

It really hadn't been that long since our teacher had quit—it just seemed like forever.

I rode into town with Grandpa every chance I got and over to Willie's a couple of times, and over to Avery's once. I even visited Mitch Turley, who had quit school as soon as he could talk his folks into it. I knew Mitch wouldn't understand my hankering to be back in the schoolroom again, so I didn't even mention it to him. Instead, I told him all about our hike up along the crik. It sounded better every time we three fellas told it.

Anyway, I was bored. Guess I was sorta getting on the nerves of the men at the farm because one day Grandpa came in and said he was going into town and I might like to pack up my things and go on back to Aunt Lou's. The latest rumor had it that a new teacher was on the way and school might start just anytime.

Well, we had heard that before and it hadn't amounted to anything, but I didn't argue. I packed up my little valise, threw it in the back of the wagon, then went back into the big farm kitchen to tell Gramps and Uncle Charlie goodbye, scooped up Pixie and we started off for town.

"Feel that bite in the wind, Boy?" Gramps said as he turned up his collar. The wind really caught a body all right when you were perched up on the high seat of that wagon. I nodded my head and turned up my own collar.

"Winter might finally be on its way. Don't know when we ever had us a fall like this one."

I nodded again and looked at the trees lining the roadway. The branches were whipping back and forth and the leaves were dancing here and there, as though scurrying about to find the right bed for snuggling down before the snow started falling.

Grandpa clucked to the horses to hurry, and then I saw him look toward the sky.

My eyes followed his, and it sure did look like snow weather all right. I purposely didn't think about the wood it would take for the fires and the extra work in choring. I smiled to myself and thought instead about sliding down snow-covered hills and skating over frozen ponds.

When we got to Aunt Lou's there was no one to answer our light rap on the door. Grandpa walked right on in, like it was our custom when he brought me back to town, sorta halloing as he did.

"Guess Lou is out—" He stopped quick-like when we heard a noise from the bedroom.

Grandpa cocked his head and listened a minute. "Lou?" he called.

"In here, Pa," came the weak answer.

We both walked to the door of Lou's room. She was laying there with flushed cheeks and the blind on the window drawn.

"Ya feeling poorly?" asked Grandpa softly, and I wondered why he even asked. Lou wasn't one to lay around in bed in the middle of the day.

She smiled, but it was kind of fragile-like.

"Not too bad," she answered, "but Doc says I'm to stay here for a couple of days."

Grandpa walked over to Lou's bed. Automatically, it seemed, his big work-calloused hand reached out and rested on Lou's brow.

"You had the doc?" he asked. I knew that fact concerned Grandpa. One did not call the doc just for sniffles or a tummy ache.

"I'm fine, Pa, really I am," Lou assured him quickly. "Why, I really don't feel too sick at all—but Doc says at my age, I best stay in bed. Measles can bring complications."

"Measles?" I guess Grandpa and I both said the word together.

Lou looked just a mite embarrassed.

"Little Sarah Smith had the measles and then her mama got them, too. I took over a couple books and some chicken soup—and—well, I guess I had no business being there. Anyway, I now have the measles and Doc says, 'Stay in bed,' and Nat says, 'Stay in bed,' so—I stay in bed."

By the way she said it, I knew staying in bed was not easy for Aunt Lou.

"You should have sent for us, honey," Grandpa was saying.

"I'm not sick, Pa. Really. I sure didn't need to go trouble someone else over it."

"Well, Josh is here now," said Grandpa. "He's right handy. He can do any running that needs being done. He can cook, too. Charlie's been teaching him a few things since he's been so bored this week."

Lou gave me a smile. "Good to have you back, Josh," she said. "I've been missing you." I knew it was more than just someone to run her errands. Aunt Lou really did miss me when I was gone—me and Pixie.

I put Pixie in Aunt Lou's outstretched arms and the little dog lay there, her small tongue busy on Aunt Lou's face. For a moment I was scared— could dogs pick up measles? And then I figured likely not and dismissed my fears.

"I'll just put my things in my room," I said.

By the time I was finished unpacking my few belongings, I could hear the kettle singing. Grandpa was busy making Aunt Lou some fresh tea. I'd noticed some laundry on the line when we drove in, so I decided I'd best slip out and get it before that storm arrived. When I had finally untangled the things that were wrapped around the string of wire, my fingers were tingling with the cold. Yep, winter sure was on its way.

Nearing the house, I could hear Aunt Lou laughing. I don't know what story Grandpa was telling her, but they seemed to be enjoying it together. I folded up the wash, enjoying the fresh, outdoorsy smell of it, and put it in the basket. By then the feeling was back in my fingers.

"Josh," called Aunt Lou, "there are cookies in the pan on the table. Mrs. Brown just brought them this morning. Help yourself and bring some in for Pa, please."

"Anything you need before I start hauling wood?" I asked Aunt Lou around the cookie in my mouth as I handed the pan to Grandpa.

"Could you run to the store for some pork chops for our supper?" she asked me. I nodded that I could and pushed the last of the cookie into my mouth so I'd have two free hands to button up my coat.

The butcher shop was always a busy place. Sometimes I had been there when I'd had to wait in line for ten or fifteen minutes. It wasn't my favorite spot. I didn't care for the smell, the mixture of sawdust and fresh meat. I didn't like to look at the cases full of chunks and pieces that used to be someone's cow or hog, either. I would have rather waited outside, but the wind was cold so I stepped in and took my place in line—for once a short one.

The butcher took care of each customer one by one, and when he had handed Mrs. Olaf her brown-wrapped hamburger and marked it on her sheet, he turned to me.

"Howdy, Joshua. I'm supposin' you've heard the good news?"

I hadn't heard any news, good or bad, that I recalled, so I shook my head.

"No, sir," I stated.

"You didn't? Well, boy, yer holiday is 'bout over. The new teacher arrived on today's train."

I guess he'd expected my face to fall or me to start to grumble or something, for he was all ready to laugh a big laugh at my expense. There must have been a little smile that crossed my lips or showed in my eyes or something, 'cause he looked real surprised and then sad, like I'd spoiled his fun or something.

"Ain't ya upset?" he asked me.

"No, sir," I answered honestly.

"Ya like school?" he went on, incredulous.

I was a little slower to answer that one. I mean, I didn't want to be thought strange or something. I swallowed. "I reckon I do," I said.

He shook his head as though to clear it of cobwebs, and then he said a funny thing. "Good for you. Maybe ya won't need to spend yer life standin' over foul-smellin' meat all day."

He handed me my package and turned to enter it on the sheet that he kept for Uncle Nat.

I didn't rightly know what to say, so I just mumbled my "thank you" and pulled open the door. Besides, I was suddenly in a great big hurry to get home. I had real honest-to-goodness news!

When I reached the house out of breath from running against the wind, Uncle Nat had arrived home from the church and was sitting by Aunt Lou, looking relieved to see her obediently in bed and visiting with Grandpa.

"New schoolteacher's here!" I gasped out to all three of them.

"Is she now?" said Grandpa with a smile. "Then the rumor was right this time."

"He," put in Uncle Nat mildly.

We all looked at him.

Grandpa's eyes returned to my red-flushed face.

"When did she get here, Boy?"

"He," said Uncle Nat again.

We seemed to catch his meaning then—at least Grandpa did.

"It's a man?"

"Right," said Uncle Nat.

"How old a fella?" asked Grandpa, and I wondered if he was thinking about whether the new teacher would be able to handle the older boys.

"Near middle age, I expect," responded Uncle Nat.

"Middle age," repeated Grandpa, seeming to ponder the information. "Did he come alone?"

"No, he has a wife and child."

"Child?" This question, too, was from Grandpa.

"A girl," said Uncle Nat, and I immediately dismissed the fact from my mind. If it had been a boy I might have been interested in his age.

"That's nice," Grandpa was saying. "Real nice. You'll be able to get back to yer studies, Boy."

I nodded and then realized I still held the brown-paper-wrapped pork chops in my hands.

Grandpa stood to his feet and gathered up the cups. "I'd best be gettin' on home 'fore that storm strikes," he said. "Josh, did you bring in the milk and butter?"

"Yes, sir," I answered him.

"Then I'd best get a-rollin'. You take care now, Lou, ya hear? Josh is here and he's happy to do yer runnin'."

Lou smiled. "I promise!" she said. "Though I sure don't *feel* sick anymore."

"I've had an awful time keeping her down," remarked Uncle Nat.

"No use takin' chances," Grandpa reminded Aunt Lou. Then he added thoughtfully, "I thought you had the measles when you were just a little tyke."

"Doc says that they were the Red measles," Aunt Lou replied. "These are the German. One is not usually as sick with them, but occasionally there are complications."

"Well, you take care." Grandpa leaned over to plant a kiss on Aunt Lou's cheek, reached out and tussled Pixie's ear, and then turned to me.

"Glad about your school, Boy," he said again with a quick pat on my shoulder.

He turned to Uncle Nat. "Any idea when classes will start?"

"I heard them say next Monday," he replied.

I was rather disappointed about that. It was Wednesday. I'd been hoping that school would take up again the next morning. I was anxious to get a look at that new teacher. I'd never had me a man teacher before.

"Guess he needs a couple days to settle in," Grandpa was saying.

He placed his hand on my shoulder again and gave it a slight squeeze like he always did when we said goodbye, and then he was off. Uncle Nat went out with him.

It was then that I finally delivered the package of pork chops to the kitchen.

Uncle Nat turned to me good-naturedly. "You can have your pick, Josh," he said. "You want to cook supper or haul the wood?"

I didn't hesitate for one minute. "I'll haul the wood," I responded and went to slip out of my good jacket and into my choring coat before leaving the warm kitchen.

The wind sure enough smelled of snow.

CHAPTER 9

The New Teacher

Over the next few days there was little time for chafing over school to start. With Aunt Lou still confined to her bed and Uncle Nat busy with church duties, I had plenty to keep my hands and mind busy. The first snowstorm came sweeping in too, and that meant more wood and coal to haul. Boy, was it cold! It seemed that Old Man Winter wanted to make up for lost time, all in a day or so—thought we'd had it warm and sunshiny for quite long enough. The snow piled up overnight and the north wind whipped it into little drifts all around the corners of the house. I had to shovel my way to the coal shed and the woodpile. It did look awfully pretty out though.

Now and then one of the fellas would drop by with the latest bit of gossip about the new teacher. I couldn't invite anyone in because of the house being in quarantine, so we'd talk through the open window or over the front gate. You'd be surprised how many things were being passed around town about the schoolmaster.

One story said he was running from the law, and another one said, no not the law, but the army, and still another said he wasn't running at all but it was his wife who was on the run. Then there were those stories that said he'd been put out of his last school for beating a boy to within an inch of his life, and another that he had lost his school because of some jealous woman who falsely accused him because he wouldn't leave his wife for her.

There were even stories about his finances. Some said he was only a step ahead of creditors, and others said he had lost his home, his horse and his holdings to the town banker where he had last taught.

Nobody seemed to know for sure where he had taught. Nobody seemed to know many *facts* at all, but the gossip kept sweeping over the gates and into the homes of the town folk. Uncle Nat was getting right put out about it all and said that someone should call a town meeting and put an end to all the foolishness. "A man is innocent until proven guilty," he said.

It was all rather mysterious. I could hardly wait to get my first look at the man. I felt quite confident that when I got that look, I would be able to tell right off just which one of the stories had any basis in fact.

By the time Monday finally rolled around, the doc had let Aunt Lou out of bed. She was right anxious to take over her own house again, and I guess Uncle Nat and I were just as anxious to let her.

My lunch pail in hand, well stocked by Aunt Lou, I left for school with a great feeling of excitement. Avery, Willie, Jack and I had agreed to meet at the corner of Main Street and all go to school together. None of us could live with the thought of one or the other of us fellas getting the first look at that new schoolmaster.

Willie and Avery were already there when I came puffing up. The air was frosty and it hurt one's lungs to run hard on such a morning. My insides felt frozen as I came wheezing up to the fellas.

We had to wait for Jack. The three of us stood there stomping our feet and clapping our hands, trying to keep warm. We were about to give up on Jack and go on to school when he came panting around the corner. His cheeks were red—I just figured it to be the cold wind. Then he grabbed my arm and squeezed it real tight.

"You're not gonna believe this," he said. "I wouldn't have believed it myself iffen I hadn't seen it with my own eyes."

"Seen what?" asked Willie, and Avery and I both perked our ears up too.

"Well, you know the new teacher moved in over near us."

We waited, wondering what news Jack had that would top the tales we'd already heard.

"Well, on Saturday Ma sent me into town for some eggs and milk, and there she was—comin' right outta their gate."

"Who?" we all said together. "Who?" I know our minds were all busy wondering where this new story was going.

Jack looked at us like we should have known "who" without asking.

"His daughter," he said. "Who else?"

"His daughter!" we all fairly exploded.

"Good grief!" said Avery. "I thought you had some *news*."

"Guess his daughter can come out of her own house iffen she has a mind to," I stated sarcastically and turned away from Jack.

"Come on," chimed in Willie. "Let's get to school before we freeze to death."

Jack looked disappointed. For some reason I failed to understand; he had been so excited over his silly bit of news.

"Wait, fellas," he said as we walked away. "Wait—"

But we didn't even want to hear about it.

Jack tried again. "Why the rush? Don't you want to hear—"

"Why should we care if his kid runs down his walk?" demanded Avery. "Is she weird or somethin'?"

Jack pulled me to a stop and the other fellas turned to look at him.

"You haven't seen her?" asked Jack.

We shook our heads, and I tried to shake off Jack's restraining hand.

"Have ya heard about her?" Jack continued.

"I heard he had a kid," I shrugged.

"Yeah, me, too," said Willie, his expression saying, "So what?" He turned away. "C'mon, let's get in there before that bell rings."

Jack let me go then but he had this funny look on his face.

"I think you boys are in for a big surprise," was all he said.

We looked at Jack like he'd lost his senses.

We pushed our way into the small hallway and shook the snow from our coats before hanging them up on our assigned pegs. I felt myself straining forward, trying to catch a glimpse of that new teacher.

Other students crowded into the entry. We exchanged a few teasing pleasantries with the other fellas and let the girls pass without comment. One or two of them looked our way and giggled a bit. Girls were awfully silly, if you asked me.

There was no way we fellas would have entered the schoolroom before the bell rang. It just wouldn't have looked right, somehow. Yet all of us were so anxious to get a look at the man who would be teaching us for the rest of the school year. From the stories that had been circulating, I didn't know whether he would have a long, curling black mustache and shifty eyes, or horns and a red tail.

Anyway, we were still standing there, straining to look around the door that wasn't opened quite wide enough for us to see into the room, when the other door opened and a gust of winter snow swirled in. Behind the snow-flakes was the most beautiful creature we had ever seen. I guess our mouths all dropped open. I mean, there she was just a few feet from us, brushing the snow from a green velvet-looking coat, her cheeks flushed a rosy pink, and blue, blue eyes peering out at us from under a white fluffy hat. She took the hat off to shake the snow from it, and brownish-red curls tumbled down all around her shoulders.

Guess Avery found his voice first.

"Who is that?" I heard his hoarse whisper.

I was too busy just looking.

She glanced again over our way and instead of lowering her eyes and flushing in embarrassment or giggling like the other girls, she gave us a flashing look with just the hint of a teasing smile in it and then she was gone through the door.

"Who was that?" Avery croaked again.

"Oh," said Jack with a real smart-alecky grin, "that's just the teacher's daughter."

"Why didn't you tell us?" asked Avery.

"You weren't interested in the teacher's kid. Remember?"

I gave Jack a withering look and pushed my way past the other boys. The bell hadn't rung yet, but I couldn't wait to see if I was dreaming or what.

I found my way to the desk I considered mine at the back of the room and managed to sit down without stumbling over anyone. My books slid carelessly onto the wooden tabletop in front of me and my eyes traveled over the room.

Sure enough. There she was. She had removed her green coat and was wearing a blue dress that brought out the blue of her eyes. Every eye in the room was on her.

Somewhere a bell rang and through a mental fog I saw other students bringing themselves to attention. A voice at the front of the room was speaking to us. Somehow the words got through to me and I suppose I obeyed the orders I was given.

I read when asked to read—answered when spoken to—worked the sums I was given—took part in a spelling bee—even said "No, sir" and "Yes, sir," and somehow made it through the morning, but my mind sure was on other things.

When we were dismissed for the noon hour, all us older fellas clustered together talking, and a good share of the talk was about the teacher's daughter. I listened but did not take part much. I mean, it seemed sorta crude to be discussing her in such a fashion.

Skeet Williams had Jack Berry by the front of the shirt. "What's her name? What's her name?" he was persisting. Jack had suddenly taken on a swaggering air, knowing he was the only one who had really seen this new girl before classes had begun.

Jack hated to admit it, but he didn't know her name.

"It's Camellia," piped up Andy Johnson, with a measure of authority.

"How do you know?" Jack challenged him, hating to grant any further knowledge of the new girl to anyone but himself.

"The teacher—her pa—called her that. Didn't ya hear him?"

Jack hadn't heard him. I hadn't either. But then, I hadn't heard much the teacher had said that morning.

"Camellia," said Avery in a sort of whisper. "That's a flower, ain't it?"

There were many knowing nods and cute comments. I walked away from it all. The way the fellas were carrying on was almost as bad as girls giggling. I just didn't like the feel of it all.

Avery followed me. I walked over the frozen schoolyard kicking up clumps of roughed-up snow, dried grass and anything at all that showed.

"What's the matter, Josh?" Avery said at my sleeve. "You mad about somethin'?"

"Naw," I said. "I ain't mad."

"You're not gettin' those there measles, are you?"

My head jerked up. "No, I'm fine—what gives ya a silly idea like that anyway?"

"Well, yer so quiet-like. Usually you join right in the funnin'."

"Funnin'!" I said sourly. "Is that what that was?"

Avery looked at me in surprise.

He started to say something back but I cut in, "I mean, it don't seem fair somehow to stand talkin' about—about people with them not even there to defend themselves or nothin'."

"We weren't saying nothin' bad," argued Avery.

"Well—'bad' all depends," I continued. "I mean, iffen she—she's a nice girl, then she might not like a bunch a fellas pickin' her over like that—like she was just somethin' to gawk at or somethin'."

Avery swallowed.

"I mean," I went on, "why don't we just forget that girl and go play Fox and Goose or somethin'?"

"You don't like her much, do you? I mean, what's she done—?"

I looked Avery square in the eye. I wanted to tell him just how dumb he was—but he was my best friend. He flinched some at my look and scuffed his feet back and forth on the solid ground.

"It's got nothin' to do with likin' or not likin'," I finally said. "I don't even know her—yet. Neither do you. Nor do any of those other fellas. But standin' around talkin' about her doesn't do anybody any good. We might as well be playin' or somethin'."

"I'll get the guys," said Avery, but before he turned to go he said one more thing—quiet and almost condemning—"You're gettin' more like your preacher uncle every day, you know that? Ever'body in town knows he won't tolerate nobody talkin' 'bout nobody," and Avery wheeled and was gone.

I knew Uncle Nat didn't care none for town gossip. He had been the butt of it far too much himself as a kid growing up in a difficult situation. But I hadn't known he had a name about town for not allowing it in his presence.

Well, maybe I had learned it from my uncle Nat. I didn't like the feel of gossipy tongues either. And I wasn't one bit ashamed of the fact.

Avery gathered up the fellas and we set us out a ring for Fox and Goose. The game got pretty lively, but I noticed fellas continually casting glances over at the girls' side where the new girl, Camellia, was playing tag.

She fit in real nice and ran about as fast as Mary Turley, who was considered a real good athlete for a girl.

The bell rang and we got to go back into the warm schoolroom. I couldn't help but notice how pretty Camellia was with her cheeks flushed and her coppery hair tousled from running in the wind.

At the close of the day all of us older fellas left the schoolyard together, and you can just guess what the topic of conversation was. But I didn't want to listen to it. It just didn't seem right somehow for them all to be talking about her and laughing and joking and all. I pulled away from the rest of them and said I had to hurry and get home 'cause Aunt Lou might be needing me.

I guess I ran all the way—I don't really remember.

When I came into the warm, fresh-bread-smelling kitchen, Aunt Lou looked just fine.

"So how was your first day back at school, Josh?" she asked me.

I answered, "Fine."

"Was it good to be back?" she questioned.

I said that it was.

"And what is your new teacher really like?"

I started to answer, then stumbled to an embarrassed halt. I suddenly realized that I had no idea. I couldn't even remember what the man looked like.

CHAPTER 10

The Storm

The next day I made a point of taking a real good look at our new teacher. I didn't want to be caught again in an embarrassing situation like I had with Aunt Lou the night before. If necessary, I would even figure out his shoe size!

His name was Mr. Foggelson, that much I knew. So Camellia's last name would be Foggelson, too. Camellia was an only child. Everyone said she most favored her ma, so I guessed her ma must be a fine-looking woman.

But I was off track again. Back to Mr. Foggelson, our teacher—he was of medium size, neither big nor small. He didn't have a long, black mustache and shifty eyes, and he certainly did not have horns and a tail. He was clean shaven and had blue eyes—well, not real blue like Camellia's but sort of a gray-blue. His hair was medium brown in color, not dark, not light, and it didn't have the rich reddish-brown tones of Camellia's hair. His chin was neither jutting in a stubborn way nor small and lost in his neckline like a mousy man's might be. He was a rather ordinary-looking man.

His voice was well-modulated and even-pitched, neither high nor low. He taught with authority without being overbearing. He seemed to know the subject matter well. He was patient with the slow learners, but seemed to show real appreciation for a good mind. All in all, I had to admit he would probably be the finest teacher I had ever had in my limited years of schooling.

Having carefully made my mental report for Aunt Lou or anyone else who might ask, I went back to letting my thoughts wander to other things—like whether Camellia liked to skate on frozen ponds or toboggan down steep, bumpy hills. I was imagining her with her hair flying in the wind and her cheeks flushed from all the excitement.

I wonder if she'd like to go out to the farm with me? I thought. I was sure Gramps had never seen such a pretty girl and would never believe my description of her.

I wondered if she liked dogs and how she would feel about my Pixie. Somehow I could picture her with Pixie in her arms, running her slim, long fingers through the soft, fluffy fur. I could hardly wait to get the two of them together, sure that it would be instant, mutual love.

Will I stutter and make silly blunders before I even have a chance to show her that I am different than the other fellas? I worried. *That I really do care about her as a person, not just a pretty face?*

And then I realized that "a pretty face" was all I really knew about Camellia. Well, I'd just have to set myself to finding out more about her.

The week rushed by—all too quickly, I thought, filled as it was with daydreams and snatched glances and "chance" encounters. I wondered just how I would manage the whole weekend without even a glimpse of her or anything. Many of my classmates lived right in town and would have the opportunity to see Camellia as she went to the grocer's for her ma, or out for a walk with her pa, or something. Me, I'd be out at the farm with the menfolk—all alone.

I didn't talk to any of my family about Camellia. Not that I wasn't thinking about her some—I just didn't know what to say or how to say it. I tried whispering a few little things to Pixie—and then felt my cheeks get hot with embarrassment.

I got through Saturday, though my mind really wasn't on my farm chores. I was looking forward to Sunday. I was just sure that Camellia and her folks would be at Uncle Nat's church, his being the only church in town. I could hardly wait to have Gramps see her. He'd notice her for sure—I mean, she stood out in a crowd, and then he'd ask me who this new girl was and I'd be able to say, "That's Camellia Foggelson, the daughter of the new teacher." I wouldn't have to say that she had the bluest eyes in the world, or the prettiest brown-red hair. Gramps would see all that for himself.

But when I crawled out early for church on Sunday morning, we had ourselves a storm brewing like I'd never seen before. The wind was howling and the snow was drifting so bad you couldn't even see the barn.

"Whoo-ee," remarked Uncle Charlie as he looked out the frosted window, "would you look at her howl!"

"Guess this here winter is determined to make up for our fine fall," stated Grandpa.

"Gonna be tough gettin' to church," I mumbled, more to myself than to anyone else.

"Won't anyone be able to get to church this mornin'," Grandpa stated as known fact. "Doubt even the town folk will make it."

You can bet I was some disappointed about that. Suddenly the long, quiet Lord's Day stretched before me empty and desolate. How in the world would we ever fill it?

The only excitement in the day was fighting our way against the wind to care for the team, the cows, hogs and chickens. They were all mighty glad to see us. Back in the house, bone-chilled and tingling, we were all glad for a good wood supply against the cold.

After our dinner together, I helped Uncle Charlie with the dishes. We settled down with hot coffee and Aunt Lou's cookies to watch the storm and play checkers. Gramps took on Grandpa and Uncle Charlie challenged me. My mind wasn't on the game too much and I didn't play as well as I should have.

"I think I'll have a nap," stated Gramps, who often had a nap in the afternoon.

"Me, too," I said, standing up and yawning, and all eyes turned to look at me.

"Been studyin' too hard, Josh?" asked Grandpa.

"Well, no, not too hard," I stammered. "But I do need to study a fair bit to make up for all that time we lost."

I could tell all the menfolk approved of my statement.

Fact was, I *had* been studying hard. I guess I was out to prove to the new teacher that I had a "good mind," knowing he admired one and all. I wasn't sure how Camellia felt about a good mind, but I didn't think it would hurt my cause none to impress her father.

"Might as well have yer nap," Uncle Charlie said. "Nothin' better to do."

I did go to my room and lie down—but I couldn't sleep. I just lay there, tickling Pixie under the chin. I promised her we'd get back to town all right—before too long too.

I don't think Pixie was as interested in town as I was. I worried about Camellia and her folks maybe being caught short of wood or something and not making out well in the storm. I worried about other fellas maybe going over to check on how they were and making a good impression on her. I knew if I'd been in town, I sure would have been over there at her house, checking to see if there was anything I could do for them.

Thinking didn't help and sleep would not come. I pulled out one of my old storybooks from a trunk I had my "treasures" in and tried to read. Either the story had changed—or I had. I couldn't get interested in it—and it had been my favorite.

I finally gave up and just lay there listening to the wind howl. Would Aunt Lou and Uncle Nat be worried that we might try to come into town in the storm and then fret when we didn't arrive? No, they knew my grandpa better than that. He had far too much sense to head out into this storm.

When I heard voices down below, including Gramps, I knew all three men were around and stirring again. Then I heard the rattle of dishes—one of them was preparing our supper. I figured it must be chore time again, and I was glad for a good reason to leave my bed.

For two more days the wind howled and blew the snow around. In some places the drifts were higher than my head. I didn't recall ever seeing a worse blizzard. We managed to keep ourselves quite busy, shoveling our way to the stock and chopping and hauling. Even so I chafed some.

On Wednesday the weather finally broke and the sun came out. But you could see it would be unwise to try to push a team through those drifts to town.

It turned out that I missed the whole week of school. I studied at home. It gave me something to do, and I sure didn't want to get behind the rest of my classmates.

On Sunday morning we did bundle up and head for church. Grandpa was worried about what Aunt Lou and Uncle Nat had been eating. They always got farm produce from us, like their milk and eggs and cream. Their extra garden vegetables and fruit were kept at the farm in the root cellar, too, and

Grandpa always supplied them with fresh meat and poultry that was either just butchered or kept on big ice chunks in our sawdust-filled ice house.

"They do have 'em stores in town," Uncle Charlie reminded Grandpa.

"No reason to spend money when you don't need to," was Grandpa's response, so the sleigh was loaded with food, and we bundled up well and headed for church.

I put Pixie in her box in my bedroom when we got to Aunt Lou's and then helped unload the sleigh before we went to church. Uncle Nat was already over at the church, building up a good fire to take the chill off the cold room.

Aunt Lou said they had fared well during the storm, though Uncle Nat had fretted a bit about some of the parishioners, especially the older ones. He was afraid they might not have been prepared for the cold weather.

He had even brought Old Sam home with him and kept him on the living room couch, but Sam had left again some time during the night on Friday. Uncle Nat had supposed he had gone in search of a bottle.

Old Sam was the town drunk. I suppose there are nicer ways of stating it—but that's the plain fact.

He had been in our town for as long as I could remember. I don't recall ever having heard a last name for him. Everyone just called him Sam, or Old Sam.

He had worked at odd jobs here and there when he had been a younger man and before the bottle took complete control of his life, but he didn't even try anymore. I don't know where he got money for booze. He sure never had money for food. Some of the town people gave him a meal now and then just out of charity. He didn't have money for clothes either. Uncle Nat watched that department and tried to keep Sam dressed so he wouldn't embarrass folk or freeze to death in the cold weather.

Truth was, Old Sam was as much a part of our town as the butcher or the grocer, and everyone sort of used him as the example of complete godlessness and waste. Mamas would say to their sons, "You don't want to turn out like Old Sam, do you?" The menfolk would say about their lazy employees that "he's about as useless as Old Sam," and angry fellas would say to one another, "Why don'tcha go join Old Sam, where ya belong?" or "You smell as bad as Old Sam"—but nobody could do anything to change Sam from what he was.

Uncle Nat had tried. Boy, had he tried. He was always trying to clean Sam up and feed him nourishing food. He tried even harder to get him to know that the only way he could *really* clean up his life and make something of himself was to give his life completely over to the Lord Jesus. I had heard Uncle Nat tell Sam that many times myself. But Sam would just whimper that it was too late. Nothing could be undone that was done. And then Uncle Nat would insist, "Jesus can do it, Sam. He can make a new man of you if you'll let Him. No sinner is too black for the Lord to wash clean as snow. No sin is too great for God to forgive," but Sam would just shake his head, clutch his bottle and whimper.

I knew, without even asking, that Uncle Nat had probably already been looking for Sam in all of his favorite hangouts—like the livery stable, the back porch of the grocer's, the shed in the schoolyard, and the little barn out back of the town hall. I knew, too, that as soon as the morning service was over, Uncle Nat would be out looking for Sam again.

When we entered the small church my eyes quickly scanned the room, but the Foggelson family was not in attendance. I was keenly disappointed. I sincerely hoped nothing had happened to any of them during the storm.

Avery and Willie came over to me and started talking about the blizzard here in town—the Smiths' chimney fire and the Bases running out of firewood and needing to burn some of the furniture, and how Mitch Turley froze the tip of his nose and needed to see the doc.

I wasn't too interested in all the news. I was still wondering about the Foggelsons.

It turned out that I really hadn't missed much school. It was Thursday before classes were held, and then only a few of the students braved the weather. More measles were going around. Folks hoped the cold weather would put a stop to the spread. Only one patient had been really sick—the little Williams girl. The doc was hoping she was now on the mend; but there was some concern about her eyesight, for some reason none of us really understood.

After the service we shared dinner at Aunt Lou's, and before we even had time for a visit Uncle Nat excused himself from the table. I knew he was off looking for Old Sam again. I pushed back, too, and went for my heavy coat.

"I'll help you," I said. "I'll take the road down past the school."

Uncle Nat nodded, appreciation in his eyes. We left the house together, while the three older men visited with Aunt Lou over coffee before helping her with the dinner dishes.

I hadn't bothered to explain to Uncle Nat that the Foggelsons lived down the school road. Here was a ready-made opportunity to check and be sure that everything was fine there.

When I got to the Foggelsons', I was relieved to see smoke curling briskly from both their chimneys. The house didn't look like it had suffered any from the storm, but I walked up to the back door and knocked anyway, practicing in my mind what I would say, depending on who answered. It was Mrs. Foggelson—at least I figured it must be her. She did look a lot like Camellia, with the same blue eyes and clear skin and hair almost as pretty, though she wore it all piled up on top of her head.

"Yes?" she said rather hesitantly.

"I'm Joshua Jones," I said quickly, to explain myself and keep her from shutting the door. "I'm one of your husband's students, and I just wanted to check to see that you're not needin' anything—I mean with the storm and all—I thought that—"

But she interrupted, "How sweet," sorta dragging out the words and smiling nice as she said them.

I stammered then. My planned speech went flying right out of my head and I couldn't think of one sensible thing to say.

"We are fine, Joshua," she was saying. "But we do thank you for stopping by. The storm was a nasty one, wasn't it?"

"I'm right glad," I stumbled, my face beginning to redden. "I mean, I'm glad you're fine."

"Would you like to come in?" she was asking, holding the door wide open for me.

Boy, would I have loved to have gone in, but I found myself saying, "Thank you, no, I've gotta get. I mean—I'm helpin' Uncle Nat look for Old Sam. I mean, well—he always worries that he might freeze to death—or somethin'." Then I hurried on, blurting out some further explanation that didn't need to be made, "He's not our kin or nothin'; it's just that Uncle Nat always worries over folks—I mean, he's the preacher and his job—" But I finally stopped, feeling more embarrassed than ever.

"I see," said the pretty Mrs. Foggelson, giving me another melting smile. I wasn't sure if she did see or not, but I knew I had to get out of there before I said something even dumber.

I mumbled a goodbye, placed my cap back on my cold head, and started off almost on the run.

It turned out I was the one to find Old Sam. He was huddled in a corner of the woodshed behind the town hotel. His teeth were chattering and his beard was matted, and even in the crisp cold winter air, he smelled bad. He was still clutching a bottle, though it was an empty one. I couldn't figure out why he wasn't dead. Guess maybe all the alcohol maybe preserved him, like cucumbers in vinegar, or something. I knew I couldn't move him all alone, and I didn't know what to do with him anyway, so I went home for help.

Uncle Nat was still out, so Uncle Charlie and Grandpa hitched the team and went off for Old Sam. When they got him back they put him to bed on a cot in the living room, and Aunt Lou made some hot soup to try to get down him. I left the rest of them fussing over him and went to my room. I figured I had already done my part. I wasn't too crazy over the dirty old coot anyway. But I knew Uncle Nat would be powerful glad to see he was still alive. I guess I was glad for that fact too.

CHAPTER 11

Camellia

Every fella in our school—every one in his right mind, that is—was sorta sweet on Camellia. As you can probably tell, I was no different. Some days I had so much trouble keeping my mind on my work that I scarce understood the words in my lesson books. This was new to me, having always being considered a good student and enjoying the work and all.

I managed somehow to keep up with the rest of the class, but I guess I picked up the new knowledge subconsciously or something, for I don't really remember learning it.

Every recess and noon hour we fellas spent our time trying to get Camellia's attention, though none of us would actually admit to it. Some were a little bolder than others. Me, I hung back trying not to look too forward, trying not to look too obvious, but all the time thinking of little things that I might do or say if I got the opportunity.

The opportunity came in rather a strange way.

For some reason I didn't understand, Camellia's pa seemed to take a liking to me. He talked with me a lot and often asked me to stay after classes just to chat about some book or some new idea. On several occasions he made a pleased comment about my "good mind."

Anyway I got the surprise of my life one day when Mr. Foggelson, Camellia's pa, asked me to stay after class again. As I explained, staying after class was nothing new, the fellas were already teasing me some about that, but Mr. Foggelson's words sure did surprise me.

"Joshua," he said—he always called me Joshua, real proper-like—"Joshua, I wonder if you would have time to help me out."

I certainly wanted to help the Foggelson family if I could, but I wasn't sure about the time part. I did have a lot of chores to do at home, and I would need to check with Aunt Lou before I could give an answer. I figured Mr. Foggelson must have some wood that needed chopping or something like that, which could take a lot of time, all right.

Mr. Foggelson went on, "Camellia is having a bit of trouble with that new concept in geometry, and you have grasped it thoroughly. I thought she might find it easier to understand from one of her fellow students than she does when her father tries to explain it. I have a tendency to be a bit impatient with her at times, I fear. Do you think you could find the time?"

I would find the time. My head was nodding yes before I could even discover my voice.

"Very good," said Mr. Foggelson approvingly. "Would Wednesday after school suit you?"

I was nodding again and then my head began to clear, and I knew I'd better do some real thinking on the issue.

"I'll need to ask my aunt Lou," I managed. And then I even had the presence of mind to say, "Wednesday might not work. I have a lot of chorin' to do, and I need to get it all finished by prayer meetin' time."

"I see," said Mr. Foggelson rather slowly, a slight frown on his face.

"Oh, I'll do it," I hastened to inform him. "We'll arrange something, Aunt Lou and me—and I," I corrected myself quickly.

"Good," he said, his frown replaced by a somewhat distant smile.

"I'll check with her tonight and let you know in the morning, sir," I said, and with his nod of agreement I felt I was dismissed.

I left then as dignified as I could manage, careful not to put on my cap, or hoot, or run until I had left the schoolhouse steps.

I guess I ran all the way home, and when I got there I was so out of breath I couldn't even tell Aunt Lou my good news. I just sat there gulping air, my face flushed from the cold air and the run.

She laughed at me as she put the milk and cookies in front of me. She knew I had something exciting to share, and that I was near to busting for the want of telling it.

"Take your time, Josh," she said, patting my shoulder. "I'll be here when you catch your breath."

Pixie pushed against my leg, wanting up on my lap, and I scooped her up and shared a bit of my cookie. I thought Pixie would be interested in my news, too, but I couldn't tell her yet, either.

Aunt Lou went to the back porch to get more wood for the fire. She seemed to take a little longer than usual, and I wondered if she was doing it on purpose to give me time to catch my breath.

When she came back, she started chatting right away—I think to give me even more time.

"I was just thinking, Josh, it is only three weeks till Christmas. Seems funny. I haven't even gotten in the Christmas mood yet, though we have been practicing the Christmas music for the church program. Still, it's coming soon, ready or not."

I nodded my head and washed down my mouthful of cookie with the cold milk.

"Anything special you want for Christmas, Josh?"

I hadn't been doing any thinking on that. I shook my head, trying at the same time to come up with an item so Aunt Lou would feel good about getting me something I "wanted."

I came up empty. Fact was I really had everything I needed. And Camellia's special friendship was about the only thing I was wanting, and I supposed Aunt Lou couldn't do much about getting that for me. I was rather on my own there.

I emptied the last of my milk and Aunt Lou pulled out a chair at the table and sat down.

"Can you talk now?" she asked, a bit of a twinkle in her eyes.

"Mr. Foggelson asked me for some help," I blurted out.

"Help?" Aunt Lou responded, curiosity in her face.

"With geometry."

"Help *him* in geometry?" teased Aunt Lou, but I knew she didn't need an answer to that.

"Sort of coachin'—or teachin'," I went on to explain.

"Oh—h," responded Aunt Lou, and she gave me one of her shining smiles as only Aunt Lou could when she was very pleased with me.

"You must be doing very well, Josh, for the teacher to pick you to tutor another student. I'm proud of you." And she reached out and placed her hand on my head for just a moment.

"Then I can do it?"

"Of course. I think it's an honor—and will also be a good experience for you."

"He suggested Wednesday night," I continued, "but I told him it takes all my time to get my chores done before prayer meetin'."

"Will another evening work?" Aunt Lou asked, genuinely concerned. "I mean," she went on, "if no other night works, I could help with the chores or—"

I stood up quickly, almost forgetting Pixie on my lap. I was shaking my head as I grabbed for Pixie.

"I'm sure we can work somethin' out for another time," I said, not wanting Aunt Lou to even consider choring when she had me around.

"Talk it over with your teacher," suggested Aunt Lou. "We certainly will co-operate in any way we can." I knew she and Uncle Nat would do their best to work it out so I could do the "tutoring."

I was turning to go get changed out of my school clothes when Aunt Lou's voice stopped me.

"Who's the lucky student, Josh?"

I turned, not understanding her for a moment.

"Who's the lucky student?" she asked again, "to have you for a tutor?"

Without me being able to stop it the red began to creep into my face. I wanted to turn away to hide my embarrassment but I knew that would be rude. I tried to keep my voice even, though the thumping of my heart was far from normal.

"Camellia," I stated as matter-of-factly as I could, trying hard to put no special emphasis on the name.

"Camellia?" said Aunt Lou.

"Camellia Foggelson," I stumbled on.

"Oh, the teacher's daughter. Then it *is* an honor, Joshua. If the teacher picked you to teach his own daughter, then he must have a high regard for you."

I stood there, still blushing, not knowing what to say and wishing to escape to the quietness and privacy of my own small bedroom.

"Is she a poor student?" queried my aunt.

"She's 'bout the best in the class," I blurted out too quickly. "She always leads everyone in English and Social Studies. She's real good at Art and Readin' and everything. She even beats me in Arithmetic an'—" I stopped. I realized I was sounding like I thought Aunt Lou had insulted her. I also realized Camellia was a good student. A very good student. She led the class in almost every subject. So why was I being asked to tutor her? I hadn't given it a thought before, I was so excited over the possibility of just being with her. And if I did take on tutoring her, could I keep my thoughts on the geometry problems long enough to be of any help to her? Some strange doubts and feelings began to flood over me. I turned to go to my room.

Aunt Lou must have sensed my confusion, for she did not question me further or try to stop me.

All the time I was changing into my clothes for chores, my mind wrestled with the problem. Why was Mr. Foggelson asking me to tutor his daughter who clearly needed no tutoring? Was *I* failing geometry? Was this a way to help me without me feeling embarrassed over it? No, that didn't make sense. I was having no trouble with the work. In fact, I had just gotten a grade of 98% on my last test. Was Camellia really having trouble with this part of the work? Well, maybe. Maybe she hadn't gotten her usual high-nineties score last time. I was sure Mr. Foggelson expected only top grades from her. Perhaps he really did want tutoring help for Camellia.

I tried to push the weighty problem to the back of my mind and think on other things, but it kept popping to the front again, insisting on my full attention.

I picked up Pixie and headed out through the kitchen to get my heavy coat.

"You'd best stay in," I told the little dog. "It's too cold out there for you tonight."

Aunt Lou, busy peeling the supper vegetables, gave me a smile as I walked by, but said nothing further about my tutoring. I was glad. I wasn't quite ready to discuss it yet. I had to do some more sorting out first. I had been so excited about it and was nearly bursting to share it with some of the fellas. Now I just wasn't so sure. Maybe I wouldn't say anything about it at all. Might be better if I sorta kept it to myself, at least until I had it figured out.

CHAPTER 12

The Tutoring

Mr. Foggelson's eyes met mine the next morning as soon as I entered the classroom. I could not avoid him without being rude, so I sorta smiled and nodded my head slightly, and he understood that I had talked to my aunt Lou and uncle Nat.

Fact was, we'd had quite a discussion about the matter. After the chores were all done, the evening meal over and we'd had our evening devotions together, Aunt Lou brought up the subject again.

"Josh has had quite an honor today," she told Uncle Nat. "The teacher has asked him to help his daughter, Camellia, with some geometry that she is not quite understanding."

Uncle Nat's eyes lifted from the Bible he was replacing on the small corner table.

"That so?" he said. "Good for you, Josh," and he gave me a smile and a playful slap on the back.

I blushed a bit and shifted my feet some.

"When?" asked Uncle Nat.

"We haven't worked that out yet," I stammered after Aunt Lou waited for me to answer the question. "He had suggested Wednesday, but I told him I couldn't get my chores done soon enough. It's all I can do to get finished in time for prayer meetin' and I sure wouldn't have time—"

"If it's the only night that will work for them, we probably could work something out," said Uncle Nat. "Maybe a bit more wood chopping other nights, and on Wednesday I could try to get home earlier and—"

"Ain't no sense you takin' on more," I found myself saying. I knew that Uncle Nat was already too busy. He hardly had any time at home.

"I'm sure another night will work just fine," I continued. "I'll talk to Mr. Foggelson tomorrow."

"We'll co-operate in any way that we can," said Uncle Nat as they both smiled at me, and I knew they would.

Then Uncle Nat turned very serious. He spoke slowly and deliberately, "This might be an answer to my prayers, Josh. I called on the Foggelsons as soon as they moved to town and invited them to join us in worship." Uncle Nat paused for a moment, and I knew he was carefully choosing each word. "Mr. Foggelson said they had no need nor interest in church. That it was for the deprived and unlearned—as a crutch—that educated men had other things than myths and fables to give their attention to. He also said his wife and daughter were free to make their own decision, but when his wife looked up after his comment, I got the feeling that the decision had already been made for her, too."

There was silence for several moments.

"Maybe God can use you in some way, Josh, to bring His light to this family."

The thought kinda scared me. I was no preacher or anything. If Uncle Nat had failed to convince the man, then surely there was nothing I could do. I mean, it was real scary—to have someone's eternal destiny, so to speak, resting on my shoulders. Actually, I expected to take that responsibility someday. I was sorta thinking about being a preacher like Uncle Nat. I really respected him—and so did the other people of the town. Wherever he went folks greeted him and doffed their caps and listened to what he had to say with real respect. And he was the one they called on when there was sickness or an accident or trouble of most any kind. I bet there wasn't a fella who got called on more—unless it was the doc. Even then the two of them most often ended up in the same house, for the same need—doc with his black medical bag and Uncle Nat with his black Book.

Well, even if I did hope to one day be a preacher too and looked up to by the people, I wasn't quite ready for that responsibility yet, and the thought of being the one to help some family, especially the family of my teacher, see the need for Christ and the church—well, I didn't know if I could do that. Still, I said nothing. Just squirmed a bit.

"Let's pray," suggested Uncle Nat.

We had just finished praying, but after a brief glimpse at Uncle Nat, then Aunt Lou, I bowed my head like they were doing.

"Dear Lord, our Father," began Uncle Nat. "We thank you for this opportunity that has come to Josh to enter the home of the Foggelsons. Help him to be sensitive to your leading and to let his light shine for you. May he be used of you, Lord, and be instrumental in bringing this family to the place where they realize that education, as good as it is, is not enough to prepare one for life after death. That one cannot better the mind sufficiently to redeem the soul—that only through the death and life of Jesus Christ can we have our sins forgiven and our lives changed. Amen."

I gave a great deal of thought to Uncle Nat's prayer. I had never considered the possibility of a man like Mr. Foggelson being denied heaven. I mean, he was decent, intelligent, and a gentleman. Everyone nodded to him and greeted him with respect. Yet here he was, not believing in God and not ready for heaven. If he should have an accident or a sickness and die—I didn't even want to think of it. It was easy for me to understand about Old Sam. He was wicked. The fella was always drunk. He couldn't even care for himself properly. He didn't wash, he didn't change his clothes. He didn't even eat most of the time. Uncle Nat had to look after him constantly and pour soup down him or he wouldn't even have survived from week to week. But Mr. Foggelson? It was awfully hard for me to put the two men in the same category—"lost."

So that's how I came to be back in class, trying not to let on to Mr. Foggelson that I knew he was a sinner, that he would not be allowed into heaven unless he chose to repent of his sin. It wasn't my rule, it was God's rule—it was that simple, that straightforward. There was no middle road. No other option. There was only heaven and hell, and heaven was for those who called on the Lord God to forgive them for their wrongdoings. If one chose to ignore God or deny that He had a right to direct one's life, that person would not be allowed into heaven, no matter how good other people thought he was.

I was glad we went right to our history lesson so I could lower my eyes to my book.

At recess and lunch time I didn't say anything to the other fellas about tutoring Camellia. Not even to Willie or Avery. I tried to join in with the games as usual, but it was difficult. My mind just wasn't on them. I think the others noticed my lack of concentration and my quietness—I caught a few glances my way, but no one said anything, for which I was glad.

I also noticed a few glances from Camellia. She looked over my way several times and once even smiled before I could turn away. My stomach gave a flop and I missed the tag on Avery. I tried to fake a trip so the fellas wouldn't guess what had really happened. I don't think I brought it off very well.

After school I knew I would be questioned by Mr. Foggelson, so I didn't even try to hurry putting away my books and gathering up my lessons to take home.

He came with a big smile.

"Well, Joshua, did you get permission from your aunt and uncle?"

"Yes, sir," I answered, swallowing hard and trying to raise my eyes to Mr. Foggelson's face.

"Good," he beamed. "When can you begin?"

"Thursdays seem to be best, sir. Right after school, if that suits you."

"That suits me just fine. And Camellia, too. She's happy to hear you can help her."

I blushed, hating myself for doing so.

This was Wednesday and I had to get right home to do the chores. I was glad for an excuse to get away quickly.

I gathered my books and nodded at Mr. Foggelson.

"I'll plan on tomorrow then. Right after school."

"Fine," he said and reached out and placed a hand on my shoulder. It was the first time he had touched me, the first I had seen him touch any of the students. Not even Camellia, though I was sure that in the privacy of their own home there must be father-daughter contact. I felt a bit embarrassed, though I did not know why. I was used to a great deal of touching. Why, in my family we were always hugging and slapping one another on the back and patting on the head and squeezing the hand and all sorts of nice family things.

Still, it wasn't like your teacher laying his hand on your shoulder, like you were someone special to him—and you weren't just sure what the "special" was. I didn't know what to say or do, so I just cleared my throat and looked down at my books again.

"I'll see you tomorrow," I said awkwardly and headed for the door.

I both dreaded and anticipated the day for the first tutoring and, boy, can that ever mix you up inside!

I did have the sense to set aside my geometry book after class the next day. I fumbled around at my desk, pushing books around, sorting and resorting until I was sure the fellas had left the room.

I finally dared to look up, half expecting Mr. Foggelson to be standing at my desk with instructions on how I was to teach his daughter. But it was Camellia's deep blue eyes that met mine. She gave me a wonderful smile, and I nearly dropped the geometry book I held in my hand. I looked down again, fumbled some more with my book and nearly choked mid-swallow.

"Are you ready?" she asked nicely and I nodded, then let my eyes wander to the boards that Mr. Foggelson was meticulously cleaning.

"Papa will be home later," she said in answer to my unasked question. "He always stays to clean the chalkboards and put some lessons on for the next day."

I nodded again, but I felt like I was rooted to my spot.

"Let's go then," she offered. "Papa said you have lots of chores after school so I mustn't waste your time."

I forced my wooden legs to move and followed her out of the schoolroom. We were halfway across the yard before I realized she was carrying a load of books. I mumbled some kind of apology and reached to take them from her.

"Thank you, Joshua," she said with just a hint of appealing shyness, dropping her long, dark eyelashes. It rather threw me. I had never had a girl flirt with me before. At least not one like Camellia.

When we got to her house her mother greeted us warmly and waved us toward the tea and fancy pastries placed on the table. I was not a tea drinker. I didn't care much for the stuff and I had always been encouraged to drink milk, a growing boy needing lots of it to make his teeth and bones strong and all, but I would have died before I would have admitted that to Camellia or her ma.

"Do you care for cream or sugar?" asked Camellia courteously, about to pour.

I tried to remember what Aunt Lou or Grandpa took in their teas but my mind went blank. "No, thank you," I finally mumbled. "Just bare."

Camellia's eyelashes fluttered softly as she glanced at me, and I knew I had said something dumb. What was it that one said about tea anyway? I knew Gramps always had his coffee "black," but tea wasn't black. What was it, anyway?

"I like a little cream in mine," Camellia was saying. "Papa's always teasing me, saying it will make me fat someday, but I use it anyway." She laughed merrily.

I couldn't imagine her fat but didn't know if I should say so.

She passed me a pastry then. It looked about the size of one mouthful, but I knew better than to take two. Besides, I wasn't sure just what the thing was and how one went about eating it. I laid mine down on the small flowery plate that sat on the white tablecloth and waited for Camellia to lead the way.

She picked hers up nimbly in her fingers and took a dainty nibble. I followed suit. Only for some reason mine didn't work quite like hers had. I don't know if I had gotten a faulty one or what, but just as I went to take a teeny bite from the side like Camellia had done, the fool thing crumbled in my fingers and fell all over the tablecloth, leaving me with empty air and a red face.

I felt like a dolt, that's how I felt, but Camellia pretended not to mind.

"I've always told Mama that those dainty little pastries were not made to be held in the strong hands of a man," she said. "Their fingers are just too used to a firm grip on things." And so saying she leaned right over toward me, swept the crumbs into her own plate and took them away from the table. When she returned she brought with her a small fork with a short handle, and she passed me another pastry.

"They are difficult to eat with a fork, too," she whispered confidentially, "but it might be a little easier."

I somehow managed to get most of that pastry to my lips. By the time I was finished I was glad the thing hadn't been any bigger. I was almost sweating with the effort—and I still had that cup of tea ahead of me.

The teacup with its little handle was not much easier to manage than the pastry had been. It must have been designed for a creature with only one finger and a thumb. I didn't know what to do with the other three—no matter how I held the cup they all got in the way.

Camellia tried to put me at ease and I appreciated her effort. *Not only pretty, she is sensitive and caring, too,* I thought, and that made me like her even more.

"We will study in the sitting room," she informed me when we had finally freed ourselves of the tea and dainties, and with great relief I followed her away from that table with its linen cloth and china cups.

The sitting room was comfortably furnished, and we chose a settee by the large window and spread our books out on the small table before it. Somehow I had the feeling that the table had been placed there purposely for our use.

"What part you wishin' to study?" I began, opening my text.

"None of it," she responded. I'm sure I couldn't have looked as astounded as I felt, but she giggled, softly and bubbly, like our little crik when it splashes over pebbles on a sandbar.

Now, I had never cared much for girls giggling, but Camellia's was different. It made me feel like giggling, too, and I had to check myself before some dumb sound came out of my mouth. Instead, I just smiled, a blush making my cheeks hot. I knew there was a secret joke here, but I wasn't sure just what it was.

"One is supposed to be honest, isn't one?" Camellia was saying pertly, her blue eyes twinkling with merriment.

I nodded. Certainly one was to be honest.

"Well, I'm honest. I wish we didn't need to study."

"I'm sorry," I began. "I didn't know that your pa was *makin'* you—"

But I got no further.

"Oh, Joshua," she stopped me, reaching out one soft hand to lay gently on mine. "This wasn't Papa's idea."

I was totally lost. If it wasn't her pa's idea that we study and she didn't wish to study, then what was I doing in her house?

"I coaxed Papa to ask you," she said frankly in response to my perplexed look.

"You did?" I stammered.

"Yes," she said with a flip of her coppery curls. "I did."

"But why?"

"Why?" She seemed a little annoyed at my question.

"Why—if you don't want to study—?"

She looked at me like I was a child. But then she tossed her hair again and fluttered those long eyelashes.

"I just wanted to get to know you better—to talk."

I was dumbfounded. I stared at her, my mouth open and my heart pounding wildly. I wanted to ask "why?" again but I didn't dare. Camellia would expect me to know the answer, and I didn't—not yet at least. It might take a good deal of sorting out.

I swallowed hard and turned back to the book, thumbing through the pages.

"Well—well—" I began, "guess we can talk and study, too."

She rewarded me with a flashing smile and slid over so we could both share my geometry text. Hers lay on the table, unopened.

We started through the text page by page, and I found there was little if any help needed by Camellia. She understood the concepts most as good as I did.

It was nearly time for me to be hurrying off home when she looked up from the text. "Do you have any brothers or sisters, Joshua?" she surprised me by asking.

I shook my head.

"Me neither." There was silence for a minute. I guess we were both thinking some on that.

"Does it make you angry?" she asked in a quiet voice.

"Angry?" Though I missed having a brother or a sister, I had never thought of being angry about it.

"Yes. Angry."

"Guess not. Why?"

Her brow furrowed in deep thought or consternation, I wasn't sure which. "Sometimes it makes me angry," she confided. "It used to make me terribly angry. I didn't think it was fair at all. Everyone should have more family than just a mother and a father. Don't you think?"

I shrugged my shoulders carelessly. I wasn't sure I was ready to tell Camellia the fact that I didn't even have that much family.

"But I don't get as angry anymore," went on Camellia. "In fact, I guess there are some good things about being an only child."

"Like?" I asked.

"Well—" she said slowly. "Like you."

"Me?"

"Sure. If I was not an only child, then I probably wouldn't get my own way all the time, and Mama and Papa might not have agreed to let you tutor me."

I felt my mouth drop open again.

"It wasn't hard to convince Papa. He gives me anything I want," said Camellia, "but Mama can be awfully stubborn sometimes."

I had never heard a person talk like that about their own parents before, and I must confess I was a bit shocked. But Camellia said it so innocently, so frankly, that I found myself excusing her.

"Do you always get your own way, Joshua?" she asked me.

"I—I don't know," I said truthfully. "I've never thought on it before. I guess I'd never thought to even try."

"You haven't?" The idea seemed preposterous to her.

"Well—ah—well, they let me have my dog, Pixie, an'—"

"You have a dog?"

I nodded.

"Oh, you're so lucky. I've always wanted a dog, but Mama says, 'Positively not.' She has allergies. And she is so—so—"

"Stubborn," I whispered, and we both burst into laughter.

The laughing must have jerked me back to reality, for my eyes traveled to the clock on the mantel.

"I've got to get," I said, jumping to my feet. "I'll never get my chores done if I don't hurry."

She looked like she wanted to ask me to stay longer, but she bit her lip and didn't say anything.

"Thank you, Joshua, for your help," she said instead. "I'll see you next Thursday."

Her comment brought me up short. I hardly knew what to say or how to say it.

"Camellia," I began, "you know the geometry as good as I do. I really didn't help you none."

"But you did!" she insisted. "Please, Joshua. You promised. Please say you'll come again."

That part was right, I had promised. The whole thing didn't make much sense. It wasn't that I didn't want to come. And maybe—maybe I had helped her some.

I smiled.

"Sure," I agreed. "I promised. I'll see you next Thursday."

"Joshua," she said with a big smile, "could you show me your little dog sometime?"

"I'd love to. She can do all kinds of tricks and everything."

"But you can't bring her here," she frowned, "on account of Mama's allergies."

"Then you can come home with me and see her. Ask your folks. Aunt Lou would love to meet you."

She smiled again—and I took that smile all the way home with me.

CHAPTER 13

Good Old-Fashioned
School Days?

When I got to school the next morning, the word had already gotten around that I had been seen carrying Camellia's books home. I never did find out who saw me and passed the news along, but it seemed to have done a bit of growing with its travels.

Avery met me by the path that leads up to the school, just below the bare, gnarled branches of the old maple tree the town fathers had planted there so many years before our time.

His first words were, "Is it true?"

"Is what true?" I responded innocently.

" 'Bout you and Camellia?"

My face started to redden. I had no idea what Avery had heard, but I had me a sinking feeling that some of it might be based on facts.

"I dunno," I said slowly, moving past Avery to continue up the path. "What've ya heard?"

"That you went home with Camellia."

I nodded, agreeing that I had. "Her pa asked me to help her some with her geometry." That sounded reasonable enough to me, but it didn't to Avery.

"Camellia?" he snorted. "Camellia? Camellia don't need help with nothin.'"

Just then Willie and Jack sauntered up.

"Hey, listen to this, fellas," Avery called out before they even joined us. "Josh here went home with Camellia to *help* her with her *geometry*." He emphasized the words "help" and "geometry," and just as he had expected, the other two fellas stopped short and howled.

"Camellia?"

"Help with geometry?"

"Very funny, Josh!"

"Honest!" I argued as I was slapped on the back and punched on the arm, my face getting redder by the minute. "Her pa asked me to."

"Oh, come on, Josh," said Jack scornfully. "We're not dumb enough to believe that story."

"What really happened?" demanded Avery.

But before I could even answer, Jack was continuing. "I s'pose that's why you carried her books and held her hand, too."

"I did not," I denied hotly.

"An' I s'pose that's why you stayed at her house till almost dark," went on Tom Foster, who had just joined the inquisition.

"An' here you were pretendin' to not even be interested in her," went on Jack. "Whenever we'd talk about her or somethin', you'd hush us up, or move away from us, or change the subject or somethin'. 'We shouldn't talk about people behind their back,' you said. All you really wanted was to have her all to yourself." Jack's tone was so sarcastic, all I could do was stare at him.

But Willie was laughing. He was in the mood for doing a little teasing.

"An' I s'pose you had 'tea' with her mother," he said, and he held his fingers in a ridiculous pose and pretended to sip from a dainty cup.

"I did not," I denied, and then remembered the small cups and the flimsy pastries. Well, it hadn't been with her mother.

"An' her pa said, 'Josh-u-a, my boy, are your in-ten-tions hon-or-able?' " went on Tom, exaggerating every word and mannerism.

He somehow managed to catch the look of Mr. Foggelson and I suppose even I would have laughed had not the joke been on me. Willie and Avery howled. Then I noticed that Jack didn't join the laughter. His face looked about as red as mine felt. It took me a moment to realize why.

Jack was sore. I knew he had been making quite a fuss over Camellia, but I sure hadn't expected him to carry on in this fashion.

My face was getting redder too, a lot of it from the anger churning away on my insides. I didn't know where to start with my denying; so much of what was being said was the truth that it was hard to sort it out from the errors. I knew then why Gramps had tried to explain to me how dangerous half-truths are. A downright lie you can dismiss in a hurry, but when it gets all tangled up with a smattering of truth, it is awfully hard to untangle.

I was genuinely saved by the bell. I had never been so glad to hear it ring in all my life.

We ran toward the schoolhouse, but even as we tore over the schoolhouse yard, I was aware of Jack's angry glances my way. When we jostled our way out of the boys' cloakroom and Camellia was just leaving the girls', her bright hair tossing about her shoulders and her cheeks flushed pink from the chill morning air, Jack gave me another black look. And then, to make matters even worse, Camellia flashed me one of her dazzling smiles and said, "Good morning, Joshua," very softly, but it wasn't soft enough for the other boys not to hear.

Willie and Avery were fit to be tied. They jabbed me with their elbows and sniggered behind their wind-cold hands. Tom stuck out his foot to trip me and almost succeeded. But it was Jack that bothered me the most. He glared at me like I was suddenly his worst enemy. My face flushed red and my head clouded with confusion. What was all of this about anyway?

The day didn't improve much. The boys teased me every chance they got. Camellia flashed little smiles and fluttered her long eyelashes. Her silent signals made shivery feelings go slithering up my spine, but I hoped with all my heart that no one else was catching her at it.

By noon it was not only the boys but the girls as well who were teasing me. They weren't as bold about it, but the glances, the giggles, the laughter, all made me most uncomfortable. I was beginning to wish I had never seen or heard of Camellia Foggelson.

But, no, that wasn't fair—nor true. I knew that deep inside me, every time I stole a brief look at Camellia.

Near the end of the class, Mr. Foggelson caught my eye and gave me a bit of a nod, which I had come to recognize as his signal that he wanted me to remain behind after class. Of all days to be doing that! The fellas would really make a case of it.

At last the room seemed to be empty. I was still shuffling books around and pretending to look for something I couldn't find. Mr. Foggelson moved from the chalkboards back toward my desk. I knew I had to look up. But, boy, it was hard to raise my eyes.

"How's the tutoring going, Josh-u-a?"

He really did say my name that way. I hadn't noticed it before.

"Fine, sir," I responded as clearly as my dry mouth would allow me.

He nodded. "Camellia seems to understand the concept much better now."

I let the words settle about us, wondering just what to say next. We were both silent. It seemed like hours.

"Then she won't need any more help?" I asked, wondering if that made me sorrowful or relieved.

"Oh yes," he cut in quickly. "I'm sure she would appreciate a little more of your time—if you can spare it."

I wondered if he could hear my heart pounding, and then blushed at the thoughts of my classmates' taunts. I swallowed again, then slowly nodded my assent.

Mr. Foggelson sat down on the desk in front of me, a place we students were forbidden to sit. Slowly he brushed the chalk dust from his fingers. Then he pulled a white handkerchief from his pocket and wiped his hands clean. He had a strange look on his face—like disdain or disgust or something.

"Fool dust," he muttered. "Gets on everything. Your hands, your clothes— even up your nose."

I didn't know how to respond so I didn't say anything.

"Don't ever be a teacher, Joshua," he said, still pronouncing my name like each syllable stood alone. He surprised me with the intensity in his voice as he stared over my head at some spot in the back of the room. "Poor pay, long hours, and a tough job. Day after day trying to pound a few facts into dense, uncaring little heads."

I wondered if he remembered I was still in the room. He seemed to be talking to himself—and he sounded bitter and depressed.

I still did not make any comment.

Suddenly he swung back to me, carefully tucking the handkerchief back into his trouser pocket. His expression changed and his eyes looked alive again.

"You have a good mind, Joshua. The best I've ever had the privilege of working with. I can see your face light up with understanding and appreciation. You can go far, Joshua. Be anything you want to be."

I knew that somehow my ability to learn had brought some strange joy to Mr. Foggelson. I couldn't understand just why, but it was enough to know that I had pleased him. I knew he was paying me a high compliment, yet I didn't know what to say in response.

"How would *you* feel about some special tutoring, Joshua?"

I licked my lips and swallowed again. I wasn't sure just what he meant by his question. Was he proposing now that *Camellia* tutor *me*? Boy, that would really make me the laughingstock of the school.

"I have a good library of sorts, Joshua. Oh, it's not big or grand, but it has some good basic books—books that would provide you with a great deal of information. I would no more consider bringing my books into the classroom for all of the students to paw over and mutilate and soil than—than throwing my daughter to the lions. But I would be happy to allow you the privilege of studying them—in my home—and of discussing the contents with me if you desire. What do you think?"

I'm sure my mouth, as usual these days, hung open. I didn't know what to think. I did love books, I did love learning new things—but Mr. Foggelson's private collection? Would I be careful enough? Would I understand them? Would I find the time? It all made my head spin. And what about the fellas? If I spent even more time at the Foggelsons', it was bound to mean more jokes.

I knew Mr. Foggelson was waiting for my answer, but I still wasn't sure what it should be.

I swallowed nervously and forced myself to begin, even though I still wasn't sure what words my voice would form.

"That's very kind, sir. I'm much obliged. I don't really know what to say. I mean—well, I—I . . ."

I stammered to a halt and Mr. Foggelson took over.

"You do enjoy books?"

"Oh yes, sir." That was not hard to answer.

"Then why the hesitation?"

"Well, I—I," I stumbled on, "I never thought of having so many books at one time—to learn from—an' these are your own special books. I'd hate to mess 'em up or anything."

"I wouldn't be afraid of you soiling my books, Joshua," said the teacher. "I know you will give them your full respect."

"Yes, sir," I hurriedly assured him.

"Well—?"

"I'll need to check at home. I mean—I have . . ." I fumbled for words again.

"Your chores. I know. But I'm sure we can work out something. Perhaps you would have some free time on Sunday afternoons."

I must have blinked. Studying was not done on Sundays at our house— not even studying for enjoyment.

"Not on the Lord's Day, sir," I blurted out before I could even think about my selection of words.

Mr. Foggelson's eyes darkened. "I see," he said, but I wondered if he really did.

"Saturday?"

"I always go home to the farm after school on Friday night or else early Saturday mornin'. Grandpa comes for me. I stay all day Saturday and most of Sunday with the menfolk."

"And chores every night?" questioned Mr. Foggelson.

I nodded.

Mr. Foggelson stood up, still brushing imaginary chalk dust from his hands.

"So we have a problem?"

"I'll ask," I cut in quickly. "I'll talk to Aunt Lou—it's gonna be hard to work it in. But I'll ask."

"It's not that I want to be pushy, Joshua. It's just that in my years of teaching I have never found a mind like yours. It would be—it would be a shame to waste it. Both for your sake—and for mine."

I didn't know exactly what Mr. Foggelson was trying to say, but I nodded anyway. I did appreciate the fact that he was going out of his way to be kind to me and to encourage me to use the mind that God had given me. I smiled my thanks and began to gather up my books, but Mr. Foggelson was not done yet.

"Have you given consideration to what you'd like to do with your life, Joshua? A lawyer? A surgeon? An architect?"

I hadn't given much thought to any of those things. But I had thought about what I might like to do with my life, all right.

I smiled confidently at my teacher as I answered, "Yes, sir. A minister."

"A minister?" Mr. Foggelson shook his head slightly as if to clear cobwebs. I thought perhaps he had not understood me.

"A minister—like my uncle Nat," I explained to him.

"Nat? Oh, yes. Nathaniel Crawford is your uncle, isn't he? I had forgotten."

"Yep," I said with a great deal of pride, "he's my uncle."

I guess I had expected Mr. Foggelson to greet my announcement with a great deal of enthusiasm. He didn't. He didn't seem pleased at all. I couldn't understand it. But then, I remembered, Mr. Foggelson did not attend church. He most likely did not understand much about being a pastor. Maybe I could bring a few of Uncle Nat's precious books with me when I came to read from Mr. Foggelson's library.

I looked up. Mr. Foggelson was clearing his throat. Then he said a very unusual thing—more to himself than to me. "We'll see," he said. "We'll wait and see."

Revenge

I was still getting a great deal of ribbing at school. The fellas got a lot of laughs from it but they meant no harm. It wasn't that way with Jack Berry. He had been my friend, a close friend. Now he rarely even spoke to me, just about me—and everything he had to say was mean and cutting.

I was really sorry about this. I didn't like having an enemy. I'd never had one before. Was he sore, too, about not getting to go on the camping trip? I just didn't know what to do.

I knew what the Bible said about enemies—that we are to love them, to do good to them. But, boy, it sure was hard to be nice to Jack Berry. He seemed to spend his nights thinking up mean things to say about me, and his days saying them.

I tried to ignore the insults but it sure got tough. Even the other fellas were beginning to get on me about the situation. They said I shouldn't allow Jack to say those things, that I should stand up to him. I tried to shrug it off.

Willie was the only one who really understood how I was feeling.

"It's tough, Josh," he said. "Doing what you know Jesus would do is really tough sometimes."

"Turning the other cheek" was what Willie said the Bible called it. Though he acknowledged that not defending myself was tough, that was exactly what Willie expected a follower of Jesus to do.

Then one Thursday everything all broke loose.

I had gone again to Camellia's house and, after our tea and pastries—which I still didn't manage too well—we spent some time studying. I would have stuck with it longer, but after a few minutes of working over the geometry text, Camellia started talking about other things.

She was bright, lively, exciting, and it was fun talking to her. It was easy for me to just let the book slide to the table and listen to the music of her voice. When I finally pulled myself away, gathered up my books and my coat and left her house, I was in a big hurry. I was later than I should have been and I had chores waiting for me at home.

I was just running by the darkened schoolyard, my breath puffing out ahead of me in cloudy little spurts of frost, when I heard an unexpected shuffling sound. Before I could even turn to look, someone grabbed me and a fist whirled through the air and hit me right in the face.

I hollered out with surprise and fright and my book went flying through the air and landed somewhere in the dark bushes just beyond me.

The fist hit me again, and this time pain streaked through my right eye. It made tears stream down my face so I couldn't even see my assailant.

I had never fought before in my life, but suddenly I was fighting as if my very life depended upon it—for all I knew, maybe it did.

As we traded punch for punch, I could tell whoever had jumped me was about my size and weight. I still couldn't see, so I had to cling to him with one hand and swing with the other. Most of my punches missed, but a few of them were solid hits. The other fella responded in grunts or cries of pain that made me fight even harder.

It was hard and slippery under foot because of the frozen ground, and as we tussled and pulled at one another, swinging whenever we could get a hand free, our breathing became more and more labored. Once or twice I heard a tearing sound but I didn't know, nor care, whose clothes were being ripped in the exchange. I was far too busy trying to save myself from who knew what.

I stopped worrying about who I was fighting and why, just kept on swinging as hard and effectively as I could. And then a solid blow caught me right on the chin, and I felt my knees turn to mush.

I didn't realize it at the time, but it would be several weeks until I was able to remember and sort out exactly what happened after that. Reconstructing events later, I recalled I had tried to stay on my feet, but the slippery ground and our tangled legs didn't help my sense of balance any, and I felt myself slowly going down.

"That oughta teach ya!" a familiar voice ground out between gasps for air, and I knew that it was Jack Berry who had attacked me.

A fiery anger went all through me like a knife blade. I tried to force my weak legs to work so they would hold me up long enough for another punch. But I couldn't stay on my feet. My head hit something solid and everything went black.

When I came to, I forced my eyes open, wondering where I was and what had happened to me. Darkness had totally taken over our small town. I did not know how long since I had left the Foggelsons. I did know that I hurt. My knuckles hurt, my face hurt, and my head hurt worst of all.

Realization flooded over me as I lifted my hand to my face. Even that movement made pain shoot all through me. I could feel a damp, sticky substance wetting my fingers. I felt a cut above my eye and knew my nose had been bleeding. Beyond that I didn't think I was hurt too bad except for my pounding head. If only I could get my legs under me again. But they just wouldn't co-operate.

I could feel the chill of the frozen earth beneath me seeping through my school jacket, and I found myself shivering with cold and wishing for my good, old, warm chore coat.

I should be home, I'm late for my chores. Aunt Lou will be worrying, were my fuzzy thoughts.

I was still lying there, trying to get my frozen fingers to button my jacket when I heard shuffling feet again. I gathered all my strength in one more effort to get to my feet. Then I heard the unmistakable mutterings of Old Sam. I could tell he was drunk as usual. And then there was a loud hiccup and Old Sam was stumbling over me to end up on the frozen ground.

He mumbled a few unrepeatable words, and struggled to get to his feet. His legs didn't seem to work much better than mine, and he sprawled out on top of me again, banging my aching face with one boney elbow.

"Ohh," I groaned. "Watch it, Sam, will ya?"

"Joshsh?" questioned Sam in the darkness. "Joshsh?" he muttered again. Another hiccup followed. "Joshsh, that you?"

"Yeah, it's me."

I tried to roll Sam off so I could get to my feet. I couldn't do either. He made no attempt to help me. Just lay there like a limp sack.

"Sam," I implored helplessly, a hint of anger in my voice, "get up, will ya? At least get off me."

With a loud "hick" Sam rolled off me, mumbling to himself as he did so. Sam's mumbling was sort of a town joke. We fellas had never been able to figure out if he was trying to talk or sing.

Then he was on his knees fumbling around in the darkness, and I knew he must have lost his precious bottle.

I finally managed to get myself to a sitting position. My head was throbbing and spinning. I still couldn't pull myself to my feet. In fact, I wasn't too sure where my feet were.

Old Sam, still searching for his beloved bottle, muttered something about a "dumb book," and something clicked in my mind.

"That's my book," I said quickly, afraid Old Sam would throw it away.

He shoved my book toward me and went on feeling around on his hands and knees. He must have found what he was looking for, for he sighed and mumbled in his funny sing-songy voice, and then I heard him swigging from his bottle again.

He probably emptied it because he turned his attention back to me.

"Ya hurt, Joshsh?"

I thought that was quite apparent, but for someone like Sam who spent a good deal of his time on the ground, perhaps it was a reasonable question.

"Yeah," I said, trying to keep the moan from my voice. "Yeah, I'm hurt."

"What'sh happened?"

"Guess—guess I hit my head."

I hoped Sam would ask no more questions.

"I'll help ya home."

It made me want to laugh. In his present state, Sam probably didn't even know which direction my home was.

"Just help me up," I told him. "I'll make it home."

That statement was a bit presumptuous. Even with Old Sam's help I had a hard time getting to my feet, much less putting one foot in front of the other. Of course his wasn't the steadiest help ever offered. Our first try landed us both back on the ground. But you had to give Old Sam credit for persistence. He kept right on tugging and pulling until somehow we were both on our feet again. I wasn't sure who was holding up who.

I found my book and tucked it under my coat and we started off, our arms around one another in some strange way. Shuffling our feet along, we felt our way down the street. The only light to guide us was the anemic splashes from small windows in the town dwellings.

My body was shaking with cold and shock. Sam did not seem to notice the cold, though the coat Uncle Nat had provided for him was not much warmer than my own.

We stumbled along together, me confused and aching, and Sam likely wondering where he could find another bottle.

Then I realized it was snowing. Large, flowery flakes drifted down to cover our head and shoulders. Even in my present state I enjoyed the snow.

"Almost home," Old Sam was muttering—and, squinting through the flurries, I could see that we were. Somehow, even in his drunken condition, he had found the way.

I still remember the flood of yellow lamplight and the rush of warm air when Old Sam pounded on the door with one foot and it opened to us. I remember hearing Aunt Lou's little cry of "Josh!" But that is all I can recall.

The next thing I knew Doc was bending over me and I was safely tucked in my own bed, with Aunt Lou and Uncle Nat hovering nearby.

From the parlor came the snoring sounds I had heard many times before, and I knew Old Sam had been "souped" and "bedded" and would be spending at least this night sheltered from the winter's cold.

CHAPTER 15

Questions and Answers

I awoke the next morning with a bad headache. My mouth felt dry and sore and one eye was swollen shut.

Aunt Lou was stirring about my room and the lamp was still lit on the bedside table. At the time, I couldn't even think properly to wonder if she had been there all night.

She moved close to my bed and bent over me. From the next room came the familiar sounds of snoring and someone else, likely Uncle Nat, tending the fire.

"How're you feeling?" Aunt Lou asked softly as though the sound of her voice might make me suffer even more.

I tried to shake my head because I didn't feel like I would be able to talk, but it hurt too much to move.

"Can I get you anything?" asked Aunt Lou, and I somehow got the message to her that I would like a drink.

"Just a sip," she told me. "Doc says you have a concussion and shouldn't put much in your stomach in case it won't stay down."

I sipped. The water had barely touched my parched lips when Aunt Lou withdrew the cup. I wanted to protest but the right sounds didn't come.

"Doc said that you'll be just fine in a day or two," Aunt Lou was assuring me.

I tried to nod in agreement, but stopped myself.

"Nat rode out to the farm last night to let them know," Aunt Lou told me. "They wanted to come right in, but Nat convinced them that Doc was taking good care of you and that it would be fine for them to wait until this morning."

"What day is it?" I managed to ask through swollen lips.

"Don't you remember? This is Friday."

Friday. Then I should be in school. In the afternoon Grandpa would be coming for me. I wasn't sure if I would be quite ready to go.

"Nat will stop by the school and tell your teacher that you won't be in class today," Aunt Lou was continuing. "We hope that by Monday you'll be just fine again."

Did she mean I would not be going to the farm? That I would spend the entire weekend confined to my bed?

"What happened?" I mumbled.

"We were hoping you'd be able to tell us that," said Aunt Lou. "Don't you remember anything about it?"

I tried to shake the fog from my brain.

Nothing was clear and I didn't want to try to think. My head hurt me enough with just the effort of laying it on my pillow.

"Doc left you another pill," Aunt Lou said. "Let me help you," and she placed the pill between my swollen lips and lifted my head slightly so I could swallow it with a sip of water.

I slept again then. When I awoke my head ached a little less. Gramps was sitting in my room holding a book on his lap and looking out the window at the snow gently sifting down.

I stirred so I could see the snow better and with the movement came sharp pain. I groaned and Gramps was immediately beside my bed.

"You okay, Joshua?" he asked me, his eyes filled with concern.

I gave my head a moment to settle down again.

"Yeah," I mumbled. I tried to lick my lips but that stung even more.

"Have a sip of water," Gramps offered and he held the cup to my mouth just a second longer than Aunt Lou had.

From the kitchen I could hear the sound of quiet voices, and I knew the rest of the family were gathered waiting for me to return to wakefulness.

"You've been sleeping for some time, Joshua," Gramps was saying. "Are you feeling any better?"

I wasn't sure. My head still hurt pretty bad but it was tolerable if I held it still.

"It's almost time for another tablet," Gramps went on.

"It's snowin'," I murmured. "How much?"

Gramps smiled. I think that simple question was a great relief to him.

"We've had about three inches already, Joshua, and it looks like we're going to get lots more."

"Good," I said. "We can have Christmas."

The earlier snow was already rutted, splashed with the dirty stains of shuffling feet and wagon wheels. I had never felt that such snow was fit for Christmas, even though I realized a messy ground would not keep Christmas from coming. But for me a "real" Christmas, Christmas the way it should be, meant white freshness covering our world.

I guess Gramps understood, for he grinned widely.

"We sure can, Joshua," he said. "We sure can."

My door opened a crack and Grandpa peeked around it. He probably had done the same thing many times over the last hour. At Gramps' nod the door opened farther and Grandpa came in.

He stood looking down at me for a long time, his throat working and his gray mustache twitching slightly. His eyes were shiny with wetness.

"How are you, Boy?" he finally asked.

"Okay," I managed as he reached out a calloused hand and laid it gently on my forehead.

There was a flash of movement through the door and Pixie bounded up on my bed.

"Forgot to shut that door," Grandpa muttered in apology, moving to lift Pixie down from my bed.

"She's okay," I quickly informed him and reached out a hand to fluff the silky fur on her head. Even that movement hurt and I scrunched my eyes tightly against the pain.

Pixie was in a frenzy of excitement as she licked at my fingers, my hand, and even my battered face.

Aunt Lou was there then. "How did that dog—?" she started to ask, but Grandpa broke in to explain.

"Forgot to close the door, and she dashed in and was on the bed quick as a wink."

I figured keeping Pixie out of my room must have been quite a chore.

"How are you, Josh?" Uncle Nat was asking.

"Okay," I said again, trying to calm Pixie down by gently stroking her so they wouldn't take her away.

"Good," said Uncle Nat. "You had us worried some. You've near slept the day away."

"You should have another pill now, Joshua," said Aunt Lou and lifted my head so I could swallow the tablet and the drink of water.

Uncle Charlie poked his head in the door. His eyes held his questions but he did not voice them. "Don't tire 'im," was all he said.

They left me then to rest and went back to the kitchen table. I could tell where they were and what they all were doing simply from the sounds in the house.

I lay quietly and let my hand rest on Pixie's head. She slept beside me, occasionally lifting her head and licking my fingers with her warm little tongue.

Soon the medicine began to take effect, but instead of sleeping deeply as I had done before, I began to do some thinking, now that the pain was dulled.

What happened anyway? Why am I here in bed? I mulled over in my mind.

Jack Berry—Jack Berry kept flashing through my thoughts but I had no idea why. What did my being in bed have to do with Jack Berry? I couldn't work my way through the fog to come up with the answer.

I lifted a hand to my face and felt the bandage on the cut over my eye. I felt my swollen nose and touched my bruised lips with my tongue.

Jack Berry, Jack Berry pounded through my brain.

Jack had been pretty nasty lately. Mad because Camellia had invited me instead of him to her house. But no girl in her right mind would invite Jack Berry to tutor her in geometry—or anything else for that matter. Jack was barely making it through his studies himself.

I tried to settle myself and piece together the events of yesterday.

I had gone to school—been teased as usual because the fellas all knew that it was the day I would again go to Camellia's house. Had I gone? I couldn't remember.

Slowly, oh, so slowly, I began to relive the day. Class by class I went over each part of it. I remembered reading—we were working on Dickens' *Christmas Carol*, it being near Christmas and all. I remembered spelling, and nearly missing the silent "e" in "maneuver." I remembered the recess break. We had wanted to play Fox and Goose but there was no clean snow to make a ring. Our whole schoolyard was a mess of trampled snow—we needed a fresh fall to make trails for the game.

I could remember the rest of my classes, right up to dismissal. I even recalled the chat with Mr. Foggelson. He said I could read the books in his library.

Did I go to Camellia's? Yes—it was beginning to take shape for me. We had tea again, as well as funny little pastries with a filling in the middle. I had nearly dropped mine in my lap. Then we studied—but mostly talked. And then I left for home—in a hurry because I was late.

Was it snowing when I left Camellia's? I couldn't remember. I left alone—to run on home—and here I was in bed with the worst headache of my life and a cut, battered face to go with it.

Jack Berry. Jack Berry.

I pushed it away. Sure, I was upset with the guy. He had been acting like a jerk lately. But it sure wasn't worth troubling myself over. I turned my eyes back to the snow and watched it fall like feathery petals. *This is great to have the freshness and cleanness for Christmas*, I thought sleepily.

"Are you feeling any better?" came a soft voice and Aunt Lou was back in my room.

I even turned my head slightly on my pillow and the pain did not sweep through me with the same intensity.

"Yeah," I answered. "Lot's better."

"Good! Are you up to visitors?"

"Sure."

Mr. Foggelson and Camellia entered my room. She looked at me and her face went white, but she came right over to my bed.

"What happened, Joshua?" she asked me, her eyes wide with the terror of it.

"I don't remember," I said honestly.

"Nothing?" asked Mr. Foggelson, as though he found that hard to believe.

"Doc said he hit his head on a rock when he fell," said Aunt Lou. "Sam took Doc back to the spot where he found Josh. The snow had covered the ground so Doc couldn't learn much, but he said there was a large rock on the ground beneath the maple tree."

Sam? Old Sam? It must be. Vaguely I remembered Sam helping me home, but nothing further would come clear to me.

"But your face—?" quizzed Mr. Foggelson. "Surely your face wasn't hurt like this in the fall."

"I don't remember," I said again, a bit stubbornly.

Camellia reached out a soft hand and gently touched the bandage over my eye.

"Does it hurt terribly, Joshua?" she asked me, wincing with the words.

"Naw," I said bravely. "I hardly feel it."

And it was true. My head had been hurting so fiercely that I hadn't really felt the cut above my eye.

"Good," she said and smiled. For a moment I didn't feel any pain at all.

"Oh!" Camellia squealed, reaching over me to gently stroke Pixie. "Your little dog. She's a darling."

Pixie responded by sending out greetings with her little pink tongue.

Camellia squealed again.

"May I hold her?" she pleaded. No wonder she got whatever she wanted from her pa.

"Sure," I said. I watched proudly as she scooped up my little dog and held her close against her cheek for a moment. Then she sat on a nearby chair with Pixie on her lap, patting the soft head and stroking the silky fur.

It was quite a sight the two of them made there together.

Mr. Foggelson broke the spell.

"We mustn't tire Joshua, Camellia."

I noticed again the way he pronounced each syllable, and the teasing of the fellas came back to my mind. With it came the haunting rhythm of *Jack Berry, Jack Berry.* I pushed it away again and tried to thank my visitors for coming.

"Can I come again tomorrow?" Camellia begged.

"Now, Camellia," her pa objected. "You know the doctor has said that Joshua must have his rest. We do want him back in school soon."

"But, Papa—" she cajoled him, "I won't stay long. Promise."

"I'm fine," I joined in. "Likely be out of this bed by tomorrow."

"Oh, no you won't." Aunt Lou's voice came from the door. "Doc says we are to keep you here at least until Sunday afternoon."

Then she turned to Camellia and gave her a bright smile. "But I'm sure Josh would be glad for your company for twenty minutes or so—if it's okay with your folks."

Camellia rewarded her with a dazzling smile. She didn't even turn to her pa, assuming that the issue was settled.

"I'll bring a book and read to you," she promised as she put Pixie gently back on the bed beside me and the Foggelsons left my room.

One by one the family members came to see me. I guess they felt that all of them at one time would be too much for my poor head. They visited for a few minutes each, always the same questions in their eyes if not voiced. What had happened? How had I been hurt on my way home from Camellia's house? Why had Old Sam found me lying on the ground?

I still had no clear picture of the evening, only bits and pieces that made no sense. I knew that I felt anger flood through me when I thought of the night before. But I had no idea why. *Jack Berry, Jack Berry* played over and over in my head, and I couldn't imagine why that should be.

Eventually Grandpa, Uncle Charlie and Gramps went on home. I envied them their trip through the new snow, but I knew better than to coax to go with them.

Doc stopped in again before nightfall. He seemed pleased with my progress and told Aunt Lou that I could have a few more of the pills if the pain was too bad.

Uncle Nat came to chat after he had done up my evening chores. I told him I was sorry about his needing to take over for me, but he brushed it all aside, saying that the exercise was good for him.

That night we had our devotional time in my bedroom so I could share in it. In Uncle Nat's prayer he gave special thanks to God that I had been found and helped home the night before. When Aunt Lou prayed, thanking the Lord I was safe and home, I realized how worried she had been. Uncle Nat had been away at the Browns'. One of their daughters was planning a New Year's wedding, and he was counseling her and her beau. So Aunt Lou had been alone with her concern. I could imagine her going often to the front room to check the street for my return. Pixie would have been whimpering about her ankles.

I smiled as cheerfully as I could at her when she gave me a pill, tucked the blankets around me and kissed me good night. The pain in my head was much subdued. I slept.

CHAPTER 16

Christmas

Christmas was one of my favorite times of the year. We always went out to the farm. I don't know what part of it I liked best. I loved the smell of the spices while Aunt Lou baked savory cookies and pies. I loved the tangy odor of pine as the tree from our pasture woods was set up in a corner of the big farm kitchen, decorated with paper chains and popcorn strings. I loved the mystery of hidden gifts that a person could accidentally stumble across if he happened to be looking for something in out-of-the-way places.

I even loved the Christmas program at the church, though it took a lot of time and patience from those like Aunt Lou who worked to get it to finally come together for the night of presentation. It took a lot of hounding by the mothers—in my case, my aunt Lou—to get us to memorize the parts.

But in the end, it always came off quite well and folks enjoyed it and praised our efforts until our heads puffed up with thinking about how good we were. When it was all successfully behind us, Aunt Lou heaved a sigh of relief and put her program ideas away for another year. But she still had her books out for this year 'cause the program was yet to come.

Like I've explained, I loved the snow of Christmas. It made the world look fit to welcome the King of Kings—even if He did come as a tiny baby and likely didn't even notice if there was snow or not. But I couldn't imagine Christmas without snow. Once when a visiting speaker at our church said that there most likely was no snow in Bethlehem on the night Jesus was born, I wanted to argue back that the fellow must be wrong. To think of Christmas with no snow—a dirty, bare, sordid world to welcome the Christ-Child—just didn't seem right.

Yes, I waited every year for a Christmas snowfall. It was like a hallowed sacrament to me—the covering of the drab, ugly world with clean freshness right from the hand of God himself. The unclothed trees, the dirty rutted yard, the bare, empty fields—all were suddenly transformed into silvery, soft images, always making me think that something truly miraculous was happening before my very eyes.

I had been allowed to return to school the Tuesday after my accident—or whatever it was. My face was still a bit swollen and my eye discolored, but other than that, I felt quite good. The doc insisted that I not be active in any of the boys' games, so I stayed in at recess time. I felt like a jerk—like some kind of sissy. But it did prove to be an opportunity to spend some time with one of Mr. Foggelson's books. He brought it for me and kept it locked in a corner cupboard. He brought it out only after the rest of the students had left the room, and returned it to the cupboard again before he rang the bell.

My head gradually stopped aching and I seemed to be back to normal. I felt awful about Uncle Nat doing my chores, but the doc insisted that for at least two weeks I was to do nothing strenuous. Two weeks would take us past Christmas.

I still had this troubled feeling about Jack Berry. He wasn't at school either, and word had it that he was down sick with the flu. That would keep him out of my hair for a while. By the time he was back, my eye and bruised nose and lips would be back to normal again and he would not have further occasion to goad me.

Camellia kept fussing over me. She said she felt to blame, seeing that I was on my way home from her house—but that was ridiculous. The attention was embarrassing, but sort of special, too.

As I watched this Christmas quickly approaching, I was filled with all kinds of mixed emotions.

I had been storing away every nickel and dime I could get my hands on for shopping for my Christmas gifts. It would have worked out just fine, too, if Camellia hadn't entered my life when she did.

Most every day I went back to my dresser drawer and counted those coins. They sure didn't multiply any. I still had the same four dollars and fifteen cents.

I'd figured on paper just what I would get for each family member and had it all worked out just fine until I decided that the only right thing to do was to get Camellia a gift as well. I mean, she had been so nice to me and all.

I reworked my list a dozen times but I couldn't get it to work out.

If I'd been healthy, I mean, if Doc hadn't made his silly pronouncement that I wasn't to "exert" myself, I could've been hustling around town looking for odd jobs. But with things as they were, there wasn't a hope in the world that I could get ahold of any more money before Christmas. So I wanted Christmas to come, but I didn't know what to do about gifts.

I window-shopped one more time and came up with decisions about family gifts that would leave me with fifty-five cents! With excitement coursing through my veins and joy in my heart, I went looking for a gift for Camellia.

The joy didn't last long. There was nothing that would do for a girl like Camellia that could be purchased for a mere fifty-five cents. Nothing.

I went home with a heavy heart, my feet dragging across the snow-covered ground.

Pixie met me at the door. I pulled her into my arms and held her close while she licked my face. *Pixie!* I could give my dog to Camellia! There was likely nothing on earth I could give her that she would like more. I remembered the time when she had come to read to me when I was in bed. She had loved my little dog and never tired of holding her or of watching her playful antics or her puppy tricks.

But how can I give Pixie away? I moaned. Never was a fella so torn. I loved Pixie more than I had ever loved anything—except for family, that is. As a matter of fact, it was awfully easy to think of Pixie as family. I held her so close just thinking about it that she started to whine.

But Camellia? She was pretty special too, and if you really cared about someone, weren't you supposed to put that person's wants and needs before your own?

I was still battling it through in my mind, this way and that, when it dawned on me that Camellia said she couldn't have a dog because of her ma's allergies. I hugged Pixie even tighter and breathed a prayer of thanks.

Boy, was I glad for that allergy. I sure wouldn't have been able to decide that tough one on my own.

Without even knowing, Uncle Nat solved my problem about a gift—though he did sort of leave it until the last minute.

I knew he had been secretly working on a cedar chest for Aunt Lou for her Christmas present. He kept it hidden at the farm, and he slipped out and spent time on it for an hour or so when he'd finished his pastoral visits and duties.

The first weekend I was allowed to go home to the farm—the only weekend before the Christmas break—Uncle Nat came out on Saturday morning, determined to get the chest finished.

It was a beautiful piece of work. Uncle Nat didn't have many fancy tools, but he had a lot of love for Aunt Lou. He did want the chest to be just right, so he toiled over it, careful to make every board fit perfectly.

It smelled good, too. I loved the smell of the cedar.

I guess I said some nice things about the chest and about the smell of the wood, for Uncle Nat, without even looking up from his work, said, "There's a bit of lumber left over, Josh, some board scraps and things. You're welcome to them if you'd like them for anything."

"Thanks," I said without too much enthusiasm, "but I wouldn't know what to do with 'em."

"You could always make a little jewelry box or a treasure box."

I was about to ask him who that would be for, knowing that Aunt Lou already had a jewelry box, when I thought of Camellia.

"Could you help me?" I asked instead, unable to hide the eagerness in my voice.

"I guess I could—I don't think it'd take too much time."

I couldn't believe my good luck. I went right to work on it. With Uncle Nat's guidance in measuring and sawing, and help from Uncle Charlie in the sanding and Gramps in the varnishing, I got the small box finished in time for Christmas. It looked just fine. I could hardly wait for Camellia to see it.

That Sunday, December twenty-second, we had our Christmas program in the evening. I had hoped Camellia would attend. I mean, she knew I had an important part in it and had been studying on it for weeks. But she wasn't there.

I tried to put her from my mind and think about other things—like how my lines went—but I have to admit that I was deeply disappointed.

The program went all right. I can't say it was perfect. But it was close enough for folks to overlook the little things and compliment us all on our efforts after it was over.

Aunt Lou went home tired that evening and placed her hat on the hall closet shelf.

"I'm glad that's over," she said with a sigh as she always did, and Uncle Nat gave her an impromptu hug.

"You did a great job," he assured her.

The next morning Aunt Lou was back in true form again, scurrying around doing the work of three people. Christmas was just two days off.

The next morning I took my four dollars and fifteen cents and went to the store to purchase the family presents I had planned to buy in the first place since I didn't need the fifty-five cents for Camellia. Then borrowing some bits of paper from Aunt Lou, I got them all wrapped up.

I had to ask help from Aunt Lou in wrapping Camellia's present. I wanted Camellia's gift to look especially nice.

I took the gift over to Camellia's house when I knew she would be off to Miss Thompson's house for her weekly piano lesson. I gave the package to Mrs. Foggelson and asked her to place it under their tree on Christmas Eve, and she promised to do that for me.

I felt real good about it all. When I got back home I gave Pixie a big hug, feeling that I hadn't compromised a bit.

On the twenty-fourth we were up early and packed into the cutter with boxes and bags stacked in all around us. We were off to the farm for our annual Christmas festivities. I had never called them "festivities" before, but that was what Camellia's ma called them.

"Where will you celebrate your Christmas 'festivities'?" she had asked me.

At first I didn't know what she meant.

"Don't you celebrate Christmas?" she asked, looking puzzled.

"Oh, sure," I said, the light beginning to dawn. "We always go to the farm and have it all together."

"The farm?"

"My grandpa's. Him and Uncle Charlie and Gramps live there. Uncle Nat and Aunt Lou and me—and I—go on out there and join 'em."

"That's nice," she said, "—a real old-fashioned Christmas."

"Yeah," I answered, "yeah, a real old-fashioned Christmas."

So now we were on our way to our "festivities" and I was all excited inside, just like I was every year.

It was a good Christmas, too. We had the best-tasting turkey I can ever remember, and I got the nicest presents, too. There was a new store-bought sweater from Grandpa, a real fishing rod from Gramps, a shirt from Uncle Nat and Aunt Lou that she had made, and a brand-new five-blade knife from Uncle Charlie. There was even a surprise gift. A large, colorfully illustrated book from Camellia titled *How the World Began* was full of the strangest pictures and diagrams. I could hardly wait to read it and find out what it was all about.

I wondered what she had thought of the "treasure box" from me. I sure hoped she liked it.

After the paper had been pulled from all of the presents and each one had told the others how much we liked their gifts, Uncle Nat went out and brought in the chest for Aunt Lou. It was about all that one man could carry, and when she heard the thumping behind her and wheeled to see what was going on, her breath caught in a little gasp and tears filled her eyes.

She nearly bowled Uncle Nat over when she threw herself into his arms and wept against his shoulder. I kept checking her face to be sure, but the tears were for joy, not sadness. I had never seen a woman quite so "joyous" before.

"It's lovely! It's perfect!" she kept saying over and over, and Uncle Nat just held her close and patted her shoulder.

Then Aunt Lou turned to all of us. The tears were still sliding down her cheeks, but she had the brightest smile that I have ever seen her wear.

"I already have plans for its use," she said, "and I can hardly wait to fill it. The chest is going to be for our baby's things."

A real commotion took place then. Everyone seemed to be hugging everyone else, and more than just Aunt Lou were shedding tears. I couldn't make much sense out of any of it until I heard Grandpa asking, "When? When?"

"In July," said Aunt Lou. "Oh, Pa, I'm so happy I could just burst!"

I understood it then. My aunt Lou was having a baby! I was getting a new cousin. Imagine that! Me, a cousin! I'd be able to help take care of it and everything.

With a whoop I was across the room and hugging Aunt Lou as tightly as I dared. I wasn't sure, but I thought there might be some tears on my cheeks, too.

Back to School

I was anxious to get back to school again after our Christmas break, and not just to find out what Camellia had thought of my Christmas gift. I also wanted to tell the fellas about the nice gifts I had gotten and how much stuffed turkey and apple pie I had eaten and all. It was the same every year.

I guess they were just as eager to share their Christmas news—they were all there waiting at the corner of the schoolyard when I arrived.

We all talked at once and no one really listened much, but I did get the feeling that they all were pretty happy with the Christmas they had just shared with their family.

Willie had some other news too. Jack Berry had dropped out of school. It shouldn't have surprised us any, and I guess that it didn't much. I mean, Jack Berry had never been fond of school. It was his pa's idea that he keep on going. Well, with him missing so many days before Christmas with the flu and all, I guess Jack decided he didn't want to work so hard to catch up to the class, so he finally talked his pa into letting him quit.

I wouldn't have said so to the fellas, but I wasn't going to do much crying over Jack being gone. He had been acting so nasty of late that I figured school, at least for me, would be a better place without him. No, I wasn't prepared to be missing Jack Berry much at all. I was content to let the matter drop.

I felt pretty good about life when Camellia told me she really liked my Christmas gift. She said she was going to keep her hankies in it and, not wanting to argue none with her, I didn't tell her I thought hankies to be rather strange "treasures." They sure weren't treasures in my book.

I knew Aunt Lou wouldn't be too happy with me spreading the news of the coming baby among all of my school chums yet, so I held my tongue; but it was awfully hard to keep the excitement to myself. We had never welcomed a little one into our family since I had arrived, and of course I didn't remember anything about what happened at my own coming.

There were some days when Aunt Lou didn't feel too well. I could tell it by looking at her, but she never made any mention of the fact. I guess Uncle Nat and I were both watching for signs. I tried to keep the woodbox a little fuller and made sure there was plenty of water on hand from our yard pump. Uncle Nat was watching for ways he could ease her load as well, but she usually laughed at our anxieties and assured us that she was just fine. She did look a little tired at times, though, and I knew she skipped breakfast some mornings.

Still, things seemed to settle down and the household pretty much ran as it had before, except for the underlying current of anticipation that we all felt.

I started "tutoring" Camellia again. We spent most of the time poring over her pa's books, discussing interesting things that we found.

I had read the book that Camellia gave me for Christmas. It was rather a strange one. Parts of it I couldn't make much sense of. I mean, it said, bold as brass, that man sort of oozed into being, coming up out of the muck and mire and then went from a primitive stage to a more progressive stage of development. As I say, it puzzled me at first because I knew how man really had come into being, and I scratched my head a bit until I realized that the book must be some new sort of book of fancy. Then I settled back and tried to let the imaginings of this writer interest me.

It was quite a tale. All about how this new man creature "evolved" until finally he discovered how to walk up on his two hind feet and use his forefeet to grip things. He did this so much that finally his forefeet turned into fingers for gripping, and then he learned new skills and lost his shaggy fur so he had to make clothes to protect himself and build homes to live in and plant crops for food that he learned to store and preserve.

Even though the whole book was a fairy tale sort of thing, I couldn't make out the reasoning behind it. What I mean is, each stage that this man "advanced" seemed to bring him a lot more troubles and complications instead of simplifying things for him. So why did the teller-of-the-tale bother with the advancing?

It must have been that some folks thought it made interesting "supposing," but I preferred fanciful stories to make a bit of sense. Anyway, I guessed that the Foggelsons liked this kind of fairy tale and wanted me to become acquainted with it, too. I certainly didn't plan to tell Camellia what I thought of her book.

Then one day when we were reading some of Mr. Foggelson's other books, we came on the same kind of tale again.

"Here's another one," I mumbled more to myself than to Camellia.

"Another what?" she asked.

"Another fairy tale about man creepin' up outta particles of something or other and startin' to live on his own."

"Joshua," said Camellia, surprise in her voice, "that's not a fairy tale."

I just looked at her. I didn't know what to say.

"What do *you* call it?" I finally asked, thinking that Camellia must know a new word for a fanciful tale that I didn't know.

"Evolution," she answered, as though surprised I didn't know the word already.

"Evolution. Oh!"

I let the matter drop, but I repeated the word several times to myself so I wouldn't forget it. I intended to look it up when I got home so that next time I could impress the Foggelsons by naming the tale by its proper name.

Even before I sat down with my cookies and milk when I got home, I looked up the word. Old Webster was a good friend of mine, and I guess I depended on him to know the meaning of most every word there was. I found "evolution" and his meaning for it. Webster said a number of things about evolution that didn't seem to fit. He talked about development and growth, about movement of troops in marching or on the battlefield, and about arithmetic and algebra. None of those meanings made sense when I connected them with the Foggelson books. Then he said, "The gradual development or descent of forms of life from simple or low organized types consisting of a single cell."

I still couldn't understand it. I tossed the words around in my mind all the time that I was choring, but I never did get them sorted out.

After supper was over and we'd had our Bible reading together, I again pulled out Webster's dictionary. I read it over again, but I still couldn't get the meaning, so I let my eyes travel down the page a bit and checked some other words, hoping that that would help. "Evolutional" was pertaining to evolution. That sure didn't help me any, and then I read through the lengthy explanation of "evolutionist" until I came to the part that said, "The theory that man is a development from a lower order of creation; a teacher or advocate of Darwinism."

I read it again. Surely no one really believed that man "developed" that way. Why, that wasn't anywhere near what the Bible said. I may not have listened to preachers as much as I should have, but I had listened enough to know how man came into being, and how they had gotten to their sorry state of sinfulness, too.

Before closing Webster up again, I got a stub of a pencil and a piece of paper and wrote down the words from the printed page. I needed to do some thinking about this and talk to Mr. Foggelson and Camellia. Did the fact that they weren't churchgoers mean that they had never heard how things *really* happened? I couldn't believe that someone could have missed out so completely on the facts.

I wasn't sure whether I should make use of Uncle Nat's help on this or not, but I hated to bother him with my problem. I knew he had plenty of his own—and other peoples'.

Gramps and I had a chance for some checker games that weekend. The weather was stormy and cold, and it didn't make much sense to go out in it unless one had a good reason for going. So Uncle Charlie and Grandpa spent some time working on harness mending and drinking coffee, and Gramps and I read and played checkers.

Gramps beat me, which wasn't unusual. He had won three games before I pushed the board back a bit and stood to stretch.

"Mind not on the game, Joshua?" he quizzed me.

I grinned. "You 'most always beat me," I answered good-naturedly. "Can't always blame it on my mind bein' elsewhere."

"No not always—but this time I think we can."

I stopped my grinning. "Maybe so," I admitted, and sat back down again.

"Just thinkin' on some of my studies. Been reading some real interestin' books. Lots of new things to learn—new ideas. Some of them I understand, some I don't."

"Like?" said Gramps.

"Well, like—like—well, evolution."

I expected I would have to stop and explain the word to Gramps, and my hand started into my pocket to pull out the paper I had written Webster's words on, but Gramps surprised me.

"Hogwash!" he said with sort of a snort.

My eyes popped wide open.

"Pure hogwash," Gramps said again, and I knew he felt pretty sure of himself.

"What's it all about anyway?" I asked him.

Gramps didn't even hesitate.

"This man, Darwin, got these funny ideas of where man came from—where everything came from," he said. "He saw the similarity in the animals and birds and fish, and decided that they had a common source."

I nodded.

"Well, he was right," went on Gramps to my surprise; "they do have a common source. A common Creator. Only thing is Darwin got mixed up about the beginnings. He thought that because this 'common' bond, this thread, ran through all creatures, the one came from the other. He decided that he knew more about things than anyone else who ever lived and threw out what the Good Book said about God creating all things in the beginning. Got himself in a heap of trouble, because try as he did to make all the pieces fit, he never did get them untangled.

"But others jumped on that theory and they too kept trying to come up with 'proofs' for what they thought they found. They haven't let it die yet. Been lots of books written on it and some places now teach Darwin's theory as if it were fact. Don't let it throw you, Joshua. It still is theory. No facts have proved it yet—and they never will. What God has said still stands. Remember that. God was the only one around at the time, so I'm willing to take His word on just how it all happened."

I guess I took a deep breath. Gramps stopped his talking and his eyes pinned me down.

"That new teacher been trying to teach you evolution?"

"Not in school, no," I said quickly.

"Then where'd you get this stuff?"

"Camellia gave me a book for Christmas an'—" I hated to lay the blame on Camellia.

Gramps just nodded.

"Her pa is letting me read his library books. I found the same thing in them, and Camellia says that—"

"Don't you believe it," Gramps cut in. "Not one word of it."

I nodded and swallowed hard. It was a relief to me to have some solid ground under my feet again.

With my beliefs about creation and the Creator securely intact again, I felt an obligation to pass on my knowledge to Camellia.

The next Thursday when we settled ourselves to study after having our tea and those messy little pastries, I brought up the subject.

"You know those books," I began, trying to choose my words carefully, "well, they are a bit mixed up on things."

"What books?" she asked me.

I didn't want to come across as a know-it-all, but I did feel that Camellia should know the truth.

"The ones on evolution," I said hesitantly.

"Mixed up? How?" she asked.

"That's not the way things really happened," I stated firmly. "The Bible has it all in here," and I pulled my Bible out from under my sweater and proceeded to open it to Genesis, chapter one.

"Oh, Josh," Camellia said, playfully pushing at my hand that held the Book. "Don't tease."

I blinked.

Camellia was entertaining herself in silvery gales of laughter.

"I'm not teasin'," I finally said, my voice low and serious.

Camellia's laughter died then and she looked at me, her face wearing a look of total disbelief.

"You're not?"

"No, I'm not. See? It's all right here. Nothing evolved. God created everything."

"You don't really believe that?"

"I do—I most certainly do. And you would, too, if you'd just read what it says. See—"

"But it doesn't make sense. I mean—"

"*Evolution* doesn't make sense," I countered rather hotly. "Why would things 'evolve' when their present state was not nearly as demanding? Why—"

"Oh, Joshua—think! Don't just fall dumbly for those old superstitions that have been passed down from generation to generation. We are enlightened now! No one who is a scholar believes that Bible gibberish."

I looked at her in silence, my thumb still held in the page I had wanted to show her.

"You know what it says?" I finally asked.

"Of course I know what it says. Papa taught me all about the false statements that are in there so I might know how to refute them."

"You don't believe the Bible?" I asked in amazement. I could not understand how anyone could possibly know what was written in its pages and still not believe what it said.

Camellia stood up and came slowly to me. She was no longer smiling, but she had a soft, pleading look about her now, like a woman placating a spoiled or sensitive child.

"Look, Joshua," she said, "we understand that this is hard for you, being raised in the church and—and—well, we are willing to take it slowly—to help you to understand. That's why Papa has given you the use of his library. With scientific data at your disposal, you will discover the truth for yourself. You have a good mind, Joshua. Papa is most pleased with it. I am proud of you. You can be anything you want to be. There is no limit, Joshua."

"I'm gonna be a preacher," I said quietly.

"But *anybody* can be a preacher," Camellia moaned. "Can't you see?"

I shut my Bible with a slam I had never used on it before and immediately felt ashamed of myself. Unconsciously I reopened it and closed it tenderly.

"I'm afraid I don't see," I said to Camellia.

"Well, Papa said that you have potential. More potential than any student he has ever had. He will help you make something worthwhile of yourself if only—"

"An' you were helping him?" I asked coldly.

"Of course." The words were out before Camellia realized what she'd said. She caught herself and flushed. "Well, not the way you mean. I like you, Joshua, I do—"

"I think I'd better go," I said, feeling all mixed up inside. I couldn't understand all of this, but I didn't like it. Not one bit. I moved to the door, but

Camellia was there before me. She faced me, with cheeks flushed and her eyes sparking angrily. Even then I was aware of how pretty she was.

"Joshua," she said, "if you go like this—just up and walk out in a rage—can't you see what it will do to my father? Hasn't he suffered enough already? He lost his position in his last school—a good position—just because he tried to help some capable students understand science, true science. And now you are going to—to spurn his help and—"

I had stopped. I couldn't very well push her aside and force my way out of her home.

"Don't you see," she went on. "He just wants to help you."

"By takin' away the truth—and makin' me believe a lie?"

"I can't believe this, Joshua," she said hotly. "You have a good mind. How can you just accept everything that they tell you—without thinking it through or anything."

"But don't you see," I replied, "that is what you've done. I mean, just because you love your pa, you believe whatever he tells you without even having proof. The Bible has been proved over and over, and it never comes up short with pieces all missin' and—"

Camellia moved away from the door. Her eyes were dark with rage.

"If you go now," she said through tight lips, "don't ever come back."

I nodded my head, my throat workin' hard on a swallow. I wanted to invite her to church. I wanted to say that I'd pray that she might learn the truth. I wanted to say that I was sorry—for—for how everything had turned out, but I couldn't find my voice to say anything, so I just nodded and left.

That heavy lump in my chest stayed with me as I made my way home. My feet dragged, and the short distance had never seemed so long before.

Hard Days

The next morning, after a restless night, I wished with all of my heart that I could just stay in bed and not ever go to school again. I knew Aunt Lou would soon be in my room fussing over me if I was even late getting up, so I reluctantly crawled out and made my usual preparations. I sure didn't want Aunt Lou fretting about me for fear it might cause some kind of harm to the coming baby.

I dressed and washed at the kitchen basin and slicked down my hair good enough to do. We had our breakfast together, Uncle Nat telling Aunt Lou his plans for the day. I was glad I didn't need to enter the conversation much.

In no hurry at all to get to school, I sort of dawdled along until I heard the bell ring. I had never been late for school before and I found myself running now. I didn't want a "tardy" mark on my report card.

Most of the kids had already hung up their coats and shoved and pushed their way into the classroom by the time I arrived, puffing from my run. I hurriedly threw my jacket at my hanger and, fortunately, it stuck. I picked up my books and my lunch bucket and hurried to my place. I almost ran smack into Camellia in the hall. I guess we both got red. Me, from embarrassment. From the way she sniffed and flung back her long, silken hair, I guessed her redness was from anger.

I stumbled my way to my desk and got out my Dickens like I was supposed to do.

There were no flashing smiles across the room, no waiting at the door just to walk out into the schoolyard with me. I tried not to even look her way, and I suppose she tried not to look mine.

Mr. Foggelson did not call on me to recite or give an answer all day long. In fact, I might as well not have been there for all I was noticed.

The fellas must have realized something was up. At recess time their teasing took a new tack. "What happened, Josh—drop all her books in the snow?" and so on. I tried to ignore them, but it was pretty hard to hide the fact that things were different now.

When school was over for the day, I breathed a sigh of relief, ready to hurriedly slip from the school building and run for home. But Mr. Foggelson's voice stopped me. He hadn't used the raised eyebrow trick, and I had been sure I was going to be able to slip off without a confrontation. Now his soft-spoken call of my name stopped me mid-stride.

I turned slowly, half hoping I was only hearing things. I wasn't. There stood my teacher beside my desk, the chalk brush in his hand and his eyes on me.

I retraced my steps slowly.

"You—you wished to see me, sir?" I said after swallowing two or three times.

"Yes, Joshua." He pointed to my seat.

I sat down, somewhat glad that I didn't need to stand. On the other hand, I knew I wouldn't be able to bolt for the door from a sitting position, and I sure did wish I could bolt.

Mr. Foggelson laid aside the brush and pulled out a handkerchief to wipe his hands. The actions were slow and deliberate and I waited, wishing to get this over.

"Camellia tells me that you and she had an unfortunate little misunderstanding last evening," he said slowly. He waited for me to acknowledge his words and I finally found my voice.

"I don't think so, sir," I said respectfully.

His eyebrows shot up.

"You didn't have a misunderstanding?"

"No, sir. I think we understood one another very well."

He paused and stared at me. I tried not to let my eyes waver.

"You'll have to explain that, Joshua," he said then. "I don't believe I follow you."

"Well," I said, shuffling my feet under my desk and dropping my gaze, "Camellia believes that stuff about evolution, and I believe what the Bible says."

"Have you studied evolution, Joshua?" he asked me, knowing that I would have to say no.

"No, sir. Not really. But I've read enough—"

"Perhaps you are making your judgment too hastily," went on Mr. Foggelson reasonably. "Don't you feel that you should acquaint yourself with all of the facts before making your decision?"

I had dropped my gaze but I raised my eyes again so I could look squarely at him. I tried not to flinch.

"No, sir," I said, rather quietly.

"And why not?" he quizzed me. "Are you afraid of the truth?"

I answered that one quickly.

"No, sir."

"Then why did you refuse to look at what other learned scholars have arrived at after years and years of scientific study deductions?"

"Because—" I swallowed again, "because, sir, it disagrees with the Holy Scriptures."

"Have you ever considered that the 'Holy Scriptures,' as you call it, could be wrong? That it could be a mere invention of man to satisfy his superstitious need for a god to cling to?"

"No, sir."

"Then perhaps, Joshua, it would do you well to carefully consider the possibility. How do you know that your 'Bible' is as accurate as you have been made to believe? How do you know that it isn't a book of fairy tales? Do you have proof, beyond all doubt?"

I didn't answer. I just sat there and shuffled my feet and swallowed and awkwardly thumbed the pages of my geography book.

"I want you to think about it, Joshua. A good mind is not to be wasted. I would feel a failure if you, my best student, closed the covers of scientific books because you dared not challenge the teachings that you have had thrust upon you since babyhood. If the Bible is really true, then it should bear the scrutiny, right?"

That sounded reasonable. I nodded dumbly.

"Well, then," said Mr. Foggelson, giving me the token of a smile, "I am glad we have had this talk. My library is still at your disposal. I hope you will use it, and open your mind up to all truth."

He nodded and I understood that meant I was dismissed. I gathered up my books and stood to my feet.

"Good night, sir," I had the presence of mind to mumble and left the room, gathering momentum with each step.

A lot of troubled thoughts were tumbling around in my head, but of one thing I was sure. I would not be going back to the Foggelsons' to use the books in the library. There was too much in them that I wasn't ready for yet. Someday—maybe someday I would need to grapple with the theories they presented as fact, but not now. I wasn't ready to face them head-on, and I had the sense to know it.

And I wouldn't be going back to "tutor" Camellia either. The tutoring was just a ruse. I had liked her. Had enjoyed hearing her laugh, her chatter, had liked to watch her toss her mane of shiny hair, had found her exciting and interesting, but I wouldn't be going back. She left me with such confusing thoughts when she challenged my belief in the Bible, my desire to be a minister. No, I would not spend time with Camellia again.

And the tea and pastries I could sure do without. Aunt Lou's milk and cookies were far more filling.

No! I was most definite in my decision. I would not be going back to the Foggelson house.

CHAPTER 19

Spring

I was glad to put the difficult months of January and February behind me. By March I was feeling more comfortable at school. Mr. Foggelson had obviously given up on me, for he never asked me to come over to the house or stay and chat after class. I felt sorry about it in a way, but I was relieved, too.

He hadn't given up on some of his theories though, about "religion" being an escape for shallow minds or evolution being the "true" science. Often he inserted sarcastic little comments into his class lectures. At first I could often feel Camellia's eyes on me at such times, but then she too seemed to put me out of her mind entirely.

Word began to circulate through town that Jack Berry was doing a lot of visiting at Camellia's house. I don't know why that bothered me, but the haunting old chant of *Jack Berry, Jack Berry* was hammering away in my brain again. I tried hard to shove it aside but it kept hanging in there. I didn't understand it. Why was it haunting me again?

By the time March arrived, things had pretty well returned to normal—that is for Willie, Avery and me. We tried a bit of kite flying on the windy days—and there were lots of them. Not all of the snow had left us yet, but that didn't slow us down none. We were used to trying to fly kites with snow still on the ground. Truth was, I guess we just couldn't wait for real spring to come.

It was obvious now to the entire congregation that Aunt Lou was expecting her first baby. When news started to circulate about the coming big event, young women exclaimed with red-flushed cheeks, girls tittered and got all excited and matronly ladies had lots and lots of advice to give to the mother-to-be. Aunt Lou took it all good-naturedly. I think she loved the attention. I do know for sure she was plumb excited about that baby. Already she was busy filling the cedar chest with all sorts of special little tiny garments. Made me think about my ma—had it been that way with her when she knew I was on the way?

All the menfolk at the farm were talking about that baby, too. Grandpa was busy fashioning a wooden cradle, and every weekend when I went home, he would show me how far along he was on his project. He worked on it in the near-empty parlor, and it was coming along very nicely, too.

Uncle Charlie had a project of his own. He was making a woven hamper for Aunt Lou to keep all of the baby's soiled laundry until washday. He couldn't do too much with wood, he said, but that laundry hamper sure did look nice.

Even Gramps was busy. His project I found the most interesting of all. He was piecing together a quilt just big enough for the baby's bed.

"If your great-grandmother were here, she would insist on a homemade quilt for that little bed," Gramps told me. "She could do the most beautiful stitching, your great-grandmother. Well, I can't do it as fine as she could have done, but that baby is going to have a quilt anyway," and he went to town and purchased materials and started to work on that quilt. I guess he must have watched Great-grandmother do the job many times, for he seemed to know just how to get on with it.

I wanted to do something for the new baby, too, but I didn't know just what it would be. I couldn't work with tools much, and I didn't have any idea how to weave. I wasn't about to have the fellas find out I was sewing— I'd had my fill of teasing for the year—so quilting was out of the question. I finally decided to see what I could find for odd jobs so I might earn myself a bit of money to buy something for the baby.

There really wasn't that much opportunity for paying work in our small town, but I did hang around the stores all I could and let it be known that I was willing to run errands or do some sweeping up or whatever else came about.

It was while I was sweeping the sidewalk in front of the downtown hotel one sunny spring day in mid-April that Mrs. Foggelson came along. She smiled nicely at me and I doffed my cap like I had been taught and smiled back at her. After all, she had been awfully kind to me.

"Good afternoon, Joshua," she said, and then remarked about what a fine day we were having.

I agreed and moved aside so she could pass more easily. It was then that I noticed that her arms were full of packages. I was finished with my sweeping and had a few extra minutes before choring and I knew what Aunt Lou would wish me to do.

"I just need to give Mr. Powell back his broom," I said to Mrs. Foggelson, "an' I'll be glad to help you home with your packages."

"How thoughtful of you, Joshua," she said, giving me another smile.

I ran to report to Mr. Powell and was soon back out on the sidewalk again. I eased some of the packages from Mrs. Foggelson's arms and we started out together.

"I've missed you, Joshua," she said to me.

I didn't know quite how to respond so I said nothing, just sort of pretended I didn't hear her. We walked along in silence for some minutes, talking only now and then about the sunshine, the spots of new green grass and Mrs. Jones's daffodils that were nodding golden heads in the slight breeze.

We were almost home when Mrs. Foggelson spoke again.

"I know that it must have been very difficult for you, Joshua. I'm sorry about it."

I was about to assure Mrs. Foggelson that I did not blame her in any way for what had happened, but she went on in a quiet, sad voice, "When I married Mr. Foggelson I was a believer, too. I wasn't strong like you, Joshua. I didn't stand up to him. His arguments sounded so logical, so profound. How could I, a mere girl turning woman, with no education higher than the eighth grade, possibly know more than this man who had trained in one of the country's best colleges? I gave in and I shouldn't have. I lost far more than I realized at the time."

I just sort of stumbled to a stop and looked in the sad face of this distressed woman. I had no words of comfort or of counsel.

"But it's not too late," I finally stammered.

"Oh, it is, Joshua, it is," she said with a resigned sigh.

"But—" I started to protest, wishing that Uncle Nat was there and hardly able to wait to get home to talk to him about Mrs. Foggelson and her problem.

She stopped me.

"I have shared my little secret with you, Joshua, because I know what you are feeling—because I admire you for standing strong—but, please, please, keep our secret. Promise me, Joshua?"

I had to promise. Standing there facing Mrs. Foggelson with the tears just ready to slip from her eyes and course down her cheeks, I could do nothing else. But it was a hard promise for me to make. Now I would be unable to tell Uncle Nat or Aunt Lou about her, about how she needed to be helped to understand that she could still come back to the church, and to her God.

"I—I promise," I reluctantly agreed.

She lifted a gloved hand to carefully wipe away the unwanted tear and then smiled again. No one would have known that she had been so sad looking just a moment before.

"Thank you, Joshua," she said in almost a whisper. "Thank you for sharing my load—and my groceries."

We were at her door then, and I waited while she took in the things she was carrying and returned to take the parcels from me.

She smiled at me again and said another thank you and I doffed my cap and hurried back down the walk. I didn't especially want to meet Camellia or Mr. Foggelson.

I was just leaving the yard when I unexpectedly ran into Jack Berry. And I mean just that. I wasn't paying very close attention to where I was going, I guess, and I swung around some shrubbery and smacked right into someone starting up the Foggelson walk. We both started to mumble our apologies and then Jack got a look at who he was talking to.

Before I knew what had happened he had a fist full of my shirt front and he was pulling me toward him with his face going red with anger.

"You been sneakin' around callin' on Camellia?" he hissed.

I attempted to get my shirt front back.

"I have not," I hissed back, and jerked on Jack's hand.

"Are you sure?" he shot back at me.

"I don't lie an' you know it!" I spat at him. "Let go of my shirt."

He did let go but his face was still red and angry.

"I'll ask Camellia," he assured me, "an' if you have, you're gonna be sorry. Next time you won't get off with just a bump on your poor dumb head."

I pushed past Jack and started for home, inwardly raging. My shirt wasn't damaged badly but one button hung loose. Stupid Jack Berry! *I never did care too much for the guy*, I told myself, but I quickly amended the thought. It wasn't true. There had been a time when I counted Jack Berry as one of my friends.

But that was before Camellia had come to town and he had gone off with his craziness over the girl. He acted like one who had lost his mind or something, the way he carried on. Well, he could have Camellia. I didn't care. No, that wasn't quite true, either. I still thought she was the prettiest girl I had ever seen. I still enjoyed her silvery laughter and the toss of her coppery curls. I still prayed for her every night when I said my prayers. I prayed for her pa, too, and now that I knew the situation I would pray for her ma most of all.

I continued on home, still riled by my encounter and trying to sort through the whole silly mess. Life sure could get complicated. How did one ever get it all put together anyway?

In the back of my mind the old chant started again. *Jack Berry, Jack Berry.* The whole thing just made me feel madder. And now I was a little late for choring as well. I knew Aunt Lou would understand when I told her my reason, but that wouldn't help my chores to get done any faster.

I was just passing by the schoolyard when I met Old Sam. He was stumbling along, the coat Uncle Nat had found for him open and flopping back and forth with each staggering step. It looked to me like it had all of the buttons torn from it, but Sam didn't seem to mind. He was muttering or humming to himself and clutching a nearly empty bottle close against his chest as though he was afraid someone might try to wrest it from him.

He waved his bottle in the air when he saw me. I guess he knew it was safe enough. I wouldn't be wanting it.

"Hi, Joshsh," he slurred his greeting to me and hiccupped.

"Hi, Sam," I answered without stopping.

"Now, don' ya go fall ag'in, Joshsh," he said and chuckled. Without even meaning to I looked aside and there, sure enough, was the big rock that I was said to have hit my head on.

Jack Berry, Jack Berry chanted my mind. What had Jack just said? Next time I wouldn't get off with just a bump to my dumb head. Suddenly, without warning, everything fell into place. *It was Jack's voice I heard that night!* We had fought. He had hit me and I had stumbled. That was when I must have hit my head. And good old Jack Berry had run off and left me there, knowing full well I might die of cold before I was ever found.

An anger took hold of me such as I had never felt before. It was all that I could do to keep myself from turning around and heading straight back to the Foggelsons' to confront the dirty, yellow good-for-nothing Berry right on the spot and make him pay for what he'd done.

I likely would have, too, had it not been for Aunt Lou. Somehow the fact that she needed me, needed me to haul the wood and water, and needed to not worry about where I was, kept me heading for home. There was no way I wanted to cause any anxiety for her—especially with the birth of that baby getting closer and closer.

CHAPTER 20

Pain

Spring slid from April through May and into June. After everything that had happened to me, the days seemed lazy and uneventful. At school, Mr. Foggelson's attitude toward me was to either ignore or avoid me, and I preferred it that way. Camellia was too busy telling secrets to the other girls to pay much attention to any of us fellas. We all knew that Jack Berry was still a frequent visitor at Camellia's house.

I no longer cared. I still burned with anger every time I thought about Jack. Since my memory had come back, I had never discussed with anyone the details of the night he had laid ambush for me. Maybe I was afraid someone would try to talk me out of my anger, I don't know. Anyway, I nursed my anger and conjured up all sorts of evil and torturous things that I hoped would one day happen to Jack Berry.

By June the sun became warm in the sky. Old Sam no longer wore his ragged, buttonless coat, not even in the cooler evenings. Uncle Nat still watched out for him, but Sam seemed to fare well enough. I had the impression that he was without any normal feelings for hot or cold, right or wrong, and I dismissed him from my mind. Uncle Nat didn't though—not for a moment. I couldn't really understand his deep concern. The old man seemed content enough in his drunken state of fantasy.

June arrived bringing yellow splashes of sunlight, young rhubarb pushing its way up in a corner of Aunt Lou's garden, and new calves and foals frisking in the fields along the road leading to the farm. I was thinking that spring must be about the best time of the whole year—and then I thought about harvest and knew I really liked that even better. And then of course there was Christmas . . . Well, anyway, I liked spring a lot.

I had some extra chores after school each day, but they didn't bother me none. It stayed light much longer now and so choring was no problem. The extras involved Aunt Lou's garden patch. The long rows of vegetables were sending up little spikes of green that gradually unfurled to be a pair of leaves, then four, then six, until a new plant was born and reached up for sunlight.

As you may have guessed, along with the plants came the weeds. It was my job to get them out of there. I didn't mind the hoeing, but I wasn't too keen on getting down on my knees and shuffling my way through the dirt to pull weeds. I did it though. After all, I sure didn't want Aunt Lou out there doing it with that new baby's birth only about four weeks away.

Aunt Lou loved her garden, and it was hard for her not to be out there picking weeds herself, but the doc had told her she would be wiser to let me do the pulling for this year. Reluctantly she agreed.

We were all counting the days till that baby joined us. The new crib Grandpa had fashioned was already in a corner of the little room that Aunt Lou called the nursery, the woven basket for the baby laundry beside it. Aunt Lou had made new ruffly white curtains and hung them at the window and framed a few pictures of somebody else's chubby babies to hang on the wall. Uncle Nat had bought a used rocking chair and revarnished it, and it sat there all ready for use with a knitted baby afghan tossed over one arm. The little chest was filled with baby clothes that Aunt Lou had sewed on her old machine, and on the crib, looking as good as any woman could have done by my way of thinking, was the baby quilt that Gramps had sweated over.

I stopped at the door and looked in on that little room 'most every time I walked by. We spent our time around the kitchen table discussing names and stating why we thought the baby would be a girl or a boy. It was fun planning together for the baby like that, and I think each one of us grew to love one another even more than we had before.

I was out there weeding in the garden late one afternoon when I got an awful urge for a cold drink of water. The afternoon sun could really beat down hot and made my throat dry and my skin prickly awfully quick. I stood up and stretched a bit and eyed the row ahead of me. I would easily finish it by suppertime.

When I got to the kitchen the potato pot was still sitting on the table with a half-peeled potato laying beside it. That was strange. Aunt Lou always had the potatoes cooking at this hour.

I listened, wondering if Aunt Lou had been called away for some reason. Then I heard a strange stirring from the bedroom, followed by a groan and my whole body went weak with the sound of it.

Aunt Lou lay on her bed, her face covered with her hands and a strange agony showing in the rigid way she was holding herself. Before I could even speak, another groan had escaped her and I ran to her side.

I was afraid to even touch her, so I just stood there, shaking, wondering what I should do and how soon Uncle Nat would be home.

Then she relaxed somewhat and took great gulping breaths of air. Her hands slipped down to rest on her full abdomen and I saw that her eyes were teary and pained looking.

"Aunt Lou?" I whispered.

She turned her head toward me and tried a weak smile.

"Oh—oh—Josh. Sorry, I—I'm not feeling so good."

"Should I find Uncle Nat?" I asked, wondering if I dared to leave her.

She nodded. Then she put out a hand to stop my dash.

"Get Doc first," she managed before another moan took hold of her.

I ran like I'd never run before, praying all the time I was running. *What if Doc isn't home, Lord?* I prayed. *What ever will I do?* Aunt Lou needed him, and she needed him *now*.

Doc was home. He was busy stitching up a cut on little Jeremy Sweeden's hand when I burst into his office room, calling out before I even reached him.

"Doc, come quick! Aunt Lou is awful sick."

Doc looked up from his stitching, his eyes showing immediate concern. But he didn't jump up and grab his black bag like I thought he should. Instead he said, "What is it, Joshua?"

"Aunt Lou," I said again, puffing out each word. "She's awful sick. She needs ya. Right now!"

"I'll come," he answered and turned back to his stitching.

"Right now!" I repeated almost shouting. I wanted to grab him by the arm and drag him to Aunt Lou's bedside.

"Yes, Josh. I'll be right there. Soon's I finish his hand."

It made me mad. I reckoned the hand wouldn't fall off or nothing if he left it, but who knew what might happen to Aunt Lou?

"You go on home and make sure there's a fire going and a kettle of water on," Doc told me. "I'll be right behind you."

I ran back to Aunt Lou, glad to have something to do. She was still groaning and tossing when I entered the house, and I nearly went wild with panic.

I guess it wasn't long till Doc joined us, but it sure did seem like forever. He didn't even stop in the kitchen to check on the fire or the water or nothing but went right on into Aunt Lou's bedroom and shut her door. I could hear the two of them talking in between Aunt Lou's groans. I checked the fire again to be sure it had lots of wood and then left again on the run. I had to find Uncle Nat, and I had no idea where he might be calling.

I ran all over the little town. I did find a few folks who said they had seen Uncle Nat earlier that day, but no one who knew where he was presently. At last, all tired out and panting, I turned for home. That was when I found Uncle Nat—at least signs of him. Poor old Dobbin stood at the hitching rail looking tired and hungry. Uncle Nat had deserted him and I was sure he was now in with Aunt Lou.

I took care of Dobbin, glad to be busy. I was very relieved that Doc and Uncle Nat were both with Aunt Lou.

After giving Dobbin his oats and brushing him down, I went to do my other chores. The woodbox still needed wood and the kitchen needed water even if Aunt Lou was sick. I left the unfinished row in the garden. I had no heart for it. The weeding could wait.

When I couldn't think of any more chores that needed doing, I returned to the kitchen. I wished there was some way I could just stay outside, but it was dark now and there was no reason for me to not go in. I hated the sounds of Aunt Lou's moaning. It made me hurt all over just to hear her.

I rumbled around in the kitchen peeling the rest of the potatoes and getting them on to cook. The smell of a roast baking was already coming from the oven. I didn't know what else she had planned to have for supper, so I went down to the cellar and took a jar of her canned beans from the shelf.

When I got back to the kitchen, Doc was sitting there on a chair at the table.

"Know how to make coffee?" he asked me, and I nodded that I did.

"Put on a pot, would you, Josh?" he asked me. "We could be in for a long wait until that baby decides to join us."

I stopped in my tracks, nearly dropping the jar of beans.

"Baby?" I said. "It's not time yet for the baby. It's not to be born until July."

"That's what we thought, but the baby has other ideas," said Doc knowingly.

"But it's too early," I continued to argue.

Doc sighed and drummed his fingers on the oil-clothed table. He raised his eyes to me and there was both sadness and hope there. Still he said nothing.

"Will she be okay?" I asked shakily. I was one who had voted for a baby girl. I wanted her to be just like her mother—so I would have a tiny Auntie Lou whom I could love and care for, just like Aunt Lou had cared for me when I was a baby.

"Can't say," said Doc quietly, and the whole inside of me trembled.

"Can't you stop it?"

Doc just shook his head; then he sighed a deep, sorrowful sigh.

"I've done all I can, Josh, but it's no use. This baby's going to come now."

I wanted to scream at him. To tell him he wasn't much of a doctor if he couldn't stop a tiny baby from coming before it should, but the words didn't come. Everything inside of me seemed to sort of freeze up.

Doc must have known how I felt. He cleared his throat and began to speak.

"We might have missed on the time, Josh. It happens. Remember, your aunt Lou was sick about then. But even if we didn't, and the baby is rushing things a bit, well, it still might be okay. Lots of babies have made it just fine even as early as your aunt Lou's will be. We just have to do everything we can—be ready to give him the best of care, and leave the rest to the Maker."

I somehow managed to put on the coffee Doc had asked for. I don't know how it tasted but Doc drank it anyway. He had probably tasted some pretty bad coffee in his day.

We had our supper. No one felt much like eating. Doc fixed a plate of food and took it to the bedroom for Uncle Nat, but it came back nearly as full as it had left the kitchen.

Along about eleven o'clock there was a knock on our door. It was unusual for someone to be calling at that time of night, and I didn't know just what to expect. It was Tom Harris. I knew he had been running pretty hard, in spite of the darkness. His eyes were sorta wild and he had a hard time talking because of his panting.

"Is Pastor Crawford here?" he asked me. I nodded my head that he was.

"We need him, right away," puffed Tom. "Old Sam is dyin.'"

"What?" I couldn't help my question.

"Old Sam," went on Tom between gasps of air. "He's dyin'. He wants to talk to the parson."

"He can't come now," I told him frankly. "Aunt Lou is havin' her baby."

"But he's gotta! Old Sam won't last long. He said he has to see the parson."

I was about to shove Tom out the door when I heard Uncle Nat's voice behind me. "What is it, Tom?"

Tom told his story again and I watched Uncle Nat's face as he listened. I could see the agony deeply etched there.

"I'm sorry, Tom," Uncle Nat was saying, shaking his head. "I'm sorry, but I can't leave just now. Lou needs me here, I—I—I'm sorry."

Tom stood looking bewildered. He didn't leave like I figured he should have.

"He said not to come back without ya," he insisted.

"Where is he?"

"At the livery stable."

"You can't get him here?"

"He won't let us touch him. Says he'll die for sure iffen we try to move him."

"I'm sorry," said Uncle Nat in a tired, hurting voice.

Tom left then, slowly, sadly.

It wasn't long afterward that Uncle Nat came from Aunt Lou's room with his hat in one hand and his black Book in the other. I knew he was going to see old drunken Sam, our useless town bum.

"I'll take Dobbin," Uncle Nat said to himself as much as to me. "I'll be right back as soon as I can."

I guess I nodded or maybe even made some reply, I don't know, but deep inside me there was a feeling that this was wrong—all wrong.

CHAPTER 21

The Baby

Doc stayed in the room with Aunt Lou, and I paced back and forth in the kitchen. I guess I prayed. I don't really remember. I do know that I was hoping Uncle Nat would get back quickly.

I was annoyed with Old Sam. After all, Uncle Nat had talked with him many times about making things right with his Maker, and he never would pay him any heed, and here he was now, sick and dying and deciding that it was time he clean up his life.

Now, I didn't blame Sam none for not wanting to face God in his present state, but it did seem to me he could have picked a better time to start getting sorry for all his sins.

I guess I was a little annoyed with Uncle Nat, too, but I had the sense to know he had really been caught in a fix. I knew he really wanted to be here with Aunt Lou, and I sure knew that was right where Aunt Lou wanted him. I had heard little comments many times between them about how the two of them planned to share together in the birth of their baby. And now Aunt Lou was facing it alone.

The minutes kept ticking by. It was taking the old kitchen clock an unusually long time to move forward. I even thought about pouring myself a cup of coffee to give myself something to do, but I changed my mind. I never had cared for the stuff and often wondered how older folk managed to drink it.

It was right around midnight when I noticed there seemed to be more activity in the bedroom. I could hear Doc's voice talking to Aunt Lou. I couldn't tell if he was comforting her or instructing her. Soon I heard Aunt Lou give a little high-pitched cry, and then there was silence.

I strained to hear something, but there was nothing. The quiet was even worse than the moans had been. I walked slowly toward the closed bedroom door. I was almost to it when I heard Doc's voice again. I couldn't hear the words, but I could hear the tone and it made the fear run thick all through me.

Then there was a cry from Aunt Lou. It sounded like she said, "Oh, no! Please, dear God, no!" and then she started to sob. I could hear the loud crying right through the bedroom door and I wanted to fling it open and rush in to her. I didn't. I just stood there rooted to the spot, shaking and sweating and willing Uncle Nat to get back in a hurry.

He didn't. It was almost one-thirty and he still hadn't come. Doc had spent most of that time with Aunt Lou. She was quiet now and when Doc came back out to the kitchen, he looked old and tired.

"She's sleeping now," he said.

He knew very well that I wanted to know more than that.

I couldn't ask. As much as I wanted to I couldn't ask.

"The baby didn't make it, Josh," said Doc, and that's all he said.

A thousand questions hammered at my brain, but I didn't ask a one of them. I couldn't. No words would come. I wanted to cry, but tears wouldn't come either.

"You should go to bed, Josh," said the doctor and he poured himself another cup of the strong black coffee with a rather shaky hand.

I didn't think I could sleep but I decided to go to bed anyway. I had to get out of that kitchen, to get off by myself somewhere. I turned to leave. Doc was stirring around in his black bag. He came up with a little bottle. He unscrewed the lid and a small white tablet fell into his hand.

"Take this, Josh," he said. "You'll sleep better."

Like a sleepwalker, I woodenly moved to do the doctor's bidding without giving it conscious thought. I put the pill in my mouth and lifted the dipper with water to my lips to wash it down, then headed for my bedroom.

Why isn't Uncle Nat back? Where is he anyway? If Old Sam is dying, he should have done it by now. My thoughts churned through my brain. I felt angry at both of them. Aunt Lou needed Uncle Nat. Or at least she *had* needed him. It was too late now. The baby was already dead. Aunt Lou had faced all the pain of it alone. She was sleeping now. *Most likely won't even hear Uncle Nat come in. What is keeping him anyway?* I raged.

Just as I reached the door I heard Doc's voice. He had lowered himself into one of the kitchen chairs and was sipping at the hot coffee, but he was talking to me.

"It was a girl, Josh. A baby girl."

I almost ran then, choking on the sobs that shook my whole body. I didn't even wait to undress, I just threw myself on my bed and let the sobs shake me. I cried for myself, for the loss I felt in not being able to love and care for that little baby. I cried for Aunt Lou in her pain of losing a child. I cried for the little baby, the tiny girl who would never know sunshine or flowers or the love of her family. And after I was all cried out, the bitterness began to seep into every part of me.

I was angry. Deeply angry. *God could have stopped all this.* At least if He was going to take Aunt Lou's baby, He could have left Uncle Nat with her to share her sorrow. But, no, Uncle Nat was gone. Out caring for some old drunk who had never listened to Him in all the months he should have been listening. So Aunt Lou had been all alone. Why? Didn't God care? Didn't He look after those who followed Him? After all, Aunt Lou and Uncle Nat were serving Him—were working in His church.

One thing I knew for sure, I would never be a minister. Not for anything. If a man couldn't even count on God to be with him and look after him, then what was the point of spending your life serving Him?

Maybe Mr. Foggelson was right. Maybe the Bible was a book of myths. Maybe the whole thing didn't make any sense. *How do I know?* was my last hopeless thought. In a state of confusion and rejection, the small white tablet claimed me for sleep.

When I awoke the next morning, I was still in turmoil. I was still angry, too. I was not undressed, but someone had thrown a blanket over me some time during the night.

There were voices coming from the kitchen, and I forced myself to get off my bed. I wasn't too anxious to leave my room, but I couldn't just stay where I was. Reluctantly, I pushed open my door and stepped from the bedroom. I knew the voices then. I could hear Grandpa, then Gramps, and they were talking in soft tones to Uncle Nat.

When I finally forced myself to enter the kitchen, I saw that Uncle Charlie was there, too. There were coffee cups sitting on the table, but at present no one was drinking coffee.

A hush fell on the room when I entered, and I was embarrassed. I knew I looked a mess. My clothes were crumpled, my hair standing on end, and my face swollen from crying myself to sleep.

"Mornin', Boy," said Grandpa and he reached out an arm and pulled me to himself. I almost started crying again. Grandpa just held me close, like the holding would somehow lessen our pain.

Uncle Nat was there. I don't know when he returned. I didn't even care to ask him. Whenever it was, it was too late, by my way of thinking.

"You'll be happy to hear that Sam asked God to forgive him last night," said Uncle Nat, and I knew he considered that very good news.

I looked at the faces around the table and I could see that all of them shared Uncle Nat's feeling.

I nodded. So Old Sam had made his peace with God before he died. I knew that was good, but I just couldn't get too excited about it.

"Doc is carin' for him now. He's much better this mornin'."

"He didn't die?" I sputtered in bewilderment.

A gentle chuckle rustled from man to man around the table.

"No, he didn't die," said Uncle Nat. "He had himself a good scare though."

So he didn't die! He had called Uncle Nat away from Aunt Lou and then not even had the common decency to die. And as soon as he was back on his feet and able to stumble around the town, he'd be right back to his sinful ways too, I'd wager. It made me even angrier. I turned from the men at the table.

"I gotta get ready for school," I muttered.

Grandpa cleared his throat.

"Boy," he said, "iffen you're not up to it, you don't need to be goin' to school today."

I didn't want to go, but I didn't know what to do if I hung around at home, either. Seemed to me there wasn't much for choices. Then I thought of Aunt Lou's garden. It still had some weeding to do. I mumbled a thanks to Grandpa and went to wash for breakfast.

It was a long, bitter day for me. The work in the garden helped, but all the time I weeded I could hear the saw and hammer, and I knew what was going on in Uncle Nat's shed. All four of the men were in there and they were working on a tiny coffin.

Every few minutes Uncle Nat would break from the others and go into the house to see how Aunt Lou was faring. If she was awake he would stay with her, but if she was sleeping he would come back out and help the men some more.

Doc called twice. Once in midmorning and once in the afternoon. He talked quietly to Uncle Nat, and I heard him say something about Aunt Lou being "as good as could be expected," and then he said that she was "accepting it well."

I finished the weeding and looked for other things to do. I cared for Dobbin and cut lots of firewood. Then I hauled water until I had all the buckets full.

The long day began to draw to a close. The menfolk took turns peeking in on Aunt Lou. I knew she welcomed the support of her family, but I just wasn't ready to see her yet.

The three men left for the farm, chores needing to be done. They said that they'd be back again in the morning.

Uncle Nat spent most of the evening with Aunt Lou and that left me pretty much on my own. About the only thing I had to do was to answer the door. Already word had gotten around about Aunt Lou losing her baby, and pies and cakes and casseroles began to arrive at the house along with the condolences of the people of the parish. Even some of those who didn't go to church stopped by with a batch of cookies or a chicken pie and expressed their sorrow.

I was glad when I could finally shut the door, extinguish the light against more callers and go to my room. I was exhausted. I hadn't had much sleep the night before, and it had been a long and difficult day.

I must have gone to sleep fairly quickly. At least I don't recall laying and thinking none. I didn't want to think. And I sure didn't want to pray. I couldn't see much reason to keep on trying to be friends with a God who wouldn't care for His own.

CHAPTER 22

Adjustments

Somehow we got through the next few days. People came and went. The menfolk lined the small coffin with a soft blanket, and a service was held in the church with family members, parishioners, and many neighbors and town people. I'm sure it must have been especially hard for Uncle Nat, conducting the funeral for his own firstborn.

Aunt Lou was unable to attend the service, so Grandpa stayed home with her. I don't know what words he could say for comfort, but then maybe she didn't want words. When I walked by the door and glanced in, Grandpa was just sitting there by the bed, holding tight to Aunt Lou's hand.

I went back to school. The girls talked in hushed whispers as I walked by, and it angered me rather than bringing any solace. I wondered just what they knew about grief, and if they had ever lost someone that they had looked forward to seeing for so many months.

At home, the door to the little room known as the nursery was closed. I hurried every time I needed to pass it. Aunt Lou didn't. I saw her almost stop many times, as though to listen for the crying of a baby or the even breathing of a sleeping child. I wondered if she ever slipped in there when she was all alone and handled the tiny garments or straightened the quilt on the baby bed.

School was soon out for the summer and I was glad. A change of routine sounded good to me.

Under usual circumstances I would have gone right out to the farm. But Aunt Lou was just beginning to get back on her feet again, and Grandpa felt I should stay around for a few more days to help her.

I didn't mind helping Aunt Lou, but I sure missed the farm. The open fields with wild strawberry patches, the crik with its fish holes, the clear, clean sky—all seemed to call to me. I needed to get away from town, I needed to get away from the little parsonage, I needed to get away from people. I would even have gotten away from myself if I could have thought of any way to do so.

There was no use fretting about it, so I just settled in and tried to make myself as useful to Aunt Lou as I could. She was getting stronger. She was even up and about in her kitchen. We still wouldn't let her out in her garden though, so I kept the weeds out the best that I could.

One day I went to the grocery store for Aunt Lou and nearly ran into Camellia on my way out. I could feel the red creeping slowly into my face and couldn't think of one thing to say to her, but she seemed composed enough. In fact, she even stopped and gave me one of her special smiles.

"Hello, Joshua," she said kindly. "How is your Aunt Lou?"

She sounded like she really cared, so I nervously shifted my package to my other hand and stopped to answer.

"She's getting lots better, thank you. She is even up now."

"Good," she said and then gave me another nice smile.

I looked around. I guess I expected Jack Berry to be lurking somewhere close at hand.

I was about to turn and go on my way when Camellia stopped me again.

"Would you care for some ice cream, Joshua?" she asked. Coming from anyone other than Camellia I would have considered that a pretty dumb question. Of course I liked ice cream.

"Papa gave me some money for a treat," Camellia went on, "and I do hate to eat all alone."

"Sure," I said, shuffling a bit awkwardly. "I'll have some with you."

I stopped thinking about Jack Berry. He really wasn't worth worrying about anyway.

We walked together to the sweet shop, and I held the door for Camellia. We settled ourselves at the counter on one of the high stools and gave our order. Vanilla for Camellia, chocolate for me.

Of course I had no intention of letting Camellia pay, and I was thankful that before leaving the house I'd had the good foresight to drop some coins into my Levi's.

"I suppose you've heard I am no longer seeing Jack," Camellia said casually. My head jerked up. She was looking down demurely and her lashes laid dark and soft upon her cheeks. I had almost forgotten just how pretty Camellia was.

I shook my head that no, I hadn't heard that.

"Well, it's true," she continued. "He was just so dull. Papa never could endure him. Papa just detests a person with no wits, and Jack was certainly witless."

I couldn't have agreed more, but I didn't say so.

"Papa says he thinks that Jack has chalk dust where his brains should be," Camellia laughed. "He was just so boring. He couldn't reason a thing out for himself. Why, he couldn't even follow the thinking of a person who could reason. He never will make anything of himself."

She shrugged her shoulders carelessly. "So he has gone off to the big city. He said he's going to find a job and make all kinds of money and then I'll be sorry." She laughed again as though she found that hard to believe.

I sat there, not saying anything. I hated Jack Berry. Yet somehow it didn't seem right that Camellia, who had supposedly liked him, sat there and said such harsh things about him. But I pushed it all from my mind. What did I care about what had happened between Camellia and Jack, anyway? I looked at Camellia. She was as pretty as ever. Maybe even prettier.

She turned to me and said, "So what have you been doing, Joshua?"

I shifted nervously. "Oh, dunno. Nothin' much, I guess. Been helpin' Aunt Lou."

"I thought you might be at the farm," she commented.

"I will any day now. Grandpa thought I should stay a few more days till Aunt Lou gets a bit more of her strength back."

Our ice cream arrived—which I paid for—and we took a few bites before Camellia turned those blue eyes on me again.

"I've missed you, Joshua," she said softly and I nearly choked on my spoon. "Mama has missed you, too," she hurried on. "She has always said that you are the nicest and the bravest boy she knows."

I thought that that was awfully kind of her mother. I took another spoonful of ice cream so I wouldn't be expected to say anything.

"And Mama keeps telling Papa that being a preacher really isn't that bad," Camellia added.

"I've kinda changed my mind on that," I said rather slowly. "I don't think I want to be a preacher after all."

Camellia's face lit up.

"You don't?"

"Naw. I kinda got to thinkin' that I might like to be a lawyer. Or a university professor, maybe. I don't know for sure yet."

Camellia was giving me her biggest smile, her lashes fluttering as she did so. I knew she was pleased with my new direction in life.

I finished my ice cream and suddenly remembered why I had been sent up town.

"I've gotta get," I said. "Aunt Lou's waiting for this yeast."

I gathered my package and my cap and prepared to take my leave.

"Thank you, Joshua, for the ice cream," Camellia said, and then added so softly that only I could hear her words, "You're welcome to come over—any time."

I blushed and rushed from the sweet shop, sure that everyone must be staring after me. I glanced back at Camellia from the door. She was still sitting on the high stool, rhythmically swinging her legs back and forth. She gave me another of her smiles and then I was gone.

I was about to place the package on the kitchen table and run back outside but Aunt Lou stopped me.

"I have some fresh cookies, Josh. Would you like some?"

Now, normally I would not turn down such an offer. Aunt Lou prided herself on her cookies and I liked them, too, but I'd just had me a dish of ice cream. Still, I didn't want to refuse her, so I grinned, said, "Sure," and threw my cap in the corner.

Pixie always insisted on sharing my cookie time. I didn't object but held her close and fed her little broken-off nibbles now and then. These were the first cookies Aunt Lou had baked since—since she had been sick, and they sure did taste good all right.

"They're great," I enthused to Aunt Lou around the cookie that was in my mouth.

"I'm glad you like them," she answered and sat down in the chair next to me at the table. "Maybe now I'll be able to bake regularly again."

I sure was not blaming her for not keeping up with the baking, and I wanted to tell her so. But I didn't know quite how to say it, so I just reached for another cookie and fed Pixie another nibble before I popped the rest into my mouth.

"I haven't really talked to you about the baby, have I, Josh?" Aunt Lou said then, and I looked up, hoping that she wouldn't want to talk about her even now.

"You didn't even see her, did you?"

I shook my head. I'd had no desire to see Aunt Lou's baby.

"She was so tiny. So tiny. Why, she was almost lost in her nightie and blanket."

I could tell by Aunt Lou's voice that the memory of her little baby was both painful and pleasureful to her.

"We were wrong about her birthing time, Josh," Aunt Lou went on quickly. "She was full term."

My head came up then and I looked directly at Aunt Lou.

"Then why did she—?" I stopped short. I just couldn't say the word "die."

"Why did she die? Because she had some terrible deformities. You see, we didn't know it at the time, but Doc says now that I was already expecting the baby when I had the measles. You remember the measles, Josh? Well, measles can be bad for babies in the first few months—I mean, if the mother gets them. It can cause abnormalities—serious ones. We haven't talked much about it to folks because we don't want the Smiths to feel bad that I caught the measles while helping them. I didn't know about the baby then, or I would have stayed away."

I just sat there letting Pixie lick the crumbs of cookies from my fingers.

"Every day I thank God that He took our baby home to be with Him," Aunt Lou continued, and tears filled her eyes now. "Every day."

Aunt Lou is thankful that her baby died? I couldn't believe it.

"But—but I heard you," I stated rather sharply. "I heard you that night. You said, 'Please, God, no.' "

"Yes, I did," agreed Aunt Lou, and even though she was seated with me at the table, she somehow seemed far away. "My faith was small, Josh. I admit that to my shame. When I saw the baby and was afraid that she would live with her handicaps—her deformities—I said, 'Please, God, no'—not because I was afraid she might die, but because I was afraid she might live. Josh, I know that you won't understand this, and I'm ashamed to tell it, but I—I cried out to God to take her. I was wrong, Josh. I shouldn't have done that. I should have been willing to accept from God whatever was right for us and our baby."

The tears were running freely down Aunt Lou's face now. I'm not sure, but there might have been some on my cheeks as well.

"I did pray for the strength to accept God's will—later," went on Aunt Lou. "And I was finally able to honestly say, 'Thy will be done.' In just a few minutes after I uttered the prayer, God took her to be with Him."

I couldn't understand it. Not any of it.

"I am so thankful. So very thankful. Not for my sake, but for hers. Our baby is perfect now. She is no longer deformed. She will never be teased or tormented or made fun of. She will never suffer because of her handicaps or need to endure surgeries or painful hours. I do thank God for taking her."

I had eaten as many of Aunt Lou's fresh cookies as I could hold, so I just sat there ruffling the fur on the back of Pixie's neck.

"If she had lived, Josh, I would have found a way to thank God for that, too. I think that's some of the meaning in the word 'grace.' The Lord gives His grace to take what comes with thanks and faith. Do you understand that?"

I wasn't sure, so I didn't say anything.

"We called her Amanda, the name you had picked. Did you know?"

I did. I had heard.

"It hasn't been easy," Aunt Lou confided, "but I am glad to have a little jewel in heaven. Amanda. Amanda Joy. She did bring joy, even during the months we were planning and preparing for her. And it brings us joy to know she is safely in heaven, too."

Aunt Lou stood up and brushed away the last trace of tears with her apron.

"I know this has been hard for you, too, Josh," she said. "Why, you wanted that baby 'most as much as Nat and me. It's hard to give her up, I know that Josh, but we can be glad she is safe and loved and cared for by God himself." There was a brief pause, "And as soon as I am completely well and strong again, we are going to have another baby. We won't need to worry about the measles this time—that's over now. I know it seems like a long time to wait, but the months go quickly and before you know it, you'll have that little cousin you've been wanting."

Aunt Lou reached out and ruffled my hair, her smile back.

"We'll make it, Joshua," she said. "With God's help, we'll all make it."

I got up to go. I had wood to split and haul. I was glad, too, to be out of the kitchen.

I was really confused now. We had lost our baby—our Amanda Joy, but Aunt Lou said she thanked God every day for His mercy in taking her. How could I have known that God—in His will—had been answering Aunt Lou's prayer when He took Amanda Joy to heaven?

But I was still upset about Uncle Nat being away. If God wanted to care for Aunt Lou, He could have had Old Sam get sick at a different time—or the baby born earlier or later or something. There was no reason Aunt Lou should have been left to face the delivery of a severely deformed child, then the loss of it, all alone. Surely God could have worked things out much better than that.

I was really confused, but my anger still hadn't left me.

CHAPTER 23

Picking Up the Pieces

I visited Camellia once before I left town for the summer. I'm not sure how I felt about the visit. It was fun to sit and read books and chat about ideas again. It was great to be able to handle some of the interesting, colorful texts from Mr. Foggelson's library. It was good to see Mrs. Foggelson and get her pleasant smile of approval. I even enjoyed the tea and pastries—sort of—but all the time I was there I had this funny, nagging feeling deep down inside that I wasn't doing the right thing. I tried to ignore it, but it wouldn't go away.

Mr. Foggelson sort of hung around for a while talking about good books and showing me special pages that I should read. He even read a few paragraphs from a history book aloud to me to be sure I wouldn't miss them. Then he talked about the passages, asking me what I thought about this idea or that concept. I tried to answer the best I could, but some of them were things I had never heard of before.

I think Camellia and I were both glad when he finally left us on our own. Camellia told me over and over how "dull" she had found Jack Berry and how much she had missed my visits. I almost got to believing her. I did wonder why it had taken her so long to discover the fact of Jack's "dullness," but I didn't say so.

I still wasn't much taken with talk about Jack Berry. I hadn't forgotten what he'd done to me. It was my right to feel pretty strongly about him, and I managed to keep quite a "hate" for him going.

In fact, whenever I wanted to spend some time feeling sorry for myself or getting mad about something, all I had to do was think of Jack Berry. I would let that little voice play over and over in my mind, *Jack Berry, Jack Berry*, and then I would think of the fist coming at me in the dark and the taste of blood and the sting of knuckle cuts and I would lather up real bitter feelings. Actually, I kind of enjoyed it. I must have—I did it often enough. It was the first time in my life that I had a really good excuse to get mad at the world.

Oh, I had been mad or upset about things in the past to be sure, but always I listened to this little voice saying, *Josh, this isn't right. You're not as bad off as you pretend to be.* But when it came to Jack Berry nearly killing me, I felt I had real good reason to nurse my anger.

Well, I only got that one chance to go over to Camellia's house and then Aunt Lou announced that she was feeling well enough that I should go on out to the farm like I usually did. She knew how much I missed it. Grandpa promised her that we'd slip into town every few days and see that she wasn't wanting for anything. Uncle Nat said that he'd see to it that she didn't do any water hauling or hoeing in her garden for a while yet, and I set off for the farm, anxious to get back to the familiar surroundings of green fields and wooded pastures.

Pixie was almost as glad to be back as I was. She spent the first ten minutes running round and round in circles and the next ten minutes checking out everything around to make sure it was just the same as when we had left it.

We all laughed at her, but I knew just how she felt. I was a little anxious to do some checking on my own, as well.

The place where I was heading was the crik, but I didn't want to appear too eager—just up and run for it the minute I got in the yard. But my family knew me well. I had just put my things in my room and returned to the kitchen when Grandpa turned to me.

"You suppose you might be able to catch us a fish or two for our supper, Boy?" he asked. I grinned and nodded.

"Hear they've been biting pretty good," added Uncle Charlie.

"What about my chores?" I asked.

"Reckon we can handle things for 'nother day," Grandpa assured me. "Catchin' us our supper will be your job for today."

"If you get some big ones," said Gramps with a wink, "then I'll go with you tomorrow."

So I was soon off to the crik.

My family must have known I needed this trip—and alone. I'd always enjoyed the company of Gramps. I would look forward to having him go with me on any of the days throughout the summer—except this one day. After so many things had happened, tearing me all up inside and confusing my thinking, I felt that my head was spinning. This day I needed to be alone.

The crik was about as pretty as I had ever seen it. The water was silvery ripples, almost as clear and clean as when it first splashed out of its hard rock bed at the spring up in the hills. The leaves were new green and they dipped and swayed in the afternoon breeze, flipping snatches of sunshine back and forth on the soft, still air. The birds were all atwitter. They had finished their nest building and were busy now caring for young. Nearby a nest of baby robins called loudly to be fed, reminding me of the two babies at the last church picnic who had thumped on their high chairs with their metal spoons, making one awful commotion.

The thought of babies turned my thinking back to Aunt Lou and little Amanda. I still hadn't sorted through the hurt of it all. Aunt Lou was thankful that her little baby, her helpless little deformed baby, had been taken to heaven where she could be whole and without pain.

I knew Aunt Lou loved her baby so much she was willing to bear the pain of losing the little one if it meant something better for the baby. I knew that Aunt Lou hurt deeply. She said many times how much the prayers of the people kept her bearing that pain each day, and how she depended upon them. Well, I was glad that the people were praying for Aunt Lou. I wanted her to have all the help God could and would give her.

I still had some questions, though, and they wouldn't go away. Why did God let Aunt Lou get the measles in the first place? And why did He work it so Aunt Lou was without Uncle Nat when the baby was born and died? If God was really a God of love, why didn't He care for her better than that? I sure wouldn't treat someone I loved in such a fashion.

No, I just wasn't ready to forgive God. He could have worked it out much better. I didn't understand His ways at all. Did He *plan* for His people to hurt? I had heard preachers say that it was in such times that people learned to "trust" and to "grow." Well, there must be a better way than that. They were just trying to excuse God for His thoughtless actions, according to my way of thinking. I still had my mind made up. If God treated His good servants that way, then I sure wasn't going to be one of them.

I didn't know if He'd miss my service or not, but I guess I hoped that He would feel pretty bad about it. After all, that was about the only way I had of getting even.

I caught two nice-sized fish and felt pretty good about myself when I hurried home to show them off.

"Well, Boy," beamed Grandpa, "I guess you've earned your supper, right enough."

Uncle Charlie grinned too and took the fish to fillet them for supper.

"Do we have a date for tomorrow, Joshua?" asked Gramps. "I sure would like to catch one of those. I've been wanting to go fishing, but somehow it just isn't much fun for me to go on down to the creek without you. You willing to take an old man with you tomorrow? Is it a date?"

"Sure," I answered, nodding my head in agreement. "It's a date."

"Good!" said Gramps. "I'll get my hooks all cleaned up and ready."

Boy, did those two fish taste good. Even Pixie got in on it. I fed her tiny pieces of the fish after making good and sure there weren't any bones in them. She licked her little chops and begged for more. I let her lick at my sticky fingers instead.

We all went to bed early. I felt tired, though I couldn't understand why. I had worked lots harder on many days and not felt so all done in. *It's the excitement of coming home again,* I decided. I cuddled Pixie close on one arm and settled down to sleep. By now it didn't even bother me much that I hadn't taken time to say my prayers.

Willie rode his old horse Nell over for a visit one day. She was fat and lazy and a little clumsy, but Willie wouldn't have stood for anyone saying anything mean or teasing about her. He had ridden her since he had been just a kid in first grade, and he loved her just as much now as he had when she'd been a spirited young mare with her head held high and a prance to her step. I knew better than to make any cracks about old Nell.

We spent our time rubbing down the old horse and talking some boy talk about things we wanted to do with our summer. Already we were talking camping trip again. The further behind us our trip up the crik got, the better our memories of it. We were ready to go again the first chance we got. This time, though, we wouldn't try to shortcut through the Turleys' pasture.

"You know," remarked Willie, "I sure understand Avery lots better since that trip. He's a good kid, too. We spend lots of time together now. Was a time when I couldn't really understand what you saw in the fella. Used to make me kinda sore that you thought him your best friend 'stead of me. Now that I know him, I really like him."

I was a little surprised at Willie's words—not about his liking Avery now that he knew him better, but about him feeling kinda jealous because I had liked Avery a lot.

"His ma is feelin' lots better now," Willie went on. "An' I think Avery feels better about things, too. You know, Josh, he's grown a lot closer to God now that he isn't so scared an' he feels more sure of himself an' all. I think God really worked out that trip so's I could get to know Avery better and he'd have one more good friend."

Willie stopped and thought for a few minutes in silence. I guess I was doing some thinking, too. I had a feeling that Willie might be making a much better friend for Avery than I had ever been. Willie was helping him to understand God better. I had left Avery to do that sorting out all on his own.

"I'm not sure how it works," Willie suddenly said. "Do you get closer to God when you are not so scared about other things, or are you not so scared about other things because you are closer to God? What do you think?"

I looked at Willie's serious face, then shrugged my shoulders carelessly. How should I know which came first—if either?

I showed Willie all of Pixie's tricks, and then he wanted to see if she'd do them all for him. When she did some of them, he was real pleased with himself. He'd always wanted a dog of his own, he said.

We sat under the big poplar tree in the yard and ate cookies and drank some of Uncle Charlie's fresh lemonade until our sides ached. Then we decided to go down to the pond and try skipping rocks.

"Did ya hear that the School Board is lookin' for another teacher?" Willie asked off-handedly, slicing his rock against the surface of the pond.

I hadn't heard and my thoughts immediately went to Camellia rather than to her father.

"Why?" I asked Willie.

"They didn't like all the stuff he was teachin'. Like evolution an' everything."

I could believe that. I didn't think Grandpa would have been too happy either if he'd known what was being taught.

"That's why he got kicked out of his last school, ya know," went on Willie.

"Yeah," I replied as matter-of-factly as I could. "I heard." I didn't explain.

"When are they leavin'?" I asked next.

"He's still tryin' to convince the Board to let him stay," Willie answered. "Don't think there is much chance, though. Some of the members are really upset about it. They say it wouldn't have been so bad if Foggelson had taught it as theory, but he's been teachin' it as unquestioned fact—like it was the only way it could have happened. That's what they don't like."

"What do you think?" I asked.

"I don't think he should teach it as fact either. It mixes up some of the younger kids an'—"

"I don't mean that," I cut in.

"What do ya mean?"

"I mean, do you think it coulda happened that way? Like evolution?"

"Things just happenin' instead of God makin' them?"

"Yeah. Do you think it coulda?"

"Isn't what the Bible says. Sounds crazy to me. Actually, it's a lot harder to believe in evolution than in a Creator. What do you think?"

"Yeah," I agreed a little slowly. "It does sound rather crazy."

"You hear about Old Sam?" Willie said next.

"What?"

"He asked to be church custodian—without gettin' paid—just as a thank you to God for cleanin' his life up while there was still time. He's over there cleanin' an' polishin' every minute he gets. He's doin' a good job at the livery stable, too. They gave him a raise already."

"A raise?"

"Yeah—a little bit more money. They wanted to see first if he'd really be dependable—or iffen he'd just go off drinkin' again when he got his first wages. He didn't. An' Mrs. Larkin says he's a good boarder. Keeps himself an' his room nice and tidy an' comes to meals on time. He even helps some around the place."

I stopped throwing rocks and looked at Willie.

"Well, if that don't beat all," I declared, feeling some grudging gratitude toward Old Sam. I knew it sure would help Uncle Nat out a powerful
amount. He'd been doing the janitorial duties at the church along with all
his other work.

We threw rocks until we spotted an old mother duck bringing her new
hatching of ducklings to the pond for a swim, and then we flopped down on
the warm, moist ground to watch them play around in the water.

I was still thinking of Camellia and questioning if she'd have to move
away and wondering what she thought about it all when Willie cut into my
thoughts again.

"Guess you must feel kinda special glad about Old Sam," he said.

"What do ya mean?" I asked.

"Well, about him making things right with God. None of us thought it
could ever happen. We thought that Old Sam was too bad a sinner for God
to even care about. Guess we thought he was goin' straight to hell. But there
must have been some spark of conscience in him, for him to stop and help
you when you fell in the dark and hurt your head like that, so you must feel
good—"

I'd heard enough.

"I didn't fall!" I hissed, anger making my voice brittle.

Willie looked at me like I had lost my senses.

"I didn't fall," I said again. "It was that stinkin' Jack Berry—"

"What ya talkin' about?" exclaimed Willie, raising up on one arm so he
could look me full in the face.

"Jack Berry," I repeated hotly. "He was there waitin' for me under that
tree in the schoolyard. He was mad 'cause I was seein' Camellia and he liked
her. He grabbed me and started punchin' me in the dark. I couldn't see who
it was or anything. I tried to fight back—and I got in a few good punches,
too—and then he hit me again and I slipped and ended up fallin' and hittin'
my head on that rock, and that yellow coward ran off and left me there to
freeze to death, for all he cared."

Willie sat right up and looked at me like I'd gone plumb crazy or
something.

"Where'd you get that wild idea?" he asked.

"What d'ya mean?" I snapped back. "I was there, wasn't I?"

"Yeah, but you didn't say anything about any of that after you were hurt. You said you musta fallen. You said you couldn't remember."

"I couldn't. Not for a long, long time—an' then once after Jack started to see Camellia, he admitted it himself. Said he'd beat me up even worse the next time if I saw Camellia again."

Just thinking about it made my blood boil.

"Why didn't you say somethin'? I mean, after you remembered? Why didn't you tell us?"

"What good would that do?" I asked bitingly, and Willie nodded. He wasn't as riled up about the whole thing as I was, but still I could see it all troubled him. After all, he did consider me one of his best friends.

"That's about the most rotten thing I've ever heard," he stated at last. "How could Jack do such a thing?"

"That's good ol' Jack for ya," I said sarcastically.

"Did he ever say he was sorry?"

"Are you joshin'?" I scoffed. "He wasn't sorry, not ever. He would have done it all over again if he'd had the chance."

"That's rotten," said Willie. "Really rotten."

There was silence for a few minutes while Willie plucked at the grass and I hammered one little rock against another. I guess I was wishing I had Jack Berry's fingers between them.

"No wonder he didn't dare show up back at school," Willie remarked thoughtfully.

It was the first time I had thought about that, and I realized Willie was right. Jack likely did quit school because of the fight. Somehow the fact that he had lost something in the exchange brought me satisfaction.

"There's talk in town about Jack, too," Willie went on and his voice sounded a bit sad.

"What?" I asked, wondering if I was even interested.

Willie lowered himself back onto his elbow and started pulling up little bits of grass that he threw to the side. He was stalling.

"What?" I asked again.

"You knew that Jack left town, went to the city."

I nodded. Camellia had told me that.

"I guess he and Camellia had a fight or somethin'. Least that's what the talk says. I don't know anything about it or what they was fightin' about," went on Willie.

"Maybe they didn't even fight," he surmised. "Maybe she just changed her mind, I don't know. Seems that Camellia, or her pa—I don't know which—thinks a fella should be smart an' make lots of money if he wants to call on her. Anyway, Jack left, an' he was plannin' to make himself rich real fast to impress Camellia or her pa. Well, I guess he tried—but not in the right way. Not many folks know much about it yet, but Jack landed himself in jail."

Willie looked so mournful when he said the words, like we should all be grieving over good ol' Jack or something. The whole thing hit me as funny—funny and terribly just. I threw back my head and laughed.

Willie looked up in surprise and then threw his next handful of grass at me.

"What's wrong with you, anyway?" he said hotly. "What's so funny about a fella bein' in jail."

"Nothin'," I answered, trying to control myself; "only it couldn't have happened to a nicer guy."

Willie gave me a stern look and pulled himself to his feet. He looked upset and Willie didn't get upset often.

Suddenly I was upset too. I sprang to my feet beside Willie.

"Oh, come on, Willie," I argued. "The guy jumped me in the dark and could've killed me. What do you expect me to say?" I changed my voice to a whining sing-song, "Poor, poor little Jackie. Someone has done him dirt."

Willie turned and looked at me, not pleased with my little charade.

"This is the real world, Willie," I continued, really in a lather; "the fella only got what's comin' to 'im."

Willie stood and looked at me for a long moment. "It doesn't hold up, Josh," he said, his voice even and controlled.

"Whatcha talkin' about?" I threw back at him, angry that he was now calm and I was still upset.

"You know what Scripture says about forgivin'."

"The jerk jumped me in the dark!" I insisted hotly. "What do you expect? That I'm just gonna say, 'I forgive you, Jackie. I know you didn't mean no harm'?"

" 'Course he meant you harm," agreed Willie. "Iffen what you say is right—an' I have no reason to doubt your word, Josh. 'Course he meant you harm. But is that what the Bible says? 'Forgive them only if they meant no harm'? No. It says 'forgive them.' Period. That's what Jesus did. Do you suppose Jack did you more harm than the mob did to Him?"

It was a silly question and we both knew it.

"He doesn't deserve forgiveness," I said, not ready to give in. "Anyone who would wait in the dark—and—"

Willie didn't even wait for me to finish.

"It's got nothin' to do with what he deserves. Can't you see that? You don't answer for Jack Berry; you answer for Josh Jones. The wrongs of Jack have nothin' to do with you. Aw, come on, Josh! What Jack did was pure rotten. Nobody's arguin' that Jack *deserves* your forgiveness, at least not in man's thinkin'. But God doesn't reason like that. Whether you forgive Jack or not really isn't goin' to hurt Jack Berry. It only hurts you, Josh. You happen to be my friend, an' I think that *you* deserve forgiveness."

"Me?" I said in shock. "What did I do?"

"Hate! Plan revenge! Hold bitterness! All those things are wrong and need forgiveness, too. God says He will only forgive us as we forgive others. I don't want you to be unforgiven, Josh." His voice broke.

Willie, my best friend, had tears in his eyes. He turned from me and kicked at a stone. I knew he was fighting to get back some control.

As I watched him, his words, and the truth of them, kept pounding through my brain. Wow! I hadn't thought of all that.

Willie was still swallowing hard. When he turned back to me, he was a bit pale and his voice trembled as he spoke.

"I gotta get home, Josh. I'll see ya Sunday," and Willie turned and left, traces of tears still in his eyes.

I watched him go. Inside I was all mixed up. I was still angry with Jack Berry. I still couldn't feel sorry that he had gone and got himself thrown into prison off in some big city somewhere.

Then I started to think about what it would be like to be in a big city all on your own and in some jail somewhere locked up, not knowing anyone and being shut away from the green grass and the blue sky. I guess I wouldn't like it much. *But he deserved it,* I kept telling myself. And then my mind flipped to some of the things that *I* deserved. I thought about my anger, hate, evil thoughts, selfishness—as bad as what Jack was in jail for.

The whole thing was so confusing. I didn't know what to think about anything anymore. I turned to the pond again and started throwing rocks, but my heart just wasn't in it. None of them "skipped." They just smashed into the blueness of the pond, then sunk to the bottom.

CHAPTER 24

A Fishing Trip

Gramps and I did go fishing a number of times. We usually took along a bucket with some lunch so we could sit and snack alongside the stream. In the clear, warm summer air it was cozy and relaxing and fun. Grandpa called it "lazy" weather. One sure didn't feel like doing much. You could use up a whole afternoon just laying on your back looking for funny shapes in the clouds or watching the new ducklings on the pond or something.

On one such afternoon as we headed for the crik again, Gramps looked up at the almost cloudless sky. "Ah-h, summer," he said. "Seems that God is always closest to earth in summer."

I wasn't sure if I shared Gramps sentiment, but I wasn't about to spoil our day by saying so.

We took off our shoes and socks, rolled up our pant legs and waded the crik to get to our favorite fishing hole. We spread our belongings out around us on the bank so we wouldn't have to get up for anything, then set about getting our lines in the crik water.

Before we even had time to drop a line in, a shadow swept slowly past in the water in front of us. We both nudged one another at the same time and leaned as far forward as we dared, to get a good look. It was all I could do to keep from jumping right in and trying to grab that big fish with my bare hands.

"Wow! Did you see him?" I whispered in excitement to Gramps. Almost at the same moment he said, "Did you see him? Biggest fish I ever saw! Oh, boy, Joshua, this is going to be fun!" and we both got serious about it, too excited to even think about munching on our sandwiches and brown sugar cookies.

Sorry to say, we never did see that big fish again, but we caught three others—two of them a nice size and the other a rather scrawny little thing. We kept it anyway. It would taste just as good as its bigger brothers and, anyway, its mouth was torn from the hook and we didn't want it to suffer.

Fishermen aren't much for visiting. I mean, you go fishing so you have you some thinking time. The notion that talk might scare the fish is just a ruse. What fishermen are really saying is, "Please don't interrupt the solitude. I'm communing with myself and nature out here."

When the sun swung to the west, we decided we should be getting on home, so we picked up our belongings and waded the crik again. Drying our feet on the grass, we sat down to slip back into our shoes and socks. We picked up all our gear and our empty lunch bucket and started down the trail to the farmyard. I was thinking of Camellia and how she might look at this quiet place when Gramps interrupted my thoughts.

"How's little Lou?"

I was surprised at his question. He had seen Lou just the day before, and I supposed he would have seen how she was most as good as anyone.

But Gramps went on. "You know Lou about as well as anyone does, Joshua. How do you think she is doing? I mean, way down deep inside?"

I thought I understood the question then, but I hesitated some before I answered.

"Good," I finally responded. "Quite good, I think."

"Thank God!" said Gramps and I knew he meant it from the bottom of his heart.

"Has she talked about the baby?"

"Yeah. Just a few days before I left to come home."

Gramps raised his white, bushy eyebrows. "What did she say?"

"Said she thanks God that He took the baby. Said that Amanda"—it was hard for me to call the baby girl by her name—"that Amanda is better in heaven. That she would have suffered a lot if she'd lived—and been made fun of, too."

Gramps shook his head slowly, then sighed deeply.

"She's right, Joshua. She's right."

Then Gramps said something I thought very strange.

"There are many things worse than death, Joshua. Many things. Oh, I know it is hard for those left behind. I still miss your great-grandmother terribly. Some days I think I just can't go on anymore without her, but God helps me and gives me strength and grace for each day." Gramps stopped to wipe his eyes, and then he went on, "That's not just a pretty phrase, you know, 'strength and grace for each day.' No, those are words with a lot of meaning. A lot of truth."

We walked on. I tried to tick the tree branches with the tip of my fishing pole without getting myself hung up on any of them.

Gramps went on. "When one is ready to meet his Maker, prepared and forgiven, then death is a welcome thing. I would not wish your great-grandmother back to endure the suffering of this world. Not to bring me comfort for even one day, one hour. I love her far too much for that."

It sounded strange to me, but I knew Gramps meant it.

"Lou is right about her little girl. She is much better off in heaven."

There was silence for many minutes. I thought Gramps had put aside his thinking on death, but he hadn't.

"When it comes time for me to go, I hope folks remember that I have finally had my hopes realized. That I have been taken home. I've felt lonesome for heaven for a long time now, Joshua. Ever since your great-grandmother left ahead of me, I guess. I can hardly wait to get there—can hardly *wait* to get there! Every day I have to ask the Lord for patience—for just a little bit longer. No, Joshua, I hope that no one, *no one* will ever grieve long for me."

My eyes were big and my heart thumping as Gramps said his feelings. I hoped with all my heart that God wasn't listening. He might decide to answer Gramps prayers right then and there. The very thought of it scared me half to death.

I started to try to voice a protest but Gramps kept right on talking. "Your great-grandmother's passing did bring about one good thing, Joshua." He paused and reached a soft, once work-roughened hand out to lay it on my arm. "If she hadn't left me, I might never have gotten to know you."

I swallowed hard. It was true. I blinked back tears when I thought of how I had fought against the idea of Gramps coming to join us—at first, that is. Now that he was here I wondered how we had ever gotten along without him.

"It's been good, my boy." Gramps had never called me that before. "I have loved our checkers, our chats, our choring," and he ruffled my hair, "and most of all our fishing."

I bit my trembling lip.

"You're a good boy, Joshua. I'm mighty proud of you."

There were so many things I wanted to say to Gramps. Like how I loved him, how much I enjoyed his companionship, his help, his just *being there*. Like how much more fun it was to come home to the farm knowing that he was there. But I didn't say any of them. I just didn't know how to put all those things into words.

"I'm getting to be an old man now. I've lived a full and good life. It won't be too much longer until the Lord calls me on home to join your great-grandmother. I won't need to be patient for much longer now." There was another pause. We were almost to the farm buildings now, and I guess Gramps figured that whatever else he had to say to me had to be said quickly.

"You are still very young. Your life stretches out before you. Don't waste it, Joshua. A life is far too precious to waste."

Mr. Foggelson had said that too, only a little differently. He had said that a mind was too precious to waste—a good mind.

"The most wasteful, shameful thing that one can ever do is to fight against our Maker. He has only your good in mind, Joshua. His plan is the best possible plan for you to follow. Now, I don't know what that plan is. Only God knows. But whatever it is, Joshua, don't waste time and energy fighting against Him. Life is too short for that—even though right now it looks to you like you have almost forever. I'll be there waiting for you, Joshua, but when you come, I want you to come triumphant, because you have served God with all your energy, all your years, all your manhood—not head-hanging and ashamed. Do you understand me, son?"

I nodded. I thought I did.

"Let Him lead you, Joshua—every step of the way. Don't ever question Him and don't ever detour off His path. It's far too costly."

I nodded solemnly. I wondered if Gramps had been reading my mind. It made me feel a mite uncomfortable.

By then we were entering the path that led up to the house. I knew that Gramps had no idea of the turmoil that was going on inside me. I was glad. I wouldn't have wanted him to know. He would have been ashamed of me. Of the way I had been thinking and feeling.

I was glad we were home, that I had chores to do. I was anxious to slip away by myself so that my feelings wouldn't show. I was swallowing hard to keep the tears from coming. I knew Gramps hadn't said his words to upset me. He loved me and had no idea of the thoughts I had been burying deep inside. The thoughts of hate for Jack Berry. The doubts and frustrations about the Bible and evolution. The bitterness about little Amanda Joy. The feelings about God not caring for His people. I was glad Gramps couldn't see my heart. He would have been saddened by what he found there. I loved Gramps and would have died before I would have intentionally hurt him.

I tried to give Gramps a smile before we parted company but it was a bit shaky.

He patted my shoulder once more and gave me one of his big smiles that twitched his trim mustache and made his eyes twinkle. I loved Gramps. I hoped he would be with us for many years to come. I just couldn't imagine what life would be like without him.

CHAPTER 25

Lessons in Living

I did a lot of thinking during the next few days. The conversations I'd recently had with Willie and Gramps kept playing over and over in my head. My conscience told me that what they had said was true. I knew I had no rights that gave me the privilege of hanging on to anger and bitterness against Jack Berry. God had commanded us to forgive others, even when they had given us cause to hate instead.

I knew, too, that baby Amanda truly was better off in God's heaven. Grandpa had talked with me about some of the severe abnormalities of the baby. If she would have lived—and Doc could see no way that she could have possibly survived, but if by some miracle she had—she would have needed hospitalization and many operations to make it possible even to feed her. We would have loved her, we all knew that, but she would have suffered terribly, both physically and from mistreatment by others.

But I still blamed God. Not only for the fact that baby Amanda was born as she was, and then died so quickly, but because Aunt Lou had needed to face it all alone.

Old Sam hadn't gone back to his drinking like I was sure he would. He was still holding down his job and keeping himself and his rented room neat as could be. He was taking good care of the church as well, and sang, intelligibly now, as he worked.

I went to town at least twice a week, stopping in to see Aunt Lou and to help her with her garden. I split and carried the wood for her, too. Aunt Lou was getting stronger every day, and though she still grieved over her baby, the anguish was gone from her eyes. She could smile again and she could even laugh. I loved hearing her sing the old hymns softly to herself as she went about her daily tasks.

"Isn't it wonderful to watch Sam polish up the church?" she said to me one day as I sat at the kitchen table. She probably thought of that 'cause I was polishing up a new fishhook I was dying to try. "Whoever would have believed that God could change him so much." She went to stand at her kitchen windows, one hand holding back the lacy curtains so that she could watch Old Sam washing the church windowpanes. She laughed softly.

"That's silly, isn't it? Of course God can change a man. He changed me when I asked for His forgiveness. It just shows up in different ways, that's all."

She let the curtain slide back into place and returned to her bread-baking.

"When I think how Nat nearly didn't go that night, it scares me."

I looked up then. Aunt Lou noticed and continued.

"Oh, Nat wanted to go. He wanted to go very much, but he didn't want to leave me and Amanda." Aunt Lou was finally at the point where she could talk about Amanda, even call her by name, without weeping.

"He knew he should go and he longed to go, but he wouldn't leave me. It was awfully hard for Nat. I had to *insist* that he put his calling to the ministry before his family. God was asking him to go to Sam! There was no one else to go, and an hour, two hours, might be too late, forever. Doc was with me. I knew I'd be all right."

Aunt Lou gave the bread one more brisk roll, then plunked it back in the pan and gave it a firm pat. She recovered it with the clean, white kitchen towel and pushed it back out of her way.

I was still chewing over her words. *Aunt Lou* had insisted that Uncle Nat go to Old Sam. I hadn't known that.

"How did Uncle Nat feel when he got back?" I asked, trying not to let Aunt Lou know that the question was loaded with all sorts of implications and accusations.

"Poor Nat," she said, her eyes clouded. "He felt just terrible. Not only was he grieved with losing our baby, but he was so sorry he hadn't been there with me."

I nodded. *He should have felt that way,* I reckoned. And God could have done something about the whole thing.

"I told Nat that it was okay. That I knew why he was gone. I prayed for him the whole time he was away that God would give him the right words, so Sam would understand how much God loved him in spite of his sin—that God was waiting to forgive him if he'd just ask.

"And—" Aunt Lou hesitated. "This is hard to put into words, Josh, but it was the strangest thing. I didn't miss Nat. I mean, I felt like I was there with him, sharing in his ministry to Sam, and I felt that he was here with me, sharing in the birth of our first baby. I think it was God—I mean, I think because God has made us one, and because it was a special time for both of us, that God sorta bonded us together in love even though we were apart."

Aunt Lou reached out a hand to my shoulder and smiled.

"I'm sure that none of this makes much sense to you, Josh. Maybe some-day, when you grow older and fall in love and marry some sweet girl, you will know more what I am talking about."

"You're right," I nodded. "It don't make much sense. I thought you wanted Uncle Nat right there with you."

"Oh, I did," she quickly responded. "And if it would have been for any other reason that Nat wasn't there, I would have been really upset. I mean, if he'd been off fishing or just off with the menfolk chatting or something—but it was his duty, not his desire, that took him away from me, and I can understand and accept that."

"His duty?" I muttered.

"Yes, he had to go. Sam needed him."

"You needed him, too. He left you all alone—"

"No, not alone. Never in my life had God seemed so close. He was right there with me, wrapping me in His love, holding me tight when I needed comfort."

Aunt Lou stopped for a moment as though once again sensing the special feelings of those hours spent with God. Then she went on again. "No, Josh, it was Sam who needed Nat. He might have died without his sins forgiven and gone out into eternity without God."

"He didn't even die," I reminded her.

"How were we to know that? At least he was ready that night when he was afraid he might die, ready to call on God for forgiveness. If Nat had missed the opportunity, Sam might have thought that Nat really didn't care and he might never have become a believer."

"I dunno," I said carelessly, still polishing the new fishhook. "Seems like pretty bad timing to me."

Aunt Lou crossed back to the window and lifted the curtain again. She stood there watching Old Sam, her eyes brimming with tears. They spilled down her cheek and she didn't even bother to wipe them away.

"Seems like perfect timing to me," she said in almost a whisper. "At the same moment I was losing the child that I wanted and loved, God was reclaiming one of His children for His very own. He loves Sam as much—no, even more—than I love Amanda Joy. Every time I think of little Amanda, I am reminded of the night, the very hour, when Sam came back to the Father."

Aunt Lou just stood there, the tears still unchecked on her cheek. Then she let the curtain drop again and turned to me with a trembly smile.

"God received two children that night, Josh. One through death, one through rebirth. It's beautiful, isn't it?"

Summer slowly crept toward autumn. The School Board decided to let Mr. Foggelson have one more chance and school started as usual. I only missed the first week to help with the harvest. Then it rained so I hustled to town to try to catch up on my schoolwork.

I didn't admit it to anyone, but I was relieved that Camellia wouldn't need to move away. I went to see Camellia again on Thursday. I felt rather funny and uncomfortable about it, but because I enjoyed her company I went again the next day before I headed to the farm for the weekend. Mrs. Foggelson joined us for tea. I tried to relax and enjoy her tea and pastries, but I felt her sharp blue eyes upon me, as though they were trying to pierce through me to find some answers. Was I going to compromise like she had done? Would I let her down? Had Mr. Foggelson, with his sharp mind and his eloquent tongue, gotten through to me just as he had to her?

Later, Camellia and I tried to talk about books just like we had always done. It was hard for me. I had so many things churning around inside of me. On the one hand were all my doubts. On the other hand were the Bible truths I had learned from the time I was a child. I couldn't really swallow evolution and the supposed facts that it presented. It was like Willie said. It was just too unbelievable.

No, try as I might, I could not believe that things just happened. I did believe in God. *There has to be a God*, I concluded. I guess I had never really doubted that, not even for a minute. What really had been troubling me was how God related to folks as individuals.

Was it true what we had learned in church? Was it true that God knew the best for each life, that He cared for those who followed His way? I had thought He had let Aunt Lou down. But Aunt Lou said that He hadn't. She said that she had never felt God's love as strongly about her. That was rather peculiar. To be going through such pain and yet feeling God's love the most.

And then there was this thing about Jack Berry. I hadn't shaken Willie's words. He said that whether Jack deserved forgiveness or not, I did, and the only way I could find that forgiveness, for my hate and my bitterness and my desire to get even, was to ask God to forgive me.

Boy, it had me all mixed up.

I stole a glance at Camellia. I had never really faced it before, but she was my other problem. I knew Camellia and her pa had their hearts set on a smart young man who could make lots of money and buy her lots of nice things. I knew Mr. Foggelson thought that a fella who believed the things that the Bible said couldn't be all that smart, and therefore he likely wouldn't make much money and so he'd never make his daughter happy.

I thought Camellia was pretty special. I knew that my faith in God and my choice of a friend weren't very compatible. Not that I was thinking on getting married or anything. I mean, I wasn't even sixteen yet—neither was Camellia, but well—she was really pretty and . . .

If I told Camellia that I believed what the Bible said was true, she'd tell me not to bother coming back, I was just sure of it.

Then another idea came to me. I'd pray. I'd pray that Camellia and her ma and pa would change their thinking. That they would start to go to church and believe the things the Bible taught. Then Camellia and I could still go on seeing each other.

Even as I got excited about the thought, I knew it was wrong. Sure, I should pray for Camellia. And for her folks, too. But not so I could go on seeing her. That was the wrong kind of an attitude. I should pray for her because I cared about her, and because I cared about her ma and her pa, too. They needed to turn to the Lord. They needed to recognize that things didn't just accidentally fall into being, that there is a Creator. Things didn't just evolve. And because God really was God, He had the right to ask His creation to walk in His ways.

Wasn't there some way I could hang on to God, my anger and Camellia, too? Did a person have to turn over *everything*—every part of life when he asked God to direct his ways? Wasn't there some way I could still choose some areas where I could still be in control?

And then I started thinking on Gramps' words. Gramps seemed pretty sure that wanting to take things in your own hands was fighting against God. And Gramps felt pretty strongly that doing so was not only stupid and wasteful, but sinful and disastrous.

The whole thing had my head spinning.

But I couldn't chat with Camellia about her pa's books and be working that all out, too, so I tried to push all the conflicting thoughts from my mind.

"Do you or don't you, Joshua?" Camellia was asking.

"Huh? I mean, pardon? I guess I was thinkin'—"

"About something else. I know. I just hope it wasn't another girl," teased Camellia.

" 'Course not," I said, blushing to the roots of my hair.

"I wanted to know if you'd like to come with us for a picnic on Sunday. We are going to the lake."

"Oh!" I answered. "Oh, no, I can't. It's church."

Camellia looked hurt.

"Can't you skip church for just one Sunday?" she pouted. "You go to your old church all the time. 'I can't come over on Wednesday, Camellia. I have to go to meeting. I can't see you on Sunday, I have to go to church,' " she mocked. "I'm beginning to think—"

"I'm sorry," I interrupted.

"Then you'll come?"

I looked at her steadily. I think I realized at that moment that Camellia would never understand me—not really.

"No," I said firmly. "No, I can't come. I'm going to church."

Her temper flared. "Well, if your old church is more important to you than I am, then you—"

"I'm sorry," I said rather sadly. "I'm sorry, but I guess it is."

I thought Camellia would strike out angrily. But she didn't. In fact, she changed her approach completely, even giving me a smile.

"I'm sorry, Joshua," she said almost sweetly. "Let's not fight. If it is that important to you, then, by all means, go ahead. I'll tell you all about the picnic when you come over next week."

I reached for my cap and fumbled it around and around in my hands. It seemed a long time until I was brave enough to say it, but I finally managed.

"I'm sorry, Camellia," I said in a low voice. "I—I won't be comin' next week."

"What do you mean?" Her voice sounded angry and almost frightened.

"I won't be comin' back. I shouldn't be here now. I—I can't agree with your pa's books about evolution an' all those other things. I can't agree that bein' smart is the greatest thing in the world either. I don't think that makin' lots of money is the only way to live. I—I think different from you. I—I believe that church is important. I believe that God is important. I know I haven't been livin' like it but—but—"

I fumbled with my cap some more.

"Right now I'm all mixed up. I've been tryin' to hang on to God and live for Josh Jones, too. It doesn't work so good." I looked down at my cap. It was a while before I could go on. "I've got a lot of things all mixed up. I need some thinkin' time," I finished lamely. Then I made myself move quickly to the door before I could change my mind or Camellia could protest. I was anxious to get back to the freedom of the farm and the busyness of the harvest fields and the familiar chores.

"Bye, Camellia," I stammered and I almost ran from the room, anxious to get away, somehow thinking I could escape also from all of the conflicting thoughts that were tearing away on the inside of me.

CHAPTER 26

The Beginning

I awakened earlier than usual the next morning—not by my choice. I had slept poorly the night before, still wrestling with some of my conflicts. I knew that my life really belonged to God. I knew that I would most likely be happier, be at peace inside, if I let go of all my self-will and let Him direct me. But for some strange reason I just didn't want to do that.

So I was still needing more sleep when a commotion in the big farmhouse awakened me. It took me a few minutes before I could get myself awake enough to sort out the noises. It was Grandpa.

"Charlie!" he called. "Charlie—get down here quick!"

I heard Uncle Charlie as he hit the wooden floor in his bedroom and hurried to the steps. It sounded, by the strange thumping noises, like he was trying to get into his trousers and run at the same time.

"What is it?" he called back to Grandpa from the head of the stairs.

"It's Pa," said Grandpa.

The words sent a chill all through me. "Pa" to Grandpa was "Gramps" to me, and I didn't like the way Grandpa had said the word—his voice tight with emotion.

I was out of bed in a flash, and I never even stopped to pull on my pants, just grabbed them and somehow worked them on as I ran.

Uncle Charlie and Grandpa were already in Gramps' room. I came running up behind them and tried to push my way between them. Grandpa put out a hand to stop me, but I put my weight against it and forced my way by.

"What's wrong?" I demanded. "What's wrong with Gramps? He sick or—?"

I stopped abruptly. Gramps lay still on his bed, his eyes closed, a faint hint of a smile on his relaxed face. There was no gentle lifting and falling of his chest with his breathing. All was quiet. Too quiet. Grandpa moved close behind me and placed a hand on my shoulder.

"Yer Gramps is gone, Boy," he said, and his voice trembled.

"No!" I shouted. "No!" and I brushed away Grandpa's restraining hand that was meant to comfort me and dashed from the room.

I don't know how I got to the fishing hole. I don't know how long I lay there on the cold damp grass. I only know that when I had finally cried myself all out, that's where I was.

I didn't even try to get up. The grass was dew-wet and the morning foggy and cold. Suddenly a shiver made me realize just how cold I was. Laying right beside me was my choring jacket and my flannel shirt. Someone had visited me—and I hadn't even noticed.

I crawled awkwardly into my clothes, shivering as I did so. My body was damp from the wet grass, and the flannel felt good on my back.

I tried hard to pull myself together, but it was tough.

I walked down to the crik and bent low to splash cold water on my puffy face. Just as I bent over the cool water, a dark shadow approached, then just as quickly disappeared beneath some low branches hanging from the willows at the crik's edge. It was that big northern again—the one Gramps and I had seen on our last fishing trip together.

The sight was too much for me. I lowered my body to the sandy bank and let my mind drift back. The sobs overtook me again. It had been fun to fish with Gramps. He was great company. I would miss him. Boy, would I miss him! He had talked to me man to man. Just like we were equals.

My mind filled with some of those things Gramps had shared. He had said that he was lonesome. That he wanted to go home to heaven. That it was hard for him to be patient, knowing that Great-grandma was waiting for him there and all.

He had said something else, too. He said, "I don't want anyone grieving long for me." Strange he should say that—just a few short days before he went home, too.

I sorted through my memories to try to remember all of Gramps' words. He had talked quite a lot about death that day. I hadn't paid much mind to some of what he had said at the time. I didn't like thinking about death.

But he had talked about more than death. He had talked about life, too. About how to live it. That I was to be sure to let God have complete control of every part of my life. That I was to be ready to die, whenever that time would come.

That meant I couldn't hang on to bitterness or anger, no matter how much I had a right to be mad. I guess I couldn't hang on to my future either and make my own plans about what I wanted to do. It meant that I couldn't blame God for things happening when they did or how they did—especially when it all turned out right and good anyway.

Either God was God—or He wasn't. There was no moving Him in and out of my life with the mood I happened to be in.

All sorts of things started to fall into place for me. I saw some things clearer than I ever had before. I think I saw Gramps—his life and what he had tried to teach me—more clearly, too. I understood what he was trying to say to me about him being there waiting for me, and how I was to join him "triumphant" because I had been obedient to God, and not with my head hanging in shame.

As I thought of all of these things, I just lay there on that cold ground sobbing my heart out. Only this time I wasn't grieving for Gramps. I was grieving for me. I sure had messed things up. I had filled myself so full of anger and bitterness and pain and doubts, and then I had turned right around and pointed my finger at God as though He was to blame for it all. I knew better. Deep down I knew better. How could a God who loved me enough to die for me turn around and be spiteful and mean?

I cried it all out to God, asking Him to forgive me and to take away all of the bad feelings I had inside. I told Him I was done making my own plans. I didn't know if He wanted me to be a preacher like Uncle Nat, but that didn't matter. What *did* matter was that I was *willing* to be one—if that's what God wanted me to be. If He wanted me to be a farmer, I'd be that. Or if He wanted me to be a lawyer, or a doctor, or even a teacher, I would try to be the best one I could possibly be.

And then I prayed—sincerely—for Camellia and her ma and pa. I prayed that God would help them to understand how much He loved them and how sad He was that they couldn't believe in Him. I prayed for Mrs. Foggelson in another way—that she might have the courage to come back to her faith.

I even prayed for Jack Berry. Not because I *should*, but because I really wanted to. All of a sudden, I felt so sorry for Jack. He had hated school, but his pa had insisted he be a doctor. He had even been tricked out of the camping trip, and he had wanted to go as much as any one of us. He had liked Camellia, but that hadn't worked for him either. He had wanted to do great things and prove himself important, and here he was, alone, in some musty jail somewhere, no one able to visit him or even caring much that he was there. I really felt sorry for Jack Berry.

I can at least write to him, I decided. Maybe if he knew I wasn't out to get him, we could be friends again. And maybe he'd believe me when I told him about God's love.

And then I prayed for my family. The sad news would need to be taken to Aunt Lou, and I knew how much she had loved Gramps. Uncle Nat would need to conduct the funeral service, and that would be awfully hard for him. He had loved Gramps, too.

And Uncle Charlie and my grandpa—they would hurt something awful. We had all grown to need Gramps among us. He had been a strength, a source of laughter. We sure were going to miss him.

I got up and washed my face again. The shadow moved. I spoke out loud.

"It's all right. You're safe, ol' northern. I'm gonna leave you there. For Gramps. He shoulda caught you. You know how excited he woulda been to have landed you? He'd a shouted all the way back to the house."

I couldn't help but laugh just thinking about it. The laughter surprised me.

And then I turned my face heavenward and laughed again. How could one feel joy and sorrow at the same time? Yet I did. I felt good inside—clean and good. And yet I hurt. Oh, I hurt bad. I was smart enough to know I would hurt for a long time to come. I just couldn't think of life without Gramps. But I wouldn't grieve. For his sake, I wouldn't grieve because he had asked me not to, because he was now in heaven where he longed to be. I loved him so much that I'd let him go.

I turned my steps homeward. A feeling of peace stole over me. Maybe that was what Aunt Lou had tried to tell me about. God's love. God's love there to hold me when I needed His comfort so much.

I took a deep breath. It was strange. The whole thing was strange. I had nearly thrown away my faith when I had lost someone that I loved—and here, at the loss of someone else I loved, I had had it restored again.

" 'God works in mysterious ways,' " I repeated to myself. I had heard Uncle Nat say those words, but I'd never really understood them before.

And then I looked at the sky above me, a soft blue with puffy little clouds drifting carelessly toward the south. The trees along the path seemed to whisper little secrets as the wind gently rustled the leaves. Early fall flowers were blooming under the branches, spreading their fragrance to make the woods a sweetly scented place to be.

I looked back at the sky, much as Gramps had done such a short time before, and repeated the words I had heard Gramps say on that day—for both of us, "Ah, summer. In summer it seems God is closer to earth than any other time of year."

I wouldn't argue with Gramps. God did seem close to the earth that summer as Gramps and I had shared our fishing trips and our chats. Summer would always be more special to me now, too.

But I had always been rather partial to the autumn. I looked about me. Already the leaves were subtly changing color, and just beyond the trees I could hear the neighbor men busily working in their wheat field. I loved autumn—and harvest.

My time of walking the path to the crik with Gramps was over. I would miss it. I would miss him! But somehow my life would go on. Gramps' life would go on, too. He was just living in a different home now, that was all. It was not the end. It was really a beginning. A new beginning for both of us.

Winter Is
Not Forever

Dedicated
to the memory of Amanda Janette,
our third grandchild,
daughter of Terry and Barbara,
and baby sister of Ashley,
who came to join our family
on June 25, 1987,
and completed her brief mission
on September 10, 1987,
taken from us suddenly by crib death.
She was such a healthy, happy,
responsive little sweetheart!
We loved her dearly and miss her greatly.
And to Amanda's grandparents
Koert and Carol Dieterman
and all readers
who have suffered through like pain.
Our loving and faithful God wipes our tears,
mends our broken hearts, and heaven
becomes a dearer place.

"For where the treasure is,
there will the heart be also."

CONTENTS

CHARACTERS

Joshua Chadwick Jones—Josh was raised by his grandfather, great uncle and young aunt after his own parents were killed in an accident when he was only a baby. Once Josh reached his late teens, he lived with his Aunt Lou and her preacher husband, Nat Crawford, and went to school in town. On the weekends he returned to the farm to spend time with the menfolk.

Lou Jones Crawford—Though she was his aunt, Lou was only a few years older than Josh. Now Lou is a parson's wife and anxious to be a mother after losing her first child at birth.

Grandpa—The owner of the farm where Josh grew up and the only father Josh has known.

Uncle Charlie—The quiet yet supportive brother of Grandpa. For many years they have run the farm and the household together.

Willie—Josh's boyhood friend. They shared many adventures and a strong personal commitment to their faith.

Camellia—Josh's first love, though he soon realized that his faith and her faithlessness were not compatible.

Mr. and Mrs. Foggelson—Camellia's mother and father. He was the local schoolmaster and raised concerns with his teaching of evolution. She had been a Christian until her marriage.

CHAPTER 1

Decisions

"Have you decided yet?"

Willie's insistent voice demanded my attention. I swiveled around to get a look at him, for the words didn't make any sense to me at all.

"What do you plan to do—after graduation?" he prodded. "Are you gonna be a minister—or what?"

Or what? my mind echoed in frustration. *What?*

I had been asking myself the same question over and over, just as Willie was asking me now. And I still didn't have an answer. Graduation was only a month away, and it seemed that I was the only one in our small town school who didn't know exactly what to do with life after the big day. It wasn't that I hadn't given it a thought. In fact, I thought about it most of the time. I prayed about it, too, and my family members kept assuring me that they were praying as well. But I still didn't have an answer to Willie's question, except to say honestly, "No—I don't know yet." And I'd been saying that for a long, long time.

I must have been frowning, and I guess Willie understood my dilemma. He didn't wait for my answer—not in words, anyway; instead he went right on talking.

"God has different timing for different people, and with a reason," he mused. "That doesn't mean that He hasn't got your future planned out. When it's time—"

I quit listening for a minute, and my mind jumped to other things. Willie already had his future clearly mapped out. God had called him to be a missionary; Willie would leave for a Bible school in the Eastern United States at the end of the summer. I envied Willie, I guess. "It must be a real relief to know what God wants you to do," I muttered under my breath.

"I still can't believe it," Willie was saying when I tuned back in. "I mean, most of my life—at least what I can remember of it—I've been goin' to school, day after day. And here we are about to graduate. I just can't believe it! It doesn't seem real to me yet."

I twitched my fishing pole as if I were trying to stir up some fish. Actually I was just thinking about Willie's words. It did seem strange. We had done a great deal of talking over the years about how glad we would be to graduate and leave the old school behind, and here we were on the brink of graduation and I didn't really feel glad about it at all. In fact, I felt rather scared. I never would have dared to tell any of the fellas how I was feeling— we always crowed about the day that we'd be freed from "prison." We'd run and holler and toss our caps in the air. I knew we'd have to do it to carry on the tradition. A fella was supposed to loathe school and be more than glad to be rid of it, but at the same time I got a funny feeling down in the pit of my stomach whenever I thought about graduation.

I mulled over Willie's words and squirmed on the creek bank, pretending to have a kink in my back from sitting in one spot for so long waiting on a fish to decide he was hungry. I wiggled my pole again and noticed that I'd lost the bait off the hook. I hoped Willie didn't notice. I didn't feel much like fishing anymore and I didn't want to be bothered with baiting my hook again. Still, I wasn't ready to head for the house yet, either.

I couldn't remember much about life without school, just like Willie had said. When I was honest with myself, I knew I'd miss the daily lessons, the recesses, the access to books. Maybe I'd miss it a whole lot, but I wasn't about to share my thoughts with anyone—not even Willie.

'Course, Willie needn't worry, I reminded myself, almost enviously. *Come fall, he'll be off to a new school, new books, and new friends.* I squirmed again.

"Here," said Willie, "lean against this stump for a while."

"Naw," I responded slowly, casting a glance at the sky. "It's almost time for chores anyway. And the fish sure aren't bitin' today."

Willie's eyes twinkled the way they did when he was trying to hold back something that made him want to laugh. I had seen the same look on his face when our teacher held his book upside down when lecturing to the class, and when Agatha Marshall took a bite of her sandwich and ate the ant that had been crawling on it, and when we tied Avery's shoelaces together as he lounged on the school grass waiting for the bell to ring.

I looked at Willie suspiciously now.

"Never seen fish bite without bait, Josh," he said, the twinkle openly showing in a grin now. "You haven't had bait on that hook for the last half hour," Willie informed me with a chuckle.

"So why didn't you tell me?" I threw at him, trying to sound miffed.

Willie sobered. "Didn't think you cared about fishin'. Your thoughts have been off someplace else all day."

I jerked up my empty hook and set about wiping it carefully on the grass and removing it from the line. Willie let me work in silence until I had finished with my fishing gear.

"You still bothered about Camellia?" he finally ventured as we picked up our gear and started down the trail to the farm.

"Camellia?" My head swung up at her name.

Willie held my eyes with a steady gaze. The question was still there, unanswered. I couldn't hide much from him, and I sure did need someone to talk to. I decided to stop playing games.

"I guess so—a little. I mean, here we are, almost finished with school— and I've been praying and praying, and trying an' trying to show Camellia that the Bible is right, no matter what her pa says, an' she still won't even listen to a thing I have to say. She'll be done with school, too, Willie, and then she plans to move off somewhere and take some training to be a decorator—"

"Interior designer," Willie corrected.

"Interior designer," I amended with a shrug. "Who knows who she'll meet or what she'll get herself into in some god-forsaken city somewhere—"

"New York," said Willie. "Her pa says New York. If you wanta learn from the best, then you need to go to New York."

"New York? That's even worse than I thought!" I raged. "That's about as wicked a city as there is."

Willie just nodded his head solemnly.

We trudged on in silence, me wrestling with the idea of Camellia alone in a city like New York. Then Willie cut into my thoughts again.

"You still care about her, Josh?"

For some reason the question caught me wrong. Of course I cared about Camellia! She was a friend, wasn't she? And we were commanded to care about—or love—everyone, weren't we? Willie knew the Bible as well as I did. He knew I was supposed to care about Camellia.

"That's a dumb question!" I threw at Willie. "We're *supposed* to care. I've been praying for Camellia for years now—Nat and Lou have been praying, too. We all—"

"That's not what I mean, Josh, an' you know it," Willie cut in. "Do you still like Camellia?"

I wasn't prepared to answer that. In the first place I didn't see that it was any of Willie's business, even if he was my friend. In the second place, though I didn't want to think about it at the moment, I wasn't sure of the answer myself. Did I still care for Camellia—as a girl, not as just a human? I had given up any special friendship with Camellia because she and I did not have the same spiritual values. In fact, Camellia declared that anything to do with religion was silly and superstitious. She didn't even believe that God existed, she said. Religion was a crutch for insecure people. But I believed with all my heart that God not only existed but had sent His Son to die for *me*, for my wrongdoings, and that He had a special plan for my life. How could I even consider a special relationship with Camellia? I couldn't, I knew, but I kept hoping and praying that Camellia would become a believer and then—then—Now, here we were at school's end, and still Camellia would not even listen to my side of the argument. There was more than one reason why graduation bothered me.

Willie did not pursue the question.

"Are you coming to town for the social tomorrow night?" he asked.

It was a church social—one of the few activities meant just for our age group, and they were always fun. Aunt Lou and Uncle Nat saw to that. Several teenagers from town had started coming to church as a result of the socials that Uncle Nat organized. Most of the young people eagerly anticipated the monthly socials, and I enjoyed them, too. At any other time I would have answered Willie with an enthusiastic, "Sure, I'll be there," but instead I mumbled, "I'll see."

"Well, sure hope you can make it." Willie shifted his pole and the one fish he had caught into his left hand so he'd have his right one free to untie his horse from the hitching rail.

I hadn't been very good company, and suddenly I felt ashamed because of it. It wasn't Willie's fault that Camellia still wasn't a believer, and it wasn't Willie's fault that I still didn't know what God wanted me to do with my life, and it wasn't Willie's fault that graduation was quickly approaching with its unsettled questions. Willie had no more control of the ticking clock than I did. I had no right to be owly and disagreeable with Willie.

I tried hard to shift my troubled thoughts to the back of my mind and bid my friend the kind of goodbye he deserved.

"Thanks, Willie," I said, and then didn't quite know how to finish. "Thanks for coming out."

I saw the twinkle in Willie's eye again.

"Sorry the fish weren't biting."

"Next time I might even try using a little bait," I teased back. "Though at least now I don't have fish to clean and can loaf a bit before chorin.'"

Willie looked down at the one fish that dangled beside his saddle. A mock frown crossed his face.

"I think I might just stop off and present a fish to Mary Turley," he said, "and invite her to the social tomorrow night." I wasn't sure if Willie was serious or not.

We both laughed and Willie moved his horse off down the lane.

"See you tomorrow night, Josh," he called back to me.

I answered as he knew I would. "I'll be there."

CHAPTER 2

The Social

That next night I hurried through my chores and ran for my bedroom to bathe and change. After adjusting my tie and slicking down my hair, I picked up my jacket and started down the stairs, avoiding the step with the worst creak.

"Big night tonight, Boy?"

The question came from Grandpa. He and Uncle Charlie were sitting at the kitchen table going over some farm bills together.

I grinned. I guess the night was no bigger than any other social night, but it still was pretty special to me. I nodded.

"Nat says the Youth Group is really growin'," continued Grandpa.

I nodded again, then added, " 'Bout twenty of us now."

"That's good," said Grandpa. "Any of the new ones comin' to church too?"

"Yeah, three of 'em are."

"Good!" said Grandpa again.

Uncle Charlie took a gulp of coffee and let the legs of his chair hit the worn kitchen linoleum with a dull thud. He looked me over carefully, from the crease in my best pants to the straight part of my hair. Then he nodded, as though I passed inspection.

"Enjoy youth, Joshua," Grandpa said. "The cares of adulthood will be upon ya soon enough."

I couldn't help but smile. Grandpa knew little about *youth*. If he thought that I wouldn't have any worries or concerns until I stepped out into the adult world, he was all wrong. Or he had forgotten. He had no idea about the things I had been grappling with lately. But I let it pass as though the only thought in my mind was a night of games and singing, followed by some of Lou's punch and cake. But at Grandpa's words I could feel my mood change somewhat. I wasn't in quite the same hurry that I had been a few minutes before.

Uncle Charlie's sharp eyes were on me again. He was searching for something, I knew. I mustered a grin and moved out of his range. I didn't want to be answering any questions. Not that Uncle Charlie would ask—not outright, anyway—but I felt the probing and had always squirmed some under it.

"I shouldn't be too late," I said as a parting remark of some kind. They knew I'd come straight home as soon as the social was over, and that it would be well chaperoned by Uncle Nat and Aunt Lou.

"Take yer time. Have fun," Grandpa responded.

The thought of Aunt Lou filled me with a bit of concern. Her baby was due in a couple of weeks, and after what had happened with her first baby I was uneasy about her. Over and over she assured me that there was no need to worry. She had lost little Amanda because she had had the measles during the pregnancy. Aunt Lou had been the picture of health all through this one. Doc had told her over and over that the baby seemed healthy and energetic. He was predicting a strong baby boy, but Aunt Lou still had her heart set on another daughter, and I guess I secretly hoped for a girl, too.

In the barn I was greeted by Chester, the beautiful bay that Grandpa and Uncle Charlie had surprised me with on my last birthday. I still couldn't believe that such a horse was really mine. I patted his shining round rump and reached for the saddle. He nickered at me and rubbed his nose against my chest looking for a treat from my pocket.

"Cut that out," I scolded him. "You'll mess my Sunday clothes!" But he didn't care about that; he went right on sniffing and blowing. I moved so he couldn't reach me and smoothed the blanket for the saddle.

I walked Chester out of the barn, closed the door securely, and mounted. Chester was eager to be on the road, even if I had forgotten to bring him his sugar lump or bit of apple. I had to rein him in to keep him from leaving the farmyard on a dead run. Grandpa didn't take too kindly to running animals, but it sure was tempting when I was up on Chester. He loved to run, and his strong legs and smooth body fairly trembled with excitement whenever he was turned toward the road.

It was a warm spring night. The sun was still lighting my way, but I knew that by the time I returned home it would be dark. Chester could find his way back to his stall in total darkness if need be, but it would be nicer traveling by moonlight. Only a few carelessly drifting clouds crossed the sky; the moon should give some light later on.

My thoughts turned back to the social, and I wondered if there would be any new young people there. Wouldn't it be something if Camellia decided to come! *Maybe if more of the girls her age . . .* I thought. But there were several girls Camellia's age who attended, and that had never influenced her before. Nothing, in fact, seemed to influence Camellia in favor of coming to church.

As I began going over the list of who might be in attendance, my eagerness to get there increased. Chester must have sensed my feelings, for before I knew it we were racing down the dusty road at a reckless pace. I reined Chester in, and he snorted in disgust. He tossed his head and pranced along the roadway, fighting against the bit while I busied myself trying to brush the dust from my dress clothes.

In spite of my intentions to be there early, young people were already milling about when I entered the churchyard. I tied Chester securely and called out hellos as I hurried to the parsonage to see if I could help Aunt Lou with any last-minute preparations.

"Josh!" she called out excitedly. "Good to see you! How are things at the farm?"

Aunt Lou always greeted me as though we hadn't seen one another for months, when the fact was that I had left town to stay at the farm only the day before.

"Fine," I responded. "Just fine. How are you?"

Aunt Lou looked down at her expanding front. She placed a hand tenderly on the growing baby and smiled at me.

"We are both just fine, aren't we, honey?" she said to her unborn child.

I smiled. Aunt Lou talked to her baby all the time. I was used to it by now. And she did look fine—her eyes shone and her cheeks glowed.

"Is there anything I can do to help?" I asked.

"Everything is already done. Nat is over at the church and we carried all of the refreshments over earlier."

"I'm sorry I was so late—" I began, but Aunt Lou stopped me.

"You're not late. Everyone else is just early. Impatient to get started, I guess. My, how this group has grown! I hardly know how much food to fix anymore."

I could tell by the smile on Aunt Lou's face that she was pleased to have such a problem.

We walked the short distance across the churchyard together. Other young people were arriving, calling excitedly back and forth.

I was lounging on the outside steps talking to some of the fellas when a rig rounded the corner and headed our way. At first I thought it must be someone new, and then I recognized Willie. Willie never drove; he always rode horseback, same as me. It *was* Willie, all right—and he wasn't alone, either.

For a moment none of us spoke. We just stood there gawking as Willie climbed down and tied the horse, and then reached a hand up to help a girl step down. She was wearing a full-skirted pink dress and she had her hair piled up on her head with little curls spilling down here and there. She looked familiar, yet I couldn't place her. Willie had tied his horse some distance away from the steps where we waited. We all stood there, straining to figure out who Willie was with.

"By jingo!" hissed Tom Newton, "it's Mary Turley—an' all dolled up, too."

It can't be, I thought. *Surely he wasn't serious!* But, sure enough, there was ol' Willie leading Mary Turley up the walkway to the church.

I wanted to laugh, to howl at Willie. My first impulse was to slap him on the back and tease him some, but I didn't. I stood there quietly and watched.

Mary had certainly changed! And so had Willie—he was so spiffed up and shining I scarcely knew him. And he seemed so gentlemanly and grown-up too. All of us were put to silence by it all, and I bet other fellas besides me were wondering why we hadn't thought of inviting Mary ourselves.

Mary smiled shyly at us as she brushed by, and Willie gave me just the slightest wink. I was sure no one else had seen it, but I caught it, just as I caught that twinkle in his eye.

Avery gave me a hard jab in the ribs that made me gasp for air, and then we all shuffled and moved on the steps and made an about-face as we followed Willie and Mary into the church.

We found some places to sit. As usual, the girls sorta lined up in the seats on the south side of the building and the fellas took the seats on the north. All except Willie, that is. He seated Mary alongside Martha Ingrim, but instead of coming over to the boys, he sat down right beside her!

Uncle Nat took charge of the meeting, calling it to order by welcoming everyone and having first-timers introduced. There was another new girl from town too, but she had come with Thelma and Virginia Brown, so none of us paid much attention.

Then Willie introduced Mary. He spoke clearly and without embarrassment. I couldn't help but marvel at the way he handled it.

"This is Mary Turley," he said. "Mary lives out our way. We—Josh and I, and several others here—went to school with Mary for a number of years."

As we played some games, there was some mixing up of the seating, and Willie and Mary got separated. But Mary seemed to be having a good time. I was glad to see that she felt at home among us.

I had always thought of Mary as a plain girl, and maybe she really was, but tonight she was pretty in her own way. She had a smile that drew smiles in return, and her eyes were deep and intense. Her manner kept my eyes wandering back to her. She seemed so grown-up and self-assured compared to most of the girls I knew.

And then I remembered why I hadn't seen much of Mary for the last several years. Her ma had been sick, and Mary had needed to take over the running of the household and the cooking of the meals. She hadn't been able to go on to school in town like she had wanted to. I hadn't given it much thought when I heard about it. But now, looking at Mary, I realized she had likely done more growing up than the rest of us who hadn't borne similar responsibilities.

Not at all somber or morose, she laughed and enjoyed the games as much as anyone at the social, but she did carry the air of one who had learned a good measure of self-assurance.

After the games were over, Uncle Nat brought out his guitar and we gathered in a circle and sang every hymn we knew by heart. Mary didn't seem to know many of the words, but she listened in appreciation and once or twice I noticed her small foot tapping in time with the music. Though I wasn't sitting close enough to her to be sure, I had the feeling that she was humming right along.

When Aunt Lou served refreshments, Mary volunteered her help. I was busy pouring the punch, so we exchanged a few pleasantries. I asked about her ma, feeling apologetic that I hadn't taken more of an interest sooner. Mary smiled when she told me that her ma was much better—even able to be back in her own kitchen again.

I thought of Mrs. Turley and that big kitchen. I well remembered the day that Willie, Avery, and I stopped by on the way back from our hike along the creek. We were half-starved, and Mrs. Turley's well-stocked kitchen had about saved our lives. I remembered Mary too, a rather gangly, freckle-faced girl at the time. I never would have dreamed that she would become the well-poised young lady that I saw before me now.

"I'm glad about your ma," I assured her.

"Me, too," said Mary. "It was hard to see her so sick."

There was no mention about the hard years that she had put in being housekeeper and nursemaid. She just seemed to have a sincere appreciation that her ma was feeling better.

"Maybe you can come to our next social," I dared venture.

"I'd love to," responded Mary and I could tell by her shining eyes that she really meant it. I wanted Mary to be a part of our Youth Group. I wanted her to feel welcome. Yet she really wasn't a believer, and I couldn't help but question Willie's actions. Here he was courting a girl who was not a Christian, and I—I had to give up my relationship with Camellia for that very reason. It didn't seem fair somehow, and yet I had no doubts about Willie and his commitment to his faith. Still—was Willie taking chances going out with a non-Christian girl? My line of reasoning directed my thoughts to Camellia and they lingered there, remembering her sparkling eyes, her long, burnished tresses. She was the prettiest girl I had ever seen. *If only*—but my thoughts were interrupted by Aunt Lou's call for me to refill the punch glasses.

CHAPTER 3

Great News

All the next week we had glorious spring weather, and folks began talking about spring fever. I don't know exactly what kind of fever hit me, but I had an awful time concentrating on my studies.

Final exams were just a few weeks away, and our grades on those finals could have a great deal to do with our being accepted into college. Maybe that was why I was having such a difficult time. Most of the others already had a college picked and a vocation to pursue as well. Daily, it seemed, someone asked me, "What are your plans, Josh?" and I would mumble, red-faced, that I still hadn't decided for sure.

For sure? That made it sound like I had several considerations. The truth was, I was about as far from knowing what the future held for me as I had been on the first day I climbed the steps of the schoolhouse.

I avoided folks as much as I could. I didn't want to answer any questions when I still didn't really have an answer.

As a result, I hung around home a lot. I pretended to be studying, and Aunt Lou and Uncle Nat certainly approved of that. I was trying, but my mind just didn't seem to want to stay with the books.

On one particularly lovely spring evening, when the fragrant smell of early spring blossoms wafted in my open window, making it even more difficult to concentrate, I sat at my small desk trying hard to think through the math computations before me, but my mind refused to deal with the equations.

My thoughts insisted on flitting about. Graduation was getting nearer with each passing day. I thought of my future still unplanned, as far as I could see. I thought of Camellia and her intention to leave for distant New York and her training in Interior Design. How would she ever manage in such a big, indifferent city? How could her father sanction such a venture?

The soft spring breeze brought a fresh whisper of fragrance to my nose and reminded me of the roses along the creek bank every springtime. I could picture the young blades of greenery poking their slim heads through the soil. I could almost smell the freshness of the gently flowing water and hear the splash of a fish breaking the surface to snatch at a fly, then slip back into the coolness of the stream again.

The call of the creek turned my thoughts to Gramps. I still hadn't gotten used to his being gone. Each time that I went home to the farm I found myself searching for signs of him. The empty chair at the table looked too forlorn, the place where his worn farm sweater had hung looked bare and dejected, the padded chair by the well-lit kitchen window where he sat to read his Bible and work his crossword puzzles looked far too lonely.

I wouldn't have wished him back; I knew that. He had gone to a far better place than his dwelling here had been. But even that thought did not erase the ache I carried around with me.

Even though I stayed here in town during the week with Aunt Lou and Uncle Nat, I loved the farm. I loved the soil. I treasured the spot that held my roots buried so deeply. I loved the springtime and the planting of the seeds. I loved the summer as we watched the green begin to appear and then mature as the weeks passed by. I loved the autumn, when it was so evident that God was good and was again supplying the needs of His people.

Even the winter months were enjoyable. I loved the frosty mornings when the steam rose from the pail of warm milk I carried from the barn to the house. I loved the smell of the warm straw I spread out to bed down Bossie or one of her stallmates. I loved the soft mewing of the barn cats as they coaxed for their morning breakfast of warm, fresh milk.

The farm was a good place to be. I guess I loved most everything about it.

And then I thought again of Grandpa and Uncle Charlie, and suddenly a new thought occurred to me. What would happen to the farm when they were no longer able to care for it? I had never thought about it before; I just assumed that they would always be there, farming, just like they had been doing ever since I could recollect. But of course they wouldn't. Couldn't. The quickly passing years were taking their toll on Grandpa and Uncle Charlie. They didn't walk as erectly or as quickly as they used to. Even I could see that. And Uncle Charlie seemed to be faring a bit worse than Grandpa. I had noticed it the last time we had chored together. He was getting much slower in movement than he used to be, even a bit clumsy with his hands. I'd had to undo the knot that tied the gunny sack of grain. He had tried but couldn't manage it.

The thought of Uncle Charlie and Grandpa no longer able to carry on the farming made me restless and uneasy. I couldn't imagine life without the farm. It didn't matter if God called me to be a preacher in some far-off city or even a missionary, like Willie, to some distant land, I still wanted to think of the farm as home. I still wanted to be able to visit it when I had opportunity, to bring my family, if I ever had one, to feel the kinship with the soil and to watch things grow. I felt that my roots would always be there in that land that Grandpa had tilled ever since I could remember. To sever those roots would in some way be losing a part of me.

My reverie was interrupted by a soft whine under my feet. "Pixie!" I said. "I didn't know you were here. I haven't been paying much attention to you, have I, girl?" The little dog wagged her tail happily and jumped into my lap. I snapped shut my math book and pushed it aside. I couldn't study now. I needed a break. Pixie jumped down as I stood and stretched. "Maybe I'll go to the kitchen for some of Aunt Lou's cookies and a glass of milk." I was about to leave the room when I sensed more than I actually heard a strange commotion in the kitchen.

It wasn't loud and it wasn't hasty. It was just different somehow. I listened more carefully; for a time I heard nothing. Pixie ran to the door and barked softly; then I heard the quick, quiet step of Uncle Nat approaching my door. I stood motionless, my hand going up to push back the hair that flopped over my forehead.

Uncle Nat didn't even knock. He opened the door gently and poked in his head. He was wearing his hat, something that Uncle Nat didn't usually do in the house.

"Lou says it's time, Josh," he said in almost a whisper. "I'm going for Doc."

My mouth went dry and my breath seemed to catch in my chest. *It was time.* The very thought sent a shiver of fear running all through me. I had known all along that we would face this eventually, yet I still wasn't prepared.

For some reason the little unknown somebody that Aunt Lou had been carrying had seemed so safe and protected as long as her body enclosed it. But now it was time for this baby to enter the world—a world where sickness and dangers abounded. Would the little one make it? To face the loss of another baby would be too much for any of us to bear.

I wanted to run to Aunt Lou to assure myself that she was all right, but my feet refused to move. I tried swallowing, but my mouth was too dry. I felt like urging Uncle Nat to hurry, but I realized we had things rather backward.

"I'll run for Doc," I managed to say. "You stay with Aunt Lou."

Uncle Nat didn't argue. He stepped wordlessly aside so I could leave the room.

I was almost to the kitchen door before he called softly after me, "No need to run, Josh. Lou says there is lots of time."

I heard him, but I was already running by the time I had reached the back door. By the time I left the parsonage yard I was in full stride.

All the way to Doc's house I prayed urgently for Aunt Lou. I prayed for the new baby. I prayed that Doc wouldn't be out in the country somewhere on a house call.

By the time I reached Doc's front door I was breathing hard. I rapped loudly and stepped back to wait. I could hear movement inside, and that was encouraging. Doc answered the door himself and didn't even make a comment when he saw me standing there, my sides heaving from running. He just reached to the hat tree by the door to retrieve his hat and picked up his black bag from the small table, all in one motion, and called out to his wife that he would be at the parsonage, and we were gone.

We didn't run. Doc's slower pace frustrated me, and I found it hard to match his methodical stride, but I did try. We walked in silence until Doc seemed to feel I had enough breath to talk.

"When did the contractions start?" he asked me.

"I dunno," I admitted dumbly. "Uncle Nat just came to my room and said it's time."

"Did Lou have supper with you?" Doc asked further.

"She—she—" I thought back. "She was at table with us, but she didn't eat much. Just sorta pushed her food around on her plate."

I hadn't paid much attention to it at the time.

"She didn't say anything," I added.

"She wouldn't," commented Doc, and he picked up speed, for which I was thankful.

When we reached the house Uncle Nat was not there to greet us. Doc knew the way to the bedroom, so after letting him in, I knew there was little else that I could do—except keep praying.

The time dragged on forever. Or so it seemed. In reality I guess that things happened in good time and order. But for me, it seemed an eternity. I paced back and forth in the kitchen, and I paced back and forth on the porch, and I paced back and forth on the front board walk that led up to the small parsonage.

At last I heard the small, funny, squeaky cry of a newborn, and I knew it was finally over. I strained with my whole body to catch any further sounds. I guess I was listening for a cry from Aunt Lou. None came. And then I heard laughter and the voice of Uncle Nat raised in prayerful thanksgiving. I breathed again and ran toward the back entrance.

Uncle Nat met me in the kitchen, his face beaming. We didn't even speak to one another, just stopped long enough for a quick embrace and then hurried on to the bedroom. I suppose there were tears on both our cheeks, tears of relief and joy.

Doc was talking when I entered the room. I wasn't sure if he was talking to Aunt Lou or the tiny bundle he held in his big hands.

"Sure surprised me," he was saying. "I was looking for a big, bouncing boy, but just look at this young'un. Healthy and hearty as you please."

Lou was smiling a contented, love-filled smile. She still looked pale to me—but, oh, did she look happy!

Doc continued speaking to Aunt Lou. "You did a fine job, little lady—and just look at your reward. Beautiful baby. Just beautiful. Reminds me of her mamma when I delivered her some twenty-odd years ago."

The word *her* caught my attention. It was a girl! Aunt Lou's dream had come true and Doc's "big boy" had been a girl instead. I grinned and suddenly felt shy and awkward. I hung back a bit, not really knowing what to do or say. Aunt Lou sensed it immediately. She raised slightly from her pillows and held out her hand to me.

"Come see her, Josh," she encouraged. "Like Doc says, she's beautiful."

I moved slowly forward just as Doc reached down and laid the precious bundle in Aunt Lou's arms. The little face was red and wrinkled and her eyes were almost squinted shut. She had a thatch of dark hair that for the moment was plastered tightly to the well-shaped little head. She really wasn't all that beautiful, as Doc and Aunt Lou were insisting, but even I knew she was very special.

And then she waved a small fist frantically in the air and went searching for it with a puckered-up mouth. Miraculously, she managed to connect the two and began sucking noisily. We all laughed and Aunt Lou held her even closer and Uncle Nat's eyes filled with tears again. She *was* beautiful.

When Aunt Lou could speak again she looked down at her baby and then up at me. "Sarah Jane," she said, "meet your cousin, Joshua Jones. He's about the finest cousin a little girl could ever have. You're a lucky little girl, Sarah Jane—No, not lucky—blessed." Aunt Lou gave me one of her special smiles. I could feel the firm arm of Uncle Nat about my shoulders, and it gave me a warm family feeling.

I looked down again at the tiny bundle in Aunt Lou's arms. Since my own folks had died, Aunt Lou had been like a mother and aunt all rolled up in one. Now I had little Sarah Jane too. I might not be all that Aunt Lou had generously boasted me to be, but I knew one thing. I loved that little bundle with all of my being, and I knew instinctively that no harm would ever come to her that I had the power to stop.

CHAPTER 4

Sharing the News

"Somebody's gotta go to the farm!" I burst out excitedly, tearing my eyes from the baby and Aunt Lou to implore Uncle Nat.

"I guess that can wait 'til morning," Uncle Nat said, and I could see he wasn't too anxious to leave his wife and new daughter.

"Morning? This news will never keep until morning. And Grandpa and Uncle Charlie would never forgive us!"

"It's pretty late," Uncle Nat continued. He reached down to lift his pocket watch. "It's almost midnight." Then he spoke to brand-new little Sarah Jane. "You missed being born on your grandmother's birthday by about ten minutes, little one."

Uncle Nat didn't talk about his ma too often, but I could tell by his tone that he would have been real pleased if Sarah had prolonged her coming just a bit.

I wasn't put off by Uncle Nat's diversion.

"Midnight or not," I went on, "someone should go out to the farm. I can go. Chester could find his way even if it was pitch dark—and it's not. Looks really light out yet. Moon must be shining—"

"Well, Lou?" Uncle Nat asked. Lou just smiled and nodded. "Bring me a pen and the writing tablet," she said, and I knew it was decided that I could go.

Aunt Lou had to have her hands free to write, so Uncle Nat lifted the small bundle of baby from her arms and began pacing the floor with her, talking softly to her all the while. I didn't listen to what he said, but now and then I caught a word. He was already telling her about God. Imagine! A tiny tyke like that, and Uncle Nat was already preaching the little one her first sermon.

Aunt Lou found it a bit difficult to write, propped up on her pillows like she was. I guess she wanted to tell Grandpa and Uncle Charlie about the new baby herself, because she seemed to write on and on. I wondered how she could find so much to say about someone she had just met, so to speak.

At last she was done and folded that paper and handed it to me and laid the tablet and the pen on the small night table by her bed. She smiled again—that contented, happy smile—but I could see she was really tired.

A movement caused us all to look at the doorway. It was Doc. I had quite forgotten about him. Guess he had been in the kitchen having himself a cup of tea while we all got acquainted with Sarah Jane, and now he was back again to check everything one more time and tuck Aunt Lou and the baby in for the night. I kissed Aunt Lou on the cheek, took one more look at Sarah Jane to see if she had grown or changed any yet. I was always hearing ladies exclaim how quickly babies did that. But she looked just the same to me, only she had fallen asleep—right in the middle of Uncle Nat's sermon.

Chester seemed to sense my mood, and once we were on the road he was ready to run. I guess he thought that this time he might be able to get away with it. I didn't let him though, for even though there was a bit of a moon and even though his night-eyes were better than mine, I still knew it was unwise to let a horse travel at full gallop in the dark.

It seemed to take an especially long time to cover the distance to the farm. Normally I would let my mind wander to many things, but tonight I could only think of the new baby. Whole and well and brand new and Doc said that she was fine, just fine.

At last I reached the farm and was a bit surprised to see the house all dark. But I should have known it would be. Grandpa and Uncle Charlie went to bed somewhere around ten each night, and this night being no different than any other as far as they were concerned, they would have followed their usual pattern.

I argued briefly with myself as to whether to flip Chester's rein over the gate post and run in with the news or to take Chester to the barn—as would need to be done eventually anyway—and then go to the house. I decided to go ahead and bed Chester down. It was hard to make myself go to the barn first but I knew I would hate to come back out to care for Chester after I had delivered the good news.

Chester was glad to see his own stall. I didn't figure him to be too hungry, knowing that he had already been well fed, but I hurriedly forked him a bit of hay just in case he had a notion to eat. He started in on it right away.

I scarcely took the time to secure the barn door before I was off to the house on the run. It was a fair distance between the house and the barn—a fact I had never particularly noted before. I was puffing by the time I hit the back porch. The back door, as usual, was not locked. I wasn't sure my Grandpa could lock it even if he wanted to. I pushed it open and it squeaked just a bit.

I wanted to holler out my news, but my good sense held me in check. If I came in shouting I'd scare Grandpa and Uncle Charlie half to death.

I climbed the steps quickly, trying not to make too much noise. I never even thought about the squeaky one until I heard it protest beneath my foot.

"Who is it?" Grandpa called out.

"Me," I answered in a whispery voice.

I heard Uncle Charlie stirring, but the noise didn't come from his bed. He was sitting near his window in the old chair. I knew then that he had watched me ride into the yard, take Chester to the barn and run for the house.

For a moment I forgot about Grandpa, about Aunt Lou, even about the new baby.

"What are you doing up?" I quizzed Uncle Charlie.

"Nothin' much," he answered evasively. "Just can't git along with my bed sometimes."

Grandpa called out again, "Be right there." I could hear the bed springs groaning as he lifted himself from the bed and began to pull on his pants.

"I take it you have some news," Grandpa said as he came out of the bedroom, a lighted lamp in his hand.

"Sure do," I beamed, my thoughts jumping immediately back to Sarah Jane.

"Well?" prompted Uncle Charlie.

"Another girl," I fairly cheered. "And she is just fine."

"And Lou?" asked Grandpa. In his heart he knew that I wouldn't be grinning from ear to ear unless Aunt Lou was just fine, too. But Lou was his little girl, and Grandpa wouldn't be at ease until he heard it said.

"Fine!" I said. "Just fine—an' happy."

"Thank you, Father!" Grandpa said softly and I understood his little prayer of gratitude. Then he began to grin. I could see his face by the light of the lamp he held in his hand. He was beaming.

Uncle Charlie had moved to join us in the hallway. He was grinning too—a wide, infectious smile. He looked about the happiest I had ever seen him. But I was surprised at how slowly he moved. Grandpa turned to him with concern in his eyes and voice.

"Another bad night?" he asked, and Uncle Charlie nodded. I didn't understand the question—or the answer. Why was Uncle Charlie having bad nights? Why was he moving toward the stairs like an old man? Why did he reach out a hand to assist himself as he descended? I hadn't known about any of this. Why hadn't someone informed me?

"Was Doc there?" Uncle Charlie asked. He knew that sometimes Doc was out on one call when he was needed elsewhere.

"Got him myself," I explained. "He was right at home when I went for him."

"Was Nat there?" asked Grandpa, and I knew that Grandpa was thinking of the last time.

"All the time," I answered.

"Good!" said Grandpa, and he beamed some more as he set the lamp on the kitchen table.

Uncle Charlie shuffled to the stove, shook it up, and put in a few more sticks of wood. The stove had been banked for the night; before long the wood caught and I could hear the blaze grow. Uncle Charlie pushed forward the coffeepot.

"Tell us about her," Grandpa was saying, excitement filling his voice.

Uncle Charlie eased a chair toward the table and lowered himself slowly onto it. He leaned forward eagerly, not wanting to miss a word.

"She's not very big," I started, indicating with my hands, much as I often did when I told a fish story.

" 'Course not," cut in Grandpa.

"An' she—she—" How could I say that she was red and wrinkled and sort of puffy? Would they understand?

"Has she any hair?"

"Lots of it—dark."

"Just like Lou," cut in Grandpa.

"What color are her eyes?" Uncle Charlie asked.

"I—I—don't really know. She didn't open them much, but they are sorta dark, I guess."

"Did Doc say how much she weighs?"

I hadn't heard him say anything about her weight. I just shook my head.

"Tell us about Lou," Grandpa was prompting.

"Well—"

"Was it a long—?" began Grandpa again.

It had seemed half of forever to me, but I shrugged and said honestly, "Doc said it was real good. Real good. I went for him about quarter-to-nine and Sarah was born just before midnight."

Grandpa and Uncle Charlie exchanged grins and nods and I understood that they were well satisfied with that.

"But Aunt Lou says that she was having some—some—"

"Contractions."

"Yeah, from about one o'clock on. But they didn't get strong until about suppertime." I didn't want them to get the idea that it had been too easy.

"But she's fine now?" This was from Grandpa again.

"Just fine," I reassured him.

Uncle Charlie eased himself off his chair and went for the coffeepot. I wasn't sure that the coffee would be hot enough yet, but perhaps Uncle Charlie needed something to occupy his hands.

He poured three cups and brought two of them, a bit of steam rising from each, to the table. He passed one cup to Grandpa and put one down in front of me. It was the first time I noticed that his fingers looked funny. I was about to ask if he had hurt his hand when I noticed that the other hand looked the same way. I shut my mouth quickly on the unasked question and looked at Grandpa, but he didn't seem to read the question in my eyes. I guess he was still too busy celebrating his new granddaughter.

"Her name," he said suddenly. "You haven't told us her name."

"It's Sarah," I told him. "Sarah Jane."

"That's nice," said Grandpa, and Uncle Charlie, who was just returning to the table with his own cup of coffee, repeated the name after me. "Sarah Jane," he said, "Sarah Jane. That's nice."

I suddenly remembered Aunt Lou's letter. I fished it from my pocket and handed it to Grandpa. He opened it eagerly and began to read it aloud to Uncle Charlie. There wasn't much more for me to say about little Sarah Jane. Aunt Lou was saying it all.

We sat and drank our coffee and chatted some more about the new baby and Aunt Lou and Uncle Nat. But watching Uncle Charlie's clumsy fingers try to lift the coffee cup to his mouth took some of the joy out of the event for me. He spilled a bit as he tried to drink. I noticed the dark liquid dribble over his fingers more than once as he raised the cup to his mouth. Maybe this was why Uncle Charlie didn't let the coffee get as steaming hot as he used to.

I thought of all the times I had watched Uncle Charlie lift the cup to his lips and take a full gulp of steaming hot coffee and somehow manage to swallow it with no harm done. But he had steady hands then. Not gnarled fingers that couldn't grip things tightly.

"I'm pretty tired I guess," I finally excused myself. "Think I'll go on up to bed."

Grandpa was still grinning but he stifled a yawn. "Me, too," he said and reached for the lamp.

"You two go ahead," Uncle Charlie waved us on. "I think I'll just sit here for a bit longer. Maybe have another cup."

I looked at Grandpa.

"Did you take one of the pills?" he asked.

Uncle Charlie nodded.

"Still no relief?"

"Some." Both Grandpa and I knew that Uncle Charlie wasn't admitting to much.

Grandpa left the lamp on the table and we climbed the stairs without it.

When we got up to the hallway I reached out a hand to Grandpa.

"What is it?" I asked in a whisper.

Grandpa didn't seem to understand my question.

"What's the matter with Uncle Charlie?" I asked then.

"What do you mean?"

"His hands—all—all twisted, and his walk so slow and—"

"Oh, that," responded Grandpa matter-of-factly. "That's just his arthritis. It's gettin' worse."

Arthritis! Worse! How come I'd never noticed it before?

"How long—how long has he been this way?" I found myself asking.

"He's had arthritis some for years," Grandpa responded. "But he has his good days and his bad days. Folks say the weather. It's steadily getting worse, though. It's really into his hands bad now. Used to just be in his knees and his back."

There wasn't much that I could say, so I let Grandpa go. "See you in the morning," I muttered and turned to my bedroom.

I lay awake a long time that night—thinking of more than our new Sarah Jane. I thought a great deal about Uncle Charlie. It scared me, this arthritis. Already it had made him into an old man. It had happened so gradually that I had missed it.

But not now. Now it was very obvious. Uncle Charlie was not a complainer, but it was easy to see that even small tasks were hard for him to accomplish. And how could he ever farm?

I fought for sleep, both to escape my uneasy thoughts and because I knew I would need it. Grandpa had said that we would leave for town just as soon as we could finish up the chores the next morning, and I knew without asking that Grandpa would start those chores a little earlier than usual.

Even so, it was a long time until I could lay aside my excitement—and my worry—and let sleep claim me.

CHAPTER 5

Graduation

It took several days for things to fall back into a normal routine. Grandpa and Uncle Charlie visited the parsonage with far more frequency than usual. I think they were a little afraid that young Sarah Jane might grow up when they weren't looking. Anyway, they came in often to check on her.

Sarah Jane greatly changed the procedures of the household. Aunt Lou didn't seem to get as much baking done as she used to, and both Uncle Nat and I found ourselves helping around the house more. That baby was either hungry or wet every five minutes.

She was a good little tyke, though. Lou kept telling Uncle Nat and me over and over what a good baby she was, and I was quite willing to take Aunt Lou's word for it. She certainly did a great deal of sleeping. Whenever I brought one of my friends in for a peek at her she was either sleeping or eating, it seemed to me, and neither one worked too well for showing her off.

She very quickly lost her redness and her wrinkles, and soon she had a soft, pinkish look and a little round head capped with dark downy hair. She opened her eyes more, too; often she would lie in my arms and look at my face as if she knew just who I was and how I fit into her life. I loved it when she looked at me that way; if no one was close enough to hear, I'd talk to her and tell her things about myself so that she really would know me. We all adored her—after all, we all loved Lou, and had waited for this special baby for a long time.

I expected that now it would be even harder to study, and in some ways it was. But suddenly it became very important for me to get good grades as I left the school system and went out into the world. I wouldn't have admitted it to a soul, but I didn't want Sarah to ever have reason to be ashamed of me. So I pitched into those textbooks like I'd never done in my whole life—and it worked, too. I ended up with the best set of marks I had ever gotten.

Willie dropped by now and then. Sometimes we studied together, and we played with Sarah, but mostly we just took a break from our books and talked. One Thursday afternoon he tapped on my window, and I could tell just by looking that he was really excited about something. I pushed back my Advanced Speller and opened the window.

"Is Sarah sleepin'?" Willie asked.

I nodded.

"Then come out." Willie didn't want to take any chances on his excitement waking the baby.

I eased the window back down quietly and headed for the back door.

"What is it?" I asked as soon as I was clear of the kitchen.

"Mary," beamed Willie. "She became a Christian."

Now I knew why Willie was excited. I was excited, too. We gave each other a big hug, pounding one another on the back. Mary had been coming to church every Sunday since she had been to the Youth Group with Willie.

"When?" I asked when I could speak.

"Just this afternoon. I came to tell you just as soon as I could."

I slapped Willie on the back again. I couldn't help but think how happy I would feel if I had the same good news about Camellia.

"That's great!" I said. "Just great."

Afraid that my tears might show, I pulled away and headed for the backyard swing that Uncle Charlie had built for Lou. Willie followed me without a word; I guess he knew I was feeling rather emotional.

Avoiding Willie's eyes, I gave a little push with one foot to start the swing in gentle motion and looked at it carefully like I had never done in the past. Uncle Charlie was skilled with simple tools. Each board was carefully fashioned and properly joined. The arm where my hand rested was polished smooth and shaped for comfort. I ran my hand idly over it, wondering if Uncle Charlie would ever be able to hold a hammer or a plane again. Then my thoughts jerked back to the present.

"What do her folks think?" I asked Willie.

"I don't know about her pa. He hasn't said much. But her ma says that it's Mary's decision and that she'll support her in her new faith. I think she wishes that she had the courage to make the commitment herself. She must have done a great deal of thinking when she was so ill."

"I suppose," I agreed.

"Mary is already praying for her ma. She says it's just a matter of time, she knows, until her ma will become a Christian too. She says she thinks that her ma has been searching for God for a long time, just hasn't known where or how to find Him. An' now that Mary knows, she can help her ma."

The excitement had grown in Willie's voice again. His eyes were shining.

"Josh," he said, "this is the first person that I have talked to about my faith, the first one to become a Christian because of it. It's—it's—well, it is the most exciting thing that has ever happened to me."

I had never had the experience myself, although I had tried—with Camellia, with her ma, even with Jack Berry in prison by letter after I finally forgave him. None of those had worked. I still prayed for all of them, though.

"Does Mary feel called to the mission field too?" I asked.

Willie looked just a bit puzzled.

"I dunno," he answered.

"Isn't that—isn't that pretty important?"

"Well, she needs to learn a bit more about being a Christian before she thinks about where God wants her, don't you think?"

"But you already know where God wants you," I pressed.

"So?" said Willie with a shrug.

"So it just might be important where He wants your girl."

"My girl?" Willie really seemed confused now.

"Mary!" I said impatiently to jog his failing memory. "The girl you just brought to the faith. Mary! If you are going to train to be a missionary, then perhaps it would be a bit handy if your girl would be one, too."

Willie looked dumbfounded.

"Mary isn't *my* girl," he said at last.

"What?"

"Where'd you ever get that idea?"

"From you," I said. "You brought her to Youth Group and you've been bringing her to church an' you—"

"But she's not my *girl*."

"Does Mary know that?" I threw back at Willie.

"Of course! We're just friends. Mary's understood that all along. We talked it over the first night I asked her to Youth Group."

"And you came together as *friends*?" It seemed preposterous to me. "You mean you brought her and talked to her and shared your faith, just as a friend? Not because you *liked* her?"

Willie shook his head as though he couldn't believe just how stupid I was.

"Josh, you don't just share your faith with girls you want to go out with." Willie couldn't hide his grin, even though he was a bit impatient with me. "I brought Mary to the Youth Group because she is a great girl, a good friend—one who has never really had a chance. She never attended church. Never got to spend time with those of us from the church. How else was she going to hear?"

"I just thought—" I interrupted. "Well, everyone thought that you liked Mary—special like."

"I couldn't court a non-Christian girl, and you know it, Josh. You know that God wants me to be a missionary. How could I be a missionary if I went and got sweet on a girl and married her and she didn't even share my faith? Why—"

"I had thought of it," I admitted. "It didn't make much sense to me either."

We sat in silence for a few minutes and then I dared to say, "Well, she's a Christian now, so if you decide you do like her—no problem."

Willie stepped from the swing, making it stop with a jarring movement. His hand reached up to smooth back his hair. I recognized the movement as one of exasperation.

"Okay, okay," I said quickly before Willie had a chance to speak. "So she stays a friend."

I got off the swing too and started back to the house.

"I guess I'd better get back to the books," I said defensively. "Only two more exams left."

Willie grinned. "I know. You want to get a 99 again."

I blushed.

"Where's it taking you, Josh?" asked Willie.

"What?" I stopped and eyed Willie.

"I shouldn't have asked it like that," continued Willie. "I didn't mean it to sound that way. I was just wondering if you knew something that you were holding back. Thought maybe you were trying for admittance in some super college where you needed great marks or somethin.'"

I shook my head. I hadn't even applied to any colleges.

"You still don't know?"

I shook my head again.

"I'll keep praying for you, Josh," Willie said, slapping my shoulder.

"Thanks." I headed back to my bedroom and the open textbook.

I envied Willie. He already knew exactly what God wanted for him. He had no problem figuring out what to do in order to prepare himself. He could just plunge right on, getting himself ready for the task.

When graduation finally did arrive, I felt all strange. On the one hand I was excited about having completed high school. There were some awfully nice and embarrassing things said about me at the ceremony, too. I noticed Aunt Lou straighten in her chair and slightly lift little Sarah Jane so that she wouldn't miss any of the compliments. I could see the grins on the faces of Grandpa and Uncle Charlie, too. Grandpa was fairly busting his buttons. So I felt a measure of honest pride myself.

On the other hand, I felt all empty inside. Here I was, finishing up my schooling without the faintest notion of what I was to do next with my life. As I already said, Willie was going off to train as a missionary; Camellia was going to New York; Janie and Charlotte were both setting out to be teachers; Avery was going to work with his pa; Polly was getting married—the list could go on and on. But Joshua Jones, head of the class, didn't have any idea of what he would do with all this education.

I still felt all mixed up when we got back to Aunt Lou's and she served punch and cake in my honor to a number of friends and our family. She bustled around, chatting about me as she served, and Grandpa boasted some and Uncle Charlie just sat in the corner, quietly rubbing his knotted hands together as he grinned my way now and then. I could see, even then, that Uncle Charlie's hands were giving him pain again, but he, as was his way, didn't make any mention of the fact.

Over and over the question of my plans came up. I brushed them aside with comments such as, I was still "sorting it through" or "looking at possibilities" or "waiting to make a decision." Grandpa and Aunt Lou strengthened my position—"Lots of time," they'd say, or, "Josh has too much at stake to decide hurriedly." It made it sound like I had all kinds of choices.

In our private conversations they had already informed me that I shouldn't rush into deciding, should take my time and consider carefully the field that I wanted to pursue or the job that I would consider of interest, as God directed me. I knew that they were all still praying. I knew that they were all behind me, but I was quite sure that none of them knew just how much the question of the future weighed on my mind.

"You can stay right here and find a job in town until you decide what God wants you to do," Aunt Lou assured me. "We won't need the bedroom for Sarah Jane for a long time yet."

And I guess that was what everyone expected me to do. I had already had offers to work in the hardware store and the print shop. I was deeply thankful for the opportunity of choice but neither job really appealed to me.

So this was *my* reception—*my* time of honor. People came and went, giving well-wishes and enjoying Aunt Lou's refreshments and the friendly conversation. There was talking and laughter and a great deal of commendation. I tried to be a part of it, but my eyes kept straying back to Uncle Charlie and his bent shoulders and gnarled hands.

Suddenly something became very clear to me. As soon as I could, I excused myself and went to my room. I began to pack my few belongings into my duffle bag. It was spring. Planting time. I could see by Uncle Charlie's hands that he was in no shape to hold the reins. Grandpa would never be able to do all the planting alone. They needed me at the farm. The sorting out of my future could wait for now. I inwardly thanked God for putting it off for a while. We could work it out later, the two of us; but for right now I had a job to do.

I hurried faster as I packed, the emptiness within me filling up with anticipation. I loved the farm. I'd plant this one crop before I moved on. There wasn't time now to get any other help for Grandpa, and he needed his crop. If I didn't help him, who would? Scripture did say, after all, that we are to honor our parents. Grandpa wasn't really my parent, but he was the only father I had ever known. I figured that was what God meant when He spoke the words.

I sure would miss Aunt Lou and Uncle Nat, and I would dearly miss little Sarah, but I'd be nearby and able to see them often. God could have asked me to go to some far-off college or to a job in some distant town. Then I wouldn't get to see them at all. This was better—much better, for now. The decision felt right to me; and I had the impression that God approved of it. I was glad that I would have this extra time with family.

It was quiet again when I came back out to the kitchen. Grandpa and Uncle Charlie were just getting ready to head for home. They looked a bit surprised to see me out of my Sunday suit and into my everyday clothes. They were even more surprised to see my duffle bag.

"Mind if I throw my things in the wagon?" I asked. "I'll ride Chester."

"Sure," said Grandpa agreeably. "You plannin' on doin' some of yer sortin' out at the farm, eh?"

"No sortin' to be done," I answered him evenly. "At least not for the time being. Right now we got a crop to plant, and I aim to help."

"But what about a job—the further education?" Grandpa puzzled.

"We'll handle all of that when the time comes," I answered confidently. And the funny thing was, I felt confident. Uncle Nat had continually been trying to tell me that God would lead me. He would show me what I needed to know in plenty of time to do it. For me, right now, it was to help Grandpa and Uncle Charlie. That was all that I needed to know.

There were expressions of surprise on the faces before me, but gradually, one by one, heads began to nod assent.

"We're going to miss you," Aunt Lou whispered as she moved close to me and let her hand linger on my arm.

"That's the joy of it," I said. "I'll be nearby. I'll need to come to town often. Got to check up on Sarah, you know." We all laughed a bit and the tension in the room relaxed.

Grandpa and Uncle Nat helped me to load my things in Grandpa's wagon. I left nothing behind; I wanted no excuses for turning back. I went in to where Sarah was sleeping and gave her a little pat as I whispered a goodbye. Then I hugged Aunt Lou and Uncle Nat and scooped up Pixie.

"You ride with Grandpa and Uncle Charlie," I told her, and handed her to Uncle Charlie.

"I'll be along shortly," I promised them. "I'm just going to drop around and thank Mr. Lewis and Mr. Trent for their job offers and tell them that I'm needed on the farm—for now."

I don't know if I imagined it or not, but Grandpa seemed to walk with a lighter step and Uncle Charlie with a bit more straightness to his back as the two of them went toward the wagon.

CHAPTER 6

Farming

Thoughts about my future sometimes tugged at me as I prepared the ground for seed and planted the crop that spring, but for the most part I enjoyed what I was doing.

I had never had much to do with the planting before. Grandpa and Uncle Charlie had been in charge of that and I had been the chore-boy, but now the roles were reversed. Grandpa and I worked the fields and Uncle Charlie, in his own slow way, did the chores—at least most of them. I still did the milking, because Uncle Charlie found the job too difficult with his crippled hands.

Uncle Charlie took care of the household duties, too. Cooking and cleaning didn't seem to bother him too much, but scrubbing the weekly laundry sure did. I sometimes winced as I watched him trying to wring out a garment. That night, to get Grandpa alone I asked him to come with me to the barn to check old Mac's hoof. "What seems to be the trouble?" Grandpa asked, bending over to lift Mac's right front foot.

"Oh, no trouble," I quickly assured him. "I was just wondering if it should be trimmed just a bit more."

Grandpa looked disgusted for a moment, but he quickly caught himself.

"Boy, you are taking your farmin' serious, aren't you?" he commented. "Never seen anyone with so many questions."

It was true. I had been asking a lot of questions. There were so many things that I didn't know about farming and planting, and I had to learn somehow. Grandpa and Uncle Charlie seemed to be my only source of knowledge.

"That's not—not really what I wanted," I began. "I wanted to talk to you, and I didn't know how to do it without Uncle Charlie—"

"Anything you got to say to me you can say in front of Charlie," Grandpa said firmly; I could tell by the tone of his voice that he wanted that straight right to begin with.

"But it's *about* Uncle Charlie," I protested. "Doesn't seem right to talk about him right out."

"What about Charlie?" asked Grandpa cautiously. "Seems to me he does the best he can."

"That's it exactly," I quickly pointed out. "He tries so hard, but some things are so—so difficult for him."

"Like?" asked Grandpa.

"Like wringing out those clothes."

Grandpa thought on that. He too had seen Uncle Charlie struggling with the clothes.

"Don't know what can be done about it," he said slowly and moved away from old Mac, slapping him playfully on his full rump as he did so. "Neither you nor I can take time to do the laundry when we're planting," he went on.

"I know, but—" I crossed to a wooden bucket and upended it to make myself a stool. "I've been thinking, and it seems that it might be the right time to get us some more modern equipment."

"Modern equipment?" Grandpa had always scorned anything that was too mechanized.

"One of those new machines for washing clothes," I hurried on. "They have a wringer thing that you just put the clothes through and turn the handle and they squeeze all of the water out from the cloth."

Grandpa knew all about washing machines. They had been around for a number of years. He had just felt that they were unnecessary—up 'til now.

I waited. I had more sense than to press the issue. Grandpa stood there chewing on a straw and thinking.

"Lou has one," I finally mentioned.

"Lou needs one," said Grandpa. "She's got all those white shirts and fancy dresses and dozens of diapers."

"Lou had a machine long before she had diapers to wash."

"It works good?" Grandpa surprised me by asking.

"Real good," I answered. "I've used it myself. You just stand there—or even sit, and work the handle back and forth, and the agitator does the washin' of the clothes. Then when you've washed them long enough, you put them through the wringer and rinse them in the rinse tubs, wring them out again and you're done."

Grandpa took the straw from his mouth and teased one of the barn cats with it. It batted and swatted, enjoying the fun but never able to hit that straw. Grandpa always moved it just a bit too soon.

"I'll think about it, Boy," said Grandpa. "Might bear some looking into."

That was as close to consent as I expected Grandpa to come to right off.

There were other changes I felt needed to be made on the farm, but I reminded myself that it would be smarter to take them one at a time. For now the most important one seemed to be to get Uncle Charlie some help with that washing.

We headed back to the house then, both of us studying the evening sky to see if we could read what kind of a day we would have on the morrow.

"How's that east field coming?" Grandpa asked.

"Should finish tomorrow," I answered, "if the weather holds."

"Looks good," said Grandpa, his eyes back to the sky. "We're getting the sowin' done in time. Should have a fair crop."

When we reached the house Uncle Charlie was still puttering with the supper dishes.

"How's Mac?" he asked.

"Nothin' wrong with Mac," Grandpa answered easily. "Josh here did ask if his hoof needed a bit more trimmin'. But it was really just a ruse."

When Uncle Charlie looked up, I avoided his eyes and washed my hands so that I could wipe the dishes.

"He was really worried about other things," went on Grandpa. "Hates to see you wringing out those clothes on washday. Thinks you need one of those fancy machines."

I cringed. The way Grandpa was putting it, it sounded like I was making Uncle Charlie out to be some kind of sissy. I hadn't meant it that way at all, and if Uncle Charlie took it that way, he'd buck the whole idea.

"I've thought about that myself," said Uncle Charlie slowly. "Watched Lou use hers. Seems like a sensible gadget."

Grandpa just nodded like he wasn't surprised at all.

"Josh says that it is," he informed Uncle Charlie. "Guess we should look into gettin' one. We got the money for it?"

Now Grandpa had never concerned himself much with the day-to-day expenses of the farm and house. That was Uncle Charlie's job. You couldn't really say that he kept the books. There were no books involved, but Uncle Charlie always knew to the penny just where the financial matters of the household stood.

"Guess we've got the money if we decide we want one," he answered honestly. "Happen to have a bit extra right now. We had talked about adding some new hogs to the pen—"

"That can wait," said Grandpa.

"Suppose we'd have enough to do both," went on Uncle Charlie, "but hate to get too low just in case somethin' should happen to this year's crop. We get hail or anythin', and it might make it tight."

Uncle Charlie went on washing dishes and I began to dry them and place them back in the cupboard.

"We don't want to be short," Grandpa said emphatically. "No sense doin' that. We can wait on those new hogs."

In all my years of living at the farm I had never heard Grandpa and Uncle Charlie discussing finances as openly as they were now.

"We've got what we laid aside for Josh," went on Uncle Charlie. "Now that he's not heading right off to college—"

But Grandpa interrupted him. "He still might go this fall, and we sure don't want to be short of funds. We'll just leave that right where it is for now."

"We've got our savings—"

"We're not touching a penny of that," Grandpa said adamantly. "We worked hard to earn it and we sure aren't gonna go spend it."

Uncle Charlie nodded in agreement. It was the first I had heard of savings, or of the money for my further schooling.

"How much does one of those there machines cost?" asked Grandpa.

"Dunno," said Uncle Charlie. "I'll check next time I'm in town."

They seemed to have forgotten all about me. I dried the dishes and rattled them a bit as I put them back on the shelf. That didn't seem to work so I cleared my throat. They still ignored me.

"If you find out that it's what you want, just go ahead and order one," Grandpa was telling Uncle Charlie. Uncle Charlie nodded.

"How long do you think it'll take to come?" Grandpa pulled back a kitchen chair and sat down, removing his work boots and pushing his feet into his slippers.

"Dunno," said Uncle Charlie again.

I cleared my throat again. I had been there when Uncle Nat had ordered the machine for Aunt Lou. I knew what he had paid and how long it had taken to come, too. But I wasn't being asked and I hated just to butt in.

"Throat botherin' you, Boy?" asked Grandpa.

I shook my head, feeling a bit annoyed and embarrassed.

Uncle Charlie turned to me then.

"Do you recollect what Nat paid for Lou's machine and how he went about choosin' it an' all?" he asked me.

By the time I finished telling what I knew, Grandpa and Uncle Charlie had picked the make they wanted and decided that Uncle Charlie would head for town come morning and order himself a washing machine. I felt good about it as I headed up to bed. I had initiated one small change for improvement on the farm.

CHAPTER 7

More Decisions

I was so busy that spring and summer I scarcely even got to town. If it hadn't been for Sundays, little Sarah Jane would have grown up without me even seeing her. As it was, she seemed bigger and stronger and a little more attentive each time I saw her.

She soon learned to smile when she was talked to and to coo soft little bubbly noises. Soon she was content to lie there and talk. Her dark hair got lost somewhere, and when her new hair thickened and lengthened, it was a soft golden brown. Her eyes changed, too; they weren't as dark now and were showing definite blue.

As Sarah was growing physically, Mary was developing spiritually. Willie still picked her up for church, but now he was bringing her ma along, too. Mary was really excited about that, and Mrs. Turley seemed to enjoy the church services.

Willie was all excited about leaving in the fall for school. He kept getting letters telling him about the courses and what he was to bring, and every time he got one he'd rush right over and show it to me. He'd usually bring it out to the field where I was planting or cultivating or cutting hay.

We kept talking about fishing but we never did get around to going. There was just so much to do that we never had time. When I finished one job I was already behind in taking on the next one. I hadn't realized that farming kept a man so busy.

Grandpa said I should slow down a bit, but I kept seeing things that needed to be done. I hadn't been around long before I realized that some areas had been rather neglected in the last few years. I guess the farm had become too big a job for Grandpa and Uncle Charlie. I could remember a time when neither of them would have let such things go unattended.

Aunt Lou and Uncle Nat were pretty busy with church affairs and didn't get out to the farm too often. One Friday night they joined us for supper, and Aunt Lou did the cooking. Boy, was it good, too. Uncle Charlie did his best, but his meals were mostly boiled potatoes and meat.

"How's the work coming, Josh?" Uncle Nat asked after I had finished off a second piece of lemon pie.

"Good," I said, feeling kind of grown up and important. "We're haying now."

"How's it look?" Uncle Nat had been in a farming community long enough to know how important a good hay crop was.

I sobered a bit then. "Not as good as I had hoped," I said honestly. "Don't really understand. We got lots of rain, but it still looks a bit skimpy."

Grandpa entered the conversation then. "Soil's getting a bit tired," he offered. "It's been planted for a lot of years now. That hay field has been givin' us a crop for nigh unto forty years, I guess. Deserves to be tired."

"Could you use some help tomorrow?" Uncle Nat asked. "I could spare the day."

"Sure," I grinned at him. "I sure could use someone on the stack."

"I'll be here," he promised.

"I'll send the lunch," promised Aunt Lou. "I'll need to get rid of the rest of this chicken somehow."

I looked forward to the next day as I climbed the stairs to my room that night. It would be good to have Uncle Nat's help. But more than that, it would be good to have his company.

The day was a hot one; both Nat and I sweated in the midmorning sun.

When it was time to take a break for lunch, we decided to slip into the shade of the trees on the creekbank to have our meal. We gave the horses a drink from the stream, then tied and fed them and lowered ourselves to the cool grass in the shade of a large poplar.

After Uncle Nat asked the blessing on the leftover chicken and Aunt Lou's other good things, we chatted small talk for several minutes. At length Uncle Nat looked directly at me and asked candidly, "How's it going, Josh? You liking being a summer farmer?"

"Sure," I answered. "Like it fine."

"Are you any nearer an answer?"

I hesitated. "You mean, about what I should do?"

Uncle Nat nodded and I shook my head.

"Still bother you?"

"I guess it does," I answered honestly. "If I let myself think on it, it does."

"You planning to go to school somewhere this fall?"

"That's the problem," I said quickly. "I'd thought that I'd just come on out and help Grandpa get the crop in and then I'd stay long enough to help with the hay. But as soon as haying's over it'll be time to cut the green feed, and then harvest—and on and on it goes. There doesn't seem to be a good time to leave."

Uncle Nat nodded.

"Another thing," I said confidentially. "Things need a lot of fixing up around here. I hadn't realized it before, but I guess farming is getting too hard for Grandpa and Uncle Charlie." I hoped with all of my heart that Uncle Nat would understand my meaning and not think I was being critical of the two men. After all, I was still smart enough to know that they knew far more about farming than I did.

"I'd noticed," said Uncle Nat simply.

I took heart at that and dared to go on. "This hay crop, for example. I think Grandpa is right; the land is tired. But it's gotta do us for years and years yet. There isn't any more land than what we've already got, Nat. We've gotta make this do for all the years God gives us. What do we do about it? Do we just wear it out?"

It was a hard question, one I had been thinking on a good deal lately.

"There are ways to give it a boost," said Uncle Nat, reaching for another sandwich.

I perked up immediately.

"Like what?"

"Well, not being a farmer I don't know much about it," Uncle Nat went on, "but I know someone who does."

"Who?"

"There's a fella by the name of Randall Thomas who lives about seven miles the other side of town," went on Uncle Nat. "I was called out there to see his dying mother. She wanted to talk to a preacher. Don't know why. She had things to teach *me*. A real saint if ever I met one."

I wasn't too interested in the saintly woman who probably had gone Home to glory by now. I wanted to hear about the farmer.

"Well, this farmer has been busy studying all about the soil and how to— what did he call it?—'rotate' crops to benefit it. Real interesting to talk to."

I was all ears. So there *was* a smarter way to farm the land!

"You think he'd talk to me?" I asked, very aware of the fact that I was still only a boy in some folks' thinking.

"I'm sure he would. Said if there was ever anything that he could do for me in return for calling on his mother, just to let him know."

I took a deep breath.

"So when do you want to see him?" asked Uncle Nat.

"Well, I don't know. Hafta get the hay off, and then the green feed—"

"And then the harvest," put in Uncle Nat.

"But I would like to talk to him," I continued. "I'd like to get the crops planted right next spring an'—"

Uncle Nat was looking at me.

"So you plan to farm again next year?"

I shrugged. "I guess so. I mean, I still don't know what else I'm supposed to do, and Grandpa still needs me an' . . ." It tapered off. There was silence for a few minutes and then I found my voice again.

"Do you think I'm wrong? Do you think that I should be tryin' harder to find out what God wants me to do with my life? It's not that I don't want to know, or don't want to obey Him."

"Are you happy here?" Uncle Nat asked me again.

"Yeah, I guess I am."

"You don't feel uneasy or guilty or anything?"

"No." I could answer that honestly. I was still puzzled, still questioning but I didn't feel guilty.

"Then, Josh, I would take that as God's endorsement on what you are doing," said Uncle Nat. "For now, I think you can just go ahead and keep right on farming. If God wants to change your direction, then He'll show you. I'm confident of that."

It sure was good to hear Uncle Nat put it like that.

We tucked away the empty lunch bucket and moved to the creek for a drink of cold water.

"And, Josh," said Uncle Nat just as we turned to go for the horses, "while you are here, you be the best farmer that you can be, you hear? Find out all you can about the soil, about livestock, about production. Keep your fences mended and your buildings in good repair. Make your machines give you as many years of service as they can. Learn to be the best farmer that you can be, because, Josh, in farming, in preaching, in any area of life, God doesn't take pleasure in second-rate work."

I nodded solemnly. I wasn't sure how much time God would give me to shape up Grandpa's tired farm before He moved me on to something else, but I knew one thing. I would give it my full time and attention until I got His next signal.

CHAPTER 8

Sunday

Willie came over to say goodbye before boarding the train that would take him away from our small community to the far-off town where he would continue his education. He was so excited that he fairly babbled, and for a moment I envied him and his calling. I would sure miss him, I knew that. It wouldn't be quite the same without Willie.

"You'll write?" Willie asked.

" 'Course I will."

"I'll send you my address just as soon as I'm settled," he promised.

"Let me know all about your school."

"I will. Everything," said Willie.

"What happens now—with Mary?" I asked suddenly, feeling concern for Mary and her mother.

"What happens? What do you mean?"

"For church? How will they get to church?"

"Mary is going to drive. I suggested that you might not mind picking them up, but Mary insisted that she'd drive them."

"Good," I said, and then hastily added, "but I sure wouldn't have minded taking them."

"I was sure you wouldn't, but Mary is quite independent."

We were quiet for a few moments; then Willie broke the silence. "Take care of her, Josh. She's a pretty special person."

I looked at Willie, my eyes saying, "I told you so," but Willie didn't seem to catch the look.

"She's my first convert, you know," he went on, and then added quietly, "She often surprises me. She knows some things about being a Christian that I still haven't learned in all my years of trying to live my faith."

I nodded. Mary certainly was putting many of us to shame.

"I saw Camellia off yesterday," Willie said, and my head jerked up. I had hoped to learn of Camellia's parting date so that I could see her off myself, but I had been so busy with the farm. A funny little stab of sadness pricked at me somewhere deep inside. I couldn't even answer Willie.

"She sure was excited," Willie went on.

Yes, Camellia would be excited.

"Her pa seemed excited too, or proud or something, but her ma didn't seem to be too sure that they were doing the right thing."

I wanted to ask Willie how Camellia looked, how she was wearing her hair, what her traveling dress was like, all sorts of things so that I could sort of picture Camellia in my mind, but I didn't.

"She had more trunks and baggage than would be necessary for ten people," Willie was laughing. "I think her ma even packed her a lunch."

I still said nothing, and Willie thought that I'd missed his point. "They feed you on the train, you know."

I hadn't known. I had never traveled by train in my life, but I didn't admit my ignorance to Willie.

"She hasn't decided if she will get home for Christmas," Willie went on, answering the question that was burning in my mind.

"Will you?" I asked, making it sound like that was the most important thing in the world to me at the moment.

Willie shook his head slowly. There was concern in his eyes. "I wish I could, but it's far too expensive to travel that distance. I'm sure I will be ready for some familiar faces by then. Four months away is about long enough for the first time from home, don't you think?"

I nodded.

"Well, I'd best get going." Willie reached to shake my hand. I extended mine, and then we both forgot that we were grown men saying goodbye to each other. We remembered instead that we were lifetime buddies, and the months ahead would be very long. Before I knew it we were soon giving each other an affectionate goodbye hug.

After Willie left I tried to get back to work in the field, but it was hard. Seeing my best friend riding off down the road, knowing that he would soon be on his way to Bible school, gave me an empty feeling in the pit of my stomach. Besides, Willie's news that Camellia had already left on the train for New York without my having the chance to tell her goodbye didn't do much to cheer me up. I had never felt so lonesome in all my life.

It wasn't long until Willie's first letter arrived. He was so full of excitement that he wrote pages and pages. I read it over and over, trying to get the feel of how it would be to be away from home.

I wasn't expecting any letter from Camellia, though I would have welcomed one. I did take a bit of a walk one Sunday while the rest of the family lingered over another cup of coffee after Aunt Lou's dinner. I went by the Foggelsons', hoping that I might accidentally meet Camellia's mother. It took quite a while and quite a few trips past their place, but eventually I did see her. She was watering her marigolds and I tipped my hat and greeted her like a mannerly boy was supposed to do. Then I casually asked her about Camellia.

Tears came to her eyes and she fought to control them. It frightened me. For a moment I was afraid that something dreadful had happened to Camellia, but when she spoke I realized that it was just the loneliness of a mother for her child.

She tried to smile.

"She is very excited about—about being on her own and the city and her classes and new friends." Then she added thoughtfully, "She—she hasn't said so, but even though she sounds cheerful, I think she has been just a bit lonesome."

The tears came again and Mrs. Foggelson attempted to smile in spite of them.

"I hope she is," she said wistfully, as though to herself. "I am."

I waited for a minute and then asked the question that I had really come to ask.

"Will she be home for Christmas?"

"No. Her father decided that she needs to make the adjustment to being on her own, away from family. It's much too far to travel, he says. I suppose he is right, but—Oh, my! How I dread the thought of Christmas without her!"

I was surprised somewhat that Mr. Foggelson, who doted on his only daughter, could consider Christmas without Camellia.

Mrs. Foggelson continued. "Mr. Foggelson needs to make a business trip east the last week of November. He will travel on to New York and take Camellia's gifts, and check to see how she is doing. He says that's quite enough."

My feelings for Mr. Foggelson hit an all time low. He had always felt that Camellia was his individual possession, but how could he do this to the girl's mother? And her friends? And how could he do it to Camellia? If she was really homesick, did he think that the sight of "dear old dad" was all she needed?

I couldn't even speak for a few moments. The angry thoughts were churning around inside of me. I looked away from the tears in Mrs. Foggelson's eyes and studied the distant maple tree, its bare arms empty as they reached upward against the gray autumn sky.

At last I found my voice. I even managed a smile. I guess I felt more compassion for Mrs. Foggelson at that moment than I had ever felt before. This man, her husband, had robbed her of so much—her faith, her self-esteem, and now her only child. I wondered just what kind of account he would give before God on the Judgment Day.

I smiled and touched my hat again. "I'll keep in touch," I promised, and then stammered, "If that's all right."

"I'd love to see you, Josh. I need someone to talk to, and one of Camellia's friends would—"

She didn't finish, but I thought I understood. And her words, "one of Camellia's friends," echoed in my mind as I tipped my hat again and started back down the sidewalk toward home.

"Josh," Mrs. Foggelson's soft voice called after me.

I turned to look back at her.

"Keep praying—please," she almost pleaded.

I nodded solemnly and swallowed hard. I wasn't sure if she meant to pray for Camellia, or for herself, or that she would soon see Camellia again— or all three, but I'd pray. I'd pray lots and often. Living with a man like Mr. Foggelson, I felt that she really needed prayer.

I still hadn't controlled my anger toward Mr. Foggelson by the time I reached Aunt Lou's. I thought of walking right on by and spending some more time alone with my thoughts, but the realization that I didn't have too long until I'd need to go home for choring prompted me to turn into the yard.

Baby Sarah had just been fed when I reentered the house. She was in a happy mood, and Aunt Lou passed her to me, knowing that I would soon be asking for her if she didn't. She gurgled and cooed and even tried to giggle. Then she did the unforgivable. She spit up all over my Sunday shirt.

Aunt Lou jumped to run for a wet cloth, and Uncle Nat reached out to quickly rescue Sarah. I loved Sarah, but I sure did hate the feel and the smell of being spit up on. I guess I made some faces to show my disgust, and they laughed at me and ribbed me a lot.

Aunt Lou cleaned me up the best that she could, apologizing for the mess. She offered to wash my shirt, but I didn't have anything else along to wear and I figured I ought to be man enough to put up with a little bit of baby spit-up.

The need for laundering brought our thoughts back to Uncle Charlie and his washing machine.

Uncle Nat agreed to order the machine, and Grandpa and I both felt good about that. Now laundry wouldn't be quite so hard for Uncle Charlie— especially after my Sundays with little Sarah!

After a while I unobtrusively left the dining room and wandered down to the room that had been mine for so many years. The door was open, and it sure looked different. Aunt Lou had everything so neat and tidy, with new curtains on the window—white and frilly, not the kind of curtains a boy would have enjoyed. I had preferred my old tan ones, but these did look real nice. Little throw cushions were propped up against the pillows, too. I would have found them to be a nuisance.

I stood there for a few minutes looking around me and thinking back over the years; then I reached out with a toe and pushed the door shut. I knelt by the bed. "Father," I began, "you know how I feel about Camellia, and how sorry I am for Mrs. Foggelson. Well, I'm too angry right now to pray for Mr. Foggelson, but I do want to ask you to take care of Camellia and bring her into a relationship with Jesus. . . ."

As I prayed for Camellia and her mother, my anger began to subside, and I began to realize how wrong my own attitude had been.

"Lord, Mr. Foggelson is a possessive and selfish man, and he's done some terrible things to his family. But I guess he needs you about as much as anyone I know. Help him find you too, Lord—and help me forgive him."

By the time I finished praying, I could think of the Foggelsons without feeling that turmoil of anger inside.

I rose and left the room, peeking into Aunt Lou and Uncle Nat's bedroom, where little Sarah now slept peacefully in her crib. She looked sweet, one little hand clutching the edge of her blanket and the other curled up into a tiny fist by her cheek. Her soft lashes against the pinkness of her skin looked so long and thick. Her hair, a little damp, curled closely to her tiny round head. It was getting lighter in color all the time; eventually it might be the same color as Aunt Lou's.

I reached down and smoothed out her blankets, then stroked the top of her head. She didn't even move. When Sarah slept, she really slept. Aunt Lou was thankful for that. There were many interruptions in the parsonage, and if the child had been a light sleeper, she might have never gotten a decent rest.

I heard stirring in the kitchen then and I knew that Grandpa and Uncle Charlie were preparing to leave for home. I whispered a few words to the sleeping baby and went out to get the team while they said their goodbyes.

CHAPTER 9

Winter

I was kept so busy that fall that I scarcely had time to miss Willie and Camellia. It seemed that I should have been in about three places at one time. There was so much to do, and only Grandpa and I to do the farming.

Grandpa had slowed down a lot, too. I hadn't realized until I was working with him just how difficult it was for him to put in a full day's work at the farm. I should have never left them alone while I went to school in town; I should have been there sharing in the responsibility. Maybe then things wouldn't have gotten so far behind.

But inwardly I knew that they never would have agreed to my staying at home. Even now, comments were made about my "calling" and I was reminded that I was not to hesitate when I felt God was prodding me on to what I "really should be doing" with my life.

I asked myself fairly frequently if I felt Him prodding, but I also found myself bargaining with Him.

"Can I wait, Lord, until I get the pasture fence mended?" I'd pray. "God, would you give me enough time to get in the crop?" And each time I asked His permission, I felt like I got His nod of approval.

Uncle Charlie's washing machine arrived in mid-October. I hadn't realized how much it meant to him until I watched him grinning as he uncrated it. He stroked the wringer lovingly, then gave it a few cranks and grinned some more. It was going to be a good investment.

The weather didn't cooperate that fall. The fields would dry just enough for us to get back at the harvest; we'd work a few hours, and then another storm would pass through, delaying us again. In my frustration I would go to fence-mending or repairing the barn or cutting wood for our winter supply.

I went to bed worn out every night and slept soundly until morning. Then I got up, checking the sky for the day's weather before I even had my clothes on, and started in on another full day.

It was late November before the district threshing crew moved in for the last time and we got the final crop off. Because of the rain, it wasn't as good a quality as we had hoped it would be, but at least it was in. Our hay crop of the year had been scant and poor, also.

Grandpa relaxed a bit then. The lines seemed to soften on his brow. Grandpa had too much faith for worry, but he was a little less concerned than he had been with the crop still in the field.

Uncle Charlie seemed to feel the lessening of tension too. For one thing, I knew that he was relieved to have his kitchen back to himself. We'd had a neighbor woman and her daughter in helping to cook for the threshing crew. Uncle Charlie needed the help, we all knew that, but he sure was glad when the last dish was washed and put away and the women went home.

I turned my attention to other things—cutting wood, fixing door hinges and banking the root cellar. And I talked to God some more.

I had thought I might be ready for His call at the first of the year, but now I realized that I would never be caught up enough to turn the farm back over to Grandpa and Uncle Charlie that soon. I needed more time to get things back into shape. God seemed to agree. I did not feel Him nudging me to hurry on to other things. Instead, He seemed to give me assurance that my job on the farm wasn't finished yet.

And so I worked feverishly, trying to get as much as I could done before the snow came. When it did come, it came with fury. The thermometer dropped thirty degrees overnight, and the wind blew from the north with such intensity that it blew down several trees. The snow swirled in blinding eddies. I was thankful that I had repaired the chicken coop and lined the floor with fresh warm straw. I was glad, too, that the barn was ready for winter. But I still hadn't gotten the pigpens ready. I worried about the pigs, especially the sow that had just given birth to eight little piglets. I struggled against the wind with a load of straw for bedding.

It was useless even to try. The wind whipped the straw from my pitchfork as soon as I stepped from the barn. After trying several times, I tossed my fork aside and gathered the straw in my arms. Even that didn't work well. As I fought my way toward the pigpen the wind pushed and pulled, pulling the straw from me. By the time I had reached the pigpen I had very little left.

I tried again, over and over, and each time I arrived at the shed with only a scant armful of straw.

At last I gave up. I was winded and freezing as I bucked the strong gale. I hoped that the bit of straw I had managed to get to the pigs would help to protect them against the bitter storm.

I spent most of the day fighting against the wind, trying to ease the discomfort of the animals. Several times Grandpa and Uncle Charlie came out to assure me that I had done all I could, that the animals would make it through on their own. But I wasn't so sure, so I kept right on fighting.

When the day was over and I headed for the house with a full pail of milk, I was exhausted.

The kitchen had never looked or smelled more inviting. The warmth from the cookstove spilled out to greet me, making my face sting with the sudden heat after the cold. The aroma of Uncle Charlie's hot stew and fresh biscuits reminded me of just how hungry I was.

Grandpa took the pail from me and went to strain the milk and run it through the separator. I didn't argue, even though it was normally my job.

Pixie pushed herself up against me as I fought with cold-numbed fingers to get off my heavy choring boots. She licked at my hands, at my face, anywhere that she could get a lick in. I guess it seemed to her that I had been gone for a very long time.

When I went to wash for supper, Uncle Charlie spoke softly from the stove where he dished up the food.

"Your face looks a bit chilled, Josh. Don't make the water too warm. You might have a bit of a frostbite there."

I felt my nose and my cheeks. They seemed awfully hard and cold. I heeded Uncle Charlie's advice and pressed a cloth soaked in cool water up against them. Even the cold made them burn.

Over the meal we discussed the storm and all I had done to try to prepare for it. I noticed that the woodbox was stacked high. Grandpa had been busy, too.

"Looks like it could be with us for a while," commented Grandpa. "Sky is awful heavy."

I didn't know much about reading storms, and I hoped that Grandpa was wrong. One day of this was enough.

We listened to the news on our sputtering radio while we warmed ourselves with coffee. The forecast wasn't good. According to the man with the crackling voice, the storm could get even worse during the night and wasn't expected to blow itself out for at least three days.

I could sense even before I awoke the next morning that the radio had been right. The storm was even worse than the day before.

When I went out to face the wind and the cold, the range cows were pushing tightly around the barn, bawling their protest against the storm. I knew that they needed shelter; I also knew that they could not all fit inside. The barn was reserved for the milk cows and the horses. I felt sorry for those poor animals. We really needed some kind of a shed to protect them against such storms. *That's one thing I'll do first thing next summer,* I vowed to myself.

The next day was a repeat of the two that went before it. All day the wind howled. Then, near the end of the day the wind abated and the snow slackened. The temperature dipped another five degrees.

Even in the farmhouse we were hard put to keep warm. Uncle Charlie lit a lamp and put it down in the cellar to keep Aunt Lou's canned goods from freezing. We added blankets to our beds and set an alarm so we could get up in the night to check the fire.

The next morning arrived clear and deathly cold. The water in the hand basin in the kitchen was skimmed with ice. I lit the lantern and started for the barn, hating the thought of going out to face the intense cold. My breath preceded me in frosty puffs of glistening white. Even the moon that still hung in the west looked frozen into position.

Now that the wind had died down, I really had work to do. The animals outside hadn't really eaten properly since the storm had begun. It had been just too hard to fight the wind. Now they stood, humped and bawling, hungry and thirsty, and nearly frozen to death.

By the time the storm had passed and the temperature was back to normal again, we had lost three of the piglets, two of the older cows, and half a dozen chickens. Three cows had lost the lower portions of their tails to frostbite, and our winter supply of feed had already been seriously depleted. If the winter continued this way, we would find it difficult to continue feeding all of the stock. Even so, we fared much better than some of our neighbors. The storm had killed a number of the animals in some herds.

As Christmas approached, I was eager to spend time with Aunt Lou and Uncle Nat. Little Sarah was sitting by herself and even attempting to pull herself up. And the opening of the Christmas gifts was, of course, even more fun with a baby in the house. We all had a gift for Sarah, and we took her on our laps and pretended that she was taking part in the opening of the present. We also pretended that she was excited about each new rattle or bib. She wasn't; in fact, she liked the rustle of the wrapping paper better than anything else.

I even brought Pixie with us. In the colder weather I usually left her at home when we went to town, but today I tucked her inside my heavy coat and she managed just fine. Sarah loved her, and I put Pixie through all of her tricks just to make Sarah squeal and giggle. She seemed to like it best when Pixie "spoke" for a little taste of turkey. Then Sarah would wave her chubby arms and squeal at the top of her voice. We all had a good laugh over it.

In the afternoon I slipped out and hurried over to the Foggelsons'. I wanted Mrs. Foggelson to know that I was thinking about her—still praying for her, too. Besides, I was a little anxious to hear any news about Camellia.

Before I went up their walk, I could see that there was no one home. The heavy curtains were pulled shut and no one had cleaned the snow from the walk for several days. The shovel was leaning up against the back porch, so before I headed home again I decided to clear the snow from the walk. I didn't know when the Foggelsons would be back again or if it would even be evident to them that someone had been there, but I did it anyway.

I wondered if there was some chance that Mr. Foggelson had changed his mind and they had gone together to see Camellia. I hoped so. It would be a lonely Christmas for both Mrs. Foggelson and Camellia if they were to spend it apart.

I thought of Willie, too. I had received a letter from him just a few days before Christmas. "I really miss the family and friends," he wrote. "As exciting as my studies are, I'm lonesome, even weary. But I've been invited home with one of the guys from the college who lives nearby." I was glad that Willie had somewhere to go.

When I was younger, I had always thought that as soon as Christmas had come and gone, we should be working our way toward spring. I hoped that it would be true this year. I had loved winter as a boy, but then I hadn't had the responsibilities of seeing that everything and everybody made it through without mishap or suffering. Winter had simply been a time of sport—sleigh rides, tobogganing, ice skating, snowfalls and snowmen. I had loved it. Now winter was a time of struggle against the intense cold, the biting wind, the deep snow, the shortened days. The weather made it harder to chore, and the supply of winter feed and cut wood seemed to evaporate before my eyes.

Thinking of all this as I walked back to Aunt Lou's, I began to feel rather dejected. Then, it began to snow again—huge, soft, gently falling flakes. I looked up toward the sky to see the snow drift toward my face and marveled anew at the beauty of it. It might not be easy to live with winter, but it certainly was beautiful when I just took the time to look closely at it.

C H A P T E R 1 0

Making It Through

I may have been ready for spring as soon as Christmas was over, but I guess no one thought to tell Mother Nature. She stormed and fretted and gave us a hard time all through the month of January. I looked forward to February—surely things would improve!

But they didn't. When we couldn't get to church a couple of Sundays, I missed the church service, the good dinner, and the brief visit with little Sarah.

And the bad weather didn't help Uncle Charlie improve, either. His arthritis seemed to twist his fingers off to the side more and more each day. I inwardly ached for him when I watched him trying to accomplish some simple task. But he was independent and needed to feel that he was carrying a full share of the workload.

About mid-February Grandpa came down with a bad cold. He struggled along trying to treat himself for several days but got no better.

"Grandpa!" I insisted. "You're just getting worse. I'm gonna fetch Doc to take a look at you."

"Bah!" he sputtered. "Doctors can't do nothin' I'm not already doing."

When it got worse and he had a hard time breathing, I saddled Chester and headed for town—over Grandpa's protests.

"Sure enough," Doc murmured. "Pneumonia. You get that girl of yours out here to take care of you 'til you get back on your feet."

So Aunt Lou and Sarah moved out to the farm to nurse Grandpa back to health. Doc had sent him to bed with orders that he was to follow; Aunt Lou and I both knew he wouldn't obey if she wasn't there to insist.

I was sorry that Grandpa was sick, but it sure was a treat to have Aunt Lou and Sarah. Uncle Nat came out as often as he could. He missed his "two girls," as he called them, but he was awfully good about it.

It took Grandpa a couple of weeks before he was out of bed, and even then he had to lie down often because he was too weak to do much. In that time Sarah, crawling incessantly, had learned how to stand by herself. One morning I came into the kitchen, and she deserted her toy to crawl to me and pull herself up by my pantleg.

"Hey! You'll be running footraces soon!" She laughed, bouncing up and down on pudgy baby-legs.

I was really sorry to see Aunt Lou and Sarah leave for town again. The house would seem strange and empty with them gone.

By March winter had still not given up, and we were short of feed for the livestock. I worried about it each time that I doled out the hay and oats.

Grandpa must have sensed it, mentally measuring the feed each time I went out to chore. I didn't say anything to him about it but one morning at breakfast he surprised me.

"About enough for two more weeks, eh, Josh?"

I nodded silently.

"Can you cut back any?"

"I think I've already cut back about as much as I dare."

"Any chance of buying some feed off a neighbor?" Uncle Charlie asked.

"I've asked around some," I admitted. "Nobody seems to have any extra."

"We'll go out an' take inventory and see—" Grandpa started to say, but Uncle Charlie cut him short.

"You'll do nothin' of the sort!" he snorted. "Doc says yer to stay in out of the cold fer at least another two weeks."

"But Josh needs—" Grandpa began and Uncle Charlie waved his hand, sloshing coffee from his coffee cup.

"I'll help Josh," he said. "Nothin' in here that needs doin' today anyway."

Grandpa didn't argue any further, and after Uncle Charlie had washed up the dishes and I had dried them and set them back on the cupboard shelf, we bundled up and set off to take inventory.

It didn't take much figuring to know that we'd be short of feed. Uncle Charlie said what we were both thinking.

"If spring comes tomorrow it won't be in time."

By noon we had completed our calculations and headed back to the warmth of the kitchen. Grandpa had fried some eggs and sliced some bread. That, with cold slices of ham and hot tea, was our noon meal. I inwardly longed for Lou's full dinner meals again.

While we ate, Grandpa and Uncle Charlie juggled numbers and shuffled papers until I felt a bit sick inside. I wasn't sure where this all was leading us. I had never remembered a time when Grandpa and Uncle Charlie had had a tough time making it through the winter—but maybe it had happened and I just hadn't known.

In the end I was dispatched on Chester to take a survey among the neighborhood farmers. If there was any feed for sale, our dilemma would be solved.

But it wasn't that easy. Everywhere I stopped I found that the other farmers were in the same fix as we were. There just wasn't going to be enough feed to make it through this extra-hard winter.

With a sinking heart I headed for home. I decided to stop at the Turleys' on my way, more to see how Mary and her mother were doing than to check for feed. Mr. Turley fed several head of cattle and he didn't raise much more feed than we did.

When Mary opened the door, she looked genuinely glad to see me. I was even a bit glad to see her.

Mrs. Turley was busy darning some socks, and she sat there near the fire rocking back and forth as she mended. She seemed quite content and peaceful, even though she must have known that her husband, too, was facing a tough time.

"God will see us through, I feel confident about that," she assured me. "He always has—even when we didn't have enough sense to turn to Him— and I'm sure that He won't desert us now that we are His children."

My mouth must have gaped open at her words, for she looked at me and laughed softly.

"Don't look so surprised, young man. You young folks aren't the only ones who need converting, you know."

"Mother has become a believer, too," Mary whispered, a sense of awe filling her voice.

"Yes, praise God, thanks to the changes I saw in my Mary here, after she took up with your friend Willie—and his friend, Jesus."

"That's wonderful, Mrs. Turley," I stammered, still amazed at her words. "And you're right—we do need to trust Him."

Mary fixed some hot chocolate and cut some cake and we sat at the kitchen table and shared bits of news from the church and community. It seemed that she had chafed as much as I had over the snowed-in Sundays.

"Did you hear the Foggelsons are moving?" she surprised me by asking.

"They are? Where?"

"Mr. Foggelson has found a teaching position in a small college somewhere near New York. He went there to see about it in November and then he went back again over Christmas."

"Did Mrs. Foggelson go with him?" I cut in.

"No, he went alone."

"But she was gone—" I started to say, thinking back to the empty house and unshoveled walk.

"She went to her sister's. She didn't want to be alone."

"I don't blame her," I muttered, annoyed again with Mr. Foggelson.

"Camellia said her ma enjoyed her visit even if—" started Mary, but I cut in again.

"Do you hear from Camellia?"

"Oh, goodness no," she answered, shaking her head as though the thought were preposterous. "I hardly know her. I've just seen her on the street, and she would never have anything in common with the likes of me."

Then Mary blushed as though she were afraid that her words had somehow put Camellia down.

"I mean, well—we are—she's educated and all, and I—"

I rescued Mary from her embarrassment.

"Where did you hear about her?"

"From Willie. He wrote all about it. He keeps in touch with Camellia."

"Oh-h," I said. But it was rather an empty sound. I heard from Willie—often—but he had never informed me of all of Camellia's plans.

"Does Camellia like school?" I asked, because I was sure that Mary was expecting me to say something.

"Hadn't you heard?" asked Mary, taken aback. "She quit."

"Quit?" Now I was really surprised.

"She was only there for a couple of months when she quit."

"Then what is she doing? Why didn't she come home?"

"At first she was afraid to tell her pa. And then she left New York and managed to get some kind of job. A telephone operator, I think, out East. So she stayed."

What a disappointment that must have been for Mr. Foggelson. And then I thought of Mrs. Foggelson. She would have been disappointed too, but not that Camellia had dropped out of Interior Design. Her disappointment would have been that Camellia didn't come back home.

"Well, Willie says that she likes her job just fine."

"So she writes to Willie?" For some reason, the news was both encouraging and threatening at the same time. I wished with all of my heart that Camellia felt free to write to me, but at the same time I was glad that Willie was keeping in touch. He had led Mary to become a Christian. Now it seemed he was working on Camellia. Inwardly I prayed for Willie's success.

But Mary was speaking again, with a bit of a laugh. "Oh, she doesn't need to write. Her job is right there in town."

"Right where in town?" I asked stupidly.

"Where Willie goes to college. She is right there, working on the town switchboard. Willie found the job for her."

Well, that was news to me. *Why hadn't Willie mentioned it to me in one of his letters?* And then I smiled to myself. Willie knew that I was already praying for Camellia. But he didn't want me to get my hopes up too soon. Her father had influenced her so strongly that it might take many weeks, even months, before she would see the light after so many years of antagonism toward Christianity, and I wouldn't ask any questions of Willie. He'd share with me when he felt that the time was right.

I suddenly realized that I had been sitting at Mary's table for longer than I had intended. It was already getting dark and there were chores to do. Besides, Grandpa and Uncle Charlie would be anxious for my report—even if I wasn't returning with good news.

"I've gotta get," I said to Mary and rose from the chair, reaching for my coat and cap all in one motion.

Then I thanked her for the refreshments, told her mother goodbye, and was on my way.

Mary saw me to the door.

"I'm sorry, Josh," she said quietly.

"About what?" I asked, startled.

"About the winter being so hard and all," she went on. "It's been a tough year for your first year farmin'—it was such a long, hard fall, and then—and then this," she finished lamely.

I was relieved at her words. I had been afraid that she had been going to say something about the Foggelsons. I had counted the days until Camellia would be done with her schooling and come back to our little town, and now with her folks moving, it didn't look like there was much chance of that happening. But I was relieved that Mary couldn't read my mind.

"Like your ma says," I returned, trying to sound brave and full of faith, "it'll turn out all right. God won't forsake us."

Mary gave me a big smile. She really had a very pretty smile, with white, even teeth and a dimple in each cheek.

I found myself smiling back. Maybe it was just that Mary's smile was contagious, or maybe I hoped she'd smile again. But for whatever reason, I did feel better as I mounted Chester and headed through the chilling weather for home.

CHAPTER 11

A Visit

We had to sell several head of cattle and all but two good sows. It would be a long time until we would get the herd and the pigpens built back up again, and I wondered if Grandpa and Uncle Charlie's decision was the right one. What if spring was just around the corner, and the new grass would soon be available? Maybe we would have been able, with careful rationing, to make it through.

It turned out that they had done the right thing. Another and then another storm struck, making it difficult to feed the few head of stock that remained. Neighbors who were trying to ration feed and make it through without selling off livestock lost most of their herd, and they didn't have cash from a sale to help them in rebuilding.

Our own stock diminished, and we lost one of our best milk cows when she got weak after giving birth to a fine calf. Grandpa and I sat all night with her, trying to keep her warm and pouring warm mash down her throat, but we lost her. I was sure we would lose the beautiful little heifer too, but Grandpa told me to carry her up to the kitchen, and Uncle Charlie took over from there. I don't know how he did it, but he pulled that little calf through. We all knew that she would be important in building up the herd again.

It seemed that all our days and nights were taken up with fighting to save what Grandpa and Uncle Charlie had worked so many years to build. It just didn't seem right.

As soon as the weather began to warm some and I had a bit more time, I went off to town to see Uncle Nat.

"You know that fella you told me about who changes his crops around and such?"

He nodded. "Crop rotation."

"Yeah, rotation. Well, I was wondering if I might go and see him," I went on. "I've been wondering how he made it through the winter."

"Haven't heard," said Uncle Nat. "They mostly shop in Gainerville. Don't come here too often."

"Could you tell me how to get to his farm?"

Uncle Nat gave me directions. They sounded simple enough, and I headed Chester out of town. The day was bright, and the warmth of the sun shone down on the snowbanks. Chester was tired of winter and being shut up; he wanted to run, but I held him in check. I didn't want him to get all lathered up and then catch pneumonia. We had enough problems without losing Chester.

I found the farm without any trouble, though it took longer to get there than I'd thought it would. No wonder the family shopped in Gainerville— they were quite a ways from our small town.

Mrs. Thomas welcomed me cordially enough and informed me that her husband was down at the barn, so I declined her invitation into the kitchen and told her that I'd just go on down there to see him.

The Thomases were a big family. I saw three girls of varying sizes through the open kitchen door, and when I got to the barn there were four boys working along with their pa.

Randall Thomas was a big man, about forty, with a firm handshake and a kind twinkle to his eyes.

"Pastor Crawford's nephew, you say? Well, right glad to know ya, son," he said. "Sure did appreciate the trip yer uncle made out here to see Ma."

We chatted for a few minutes, my eyes traveling over the barn and feed shed all the time I was talking or listening. It didn't look to me like there had been a feed shortage at this farm.

At last we got around to talking about the winter that we hopefully had just passed through.

"Sure a tough one," the big man said. "Worst I remember seein."

I agreed, though it was evident that I hadn't seen quite as many winters as Mr. Thomas had.

"Looks like your stock made it through just fine," I said, nodding my head toward a corral holding some healthy looking cattle.

"Sold some of 'em way last fall," he surprised me by saying.

"You did?"

"Didn't want to wait until they only made soup bones," he went on. "A farmer has to think long-range. You figure about the worst that a winter can do to you and then plan accordingly. I figured out the feed I'd need to git each critter through to the end of May. By then the new grass should be helpin' us out some, even in the worst of years."

"We didn't have near enough feed to take us that far," I commented. "We had to sell several head."

"Too bad," he said sympathetically, shaking his head at our misfortune. "Heard some folks lost a lot of stock before they could even sell 'em."

"Grandpa sold early, before things got too bad," I informed him.

"That was smart thinkin'," went on the man. "The way I see it, a few real good, healthy head of stock are better'n a whole herd of weak, half-starved ones."

I could see his point.

"A herd can get themselves into pretty bad shape if you don't keep upgradin' 'em," he went on. "Then they can't take much cold an' poor feed."

I looked at his sleek cattle. They didn't look like they had just been through a tough winter.

A bird overhead drew my attention to the sky. The sun had already moved far to the west, losing much of the warmth of the day. It was a long ride back home, and I knew I should soon be making it.

"I really came to see you about your crops," I told Mr. Thomas. "I've a feeling that we would have fared much better this winter if our land were producing like it should be. Seems to me the hay that we took off was only about half as high or heavy as it could have been."

His eyes glinted with interest as they met mine.

"You just startin' to farm?" he asked.

I nodded, then corrected myself. "Well, I was raised on that farm but until this year I've been doin' the chorin', not the farmin'. Grandpa and Uncle Charlie have been farmin' the land. They aren't able to do it all now so—"

He cut in. "So you are farmin', and you wanta start out right?"

I nodded again.

"Well, yer a smart boy." His hand fell to my shoulder and he gave it a squeeze.

"A man can farm his land right out iffen he plants the same crop year after year. Only stands to reason. Why, even way back in the time of the Israelites, God gave a command that the land was to get a rest ever' now an' then. Same thing now. The land needs to rest—to build up its reserves agin." And then he began an enthusiastic explanation of how that was to be done.

I listened attentively. But the sun was moving on, and there was so much to learn. I felt frustrated and tense, and I guess that the man sensed it.

He stopped and his eyes followed mine to the sky. "There's too much to learn in one afternoon," he told me. "You come on back—as often as you like—and we'll pick it up from here."

I was glad he understood my need to be on the road and for the invitation to come to see him again.

"Tell ya what," he continued as we walked toward Chester. "You draw up a plan of yer fields. Mark what's been growing in each for the last seven, eight years, and then come see me agin. We'll see what ya should be plantin' come spring."

I could only stammer my thanks. I hadn't expected that kind of help.

"It's important to get good seed, too," the man continued. "Some farmers try to skimp on the cost of seed. But that costs 'em more than it saves 'em. Just like it is with livestock. The Bible says, 'Ya reap what ya sow.' Now I know that wasn't talkin' 'bout the grain and the stock as much as it was what ya sow in life, but the same holds true."

I hadn't thought of it that way before, but it made sense. It was a totally different approach to farming than I had been used to, but I promised myself that I would learn all I could about it. I thanked the man for his kindness and mounted Chester.

"Now that," he said appreciatively, running a hand over Chester's thick neck, "is good breedin'. Where'd ya get a horse like this, son?"

I explained that Chester had been a gift and reached down to rub his neck myself.

"First-rate horse!" the man exclaimed, making me beam with his praise.

On the way home I let Chester do a bit of running, though pacing him so that he wouldn't get too heated. But, like the man had said, Chester's good breeding showed. He could run a lot without getting winded or sweated up.

I had so much to think about that my head was swimming. Good seed, good blood lines, crop rotation—those were things that spelled out productive farming. And if a man was going to farm—even if it was just until God called him into his real life's work—then he ought to try to do a good job of it. I determined that I would find out all I could about doing the job right. Maybe the next time we had a bad winter we wouldn't need to suffer such serious setbacks.

CHAPTER 12

Looking for Spring

As my interest in farming techniques increased, I found some farm magazines with articles about crop rotation and pored over them. I sent away to the Department of Agriculture for free information that was mentioned in one of the magazines. I also asked them for information about building up the herd with proper blood lines. Soon pamphlets and sheets of information were coming back through the mail. I hadn't realized that there was so much to farming—or that the government had information available to help farmers. There were even agricultural courses that a fella could take at home. I had always thought that a man became a farmer because he had been born and raised on the farm and his pa needed help.

"You been gettin' an awful pile of mail lately," Grandpa remarked, glancing at the three brown envelopes and a magazine on the kitchen table.

"There's a lot more to this farming than I ever knew from just growing up on one," I commented. "You and Uncle Charlie made it seem so easy—"

"Oh, we did the best we knew how, and it worked pretty good most of the time," Grandpa interrupted, "but it looks to me like yer findin' some real important things 'bout farmin' in those magazines and booklets of yers. Charlie an' I've been readin' some of them, too," he said to my questioning look. "We're real glad yer learnin' some new ways to do things." From the shine in his eyes, I knew he meant it.

All through the chill of spring I worked with the stock, trying to keep them comfortably warm so their energy could be reserved for putting fat on their bodies. I still couldn't feed them the way I would have liked, but I made a warm mash for them on the cooler days, and kept the animals in the barns all I could. It meant more barn cleaning, but if the stock benefited, then it would be worth it.

On the sunnier days I let them out to pasture. The snowdrifts were slowly melting down and the horses led the way for the cattle, pawing back the snow in order to get to the left-over grasses from last fall. They even began to discover some fresh new blades of grass and that increased their desire to forage. The cows followed along behind, eating from the open spots the horses had left.

Every day I watched the sky, the snow patches, the weather, mentally measuring the feed I had left with the number of animals.

At night I read the magazines and information booklets, and I began to see what Mr. Thomas had been trying to tell me—there was a *system* to good farming.

I drew out a map of the fields, and Grandpa and Uncle Charlie and I went over them one by one. It was hard to remember every field back for seven or eight years. Sometimes Grandpa and Uncle Charlie disagreed about the crop that had been planted in a particular field and then they would have to sort through their thinking, trying to figure out which one was right. I decided then and there that an accurate account of each field would be kept year by year, along with the yield and any other information I might come up with.

Daily I checked my feed rations; I was still anxious that we wouldn't make it to the end of May. Finally we held a consultation and decided to sell off two more young heifers. They looked small-boned, and we wanted to build up our herd with larger animals.

Instead of going to see Mr. Thomas alone, I suggested to Grandpa and Uncle Charlie that they come with me. I wanted them to hear first-hand what the man had to say, and to catch some of the excitement that he generated.

Thus on a mild day that held a promise of spring, we hitched the team to the wagon. The road was rutted and messy with dirty puddles of half-melted snow. The ground had not yet yielded up its frost, but still it was hard pulling for the team, and we didn't travel very fast. I drove and Uncle Charlie and

Grandpa just sat there and soaked in the warmth of the sun. It had been a long time since they had been able to feel the sunshine.

It was just as I had hoped that it would be. We were welcomed with a handshake that made my hand tingle. I thought of Uncle Charlie and his arthritis and almost said something, but Mr. Thomas must have noticed the crippled hands, for he took my uncle's hand very carefully and didn't squeeze at all.

This farmer's enthusiasm was contagious. He talked about the importance of good seed, of planting in weed-free fields, of rotating the crops so that the soil wouldn't become depleted, and of fertilizing properly each year.

With the livestock kept in so much of the winter, at least we wouldn't be short of fertilizer. But I winced as I thought of the unpleasant task of scattering it over the fields.

With the help of Mr. Thomas, we analyzed our field situation and determined what crops should be planted where and which field should go fallow. The next step was to find a source of good seed grain. We were in the favored position of being able to afford a bit of good seed. Before we left, Mr. Thomas promised to come out and take a look at our livestock. He would help us sort out the best that we had and then figure out how to start developing better stock.

My head was whirling by the time we put down our coffee cups and headed home. We had so much to think about and so much to get done—even before planting time.

All the way home I was planning the days ahead. Even if spring was slow in coming, I still didn't think we'd be ready for it. There was so much to do to prepare the ground for the coming crop year.

Because I knew I would be more than busy once we could drive the wagon out to the fields, I decided to call on Mrs. Foggelson before I got too rushed. I was sorry to hear she would be leaving us. I guess I was even a little sorry to hear that he would be going. I wished with all my heart that he could realize that there was a God—a God who was in charge of the universe. How could someone with such a brilliant mind be so wrong about something so important?

With the move, I wouldn't be seeing Camellia again. I had hoped the day would come when both she and her mother would become believers. Mr. Foggelson, I knew, would be hard to convince after so many years of resisting the truth.

When I got to the Foggelsons' the snowbanks had almost disappeared off their front lawn. Little shoots of spring plants pointed up through the final snow covering the flower beds. I knew that Mrs. Foggelson dearly loved her flowers, and I wondered who would be caring for them after she had moved away.

In answer to my knock, Mrs. Foggelson came hesitantly to the door. When she saw me, her face lighted up and she flung the door open with a welcoming smile.

"Josh! So good to see you," she said, sounding glad that I had come. I sat twisting my cap in my hands in her parlor while she rushed to the kitchen for tea. Once we were settled with our cups, Mrs. Foggelson chatted about spring, about her garden, about the hard winter, and finally about Camellia.

"Did you know that Camellia quit studying Interior Design?" she asked. I had to admit that I did.

"Did you know that she is working as a telephone operator?"

I nodded again.

"I am so glad," went on Mrs. Foggelson. "I was so worried about her in New York. She got in with the wrong choice of friends almost immediately, and I was so worried."

I hadn't known about that.

"Does she like her work?" I asked.

"Not really. But it is good clean work with good people. That's the most important thing. Camellia might be smart, and she might be independent, but she has had no experience dealing with people. Especially the kind of people who would lead her into—into wrong living."

I hardly knew what to say. I just nodded my head in understanding, trying to balance the light flakes of pastry that didn't want to stay on my fork.

"I'm glad she's no longer in New York." Mrs. Foggelson sighed with relief.

I nodded again, then ventured, "But you must be sorry that she won't be close by when you move."

Her eyes dropped and she was silent for a few minutes. When she looked up again, her voice was very soft and low.

"I won't be moving," she said.

"There's been a change of plans?" I asked hopefully.

She just shook her head.

"But—but I was told that Mr. Foggelson got a teaching position in a small college—somewhere near New York City."

She let her eyes look evenly into mine.

"Yes," she said, "he did."

Silence.

"Well," I prompted, "then he has changed his mind after all."

"Oh no. He'll be going as planned."

"But—" I felt that we were talking in riddles. I stopped and waited for her to enlighten me.

"Mr. Foggelson will be going as he has planned," she said carefully, "but I will remain here."

I must have looked as shocked as I felt. I lowered my fork, scattering the last of my flaky pastry onto the white damask cloth. My face flushed hot with embarrassment.

Mrs. Foggelson reached over to pour me some more tea. I didn't have a voice to refuse it, even though I didn't think that I could drink another drop.

"Did you notice that the early tulips are already showing some?" Mrs. Foggelson asked, as though flowers were all we had been discussing since I had come in.

I nodded and cleared my throat again.

"I do so hope that we have a nice spring," said Mrs. Foggelson. "We can't have an early one—it's already too late for that, but I do hope it's a nice one. I am so tired of the dreary winter."

My eyes drifted to a picture of Camellia on the corner table. Mrs. Foggelson had lots of pictures of Camellia. Or were they Mr. Foggelson's? I looked about the room, my mind busy with embarrassing thoughts. Who would get the pictures? Who would get the brocade sofa? Who the silver tea service or the china cups?

What did folks do when they separated company, anyway? How did they ever go about portioning out a house? A home? I knew absolutely nothing about such things. But surely some rough days lay ahead for the Foggelsons.

Then another thought quickly came to my mind. With Mrs. Foggelson staying, maybe—"Does Camellia plan to stay on in the little town where she is, or—or might she come back home again?"

For the first time I saw the tears threaten to form. Mrs. Foggelson shook her head slowly, and suddenly her lovely, gentle face looked old.

"I don't expect so," she said candidly. "Camellia does not approve of my staying here. She has always been her daddy's girl, you know. If she goes to anyone, it will be to him."

I pushed back my chair and got to my feet. I felt so sorry for Mrs. Foggelson, but there was really no way I had of telling her. What could a young fella like me know about the way she hurt? How could I understand her reason for doing what she was doing? And yet, from the expression in her eyes I knew that her decision to remain behind was not made lightly.

"I'd best be going," I said hoarsely. "I still have things to do before I head for home."

She nodded in understanding and smiled. "You drop in anytime you can, Joshua."

I worried about her as I left. The tulips were appearing. Mrs. Foggelson would do just fine tending her beloved spring flowers. But who would be responsible for the many other things that needed tending?

The school year was almost over, and Mr. Foggelson would undoubtedly leave as soon as he was finished with his teaching obligation. That would leave Mrs. Foggelson totally on her own. She hadn't made many friends in town, either. She would need someone.

I had been brought up to not take kindly to neighborhood gossip, but I knew I had to talk to Aunt Lou. I knew she was busy with all her housework, the church, and baby Sarah, but Mrs. Foggelson would need some lady to talk to, and I figured that Aunt Lou would be just the one. I would help Camellia's mother all I could. I wouldn't be able to do much, but I'd pray. And I'd get Aunt Lou.

CHAPTER 13

Building

Days passed into weeks, weeks to months, and months to years. During those two years I worked hard, occasionally wondering if God would suddenly make up His mind about what He wanted me to do and move me on before I had things under control at the farm. If I had thought it through at the time, I would have realized that our heavenly Father doesn't do things that way.

With the help of Mr. Thomas, we got the quality seed that we needed and began our crop rotation. But there were no miracles. The land did not turn more productive overnight. By the end of the second year of our new program, Grandpa and I both hoped we were seeing some improvement in the yield—but maybe it was just that we had a wonderful summer for growing.

The herd, too, was slow to increase. We were able to purchase a few good animals from Mr. Thomas, and with the best from our own herd, we began to build for the future. But there were no quick profits on our investment, and we had to watch the farm budget carefully so we wouldn't overextend ourselves. The calves of that spring were the first real return we saw on our experiment; even Uncle Charlie had to come out to the barnyard to have a look as each one arrived. One of the cows had twins—both little heifers that would one day greatly strengthen our herd.

Aunt Lou's family was increasing, too. Jonathan Joshua joined Sarah at the parsonage. Sarah, at two years, was so excited that she could hardly contain herself. She called him "my brudder," and squeezed him each time she came near him. She wanted to share everything with him, from her fuzzy teddy to her breakfast toast. Aunt Lou had to watch her closely.

Willie came home the first summer, excited about how God was helping him with his studies and also his finances. He was just bursting with it all. But he ended up getting a summer job at Gainerville, so I didn't get to see him nearly as much as I would have liked.

He did talk with me about Camellia, however. She was still angry about her ma staying on in town. Willie said that Camellia had, at one point, become quite open and willing to listen to him as he tried to explain his faith. Then when she got the word about her folks, she completely turned it all off again. Willie said he didn't dare raise the subject after that. Every time he attempted to say anything about Christianity, Camellia would remind him that her ma had at one time professed faith, and look what she had done to her pa. It wasn't fair of Camellia, we both knew, but people can reason in strange ways sometimes. Willie urged me to keep on praying, and I promised I would.

Mrs. Foggelson didn't stay on at the big house after Mr. Foggelson left town. She moved the few things that she still called her own into a single room at the boardinghouse in town and started to take in sewing. There were no silver tea services, no sets of fine china, no flower beds of tulips and roses—nothing but a sewing machine and the bare necessities of life.

But Aunt Lou did befriend her, and she responded. She often walked over to the parsonage for a cup of tea. Aunt Lou was even able to get her to start reading her Bible again—but she still wouldn't agree to come to church.

Willie didn't even come home the next summer. He had a job there near the school. I missed him, but I was really too busy to think much about it.

The harvest weather was better and the crops were in on time. The next winter was milder, too, and our few animals fared much better.

When spring returned, we planted again—this time with some of our own seed. We had chosen the best, spending many of our winter evenings gathered around the kitchen table carefully sorting out seed for planting. For Uncle Charlie it was difficult; his twisted hands found it almost impossible to handle small things.

That third year on the farm, the crop that we planted gave us the best yield we had seen for some time. The hay did especially well, and the pruned-back fruit trees began to bear again like they hadn't in years. We'd have several pigs ready for fall market, and the cattle, though slow to make a comeback, showed good quality in the small herd we were developing.

We were even able to put out money for paint, and in between the haying and the harvesting I was able to paint the buildings, including the house. It sure did make the whole farm look better.

I even began to think about a tractor, though I didn't mention it to Grandpa and Uncle Charlie. I knew they would be likely to think I was moving a bit too fast.

The crop was all in, and I had just celebrated my twenty-first birthday when I got a letter from Willie. We hadn't been writing quite as often as we once had, and I was pretty excited when I saw his handwriting. Willie was now in his final year at the college and would soon be a mission candidate. I knew he was excited about finding which foreign field God had in mind for him. I would have been excited too, but the thought of Willie graduating was a reminder to me that I was already four years behind in my preparation time. It would take a good deal of extra hard work once God showed me what He wanted me to do with my life.

I just had to write, Willie said, *and share with you the most exciting news. Camellia has become a Christian. I won't tell you any more about it than that, as she wants to tell you all about it herself when we come home for Christmas. Yes, you read that right. She is going to come home to see her mother. She knows that they must get some things straightened out between them.*

I couldn't believe it! It was just too good to be true. And yet I didn't know why I found it so hard to believe. I had been praying daily for several years for that very thing to happen. The tears began to fill my eyes, and I brushed them away with the back of my hand.

Camellia was a Christian! Camellia would be coming home at Christmas! It all seemed like a miracle. Praise God! Bless Willie!

I read on, the pages blurred now from the tears in my eyes.

We'll be there on Monday's train, Willie went on. *It arrives at 11:35 A.M.— or is supposed to. Remember how we used to go down to the station to watch for the train—not to see the train as much as to watch the people? Remember how some of them would get so irate because the train was always so late? Well, if it's that late on Monday, the 21st of December, I might understand for the first time why they acted as they did.*

My eyes slid to the calendar. The twenty-first was twelve days away. How would I ever be able to stand the wait?

Then I let out a whoop and raced the stairs two at a time to tell Grandpa and Uncle Charlie the good news.

CHAPTER 14

Sharing the News

I daydreamed my way through the rest of the day and tossed my way through the night. After such a long time, I would see Willie and Camellia again! Camellia had become a Christian!

The next morning I saddled Chester and headed for town. I couldn't wait to tell the good news to Uncle Nat and Aunt Lou.

Sarah saw me coming and met me at the door. "Hi, Unca Dosh!" she shouted before I even had time to dismount. She was still having trouble with her *j*'s. And I was still waiting for the day when she could properly say uncle, though I must admit that I secretly thought "Unca" sounded pretty cute.

I picked her up and gave her a kiss on the cheek. "Hi, sweets."

"Have you been to da store?" she asked coyly.

"No, I came straight here to see you." I kissed her cheek again. Sarah knew that only shopping brought us to town midweek.

She squirmed to get down and I set her on her feet.

"Can I go wif you?" she asked, her big blue eyes pleading.

"I don't need to go to the store this time," I replied, feeling quite flattered that she wanted to be with me every moment that I was in town. "See?" I continued, pointing to Chester, "I didn't even bring the wagon—just Chester."

Sarah's lower lip came out, and I thought for a moment that she would cry.

"I'm not going to the store," I repeated quickly, crouching down to her level.

The tears came to her eyes then, and she looked at me as she tried to blink them away. "Then how can you get candy?"

For a minute I didn't quite understand. Then it dawned on me. We came to visit *after* shopping, and we always had a small bag of treats for Sarah.

I couldn't help but laugh. The little beggar hadn't done a great deal for my ego, but at least she was honest and forthright.

"No candy this time," I said, tousling her curly hair. "Too many sweets aren't good for you. Where's your mamma?"

"She's wif brudder." The tears were already disappearing.

"Where?"

"In the kitchen."

"Is she feeding him?"

"No," said Sarah, shaking her head, "baffin' him." Then she suddenly seemed to remember that she was missing one of her favorite parts of the day. She turned from me and ran back through the porch into the kitchen, calling as she ran, "Mamma! Unca Dosh is here."

"Good," Aunt Lou answered, "come right on in, Dosh." I could hear the chuckle in her voice.

I wasn't really uncle to Sarah and Jonathan, of course—I was cousin. But Aunt Lou was training the children to call me uncle since our relationship fit with that title better.

Sarah ran ahead of me and climbed up on a kitchen chair beside the table before I got there.

"See!" she pointed excitedly. "Brudder can sit now."

I couldn't believe how much he had grown just since the last time I'd seen him.

Aunt Lou smiled at me. "I'll be done here in a second; then I'll fix you some—whatever you want. Coffee, tea, milk, lemonade."

I nodded, reaching to chuck Jon under the chin. "How ya doin', big fella?" I asked him. He rewarded me with a grin.

"He's got a tooth already!"

"Two," corrected Sarah. "Mamma say two."

"Two is right," informed Aunt Lou. "Another one is just coming through."

Aunt Lou finished dressing Jon and handed him to me.

"Will he spit?" I would have taken him even if she had assured me that I was bound to get spit up on.

"He's good about that," she said instead. "Hardly ever spits up. And I haven't fed him yet, so you're safe."

Sarah and I played with the baby while Aunt Lou made hot chocolate and cut some slices of lemon loaf. "So, how is everyone?" she asked.

"Fine."

With her question and my reply, my good news again came foremost in my thinking.

"Uncle Nat here?" I asked. I had hoped to tell both of them together.

"No, he went out to the Lewises'. Mr. Lewis is the new Church Board Chairman and they have some things to discuss."

I was disappointed, and it showed.

"Did you need him?" asked Aunt Lou.

"Oh no. I—I just got some great news, and I wanted to tell both of you."

Aunt Lou's head came up from the stirring of the hot chocolate. Her eyes searched mine. "Well, you aren't going to make me wait just because Nat isn't here, are you?"

I grinned. "Naw," I said. "I wouldn't be able to stand it."

"Good!" she said emphatically and set the two cups of hot chocolate on the table. Then she reached for a glass partly filled with milk for Sarah.

"So?" she asked, passing me the lemon loaf.

"Just got a letter from Willie," I began.

"Did he get his assignment?"

"Nope. Even better than that."

"He's coming home?" said Aunt Lou, knowing I would be pretty excited about that.

"Yeah, for Christmas—but there's more."

I was really enjoying this little game. We had played it many times over the years, savouring some bit of exciting news and making it stretch out just as much as possible.

"And?" prompted Aunt Lou.

"Camellia is coming, too."

"Camellia?" Aunt Lou sounded almost as excited as I had been.

I nodded, my face flushed with the wonder of it all.

"Here?"

"Here! To see her ma."

Aunt Lou surprised me then. She started to cry. I think she started to pray too. She was talking softly to someone, and I knew it wasn't me.

I sat there hardly knowing how to respond; then I got up from my chair and gently laid Jonathan in the small bed that stood in the corner of the kitchen. I had the feeling that Aunt Lou might need me, but I still didn't know just what move I should make. Sarah brought me back to attention. She reached for Aunt Lou's hand, concern in her eyes.

"Mamma," she said. "Mamma, why you cry?"

Aunt Lou's face changed immediately and reached out to gather Sarah to her. She began to laugh softly. "It's all right, sweetheart," she assured Sarah. "Mamma is crying for joy. I'm fine. Really. It's all right."

Then Aunt Lou turned to me. "Mrs. Foggelson will be so happy. I told her I'd pray that Camellia would forgive her for what she had to do."

Had to do? The words echoed and reechoed in my mind. But I didn't ask questions—at least not then.

Then Aunt Lou put a hand on my arm and, looking at me with tears starting again, pleaded, "Oh, Josh! We've got to pray like we have never prayed before. We've got to pray that this time together might be a time when Camellia and Mrs. Foggelson will realize how much they need God in their lives."

"Well," I began, then abandoned all caution and rushed on, "that's the rest of the good news. Camellia has already realized that."

Aunt Lou's eyes got big and she searched my face to see if I had really said what she understood me to say.

"You mean—?" she began. I nodded and then I gave a whoop and reached out for Aunt Lou and we laughed and cried and praised together.

"I've gotta go," I said to Aunt Lou finally. "I really didn't have time for a trip to town today, but I just couldn't wait to tell you."

"Oh, Josh," she said, "I'm so glad you came. That is the most exciting thing that has happened since—since Jonathan," she ended with emphasis, and turned to her little son.

Jonathan sucked his fist noisily, reminding his mother that he was still unfed. Aunt Lou kissed his forehead and murmured something to him.

I heard a deep sigh from the chair beside me and looked down into the forlorn face of little Sarah. She sighed again, gave her little shoulders a shrug and turned her small palms up.

"Nonny sweets," she said. "Nonny" was Sarah's own word. As far as we could figure out, she meant "not any" or "none" when she used it.

Both Aunt Lou and I laughed.

"Here," I said, fishing in my pocket. "Here's a penny for your piggy bank."

Her face immediately lit up and she took the penny from me, scooted down from her chair and called as she ran toward her room, "T'anks you, Unca Dosh."

We heard the penny clink as it joined the others in her bank. I grinned as I shook my head.

"That's an awful little beggar you're raising there, Lou," I said.

"Me?" responded Lou. "*Me?* Seems to me her begging has something to do with three men in her life."

I shrugged my shoulders, turned my palms upward, "Nonny sweets." I grinned and left.

CHAPTER 15

Homecoming

I suffered terribly waiting for the twenty-first. I kept trying to imagine what it was going to be like to see Camellia again. I wondered what the *new* Camellia would be like. She was a believer now. She would undoubtedly have a new softness, a new understanding, a new gentleness to her.

On the other hand, I hoped she hadn't changed *too* much. I would have been terribly disappointed if she had put her beautiful coppery hair into some kind of a tight bun or something. And I couldn't imagine her in strict, plain dresses either. Somehow they just wouldn't suit Camellia.

And Willie—it seemed like such a long time since I had seen him. He was bound to have changed. I thought I had grown away from Willie; that after my first awful months of missing him so, I had finally learned how to get along without him. But now that he was due home, all the old memories of our friendship returned, and I missed him more than I ever had.

A glance in my mirror told me that I had changed over the years, too. I tried to think back to how I had looked at eighteen and I couldn't really remember. I knew I had filled out since then. The clothes I had worn as a teenager just hung in my closet, waiting for someone to sort through them and discard them. But somehow it felt comfortable to have them still hanging there day after day, month after month, even though I knew I would never be able to wear them again.

I looked at my muscular arms. Shoveling the grain on the wagon and shoveling the fertilizer off had made me quite well developed, not the skinny teen I had been.

I rubbed the outline of my jaw. At seventeen I had shaved a few times, but not really because I had needed to. It made me feel rather grown-up to pull the razor over my face. But now I had to shave, and to my surprise it hadn't turned out to be nearly as much fun as I had dreamed it to be.

But apart from growing up and filling out and needing to shave rather than just wanting to, it seemed that there really hadn't been that much change in me. I was still the same farm boy that I had always been. And now Willie would be cityfied and book-learned.

I thought of other changes. We had all been a lot younger in more than years when we had last seen one another—kids, still thinking that life had only good things in store for us, I guess. Willie had his dream of being a missionary, and looked like he was about to realize that dream. Camellia had high hopes of becoming someone important in the field of Interior Design; for some reason I had never been told, her dream had gone sour. She had quit and taken a somewhat mundane job.

And I was still "treading water" as far as what I was to do with my life. After I finished straightening out the farm and getting Grandpa and Uncle Charlie cared for, that is. It was taking much longer than I had first thought, but things around the farm were slowly improving.

The only problem was, Grandpa and Uncle Charlie weren't improving. Grandpa was no longer a young man. Slightly stooped, he grumbled some when he went to climb anything and he grunted when he leaned over. I knew Grandpa had neither the strength nor the desire to run the farm again.

And Uncle Charlie really worried me. Week by week it was more difficult for him to handle the household chores, things like the hot pots and peeling the vegetables. More and more Grandpa was needed to help him in the house. For now I could handle the chores and most of the farm duties myself, but what would happen after God had directed me into my life work?

It weighed heavily on my mind. But Uncle Nat had told me time and again that God would make things clear to me one step at a time. When it was time for me to pursue my life's calling, God would have someone else to care for Grandpa and Uncle Charlie.

Still, I couldn't help but speculate just how God might do that. He could arrange for hired help. But that was so costly. Unless the farm really did *much* better on the new program, I didn't see how that plan would work. He could have one of the neighbors sharecrop the farm. The Turleys were our closest neighbors, and they were really struggling after the setback of the hard winter when they lost most of their stock. They wouldn't likely be able to afford it.

Or He could direct Grandpa to sell the farm. That thought really bothered me. I knew that after having put so much time and energy into making the farm more productive, I would have a tough time watching someone else take over—especially if that someone let it go back to the way I had found it! I'd have to do a lot of praying to be able to accept the sale of the farm.

But as much as I pondered the questions about the farm, even that failed to occupy my thoughts in the days prior to December twenty-first. Most of my thinking was of my two school friends and how we would feel about each other after so many years and so many changes.

I couldn't, of course, expect Camellia to come back home and consider me her beau. I mean, I had called it all off when she didn't believe as I did. Now it would take some time and some getting reacquainted to get things back to where they had been.

I was prepared for that. In my mind I began to list all of the things that young fellas do when they court. Flowers were hard to come by this time of year, but candy was readily available. A fancy necklace or a bracelet might be nice. I might even be able to find one that would match the ring I planned to buy later on.

One thing troubled me. I didn't know how long Camellia expected the courting to take. Would she expect me to come calling for a number of months, or could we take a shortcut since we had once been sorta sweethearts? I decided that I would just have to play that part by ear.

But the wait seemed forever.

I checked out the time of that train. Three times, in fact, I had checked just to be sure. I shaved especially carefully that morning and shined my Sunday shoes and pressed my shirt. Uncle Charlie had already ironed it, but he couldn't do the job that he used to do.

After getting myself dressed I fussed and polished and smoothed and patted and all the time I kept an eye on the clock. I caught Grandpa and Uncle Charlie exchanging grins and winks now and then, but I paid no mind to them.

I had intended to ride Chester; then I thought that maybe Camellia would be anxious for a chat. We could go for a little drive if I had the sleigh, so I harnessed up the team instead. I threw in a warm blanket so Camellia could bundle up and keep warm, then finally headed off for town.

I was still early, but I couldn't bear to wait another minute. Besides, I had to stop at the store to pick out a box of candy. I had looked a couple of times before but hadn't been able to make up my mind.

When I reached the store I tied the team and went back to the candy counter. The girl behind the glassed-in goodies looked at me with a friendly smile on her face. She was new in the store, but I recognized her as one of the Tilley girls. We had gone to school in town together but she was younger, so I hadn't paid much attention to her. I didn't know if she expected me to greet her now or not. I said "Howdy," but I kept it very impersonal.

I still didn't know which candy to buy, and after trying to sort it out in my thinking for some time I finally blurted out, "If a fella brought you candy, what would you like best?"

She smiled rather coyly and picked out a large box of assorted flavors. "That one?"

She nodded.

"I'll take it," I said and started to count out the money.

"Could you wrap it nicely for me please?" I asked, and she nodded and went into a back room. When she returned and handed me the package, I could see she had done a good job with the wrapping. I smiled and thanked her, took the package, and left.

It wasn't far enough from the store to the station to justify driving the team. Besides, some horses spooked at the train as it whistled and chugged its way into town. I didn't want to have my mind worried with skittery horses.

I kept checking the watch that Aunt Lou and Uncle Nat had given me for my twenty-first birthday. At one point I was sure it must have stopped, but when I put it to my ear it was still ticking.

"I'll just explode if it's late," I said to myself, kicking a small pile of frozen snow near the walk. I was immediately sorry. The snow splattered all over the toe of my boot, and I had to get down and wipe it off with my handkerchief. I hoped that the handkerchief wouldn't be needed any further. It sure wouldn't do to pull it out in public all smeared up like it was now.

My impatience reminded me of the childhood game Willie had referred to in his letter, and I smiled at the memory. We loved to watch the reaction of people in trying circumstances; only we had never realized that waiting for a late train was so trying.

I had been vaguely aware that the platform was crowded, but I hadn't really looked to see if I knew anyone. In fact, I hadn't really paid much attention at all until I heard a shout, "It's coming!" and then I saw Willie's folks lined up on the platform just down from me. Most of the other folks I knew, too, at least by sight. I spotted Mary Turley and I smiled to myself. Willie might insist that they were "just friends," but didn't her presence verify my suspicions?

That's nice, I thought to myself. *Mary would make a wonderful missionary's wife. She's kind and caring, even attractive in her own way.*

The train blew its whistle then and I forgot all about the crowd of people. I forgot all about Willie's family and even Mary Turley. All I could think about was Camellia. My throat got dry and my eyes moist and my knees felt so weak I felt that I might go down in a heap.

I saw Willie first. He looked about twice as big as I had remembered him. He had on a new coat. I unreasonably thought it strange to see Willie in clothes I hadn't seen before. He looked taller and broader and much more grown-up. But his smile was the same. He yelled, "Hi, Josh!" my direction; then he saw his folks and he turned from me and wrapped his mother in his arms.

I searched over the tops of heads to watch for Camellia to appear on the train steps. I was beginning to fear something had happened and she had changed her mind. Folks seemed to have stopped coming from the train, and then Willie broke from his folks and dashed back up the steps again and when he returned he was carrying a large suitcase and an armful of parcels. Just behind, looking even more beautiful than I had remembered, was Camellia.

Her coppery hair was still wisping about her face, but in a much more grown-up style than the flowing waves of her girlhood. Her coat was a soft green color and it accented her creamy cheeks and her beautiful eyes. For a moment my breath caught in my throat, and I couldn't move or speak. Her eyes sorted through the crowd that was left; then she looked directly at me and cried, "Josh!"

Somehow I managed to get my feet going, and I moved myself forward toward Willie and Camellia. Willie grabbed me first and as we hugged one another, I remember thinking that he was likely making an awful mess of the box of candy I held in my hands.

Then he let go of me and I was standing there facing Camellia. She laughed softly and reached up to my shoulder.

"You've grown, Josh," she said in a teasing voice. I just nodded dumbly.

Then she pushed herself up on her tiptoes and with one hand on the back of my head to tip it forward, she kissed me right on the cheek. I wanted to reach out and pull her to me and kiss her again, but I couldn't move. She moved back rather quickly and looked at me again.

"I gave Willie permission to tell you the good news, but I want to fill in all the details myself. I know you've prayed for me for a long time, Josh—and I thank you. But I still need your prayers. It isn't going to be easy to see Mamma."

I nodded again. I still hadn't managed to speak a word to Camellia.

"I wrote Mamma that I was coming, but I asked her not to meet the train," Camellia went on. "I have a feeling that our meeting might be a bit emotional."

I just nodded again.

"I promised her that I would go directly to her."

I swallowed and nodded the third time. Her plans were reasonable enough.

And then she laughed again and her beautiful hair swirled as she flipped her head. "We have so much to talk about," she said. "Can you come over about three-thirty? I'm just dying to tell you everything." She stopped and looked at me again. "And to hear how things have been going with you," she concluded.

Willie and Mary were chatting excitedly beside us, but I didn't hear a word they said. I was too filled with the sight of Camellia.

I finally found my voice. "Three-thirty," I promised, then remembered the box of candy that I still held in my hand. I thrust it forward. The bow was lopsided and the paper a bit crumpled, but I guess Camellia understood.

"Welcome home," I managed.

"It's so good to be home," she said softly, and her eyes were misty with unshed tears.

Before I could say anything more, Camellia and Willie were moving away. Camellia was being greeted by his family, and I knew that she and all of her belongings would be loaded in the waiting sleigh and driven off to see her mother.

I berated myself for not having the foresight to bring the team right to the station. *I* could have been the one taking Camellia home.

But three-thirty really wasn't that long to wait. And I had some shopping to do. Now the fancy jewelry not only seemed like a good idea, but a must. I hurried off down the street to give myself plenty of time. I couldn't remember being so excited or so happy in all my life.

CHAPTER 16

The "Call"

It took me quite a while to find the piece of jewelry that was just right for Camellia. There wasn't a necklace or bracelet in town with a ring to match, so I had to settle for something else. I finally found a chain with a cameo so delicate that it looked like it had been made just for her. It still wasn't as pretty as the wearer would be, but nothing could hope to compete with Camellia.

I had the clerk wrap it prettily, and I carefully tucked it into the inside pocket of my coat. I didn't want to take any chances on this special package getting messed up.

I finished my shopping shortly before three-thirty; feeling generous and a bit lightheaded, I decided to go buy Sarah some peppermint patties. Pocketing the candy, I headed for Aunt Lou's.

Sarah came running to meet me. "Hi, Unca Dosh," she called, then stopped and with great concentration started over. It was obvious that some-one had been schooling her. "Unca-le-J-dosh," she managed, quite proud of herself for including the proper consonants. I picked her up and kissed her, congratulating her profusely for her accomplishment. She grinned, obviously pleased with the effect of her speech.

"You come to see us?" she asked.

"No, not really. I'm going to see another—lady." I blushed even as I spoke the words.

"But you're here," she corrected me.

"Not for long. I'm going to leave again."

"Why?" she asked, looking about to cry.

"Because," I answered gleefully, and even young Sarah should have caught the excitement that I felt.

"Mamma's in the bedroom feeding my brudder," she informed me.

"Well, I didn't come to see Mamma either," I answered.

"Why?" she asked again.

"Because," I said, drawing out the small bag of peppermint patties, "because I've been to the store."

She squealed when she saw the bag, knowing it was for her.

Aunt Lou called from the bedroom, "I'll be right out, Josh."

"Don't hurry," I called back. "I can't stay. I just dropped by with something for Sarah."

"You're heading home?"

I couldn't keep the excitement from my voice. "No, I'm on my way over to Camellia's. She wanted to see her ma alone first."

Aunt Lou was silent for a minute; then her voice came back softly to me.

"I'll be praying for you, Josh."

I didn't feel that I needed much prayer at the moment. All my prayers— and my dreams—had finally been answered. With a light step I started out for Camellia's, leaving the team tied in the churchyard. There wasn't much room for hitching horses outside the boardinghouse, and in the middle of the business day I was sure all of the room would be taken. I had been to see Mrs. Foggelson several times over the years since she had taken up residence in the rambling building.

I paced myself so that it was three-thirty-one when I was let into the boardinghouse hallway, and a moment later I was knocking on the door marked Number Four, my heart knocking just as hard on the inside.

Camellia answered the door. She took my hand and drew me in, exclaiming as she did so, "Mamma has just been telling me how kind you've been over the years, Josh. I will never be able to thank you."

But Camellia was wrong. The light in her eyes was more than enough to thank me for the little I had done.

She led me into the small, crowded room that served as Mrs. Foggelson's parlor, sewing room, and living quarters. It was even more crowded now, with Camellia's luggage and packages littered about the room.

"Please excuse our mess," Camellia said with a wave of her hand and pushed aside enough packages for me to find room on the sofa.

"I haven't had time to put things away," she explained, then sighed deeply. "And I have no idea where I'll find room to put it when I do get the time." A silvery laugh followed the words. It was so much like Camellia, so vitally alive—and unpredictable.

She turned to me then and looked me over carefully again. I blushed under her frank scrutiny and shifted uncomfortably.

"Oh, Josh," she began, "it is so good to be home."

I looked at this beautiful girl-turned-woman. All the things that I longed to be able to express died in my throat. I could only nod and mumble something about it being good to have her home again.

The dress she was wearing was unlike anything I had seen before. The collar was high and shaped to highlight her face; the bodice fitted her well-shaped waist and then flared out in a skirt that swirled as she moved. The sleeves came down to her wrists and tapered to a point over the back of her hand. The color was a soft blue-green, and it accented her hair and eyes beautifully.

"Where do we start?" she was saying. "We have so much to catch up on."

Then she swung toward me. "Oh, my! My manners. Let me take your coat and hat."

That special gift was secreted carefully in my coat pocket. I was twirling my hat nervously in my hands. She laid them both on a chair nearby.

"Would you like some tea?" she asked.

I nodded and said that would be nice. I really didn't care for tea, but I hoped by drinking it my tongue might be loosened.

"Mamma had to deliver some sewing," Camellia informed me as she went about putting the kettle on to heat on an electric plate on a small corner table. I hadn't even thought to wonder where Mrs. Foggelson was.

"She said she wouldn't be long."

I hoped that Mrs. Foggelson didn't hurry too much.

I watched Camellia as she put the tea in the pot and tapped her trim foot impatiently, waiting for the kettle to boil. Then she poured the water, drew two plain white cups from a small shelf, and set them on the table. There was hardly room for the cups and saucers, so after Camellia had poured the tea she brought me my cup.

"So, Joshua Jones," Camellia said in a teasing voice as she settled herself on the sofa beside me, "what have you been doing with yourself in the past million years?"

She emphasized the *million*, and I found myself agreeing. In fact, the last twelve days had seemed about that long.

"Nothing, really," I answered. "Farming."

"Mamma says that you are really knowledgeable about farming. That you are trying new things and—"

Secretly I blessed Mrs. Foggelson for saying something nice about what I had been doing at the farm. I was also excited to know that the two of them had been talking about me.

"Some," I cut in modestly. "But mostly I've been just waiting—an' praying."

Camellia's teasing eyes sobered.

"I know," she said in not much more than a whisper. "And I thank you."

She sipped her tea slowly and then set her cup aside. I was surprised to see that tears had gathered in her eyes.

"I honestly don't know why you and Willie didn't give up on me long ago. I was so stubborn. So blind. I don't know why I couldn't see that you were telling me the truth all the time. That you were only interested in my good.

"Do you know what I used to think?" she said after a pause. "I used to think, 'These people are dumb. They are unlearned and they have one thing in mind only. To get me to be just as dumb and dependent as they are so that they can chalk up points for saving the most people.' That's what I actually thought. It was a long time until Willie could convince me that he was really concerned about *me*. That he knew that without God I was lost, doomed for eternity, and he cared about *me*."

Camellia twisted a coppery curl around a finger as she spoke. With all my heart I wanted to reach out and take one of those curls in my fingers but I held myself in check.

"And then this—this thing with Mamma and Papa happened. I couldn't believe it. I just couldn't bear to think of them living in two houses, many miles from one another.

"I had always been a daddy's girl. You know that. Well, I was sure that this whole thing must be Mamma's fault. I hated her. Honestly, Josh, I hated her. I couldn't understand why she had done this to Papa. I knew that she had at one time believed in God. I decided if she could do that to my papa and still pretend to have known the truth—even if Papa had forbidden her to go to church—then I wanted no part of religion."

She sighed and flipped her hair back from her face.

"Well, Willie still wouldn't give up. He kept inviting me to Bible studies and to church and we had lots of talks and arguments—" She stopped and laughed as she recalled.

"Then one day I did—I'll never know why—I did agree to go to a Bible study with him. Well, that was the beginning." She laughed again.

"And who would have ever dreamed the end?" she said and her eyes shone. "I was home alone in my room one night, reading over again the portion we had read in Bible study. It was John 5:24: 'I say unto you, He that heareth my word, and believeth on him that sent me, hath everlasting life, and shall not come into condemnation; but is passed from death unto life.' Suddenly I believed it. I really believed it! Somehow I understood. I was evil, I knew that, but I could, by believing and accepting, pass from death to life.

"I have always been afraid of death, Josh. I wanted life. So, alone there in my room, I turned my life over to God, thanking Him that His Son had taken my condemnation, just as the verse said. And now I am enrolled in Willie's Bible college instead of working at the telephone office."

"Really?" I said excitedly. "I didn't know that."

"Really! And I am learning so much, but there is so much that I don't know. Now I wonder how in the world I could have been so—so stupid as to believe all of those lies."

"Blinded," I corrected.

"Blinded—and stupid," she finished with a laugh.

I set my cup aside. I had wanted to hear all about Camellia's conversion, but I wanted to talk about other things, too. If she was enrolled in college then—

"So you aren't staying home here, with your ma?" I asked. I didn't know if I was ready to hear her reply.

"Oh no," she answered quickly. "We only have a week."

"We?"

"Willie and I."

Of course. I had forgotten that they were both going to the same school now. They would need to be back to classes at the same time.

"Willie should be here any minute," she said, eying the clock impatiently.

"Willie?" I puzzled.

She looked at me with a twinkle in her eyes. "We have something to tell you," she said. "Willie made me promise not to tell until he came."

So Willie was coming. I thought of the gift in my coat pocket. If Willie was expected soon, I'd best get some business done. I cleared my throat.

"I was wondering," I began cautiously. "I mean, well—I've missed you so much—being friends—and I was wondering, seeing you won't be here long and will need to get back to classes, if we could make the most of the days you have, sorta get to know one another again?"

It was a long enough speech for a fellow as tongue-tied as I was, but not too articulate.

"Oh, Josh!" Camellia cried, clapping her hands together. "I was hoping we could. I might have been bullheaded and mean, but I did appreciate you, and the Christian stand you took, and your prayers over the years. I was hoping—"

"How about tomorrow?" I cut in. "Would you like to go for a ride tomorrow? Maybe visit the farm?"

Her face fell.

"Oh, Josh. I'm sorry, but tomorrow I am to go to visit Willie's folks."

Willie's folks!

"Sunday?" I asked.

She made a face. "And Sunday Willie is coming here to have dinner with Mamma and me."

It seemed that a good share of Camellia's time had already been spoken for. I was a bit annoyed with Willie. He could have her company when they got back to school. Still it was understandable that he should want his folks to spend time with her. They had been praying for her, too.

"Well—" My next invitation was interrupted by a knock at the door. And I still hadn't had opportunity to give Camellia her gift.

Camellia sprang to answer the door, and just as we had both expected, Willie stood there, a big grin on his face. Camellia took his hand, much as she had taken mine, and drew him into the room.

Only she didn't drop Willie's hand. She stood there holding it and I saw Willie's fingers curling possessively around Camellia's.

"I haven't told him," she glowed. "It was so hard, but I kept my promise."

Willie dropped Camellia's hand, and his free arm stole around Camellia's waist, drawing her to him.

"Josh," he said, "because you are so special to both of us, we wanted you to be the first one to know."

I felt my throat go dry.

"Camellia and I are going to be married," beamed Willie as a radiant Camellia reached up to place a hand lovingly on his cheek.

I was glad I was still seated on the sofa. I knew that my legs would never have held. The room seemed to whirl around and around, and I was being swept along helplessly by the tide of a dark, bottomless sea. Then, just before my head went under, I realized that I was being watched, that someone was waiting for an enthusiastic response from me regarding the announcement that had just been made.

Christmas

"I do believe that we took Josh totally by surprise!"

Willie's voice roused me from my stupor. I looked toward the sound and saw Willie with his arm still around Camellia, his face lit up with a broad grin.

Camellia was smiling, too. She turned to give Willie a kiss on the cheek and then moved from his arm and came toward the sofa where I was sitting.

"Isn't it wonderful?" she enthused. When I was unable to answer she continued, "Didn't you even guess?"

I shook my head slowly, still unable to express myself in words.

Willie had joined Camellia and reached out his hand toward me.

"We wanted our good friend to be the first to know—after our parents, that is. I told my folks and Camellia told her ma, but that's all. We knew that you would be—"

"Oh, Josh," cut in Camellia, "I could hardly keep our secret. If it hadn't been for you, all the years of telling me that I was wrong, all the years of praying, I might never have become a believer."

"And I would be going to the mission field all alone," Willie added rather soberly.

The spinning room was beginning to slow down. I could hear all the words that were spoken to me, but they still seemed unreal, and I wondered momentarily if I was having a bad dream.

Willie reached down and pulled me to my feet. He thumped me on the back and squeezed my left shoulder, and the pounding seemed to start my blood flowing again.

"I want you to be my best man," he was saying.

I found my voice then. I even managed some kind of a smile. "Sure," I said. "I'd be—I'd be honored."

Willie slapped my back again. "Caught you by surprise, eh?"

I nodded. "Sure did," I was able to respond honestly. "Sure did."

And then Willie, interrupted often by Camellia, began a full account of their courtship and Willie's proposal and Camellia's acceptance. I didn't want to hear it, not a word of it—but I could hardly get up and walk out on my two best friends. I grinned—shakily, I'm sure—and nodded from time to time, and that seemed to be enough to satisfy them.

I wondered how soon they would be married, but I didn't ask. I figured that I'd find out eventually.

"And we're going to be married right here, in our little church," Willie was saying.

I did my smile-and-nod routine. Uncle Nat would have the wedding.

"I just wish we didn't need to wait," Willie went on.

"Wait?" I echoed.

"For Camellia to finish her training. I'll be done in the spring, but Camellia is just starting. She won't take four years of straight Bible courses, but she will do a couple of semesters and then go on to take classes in nursing, so that means a long wait."

I was about to ask when the wedding would take place when Camellia cut in.

"It's going to seem such a long, long time," she moaned, "but I know God can help us. Willie will put in one term on the field; then when he comes home for furlough we'll be married, and I will join him."

"How long is a term?" I found myself asking.

"Four years," groaned Camellia.

"*Four years?*" I didn't mean to say the words. They just popped out.

Willie's arm went around Camellia again. "Four years," he repeated. "A long time—but I can wait."

I didn't see anything particularly heroic about that, though I didn't say so. I would have waited four years for Camellia, too.

"Jacob waited seven years," Camellia reminded us, and Willie added quickly, "And then worked another seven."

They looked at one another and smiled. The whole scene was getting to me. I knew I had to get out of there. I pulled my watch from my pocket and studied its face. The time really didn't register, but I tried to look surprised and mumbled something about the fact that I really had to be going.

"I know you're awfully busy," said Willie, "but we have a whole week here at home. I hope we can get together often while we're here. We really would love—"

So that's the way it was. Willie and Camellia. It was no longer *me* for either of them. It was *we* now, and I was still just *me*.

"Yeah. Sure," I said. "Lots of time. We'll—we'll get together."

"That sleigh ride, Josh," cut in Camellia. "That sounds like so much fun. I hope we can work that in."

"Sure," I said. "Any time. Just let me know when it will work out."

"Hey," said Willie, pounding me on the back again as I shrugged into my coat, "I've got an idea. Why don't we ask Mary to join us? Make it a foursome? What do you think?"

Camellia was already clapping her hands. "That would be so much fun!"

"Sure," I said, trying hard to grin. "Sure—whenever you can make it."

I managed to escape then. I found my way out of the boardinghouse into the crispness of the winter afternoon. The cold air helped me get my bearings. Already the sun was hanging very low in the sky. Snow was beginning to fall in light, scattery flakes. The cold wind promised that choring would be much harder over the next few days.

But I didn't care. In fact, I welcomed the extra work. Something good and solid and demanding would help my whirling brain to sort through the news that had just been enthusiatically shared.

I still couldn't grasp it. Here I had waited and prayed for years for Camellia to become a Christian so that—so that I could feel right about asking her to be my girl. Then she finally becomes a Christian, and what happens? My friend—my best friend Willie gets there first.

I shook my head to clear it; then I realized that I was hurrying down the street in the dead of winter with my coat flapping in the breeze instead of buttoned like it should be. I fumbled with the buttons. There seemed to be a bulge in the right pocket. Then I remembered—the cameo! My special gift to Camellia. My face felt hot, even with the wind blowing cold against it. *I would have given it to her, too!* exploded through my mind. If Willie hadn't come when he did, I would have made a complete fool of myself. To think I had been dumb enough to look for a piece of jewelry with a ring to match. My face burned with humiliation.

Aunt Lou called to me as I unhitched the horses from the churchyard, but I just waved at her and shouted that I didn't have time to stop.

The horses were in a hurry to get home to a warm barn. They had been standing in the cold for too long. I let them pick their own speed and didn't even bother driving them much.

Grandpa and Uncle Charlie were both in the kitchen when I came in from settling the horses to change my clothes for choring. They seemed to look me over real good, and I was determined that I wasn't going to let anything show.

"Your friends get home?" asked Grandpa.

I nodded.

"How's Willie? Changed much?" put in Uncle Charlie.

I shrugged. "Some," I said.

"Like how?" This was Grandpa again.

"He's—he's bigger. Broader. Almost done his schooling. More grown-up, I guess."

"Grown-up," chuckled Uncle Charlie. "Never thought that Willie would actually grow up."

I defended Willie then—after all, he was my friend. "Well, he is," I said stubbornly. "He's even gonna get married."

"Willie?"

"To whom?"

"To Camellia," I stated boldly.

I hadn't wanted to say that. In fact, I hadn't even been able to admit that truth to myself yet, and now saying it out loud made me feel like I was shutting and bolting a door to a beautiful room.

"Camellia?"

"You mean, the teacher's daughter? The one that just became a Christian?"

I nodded, my eyes dropping to my boots.

I could sense Grandpa and Uncle Charlie both studying me, and then their eyes turned back to one another. I didn't even look up, just moved toward the stairs.

"I gotta change for chorin'."

I heard a chair scrape behind me and knew that Uncle Charlie was shifting his position. Then he called after me, "When?"

I didn't even turn around, just kept right on toward the stairs. "Not for four years."

I heard Uncle Charlie shift again and Grandpa give his little, "Whoo-ee," and then I heard Grandpa say plain as day, though I knew he wasn't speaking to me. "Lots of things can happen in four years." But I kept right on going up the stairs and didn't even look back.

Not until I finished with chores and supper, alone, in my own room in my own bed, did the truth of it all really hit me. *Camellia is getting married. Getting married to Willie.* There would never, never be a chance for her to be my girl. I had no right to even think of her in that way again.

Before me flashed her beautiful face framed by coppery curls. Her eyes flashed excitedly and her cheeks dimpled into a winsome smile. I turned away from her, shutting my eyes hard to blot out the image, and I buried my face in my pillow and cried like I hadn't done since I'd been a kid.

And after I had cried myself into exhaustion, there was nothing else for me to do but pray.

For seven days I would be forced to see Willie and Camellia—together. For seven days over Christmas. There would be special parties, special services, extra outings—and I would be expected to be there. They would be there, too, arm-in-arm, smiling. There was no way to avoid them.

I thought of faking illness, but I knew that wouldn't be honest. I thought of not going, but that would get me nothing but questions to be answered. I thought of saying I was too busy, but the farm work was so completely caught up that I could hardly use that excuse. In the end I did what I knew I had to do. I went. I went to the Christmas program, the Carol singing, the party at Willie's. I even took that sleigh ride with Willie, Camellia, and Mary Turley. Somehow I managed to make it through.

We spent Christmas with Uncle Nat and Aunt Lou again. I thought about giving her the cameo, but I knew I just couldn't do that. I ended up shamefacedly taking it back, exchanging it for a brooch for Aunt Lou, cuff links for Uncle Nat and a tie bar for Uncle Charlie. That just about finished off my Christmas shopping. I added a tie and suspenders for Grandpa and then went looking for something special for Sarah and Jonathan.

I didn't call on Mrs. Foggelson on Christmas Day. I knew she was having her own Christmas that year. With Camellia home, she sure didn't need me. It was good to see the two of them doing things together. Mrs. Foggelson had even joined Camellia in church on Christmas Sunday. It turned out to be a good Christmas, after all. Maybe God really was answering my prayers. I was even able to think about other things than Camellia—but that took some effort.

Before we knew it, it was time to gather at the train station and say good-bye to Willie and Camellia. I wasn't sure when I would see them again. Willie said that he might be going overseas right after he finished his schooling, and Camellia planned to stay right on at the school, working in the summer and then going back to classes in the fall again.

Mrs. Foggelson was at the station, too. She was awfully sad to see Camellia go. They hugged one another for a long time and cried a lot. It made me feel a bit teary too, but there was no way that I would let it show.

Willie shook my hand, then hugged me. Camellia hugged me too.

"You've been such a special friend, Josh," she whispered. "I have one more thing to ask of you. Take care of Mamma. Please. She needs someone so much."

I nodded in agreement but I couldn't help but wonder why Camellia couldn't stay and take care of her ma herself.

And then they were gone. Several people stood around watching the train pull out. Some of them, I imagined, would stand right there, like they always did, until the train was just a distant dot. I didn't. As soon as the big wheels began to turn, pulling it forward, I turned my back on it and headed for Chester. I didn't need to prolong the agony. I had been through quite enough.

CHAPTER 18

Going On

I did a lot more growing up in the months that followed. I did more praying, too. For the first time in my life I began to realize what it really meant
to turn my life—everything about it—over to God for His choosing.

As I thought about it I realized that Camellia had made the right choice.
Willie was a strong Christian, intent on service for God. At first I had a
difficult time picturing a woman like Camellia with her hair pulled back
in a strict knot, wearing a plain dark dress and high leather boots against
snakes and scorpions. Then I began to think of the real Camellia, the one
that God wanted her to be—gentle, caring, compassionate—a worthy and
life-enriching companion for Willie.

As I prayed and sorted through things, putting them in their proper
perspective, I came to a quiet peace with the way that God was working
out the situation.

I turned my attention back to the farm just in time to begin the preparations for spring planting.

I knew that we still had a long way to go in reaching maximum production, but we were on the right track. The farm looked good. The freshly
painted buildings and fences glistened with each sunrise, and the fields were
free of weeds and thistles—as much as we could possibly keep them. The

spring calves were the best-looking bunch I had seen in my years on the farm. They looked strong and healthy, and I knew they would make good stock.

So as I entered that springtime, I began it as a more mature person, physically, emotionally and spiritually.

Grandpa seemed to pick up a bit that spring as well. He seemed to feel better, and he looked better, too. Maybe he was finally getting rested and built up after so many years of carrying the load. At any rate, he did almost as much of the farming as I did, and when I protested, he just waved it aside, saying that he never felt better in his life.

Seeing Grandpa in good form made it even harder for Uncle Charlie. He wanted so much to be as involved, but he wasn't able to do much at all.

But Sarah was allowed to pay us frequent visits, and she was good for Uncle Charlie's morale. She was going on five and quite grown-up. She spent most of her time in the kitchen with Uncle Charlie, running his errands and helping him. Being with Sarah kept his spirits up—and she was amazingly helpful, too.

A late, slow spring put everything behind for the whole growing season. Aunt Lou came out and planted the big farm garden; that saved us time and worry. And it wasn't a burden for Aunt Lou, for she loved to be involved in making things grow.

At last, some warm, dry weather arrived, and the crops took off. They seemed to sprout up overnight.

I was going through the last of the summer months thinking only of farming and a very occasional trip to the fishing hole when Grandpa caught me off guard. We were heading to town for some supplies, and I was thinking ahead, looking forward to some time with Jon and Sarah and a piece of Aunt Lou's berry pie.

"Been thinking of offering to board the schoolteacher this year."

I swung around to face him and must have given the reins a fair jerk, for the team threw up their heads and switched their tails in protest.

"You what?" I blurted.

"The teacher," repeated Grandpa as though I hadn't heard. "I hear they need a place for her to board."

"And what would we ever do with a teacher?" I said tartly. "We can barely manage ourselves."

"That's the point," said Grandpa.

"You aren't expecting a schoolteacher to teach all day and then come home and cook supper for—"

" 'Course not! 'Course not!" said Grandpa holding up his hand and shaking his head.

"Then what did you mean? How's boarding the schoolteacher going to help us out any? And, besides, where would we put her?"

"We have extry bedrooms."

"Where?"

Grandpa looked at me like I wasn't even thinking. "Well," he said. "Iffen you recall, there is one just down the hall from you."

"*Aunt Lou's?*" I threw out the words as if Grandpa was considering treason.

"Was," corrected Grandpa. "Was Lou's. Don't recall seeing her use it for some time now."

He was being a little sarcastic, but I had it coming. Still, I couldn't imagine him letting someone else use Lou's room.

"Sarah uses it," I argued.

Grandpa thought about that for a few minutes before responding. Then he nodded his head. "I've thought on that," he said. "She does come now and then, an' I sure wouldn't want to be discouraging that." He chuckled. "Isn't she somethin'?" he went on. "You see the way she helps Charlie?"

I had seen all right. And yes, Sarah was really something.

Grandpa laughed again, an outright guffaw. "The other day she was even bossin' him. 'Uncle Charlie,' she says, 'I think you are making your biscuits too stiff. Mamma adds more milk.' " Grandpa laughed again.

"So what did Uncle Charlie say?" I asked, hoping to sidetrack the conversation and, thus, the ideas.

Grandpa laughed again. "He winked at me over her head and said, 'You're jest like your mamma—a little take-over.' But he loved it, I could tell."

But Grandpa wasn't ready to let his wild idea drop.

"Sarah could sleep on a cot in the corner of the kitchen," he said.

"In the kitchen? What kind of sleep would a child get there in the kitchen with you and Uncle Charlie having your coffee and talking over the affairs of the day?"

Grandpa thought about that for several moments. I had scored a point.

"You're right," he admitted at last. "I'll sleep in the kitchen."

"You?"

That idea was almost as preposterous.

"I've slept on the cot before," Grandpa informed me rather firmly.

I bit my lip. I didn't want to say something that I shouldn't.

"You still haven't listened to my full idea," Grandpa went on.

"There's *more*?" I hadn't intended to sound smart, but it sort of came out that way. I felt my face getting a bit red and knew that I wasn't fair to Grandpa.

"I'm sorry," I apologized. "Go ahead."

Grandpa cleared his throat. He seemed to feel that we were finally getting somewhere.

"You know Charlie is having a bad time getting things done around the house?"

I nodded. We all knew that. *But a teacher? A teacher would have no time and no inclination to help out three—*

But Grandpa was going on. "Well, for some time now I've been a thinkin' that what we really need is a hired girl."

A teacher? A hired girl? I didn't say it, just thought it, but Grandpa must have read my mind.

"Now, a teacher's much too busy teachin' and preparin' lessons to be able to help around the house, but to get in someone else, well that poses a problem too. Can't hardly ask a young girl to be moving into a house alone with three men, now can ya?"

I agreed, but I still couldn't follow Grandpa's line of reasoning.

I shrugged and spoke to the team. Somehow I felt hurrying them might also hurry Grandpa to his point.

"So iffen we have the teacher there; then it won't be a problem getting a hired girl," he said quickly.

"What?" Was Grandpa really proposing not one woman to live in, but *two*?

"Simple!" said Grandpa.

"And where you planning to put *her*?" I said in exasperation.

"Well, we got two spare bedrooms as I see it," Grandpa said flatly.

Gramps' room! The bedroom off the kitchen. I hadn't even thought of it—and I was surprised that Grandpa had.

I guess he read my mind again, for he kept right on talking. "A room is for use, Boy. Not for a shrine. One of the girls can have the upstairs bedroom and the other the downstairs bedroom. I don't much care who takes what. They can work that all out between themselves. Thing is, Charlie needs help, and you and I just don't have the time to spend in the kitchen. Yer ideas for better farmin' have been good, real good. But they also take lots more work to put into practice—you know that. Fella can't be two places, doin' two jobs at the same time. Now—"

But I cut in. I had better control now and spoke evenly and softly. "Have you talked to Uncle Charlie?" I felt that Uncle Charlie would be on my side.

"Not yet," said Grandpa. "Wanted to run it by you first."

Grandpa gained some ground there. It flattered me that he had chosen to confer with me. But I was still far from convinced. I thought the idea an awfully dumb one but I knew that rather than arguing with my Grandpa, I should be logical.

"What makes you think the school board would okay a teacher staying with us?"

"Already talked to the board chairman," Grandpa admitted.

"And if the teacher refuses?"

"She hasn't. Says that our place is right handy to the school and that it is easier to board where there aren't lots of kids."

So this wasn't some sudden idea of Grandpa's. He had already been working—behind our backs.

"Where could we find a hired girl?" I asked next, hoping that I'd stumped him on that one. There weren't many girls in our area old enough to know how to keep house who weren't already keeping their own.

"Mary Turley," said Grandpa simply.

"Mary? Mary is needed at home."

"Not anymore. Her ma is feelin' just fine now, and she has two younger sisters who—"

I was beat on that point. I tried for another. "Who says she'd be willing to come? She—"

"She did," Grandpa said frankly.

I felt anger starting to rise. There sat Grandpa throwing out this wild and crazy scheme; he hadn't talked to either Uncle Charlie or to me before, but he had been sneaking around arranging the whole thing without us even having the chance to have our say. I had never known Grandpa to do anything so—so *backhanded* before.

"Now wait," I said, holding up a hand just as I had often seen Grandpa do. "Do you think you've been fair? I mean here you are, making all these arrangements and not even asking Uncle Charlie or me what we think about the whole business. Don't you think you should have asked our opinions? After all—"

"I'm askin' ya now," Grandpa said smoothly.

"Well, it sounds to me like it's a little late," I continued. "I mean you've decided—"

"Nothin's decided."

"But you've *asked*."

"Just put out some feelers," argued Grandpa.

"Quite a few feelers, I'd say," I countered rather hotly.

"Two," said Grandpa. "Whether we could keep the teacher as a boarder, and whether we could hire some help."

"We haven't even talked about whether we can *afford* the help," I reminded him. "What if we don't get a crop? What if—"

He surprised me by chuckling. "That's the beauty of the whole plan," he said. "The teacher's board pays the hired girl."

I could only stare. He had thought of everything.

I shrugged my shoulders helplessly. I still didn't like the idea one bit. What in the world would we do with two women in the house? We'd been alone for so long, and we knew our own routine and our own quirks. How in the world would we ever make room and allowance for two women? How could Grandpa even think that it would work?

Yet it was still his house.

Then I thought of Uncle Charlie. It was true that Uncle Charlie found it difficult to care for the household, but at least he still had the feeling of being useful. Uncle Charlie would never agree to having a woman come in and take over his kitchen. Why, that would be admitting that he was no longer of use to anyone. Uncle Charlie would never be shelved like that.

"As I see it," I said, mustering my courage, "it's Uncle Charlie's decision. The house is his area."

"Exactly!" agreed Grandpa enthusiastically. "That's just the way I see it, too."

Did Grandpa know Uncle Charlie better than I did? I slapped the reins over the rumps of the horses.

CHAPTER 19

Arrangements

Sarah pleaded to go with me to the store, and I couldn't resist the coaxing in her eyes.

"You know your mamma and papa don't want me to buy you candy," I warned her as I led her by the hand to the waiting team.

"I know," she said cheerily. "But I like being with you anyway, Uncle Josh."

She could say her *j*'s just fine now. She could also sweet-talk. I looked down at her to read her face, but she seemed so open and honest. I gave her hand a little squeeze.

"I like being with you, too," I assured her.

"Where do we go first?" she asked me as I lifted her up onto the wagon seat.

"First the feed store, then the post office, then the hardware, and finally the grocery store."

She seemed quite satisfied with our schedule.

The feed store didn't take long; I threw the two bags of supplement feed on the wagon and we moved on.

The post office was busy, and I had to stand in line for some time before the clerk handed me our mail. But it was worth the wait. There was a letter from Willie. I tore the envelope open before I even returned to the wagon and began to scan the pages.

"What you got? A letter for you?" asked Sarah from her perch on the wagon seat. I nodded and climbed up beside her.

"Are you gonna read it?" she asked further, which I thought was rather a silly question seeing as I was already reading it. And then I realized that the questions were to remind me that Sarah was there beside me, feeling a need for a little of my attention. I reached out and took her tiny hand.

"There's a new catalog there," I told her. "Would you like to look at that while I read my letter?"

Sarah responded immediately to the arrangement.

"We'll both read our mail," she said with a grin.

The first part of Willie's letter was all about Camellia and their court-ship and their plans and what a wonderful person she was and how she was learning and growing. I skimmed quickly since it was still rather painful.

Then I came to a part that really interested me. Camellia had been to call on her pa.

It was really hard for her, wrote Willie. It was easy to understand that. I knew how Mr. Foggelson felt about religion of any kind, and I could imagine how he would respond to Camellia's becoming a believer.

But as tough as it was, she was glad that she went, the letter went on. *For one thing, it helped her to understand her ma more. When we were home at Christmas Camellia tried hard to pursuade her ma to go back to her pa. Her ma just shook her head but wouldn't say anything about the situation. It made Camellia very angry with her mother.*

You can imagine how surprised Camellia was to discover that Mrs. Fog-gelson didn't stay behind—she was left behind. Mr. Foggelson has no intention of ever resuming the marriage. He told Camellia that her mother had written him twice asking him to forgive her for not being the kind of person she should have been, and for going back on her Christian faith. She also told him that she would be willing to try again, but that she had to be free to be the person that she had been before their marriage—that is, to be a Christian.

Camellia finally realized that Mrs. Foggelson would have joined Mr. Fog-gelson again, but this time she would stand firm for her Christian beliefs. Needless to say, he would not agree. In fact, he had quite made up his mind long before he moved from town. He told Camellia that he had found someone "more compatible." It nearly crushed Camellia.

For a moment I was filled with such anger toward Mr. Foggelson that I could feel my whole body tensing. Then I remembered that he was a victim of lies and deceit. His false beliefs had taken him down a dark and destructive path. Only God could reach out and open his blinded eyes.

But I felt terribly sorry for Camellia. How shattering it must be to discover the truth about the father that she had idolized for so many years.

Willie's letter went on. *What I really wanted to share is my good news. I went before the Missions committee last week and was accepted. I am to leave for South Africa in two weeks' time. Of course, I go with mixed emotions—I can hardly bear the thought of leaving Camellia behind, but she is tremendously brave about it. She—*

And Willie's letter went on and on about the virtues of his betrothed.

A tug on my sleeve reminded me that I had company. Sarah's little eyes turned wistfully to me.

"Are you done yet?" she asked, handing the catalog back to me. "I am."

I nodded. "I'm done, too," I told her. I still had so much to think about, but now wasn't the time. I would reread the letter and digest the contents.

"Now where?" asked Sarah as I lifted the reins.

"The hardware store. I need some nails, and some rivets for fixing the harness."

Sarah waited patiently while I made my purchases; then we crossed the street to do the grocery shopping.

As I was depositing the parcels in the wagon, Sarah looked at me with big blue eyes. "Do you need anything at the drugstore?" she asked.

I shook my head and was about to lift her up to the wagon seat when I stopped. "Why?" I asked her.

"Just wondering," she said with a shrug of her slight shoulders.

A light began to dawn. "You know I told you I couldn't buy any candy today."

"I know," she said with a sigh, then added sweetly with a tip of her head, "but I didn't know if a soda counted or not."

"Come on, you little trickster," I laughed, taking her hand. "I don't know about a soda, but an ice cream cone might be okay."

Sarah skipped along beside me, her tiny face beaming.

"I want chocolate," she chirped. "What do you want, Uncle Josh?"

When I reached Aunt Lou's to drop off Sarah and pick up Grandpa, I heard part of a conversation that wasn't really intended for me. I was not trying to eavesdrop; I just came in quietly and at the wrong time.

Sarah had not come in with me. As we pulled into the yard we saw little Janie Cromstock from two houses down. She and Sarah were good playmates, and Janie called Sarah to come play on her new swing.

"Can I please, Uncle Josh?" she pleaded.

"You have to ask your mamma," I reminded her.

"Can you ask for me? Please?" Her big eyes searched mine. "You're going in anyway," she reminded me.

"Okay," I said, "I'll ask, but if it isn't okay with your mamma I'll call you and I'll expect you to come right home."

She nodded in agreement, and tripped off after Janie.

Thinking Jon might be taking his afternoon nap, I entered the back porch quietly and upon hearing my name hesitated a moment.

" . . . does Josh think?" Aunt Lou was asking Grandpa.

"He kicked about it," Grandpa said in reply and then chuckled. "But he didn't make as much fuss as I feared he might."

"So are you going to do it?"

"Have to get it past Charlie first," said Grandpa matter-of-factly.

"And do you think he'll agree?" Again Aunt Lou was questioning.

"Just depends." Grandpa sounded thoughtful. "I know Charlie needs the help, but I also know that Charlie needs to be needed. Iffen he can give up his household duties and still feel he's not just in the way, then I think he'll agree. It all depends."

I knew then that Grandpa had talked to Aunt Lou about his crazy scheme. I was about to burst in and tell Aunt Lou what I thought of the idea when I heard her say, "It would be such a load off my mind. I worry so about you— all of you. I think that it would be the wisest thing you've ever done." Then she added quickly with a chuckle, "Since you had me, of course."

I knew better than to let my feelings be known. I hesitated, made a bit of noise with the door and tapped lightly before entering the kitchen. Grandpa and Aunt Lou were sitting at the table sipping from tall lemonade glasses. Lou looked up.

"Did you sell Sarah?" she asked playfully.

"She begged to go to Janie's to try a new swing. I said I would ask your permission. Can she?"

Aunt Lou shrugged and laughed. "I guess she already has," she responded.

"Yeah, but I told her I'd call her if it wasn't okay with you."

"It's okay. At least for a few minutes. I'll call her after she's had a while to play."

Aunt Lou rose to pour me some lemonade and pushed the oatmeal cookies toward me.

"Get everything ya needed?" asked Grandpa, and I nodded.

"Got a letter from Willie, too," I said.

"Any news?"

I turned to Aunt Lou, who had asked the question. I wasn't one for sharing gossip, but I felt that she had to know some of the information Willie's letter had contained.

"I know how you have been seeing Mrs. Foggelson and studying the Bible with her and all since she started coming back to church again. I know that you are excited about the way she is seeking to let God lead in her life again." I hesitated. "But I also know that you, like me, have been a little impatient with her for not going back to Mr. Foggelson."

Aunt Lou nodded, her big blue eyes intense.

"Well, Camellia went to see her pa and found out the truth," I said. For a minute I couldn't go on. I felt like I was about to disgrace the whole Foggelson family.

I swallowed hard. "It wasn't Mrs. Foggelson's idea to stay behind. Mr. Foggelson had found a—a 'more compatible' someone."

I heard Aunt Lou's little gasp; then her eyes brimmed with tears. "The poor soul," she whispered.

"She has never breathed one word about it," Aunt Lou continued. "It must be terribly hard for her—folks all blaming her, and all."

I nodded.

Just then Jon came toddling into the kitchen. His eyes were still bright from sleep, his cheeks rosy, his hair rumpled, and his clothes slightly damp from the warmth of his bed. He dragged a lumpy-looking discarded doll of Sarah's behind him, and when he saw us his eyes lit up and he headed straight for Grandpa.

He was met by open arms and Grandpa cuddled him close and kissed his flushed cheeks.

"Thought yer goin' to sleep the whole day away, Boy," Grandpa told him. " 'Fraid I wasn't even goin' to get to see ya."

Jon pointed at the cookie plate and then squirmed to get down. I was flattered when he ran to me as soon as his little legs hit the floor. But my ego didn't stay inflated for long. It turned out I was closer to the cookie plate than Grandpa, and as soon as I picked the little boy up, his pudgy hands were grabbing for all the cookies on the plate.

I settled him back and removed all of them except one, then pushed the plate out of reach. He lay back against me, munching on his cookie.

I held him until he was finished and then Grandpa stood.

"We best be gettin' on home, Boy," he said, studying the clock on the wall.

"Have you started the harvest yet?" asked Aunt Lou as Grandpa retrieved his stained, floppy hat.

I knew that the question was directed at me. I was the one who made the major decisions at the farm now. Grandpa and Uncle Charlie, without really saying so, had handed the reins to me.

"Not yet. Hope to get going just as soon as it dries."

"Expecting a good yield?"

"Looks good so far, if the frost just stays away."

"Suppose you'll be pretty busy for the next few weeks then," continued Aunt Lou.

"Expect to be."

"We won't be seeing much of you for a while."

"Only on Sundays."

"Maybe I can sneak out and give you a hand now and then," she continued. "Sure would be nice if you had some regular help."

I couldn't help but smile. I hoped Aunt Lou didn't think that she was being subtle. It was all too obvious what she was hinting at. It was also obvious that she was on Grandpa's side.

CHAPTER 20

Changes

Grandpa didn't waste much time in presenting his idea to Uncle Charlie. I had wondered just how he would go about it. I figured he'd wait until I had gone up to bed and the two of them were sitting around the kitchen table having their last cup of coffee. I even had the notion that I'd like to slip down the stairs and sit on the step to hear his presentation.

But he didn't choose to do it like that. Perhaps he knew Uncle Charlie so well he decided that if it came to pick and choose, Uncle Charlie would side with him rather than me.

At any rate, we had just finished up the chores and the supper dishes and Uncle Charlie had hung the dishpan back on the hook when Grandpa came right out with it.

"I suggested to Josh today on the way to town that it might be a good idea to get ourselves a little help."

My mouth fell open at Grandpa's directness, but it didn't seem to throw Uncle Charlie a bit. He never missed a beat, just went right on swishing the dishrag over the checkered oilcloth that covered the table.

"What kind of help?" he asked.

"Cooking. Cleaning. Help with harvest and canning."

"Anyone in mind?" asked Uncle Charlie. I was surprised when I looked at him that he had a twinkle in his eye.

"Mary Turley," said Grandpa.

"Oh," said Uncle Charlie with the same twinkle, "then I take it yer dependin' on Josh to bring in the help, not you?"

I started to say something but Grandpa cut me short. "What're you aimin' at?"

"Aimin'? Why, I ain't aimin' at anything. I thought the way you started off that *you* was aimin' to bring a wife fer someone into this here house."

"A wife?" snorted Grandpa. "Fiddlesticks! Josh can get his own wife."

"I'm glad we're all clear on that," I said with a bit of good-natured sarcasm.

"Then what did you have in mind?" asked Uncle Charlie, giving the table one final lick with the cloth.

"A hired girl," stated Grandpa.

"Oh," said Uncle Charlie. Just "Oh."

"Mary Turley says she's willin' to work out fer a spell," went on Grandpa.

"Still think my idea is a more permanent arrangement," smiled Uncle Charlie. "How long do you expect a girl like Mary Turley—an' at her age—to be available to babysit three bachelors?"

"Ain't babysittin'!" protested Grandpa. Uncle Charlie didn't even seem to notice.

"How do we pay her?" he asked, and I held my breath. Here was the craziest part of Grandpa's scheme in my way of thinking. Wait until Uncle Charlie heard the whole story!

"We board the new teacher," said Grandpa matter-of-factly.

Those words stopped even Uncle Charlie. He straightened up as far as his crippled back would allow and looked sharply at Grandpa.

I could see the questions in his eyes, but he didn't voice them. Grandpa took the opportunity to hurry on.

"We got two extry rooms here. The schoolteacher gits one, the hired girl the other. That way neither of 'em are put off 'bout living in a house with three men. Then we take the board payment from the teacher an' pay the hired girl. Works good for everyone."

Uncle Charlie snorted. I knew he had some doubts.

"Where's the flaw?" asked Grandpa a little heatedly.

I could hold back no longer. I leaned forward in my chair and laid my hands out on the table. "It's a crazy scheme. A crazy scheme," I informed Uncle Charlie. "We've got no business filling our house up with women.

We've gotten along all of these years, and I see no reason why we still can't. They'll just come in here and start putting on white tablecloths and asking us to take off our work boots an' starching all the shirts an'—"

I hadn't run out of steam, but Uncle Charlie moved away from both of us. I thought that he was dismissing the whole crazy idea, but he was just hanging up the dishrag.

As he approached the table I started in again. "I know it's tough for a while at harvest, but harvest doesn't last long, and we can always get help. I'll bet we can get Mrs.—"

"I hope not," cut in Uncle Charlie. "Nearly drove me crazy, that woman."

"Then we'll get someone else. There are lots of women who cook out at harvest time. We'll—"

"Name me a few," said Grandpa. "Remember the time we had finding someone last harvest?"

It was a sobering fact. We'd had a tough time. All of the neighborhood women were busy with canning and their own threshers every fall.

"Well, we still don't need someone to live in, to stay here and change everything about our lives. We have our own way of doing things. Our own routine. We wouldn't feel like it was even our house anymore."

Uncle Charlie lowered himself slowly to a chair at the table. I could see that his back was giving him pain again.

"And where would we put them?" I went on. "The upstairs bedroom is Aunt Lou's and the downstairs one"—I waved at the door of the small room off the kitchen—"is Gramps."

Uncle Charlie didn't seem to be listening to me and Grandpa wasn't saying much.

"We don't even know what this here new teacher will be like. She might—she might be—disgusting."

I couldn't think of anything specific to charge her with.

Uncle Charlie raised his eyebrows at that and turned his gaze toward Grandpa. Grandpa understood his unanswered question and responded.

" 'Course I checked her out. I wouldn't want her spittin' tobaccy through the cracks, now would I?"

Uncle Charlie's mustache twitched slightly, and I knew he was hiding a smile.

"She's from a good Christian home over near Edgeworth. She's got high recommendations, and hopes to become part of our church. She asked about stayin' in a Christian home when she applied here," went on Grandpa.

Still, Uncle Charlie looked a bit doubtful for a moment. He spoke for the first time for several minutes.

"Her folks would okay her staying on here?"

"We been checked out," said Grandpa frankly.

"What family would let their young girl stay with three old bachelors?" I argued. "Surely they—"

"Let's do it," said Uncle Charlie.

I couldn't believe my ears.

"What do *you* think, Josh?" Uncle Charlie surprised me by turning to me. Hadn't he been listening to a thing I'd said?

"He said it was your kitchen, and your decision," Grandpa answered on my behalf.

"Did ya?" Uncle Charlie looked squarely at me.

"Yeah, but—" I began.

"Then let's do it," Uncle Charlie said again, emphatically. "I think it's time we had a woman here in this house."

I was stunned. I couldn't believe Uncle Charlie had let Grandpa talk him into something so foolish. Then it began to dawn on me that Grandpa really said very little. I had been doing most of the talking, and I might have just talked myself right into a corner.

I was even more sure of it when I was preparing for bed and Uncle Charlie's voice drifted up the stairs to me.

"I'm worried some about Josh," he said.

"Meaning?" asked Grandpa.

"Did ya hear 'im? Sounded like he was scared of women—or else thinks thet they are a curse rather than a blessin'. Talked all thet silly stuff 'bout them messin' up his routine."

"Yer right," sighed Grandpa. "Guess Lou is the only woman Josh has really had much to do with."

"Hope we ain't too late," said Uncle Charlie and there was genuine concern in his voice.

I reached out and closed my bedroom door. Uncle Charlie's words made me angry, but I began to feel a little scared, too. Did I really feel that way about women? Was it too late? It was true that I dreaded the thought of sharing the house with two of the opposite sex. But why? I loved Aunt Lou. I loved little Sarah. I loved—or *had* loved—Camellia. What was I afraid of—fighting against?

And then it hit me. Uncle Charlie hadn't been so fond of the idea, either. I could see it in his face. But without even arguing, he suddenly said, "Let's do it." And I was the reason. Uncle Charlie might not like a woman coming in and taking over his work and putting him aside. He might even feel useless and not needed any longer, but he was willing to sacrifice the way he felt because he was worried that I was developing unhealthy attitudes.

I decided that I wouldn't say any more about the arrangements and when Grandpa asked me straight out, I told him to go ahead and do whatever he thought it wise to do. I was pretty sure what that would be.

Mary moved in first. Grandpa went over with the wagon and fetched her. She came with a small suitcase and a worn trunk, and I helped Grandpa haul it in.

I didn't feel too uncomfortable with Mary. After all, we had known one another since we were kids and she was a member of our church and all. It wasn't like a complete stranger coming into our home. Still, it was hard to adjust to having someone else around.

She chose the downstairs bedroom because she said it made more sense for her to be close by the kitchen, seeing as she would spend most of her time there.

We didn't need to worry about Mary knowing how to do household chores. She had been tending house since she had been a young girl. She moved in and took over that kitchen, yet I had to admire her—she didn't push Uncle Charlie aside. She asked this and praised that until she had him wrapped around her little finger. Didn't take long, either. And she found him more little jobs to keep him busy than I would have ever thought possible.

They worked there in the kitchen together. I could hear them chatting and chuckling each time that I came near the house. It upset me a bit at first; then I began to realize how good it was for Uncle Charlie, and I started being thankful for Mary and her sensitivity.

Special treats began to show up at the table, too—green tomato relish and fresh butter tarts and oven-baked squash. Uncle Charlie had done his best, but Mary's best was definitely better.

Mary had been there only a week when the new teacher moved in. Mary had already busied herself cleaning Aunt Lou's room until it sparkled. She even put in a small bouquet of fall flowers and a tiny basket of polished apples.

Mary may have been excited, but I was dreading the thought of sharing a house with a finicky schoolmarm. I made myself scarce the day Miss Matilda Hopkins was to arrive. I wanted to be as far away from the house as possible. It wasn't hard to do. We were already into harvest, and I had lots to keep me busy.

Miss Hopkins was to arrive by train, and Grandpa volunteered to go to the station to meet her.

I worked late. The supper hour came and went, but I purposely paid no heed to it. It was still light enough to work the field, so I just stayed working. Even though my stomach was complaining bitterly, I disregarded it. I was in no hurry to get to a kitchen overrun by women.

When it finally got too dark to see any longer, I unhitched the team and headed for the barn. I took my time watering and feeding the horses and giving them a good rubdown. A quick check around told me that Grandpa had already cared for the other chores. Normally I would have been thankful for that but tonight it just irked me a bit. I would have no excuse to escape the kitchen.

I finally headed for the house, grumpy and dirty. I knew that introductions would be in order and I also knew that I sure didn't look my best. Well, I didn't care. What difference could it make to some old-maid schoolteacher anyway?

I stomped my way across the back veranda and pulled open the door. The kitchen was empty, except for Grandpa and Uncle Charlie.

"Working kinda late," Grandpa observed.

I stared around rather dumbly, but I wasn't going to ask any questions. I crossed to the corner basin and poured myself a generous amount of water. Then I set about sloshing it thoroughly over my hands and face. When I looked up I noticed that I had also sloshed Mary's well-scrubbed floor and spic-and-span washstand. I pretended not to notice and moved toward the table.

"Where's supper?" I asked, trying to sound casual.

"Supper was over a couple hours ago," said Grandpa, not even looking up from the paper he had gotten from somewhere.

"Yours is in the warmin' oven," said Uncle Charlie around his section of the paper.

I crossed to the warming oven and found a generous serving. I hadn't realized how hungry I was until I saw and smelled the food. Even so, my good sense told me that it had been much better a couple of hours earlier. Well, that wasn't Mary's fault, I had to admit.

"Where'd you get the paper?" I asked around a mouthful.

"Matilda," said Grandpa.

"Matilda?"

Grandpa just grunted.

"You mean Miss Hopkins?"

"She wants to be called Matilda," Grandpa spoke again.

There was silence as the two men pored over their sections of paper. We didn't often see a daily paper in our house, and they seemed to find this one awfully intriguing.

"So she arrived, huh?" I tried again.

"Yep," said Uncle Charlie; then he began to read aloud to Grandpa some bit of interesting news that he found in the paper. Grandpa listened and then they read in silence again. Soon it was Grandpa's turn to read some little bit to Uncle Charlie. I expected they had been sitting there doing that all evening, and I also expected they would keep right on doing it. Some exciting evening this was going to be!

I finished my meal and pushed my plate back. "Any dessert?" I asked.

Grandpa waved a hand that still clutched the paper. "On the cupboard," he said and never even looked up.

I found fresh custard pie—my favorite—and helped myself to a large piece. That was one nice thing about having Mary around—she sure could bake a pie! I had a second piece.

The two men still hadn't stirred except to read to one another every now and then. They were really enjoying that paper.

My eyes traveled to Mary's bedroom door. It was open a crack and I could see a neatly made bed and the small desk in the corner of the room. It was clear that Mary was not at home.

Finally I could stand it no longer.

"Kind of quiet," I said. "Where is everyone?"

Grandpa lowered his paper just enough to look over it at me. "We're here," he said simply.

I blushed and ran a hand through my unruly hair. But Grandpa still didn't pay much attention to me.

Uncle Charlie folded his section of paper carefully and laid it on the table beside him. He removed his tiny round reading glasses.

"You know," he said to Grandpa, "I think Matilda's right. A man does need to read the daily paper to keep up with what is goin' on in the world. I can't believe all the things I've learned in just one night."

Grandpa grunted his agreement and shuffled through some more paper.

I carried my empty pie plate to the cupboard and piled it with my dinner plate—more out of habit than consideration. I was about to say I was going up to bed when Grandpa looked up.

"Oh, Josh," he said, "Mary took Matilda over to her folks to introduce her. I let them hook Chester to the light buggy. Hope you don't mind."

I just stood there letting the words sink in. Not only were they taking over my kitchen and my house, but my horse as well! Anger welled up within me, but at the same time I realized how juvenile it was to feel the way I did. I calmed myself, muttered some kind of reply to Grandpa, and started to climb the stairs.

"Goin' to bed already?" Uncle Charlie called after me.

"Yeah," I replied, not even turning around. "It's been a long day."

"Sure you don't wanta read a little of the paper here?" Grandpa asked.

I was in no mood for reading Matilda's paper, I can tell you that, but I didn't say so to Grandpa. At least not in those words.

"Think I'll just go on to bed," I said instead.

But I couldn't sleep. I lay there tossing and turning and listening for the sound of buggy wheels.

They finally came. Then I could hear their whispering voices as they approached the house after putting Chester in the barn. They sounded like two young kids sneaking in the back door, but they weren't kids and they weren't sneaking in. Grandpa and Uncle Charlie were waiting right there at the kitchen table where I had left them.

I could hear the rattling of cups as Mary made them their before-bed coffee and then there was general chatter and some soft laughter and finally footsteps on the stairs, and then the house was quiet for the night.

I still couldn't go to sleep. It seemed that life was out of control. All the old familiar ways seemed to be changing. Even our familiar routines seemed to be gone.

Then I thought of Grandpa and Uncle Charlie and that last cup of coffee, and I realized that things weren't really so different after all.

CHAPTER 21

Harvest

I wasn't in a much better mood when I awoke the next morning. I hadn't had much sleep, but mostly I had my mind set to be ornery.

I got up early and went out to get a start on the chores. First, I went to check out Chester. I couldn't find anything to get upset about so I went on down the lane to let the cows up for milking.

It wasn't long until Grandpa joined me at the barn.

"Yer up early, Boy," he greeted me. "You musta had a good sleep last night."

I didn't make any comment.

"How's the cuttin' comin'?" Grandpa went on.

"Fine," I answered truthfully.

"Does it look as good as we hoped?"

I had a hard time keeping the excitement out of my voice. The crop was a good one. It looked like it would beat any yield we'd ever had.

I forgot my sour mood momentarily and concentrated on sharing the report of the field with Grandpa. His eyes took on a twinkle as I talked and his mustache twitched in satisfaction now and then.

By the time I had finished raving over the crop, Bossie was bellowing to be milked. We parted ways; I went on to slop the pigs and Grandpa grabbed the milk pail.

I had almost forgotten my dread of going in to breakfast and was thinking instead about the tractor I was dreaming of purchasing. I was walking toward the chicken coop with my head down when I unexpectedly bumped into something.

Now I had walked that path many, many times over the past years, and I knew very well that there shouldn't be anything in that spot one could bump into.

My head came up and my hand reached out at the same moment. And there, standing with her back to me and looking around as startled as I had been, was a slip of a girl.

"I—I'm sorry," I mumbled, pulling my hand back from her shoulder where it had landed. "I wasn't watching where—"

What's she doing standing there in the middle of the path, anyway?

She was shaking her head back and forth, the startled look giving way to mirth. "It's my fault. I shouldn't have been standing here in the way—I've been drinking in the sunrise."

Drinking in the sunrise? I had never heard it expressed like that before. My eyes shifted to the east and was astonished to realize the sunrise was worthy of such an expression. I stood staring at it—seeing it like it was the first time.

"It is pretty, isn't it?" I mumbled. "Could I help you?" I asked. "Are you looking for someone?"

She looked puzzled at my question, then began to laugh. "You must be Josh," she said, rather than answering my question.

I nodded, but I didn't see what that had to do with anything.

"I'm Matilda," she said simply, extending a small hand.

My mouth must have hung open at that. I had expected an older woman, with hair swept severely back from her face and a dark blue, long-skirted dress with lace at the throat and sleeves. But I was facing a girl who looked no more than seventeen, with bouncing, light brown curls and sparkling eyes. She wore an attractive dress of green calico.

"Matilda Hopkins," she said again. "The new teacher."

I still couldn't speak.

Then Matilda changed the subject completely, her enthusiasm spilling over in a candid fashion. "I love your horse, Chester. He's just bea-u-ti-ful." She stretched the word out, emphasizing each of the syllables.

"I've never seen such a beautiful horse," she went on, "and Mary says that he is saddle broken too. I'd love to ride him sometime. I'd just love to!"

She took a breath and finished more slowly, "If you wouldn't mind, that is."

I found myself shrugging my shoulders and saying "of course not," and Matilda was beaming her joy and thanking me profusely.

"But I must get in. I'll be late for school on my very first day if I keep dawdling."

And she was gone, tripping down the path in a most undignified way for a schoolteacher.

I could only stare. And then I began to laugh. What had I been so upset about? Why had I been so scared? There was absolutely nothing to fear from this child. It wouldn't be much different than having Sarah around.

I chuckled all the way to the chicken coop.

Friday night there was a Youth Group meeting at the church. Grandpa suggested, rather slyly, that I might want to break from the field work a bit early and take the girls. At first I was going to decline, and then I figured that it really wouldn't hurt. I knew Uncle Nat felt that the farm work shouldn't really come before my church commitments, so it might be wise for me to follow Grandpa's suggestion.

I should have taken the team, but I guess I just wanted to show Chester off a bit. The light buggy would be faster than the heavy wagon, but the light buggy also was very crowded for three people. It was really only made for two.

Grandpa raised an eyebrow when he saw me hitching up. I knew what he was thinking.

"Won't be a problem," I said before he could comment. "Both those girls are so small I could fit four like 'em on that seat."

Grandpa didn't say anything.

When I went in to do my last bit of slicking and polishing Uncle Charlie looked at me good-naturedly.

"Figure you might take a bit of teasin' showin' up with two girls, Josh?" he asked me.

His question caught me completely off guard.

"Girls?" I said. "One of them is Mary and the other—well, she's just a kid."

Uncle Charlie looked surprised at my assessment but he didn't say anything.

I was ready before the girls were, which was always a puzzle to me. I had put in a full day in the field, helped with chores, hooked up Chester, and still had to wait.

Mary showed first. She really did look nice, and I remembered thinking again that Willie really had missed out—until I also remembered just who Willie had ended up with.

What is taking young Matilda so long? I fidgeted mentally, and then she came down the stairs and I couldn't believe my eyes. Her hair was gathered up away from her face and her dress was much more grown-up and I suddenly realized that she wasn't a kid after all. I also realized that Uncle Charlie had been right. I might be in for some ribbing.

But it was too late to unhitch Chester and hook up the team. The girls had already expressed their delight in the light buggy. I gathered up the reins and climbed aboard. I wasn't sure how to arrange the seating.

Mary took charge.

"Why don't you sit in the middle, Josh, and one of us will sit on each side," she suggested.

I don't exactly know why I agreed, except I didn't know what else to do, so I sat down in the middle, a girl on each side of me. It was crowded, and I guess they feared they might get bounced right off the seat with Chester moving along like he always chose to do. Each grabbed an arm and hung on for dear life. I was hard put to handle the reins.

I began to sweat. I didn't know if I had the right to pray over such things or not, but I sure was tempted. I hoped there would be no fellas outside watching me arrive. But it was a warm fall night, and the fellas always stood outside and laughed and talked and watched everybody as they came.

Oh, boy, I thought, *have I gone and done it now!*

I wanted to put the blame on the girls. What did Mary go and fix herself up like that for, and why had Matilda chosen *this* night to look her age? How old was she, anyway? And why hadn't she warned me?

But I couldn't blame them. Chester and the buggy had been my idea. I'd wanted to show off my horse—and look where it had gotten me!

Mary and Matilda didn't seem to have any problem with the arrangement at all. They laughed and chatted all of the way to town, with me right there in the middle.

At one point a big jack rabbit sprang from the grass in the ditch, making Chester shy to his right. It wasn't dangerous; Chester was a well-trained horse, and it only startled him.

But it was enough to give the girls quite a scare. They grabbed hold of me with both hands. Matilda screamed. Mary was the first to recover; her face got a bit red and she released her firm grasp and mumbled some sort of apology.

Not Matilda. I think she actually enjoyed the excitement and would have been glad to repeat it again. She wasn't like any schoolteacher I'd ever had!

When we got to the church, a whole yard full of fellas were standing there waiting. I could feel my face color and knew that I was really in for it.

The girls didn't seem to notice.

"Josh!" one of the group called out. "Got your rig pretty full, don't you?" But to make matters worse, I knew I had to get the three of us down from that buggy seat. I didn't know quite how to be gentlemanly about my situation. I mean, how was I to hold Chester and assist two young women—one on each side of me—to descend in ladylike fashion?

Uncle Nat arrived to save the day. He was just coming from the parsonage to the church, and he stopped and greeted us cheerily, then took Chester's bridle and eased him in to the hitching rail. When I was able to release the reins, I excused myself and crossed in front of Mary so I could jump to the ground; then I was able to help the girls step down one at a time.

While the boys were still shuffling and gaping, Mary was calmly introducing Matilda to Uncle Nat, a job that I should have been doing.

The entire evening was pretty much what I expected. The fellas razzed me the total time. I sweated my way through the social, vowing to myself that I'd never be caught in the same predicament again.

When we were about to go Aunt Lou called me aside. "I'm so glad you brought the girls, Josh," she said. "I hope that you can do it again. Matilda seemed to fit in well with the group."

I nodded. She had, in fact, rather been the life of the party.

"And, Josh," went on Aunt Lou, lowering her voice to a whisper, "don't pay any attention to the 'pack.' " She nodded her head slightly in the direction of the boys, who had given me razzing for bringing two girls. "There's not a one of them who wouldn't give his right arm to be in your position tonight."

I looked dubiously back at my circle of friends and I began to grin. Aunt Lou was right. I walked over to the two young ladies who had shared my crowded buggy and extended an arm to each of them.

From then on things began to change at our house. My lot wasn't really so bad, after all. In fact, many would have envied my situation.

Mary was probably one of the best cooks in the whole neighborhood. What's more, she was gentle and caring and thought of many little ways to brighten the days for each one of us.

And Matilda? Well, Matilda was Matilda. She was vivacious and witty and bright—a real chatterbox, about as different from Mary as a girl could be. Each added to our household in a special way.

I wasn't chafing anymore. There were still times when our big farm kitchen seemed a bit too small and I longed for a bit more space and a little more quiet, but generally speaking we all began to adjust to one another.

And then we went full swing into harvest. All I could think about was getting that bumper crop from the field to the grain bins, and I blocked everything else momentarily from my mind.

CHAPTER 22

Fall

Harvest went fairly well that year. We had the usual weather set-backs, but nothing that lasted more than a few days at a time. As the weather permitted, the grain was cut and stooked; then we had to wait on the warm sun to do the final drying of the stooks.

It was my first year to drive a team on the neighborhood threshing crew. We traveled from farm to farm working the fields. A strict tally was kept of our days worked; we were allowed one day of labor, a man and his team, for every day that we put in. If I worked for eighteen days, I would be allowed three days of a six-man crew with no money changing hands. I figured that three good days would about finish our threshing, and that eighteen to twenty-four days would be the maximum of good weather needed to take care of all of the crops in our area.

It was hard work, and long days for both the teams and the men. It was especially hard when the farm being threshed was several miles from home. Most of the farms were bunched in within a radius of a few miles, but one of them was seven miles away and another was six and a half. On those days I had to leave home early to get there in time to start the day with the rest of the men, and on the same days I got home well after dark.

Some of the men took their bed rolls and bedded down in the stack of fresh straw, tying their teams to a nearby fence post. I didn't want to stay, but rather than driving a tired team the additional miles each day, I decided to tie Chester on behind my rack first trip out. Then I left the team resting and feeding and rode Chester home each night and back again in the morning. It worked well. Chester could shorten my time on the road and also get a bit of a workout. He got too frisky when he wasn't ridden frequently.

The threshing crew represented an assortment of fellas—big and small, old and young, quiet and loud—all working together for a common goal. There were usually about six of us at a time, plus Mr. Wilkes, the man who operated the threshing machine. Some of the men worked for two or three days at a time and then sent out a replacement so they could get on home and get their own crops cut and ready for threshing. I was lucky enough to have all my fields cut before I left home.

Mitch Turley and I were the youngest two on the crew. We had gone to school together back in our little one-room school—the very school where Matilda taught now. Mitch was Mary's older brother, so he kept asking me strange questions about Mary. I soon caught on that he was really fishing for information about Matilda. It seemed that Mitch had seen her once or twice and been quite impressed.

I wasn't sure I wanted to help Mitch get acquainted with Matilda. At one time he had attended Sunday school with Willie and me. At that point he never missed a Sunday, even though he hadn't had much encouragement from home at the time. But now he never went, even though Mary tried her hardest to talk him into it. I didn't offer him much information—or much hope.

The oldest member of the crew was Mr. Smith. I think that Mr. Smith had been threshing most of forever with Mr. Wilkes. In fact, his team of bays was so familiar with all of the nearby fields that I think Mr. Smith could have stayed at home and the team could have made the proper rounds—except that they wouldn't have been much good at forking bundles!

Barkley Shaw and Joey Smith were both on the crew part time, too. Barkley and Joey were about the age of my Aunt Lou. I had never cared that much for Barkley—always considered him a show-off. But to his credit, he had settled down a lot since he had married SueAnn Corbin and become the father of four little ones.

All of the crew were neighbor folks I had known all of my growing up years. There wasn't much said around the table about world events. Mostly it was who had lumbago, and who had the best seed grain, and who was seeing whose daughter. I learned a lot just listening to the conversation.

During the time that I worked with the crew Grandpa did all of the choring. Uncle Charlie did whatever he could, and Mary did more than was expected. Even Matilda pitched in with feeding the chickens and carrying some wood.

I didn't see too much of the household during harvest. But when I got home late at night, they would all be waiting up. Matilda would sometimes be preparing her next day's lessons while Mary mended or worked on some fancy things that Uncle Charlie and Grandpa teased her about, saying it was for her hope chest. Grandpa and Uncle Charlie would often be reading the latest edition of Matilda's paper.

They'd all ask politely about my day, and Mary would quietly prepare a snack and the evening coffee for Grandpa and Uncle Charlie while Matilda told us amusing stories about the happenings at school. As soon as we finished we'd all head for bed. Some nights I was so tired I could scarcely drag myself up the creaking steps. But then I would be off again in the morning before anyone else was even up.

For eleven days we worked that way; then it was our turn for the threshing rig. I was so nervous and excited that I could hardly stand it. This was my first year to be completely in charge of the operation on our farm. I had to make all the decisions and handle all the arrangements.

We had always hired at least two women to work in the kitchen preparing the food for the crew, but this year Mary informed me that she was sure she and Uncle Charlie would be quite able to care for things. I must have looked a bit doubtful. I remembered some of those farm homes where the food had been a little short and the unspoken disgust of the men around the table. I sure didn't want them feeling that way about us.

When Uncle Charlie sided with Mary, I decided to let them give it a try, wondering if Uncle Charlie was simply saying what he did because he hated extra women in the kitchen.

I needn't have worried. Before the three days were up Mary had established quite a name for our kitchen. Her meals were wonderful, and she also brought refreshments to the field—steaming coffee, cold milk, sandwiches, cakes and cookies. She fed the men so well, in fact, that it was a good two hours after each meal until they were really able to work well again.

The first night we went in for supper, I could see Mitch Turley straining to get a look in the kitchen window before we entered the room. At first I supposed he was looking for his sister, but I noticed that his glance slid right past Mary, who was at the stove serving up heaping bowls of corn on the cob.

Matilda appeared just then, a big white apron nearly circling her entire frame, making her look even tinier than she actually was, and I heard Mitch suck in his breath.

Mitch didn't say much at the table, but I saw him stealing glances Matilda's way. Seeing Mitch watching Matilda made me look at her a little more closely. She seemed to belong in our country kitchen, and I suppose I was getting used to her. But now I watched, and noticed that she didn't just walk, she floated around, her full-skirted dress swishing about her legs and her hair swishing about her cheeks. She served and smiled and dished out food and witty conversation, making all the men feel that they weren't quite as tired as they had been when they seated themselves at the table. Some of them even began to make funny remarks and tell ridiculous stories on one another.

Mary worked just as fast—only it didn't look that way. She moved with a quietness and grace that I hadn't noticed before. But then, I had never noticed anything about the way Mary moved. She did nothing to draw attention to herself. She had a poise—a serenity that people felt rather than saw. In fact, Mary had a way of making people feel comfortable, at home with themselves.

But Mitch never looked once at his sister—at least, not that I observed. And if Matilda knew that she was being studied, she never let on.

Mitch wore a clean, fancier shirt the next day when he came to work. Usually we wore old, patched, faded work clothes in the fields, because the work of pitching bundles was hard on clothes as well as bodies. Sweat drenched our shirts and straw stuck to them. Wagon wheels sometimes had to be greased and horses curried. A shirt could look pretty bad by the end of the day and nobody wanted to wear a shirt that he had to worry about. But here was Mitch looking like he was heading for town or going to the school picnic.

I guess the other fellas noticed it, too, and having been young once themselves, they pretty well knew the reason for his fancying up. I saw some whispering going on and heard a few laughs, and I knew that something was up. Barkley Shaw seemed to be the instigator; maybe he hadn't settled down all that much after all.

The day was almost over and we were just finishing up the last couple of loads. I had forgotten all about my suspicions by then, so I wasn't being very cautious. Mr. Smith was the second last wagon in, with Mitch following right behind him. As the other racks were all unloaded, I sent up an extra two men to help each team driver. Barkley and Joey were standing by, awfully anxious to give a hand to Mitch. I didn't think a thing of it at the time. Just figured that they were in a hurry to get in for supper.

Smith was soon unloaded and moved his rack out of the way for Mitch to pull up. The unloading went well, and before we knew it Mitch's rack was empty. Then Mitch went to drive his team on, when there was a thump and one back side of the wagon dropped down much lower than the other.

He halted his team and leaned over to look. To his surprise, his back wheel had come completely off. He said some questionable words, tied the lines securely over the middle post of the rack and climbed down. That was when Joey and Barkley both pressed in, seeming to be awfully concerned about Mitch's misfortune.

They talked about the wheel for a few minutes and then Barkley moved over to his rack and came back with a can.

"I got some real good wagon-wheel grease here," he offered. "Might make the wheel work back on a little easier."

Now if Mitch had known Barkley like I knew Barkley, he would have been suspicious right there. But he didn't seem to think Barkley was up to anything. He just thanked him and started to pry at that can to get it open.

"Here, use this," Barkley said, offering him a piece of metal to pry with. Mitch went to work. I could see the lid gradually coming loose as Mitch worked his way around it with the lever. Just as it opened, Barkley tripped forward over a rough bit of ground that had been there all of the time and smacked right into Mitch's extended arms. The can flew up, along with its contents, and Mitch stood blinking through a covering of dirty black oil.

"Oh, man!" exclaimed Barkley, snapping his fingers and shaking his head in fake exasperation at his mistake. "I must a' got the wrong can."

Mitch stood looking down at his fancy shirt. It was streaked and splotched with dark patches.

"Here, fella," spoke Joey in a sympathetic voice, "let me clean ya up some," and he grabbed a handful of straw and began to wipe at Mitch's chest.

At first Mitch just stood there silently and let Joey wipe away—until he saw that the straw also contained clumps of exposed soil. Every swipe that Joey took left a smeared streak of Jones's farmland behind.

By then others had gathered and were guffawing at Mitch's expense. I figured that things had gone quite far enough.

"Okay, fellas," I said as quietly, yet authoritatively, as I knew how, "let's not keep supper waiting."

Most of the men moved on then, and I turned to help Mitch get the wheel back on his wagon.

"I'll lend you a shirt when we get to the house," I promised quietly, then added as an afterthought, "It won't be fancy, but it'll be clean."

CHAPTER 23

Settling In

I spent several more days back on the road with the threshing crew, and then we were finally finished for another fall. As usual, after the harvest was over things settled down considerably. There still was lots to do, but we were at least allowed a decent night's sleep in between the doing. I was glad to be home instead of on the road, and I think Grandpa and Uncle Charlie were glad to have me at home, too.

As soon as the grain was portioned out—for sale, for feed, and for seed— we got out our pencils and scraps of paper and began to figure what our profits would be.

We all worked on it. Matilda was a real whiz in math and even outfigured me at times. Mary hadn't had as much book learning but she had an uncanny sense of rough calculations. More than once she surprised us at how close she came to the correct answer—in just seconds, too.

There were many reasons to be concerned with the year's profit; my primary goal was to establish whether we had made enough to be able to purchase the tractor I had my heart set on. I had discussed it with Grandpa and Uncle Charlie, and they seemed almost excited about the idea.

After a great deal of figuring and working things one way and then another to try to cover all of the possibilities, it was decided that there was money, with some left over. With the decision finally made, I could hardly contain myself.

The tractor had to be ordered for delivery and would be shipped in on an incoming freight train. While I waited, I busied myself with other things.

Matilda decided to have a school social and worked hard to talk us all into going. I really don't think that any one of us could have turned her down, but we teased along, letting her think we still hadn't made up our minds. By the time the night came she was all in a dither. It was rather a big undertaking for her first community affair. There would be games, some special music, and refreshments, and Matilda had to organize it all.

I think she was relieved to come down from her room to find us all waiting for her in the kitchen, dressed in our best and ready to go. She gave a glad little squeal and threw her arms around Grandpa's neck.

Uncle Charlie and I just looked at one another and grinned. We had known all along that we'd be going.

This time for sure there were too many of us for the light buggy, and we still didn't have snow so we couldn't take the sleigh. Taking the rather cumbersome wagon meant we had to leave early so Matilda could be there to make the final preparations. When the crowd began to arrive, we were ready.

I noticed Mitch as soon as he came in the door. He had been at our house a few times over the past weeks—to visit Mary, he said. Uncle Charlie and Grandpa would just smile and wink at that. Mary always seemed pleased to see him. I knew she was praying for him and hoping that he was ready to show some interest in church again. Tonight he was dressed all up in a brand-new suit that I figured he must have purchased with his harvest money. He looked pretty good, too. For a moment I wished I hadn't ordered that tractor. I could have done with a new suit myself.

Matilda started the evening with some "mixers" just to get folks moving about and talking to one another. Harvest had kept everyone too busy for visiting.

After spending a half hour or more playing the games, Matilda went on to her program. Several of the school children sang songs or recited pieces. Some of them were good, some not so good. But we all clapped anyway, and some of the young fellas lined up across the back of the room, whistling shrilly.

I found it awfully hard on the ears, and then I remembered times when my friends and I had done the same thing because it seemed like the thing to do. Now it just seemed loud.

The last item on the program surprised me; Matilda sang. I had no idea that she had such a voice. In fact, I could hardly believe it as I listened to her. To think such a full, melodious sound was coming out of such a little frame was almost unbelievable. I guess that others felt that way too; the room was totally quiet. Even the babies seemed to stop their restless stirring, and when it was over there was thunderous applause and more shrill whistles. People kept crying "Encore! Encore!" until finally a flushed Matilda sang us another. But she wouldn't sing a third number though, no matter how we coaxed.

When the refreshments were served, several neighborhood women gave Matilda and Mary a hand. They had all brought sandwiches and pastries from their own kitchens.

We all assured Matilda that her evening was a complete success as we bundled up against the cold and started off for home. It was a bright night with a full moon, and the horses had no trouble at all seeing where they were going.

Once again I was on the front seat driving with one girl on each side of me. Grandpa and Uncle Charlie had crawled up on the back seat and bundled themselves into heavy quilts. The cold made Uncle Charlie's arthritis act up, so Mary had made sure that we had lots of blankets along.

At first the ride was rather quiet, with only an occasional comment followed by some laughter. A shooting star caused some oohs and aahs from the girls. Mary told Matilda she had a lovely voice and begged her to sing the song again. Matilda began to sing, softly at first, and then Mary joined in, and the beautiful sound drifted out over the moon-drenched countryside. It was a well-known hymn, and by the time they got to the second verse I could hear Grandpa humming along with them. Then he stopped humming and began to sing, and then Uncle Charlie joined in, softly, shyly.

Matilda gave me a little poke, and I sang, too—a bit hesitantly at first, and then much more bravely. Soon we were all singing, full voice. We finished the song and went on to another one and then another and another. As soon as we had completed one, someone would lead out in another.

All the way home we sang. I had never had an experience like it in all my life. Somehow in the singing we had drawn closer together against the coldness and the darkness of the world around us. It all seemed so natural, so right.

For the first time I was sorry to see our farm come into view. I could have gone on and on just driving and singing and being close to those I cared about. Just as we pulled up to the house a star fell, streaking its way downward, then burned out and was gone—and the spell was broken.

Sarah came to visit. It had been a long time since she had spent time with us at the farm, and we had missed her.

"Oh no!" said Uncle Charlie in mock horror. "What am I gonna do with *two* bosses in the kitchen?"

Mary and Sarah both laughed.

I came home from town midafternoon to find Mary and Sarah elbow-deep in flour as they rolled and cut sugar cookies. Uncle Charlie sat in his favorite chair by the window working a crossword puzzle, but every now and then he would steal a peek at the activity. I knew that he was enjoying their fun almost as much as they were.

"What would you like us to make for you, Uncle Josh?" Sarah called. Without hesitation I answered, "A tractor." It had seemed like the tractor was taking an interminable time to come.

Sarah laughed at my response but Mary gave me a sympathetic smile.

"I don't know how to make a tractor," Sarah giggled.

"That's too bad," I said shaking my head. "If you could make me one I could cancel my order."

Uncle Charlie's head lifted from the crossword.

"No word?"

I shook my head in disappointment.

"I thought you didn't need a tractor 'til spring," Sarah offered as she patched up the leg on a cookie dog.

"I don't."

"Then why are you so apatient?"

She tipped her head to the side and sucked some cookie dough off a finger as she waited for my answer. I waited too. I wasn't sure how to answer her. At last I had to smile.

"I'm 'apatient,' " I said honestly, borrowing her word, "because I *want* it so much, not because I *need* it so much."

"Oh!" nodded Sarah. She could understand that.

She thought for a moment and then her face brightened. "Then I know," she said matter-of-factly. "Pray. Pray an' ask Jesus to help you wait. Before I had my birthday one time I was apatient an' Mamma told me to pray, an' I did, an' Jesus helped me wait."

It sounded so simple. Maybe it was simple. I ran a hand over Sarah's curly head. "Maybe I'll do that," I said huskily.

She seemed perfectly satisfied that the matter had been taken care of and could be dropped.

"Would you like a horse?" she asked.

"I've already got a horse," I informed her.

She giggled again. "Well, this one don't need hay, or oats, or anything," and she handed me a slightly damaged horse with crooked legs.

I ate the horse in two bites.

"Mamma don't let me do that," said Sarah seriously, her eyes big. "She says I might choke and throw up."

I wanted to tell Sarah that such talk wasn't very ladylike and then I was reminded by a little glance from Mary that I had provoked the whole thing.

"I shouldn't have done it, either," I admitted. "I promise not to do it again."

I gave Sarah another pat, grinned sheepishly at Mary and went on up to my room.

The question of where Sarah should sleep at our house hadn't really been solved. I offered to sleep on the cot, but Grandpa refused. He didn't say so, but I think it had something to do with him having gotten two boarders for our extra bedrooms. Uncle Charlie said he would, but it was hard enough for him to get a decent night's sleep in his own bed.

Grandpa ended up on the cot that first night. He looked awfully tired the next morning.

We talked again about letting Sarah take the cot. The idea didn't seem like a good one—not that the cot wouldn't fit Sarah better than it had Grandpa, but simply because she would be kept awake so late. Sarah would never go to sleep as long as there was stirring in the kitchen, yet none of the rest of us were ready for bed at seven-thirty.

Mary finally worked it all out. "Move the cot into my room," she suggested. "There's plenty of room; Sarah can go to bed at the proper time and the rest of us can keep our own beds."

"That's awfully kind of you, Mary," Grandpa started to protest, "but you shouldn't have—"

"Nonsense," she said. "I love her company and you know it."

So the cot was moved into Mary's room and Sarah was tucked in for the night. It was a much better arrangement. After Sarah had returned home the next day, I offered to move the cot out, but Mary wouldn't hear of it.

"Just leave it there," she said. "It's not in my way, and it will be all ready for the next time she comes."

The snow came softly at first, then heavier and heavier until there was a deep ground cover. I didn't like the idea of tiny Matilda heading off for school across the open field. It was already knee deep and there would be no path.

"Take Chester," I urged her.

"I'll be fine," she insisted. "A little snow won't hurt me. The walk does me good. Besides, there'll be worse storms before the winter is over. I might as well get used to it."

I stopped arguing, but I will admit I cast a glance out the window now and then until she passed out of sight, just to be sure that she would make it to the schoolhouse.

Storm followed storm, and we settled into another winter. Soon we all had adjusted to it, and I no longer fretted when Matilda left for school, her high boots clearing a way through the drifts and her arms full of textbooks.

Shortly before Christmas the tractor finally arrived. The station master sent word out to us with one of our neigbors. Mr. Smith seemed to be quite pleased to have been chosen to bear the news. There weren't too many tractors in our part.

I rushed off to town to pick it up and it looked like the whole town was there to watch me take delivery.

I had thought from reading the manuals that a tractor would be easy enough to handle. But we had a real time getting it fired up, and by the time the blacksmith came to give me a hand, my face was red and my fuse short.

Then I had to back the big monster up in order to get it turned around. That seemed to be harder than backing a horse and buggy. We had to start it twice more, because I kept killing the engine. I finally did get it heading the right direction, with all eyes of the townsfolk upon me. But then, not wanting to hog all the road, I got a little too close to the edge of the roadway. Those big steel wheels just seemed to pull me right on down into the ditch, and the tractor stalled again. When the helpful blacksmith and I did get it started, I wasn't sure how I was going to get myself out of there. But to my amazement, those same steel wheels that took me down so unexpectedly also took me back out, and I was off down the road heading home.

It was a cold ride. The thing moved along at a crawl, and it was made all of steel, so there was nothing warm about it—at least not back where I was sitting.

By the time I got it home, I sure was glad to pull it up beside the granary and climb on down. It wasn't nearly as easy to handle as a team, I can tell you that, and it took me most of the afternoon to get the chill out of my bones.

I did some thinking about that tractor that I hadn't done before. Getting the tractor was fine, but I hadn't thought much of where to go from there. I could tell just by looking that the farm machinery we had used behind the horses wouldn't work behind that tractor. We'd probably need to replace nearly all the equipment we owned.

I wrote Willie a long letter that night, the first one in a while. I'd had a few letters from him, and I knew he was just as busy there in South Africa as I was back home.

He was pretty excited about his new life. Oh, he still missed Camellia terribly—and his family and friends, too, I guess, but he sure was excited about getting into the work he had been trained to do. God had given him a deep love for the black Africans he was reaching out to. They were so friendly and open, he said, and he knew he was going to love being a missionary among them.

I had already told him about Grandpa's wild idea of moving two women into our house. I had even written later, admitting that it really wasn't as bad as I had expected. But I hadn't told him about the community social or our good harvest or the new tractor.

I told him, too, that Mrs. Foggelson was really doing well since she had reestablished her faith. Not that she was running around town preaching or singing on the street corner or anything like that, but she was growing in a quiet, maturing way.

I miss you, Willie, I wrote, *and I'll be glad to see you again. Four years, after all, is a long, long time. God's blessing on your work; my warmest regards. Your best friend, Josh.*

Winter Ills

Another Christmas was approaching. We all went together to the school Christmas program. Matilda had labored long and hard over it. The youngsters performed well, and the crowd of neighbors insisted that Matilda sing again. She sang two lovely songs and then she asked Mary to join her for one. Mary did, without protest, and the people clapped even more enthusiastically after the duet.

The program at the church on Sunday night was mostly Aunt Lou's responsibility, though she had help from Matilda as well.

Little Sarah sang her first solo, "Away in a Manger." She was doing fine, too, carrying the tune just perfectly until Jon jumped down from the bench beside Mrs. Lewis, who was supposed to be looking after him, and ran to get in on his sister's act.

Aunt Lou didn't know what to do. To dash after Jon would interrupt the song, but leaving him alone proved to be even more disruptive.

At first he merely stood beside Sarah, looking up in her face and rocking gently back and forth to the music. Then he decided to sing, too, but Jon didn't know the words. His song was "Ah-ah-ah" at the top of his healthy lungs. Sarah frowned at him, but went on singing. It wasn't long until Jon's "Ah-ahs" were drowning out Sarah's voice. She finally stopped mid-phrase.

"Go to Mrs. Lewis!" she hissed loudly at her brother.

He shook his head and started to sing again.

"Then go to Mamma," Sarah insisted, giving him a push.

Jon still refused to budge. I could hear some snickers and caught a glimpse of Uncle Nat heading for the platform, but Sarah hadn't seen him. "Go!" she insisted and gave Jon another push, a bit more forcefully.

"No!" hollered Jon. "Sing!" As he whirled around to escape his sister, he entangled himself in the decorated tree. It came down with a crash and Jon, frightened by it all, began to bellow as loudly as he could. By the time Uncle Nat arrived, his two offspring were both crying and the platform was a mess.

"Preacher's young'uns!" Uncle Nat said to the amused congregation, rolling his eyes heavenward half in jest and half in exasperation, and scooped up his two errant family members while Aunt Lou tried to restore some order to the front of the church.

On Monday we took Matilda to the train; she was to spend her holidays at home. She was in a dither about seeing her family again, but that was normal—Matilda lived life in an air of excitement. She and Mary had become very close friends, and they hugged one another over and over. In fact, the only one who didn't get a hug was me. I would have been embarrassed about it if I had. Us being right out in the eyes of people and all. I knew that few would understand how it was at our house. The house seemed a bit quiet when we returned. Mary served us a tasty dinner, washed up the dishes and then went to her room. Soon she reappeared with her small carpetbag in her hand.

"Your Grandpa has given me Christmas week off. With Matilda gone he says you can get along just fine by yourselves."

I was a little doubtful. We hadn't been doing much cooking for ourselves lately, and it would be rather hard now to fit back into the old rut.

"I've done extra baking," went on Mary. "You'll find it in the pantry."

I nodded.

"If you should need me—"

"We'll be fine. Just fine," I assured her with more confidence than I felt.

She pulled on her heavy coat, and I finally realized it was cold out, and it was over a mile to the Turleys'.

"I'll get Chester and give you a ride home," I offered.

I didn't wait for her to answer, just grabbed my coat and cap and headed for the barn.

I hooked Chester to the one-horse sleigh, and we set off. The afternoon was crisp and bright and the snow crunched under the runners.

"I'll miss Matilda," sighed Mary after a long silence.

I was on the verge of saying that I would too but checked myself just in time.

"She's so—so alive," went on Mary.

That was the truth. I was reining in Chester—as usual, he wanted to run.

"It won't be long till she's back."

"Oh, I hope not!" Mary gave a deep sigh.

I didn't go in when we reached the Turleys', though Mary asked me to. "I've got to get home and start in on the chores," I told her. Then I added, feeling suddenly shy, "We'll see you in a few days. Have a real good Christmas."

She turned to me. There were no rows of eyes watching.

"Thank you, Josh," she whispered. Then she reached up, gave me a quick embrace, and she was gone.

It turned out that we did need Mary. Two days after Christmas Uncle Charlie became ill. We could have handled that, but the next day Grandpa, too, was down. I didn't know what to do. I still had all the chores, and the two men were sick enough that they needed someone to care for them. In desperation I finally saddled Chester and headed back for Mary.

Mary flushed a bit when she saw Chester, but she laughed, too. "Well," she said, "does he ride double?"

"How stupid of me!" I blushed. "I should have brought the sleigh. He can carry two, but—"

"It's fine, Josh," she assured me. "If Chester doesn't mind, I don't."

She rode behind me, her arms around my waist as though it was the most natural thing in the world.

In the next few days, Uncle Charlie worsened, and though Mary nursed him with all of her skill and prepared him broths and chicken soup, he still couldn't keep anything on his stomach. I saddled Chester up again and went after Doc.

After a few days on the medicine that Doc left, Uncle Charlie seemed to be able to make some headway. But by the time Grandpa and Uncle

Charlie were beginning to show a bit of improvement, Matilda was back, and Christmas was over.

Things seemed to be fine for about two days, and then Matilda came down with chills and fever. School was cancelled until further notice, and Mary started her nursing again.

When it finally hit me, I couldn't believe that anyone could feel that bad. My whole body ached, and I broke out in sweats and then shivered until the bed shook. The mere thought of food was unbearable, and I was so weak that I could hardly turn my head on the pillow.

I don't know how Mary made it through those days. She did send for Mitch to do the choring, but even so, I don't think she got much rest day or night. Whenever I stirred restlessly, cool cloths were pressed against my fevered forehead and sips of water held to my chapped lips.

I drifted in and out of reality. Sometimes I had strange dreams where I was in heaven and the angels were flitting about me, brushing back my hair and cooling my face. Sometimes I was quite rational and Mary or Matilda would be there sponging off my face or back and chest. I think that Doc was there once or twice. I don't remember seeing him; I just remember his voice giving somebody instructions.

I had no idea how many days were passing by. I only knew that when I was finally aware enough to ask, I couldn't believe that so much of the month of January was already spent. From then on I had almost constant company. Mary came with broths and soups and Pixie lay at the foot of the bed. Uncle Charlie just sat there quietly and cleared his throat now and then. Matilda came with books and read to me for what seemed hour after hour in a voice filled with energy and excitement.

By the time I was able to sit up for short periods in the kitchen, Grandpa and Uncle Charlie were almost as good as new, and Matilda had been back to her classes for a couple of weeks.

I had never been that sick before in my whole life. And after those days in bed, helpless and sick and flat on my back, I was ready to admit one thing—I was glad there were women in the house.

It turned out that Mitch had to do our chores for the whole month of January and half of February. I maintained that I was well enough to get back to work, but Doc wouldn't hear of it. My recuperation time did give me a good chance to get back into some books. I had been so busy using my muscles that I had almost forgotten how to use my brain.

I discovered, too, that the daily papers that arrived for Matilda to the post office weekly weren't all that bad. To relieve the boredom, I began to sort through them and found some terrific articles under "Farm News and Markets."

There was so much more to farming than mere sowing and reaping. I could see the possibility of the farm turning a tidy profit in the future, and the thought filled me with energy and excitement. Folks like Willie needed support in order to stay on the mission field. I didn't say anything to the family yet, but I did do some talking to God. I was beginning to get a vision of the farm being used in God's work by helping meet the financial needs of missionaries—especially Willie. I intended to do all I could to make the farm produce so that he would never need to worry about support while he served on the field.

CHAPTER 25

Chester

I was sitting at the table talking to Matilda about some strange ideas, to my way of thinking, I'd found in one of her books. I heard a commotion and went to the kitchen window to look out toward the barn.

I smiled. There was nothing to be concerned about. The horses were just frisking about. I looked at the sky, thinking that another storm must be moving in.

"Why are they running?" Matilda asked at my elbow.

"Just feeling frisky," I answered. "Or could be a storm coming in. Horses often run and play before a storm." We stood there to watch them for a minute.

Chester was really worked up. He loved to run, and any excuse for him was a good enough one.

Mary crowded in on the other side of me, her face lightened by a smile. "I love to watch them."

The three of us stood there watching the horses rear and kick and race around the barnyard.

"He is so beautiful!" exclaimed Matilda. She held Pixie in her arms, gently scratching under one of the dog's silky ears. But I knew that it wasn't Pixie that she referred to. It was Chester, showing off out in the barnyard.

"Look at him, his head thrown back, his tail outstretched—" The word ended in a gasp.

Chester, who had been doing a tight circle around the end of the barn at almost full speed, had suddenly gone down, apparently hitting a patch of ice under the snow where the eaves dripped in milder weather.

I didn't even wait to comment; just turned and ran from the house. I guess I knew I should have stopped for my coat, especially since I had just been sick, but I didn't.

As I raced toward the barn, Chester was still floundering in the snow, pulling himself up, then tossing back down. His feet were thrashing, the snow flying, and as I ran I kept wondering why he wasn't back up on his feet.

I was almost to him when, with a snort and a flurry, he righted himself. I took a deep, relieved breath—and then I saw it. Chester's right front leg wobbled at an awkward angle. He had broken a leg in the fall!

I skidded to a halt and whirled around with my back to the horse. My arm came up and I buried my head against the fence, not wanting to see. Dry sobs wrenched my throat; then someone was gently nudging me. "Here put this on." It was Mary, helping me into my coat.

Then she, too, looked at Chester and I could hear her soft gasp.

I'm not sure when Matilda joined us. She came scurrying up beside us, her breath preceding her in little shivery clouds.

"Is he okay?" she gasped out.

Chester attempted to move, and I heard his pain-filled cry and Matilda's answering scream.

"No! No!" she kept saying over and over. I put my arms around her. She clung to me, sobbing convulsively.

When Grandpa came, we were all still standing in a huddle trying to comfort one another.

"Hurt bad?" I heard Grandpa ask.

I muttered in answer, "His front leg."

This brought a fresh burst of tears from Matilda. "I can't bear it!" she cried. "I can't bear to see him like that!"

I cast another glance toward Chester. He hadn't taken another step. He stood there, shaking his head and snorting, totally confused by the pain.

Somehow I got control of myself. "Here," I said to Mary. "Take Matilda to the house."

Mary led Matilda, still crying, away.

For the first time I took a good look at Chester. His heaving body was still covered with snow. He trembled with each breath he drew and his leg just dangled there, supporting none of his heavy frame.

I moved toward him and reached out a hand to run down his smooth neck. He quivered at my touch, then tried to take a step. His whole body reacted to the pain, and I thought for one awful minute that he was going to go down again. Sick at the sight, I turned from him, and wretched. The illness I had just come through probably had something to do with it. But I had to get control of myself. I had to help Chester.

Grandpa hardly knew whether to go to Chester or to me. I nodded at him that I was okay and he moved toward the horse. He spoke to him in soft tones, rubbing his neck and trying to calm him, his hand moving gently down toward the injured limb.

Chester threw himself back, and the pain of the movement made him squeal again in anguish.

I whirled and headed for the house. I didn't go to the kitchen, just to the back porch, and stopped there only long enough to check that there were shells in Grandpa's big old Winchester. I was turning to leave again when I heard the door open and close. Quick footsteps dashed after me and I could feel a hand on my arm.

"No!"

I jerked my arm free and tried to keep on walking.

"Josh, listen!" But I still didn't stop. Just as I reached the door Mary pushed herself ahead of me. She stood there, her back against the door, her slight frame heaving. She had been crying, too; the traces of tears were still on her cheeks.

She stood there, defying me, shaking her head and blocking my way.

"Don't!" she pleaded again.

I reached out a hand and pushed at her. "Do you think I want to do this?" I almost screamed.

We both knew the answer.

"Then don't," she said again, not budging from the spot she guarded.

"He's suffering!" I cried. "Can't you see that? He's suffering!"

Mary reached out and placed a hand on my coat front. Her eyes looked wide with fright and determination. "Yes," she said and her voice rose to almost the pitch that mine had been. "Yes, he's suffering. But life is full of suffering, Josh. You've suffered. I've suffered." She took another deep breath and her whole body heaved. "For years—for years I watched my mother suffer—day after day—week after week. I loved her, Josh. I loved her. But I didn't give up. I fought. I fought to save her. Chester is a fighter, Josh. A thoroughbred and a fighter. Chester isn't done yet. He hasn't given up. And we can't either—not without a fight."

With her final outburst, Mary took the gun from my unresisting hands and moved away from the door. I heard the sound of metal on metal as she hung it back on the pegs. The world was whirling around me and I was afraid I was going to be sick again.

Mary brushed past me and went out the door.

It was several minutes until I got myself under control. When I could think straight again, I thought of Mary's plea to fight for Chester's life. It would never work. Chester's leg was broken; anyone could see that. There was no way we could save him now. If we tried, he would suffer and suffer and then we would need to destroy him anyway. Better to relieve his suffering now.

I looked back at the gun and then let my shoulders droop in resignation as I turned my back on it and headed for the barn.

Somehow Mary and Grandpa had managed to get Chester into his stall. They were talking in quiet tones as I entered the barn.

" . . . a good clean break," Grandpa was saying. "No protruding bone."

"We need to keep his weight off it," Mary replied, beginning to gentle Chester with her hands and voice.

"How?" It was only one word from Grandpa, but it spoke for both of us.

"We need to construct some kind of sling—to hold him up, off his feet."

Grandpa eyed the stall. It wouldn't be easy.

"I saw Pa do it once with a critter," went on Mary. "Worked it on a pulley system."

Grandpa chewed on a corner of his mustache as he thought deeply. "Might work," he said at length.

"You keep him warm and try to quiet him, and I'll go get Pa," said Mary. I wasn't sure if she was talking to Grandpa or to me.

It was an awfully long time until Mr. Turley got there. Mary didn't come with him to the barn, but went right on to the house. I had spent the time soothing Chester. We had thrown a heavy horse blanket over him and rubbed his body down with clean straw. He was quieter. The fright seemed to have left him. He still quivered every now and then and snorted loudly when he tried to shift his weight.

Mary's pa went right to work. He called out orders so quickly that I was running to keep up. In a couple of hours we had Chester fitted with a body sling, and then with the pulley system Mr. Turley had rigged up above him, we gently hoisted him until his three feet just barely touched the floor. Chester's right front leg was raised just a shade higher so that he couldn't put any weight on it at all.

Chester, of course, didn't understand the arrangement. He snorted and pitched, trying to get proper control of his circumstances. It was some time until we were able to quiet him, and by then I was just sure it wasn't going to work.

As soon as Chester was settled down, Mr. Turley began to work on the leg. It had swollen a good deal, so it was difficult for him to feel the break. And any pressure on the area sent Chester flailing again.

At length Mr. Turley stood up. "A real shame!" he said soberly. "Such a beautiful horse."

I thought he was going to agree with my first response, to say that nothing could be done for Chester—but he didn't.

"Good clean break," he said instead. "Should heal nicely, barring any unforeseen complications."

The breath I had been holding came out slowly.

Then with the help of Grandpa and me, Mr. Turley got a leg support on Chester. By the time we were through, we were all worn out.

Grandpa invited Mr. Turley up to the house for a cup of coffee and I slumped down in the straw, my back to the manger and one hand on Chester. I just sat there—wondering, praying, hoping with all my heart that this beautiful animal would be all right.

I didn't even hear the door open.

"Josh?" It was Mary. She spoke in a whisper. "Josh?"

The barn lantern flickered with the slight movement of air from the door, the wavering flame sending the shivers of light dancing cross Mary's face. She stood there, holding out to me a steaming mug of chicken soup. I took it in still-trembling hands.

Then without another word she lowered herself to the straw beside me and laid a hand on my arm.

"He's gonna be okay," she whispered. "He's gonna be fine."

I tried a weak smile.

"How's Matilda?" I asked, wanting to forget just for a moment the pain of Chester.

"She's okay now. She's making dessert for supper. She's been praying—steady—ever since it happened."

I sighed and turned back to Chester.

"You really think he'll be all right?" I asked Mary.

Her smile was a little wobbly.

"Look at him," she said rather than making me any promises. "Pa says his leg felt real good. The bone seems straight—it's just a matter of time."

I looked at Chester. He was much calmer now. I almost believed what Mary was saying to me.

I turned to her. "Thanks," I said, taking her hand. "Thanks."

I should have said a lot more. Thanks for stopping me from doing something foolish. Thanks for riding old Maude through the cold and snow for your pa. Thanks for bringing me the hot soup. Thanks for your support. But all that I could say was "thanks."

She gave my hand a slight squeeze, rose to her feet, and returned to the kitchen.

CHAPTER 26

Willie

Chester adapted remarkably well to his body harness. Maybe he enjoyed the extra attention. I spent a great deal of time in the barn with him, and Matilda visited him often with treats of apples and sugar lumps. Mary inspected his entire body at least once a day, watching for any sores that might result from the harness straps.

The swelling began to go down in the leg, and after Mr. Turley had taken a look at it a few times, he suggested putting on a new leg brace. Chester hardly complained at all as it was done.

After a few weeks the brace was taken off altogether, but Chester was still not allowed to put his weight on it. I began to massage and exercise it. I wanted to be sure that the knee and ankle would still work well. Chester was able to move it with no problem—with my help, of course.

Finally the day came when we lowered the hammock and let him test his weight. He seemed reluctant at first and snorted his concern. I rubbed his neck and spoke to him 'til he calmed down.

We didn't leave him on all four legs for long. We didn't want to tire him. But every day he was allowed to stand for a longer period of time.

At last I began walking him. At first he had a bit of a limp, and then even that disappeared. It was almost too good to be true, but it looked like Chester was going to be just fine.

As the winter wore on, we all went about our daily chores. I fired up our new tractor every once in a while, just to make sure it was still working. Then Grandpa had the bright idea of dragging a log behind it to clear snow on our road. Uncle Charlie got in a bit of teasing about my "new toy."

We spent the evenings together in the big farmhouse kitchen, Pixie curled up contentedly on the lap of one or another. Those evenings were special times. On such nights, we were comforted by the thought of being snuggled in the kitchen, a warm fire crackling in the big cookstove. We could often hear another storm as it swept through, the wind howling and raging and rattling the loose tin on the corner of the eaves trough. Every time I listened to it, I reminded myself to fix it come the first nice day. But when the nice days came, I was always busy with something else.

Every time I went to town—and I didn't go any more often than absolutely necessary on those cold days—I picked up another bundle of Matilda's papers to help pass the boredom of the winter days. It had been several weeks since I had heard from Willie, and I had been watching for a letter from him—but the letter didn't come.

Then one day I heard the farm dog bark a greeting, and I looked out the frosted window to see Uncle Nat flip the reins of Dobbin over the gate post. He came toward the house in long, quick strides, and I wondered if he was cold or just in a hurry.

I met him at the door with enthusiasm. It had been a while since he had been out.

Mary pushed the coffeepot forward and added fuel to the fire so that Uncle Nat could warm himself a bit, and Grandpa and Uncle Charlie pulled up chairs to the table, getting ready for a good visit.

Uncle Nat sat down and indicated the chair next to him. I pulled it up and leaned forward, eager to hear how things were going in town.

"How's Chester?" asked Uncle Nat.

I beamed. "He's doing fine. I can't believe it. You should see him. He can move around almost as good as before."

Uncle Nat smiled and nodded his head.

"How're Lou and the kids?" asked Grandpa for all of us.

"Busy," laughed Uncle Nat. "Real busy. That Jonathan! Lou hardly knows how to keep him occupied in this cold weather."

We all laughed, knowing enough about active Jon to feel a bit sorry for Aunt Lou.

"You out callin'?" Grandpa asked.

"No," said Uncle Nat slowly. His head lowered and his face sobered. We all waited, knowing instinctively that there was more. He lifted his head again and looked directly at me.

"I'm afraid I have some bad news," he said. "I thought you should know. It's Willie."

"Willie?"

"He's gone, Josh."

I didn't understand.

"Gone? Gone where?"

"Word came to the Corbins by telegram this morning. Willie died a couple of days ago."

"But there must be some mistake!" I hardly recognized my own voice, hoarse with shock. "Willie is in South Africa. How do they know—?"

"The Mission Society sent the telegram."

"But there must be some mistake," I repeated, not wanting to accept or believe what I had just been told. I started to get up from my chair. Uncle Nat put a hand on my shoulder and eased me back down.

"There's no mistake, Josh," he sorrowfully assured me. "The Mission Board sent their deepest regrets. Willie is dead."

I heard someone crying, and then I realized that it was me. I buried my head in my arms and cried until the sobs shook my whole body.

"Not Willie!" my voice was saying over and over. "Dear God, please, not Willie."

And all the time a part of my brain kept saying, *It's all a mistake. You'll see. They'll soon discover that they were wrong. It was someone else—not Willie.*

In the background I could hear voices, but the words never really registered. Someone was comforting a weeping Mary. Someone was trying to comfort me.

It was a long time until I was able to get some measure of control. Grandpa was asking more questions.

"How did it happen?"

"Some kind of fever—malaria, they expect."

"Was he sick for long?"

"They still don't know."

"How are his folks?"

"Taking it hard."

It seemed so unreal, senseless. Willie had hardly arrived out there, and now he was *gone*.

And then I thought of Camellia. And I began to cry again. "Poor Camellia. Poor Camellia," I muttered over and over.

That storm passed, too, and I sat, head bowed, shuddering and hiccuping as I wiped my eyes and blew my nose on the handkerchief I found in my hands.

"Would you like to go to your room?" Uncle Nat asked, and I must have nodded. Uncle Nat helped me up the stairs and to my bed. I threw myself down there and began to weep again, but it seemed so useless. I started to pray instead. For Willie—though I don't know why. Willie was safe enough. For the Corbins; I knew the whole family would be devastated. I had to go to the Corbins. I had to let them know that I too shared their suffering over the news of Willie's untimely death.

I prayed for Mrs. Foggelson; Willie was to have been her son-in-law. But mostly I prayed for Camellia. How would she ever bear it? She was all alone at the college, preparing herself to serve with Willie in his Africa.

She would come home now, broken perhaps, but she would come home.

I went back to the kitchen and splashed water on my swollen face. Uncle Nat had already left, but Grandpa and Uncle Charlie sat silently at the kitchen table. Untouched cups of cold coffee sat before them. They looked at me without saying a word. Mary was nowhere to be seen, but her bedroom door was closed tightly.

"I'm going to the Corbins," I said quietly, and Grandpa nodded.

I wasn't sure Chester's leg was well enough, so I put a bridle on old Maude.

I didn't bother with the saddle; just grabbed up the reins and rode bareback. Maude wasn't the easiest horse in the world to ride, but maybe I took some satisfaction in my discomfort.

I found the Corbin family tear-stained and desolate. Mrs. Corbin sat in a rocker by the kitchen stove, saying over and over as she rocked, "My poor boy. My poor boy. My poor Willie." When she saw me she held out her arms and I went to her. She held me so tightly that I could scarcely breathe, and I knew she was trying to hold on to a little part of Willie.

Mr. Corbin paced back and forth across the kitchen floor, his face hard and his hands twisting together. Other family members huddled in little groups here and there, whispering and crying by turn.

And then a very strange thing happened. SueAnn, who had been crying just like the rest of them, wiped away her tears, took a deep breath and managed a weak smile.

"I know God doesn't make mistakes," she said. "There will be good, some reason in all this, even if we can't think of any right now."

They began to talk, in soft whispers at first, with frequent bursts of tears, but gradually the tears subsided and the praise became more positive. There was even an occasional chuckle as someone recalled a funny incident from Willie's life. Soon the whole atmosphere of the room had changed. Mrs. Corbin had stopped rocking and moaning, and Mr. Corbin was no longer pacing. Someone brought the family Bible and they began to read, passing the precious book from hand to hand as they shared its truths.

Later, when I left for home, the Corbin family was still grieving, but each member had found a source of comfort beyond themselves.

I waited a day or two before I called on Mrs. Foggelson. I didn't think I could manage it earlier. I still felt a dull ache deep within me, and I was afraid if I tried to talk about Willie I would break up again.

Mrs. Foggelson met me at the door. "Oh, Josh!" she said with a little cry and she moved quickly toward me, her arms outstretched.

I held her for a few minutes. She was crying against my shoulder, but when she moved back she quickly whisked away the tears and motioned me to the sofa.

We talked about Willie for a long time; we both needed it. I asked about Camellia.

"How is she?" I asked.

"Crushed!" said Mrs. Foggelson. "She's crushed—but she'll make it. We've talked on the telephone a couple of times."

"When will she be home?"

"Today. On the afternoon train. That was the soonest she could come."

There was a pause; then she added, "It seems like such a long way to come for such a short time, but we both felt it important that she be here for the Memorial Service."

"Short time? What do you mean?"

"She has to go back right away. She's writing important exams next week."

"You mean she's going to stay on in school?" I couldn't believe it. Why? Willie was no longer there to draw Camellia to South Africa.

Of course, I reasoned, *Camellia would not want to quit classes half-way through a year.* I admired her for that. *But she quit the Interior Design course before she had completed it.* I was puzzled, unable to understand the difference.

"If she doesn't write these exams, she loses a whole semester. That would set her back considerably."

I nodded, a bit surprised that Camellia still wanted to be a nurse.

I went with Mrs. Foggelson to meet Camellia's train. Some of the Corbin family were there as well. There were more tears. Camellia went from one to another, being held and comforted. When it was my turn there was nothing that we could say to each other. I just held her and let her weep, and my heart nearly broke all over again. The three of us walked on home through the chill winter air and Mrs. Foggelson set about making us all a pot of tea.

"Your ma says you need to go back soon," I said to Camellia.

She nodded slowly, a weary hand brushing back her curls.

"You're still set on nursing?"

"Willie said that is the biggest need out there—and who knows? If there had been a nurse there, Willie might not have died."

I could understand that much but not what it had to do with her situation.

"I just wish I hadn't wasted so much time," she went on as though talking to herself. "If I had started my training at the same time Willie did . . ." She left the statement hanging.

"But you didn't know."

"No, I didn't know." Her tone was tired, empty; then she smiled softly. "But at least I'll have the joy of serving the people that Willie learned to love."

It finally got through to me then. Camellia was still planning on going to Africa.

"You're going to go after *this*?" It seemed out of the question.

"Of course," she said simply, as though I shouldn't even need to ask. "They need me."

CHAPTER 27

God's Call

The three of us made it through the Memorial Service; Mrs. Foggelson asked me to sit with her and Camellia. And then we saw Camellia off on the train again. She held her mother a long, long time as the tears flowed.

"Mamma, I love you so much," she sobbed. "If I didn't *have* to go, I'd stay with you—you know that."

Mrs. Foggelson seemed to understand. She looked Camellia straight in the eyes and said earnestly, "Remember—always, always stand true to your convictions, to what the Lord is telling you."

They hugged one another again, and then Camellia turned to me.

"Thank you, Josh, for always being there. For being such a dear, dear friend to Willie and me." I couldn't say anything in reply. I just held her for a brief moment and then let her go.

I was restless over the next several days. I couldn't seem to think, to sleep, I didn't care to eat—I couldn't even really concentrate when I prayed. My prayers were all broken sentences, pleas of isolated words, fragments of thoughts.

I walked through the days in a stupor. I went through the motions of chores each day. The animals were cared for. Chester got his daily massage and exercise. I moved. I functioned. I spoke. Occasionally I even heard myself laugh, but it was as though another person were existing in my body.

I had to make a trip to town. We needed some groceries and the whole household seemed anxious for a new set of papers.

I went the usual route, picked up the papers at the post office, shuffled through the mail, and my eyes lighted up as they fell on an envelope from South Africa. It was from *Willie!* And then my whole body went numb.

But Willie is dead! Willie is no longer in South Africa!

I looked at the postmark. It was dated several weeks back. Somewhere the letter had been held up.

I put the letter in my coat pocket, *I wonder if I'll even be able to read it,* I thought. But at the same time I knew that there was no way on earth I could keep from reading it.

I didn't open the letter until after I had arrived home, cared for the team, done the chores, had my supper, and retired for the night. I didn't tell anyone about it either—I wasn't sure how its contents were going to affect me.

At last I opened it slowly and let my eyes drift over the familiar script. My hands were shaking as I held the pages to the light of the kerosene lamp.

Willie, in the usual fashion, wrote about the people he was getting to know, how they were learning to trust him and listen when he talked to them about Jesus. His love showed in every word he spoke. You could tell Willie was happy that God had called him to South Africa.

He made comments about my last letter and asked questions about my family and the community. He sent his love to Mary and even teased me a bit about having *two* eligible young ladies in the household.

Then he began to talk about Camellia. *How happy and blessed I am that God brought us together! I always cared for Camellia—right from the first day that she came to our school. I watched silently as you and Camellia became friends, both sad and happy at the same time.*

And now God has turned everything around; Camellia is going to be my wife. I can hardly believe the way I have been blessed; I hope with all my heart that you haven't been hurt. It will be a long time yet before Camellia can join me; I'm counting every hour, but God is making the busy days pass quickly, and before we know it, she will be at my side.

And then Willie said, *Josh, I don't have to tell you this, but the most exciting thing in the world is to live day by day in the will of God. He has a perfect plan, and if we are obedient to Him He will accomplish it, whether it takes fifty years, twenty years or a single day.*

A sob caught in my throat. I read the paragraph again. Then I went on.

I am thankful that God gave me a good home, a good church, and good friends so that I could learn that truth without fighting it. I know that you have often wondered why the Lord hasn't called you to the pastorate or to the mission field. The important thing isn't where *we serve, but* how. *The question is not "what does He have for me in the future?" but "Am I obedient to Him right now?" And you can walk in obedience, Josh, wherever you live and serve.*

May God lead you, Josh, in whatever He has for you. You're the greatest buddy a fellow ever had. Love, Willie.

I cried many tears over that letter. I read it so often in the next several days that I could have repeated it by heart, yet I had a hard time getting to the truth of it.

I was in the barn one morning exercising Chester when the door opened and Uncle Nat came in. After warm greetings, Uncle Nat came over to check out my horse. He was nearly as pleased as I was to see how well Chester was progressing.

"He looks real good, Josh," he said to me. "Soon he'll be running at a full gallop again."

I grinned.

"Well, I sure hope the ice and snow are off the ground before then," I said. "Don't want it to happen again."

"Oh, it will be," said Uncle Nat with confidence.

I shook my head. "Seems to me this winter has hung on and on," I said soberly.

Uncle Nat looked at me evenly. I could read questions in his eyes. He pulled forward a barn stool and sat down.

"So, how's it going, Josh?" I knew that it wasn't just a passing question or a social pleasantry.

I let Chester drift back to his own stall, and I sank onto a soft mound of straw.

"I don't know," I said honestly. "It's been a tough winter."

Uncle Nat nodded.

"Tough times make us grow, Josh," he said simply.

I thought about that. I hoped I had done some growing.

"The farm's doing well," Uncle Nat went on, encouraging me to talk.

"Yeah," I nodded, thinking of the good seed grain in the granaries, the fine stock in the pasture, and the tractor waiting for spring.

"You should be real proud of yourself," Uncle Nat continued. "I know we all are."

"You are? That's good, but I still—"

"You unhappy with farming?" Uncle Nat's question brought me up short.

"Oh no," I was quick to inform him. "I like it—*love* it. It's great to watch things grow—and change—and to know that you've been a part of it."

"But something is bothering you."

"Well, I mean—I still don't know what God wants me to do in life. I expected by now that He would show me, but He hasn't yet. By the time a fella is past twenty-two, he should have some clear direction about his life, he should know what he's supposed to do."

Uncle Nat gave me a playful poke on the arm. "I thought maybe you had girl troubles," he teased. "Couldn't make up your mind about which one of those fine ladies—"

"Naw," I answered, "not girl troubles." But I pondered Uncle Nat's words.

"I wouldn't even dare to choose a girl now," I added defensively. "Not 'til I know what God has in mind for my life."

"I see," said Uncle Nat.

We were both silent for a few minutes.

"But you enjoy farming?" said Uncle Nat, as though to clear up a point. "You don't feel any kind of guilt for being here for the last several years?"

"I *had* to be here," I said, surprised that Uncle Nat didn't understand that. "Grandpa and Uncle Charlie needed me. There was no one else to help them."

"And with your hard work and good management you have turned the farm around—it's better now than ever."

I appreciated Uncle Nat's lofty compliments, and I had to admit that there was some truth in what he said.

"And you think that the two men will be able to handle the farm now by themselves?"

It was a foolish question. Anyone could see that Grandpa and Uncle Charlie wouldn't do much farming in the future.

"You know they couldn't," I said rather abruptly.

"So they still need you?" Uncle Nat left the question hanging in the air between us. I didn't even try to answer it.

"Have you ever considered the fact that God might want you to go on farming? That farming might be His call for you?"

"*Farming?*" I paused for quite a while. Then I said, "Not really. I just supposed—" I shook my head.

"But you do enjoy farming?" pressed Uncle Nat.

"Sure I do. But it all seems kind of pointless. I've been trying hard to build up the farm so that it would be productive, make money." I lowered my head and picked absently at some straw. "I had even promised God that the money I made would be used to support missionaries—like Willie. And now—now it all seems wasted." My speech ended with a sob caught in my throat. Uncle Nat sat silently for several minutes until he could see that I had control of myself again.

"I suppose Willie's early death seems a waste to you, too, Josh."

Uncle Nat had tied up my confused feelings into a neat package. I said nothing.

"I don't understand about Willie's death," went on Uncle Nat. "It is sad and it causes us all much pain, but it wasn't wasteful. God doesn't make mistakes, Josh."

"That's what SueAnn said the day we got word of his death. But, Uncle Nat, that's really hard for me to swallow. Look at Willie—if anybody was being faithful to God, he was. So why did God let him die like that, so young, with so much ahead of him?"

Uncle Nat looked intently at me. "Josh, none of us can know for certain *why* these things happen. We may never know. Because God gave man a free will and he chose to sin, we now live in a world marred by sin—"

"But Jesus' death sets us free from sin!" I protested.

"As individuals who trust Him—yes. From the *judgment* of sin. But as long as we live on this earth, we will have to live with the effects of sin."

"Like evil?"

"Evil, and sickness, and accidents, and untimely death—all those things that don't quite seem fair. We live in a sin-damaged world, Josh. People do get sick and die. We may not understand it, but we do know—"

"That God loves us and wants the best for us," I finished for him. Somewhere, in the darkness of my grief and confusion, I felt a light beginning to dawn.

"We have to believe that or life has no meaning," Uncle Nat agreed in a soft, firm voice.

"Now, I don't know the reason for what happened. But there is a purpose. God can make 'all things work together for good'—those aren't just words, Josh. I'm sure of that. Willie's life accomplished what it was meant to accomplish. Willie was obedient to God. He was right where God wanted Him to be at the time that God wanted him to be there. He wasn't running away; he wasn't fighting God's plan. He was obedient. God can always—and only—fulfill His plan for us when we obey Him—about the daily decisions and the big ones."

Parts of Willie's letter flashed back into my mind. That was what Willie was trying to tell me. All that was really important was that I obey God now, this very moment, at this very place. Tomorrow could be left in God's hands.

Uncle Nat was talking again. "Do you feel that you are disobeying God in farming, Josh?"

"No," I was able to answer honestly. "I really don't."

"Then if you are not disobeying Him, could it be that you are *obeying* Him?"

I stared at Uncle Nat, thinking. Then I began to chuckle. "It seems so simple," I said, tossing a handful of straw into the air.

"Maybe it is. Maybe we're the ones who make it complicated."

I felt as if a great burden had suddenly been lifted from my shoulders. Uncle Nat and I hugged each other and then he held me away and said softly, "Josh, there are other missionaries who will still need to be supported. Camellia, for one."

Tears filled my eyes. I guess there was no other missionary I would rather support than Willie's Camellia. I nodded, too choked up to speak.

"You ready to go?" asked Uncle Nat.

I was ready all right. I had been spending too much of my time hidden away in the barn lately. Chester was doing just fine on his own. He didn't need me that much anymore. *At least for now, God wants me to be a farmer—the best one possible,* I thought. *Unless or until He shows me something else . . .* And I had the big issue settled. I was ready to get on with some of the other decisions that a fellow has to make. I gave Uncle Nat a smile—the first in a long time, it seemed. We left the barn and I fastened the door securely behind me.

As we headed for the house, I lifted my eyes to study the farm I loved. A distinct feeling of spring filled the morning air.

Spring's Gentle Promise

To all the men and women
of the soil,
past and present,
who have fought against the elements
and the changing times
to maintain their roots
and to pass on a heritage.
We need you.
We cheer you on.
God bless you.

CONTENTS

CHARACTERS

Joshua Chadwick Jones—The boy raised by his aunt Lou, grandfather and great-uncle Charlie. Josh is now an adult, farming the family farm.

Grandpa and Uncle Charlie—The menfolk who shared Josh's home and life.

Matilda—The neighborhood schoolteacher who boards with the Joneses.

Mary Turley—Housekeeper and neighbor girl who helps the men with the kitchen duties. In Grandpa's thinking, two girls in the house made the arrangement more "respectable."

Willie—Josh's boyhood friend who went to Africa as a missionary and died of a native disease.

Camellia—Josh's first love, but she loved Willie instead.

CHAPTER 1

A Beautiful Morning

I was whistling as I left the house. It was early. The sky had brightened, but the sun had not as yet lifted its head above the tree line that marked the border of the Sanders' place—new neighbors in our community.

Even in the dimness of early morning I could see field after neighborhood field as I let my gaze wander around me. First there was ours—I supposed I would always think of the farm as *ours*—Grandpa's, Uncle Charlie's and mine—though in truth it really was just mine now. Guess that was one of the reasons I was whistling. Just yesterday Grandpa and Uncle Charlie had signed all the official papers to make the farm mine—really and legally mine. *Joshua Chadwick Jones* the papers read, clear as could be. The full impact had yet to hit me. But I was excited. Really excited. I mean, what other fella my age had a farm of his own, title clear and paid for?

I sobered down a bit. It was a big responsibility 'cause I was the one who had to make the farm "bring forth" now. Had to support Grandpa and Uncle Charlie and myself and Mary, our housekeeper, and even Matilda, our boarder, though she did pay us some board and room.

I was the one who had to make the right decisions about which crops to plant and which field to plant them in, which livestock to sell and which ones to keep, and where to find the particular animal that would help build up the herd. I would need to keep up the fences, repaint the buildings, work the garden, keep the machinery in working order, watch out for weeds, put up the hay for winter feeding. . . . The list went on and on—but that didn't dim my spirits. It was a beautiful morning. I was a full-grown man with a place of my own.

I lengthened my stride. I'd been dawdling somewhat while I looked all around. The fields, the tree line, the wooded area where the crick passed through, the pastureland, and then the fields of the Turleys, Smiths, Sanders, the faraway hill that marked another Smith, the road to town—I knew it all. And I loved it more than I would ever have been able to say.

My roots were buried deep in this countryside I had known since a child. This was my life. My whole sense of being and knowing and living and growing were somehow wrapped up in the soil that stretched away before me.

I opened the gate at the end of the lane and took a break in my whistling to speak to the milk cows. The little jersey, one of my most recent purchases, rubbed her head against me gently as she moved to pass by. I reached out and ran my hand over her neck. She seemed satisfied then, and I smiled. *She's a great little cow,* I gloated. *Can fill the milk pail with the richest milk I've ever seen.* She was a mite spoiled though. Her former owners had treated her as the family pet.

I hurried ahead of the cows to open the barn door for them. I knew they were right behind me, anxious to reach the milking stall where their portion of morning grain waited. They also wished to find relief from the heavy load of milk that swelled their udders and slowed their walk.

I began my whistling again. A bird joined me, off to the right, and I turned my head to look for it. It was high in a poplar tree by the hen house, and by its vigorous song I imagined that it was just as happy with the early morning as I was.

From somewhere in Turleys' pasture a cow bawled and another answered. Perhaps a mother had become separated from her baby and was calling it for breakfast.

I opened the barn door for the cows and turned right back to the house for the milk pails. I knew the three cows would find their own way to their stalls and be appreciatively feeding on the chop when I returned. I could have gone the entire milking time without fastening the bars that held them in position, but I never did. I knew they wouldn't move from their places, heads between the stanchion bars, bodies motionless except for the ever-flicking tails and an occasional shift of a foot; but when I returned with the milk pails I fastened the bars just as I always had. It was pure habit I guess—but it was the way Grandpa had taught me.

The jersey gazed back at me with soft brown eyes as I hooked a toe under the milking stool and pulled it up to her side.

"What's the matter?" I chuckled. "You think I'm too lazy to bend over?"

I rubbed her side and eased myself onto the stool beside her, then reached out to brush off her taut bag, wash it a bit, and gently start the flow of milk.

"Well, maybe I am," I conceded. "But a fella has to conserve all the energy he can. I've a busy day ahead. I start plantin' today. Just as soon as I get the chores done. My own fields. Never planted 'my own fields' before."

I grinned and began the steady stream of milk that would soon fill the pail with rich, warm, foamy liquid.

I would never have been able to explain to anyone why I talked to the cow. I mean, no one would understand if they hadn't spent time in a barn at 5:00 in the morning doing the milking.

A barn cat, meowing, brushed itself against my pant leg. I didn't know if the soft sound was my welcome or an urge for me to hurry. I stopped long enough to squirt some milk in the cat's direction. It immediately sat back on its haunches, front paws batting in the air as though to capture every drop of milk and direct it toward its open mouth.

We were rather good at this—the gray tom and I. But then, we'd had a few years of practice. He sat there guzzling contentedly as I gave him squirt after squirt.

"Go on, now," I said at last. "I've got chores to do. You'll get your fill as soon as I'm done here."

The cat seemed to understand. He walked off a few feet and sat down to begin carefully grooming his spattered face.

The milking didn't take long, so after giving each cow a final pat on the flank, I left them, and carried two brimming pails of milk to the house. I would need to return for the third one, which was now hanging on a peg beyond the reach of the barn cats.

In spite of the early hour, Mary was moving briskly about the kitchen when I entered with the milk. I thought I noticed a certain gleam in her eyes—but perhaps it was just fanciful on my part. The fact that I was feeling so good seemed to be affecting my whole outlook on life.

Pixie was there too, rubbing against my legs, looking for her share of attention. I reached down and scratched her soft, silky ear. She was no longer the puppy I had learned to love. The years had passed by and Pixie was now old in dog years. She had remained behind, curled and contented, when I'd left my bed that morning. And I had been happy to let her sleep on. I rubbed her soft side and she licked at my hand.

"Mornin', Josh," Mary said cheerily. And without even waiting for my reply she went on, "My, you're up early. Don't know how you can even see out there in the barn."

"I waited for some light," I answered with a smile. "At least it was gettin' light when I went out." Then I added, "True, the barn stays dark a bit longer than the outside world, but I know my way around out there well enough that I don't need much light."

Mary smiled, adding to the brightness of the morning.

"Do you want to eat early?" she asked.

"I still have some chores to do."

Mary's eyes lifted to the kitchen clock, and mine followed.

"Guess I will be ready before the rest of them," I admitted. "Want to start plantin' just as soon as I can."

"I'll git your breakfast," Mary said simply and moved toward the pantry.

"Thanks. I—I hate for you to get breakfast twice, but I'm kind of anxious—"

I needn't have tried to explain. As Mary tied her apron around her slim waist, without even turning to look at me she answered, "In plantin' and harvest time, a man doesn't want to lose any time gittin' to his fields. An early breakfast is no problem—an' we sure don't need to be wakin' the rest of the house."

I hadn't missed Mary's reference to "a man" and "his fields," and my heart beat a little faster. Then my thoughts hurried on to Grandpa, rather old and tired out after all his years of farming, then to Uncle Charlie, all crippled up with his arthritis. I wondered sadly just how much sleep he had been able to get over the night hours. My thoughts went on to Matilda. She was testing her pupils again at the nearby schoolhouse, and I knew she had been staying up late marking papers for a number of nights in a row. I nodded my head in agreement with Mary's simple statement. They all needed their sleep, all right.

"I'll only be another half hour or so," I reported to Mary and then went to strain the milk into the bowl of the cream separator.

"You go on," Mary prompted. "I'll tend to that."

My eyes questioned her, though it was true that Mary had often stepped forward to help with such tasks in the past.

Her eyes held mine steadily, and I knew she wished to take over the chore.

"At least let me strain it," I urged. "These pails are heavy to lift."

Mary did not argue with that. Her eyes followed the stream of milk from the pail into the large bowl of the separator.

"The jersey's?" she asked me. But she didn't wait for my reply. "My, such rich milk. I think I'll separate it by itself and keep the cream aside. Just think of the butter it'll make!"

I could hear the smile in Mary's voice even though I was too busy to look at her face.

I positioned the pail under the separator for Mary and turned to go back to the other chores. On my way to the barn to pick up the remaining pail of milk, I stopped by the tractor and ran a hand over its still-shiny fender. I could hardly wait to crawl up into the seat and begin passing back and forth over my fields, dropping the seed that would mean a bountiful harvest. I lifted my eyes toward heaven, and an unspoken prayer of thanks welled up within me. I'm not sure, but there could have been a few tears in my eyes.

I turned back to the chores at hand. I was whistling a tune I had learned some time back in my childhood, a tune I had sung frequently over the years. But it swelled in my heart in a new way now: "Praise God from whom all blessings flow. . . ."

CHAPTER 2

Togetherness

I was tired and stiff when I climbed down from the tractor that evening. Already the sun was disappearing in the western sky and there was a slight chill in the air. It was, after all, still early spring. I had been riding the tractor almost constantly since sunup. Mary had brought my noon meal and an afternoon snack to the field to save me time. I was glad I wasn't driving a team that would need to stop for a rest and nourishment. The tractor didn't complain about the long hours, though I did need to stop to refuel now and then.

I was a bit surprised at the aches and pains in my back and legs. But then I remembered I'd been bouncing and jostling my way over the field for several hours, and it always took a few days for my body to readjust.

I moved toward the smell of roast beef, my feet reluctant to proceed as quickly as my stomach was demanding. I hadn't realized just how hungry I was until I smelled supper in the air.

"Are you finally stopping for the night?" Matilda good-naturedly asked.

I tried to disguise my stiffness as I stepped up onto the back porch. Matilda was seated on the porch swing, a cup of tea in her hands.

"I was beginning to think we'd never eat," she continued. "This is all Mary would let me have to tide me over till supper."

I stopped mid-stride. "Why?" I asked, surprised. Mary wasn't one to withhold victuals from anybody.

"Well," laughed Matilda. "Guess I'm exaggerating some. Truth is, Mary would have let us go ahead, but we all opted to wait for you."

"I'm sorry—" I began. "If I'd known—"

But Matilda interrupted me. "We all know how important it is to get the crop in. We didn't mind waiting." She stood to her feet and took another dainty sip of the tea, then looked at me, her eyes sparkling. "Honest!" she said frankly, and I believed her.

I held the kitchen door for Matilda and followed right behind into the aroma-filled room. Grandpa was reading a paper in his favorite chair by the window. Uncle Charlie sat on the couch along the west wall gently massaging his gnarled hands, and I knew without asking that they were paining him again. As soon as he felt my eyes on him, he stopped the rubbing and let the hands drop idly into his lap.

Mary was at the big kitchen stove spooning food into serving bowls. She turned, glanced over her shoulder and gave me a smile. I thought she would ask a question, but she didn't—at least not vocally. Maybe her eyes found their answer, I don't know, but she smiled softly again and turned back to the stove.

"We're ready as soon as you wash, Josh," she said.

I crossed to the corner sink with its big farm basin and noticed that it had already been filled with warm water. I didn't know who had thoughtfully supplied the water, but I did think, with appreciation, that I sure was well looked after.

It didn't take long to scrub my face and hands clean enough to appear at the supper table. By the time I'd re-hung the towel, the rest of the family had gathered around the table. I took my place beside them and bowed as Grandpa asked the grace.

When we lifted our heads and began to help ourselves from Mary's heaping bowls, Grandpa spoke for the first time.

"How'd it go, Boy?"

He still called me "Boy." Guess to Grandpa I would always be Boy no matter how old I grew or whether I was a farm owner or not. I didn't mind. It made me feel "belongin.'"

"Good," I replied around a mouthful of fresh bread.

"Tractor workin' right?"

I nodded, my mouth too full to venture an answer.

Uncle Charlie took a long draft of his coffee. "Thet there noise must nigh burst yer eardrums," he ventured. "Think I'd rather drive me a team."

I grinned. Uncle Charlie had a bit of a hard time adjusting to farm machinery that didn't require four-footed horsepower.

I swallowed sufficiently to make a decent reply. "It's noisier but faster, and one needn't stop for restin' or feedin' either."

Uncle Charlie chuckled a bit. "I had my eye on the field, Josh," he reminded me, "and seems to me I saw ya stop different times today to feed thet critter's iron belly."

I laughed along with Uncle Charlie. He'd made his point.

"I think I'd like to drive a tractor," put in Matilda, and I chuckled again at the picture that little bit of a woman would make up there on the seat of the big tractor.

Matilda must have misread my laughter, for her chin went up stubbornly. "I could, you know," she argued. "Bet I could. All you have to do is to put your foot on that—that thing, and move that lever now and then and turn the wheel where you want it to go."

Even Grandpa was chuckling now.

Matilda looked to Mary. "We could—couldn't we, Mary?" she challenged.

Mary fidgeted slightly. "I—I don't really know, but I—I think I'd just as soon leave the tractor to Josh."

Her eyes met mine for an instance. I noticed the slight color flush her cheeks before she lowered her head. For some silly reason I couldn't have explained, I felt that I had just been given a compliment. Mary often affected me that way—with just a look or a word she could make me feel like a man—a man in charge and capable. I felt my own cheeks warm slightly.

"Someday—" began Matilda, and I looked at her, waiting for her to go on. I was hoping to be able to tease her good-naturedly just a bit; but she would not meet my eyes, and she let the rest of her comment go unsaid.

Supper finished up with Mary's bread pudding, one of my favorite desserts. There was thick whipped cream for the topping, and I was sure this was how some of the jersey's cream had been used.

After enjoying a man-sized portion, I reluctantly pushed back from the table and got slowly to my feet. Uncle Charlie moved at the same time, and I knew he was getting set to give Mary a hand with the dishes.

"I can help tonight, Uncle Charlie," Matilda spoke up.

Now there was nothing new about Matilda calling him Uncle Charlie. Both she and Mary called him such, just like they did when talking to my grandfather. It seemed to please everyone all around. Guess we felt more like family than employer and employee and boarder. What had caught my attention was Matilda's offer. Not that Matilda didn't often help Mary with her household chores, but lately Matilda had been too busy to do anything but correct papers and prepare lessons.

"What happened to the classroom work?" I asked her.

"All done. Finally! And believe me, I feel like celebrating."

Matilda swirled around, her long, full skirt flowing out around her. In one hand she held the sugar bowl and in the other the cream pitcher.

Uncle Charlie looked at her with a twinkle in his eyes. "Seems like ya oughta find a better way to celebrate than with the cream and sugar," he teased.

"Well, Josh is always too busy to celebrate," Matilda teased back, pretending to pout. And she looked deliberately at me and exaggeratedly fluttered her long, dark eyelashes.

Laughter filled the kitchen. Matilda was always bringing laughter with her lighthearted teasing, but for some reason this time her teasing did not have me laughing. It gave me a funny feeling way down deep inside, and I moved for the peg where my farm jacket hung beside the door.

"Where ya goin'?" asked Uncle Charlie, and when I turned to look at him I caught his wink directed at Matilda. "Gonna feed thet there tractor agin?"

"I've got chores," I answered as evenly as I could.

"The chores be all done, Boy," cut in Grandpa.

I stood, my outreached hand dumbly dangling the jacket, my eyes moving from face to face in the kitchen. They all seemed to be in a jovial mood, and I wasn't quite sure if they were serious or funnin' me. It was to Mary that I looked for the final answer. She just nodded her head in agreement.

"All of them?" I had to ask.

"All of 'em," said Grandpa.

For a moment I wanted to protest. It was my farm. I could do my own chores. But then I quickly realized how foolish that was—and how tired I was—and my hand relinquished my coat to the peg again. I turned and smiled at the household of people.

"Thanks," I said simply and gave my shoulders a slight shrug. "Thanks to whoever did them."

"We all pitched in," replied Grandpa. "Little here, a little there and had 'em done in no time."

"Thanks," I said again.

"So you see," teased Matilda, fluttering her eyelashes again, "you will have time to help celebrate."

I was ready for the challenge now. "Okay," I answered, "checkers—right after dishes." And I reached for a tea towel and stepped up beside Mary. "I'll dry—you put things away," I dared order Matilda.

"Checkers?" Matilda commented. "Not exactly a corn roast or a pie social—but I guess it'll have to do," and to the accompaniment of chuckles from the two older men, she moved quickly to put away the dishes as I dried them.

When the last plate was on the shelf, Matilda and I turned to the checkerboard, and Mary picked up some handwork that always seemed to appear when she had what she called a "free moment." Grandpa and Uncle Charlie spent a little more time poring over newspapers. I wasn't sure if we had received a new one or if they were just rereading an old one, but I didn't ask. Beside us on the bureau squawked the raspy radio. I enjoyed the soft music but paid little attention to the commentary that interrupted it at intervals.

It wasn't too hard for me to beat Matilda at checkers. She had a keen mind and could have offered some real serious competition if she hadn't been so impatient. As it was, she played more for the fun than for the challenge, and for three games in a row I turned out the victor.

At the end of the third game I stood and stretched.

"Is that enough 'celebratin' for one evening?" I teased Matilda.

"It'll do," she answered with a flip of her head that made her pinned-up curls bounce. "But next time I'll insist on lawn croquet."

Matilda was an expert at lawn croquet. In fact, whenever there was a matchup, I always hoped Matilda would be my partner. Now I just smiled and tried to stifle a yawn.

Mary laid aside her handwork. "Would you like something to eat or drink before bedtime, Josh?" she asked me and started to leave her chair for the cupboard.

"No, thanks. It's been a long day. I think I'll just go on up to bed." As soon as I said the words, I realized the day had been equally long for Mary.

"You must be tired, too," I said, studying her face. "You've been up 'most as long as I have."

Mary brushed the remark aside and went to put on a pot of coffee for Grandpa and Uncle Charlie.

There was the rustle of paper as Grandpa put down what he was reading and took off his glasses.

"I'm plannin' to go on into town tomorrow, Josh," he said, folding up his glasses and placing them on the bureau beside the sputtering radio. "Anything you be needin'?"

I tried to think but my head was a bit foggy. I finally shook it. "If I think of anything I'll leave a note on the table," I promised. "Can't think of anything now."

"You got a list, Mary?" went on Grandpa. "Or would ya rather come on along and do yer own choosin'?"

I stood long enough to watch Mary slowly shake her head. "It takes too much time to ride on in and back," she said. "I'll just send a list."

I took three steps toward the stairway and then turned. "I've been thinkin'," I said, half teasingly but with a hint of seriousness; "maybe when we get in this year's crop, we oughta get us one of those motor cars. We could be in town and back before ya know it."

I don't know just what I expected, but I sure did get a reaction. Grandpa raised his shaggy eyebrows and studied me to see if I was serious. Uncle Charlie stopped rubbing his gnarly fingers and stared open-mouthed. And Mary stopped right in her tracks, one hand reaching out to set the coffeepot on the kitchen stove. But Matilda's response was vocal. "Yes!" she exclaimed, just like that, and she clapped her hands and ran to me. "Oh, yes, Josh!" she said again, her cheeks flushed and her eyes shining. "Get one, Josh. Get one." And she reached out impulsively and gave me a quick hug that almost knocked me off balance.

"Whoa-a," I said, disengaging myself from her arms. "I said 'maybe'— after the crop is off. I'm just plantin' it, remember? We've got a long time to wait."

Matilda stepped back, her eyes still shining. She clapped her hands again, not the least bit daunted. "Now, that's what I call really celebrating, Josh," she enthused, her hands clasped together in front of her.

I let my eyes travel back over the room. Mary had finally set down the coffeepot. Uncle Charlie had closed his mouth and was chewing on a corner of his mustache, and Grandpa's eyebrows were back where they belonged.

I shrugged my shoulders carelessly. "It's just something to be thinkin' on," I repeated lamely and headed for the stairs and my bed.

CHAPTER 3

Visitors

The spring planting went steadily forward. The tractor chugged on with only minor adjustments and repairs. The family continued to help with evening chores and work about the farmyard. Only one rain slowed me down and then it was just a few days—enough for me to sort of catch my breath and do a few little extras that always seem to need doing around a farm.

Matilda never gave me a moment's peace about the motor car. I began to wish I hadn't mentioned it. Still, her enthusiastic arguments in favor of the vehicle may have gone a long way toward influencing Grandpa and Uncle Charlie. At any rate, I never did hear much opposition to the idea, and everybody seemed to be holding their breath—waiting to see what the harvest would bring.

About the same time I finished the planting, the school doors closed for another year and Matilda left for her home again.

"Oh, Josh," she enthused on before departing, "I can hardly wait for fall—and the car. It'll be such fun, Josh!" She emitted a strange little sound like a combination sigh and groan.

"I haven't promised," I reminded her. "Just said I'd be thinkin' on it."

"I know. I know. And it will be such fun!" Apparently Matilda didn't want to hear of the possibility of *not* getting a car, so I let the matter drop.

As usual, Matilda and Mary's goodbye was rather emotional. They had grown to be like sisters in their affection and missed each other during the summer months.

"Oh, I'll be lonely without her," Mary half-whispered after Matilda was gone, and she slyly wiped her cheek with her handkerchief.

"Summer will pass quickly," I tried to console her.

"The house is always so—so *quiet* when she's gone," she responded.

It is quiet without Matilda's bubbly enthusiasm, I mentally agreed.

"You'll be busy with the garden," I reminded Mary.

She nodded; then after a moment of silence she said wistfully, "Maybe Lou will let Sarah Jane come visit for a while. She is 'most as chattery as Matilda."

I smiled at the thought. Sarah Jane was getting to be quite a little lady. And it was true that she was "chattery."

"Maybe," I responded, "for a few days. Lou counts on Sarah for running errands and entertaining her two little brothers."

Mary thoughtfully spoke as though to herself. "Lou does need her more than I do. It was selfish of me to—"

But I interrupted. "It wasn't selfish. Grandpa and Uncle Charlie—and me—we all look forward to her coming."

"Maybe we could have Jon come to the farm, too," Mary brightened. "That would leave Lou with just the baby."

I wasn't sure Mary wanted to take on the lively Jon plus all of the household and garden chores of farm life. I was about to say so, but she placed a hand on my arm, seeming to know just what I was thinking.

"It wouldn't be so bad," she argued. "Sarah would help with Jon, and there is lots for a boy to do on the farm, and the garden isn't ready for pickin' or cannin' yet, and he's usually not *too* rascally." She looked a bit doubtful about her last statement. "Besides," she hurried on, "it sure would make the house more—more—"

I looked at the small hand resting on my arm. It was hard for me to argue against Mary, but I did wonder if she was thinking straight to figure that Jon wouldn't take much time or trouble.

"It would help the summer pass more quickly," she finished lamely.

"Why don't you try it for a few days—to start with? Make sure you aren't gettin' in over your head," I advised.

Mary smiled, and I knew she was pleased with my qualified consent.

It wasn't that Jon was a bad boy, and it certainly wasn't that I didn't love my young nephew, but he was one of the busiest and most curious children I had ever known. His poking and prodding into things invariably got him into some kind of trouble.

"Keep him away from the tractor," I added quite firmly, remembering the time Jon had poured dirt in the gas tank.

Mary just nodded. "I'll check with Lou next time I'm in town," she promised. I couldn't help but think that a break from Sarah and Jon might be a welcome change for my Aunt Lou.

True to her word, Mary made arrangements with Lou. And before the week was out, Sarah and Jon had joined us at the farm. Sarah busied herself with copying the activities of Mary. She helped bake bread, churn butter and wash clothes. She even spent time in the garden pulling weeds—along with a few carrots and turnips—and washed dishes, very slowly, doing more playing in the soapy water than scrubbing the plates and cups. But Sarah seemed to fit very nicely into the farm life, and we all enjoyed her chatter and sunny disposition.

Grandpa and Uncle Charlie tried their best to keep young Jon entertained. They whittled him whistles and slingshots, fashioned him fish poles and found him a barn kitten. But, still, Jon seemed to be continually slipping out from under supervision, off finding entertainment of his own making.

In the few days he was with us he got into more scrapes and mischief—not out of naughtiness but "just tryin' to he'p." He dumped all the hens' water and filled their drinking dishes with hay—he said they looked hungry. He tied the farm dog to a tree with so many knots that it took Grandpa most of an afternoon to get him released again—he said he was afraid "Fritz might get runned over by the tractor." He shot a rock through the front room window with the slingshot he was not to play with around the house—he said that it "went off" when he wasn't ready. He picked a whole pail of tiny apples that were just beginning to form nicely on the apple trees—he wanted to help Mary with an apple pie. He visited the hen house and threw a couple dozen eggs at the old sow who fed in the nearby pen—he wanted to teach her a trick, "like Pixie," of snatching food from the air.

And, as far as I was concerned, the worst stunt of all was helping himself to a bottle of India ink from Matilda's supply desk and sneaking up on unsuspecting Chester, climbing the corral fence and pouring it all over the horse's back. He wanted to "surprise Unc'a Josh" with a pretty, spotted horse like one he had seen in a picture book.

We had a family council that night. I was ready to send Jon on home, but Mary argued that he really wasn't naughty and needed a chance to learn about the farm. Grandpa sided with her. How could the boy learn what he could and couldn't do if he wasn't given the chance to do a little exploring? So Jon stayed on, but we gave the four-year-old more rules and tried to watch him even closer.

I was busy repairing the back pasture fence when Jon joined me one afternoon.

"Hi, Unc'a Josh," he greeted me warmly. I looked at the bright eyes and mop of brown hair.

"Hi, fella," I responded a bit cautiously. "Does Mary know you're here?"

Jon did not answer my question but held a little red pail as high as his short arm could hoist it.

"Brought ya a drink," he announced. "Are ya thirsty?"

The summer sun was hot, and I *was* thirsty. I stopped to wipe the sweat from my brow and reached for the pail the boy held out to me.

"Auntie Mary said ya would be thirsty," Jon continued. Lou had her children refer to Mary as "auntie" as a term of respect.

My eyes shifted to the nearby farmhouse. I was close enough that I didn't need to be waited on—I could walk to the house or the well for a drink. Still, maybe Mary thought a bit of a stroll and an "errand" would do the small boy good. I sat down on the grass and pulled Jon onto my knee, one hand supporting the pail.

"Where's Mary?" I asked him, looking at the dirt streaks on his hands and face.

"Busy doin' some'pin," he answered.

"So you brought me a drink?"

He nodded.

"That was mighty nice," I complimented Jon. "Thank you."

I lifted the pail to my lips. The water was not as cool as usually comes from our deep well, and I couldn't help but wonder just how long Jon had been on his journey. At least it was wet. I took another long drink.

"So what have you been doing today?" I asked Jon.

He thought about that for a few moments before answering.

"I he'ped Grandpa hoe the garden," he said brightly and then added more soberly, "but he said, 'Thet's enough, Jonathan,' and sent me back to Auntie Mary."

I tousled his hair. "And why did he do that?" I questioned. "Did you mix up weeds and vegetables?"

Jon nodded his head, his eyes thoughtful. "I guess it was peas," he said somberly, and I had to hide my smile.

"Then I brought in the clothes for Auntie Mary," he began, but ended with a shrug of his small shoulders. "But she hada take 'em back agin. They wasn't dry yet." Then Jon added quickly as though with great relief, "But Auntie Mary din't scold me. Jest took the clothes and hung some back up an'—" His eyes lowered and then lifted again to mine. He finished with a grin that told me everything was all right. "An' washed some of 'em agin an' then hung *them* back up, too."

Poor Mary. She had enough work without re-doing the wash.

"Here comes Aunt Mary now!" Jon excitedly pointed toward the farm buildings.

He was right. Mary and Sarah were coming our way.

"We brought you something, Uncle Josh," Sarah called before they reached us.

I looked at the small container in Sarah's hands and then to Mary. Both young ladies seemed pleased with themselves.

"Do I have to guess?" I asked Sarah.

Puffing, she reached the spot where Jon and I still sat on the ground.

"It's a drink," she said proudly.

"A drink? That's nice. But Jon here"—I ruffled the boy's hair again—"he already beat you to it. But I guess another drink would—"

But I stopped. The mention of the drink brought to me by young Jon had made Mary's face blanch, her hand went to her mouth and she stood staring down at the red pail.

"Is something wrong?" I asked Mary, but it was Sarah who answered the question for me, though in a rather roundabout fashion.

"In that?" she squealed, pointing her finger at the red pail in the grass. Before I could even answer her she went on, "Jon was botherin' Grandpa in the garden—hoeing up things—so Grandpa gave him that pail and sent him to water the flowers."

That didn't sound so bad. I didn't mind sharing water with the flowers. But Mary's face was still pale and she hadn't said one word except for a gaspy little, "Oh, Joshua."

"But," went on Sarah, "Jon was dipping water from the stock trough!"

For a moment my stomach rebelled. I even thought I might be sick. The thought of the horses and cattle slurping and snorting in my drinking water made my insides heave. I looked up at Mary's white face and agonized expression. And then the whole thing struck me funny, and I pulled Jon closer into my arms, rolled over in the grass and began to tickle him and laugh. Not just little chuckles, but outright guffaws. Mary's color returned to normal, and I saw she was trying to hide a snicker behind her hand. Then she looked at Jon and me tumbling on the grass together and began to laugh right along with me. Now my stomach hurt from laughter.

When we finally got ourselves under control, we all sat down on the ground together and shared the cool lemonade Mary and Sarah had brought.

"I guess if I can drink with the cows and horses, I can use the same cup as family," I said and began to laugh again.

"We have cookies, too," Sarah informed me importantly. I think she was trying to get me to settle down. She didn't seem to understand why I thought my drink from the stock trough was so funny. I tried to respond properly to Sarah's announcement.

"Cookies? What kind? Where did you find cookies?"

"They're sugar cookies and I made 'em—myself." And then she quickly corrected her statement. "Auntie Mary and me made 'em."

"Can I have one? Can I have one, Sarah?" Jon was asking. Sure enough, there were some for all of us.

I guess the lemonade and the sugar cookies had a settling effect on my stomach. At any rate, I suffered no ill effects from drinking water out of the stock trough, though I did determine that in the future I would carefully check any food or drink offered me from the hand of my young nephew.

CHAPTER 4

Summer

Things settled down again after Sarah and Jon went off to their home. I think even Mary was glad for the peace and quiet, though she never admitted it. She had much to do, with the garden now in full swing. Her hands never seemed to be empty nor her body still.

The summer was busy for me as well. There was haying, the war with farm weeds, the continual care of the stock and fences; and before we could scarcely turn around, the summer would be drawing to an end.

I was glad for Sundays. It was the one day of the week that, with a clear conscience and no guilty feelings, one could actually take a bit of a break. It was good to be driving into town for the church service—though I must confess that as I sat behind the slow-moving team, I kept thinking more and more of the time we'd save in traveling if I had that motor car.

On a couple of Sundays we stayed on to dinner with Lou and Nat and their three. That was about the only chance we really had to catch up on the happenings of one another's lives.

Baby Timothy was growing so fast it was hard to keep up to him. He celebrated his first birthday in June and was busy with the task of learning how to walk—how to run might more aptly describe it. Timmy wanted to be in on the fun with his older brother and sister and tagged around after them as fast as his sturdy little legs would allow.

"The crop's looking good and seems to be a little ahead of schedule," I told Nat over one of our Sunday dinners. "It might well be our best crop yet," I admitted.

But I went from day to day with one eye on the sky and the other on my fields. I knew without being told that one good hailstorm could change everything, and deep inside me, I kind of wished there was some way I could make a little bargain with God. But of course I didn't try. I had the good sense—and faith—to know that He knew all about our needs and my wishes, and that in His love He would take care of our future. But oh, my, how I did hope that the future didn't include hail.

In next to no time Matilda was breezing in again. The two girls hugged and squealed and laughed like they'd been apart for years. Even Grandpa and Uncle Charlie got enthusiastic squeezes. I accepted a small hug myself, then backed up and looked at Matilda's glowing face.

"How's the crop, Josh?" she burst out before I had a chance to open my mouth. No "How are you?" or anything like that, but "How's the crop?" and I knew just what she was thinking about. I was prepared to tease her a bit.

I shrugged my shoulders and put a glum look on my face. "It might pay for the cuttin'," I informed her drearily. "That is, if we don't get any hail or such."

Matilda's mouth went down at the corners, and a sound of disappointment escaped her lips.

"Look on the bright side," I said, patting her shoulder. "With good weather and no more problems, we'll have a bit of seed grain for next spring."

Matilda looked awfully disappointed, even shamefaced.

"I told all my friends that you'd be getting a—a motor car," she said softly, her voice catching on the last word.

"Well, now, I didn't make me any promises on that, did I?" I said, keeping my expression somber. "Maybe you shouldn't'a been tellin' tales out of school." But when she looked like she might cry, I decided I had gone far enough.

"I'm just joshin'," I grinned at her. "The crop looks good. Real good." And as Matilda was about to exuberantly throw herself at me I hastened on, "Now remember, I'm still not promisin'. Just been thinkin' on that automobile. No promises."

But Matilda didn't seem one bit worried about the results of "thinkin' on it." Guess she knew me well enough to know I wanted that motor car too.

She punched me on the arm with a little fist, but her eyes were shining. "Oh, Josh," she scolded, "you're mean!"

Grandpa chuckled and Uncle Charlie just grinned.

When the school year started again, it was rather a traumatic time for Aunt Lou. Sarah Jane started off to first grade. I hadn't realized how tough it was on mothers to see their first baby go off into a whole new world. Lou wanted to be enthusiastic for Sarah's sake, but I knew that if it had been in Lou's power to turn back the clock a year or two, she could not have refrained from doing so.

Mary went into the final stages of putting up summer fruits and vegetables. As I watched the stacks of canning jars fill and refill the kitchen counter top, I wondered how in the world the five of us could ever consume so much food. Part of the answer came when I saw Mary and Grandpa load a whole bunch into the buggy and send it off to town to Aunt Lou. Lou was too busy with her little family and being a pastor's wife to do much canning of her own, Mary reasoned. Lou was deeply appreciative. After all, a pastor's salary didn't leave much room for extras, though I'd never heard Lou complain.

I began to find little pamphlets and newspaper advertisements scattered about the kitchen telling about this motor car or that automobile and the merits of each. I didn't have to guess who was leaving them about, but I did wonder how Matilda was collecting them.

I read the descriptions—just like she knew I would. In fact, I sneaked them off to my own bedroom and lay in bed going over and over them. My, some of them were fancy! I hadn't known that such features existed. Why, you could start the motor without cranking it in the front! Then I would look at the listed price. I hadn't known that they cost so much, either, and doubts began to form in my mind. The same number of dollars could do so many things for the farm. I began to realize that Matilda's little campaign might well come to nothing. It could be sheer foolishness for me to buy a car.

I went into harvest with my mind debating back and forth. One day I would think for sure that I "deserved a car." The whole family deserved a car after all the years of slow team travel. *And think of how much valuable time we'd save*, I'd reason. Then the next day I would think of the farm needs, of the church needs, of my promise to support Camellia in her missionary service, of the stock I could purchase or the things for Mary's kitchen; and I would mentally strike the motor car from my list. Back and forth, this way and that way I argued with myself. Even all of the praying I did about it didn't put my mind at rest.

It did turn out to be a good crop. Even better than I'd dared hope. I watched the bins fill to overflowing with wonderfully healthy grain. I had to purchase an extra bin from the Sanders and pull it into our yard with the tractor. I filled it, too. The good quality grain brought good prices as well. God had truly blessed us.

Now, how did He want me to spend what He had given? How could I be a responsible steward?

I was still busy with the farm duties during the day, but in the evenings I spent hours and hours poring over the account books. I figured this way, then that way. With every load of grain I took to town, the numbers in my little book swelled. There would be a surplus. But would there be enough for the motor car? And if so, was a motor car necessary? Practical? The right thing for the Jones family?

I knew everyone was waiting for my decision. Grandpa and Uncle Charlie did not question me. Mary never made mention of the vehicle, but I could sense that she was sharing my struggle over the decision. Matilda stopped cajoling me about it, but her eyes continually questioned, and I knew she was getting very impatient waiting for me to make up my mind.

I went to my room one night and took out all the advertisements again. I laid aside the one showing the shiny gray Bentley. It was far too fancy and costly for me, though I did allow myself one fleeting mental picture of me purring down our country road at the wheel. I laid aside a few more as well. As the pile of discarded pamphlets grew, a bit of the pride and envy of Joshua Jones was also cast aside. At last I was left with a plain, simple car made by the Ford company. There was plenty of money for the Ford—with a good deal left for other things we needed. I would get the Ford. My conscience could live with that.

I breathed a sigh of relief, laid aside the pamphlet and blew out my light. In the darkness of my room I knelt by my bed to pray. With the decision finally made with the seeming approval of my Father, I welcomed a sense of peace. I slept that night like I hadn't slept in weeks.

The next morning at the breakfast table I cleared my throat to get the family's attention. "I decided to get a car," I announced, and before I could go further there was a squeal from Matilda, a smile from Mary, and a nod from Grandpa. Uncle Charlie just grinned a bit. The long, jarring buggy rides were hard on his arthritic bones.

"Now wait. Now wait," I protested, holding up my hand and directing my words to Matilda. "We can afford a motor car—no problem. But I decided that it won't be a fancy one. No need for that, and it would just set us back. We'll get a simple, practical Ford—none of the gadgets and gizmos."

Matilda sobered.

"But it will have wheels—and get us to where we need to go," I assured them.

Matilda's face brightened again.

"When?" asked Grandpa, and though he tried hard to hide it, I caught the excitement in his voice.

"I'm goin' to town to order it today," I answered, and I had a hard time controlling my own excitement.

Matilda squealed. "Oh, Josh. It's so-o exciting!" she bubbled.

Uncle Charlie's smile widened.

I looked at Mary. Her face was flushed, her eyes shining. Then she did a most unexpected thing. She reached over and gave my hand a squeeze.

If Matilda had done it, I would have thought nothing of it. In fact, I would have thought nothing of it if Matilda had thrown herself wildly into my arms or flung her arms about my neck and squeezed with all her might—that was just Matilda. But Mary? That quiet little gesture of shared excitement somehow set my pulse to racing.

I flushed slightly as I pulled my eyes back to the other members at the breakfast table and rose slowly to my feet. It was a moment before I found my thoughts, my tongue.

"I—I'll order it—today, but—but I have no idea how long it might be before it comes."

Matilda brought things back to normal. "Oh, I hope it arrives *soon!*" she exclaimed, bouncing up from her chair. "I hope it hurries. We don't have much time. We need it before winter so we can learn to drive it before the snow—"

Matilda caught herself and stopped mid-sentence. Her eyes met mine and she looked like a small child coaxing for a treat. She had been using a lot of "we's," which was rather presumptuous on her part, but I just smiled and gave her a quick wink. I understood.

After we shared our morning devotions together around the breakfast table, I went back to my room and folded the Ford pamphlet and slipped it into my pocket. As soon as I had finished the last of the morning chores, I would saddle Chester and head for town.

CHAPTER 5

The Ford

Like Matilda, I was hoping the car would arrive before snowfall. I wanted the chance to learn to drive it while the roads were still clear.

I managed to keep myself busy with no problem. I must admit I made a few more trips to town than normal. I pretended that I needed things or wanted the mail, but in fact I stopped in to check—with regularity—if there had been any word on the car.

On one such trip to town I found a long, newsy letter from Camellia. She had received word from the Mission Society that she would be leaving for Africa in the spring. She was so excited that her penmanship, usually in character—neat and attractive—was rushed and almost sloppy. This letter conveyed intense excitement.

"I can't believe it, Josh!" she wrote. "After all these years I am finally going to Willie's Africa. To the people he learned to love so. I will be stationed near enough to the village where Willie served that the mission has promised a trip to the grave site. I will be able to see the spot where Willie's body is lying. I know that it might not seem like much to others, but I think you will understand. I want to personally be able to lay some flowers on Willie's grave. And it will be very special for me to be able to kneel there and ask God to help me in carrying on Willie's ministry.

"I won't be staying in the area. At least not for now. They say it is much too primitive to leave a woman all alone, and there is no other young lady available to live and work with me at present. But I am praying that if it is God's will, He will provide me with a working companion so that we might be able to live there before too long and have a chance to reach Willie's people.

"He used to write me all about them. I can almost see them. There was the chief—a small man by our standards—but, my, he had power! Willie said that the people didn't question his word for one minute. And there was one old woman—I do hope she is still there. She fed Willie from her own cooking pot, even though there was scarcely enough for her own family. Willie was sure she herself must have gone without food numerous times. And the little children. Willie said they followed along behind him, curious as to what this strange white man was going to do. And then there was Andrew. That was not his African name. That was the name Willie gave to him after he became a Christian. He was Willie's only convert. I can hardly wait to meet Andrew."

Camellia's letter went on, but I couldn't continue reading for the moment. It was some time before my eyes were dry enough to see the words on the page. If I missed Willie this much, I couldn't imagine what the loss was like for Camellia.

Camellia wrote about not wanting to leave her mother all alone. Then she chided herself. Of course her mother would not be alone—she had the same Lord with her who would be with Camellia on the mission field.

"You've always been such a dear friend, Josh, to both Willie and me. I appreciate your friendship now more than ever. And I can never thank you enough for helping with my support so I can go to Africa as Willie and I had planned. I pray for you daily. May God bless you, Josh, and grant to you the desires of your heart, whatever or whoever that might be."

Camellia had underscored "whoever," and I could picture her face with the teasing gleam in her eyes as I read the little message. I felt an emptiness inside of me. Would there ever be anyone else who would take the place of Camellia in my heart? I pushed the thought aside. Camellia was headed for Africa, and for some reason, still a mystery to me, God had chosen for me to stay on the farm.

I read the last paragraph again. "May God bless you, Josh, and grant to you the desires of your heart, whatever—"

I stopped there. I had come into town to check on the Ford again. As my eyes traveled back over the pages of Camellia's letter, the idea of a motor car paled in comparison.

"Lord," I admitted in a simple prayer, "I've got things a bit out of perspective. We need a car. I've weighed the purchase this way and that way, and for all involved it seems like the right move—but help me, Lord, not to get too wrapped up in it. A car is, after all, just a way to get places. These people— these Africans of Camellia's—they are eternal souls. Brothers. Remind me to spend more time in prayer for them as Camellia goes to minister the gospel to them."

I carefully folded Camellia's letter and tucked it in an inside pocket. I didn't even bother to go on down the street to check on the arrival of the car. It would be here when it was here! Instead I turned Chester toward Lou's. The children would welcome a little visit, and it would be nice to sit and share a cup of coffee with Lou.

When we awakened the next morning the ground was covered with snow. I won't pretend it didn't give me a bit of a start. I had so hoped. But I dismissed the thought. Surely a car could be driven in a few inches of snow.

When Matilda came downstairs, she didn't seem to be able to dismiss the snow quite as easily.

"Oh, no-o," she wailed. "What will we do? What will we *do*, Josh? The snow is already here, but the motor car isn't! Oh-h-h." She crossed to the window, swept back Mary's carefully ironed white ruffled curtain and groaned again. "We'll have to learn to drive it in the snow. It would have been so much easier—"

"Guess there's no problem," I was quick to cut in. "We don't have the car yet anyway."

"But it'll be here just any day now and the snow . . ."

But the snow had all disappeared by noon, and two days later the Ford arrived. I thought I had prepared myself for the role of motor-car owner, but when the news reached me I felt a thrill go all through my body. This was followed by a cold sweat. My hands got sticky and my mouth dry and my knees fairly shook with excitement—and just a little fear.

We hitched up the team, and Grandpa and Uncle Charlie drove with me on into town. I couldn't just ride Chester to pick the car up because I needed to drive it back.

We drove right up to Mr. Hickson's, and I pretended nonchalance as I stepped into his office and said I was there to pick up the car. I had the rest of the payment in my coat pocket, pinned in so I wouldn't accidentally lose it. I began to carefully unpin the coat in order to get at my money, but Mr. Hickson rushed right on by me, calling as he went, "It's this way, Josh, an' she's a beaut! Come on in an' git a look at 'er."

I followed, with Grandpa and Uncle Charlie right on my heels.

She was a beaut all right. Never had I seen so much shiny metal. There she stood, black paint gleaming and window glass sparkling. I slowly sucked in my breath. She was beautiful!

I was quite familiar with the few motor cars on our town streets. Several of them were quite fancy, too, but to me this Ford—this car that was mine— was the nicest of the lot.

I moved forward and ran a hand over the shiny fender. Mr. Hickson opened a door.

"An' look in here," he urged. "See them leather seats. Looka that. Looka that."

I moved to look. Sure enough, leather seats—finest black leather one ever saw. I let out the breath I had seemed to be holding. I heard Uncle Charlie say something to Grandpa and Grandpa answer, "Well, whoo-ee!" and I wheeled to look at them. Both of them were grinning. *Standin' there a gazin' at that car like they've never seen nothin' like it before*, I chuckled to myself.

"Whoo-ee," said Grandpa again, and he lifted a hand to stroke the black leather. Uncle Charlie's mustache was twitching. He reached out one gnarled hand to touch the shining glass of the window. For a moment I wondered if there could ever be anything more exciting in life than this—standing there getting a good look at your first car and brand new at that.

I came back down to earth in time to hear Mr. Hickson saying, "Just a few things to take care of, an' you can drive her right on out of here."

Mr. Hickson was moving back toward his little office, and I turned to follow, though I was feeling a moment of panic. I could "drive her right on out," said Mr. Hickson. But surely Mr. Hickson knew I had never driven a car before. Surely he wouldn't just put me in it and expect—

"Ya got some 'struction papers with this here new Ford?" Grandpa was asking Mr. Hickson very matter-of-factly, and I knew I should have asked the question.

"Of course. Of course," Mr. Hickson answered, nodding his head vigorously. "Everything thet ya need to know is right in here in the office."

Whew! Maybe I wouldn't embarrass myself after all.

"Joe Hess, down the street, has got him a Ford. Much like this one, only not as new," Mr. Hickson was saying. "He'd be glad to come on over here and take Josh for his first run."

"Thet'd be good. Real good," Grandpa agreed. Then added quickly, "Just till he gets the hang of it. He'll catch on real quick. Been driving thet big ol' tractor now fer quite a spell."

Mr. Hickson nodded his head again. "I'll send Mickey right over fer Joe," and making good on his word he called a young fellow from the back room and sent him on his way.

For some reason the rest of them seemed to have forgotten that I was the buyer. Grandpa and Mr. Hickson were busy making plans without me. But they soon turned back to me when it came time for the final payment to be made. I pulled the money from my pocket and Mr. Hickson counted it out.

"Right," he said. "Just right."

That was no news to me. I had checked the money out carefully—three times—before I left home.

By the time we finished with the paperwork Joe was there. He seemed properly impressed with the new car and walked around and around it, studying each feature, especially those that his older model did not have. He didn't say much, but he grinned and he admired and he ran a hand over the black metal now and then.

We all climbed in for our first spin around town. I sat up front with Joe so I might learn all the procedures for driving. Grandpa and Uncle Charlie settled in the back. It was hard to tell who was the most excited.

Mr. Hickson gave it a good crank, we started off with a bit of a jump, and I heard Grandpa gasp, but then we moved out onto Main Street past all the stores and people.

We made quite an impression, you can be sure of that. Heads turned, people stopped, store owners came out of their shops, curtains fluttered at windows and dogs barked and chased us on down the road.

The farther we went the faster we went. It wasn't long until we were whizzing along. It fairly took the breath out of me, but Joe seemed to know just what he was doing, and he maneuvered the car like it was no problem at all.

When we got out in open country he suggested that I give it a try. I was so nervous that my hands shook, but I crawled behind the steering wheel and did just like Joe had showed me. Well, almost. I let the clutch out a bit too quickly, and the Ford bucked like she'd been spurred. It killed the motor and Joe had to get out and give it a crank again. The next time worked better and soon I was steering down the road like I'd been driving all my life.

By the time we got back to town and dropped Joe off, I was getting pretty good. We decided to wheel around to Nat and Lou's and show off just a bit. I was hoping Nat would be home. A car like this would sure save a pastor some calling time.

Nat was there all right, and we had to show him everything on the Ford that moved. He studied it over and over again, making contented clicking noises and grinning from ear to ear. I felt my buttons pushing at my shirt front. I felt pretty proud and even more grown up than when the farm was signed over to me.

At last we pulled away from our admirers and headed back out on the street again, Jon howling behind us. He wanted to go too. I had already taken them all for a little spin, but I guess that wasn't good enough for young Jon. He wanted to go wherever the car was going.

When we got back to Hickson's, Grandpa climbed out and went to untie the horses from the hitching rail. Uncle Charlie began to climb out too, maybe a little reluctantly. I guess Grandpa must have sensed it. "Why don't you jest go on home with Josh?" he said. "Don't take two of us to drive this poky ol' team."

Uncle Charlie didn't argue. He settled back on that leather seat and took a big breath of the autumn air. Then he pulled out his pocket watch and sat studying the face of it.

"Okay, Josh," he said, and there was a glint in his eye. "Let's see how long it takes 'er to make the trip to the farm."

I grinned, then nodded. I put the Ford into gear and we started out. Once we cleared the town streets I opened her up a bit more. The breeze fairly whipped in the open windows. Way back at the edge of town we could see Grandpa just turning the team and buggy onto the road for home. Then the dust from our wheels blocked him from view, and Uncle Charlie and I were off.

We didn't try to set any records. I drove as sensibly as I knew how. But even with my caution at the wheel, the trip home took only eleven minutes and thirty-seven seconds. Uncle Charlie chuckled gleefully as he held the watch out for me to see.

We turned into our lane. I could hardly wait to show the girls the new car. Then I looked with dismay at the dust that already clung to her shiny exterior and wished there was some way I could quickly polish her up before the introduction. But I realized that would never work, for already Mary was running to meet us.

CHAPTER 6

A Caller

I had plenty of time to show Mary the car, take her for a ride, and wash and polish all the metal and leather before Grandpa pulled into the yard with the team.

I had learned one lesson on the way home. The feel of the fresh autumn air blowing in the open windows might be invigorating, but on our dusty country roads it was not practical. I decided that from now on when the car was on the move, the windows would be kept up. I said as much to Uncle Charlie as he watched me polish and clean.

After Grandpa had gone off to Mary's kitchen with the groceries she had ordered, I settled the team and went back to shining the car. Reluctant to leave the new Ford, I was finally coaxed into the kitchen for tea and cornbread.

As soon as the kitchen clock told us that school would be letting out, we all climbed into the car and set off to pick up Matilda.

"I can hardly wait to see her face when we pull into the school yard," Mary said warmly.

I drove very slowly. I didn't want to get the car all dusty again before Matilda had a chance to see it. Even so, we got a bit ahead of ourselves according to Uncle Charlie's pocket watch and had to pull to the side of the road just over the hill from the schoolhouse. We didn't want to arrive before Matilda was free to dismiss her students.

At last Uncle Charlie gave us the go-ahead, and I hopped out to give the car a crank while Grandpa pulled and pushed the necessary buttons and levers. Joe had said a man could start the car all by himself, but we weren't sure we had the hang of it yet.

We met some of Matilda's students as we chugged up the last hill to the school yard, so we knew that school was over for the day.

If we had expected Matilda to be excited, we weren't disappointed. As we pulled into the school yard, we saw her appear at the window. She probably wondered what the strange sound was. For a moment she stood as though stunned, her eyes wide and hands over her mouth. At Mary's wild waving, Matilda finally came to her senses. She fairly exploded from the door and took the front steps as though they weren't even there.

"It's here! It's here!" she was screaming as she ran toward us. "Oh, Josh, it's here." I decided not to point out that I was well aware of that fact.

She never even stopped to admire the shiny metal I had just worked so hard to polish. She didn't look at the gleaming glass windows. She never slowed down for a moment, just hurled herself at the door, climbed right over Mary in one swift motion and shuffled to settle herself right between the two of us.

"Show me!" she squealed. "Quickly—show me."

"You can't see much scrunched in here," I said a bit sourly, trying to shove over enough to give Matilda room. "You gotta do most of your lookin' from the outside," and I moved to open my door.

But Matilda was shaking her head so vigorously that her curls were coming unpinned. "No," she wailed, grabbing my hand from the door handle. "Show me how to drive."

Grandpa snorted and Uncle Charlie chuckled. Mary just shrugged her slim shoulders and smiled. I was stunned. I sure wasn't prepared to give Matilda a driving lesson in my new car. I'd barely learned how myself. I stalled for time.

"We've come to take you home," I informed her. "Are you ready to go?"

For a moment she seemed not to understand. She took a few gulps of air and then answered me almost sanely, "No, I have to get my books and clean the blackboards and lock the school."

We all piled out. Mary cleaned the blackboards while Matilda gathered her books. Uncle Charlie and Grandpa studied a map on the wall, but I just wandered around picturing the room as it had been when I was a student there.

In the row over by the windows had sat Avery, then me, then Willie—I could see him yet. His mop of unruly hair spilling over his forehead, his freckles scattered across the tip of his nose, his face screwed up in a frown as he worked on an arithmetic problem.

I turned abruptly and walked from the room. Even yet the memories were too painful.

"I'll wait outside," I said with as steady a voice as I could manage and I closed the schoolhouse door rather firmly on the memories.

It didn't take Matilda long and we all climbed back in the car and started down the country road.

We rearranged our load. Mary climbed in the backseat between Grandpa and Uncle Charlie. It was a bit crowded but they didn't seem to mind. Matilda rode in the front by me. Her eyes did not travel over the polished leather upholstery. Instead, they stayed glued to the steering wheel and the controls, watching every movement I made. I knew Matilda would never let me rest until she had been taught how to drive my car.

However, I was not ready to share the driving with anyone just yet. Not even Matilda.

"Why don't you settle back and enjoy the ride?" I urged her. "Remember, it won't be every day that we come and pick you up from school."

I guess she got the message. She sighed and did sit back. Sort of. Though I could still feel her eyes on my hands.

It wasn't long before I relented and did give Matilda a few driving lessons. We did not venture out on the road, only up and down our long farm lane. She caught on quickly, I must admit. I offered to teach Mary how to drive, too, but she just smiled and said she would just as soon let me do it.

The car was certainly an asset and time saver in driving back and forth to town. We looked forward to the family drive each Sunday. It was a bit crowded, but no one complained.

And then the winter snows came deep enough that the car was no longer practical. I drove it into the shed I had built for it and we started using the team again. Never had the trip to town seemed longer than when we were forced to travel it again by sleigh.

The dog was making an awful commotion one evening, and we all rose from our places to look out the window. We hadn't been expecting any callers. The evening was chilly, but not inhuman. There was no sharp wind blowing and the moon was bright. Still, we couldn't figure out why anyone would be making house calls on horseback at such an hour. I had a momentary pang that something might be wrong in town and Uncle Nat had come to inform us.

But it wasn't Uncle Nat. Relieved, I realized the traveler was a stranger. Well, not exactly a stranger. I had seen him once or twice, and from the greetings later in our kitchen, I came to realize that both Mary and Matilda had met him before.

But when Grandpa had answered his knock and opened the door, he didn't seem to know who the young man was. He extended his hand cordially anyway and offered for the young fella to come in.

"Don't believe I've had the pleasure," Grandpa was saying as he shook the hand firmly, and the man answered cheerily enough, "Sanders. Will Sanders. We bought the place just over yonder," and he nodded his head to the east.

"Sanders," repeated Grandpa. "Thought I'd met Sanders." Grandpa looked a bit perplexed. "Thet weren't yer pa, were it?"

"No, sir. My oldest brother. He bought the place. My pa's been gone for nigh unto seven years now."

"Sorry to hear thet," Grandpa said sincerely. "Come in an' sit ya down. Is there something we can be a helpin' ya with?"

The young man smiled easily. "Thank you, no," he answered evenly. "Just callin'." He made no move toward a chair.

All of this conversation had taken place while the rest of us looked on. I guess Will figured it was time to change all that. His eyes traveled around the room. He nodded briefly to Uncle Charlie, studied me for a moment and then turned his gaze toward the two girls. That was the first he smiled. He reached to remove his hat and with a slight nod in the girls' direction said, "Hello, Miss Turley, Miss Hopkins."

That was when I began to study the man before me.

A little taller than me, his shoulders were broader, hips slimmer. Even in the lamplight I could see the waves of dark hair and the deep-set dark eyes. His jaw was rather square and his nose straight. When he smiled he showed a row of even, white teeth. Even I was smart enough to know that ladies would consider him a good-looking man. I stirred uneasily as Mary and Matilda acknowledged his greeting. Both of them had a flush on their cheeks and shine to their eyes.

Mary was the first to move forward.

"Won't you come in, Mr. Sanders," she greeted him cordially. "Here, let me have your hat and coat."

Will Sanders passed Mary his hat and took off his heavy winter coat. Mary took both to a peg reserved for visitors' wraps in the corner.

I had never seen Matilda silent for so many minutes before.

"I didn't realize you were staying on," she finally ventured with a shy look in Sander's direction.

"Well, I had thought about going back to the city for the winter, but my brother said he could sure use some help with the choring."

I shifted uneasily again.

"Have you met Josh?" asked Mary, returning from hanging up the man's hat and coat.

The eyes shifted to me. He studied me for a moment before saying slowly, rather deliberately, "I don't believe I've had the privilege," and he smiled a bit too familiarly, I thought.

I stepped forward and extended my hand. It seemed like the neighborly thing to do. He shook it firmly. I wondered if he was trying to make me cringe under his grip. I found my fingers tightening around his. I wanted the man to know that other men had strength in their hands as well.

For a moment our eyes locked, and I could see in his expression some sort of challenge. I wasn't sure what it was all about, but I sure felt ill at ease.

After just sitting around for a spell thinking up things to talk about like weather and cattle feed, Matilda suggested that we play some Chinese checkers. We moved our chairs into position around the table. The game went well enough. For some reason I can't explain, it was very important to me that I win. I did. But just. Then the next game was won by Mary. That didn't bother me a bit, but it did bother me some that young Sanders came in second.

Mary fixed a little snack, and Grandpa and Uncle Charlie joined us around the table. Matilda carried most of the conversation. She and Sanders chatted on merrily, and occasionally he turned and offered some comment to Mary and she responded. I didn't pay too much attention to it all.

I couldn't see where it concerned me much anyway. Then a comment of Matilda's caught my ear.

"Josh has a new Ford, but with the snow so deep he has it put away for now."

I felt my pride swell a bit. Here was one area where I had an edge on the city slicker fella. But his words quickly cut me down to size again.

"I have a silver Bentley, but I left it in the city. I wasn't sure of the country roads and I didn't want it damaged. I'm thinking of bringing it on out in the spring."

I had a sinking feeling in the pit of my stomach.

Mary said nothing but Matilda swooned. "A silver Bentley! I saw one of those in an advertising pamphlet. They are just gorgeous."

The young man nodded matter-of-factly as though a silver Bentley was really the least of the "gorgeous" things he possessed.

After a lot of small talk, mostly centered on Will Sanders, he finally decided to go. If he expected an argument from me, he sure was mistaken. But as he took his leave, he promised to be back. Not "may I" or "by your leave" or anything like that. Just "I'll drop back again the first chance I get." I cringed inside.

After he'd finally gone I went up to bed as soon as I could tactfully excuse myself. Even with my door closed I could hear Mary and Matilda talking and giggling like a couple of schoolgirls. The whole thing disturbed me so much I could hardly concentrate as I read my nightly Bible passage and tried to pray. Yet I couldn't put into thoughts or words just why I felt as I did. I tried hard to shove the uneasy feelings aside and get to sleep, but it was too big a job for me. I tossed and turned until I heard the clock strike three—still sleep eluded me. I slammed my fist into my pillow and wished fervently that I had never laid eyes on the guy.

Changes

I awoke still tired and grumpy from my lack of sleep. I had never felt quite so disturbed in my entire life, and I couldn't make heads or tails of it. I knew it had something to do with that young whippersnapper Will Sanders, but what he might have done to merit such feelings on my part I had no idea. He seemed like a decent enough chap, and he certainly had behaved himself in gentlemanly fashion while he had been a guest—though an uninvited one—in our home.

No one else seemed to take offense at his sudden appearance, and *some* members of the household actually seemed to favor his visit.

Somehow I knew he had touched on a raw nerve. After pondering the situation, I realized I resented the attention that Matilda and Mary had given to him. I had no reason to resent it, but the feeling was there. I felt challenged—backed up in my own corner. But what was I trying to defend? And why did the presence of the new neighbor put me on the defensive?

I shoved the whole thing aside, for it was more than I could deal with in my present mood.

I finished the chores and returned to the house for breakfast. I was later than usual in coming in and the table was nearly cleared and empty.

"Matilda had to eat so she could get to school on time," Mary explained without a hint in her tone that my lateness had made it difficult for anyone else.

Mary dished out two plates of pancakes and bacon and poured two cups of coffee, which she brought to the table.

"Grandpa and Uncle Charlie joined Matilda," she continued. She did not comment on the fact that she had waited for me.

I just nodded to Mary, and when she joined me at the table I said the table grace as usual.

"Anything wrong at the barn?" she questioned.

For a moment I didn't follow her, and then I realized she noticed I had taken an unusually long time with the chores.

"No," I replied hurriedly. "Just the usual. Guess I was just plain slow this mornin'. I didn't sleep too good last night for some reason."

I figured the matter was explained sufficiently and could be dropped, but Mary's eyes searched my face.

"You're not comin' down with somethin', are you?" she asked, her eyes troubled.

"Me? No, just—just somethin' I ate, I s'pose. I'm not used to eating so much before I go to bed."

Mary let it go but I could still feel her eyes on me. I didn't dare leave any of my breakfast on the plate like I wanted to.

We continued the meal in silence—there wasn't much I wanted to talk about anyway. Mary, sensing it, didn't try to involve me in meaningless conversation.

"Where's Grandpa and Uncle Charlie?" I finally asked, realizing it was strange for the two menfolk to be missing from the kitchen at that hour on a wintry day.

"Uncle Charlie went back to his room. To read, he said, but I've a notion he didn't get much sleep last night either. And Grandpa went out to the shed to work on that toboggan he's makin' for Sarah and Jon. He says the weather could turn bitter any day now, and then he won't be able to work outside."

I nodded. Yes, the weather could turn bitter. We were nearing the end of November.

After some more silence, Mary removed our plates and poured fresh coffee. She returned to her chair and sipped the hot liquid slowly. Then she put down her cup.

"Mitch stopped by while you were chorin'," she said simply and my head came around, wondering if Mitch had brought bad news. It had been some time since Mary's brother had paid us a call, and he certainly wouldn't be making neighborly calls at breakfast time.

Mary met my gaze.

"He's tired of the farm," she went on evenly, but I could see pain in her eyes. I didn't know if she was thinking of Mitch or of her ma and pa.

"He's off to the city to find himself a job. Was goin' on into town to catch the mornin' train."

I forgot my own small problems for the moment. I knew Mary needed all the sympathy and support I could give her. I could see tears glistening in her eyes, but she didn't allow them to spill over. I wished there was some way I could comfort her—give assurance that I knew it was hard for her and cared that she was hurting. But I just sat there, clumsily trying to find words, not knowing what to do or say. Finally I made a feeble attempt to reach out to her, if only by letting her talk about it.

"Did he say for how long?"

Mary's eyes lowered. "He's not plannin' to come back," she said quietly.

"I'm—I'm sorry," I muttered, reaching out to take Mary's hand resting on the checkerboard oilcloth.

"Can—can your pa manage the farm without him?" I went on.

Mary turned to me and the tears did spill over then; she clung to my offered hand as though it were a lifeline. "Oh, Josh," she said in a whispery voice, "it's Mitch I'm worried about. I've been prayin' and prayin' that he might become—become a believer. What ever will happen to him if—if he gets in with the wrong crowd in the city?"

I reached over to cover Mary's hand with my other one. "Hey," I comforted, "we can still pray. Prayer works even over long distances. There are 'right' crowds in the city too, you know. Maybe God is sending Mitch to just the right people—or person—and he will listen to what they have to say in a way that he might never listen to us."

Mary listened carefully. She was quiet for a moment and then she turned to me and tried a wobbly smile through her tears. She pulled back her hand and searched in her apron pocket for a handkerchief. After wiping her eyes and blowing her nose, she had control of herself again.

"Papa will manage—I guess," she said softly. "Mitch never did care for farm chores anyway. But Mama will be heartbroken." And another tear slipped down her cheek.

I sat there thinking of Mary—thinking of her ma and pa and their concern over Mitch.

"Did they have a row?" I asked carefully, knowing full well that it was really none of my business.

Mary smiled. "That's exactly what I asked Mitch," she answered, "but he said 'no,' he just announced that he was leaving and they didn't even try to argue him out of it much. He said that Mama cried some—but he expected that."

Mary left the table and began preparing for washing up the dishes.

I thought about her words for a few minutes. There didn't seem to be much I could do about the whole thing.

Then an idea came to me. "Hey, why don't you go on home for a few days?"

Mary whirled to look at me, her eyes wide.

"Oh, I couldn't!" she exclaimed.

"Why not? We could manage for a few days."

"But—but the meals an' all—"

"We've made meals before." I was sure now that it was just the thing for both Mary and her mother.

"But—but Matilda—her lunch an'—"

"We'll fix Matilda's lunch. I'll do it myself—if she'll trust me."

"But I—I don't know what to say."

"Then go. Really. We can manage—as long as you don't stay away too long."

Mary was torn—I could see that. She wanted desperately to go to her mother, but she felt a deep responsibility to us.

"I mean it, Mary," I prompted further and left my chair to take the dish towel from her hands.

"Now you run off and pack yourself whatever you need for the next few days, an' I'll go out an' hitch Chester to the sleigh."

"Are you sure?" Mary asked one last time.

"I'm sure," and I turned her gently around and urged her toward her bedroom door.

Mary left then but turned back to say over her shoulder, "But the dishes—I haven't even finished the dishes."

I looked at the dishes that remained. Mary had already washed up from the first breakfast.

"I'll do the dishes the minute I get back," I promised her, and Mary went.

As soon as she had disappeared I lifted my winter coat and hat from the peg by the door and went out to harness Chester as I had promised. Mary was out, valise in hand, just as I pulled up in front of the house. I helped her tuck in and we were off. Chester was feeling frisky, not having been used much, and he headed for the road at a fast clip. I had to slow him down to make the turn at the corner.

Mary and I didn't talk much on the way over. But we both enjoyed the brisk run in the cutter. I could sense the tension leaving Mary's body and see the shine return to her eyes. I was pleased that the idea of her spending some time at home had come to me.

As we turned down the Turley lane Mary spoke for the first time.

"How long should I stay?"

"Well—as long as you think you should," I responded slowly.

Mary smiled mischievously. "Are you trying to get rid of me, Josh?"

"Truth is," I answered, matching her mood, "I'm sorta hopin' that you'll get to missin' us real soon."

Mary's face flushed slightly, and I couldn't help but laugh.

"Seriously?" she said when her composure had returned.

"Seriously—how about until Sunday?"

"That long? This is only Wednesday."

"I know—an' I'll be counting every day—so don't be late."

Mary flushed again.

"I was wonderin'," she said after a moment, "if Matilda might like to come join me on Friday evening. She's never spent time at my house before an'—an' I think that her—her cheery mood might be good for Mama."

I pulled Chester up to the front of Mary's house. "I'll tell Matilda," I promised. "I'm sure she'd love to come and I'll bring her over."

I helped Mary out and then lifted Chester's reins again.

"Will you come in, Josh?" asked Mary.

"I think you and your mama need to meet alone," I said thoughtfully. "Besides," I went on in a lighter tone, "I've got to get on home to those dishes, remember?"

Mary laughed softly, and then grew more serious.

"Thanks, Josh," she said. "For understandin'—an'—everythin'."

I nodded and climbed back into the sleigh.

"And, Josh," Mary called softly. I turned to look at her. A few scattery snowflakes were falling about her. Some of them rested on the hair that escaped beneath her fur-trimmed hat. Her eyes were shining, her face lightened by some impulsive but pleasant thought. I waited, thinking what a picture she made as she stood there, valise in hand.

"Josh," she said again. "A motor car is nice. Really. But—but you sure can't beat a wintry sleigh ride behind Chester, can you?"

I chuckled. Mary had summed up my own feelings.

"We should do it more often," I answered. "Remind me."

And with one last grin I turned Chester around and left the lane at a fast clip. Mary was quite right. You couldn't beat a wintry sleigh ride behind Chester, and I was all set to enjoy it to the full.

But for some reason, the ride back home wasn't as pleasant as I had anticipated.

I didn't need to do the dishes when I got home. Uncle Charlie had already washed and put them in the cupboard. He had also made a fresh pot of coffee, and Grandpa had joined him at the kitchen table for a cup. When I walked in both pairs of eyes turned to me.

"Somethin' wrong, Boy?" asked Grandpa.

I poured myself some coffee and joined them at the table before explaining all about Mitch leaving and Mary's concern for her ma.

"You done right, Boy," said Grandpa. "We been hoggin' too much of Mary's time. Her ma needs her too."

Uncle Charlie just slurped his coffee and then tilted his chair on the two back legs.

"What about Matilda?" he asked at length.

"Mary wants her to come and spend the weekend," I answered. "I'm sure Matilda will be glad to."

"This is Wednesday," went on Uncle Charlie.

"We'll manage until Friday," I assured them both, and Grandpa nodded.

"I don't have anything pressing right now. Just chores. I can help in the house," I added.

Uncle Charlie hid a smile. "Never did cotton to yer cookin', Josh," he teased.

I just grinned. "Then you cook an' I'll do dishes," I challenged him.

Uncle Charlie nodded. "It's a deal," he agreed.

"We'll manage," Grandpa concluded, but I could tell by his tone of voice that he was a mite doubtful. I guess none of us realized how much we'd come to depend on Mary till she wasn't there.

Matilda was looking forward to spending the weekend with Mary and her family. The plan was for us to have our Friday supper, do up the dishes and then I'd drive Matilda over to Mary's house.

We were just finishing the cleaning up when the dog announced a visitor. It was Will Sanders again. This time he'd come by sleigh. I grinned to myself when I saw him. He certainly hadn't lost any time in making good on his promise to return, but this time he had been outfoxed. We were almost ready to leave for the Turleys'.

Grandpa opened the door and welcomed him. He came in confidently and took in the whole kitchen scene with one sweeping glance. I don't know if I just fancied it or if he really was amused to see me wiping the dishes.

"What a shame!" exclaimed Matilda. "We are just finishing up here, and then I am off to the Turleys' to join Mary for the weekend."

"I understood that Mary lives here," he responded.

"Well, she does," hastily explained Matilda, "but she's been spending a few days at home with her folks this week. She doesn't get to see much of them even though she lives so close, so Josh sent her on home for a few days."

Matilda gave the last bit of news with a hint of pride in her voice, but I think Will Sanders might well have missed the meaning of it all. At any rate, he let it go by completely and surprised me by saying to Matilda, "Then let me drive you."

Now just a minute here, I wanted to cut in, but instead I said as calmly as I could, "I already have my horse ready and waiting in the barn. All I need to do is hitch him to the sleigh."

"But mine are already hitched and waiting. No use for you to go out in the cold when I can just run Matilda on over."

He ignored my scowl and hurried right on, "I wanted to see Mary anyway."

I couldn't argue much about that.

"That's very kind," Matilda responded. "I'm sure Josh and Chester will appreciate not having to go out."

Well, I couldn't speak for Chester, but I sure knew how Josh felt about the matter. I didn't say anything, though. There didn't seem to be much point.

"Go ahead," I told Matilda. "I'll finish the dishes."

"Oh, thank you," she responded, reaching up to give me one of her impulsive little hugs right there before the eyes of Will Sanders. I was both embarrassed and smug. *So what do you think of that, Mr. Sanders?* I wanted to say, but I bit my tongue and turned back to wipe the table and rinse the dishpan.

Matilda was soon back, bag in hand and her warm coat wrapped securely around her. I didn't even watch them go, and when Matilda called, "Good night, Josh," I only mumbled in reply.

I was grumpy all evening. It was almost nine o'clock before I remembered Chester still waiting in the barn, harnessed and ready for travel. Grumbling, I lit the lantern and pulled on my heavy coat.

"Well, fella, sorry about that," I apologized as I slipped the harness from his back. "I near forgot about you. Guess—guess you an' me sorta got—stood up."

I flung the harness with extra intensity to hang it back on its pegs, and it made Chester jump.

I crossed back to him and began to gently rub his neck and his back. The ink that Jon had splashed over him had finally faded away in the sun and rain.

"Sorry, fella," I soothed. "Guess I'm just a little out of sorts. First, we've been needin' to do without Mary. It isn't easy for three fellas to batch anymore when we've been used to somethin' else. An' then this here fella comes along and takes—just takes right over with Matilda—with Mary, too."

I don't know why I expected a horse to make any sense out of what I was saying, but I went right on talking to Chester for the next five minutes. By the time I got back to the kitchen, I had settled down enough to think that I might sleep.

"Guess I'll make it an early night," I said to Grandpa and Uncle Charlie, and they didn't seem surprised. They both said good night without really looking up and I headed on up the stairs to my room.

CHAPTER 8

Troubling Thoughts

But I couldn't sleep this time either. I tossed and turned and roughed up my pillow, but my mind just wouldn't let my body rest. Pixie got rather impatient with me. She left the warm spot where she always slept curled at my feet and scrambled up beside me. She whined softly, her little body wiggling slightly and her tail thumping. Then she took a lick at my face. I don't know if she was sympathizing with my misery or telling me to settle down and let her get some sleep, but I did find a bit of comfort in her seeming concern.

I reached out and ran my hand across her silky back. She let me stroke her a few times and then returned to the foot of the bed, turned a few times and lay down. I heard her yawn as she tucked in for the night. I guess she felt she had done all she could.

At last I stopped even pretending. I reached out to my night stand and felt around for the small container that held the matches, struck one and lit my lamp. Matilda had just received a stack of new dailies. I decided to get one from the kitchen and read for a while.

I was surprised when I started down the stairs to see the kitchen light still burning. I wondered if someone was ill. Then I thought of Uncle Charlie. He often got up and sat alone by the warm stove if his arthritis got too painful during the night. I decided I'd just join him for a while in the kitchen. Maybe make some hot chocolate or something.

But as I neared the bottom of the stairs, I heard voices and realized that Grandpa was up, too. I guess I hadn't been tossing for as long as I'd thought. It had just seemed like hours and hours.

"You think he's 'callin' ? " Uncle Charlie was asking.

There was a moment's silence before Grandpa responded; then I heard a chuckle. "Thet's the way I figure it, but I'll be hanged iffen I can figure out, callin' on *who*."

"Matilda?"

"Thet was in my thinkin'—at first—but he paid considerable attention to Mary the other night too. An' did ya hear him say tonight thet he wanted to see Mary?"

"Yeah—I heard 'im."

I heard a coffee cup being set on the table. A chair moved slightly on the linoleum floor. Then Uncle Charlie spoke again.

"Maybe he's jest sorta lookin' 'em both over."

"A man don't git hisself nowhere a doin' thet," observed Grandpa.

Uncle Charlie snorted. He'd been a bachelor all his life. Maybe he knew the truth of the statement. I had never thought to wonder if there had ever been a young lady or ladies in Uncle Charlie's life way back when.

"Nowhere. Thet's it exactly—nowhere," said Uncle Charlie.

" 'Course they're both awful nice girls," put in Grandpa.

"Yup. Both awful nice girls," agreed Uncle Charlie.

"Don't rightly know which one I'd pick myself."

Uncle Charlie seemed to be giving the matter considerable thought. I heard the coffee cups again.

"You know anythin' 'bout this here fella?" Uncle Charlie asked, and I could follow his line of thought. No good-for-nothin' was gonna come along and make things miserable for one of *his* girls, no siree.

Grandpa let out his breath in a raspy little sound. Finally he said slowly, "Checked a bit in town," then added quickly to try to justify himself, "Jest fer the record ya know. They say they're a fine family. Three boys. Lost both folks when the youngest was jest a tyke. Thet's Henry. Will is a couple years older. The oldest son an' his wife took in the two younger boys. Will went on to school an' then worked in the city fer a spell."

There was a moment of silence while the two men thought about Grandpa's information. Grandpa broke it.

"Couldn't find no skeletons a'tall," he admitted.

More silence. I didn't know what the emotions were down there in that kitchen—but my stomach was churnin' and my mouth went all dry. I hadn't realized it until my palms began to hurt, and then I noticed I had my fists curled so tightly that my nails were digging into them.

"Anyways—as I see it," went on Grandpa, "Josh better hurry an' make up his mind as to which girl he wants—or he's gonna be takin' the leftovers."

I felt all the air leave my lungs.

"Maybe he don't want neither," responded Uncle Charlie.

Grandpa snorted. "Iffen he don't," he said matter-of-factly, "he's dumber'n I took 'im fer."

I had long since forgotten about Matilda's newspapers. I had even forgotten about the hot chocolate. The conversation down below had my blood boilin' and was givin' me the chills—both at the same time.

"Hard choice," Grandpa was saying reflectively. "Real hard choice."

"Can't have 'em both," spoke up Uncle Charlie.

"Maybe it's been the wrong thing to have 'em both here," said Grandpa after a pause. "I mean, seein' both girls—so different—yet so—so special, an' gittin' to feel like they was more like family than—than young women to court." A long pause. "An' how in the world does a fella go about courtin' a girl thet lives in the same house as he does anyway?"

"Yeah," agreed Uncle Charlie, "an' when ya like 'em both, how do ya court the one 'thout the other feelin' left out an' such?"

"Well, this here Will don't seem to have 'im no problem—he's courtin', an' thet's fer sure."

There was silence for a minute.

"Do ya think the girls—?" began Grandpa but Uncle Charlie cut in.

"You seen an' heard 'em same as me. Any girl is flattered by courtin'."

"Do ya think they know which one he's picked?"

"I dunno. Maybe. Women have an uncanny sense 'bout thet," mused Uncle Charlie.

At the time I didn't even stop to wonder where Uncle Charlie got all his knowledge about the fairer sex.

A chair scraped against the floor. Someone was standing to his feet. I moved quickly to make my escape back to my bed, but Uncle Charlie—or was it Grandpa? no, it was Uncle Charlie, I could tell by the shuffling steps—just moved to the stove for the coffeepot.

I heard the coffee poured and Uncle Charlie sit back down. They sipped in silence for a few minutes, each busy with his own thoughts.

"Maybe Josh really doesn't care," said Grandpa.

"He cares," Uncle Charlie affirmed flatly.

"Yeah—'bout which one?"

"Can't answer thet. But he cares. It's nigh been eatin' his insides."

He sure seemed to know a lot—maybe more than I did.

"Hadn't noticed," admitted Grandpa. "How's thet?"

"Little things. He can spend the whole night tossin' on his bed. I can hear 'im. Then he gets up as touchy as a bear with cubs. I see 'im lookin' from one girl to the next—an' when thet there fella showed up tonight, Josh fairly bristled."

"Thet right? Thet right?" said Grandpa, and for some strange reason there was a bit of excitement in his voice.

I'd heard about enough. The whole thing was leaving me with a sick feeling. I moved back a step, intending to return quietly to my bed. Then a word from Grandpa caught me a blow right in the middle of my stomach.

"Jealous, huh?"

Jealous? Me? Of course I'm not jealous, I fumed. Jealousy was an evil emotion. It went right along with covetousness. My whole being rebelled against the thought.

"Iffen he's jealous—then maybe he does care. Or maybe he's jest plain-out possessive of 'em both," went on Grandpa.

"I think he cares."

" 'Bout who?"

Uncle Charlie thought for a minute. Then answered slowly, "I'm not sure thet even Josh has got thet sorted out yet."

"Well, he'd better start 'em a sortin'," Grandpa replied very seriously, " 'cause thet there young Will ain't gonna waste 'im no time."

"Yeah, he's courtin'. Fer sure he's a courtin'."

"He's a courtin' all right," agreed Grandpa again, then repeated on a still-puzzled note, "but I'll be hanged iffen I can figure out which one."

I crept back to my room, my stomach still churning and my body tight with tension. Pixie didn't even move as I eased myself back into my bed. I had been repelled by every word I'd heard. I guess that was what an eavesdropper could expect. Still, I hadn't planned to eavesdrop—it had just happened, and after the first few words I had overheard, I sure wasn't going to give myself away.

So Will is courtin'? Matilda? Or Mary? I sure hadn't been able to discern which one. *And if he's courtin', then we might lose one of the girls.* The thought was not a comforting one. Matilda and Mary seemed to sort of come as a set. And furthermore, they *both* belonged to us somehow.

But no. That was ridiculous. Even I knew that. The day would come—maybe much sooner than I liked to think—that we would lose one of the girls, or maybe both of them. We couldn't possibly keep the two of them forever. *Maybe we couldn't keep either one of them,* was a startling thought. Will would cart one of them off and then some other young buck would come along and take the other.

The very thought made my blood boil.

But *jealous?* Why would I be jealous? I mean, I had no claim to the girls—no personal claim. I'd never courted either one of them. And they certainly had not flirted with me. Well, not really. Only in a teasing sort of way.

I thought of Matilda's impulsive little embraces and my face flushed in the darkness. Then I remembered Mary reaching out to gently touch my hand, and the deep look of concern and understanding in her eyes as she did so, and I colored even deeper. *Maybe they do like me—sort of. Not just as family.* The thought was a new one and one that I had not consciously entertained before. But if—if they did—if there was any chance that they did—then I should do something about it. I mean, I didn't particularly enjoy the thought of spending my whole life as a bachelor like Uncle Charlie. I wanted a wife—love—a family.

But first—there came the courting.

I had no idea how to go about courting a girl. Oh, if it was like this here Will fella handled it, there wasn't much to it. I mean, he just came over whenever he took the notion and just sorta hung around and teased and complimented the girls some. Any fella could do that.

But, I knew that wasn't the way that I'd do it. A girl deserved more consideration than that. I thought she had a right to expect more than that. If I was courting I'd try to think of nice things to do that she might enjoy.

Take Matilda—*she loves flowers—an' sweet smellin' perfume—an' trips to town an' pretty new pieces of jewelry,* I listed off. *She likes music—and laughing and picnics in the country and drives in the motor car.* Wouldn't be too hard at all for me to think of ways to court Matilda.

What if I courted Matilda? How long did a fella have to "court" before he could properly ask a young woman to marry him? I mean, courting could take a good deal of time and expense. True, a fella could get a lot of enjoyment out of it. Especially if the young woman really enjoyed the courting—like Matilda would. Maybe she'd just want it to go on and on. *Matilda would like courtin' all right,* I decided.

But what about after the courting? I couldn't really picture Matilda in the kitchen, working over a hot stove, baking bread and canning the garden produce. I couldn't really see her leaning over the scrub board, hair in disarray while she scrubbed at dirty farm socks. Oh, Matilda fit into the courting picture just fine—but the marriage picture wasn't so easy to visualize.

Now, Mary—I could see Mary doing all those kitchen things. I had watched her perform all the household tasks dozens of times. It seemed so—so *natural* for Mary. She did it without fuss—without comment—and even seemed to somehow enjoy the doing. Mary in the kitchen seemed right reasonable. *But courtin'?* I couldn't think of a single way that one would properly court Mary. I mean, she never fussed about perfumes or pretty jewelry or lace hankies or anything like that. She never coaxed for rides in the motor car or asked for picnics. I couldn't honestly think of a thing that would make Mary impulsively throw her arms around my neck or giggle with girlish glee.

I lay there, struggling with questions I'd never faced before—working them this way and then that way. No matter how I tried I couldn't come up with any answers. But I knew instinctively that I could no longer just push the matter aside. I had to get it sorted out. My whole future depended on it.

Eying the Field

Even if I had wrestled with the problem for half the night, I was no nearer an answer when I got up to go choring the next morning. This much I knew, I had two girls right at hand who most young men in the area considered first-rate candidates for a marriage partner, and I had been taking them for granted.

I also knew that if I was going to choose one of them—and I figured I would be pretty dense not to—then I was going to need to decide which one and get on with the courting. The trouble was deciding. They were so different—yet both special.

Matilda's energy and enthusiasm made the house seem alive. We all enjoyed her company. Even Grandpa and Uncle Charlie counted the days until she returned from her trips home. The world just seemed like a nicer place when Matilda was around.

Then I thought of Mary. Mary was quiet—not bouncy. But Mary was—well—supportive. She was dependable and sort of comfortable to be around. I'm not sure how we would have managed without Mary.

Matilda or Mary? How was one to decide? And just what kind of tension would it put on our household if I started to court the one and left behind the other?

Now, I had no reason to think that either girl was sitting around holding her breath waiting for Josh Jones to start calling. Neither of them had led me to think they were interested in me in any other way than as a member of our household. I was maybe being presumptuous to even think that one of them would accept my small gifts and attention.

Then a new thought hit me. What if I picked a girl—Matilda or Mary— and decided to court her and she flatly turned me down? It could happen.

The thought scared me. I remembered what had happened when I had the foolish notion that I could just walk back into Camellia's life and she had announced instead that she was marrying Willie.

The idea of being rejected was so frightening that I decided, as I slopped the pigs and cared for the cows, that I would just hold back for the next several days and sorta look things over. I wanted to put out a few feelers to see if it appeared that either of the girls might favorably respond to being courted by Joshua Jones.

I was more sensitive to little things as I gathered around the breakfast table with the family that morning.

Matilda was telling a funny incident from school. One of the children had written a composition about winter. He had said in part, "The best thing about winter is that the 'moskeytoes' "—Matilda spelled it for us—"fly south to bite other people."

Matilda laughed merrily as she told it and Grandpa chuckled and Uncle Charlie grinned. Matilda was a lot of fun.

Matilda began to gather her school supplies and reach for her heavy winter wraps as soon as Grandpa had finished with our morning devotions. I had a sudden inspiration.

"Chester's in his stall," I said. "How would you like me to hitch him to the sleigh and drive you to school?"

She looked at me, her eyes big with unasked questions; then she threw her arms around my neck with a little squeal of delight.

I took that as her yes, and I grinned to myself as I shrugged into my heavy coat and headed for the barn while she finished her preparations. Maybe courting wasn't so hard after all.

It was colder and another storm was dumping more snow. I was glad I had thought of driving Matilda to school. It would have been rather miserable walking.

I tucked the heavy lap robe closely about her and we started off, Chester tossing his head and snorting, anxious to get out to the open road for a good run. Matilda leaned into the wind, anticipating the speed of the open cutter skimming over the frozen ground.

I watched her face. She loved a good run. If she had been holding the reins, she no doubt would have given Chester his head and let him run at a full gallop. As it was, I let Chester do a bit more running than I normally did, just so that I could watch Matilda's enjoyment.

When we got to the school I helped gather her things and climb from the sleigh. Her face was flushed—whether from excitement or the cold wind, I couldn't tell.

"I'll be back to pick you up after school," I promised and she flashed a beautiful smile.

I waited long enough to see her into the school building, noting as I did so the smoke curling up from the brick chimney. The Smith boy had done his work and the potbelly stove would be spilling its welcome warmth into the room.

Matilda turned and gave me a bit of a wave just before she closed the door. I waved back and clucked to Chester, who turned smartly around and headed back out the school gate.

I felt good about the little drive to school. Oh, I hadn't made any kind of open statement or anything, but Matilda certainly had not been adverse to my company. I would just sort of keep my eyes open and see what the future days might bring.

But maybe while I was waiting, I should come up with some plan to sorta "test out" Mary.

My plan might have worked just fine had it not been for Will Sanders. I mean, the "wait and see" didn't seem too practical when he turned up on our doorstep every few days.

I still didn't care much for the guy. Grandpa's midnight discussion with Uncle Charlie kept running through my head. *He's courtin' all right,* I decided—but like Grandpa, I couldn't figure out which girl he had his eye on.

I didn't have much to say when he arrived, just sat back watching the situation. He teased and flirted with Matilda, but then he turned right around and asked Mary to a Pie Social in town. It happened to be on the night of

Matilda's annual school program, so Mary turned him down. He smiled and said, "Next time" and Mary nodded her head.

When Christmas came, along with it came Will Sanders as well. He brought each of the girls a gift, a pair of warm gloves. After he finally left for home that night, the girls openly talked about it.

"I never dreamed we'd be on his Christmas list," said Matilda. "I never even thought to put his name on mine."

"Me neither," said Mary, studying the fingers of the gloves absent-mindedly. "What do we do now? I s'pose it would be terribly rude not to give a gift in return."

She looked imploringly at Matilda as though she wished her to say that it wouldn't be rude at all. Grandpa said it.

"Seems to me that one shouldn't feel obligated, things bein' as they be."

I wasn't quite sure what Grandpa meant, but I was willing to agree.

The girls kept on mulling over the problem.

"I know," said Mary suddenly. "Let's give him a gift together!"

"Together?" echoed Matilda.

"One gift—from both of us."

Matilda's face brightened. "Let's!" she squealed.

A few days later they were wrapping up a pair of socks and putting both names on the card. I won't pretend I didn't get a bit of satisfaction from the arrangement. Then it hit me—perhaps the girls didn't care too much either for the fact that Will had not openly made known whom he was courting.

On Christmas morning I unwrapped my own gifts. Matilda gave me a pair of fine cuff links. Mary gave me a hand-knit scarf and gloves set. I don't know when she ever found the time to do it without my knowing, but I sure did take pleasure in the gifts, realizing how special they were and how they bespoke the two givers.

Will Sanders, I breathed, but not aloud, *it's your turn to be jealous!*

The winter storms began to abate, and I could sense another spring just around the corner. I could hardly wait. I wanted to get back on my land. I wanted to get the Ford out again and feel the thrill of covering the miles so quickly, the wind whipping around me. As it was, I dreaded each trip to town since I had gone from the motor car back to the slow-plodding team. I put off every journey for just as long as I could.

On one such day I returned home a bit out-of-sorts because of my impatience with the snow-covered road. After caring for the team, I bundled the groceries into my arms and headed for the kitchen and a hot cup of coffee with a bit of Mary's baking.

No coffee greeted me. Grandpa and Uncle Charlie sat at the table. It appeared that they had been there for hours, not because they wanted to but because they didn't know what else to do with themselves. It was so untypical that it threw a scare into me right away.

"Where's Mary?" I asked, my eyes quickly darting about the room.

There was silence; then Grandpa cleared his throat, while Uncle Charlie shuffled his feet.

"She went on home," explained Grandpa. "Word came her ma was sick."

"Sick?" I repeated, letting the word sink in and thinking of all those years that Mary's ma had spent in bed. "How sick?"

"Don't rightly know," said Grandpa. "The youngest girl jest came a ridin' over here—nigh scared to death, and hollered fer Mary to come quick. Mary did. Without hardly lookin' back—jest jumped on up behind her an' the two of 'em took off agin."

I put the groceries down and wheeled back toward the door.

"Mary should've taken Chester," I mumbled as I went.

Grandpa called after me, "Where you off to?" Then he added as kindly as he could, "Josh, at a time like this, sometimes folks only want family."

But I didn't even slow down. "Mary's about as 'family' as you can get," I flung back over my shoulder, and Grandpa didn't argue anymore.

I didn't even wait to saddle or bridle Chester. Just untied the halter rope and led him out of his stall. In a wink I was on his back. He wanted to run and I let him. He was hard to hold in with just the halter; I guess I rode him rather recklessly. We were soon in Turleys' yard, and I flung myself off and tied Chester to the gate before hurrying to the house.

I rapped politely before entering the back porch. There was no answer so I just eased the door open and let myself in. Once in the kitchen, I took a deep breath and the doubts began to pour through me. Who did I think I was that I could intrude upon a family in such a way? Why did I dare come without invitation?

I knew instinctively that the answer to all of the questions was, "Mary." For some reason I felt she might need me. Still—I shouldn't have . . . I turned back to wait outside, but just then the younger girl, Lilli, entered the kitchen. She was wiping tears as she came, and at the sight of me she stopped short, sucking in her breath in a little gasp. Then she seemed to realize who it was and took another step forward.

"I—I'm sorry," I apologized. "I—I thought that I might—that Mary might . . . Could I go for the doc or anything?"

She shook her head slowly, the tears pouring again down her cheeks. I moved toward her but she turned her back on me, not wanting me to see her fresh outburst of tears. I hardly knew what to do or say so I just stood there, carelessly crunching my hat in my hands.

"Josh?" The little gasp that bore my name came from Mary. I wheeled to look at her, my eyes full of questions.

"Josh," she said again.

I looked into her tear-filled eyes. Her hair was disarrayed and her long skirt spattered with road grime, attesting to the fact of how she had traveled to get to the side of her ailing mother.

I moved forward. "How is she?" I asked. "Could I—"

But Mary cut me short with a tremulous voice. "She's gone, Josh."

And then I was holding her close, letting her sob against my chest. I don't know which one of us moved toward the other. Perhaps we both did.

I just held her and let her cry, and I guess I wept right along with her while my hand tried to stroke some of the tangles from her normally tidy hair. I heard my voice on occasion but all I said was, "Oh, Mary. Mary. I'm so sorry. So sorry."

At last Mary eased back from my arms. We were alone in the big farm kitchen. I looked at Mary, wondering if she was okay, wondering if I should let her go, but she just gave me a little nod and moved toward the cupboard.

"Papa needs some coffee," she said matter-of-factly, and began to put the pot on.

But Mr. Turley did not drink the coffee. I'm not sure that anyone drank from that particular pot. The whole house was too stunned—too much in pain to think of coffee or anything else.

At last I found something useful to do. I was sent to town to fetch Uncle Nat. I was both glad to go—just to get away from the intense sorrow—and sorry to go, for I hated to leave Mary in such pain.

The funeral was two days later. Mitch came home, but he stayed only a couple of days afterward and then returned to the city. Mary stayed at her home for an entire week. It seemed forever. Even when she did return to us I hardly knew what to say or do. I knew she was still sorrowing. But how did one share sorrow without probing? The only thing I could think of was to make things as easy for Mary as possible. I made sure the woodbox and water pails were kept full. I helped with dishes whenever I was in the house at the right time. I was extra careful about leaving dirty farm boots outside her kitchen—even stepped out of them before I came onto her back porch.

Whenever I saw tears forming in her eyes, I wanted to hold her again—just sort of protect her from her pain and sorrow—but it didn't seem like the thing to do. Matilda slipped her arms around her instead, and I left the room, confused and sorrowful.

Somehow we managed to get through the days until spring was finally with us again.

CHAPTER 10

Spring

I gave my full attention to the land and the planting. I didn't even have time to wonder and worry about which girl I should be courting. Except on those evenings when Will Sanders showed up at our door. He still called at least once a week. I guess getting the crop in didn't cause Will as much concern as it did me.

He asked Matilda for walks and paid Mary elaborate compliments on her pies and cakes. He suggested picnics and drives. He kept promising to bring out that silver Bentley from the city. I tried to ignore him and go about my daily tasks. I was busy enough that I didn't have too much time to fret—even about Will Sanders.

Matilda began to coax about the Ford again, so on Sundays we used it to go to church and then sometimes went for a little drive in the afternoons. Matilda always wanted her share of driving. She handled the car quite well, too. Pretty soon she was asking to take it to town on her own or to take Mary home for a visit. I couldn't think of any good reason that she shouldn't, so I let her use the car. It seemed to please Matilda mightily to be behind the steering wheel.

Mr. Turley wasn't doing too well since his wife's death. In May, Faye got married as had been planned. Mary was her maid-of-honor. We were all invited to the small wedding. Mary wore a gown of soft green that brought out the reddish highlights of her hair and matched the green flecks in her eyes. I thought it most becoming on her.

Everyone tried to make the wedding a happy occasion, but we all knew that it really could not be. It was the first "big" family event that Mrs. Turley had missed, and I guess we were all thinking of her.

It was especially hard on young Lil. She knew that she would be the only girl at home now, and I think she dreaded the thought. She also was likely wondering about when it came her turn to wed—would she feel right about leaving her pa at home all alone?

I suggested to Mary that she might want to spend a few days at home after the wedding, and without argument she accepted.

She stayed for three days, and when her pa drove her back to our farm to resume her duties, he carried a large box in and set it down just inside the kitchen door.

We were all glad to see Mary back. As soon as she removed her hat she tied on her apron. The next thing she did was to stir up the fire and put on the teakettle. Mr. Turley watched her move about the kitchen. I wondered what was going through his mind. Perhaps Mary reminded him of her mother. At any rate he sure did seem to be studying her.

When the tea was ready and Mary served it up along with what was left of her orange loaf, Mr. Turley sat a long time. Grandpa and Uncle Charlie kept trying to engage him in conversation, but he answered each query scantily. He didn't seem in any hurry to leave though, and I guessed he was just stalling, hating to return to his empty house. They had dropped Lil off with a friend for a few days, Mary explained.

"Why don't you just stay on to supper?" I heard Grandpa asking.

"Got chores," mumbled Mr. Turley, and he seemed to stir himself to leave.

"Chores work up a lot faster on a satisfied stomach," argued Grandpa.

Mr. Turley nodded and settled in again.

It ended up with Uncle Charlie and Mr. Turley having a few games of checkers while Mary fixed supper. I didn't see the games, being out with my own chores, but I understand they were played rather absent-mindedly by Mr. Turley. However, they did help to pass some time.

After he had eaten, Mr. Turley still didn't seem in too big a hurry to leave. He sat toying with his coffee cup and thinking. Finally he spoke out.

"Been thinkin' on sellin' off the livestock. Mitch is gone an' there jest don't seem to be no point in spendin' time out at the barn."

I guess we all sort of looked at him, surprised at his statement. But then, we shouldn't have been.

"Anythin' over there thet you might want fer yer herd, Josh? Got one real good milker. She's had her three sets of twins already in jest five years of calvin'?"

It sounded good. I nodded. "Might take a look at her," I agreed.

"Got one first-rate brood sow, too. Averages nine per litter. No runts. Though she's big, she's careful. Never laid her on a piglet yet. You know how some of 'em big sows just go 'plop' right down in the middle of the litter. Well, not this one. Coaxes 'em all off to the side 'fore she goes down."

That sounded impressive all right. I nodded again.

"Come over some time, Josh. See if there be anythin' ya'd like. Rather sell 'em to you than off fer slaughter."

I stood to my feet when Mr. Turley stood.

"You're sure you want to sell?" I asked. I still found it hard to believe.

He sighed deeply. "Yeah," he said at last. "Been thinkin' on it fer some time. Just don't cotton to the idee of spendin' hours out chorin' when the winds start to howl agin. Best time fer sellin' is when they're nice an' fat on summer grass. I'll sell 'em off gradual like an' be done with 'em by fall."

"Sure," I nodded. "Sure. I'll be over first chance I get."

"No hurry," went on Mr. Turley. "Come as soon as yer crop is all in."

Then he kissed Mary on the cheek, thanked Grandpa for supper and picked up his hat.

I felt so sorry for the man that I ached inside. I was glad I had more chores of my own that needed doing. At least they would keep me busy for a while and out of sight of Mary's sorrowful eyes.

When I came in from chores Mary had the big box up on the kitchen table and was carefully lifting something out from the wrappings to show Matilda.

"Oh," I heard Matilda gasp. "It's just beautiful!"

"I think so," Mary said softly. "Even when I was a little girl I used to admire them. They sat in Mama's buffet, and I'd look at them and look at them. Mama wouldn't let me touch them. She didn't want fingerprints all over them. Then when I got older Mama taught me how to handle them carefully. I was even given the privilege of cleaning each piece."

"How many are there?" Matilda asked.

"The large tray, a smaller tray, the coffeepot, teapot, creamer and sugar bowl, plus a sugar spoon and a cake server."

"They are beautiful!" Matilda said again.

I watched as Mary lovingly ran a hand over the silver pieces sitting before her on the table.

"Pa found a note Mama left in her Bible," she stated, tears in her eyes. "She said that I was to have the silver. She left Mitch her Bible, Lil her ruby pin, and Faye her china."

"Oh-h-h," murmured Matilda. I could tell she wanted to say how fortunate Mary was, but that hardly seemed appropriate under the circumstances.

We didn't have to wonder how special the silver was to Mary. After fondly gazing at each piece, she polished them all once more. Then she began to carefully wrap them in the soft pieces of cloth they had been snuggled in and, with tears in her eyes, placed them tenderly back in the box.

Grandpa cleared his throat. "Would ya like to put 'em there in the corner china cupboard," he ventured, "where ya can see 'em?"

Mary hesitated, looked across at the cupboard and then went to give Grandpa a little hug. I don't know what she whispered to him, but Grandpa's mustache twitched a bit and Mary began clearing a spot for her silver on the middle shelf. It did look pretty there, and it sure did dress up our farmhouse kitchen.

I guess we got rather used to it after a while, but I noticed Mary frequently glancing that way. She even used the set for tea when Aunt Lou dropped out one day, and the Sunday of Uncle Charlie's birthday she served us all our afternoon coffee from the shiny coffeepot when she served his birthday cake. Sarah thought it was just wonderful.

"Where did you get it, Aunt Mary?" she asked, her eyes shining. And Mary's eyes shone just as much as she answered.

"It was my mama's."

"I have never seen anything so pretty," went on Sarah. "Where did your mama get it?"

"It was her grandma's—a wedding present from an elderly lady she worked for. Mama said it was a shock to everyone. The older lady was usually sour and tight with her money, and no one could believe it when she gave Great-grandma such a beautiful gift."

Mary chuckled softly. It was the first I had heard her laugh for some time. She smiled often, sincerely, almost sadly, but she did not laugh. With the soft laughter a heavy weight seemed to lift from me deep down inside somewhere. I looked around the circle, wondering why there was no celebration, but no one else seemed to have noticed that Mary was laughing again.

Still I tucked the sound of that laughter away inside and replayed it over and over during the next days.

As soon as I finished the spring planting, I went over to see Mr. Turley. I ended up buying the cow he told me about plus a couple of her heifers. I also bought the sow along with the recent litter. We decided we shouldn't move her at the present, so Mr. Turley agreed to feed her for a few more weeks.

Mr. Turley carried through with his plans to sell off all his livestock, and neighbors dropped by to look over the animals and buy what they figured they could use. I thought it strange for a farmer to be without stock. But I guess the fields were enough to keep one man busy, and, as Mr. Turley had said, Mitch didn't seem inclined to come back home. It sounded as if he liked city life and was happy with the job he had found.

Lilli was restless, though. She didn't even plant much of a garden. Mary planted even more and prepared herself for a busy canning season. She went over to her ma's cellar and brought back some boxes of canning jars so she could fill them for her pa and Lil.

Matilda suggested to me that Mary might like another trip over to see Faye before her busy summer began. Mary didn't get together with her sisters nearly enough, I knew.

"I'll see what I can do," I nodded to Matilda as we sat idly swinging on the back porch swing.

It was the first we had spent any time together for several months, and with school almost out I immediately thought ahead to Matilda being gone for another summer. I wondered if I had allowed my busyness to interfere with courting again. *If I keep on at my present rate, I'll never get around to findin' myself a girl*, I concluded.

Maybe I'd lost my sense of urgency. Word passed around the neighborhood that Will Sanders had decided he preferred city living and had left his brother's house to return there. I felt a bit of smugness when I reminded myself of it.

My thoughts were interrupted by Matilda.

"You needn't do anything about it, Josh," she was saying. "I can drive Mary over to Faye's."

I was about to object when I realized that there was really no reason why Matilda couldn't. She could drive the car as well as I could. And Mary might not feel as rushed if I weren't hanging around, impatient to get back to some farm chores.

I nodded without saying anything, wondering if I was about to get another impulsive hug. Rather shamelessly I wondered if this time I should do some huggin' back. But the hug never came. Just then the back door opened and Mary stepped out with a tray of cold lemonade.

"Guess what?" squealed Matilda. "Josh says I can take the car and drive you over to see Faye before I leave for the summer."

Mary's eyes shone in the soft darkness, and I could see her appreciative smile. She didn't speak, but her eyes met mine and I read the thank you there. For a moment I wondered what it would be like to get a hug from Mary. And then I remembered the time when I had held her—not like Matilda, bouncing in and out of my arms with a quickness that took one's breath away. Mary had lingered, had leaned against me like a lost child, drawing strength and understanding from me. I had felt protective, needed. In spite of the sadness of that moment, I treasured the memory. Yet I couldn't really explain—

My thoughts were interrupted.

"When should we go?" Matilda was asking Mary.

Mary put the tray down and handed each of us a glass. "We don't have long," she reminded Matilda. "You have only another seven days to teach."

Had time really slipped by so quickly? It seemed that the year had just started, and here we were heading into another summer vacation.

"I know," moaned Matilda.

"I think we should go at a time when we don't have to worry about darkness," went on Mary. "Maybe Saturday."

"Saturday," said Matilda. "That sounds great!" Then she had the good grace to turn to me. "Will you need the Ford for anything on Saturday, Josh?"

I shook my head. I still had field work to do.

"Then we'll leave on Saturday morning," agreed Matilda.

Mary seemed to think carefully about it. "I guess we could," she said at last. "I could leave dinner all fixed for the men, and we'll be sure to be back in plenty of time for supper."

When Matilda went to school the next day, Mary sent a note for Faye, and Matilda sent the note home with one of the students who rode past Faye's new home. A reply stated that Faye would be watching for the two of them the next Saturday.

Saturday morning I moved the car from the shed, filled it with gas and checked the tires. One needed more air so I got out the pump and pumped it up until I was sure it was okay. Then I left the keys on the table for Matilda and went off to the field to do some summer-fallow work that needed doing.

I was interrupted midafternoon by a sudden rain squall. I studied the dark clouds for a few moments and headed in with the tractor.

I hope the girls aren't on their way home now, I thought, but the shower passed over. When the girls did not arrive, I dismissed the incident from my mind and started some evening chores.

By suppertime there still was no sign of an approaching car. I remembered Mary's words about being home in plenty of time to get supper, and I felt just a little aggravated that her visiting had put us hungry menfolk from her mind.

I went on to further chores and was surprised when Grandpa joined me at the pig barn. After making small talk for a few minutes, he turned to me. "The girls aren't home yet, Josh."

It wasn't news to me. I nodded rather glumly.

"It's past suppertime," went on Grandpa.

"Guess we can get our own supper," I grumbled. "We've done it before."

I wondered why Grandpa or Uncle Charlie weren't in the kitchen doing just that. Why should I need to do the chores, then—?

But Grandpa kicked at a fluff ball; then his eyes met mine. "It's not like Mary, Boy."

It finally got through my thick head. Grandpa was worried. I threw a look at the sky. It *was* getting rather late. *I* should have been worried. I just hadn't been thinking straight.

"I'll get Chester," I said, throwing my slop buckets down beside the pig pen. But I hadn't even gotten the saddle on Chester's back before I heard voices. Someone was "yahooing" my grandpa. I left Chester and went to see who had come and what news he had brought. It was one of the young Smiths, but he had already delivered his message, whirled his horse and was on his way back down the lane.

I started to holler at him to come back; then I noticed Grandpa still standing there, his hands lifted helplessly to the gatepost as though to steady himself. I hurried to him. His face was shaken.

"The girls—" he choked. "There's been an accident. The car flipped."

CHAPTER 11

An Awakening

I just stood there, staring at Grandpa, trying to get his meaningless words to make sense to me. I couldn't get them to connect somehow.

"Wh-what?" I finally heard myself stammer.

There was no response from Grandpa. He still clung to the post, weaving slightly as though fighting against a strong wind.

Uncle Charlie seemed to bring us both back to reality. He had hobbled out with his two canes to see what the commotion was about. He had heard the galloping horse—and I knew he realized it meant some kind of trouble. I could read it in his face when he demanded an explanation.

"What is it? Is it the girls?"

"They—they flipped the car." I mouthed the words but still did not really understand them. "The Smith kid—" But that was all I knew. I reached out a hand and squeezed Grandpa's arm.

"What did he say?" I insisted.

Grandpa shook his head as if to clear it. Still, it was a moment—a long moment—before he got his dry lips to form words.

"He said they—flipped the car."

"I know—I know," I heard myself agreeing impatiently, "but are they hurt?"

My own common sense told me that they would be hurt. I began to shake. "How—how badly—?" but I couldn't finish.

"I—I don't know," Grandpa said with a shudder. "The older boy went fer Doc. Thet's—thet's all he said."

I came alive then. Spinning around I ran for the barn, calling over my shoulder, "Where are they?"

Grandpa called back, "At Smiths," and I raced to get to the barn and Chester. My insides felt as if they were in a vice. I was frantic for both girls, but I heard only one word escape from my lips. "Mary!"

Maybe it shouldn't have surprised me, I don't know. I probably should have been smart enough to know it all along, but it was painfully clear to me as I ran that if anything happened to Mary, I—I wouldn't be able to bear it.

Chester had stood stock-still. I guess he sensed I hadn't finished the job of properly putting on his saddle. If he had moved at all it most certainly would have fallen down under his feet somewhere. I jerked it off and thrust it aside now. I sure wasn't going to take the time to fuss with a cinch.

I threw myself across Chester's back even before we left the barn, ducking low to miss the crossbeam of the barn door. I didn't stop even to fasten the door behind me as I had been taught. I put my heels to Chester, and we were off down the lane.

It was the first time in my life that I let Chester run full gallop for any distance, but I didn't check him. He seemed to sense my agitation and took advantage of the situation. But even with the Smiths being fairly close neighbors and Chester running at full speed, the trip still seemed to take forever.

I wanted to cry but I was too frightened—too frozen. Even the whipping wind failed to bring tears to my eyes. All of my being seemed shriveled and deathly cold with fear. All I knew was that Mary had been hurt—maybe badly hurt—maybe even—*I need to get there—need to get to Mary!* my mind screamed at me.

When we came to the Smiths' lane, I forgot to rein Chester in and we very nearly didn't make the turn at their gate. Because of his speed, Chester swung wide when I turned him and ended up almost running into the fence rails. That near-accident sharpened my senses a bit, and I began to think rationally again.

I pulled Chester in and was able to get him under control as we entered the farmyard. I flung myself off his back and flipped a rein carelessly over a fencepost. I could see Doc's horse tied to a post down by the corral. I breathed a prayer for him and the girls as I raced toward the Smiths' back entry.

I guess I didn't knock—I don't know, but there I was in the Smiths' big kitchen. Mrs. Smith was clucking over the tragic event.

"—such a shame," she was saying. "Such nice young ladies, too. Just to think—"

"Where are they?" I cut in, completely ignoring any manners.

"Doc is with them," she replied, not seeming to take any offense at my rudeness.

"How—how—?" But I still couldn't ask the question.

Mrs. Smith just shook her head, motherly tears of concern filling her eyes. I couldn't stand it any longer. I wanted to scream. Mrs. Smith was busy pouring a cup of coffee, and I knew without her even saying so that she expected me to sit down at her table and drink it. I turned my back on the table and the coffee cup, biting my lip to get some kind of control. I had to know! I had to know!

"Where are they?" I asked Mrs. Smith again, fighting to control my voice.

"The young schoolteacher, Miss Matilda, is in Jamie's room," she said slowly. "We thought that—"

"Where's Mary?" I cut in.

But I didn't get an answer. Right at that moment Mr. Smith entered the kitchen. He eased himself to a chair at the table and took the coffee that had been poured. Mrs. Smith just reached for another cup.

"A shame, Josh, just a shame," Mr. Smith said, shaking his head in sympathy. "Here ya only had thet there new car fer such a short time, an' I'm afraid thet it won't never be quite the same." At the look of horror on my face he hurried on. "Oh, Jamie and me pulled it outta the ditch with the team. Got it back right side up—but the frame—"

I couldn't believe it. Mr. Smith was bemoaning my motor car, and the girls were somewhere in the house in a condition I could only guess at, with the doctor trying to piece them back together.

"I don't care none about the car," I fairly exploded and then knew I wasn't being fair. "I—I'm sorry," I apologized. "It's just—just—what about the girls? You see," I went on, nearing Mr. Smith's chair as I spoke, "I don't even know what happened. How badly—?"

"I'm sure Doc will—" started Mrs. Smith, but I didn't even turn to hear the rest of her sentence.

Mr. Smith interrupted her. "Near as we can figure it," he said, "they was headin' home when thet there storm hit. The road likely got slippery. You know how it gets."

I nodded and Mr. Smith stopped for another sip of coffee.

I urged him on with another nod. *That storm was hours ago!* my brain was telling me.

"Well, they went off the road. The car flipped over. Miss Matilda wasn't able to go fer help. I suspect thet she has a broken leg—along with other things."

"Mary?" I asked numbly.

"She—she was pinned under the car—she couldn't go fer help either."

Pinned under the car. The words sent my world spinning. She was pinned under the car. She might be—she could be—

"Mary," I heard myself say again, but this time I was pleading. "Please, dear God, don't let Mary—"

"Too bad they had to lay there in the wet fer so long," Mr. Smith was saying. "Not many folks travel along thet road. Jamie an' me jest happened to—"

But I couldn't stand it anymore. I knew the rules. One was supposed to wait patiently until the doc had finished with the patient and given permission for you to go in to call at the bedside. *But this is Mary!* I had to know.

I headed for a door that would lead me to the inner part of the house. There were no sounds coming from anywhere but the kitchen, so I had nothing to guide me. "Josh," Mrs. Smith was calling from behind me, "Josh, you should—"

There was a stairway—and I took it. It led me to a hallway with doors leading off it. Four doors, in fact. I assumed them to be bedrooms and opened the first one. No one was in the room. I hurried on to the second. Doc was there. He was bending over the bed where someone lay quietly. I moved forward, part of me demanding that I turn tail and run.

It was Matilda. Her hair was wet and matted. Her face was bruised and had several tiny bandages. One leg, which lay partly exposed outside her blankets, was wrapped in whiteness. I guessed that Mr. Smith's diagnosis had been right.

I had never seen a human all bruised and broken before. She looked just awful.

At the sight of me she began to cry. "Oh, Josh. I'm so sorry," she sobbed. "The rain—the road just—"

Doc didn't scowl me out of the room. He even moved aside slightly. I knelt down beside Matilda and ran a hand over her tangled hair.

"It's all right," I said hoarsely. "It's all right. Don't cry. Just—just get better. Okay?"

I wanted to cry right along with Matilda, but I couldn't. My eyes were still dry—my throat was dry. I could hardly speak. I just kept smoothing her hair and trying to hush her.

Matilda seemed to quiet some. I stood to my feet and looked Doc straight in the eye. "How's—" I began. "How's—?"

"Mary?" he finished for me.

I nodded mutely.

"She's in the room across the hall," Doc said and turned his attention back to Matilda's arm.

I swallowed hard and turned back to the hallway. The first few steps made me feel as if I had lead boots. I could hardly lift my feet, and then I almost ran.

The door was closed and I shuddered as I turned the handle. Seeing Matilda had really shaken me. How might Mary look? She had been—had been *pinned* under the motor car. I didn't want to go into the room—but I had to know. I had to be with her.

I opened the door as quietly as I could. A small lamp on the dresser cast a faint light on Mary's pale face. There was a large white bandage over one eye, and another covering most of an arm lying on top of the sheets, which were pulled almost to her chin. Two heavy quilts were tucked in closely about her body. *What are all those blankets hiding?* I asked myself. *She was pinned—*

My eyes went back to her face. So ashen. So still. Her eyes shut. Was she—? *Is she already gone?* And then I saw just the slightest movement— almost a shiver.

In a few strides I was beside her, kneeling beside her bed, my hand reaching to gently touch her bruised face.

"Oh, Mary, Mary," I whispered.

Her lashes lifted. She focused her eyes on my face. "Josh?" she asked softly.

"I was so scared," I admitted as I framed her cheek with my hand. "I was afraid I'd lost you—that—"

"I'm fine," she whispered, moving her bandaged arm so that she could reach out to me.

"Don't move," I quickly cautioned, fearing she might come to more harm.

"I'm fine," she assured me again in a whisper.

"But—but you were pinned—"

"Miraculously pinned," Mary responded and she even managed a weak smile. "Oh, it caught me a bit on the arm—but it was mostly my coat sleeve. Doc says I'm a mighty lucky girl."

"You're—you're not hurt?"

Mary moved slightly, and groaned. "I didn't say I'm not hurt," she admitted; then seeing the look of panic in my eyes, she quickly went on, "But nothing major and nothing that won't heal."

"Thank you, God," I said, shutting my eyes tightly for a moment. Then I turned my full attention back to Mary. "I was so scared—so scared that—that—I didn't even know until—until Billie brought the word—"

"I'm sorry, Josh. We had no way of getting help. No way of letting you know. We couldn't get to a neighbor's. Couldn't even get to the road an'—your supper—?"

I stopped her. The memory of my impatience over our meal not being ready made me flush with shame. I looked at Mary's face, swept soft and pale in the lamplight. "I should have known. I should have realized before," I admitted. "I don't know how I could be so dumb."

"You had no way of knowin'," argued Mary. "Sometimes we are later than we plan. Things—things just happen that delay us. But to miss the supper hour—No one could have guessed that we were lyin' there in the ditch," Mary explained and I realized that once again she was finding excuses for me. She was always doing that. Getting me off the hook when I did or said something stupid.

I brushed a wisp of hair back from her face. "Maybe deep down inside I knew all the time," I murmured, "but it took something like this for me to realize—"

Mary's eyes were puzzled. "You couldn't have known 'bout the accident," she said.

"No," I answered. "I'm talkin' 'bout me—us. I was scared to death, Mary, that I'd lost you—before I'd really found you. I didn't realized until—until—" I stopped with a shudder.

"Josh," said Mary softly but insistently, "what are you talkin' about?"

I looked at her—my Mary, lying there white and quiet on the neighbor's borrowed bed. *She could have been killed!* My heart nearly stopped even at the thought. *I could have lost her. But she is still here—*

I tried to speak but I choked on the words. I swallowed hard and tried again, looking directly into Mary's eyes.

"I—I love you," I managed to blurt out. "Maybe I always have—at least for a long time, but—but I was just too blind to see it—until now. I—"

But Mary's little whisper stopped me. "Oh, Josh," she uttered, her hand coming up to touch my cheek, and I could see tears filling her eyes.

My own tears came then. Sobbing tears. I laid my head against Mary's shoulder and wept away all the pent-up emotions of the past dreadful hours. Mary let me cry, her hand gently stroking my head, my shoulder, and my arm.

I didn't bother to apologize when I was finished. Somehow I knew Mary wouldn't think an apology necessary.

"I love you," I repeated, conviction in my voice.

"Bless that ol' car," Mary said with a little smile.

"What?"

"Bless that car. An' the rain. An' the slippery road. An' our upendin'." Mary was smiling broadly now, but her words made no sense at all. I wondered if she maybe was hallucinating.

"Oh, Josh!" she exclaimed, her eyes shining, "you don't know how long I've wanted to hear you say those words."

"You mean—"

"I have loved you—just *forever*," she stated emphatically. "I began to think that you'd never feel the same 'bout me."

I felt as if there was a giant explosion somewhere in my brain—or in my heart. *I love Mary. Mary loves me back!* She would get better. We could share a life together. I could ask Mary to be my wife.

I had to put it in words—at least some of it. "You love me?"

Mary nodded. "Always," she stated simply.

"And I love you—so much."

Mary nodded again, her face flushed with color.

"Then—" I began, but stopped. I hesitated. It didn't seem fair to her somehow. Slowly I shook my head.

"No, no," I said. "I'm not gonna ask you now. Not yet. I'm gonna court you properly. Give you a little time."

A small question flickered in Mary's eyes.

"But not much time," I hurried on. "I couldn't stand to wait long now—now that I know. And one thing you can be sure of—I'm gonna come askin'—so you'd best be ready with an answer."

"Oh, Josh," Mary whispered.

Doc's timing couldn't have been worse. I had just kissed Mary—for the first time—and found it quite to my liking. Knowing now that she wasn't seriously injured, I drew her a little closer. Mary's eyelashes were already fluttering to her cheeks in anticipation of another kiss, her arms tightening about my neck. I don't know if it was the opening of the door or Doc's "Ahem" that brought me sharply back to reality, but I sure did wish he could have delayed just a few minutes more.

CHAPTER 12

Courtship

When I got back down to the kitchen, Grandpa and Uncle Charlie had arrived as well as Uncle Nat. Everyone was concerned about the girls, and the talk in the room was hushed and stilted.

But I wanted to shout and skip around the room like Pixie used to do. It seemed impossible that just a half hour earlier I'd had the scare of my life. Now I was walking on air. With all my heart I wished that I could share my good news—but I knew that wouldn't be right. Especially when Mary couldn't be with me. Yet I was fairly giddy with my new-found love. I felt several sets of eyes on me, and I wondered if they could see right through to my heart. I fought hard for some composure.

"They're fine," I said as nonchalantly as I could. "Both of 'em. Only scratches and cuts and bruises and a broken leg."

I knew that description didn't exactly go with "fine"—but I guess the group around the kitchen table was willing to chalk it up to my relief.

"Thank God!" said Grandpa, and Uncle Nat echoed his words. Then we were all bowing our heads while Uncle Nat led us in a prayer of thanksgiving. As soon as we had finished our prayer they wanted a more complete report.

"So Miss Matilda's leg *was* broken," Mr. Smith pointed out with a knowing glance around the room.

I nodded.

"What else?" prompted Grandpa, referring to Matilda again. "What other injuries? Is she hurt bad?"

"Just cuts and bruises. Nothin' that won't quickly heal. She was worryin' about the motor car." I was still uncomfortable that she would even think about that when all I wanted was for the two girls to be alive and well.

"An' Mary?" asked Uncle Charlie, his voice quivering a bit.

At the mention of Mary's name, my heart leaped in my chest and I was sure my face must be flushing.

"She's fine—just fine." I couldn't keep some excitement from creeping into my voice no matter how hard I tried. "She—she has some cuts—one above her eye, one on her arm. Lots of bangs and bruises—but not even a broken bone." They were all so intent in their worrying over the girls that they missed my intensity. Anyway, no one looked at me like I expected them to look. They just muttered words of relief and joy and glanced at one another with a great deal of thankfulness.

"She was pinned," insisted Mr. Smith, who must have told them that Mary, having been pinned under the automobile, could be in serious condition.

"Doc says she was lucky," I explained. "It was mostly the sleeve of her coat that was pinned to the ground. Oh, her arm is cut some—but it could have been bad—really bad."

There were murmurs again.

"Now, Josh, you just sit yerself right down here and drink a cup of coffee," Mrs. Smith was saying. "You are 'most as pale as a ghost."

All eyes turned back to me. And then the funniest thing happened. The whole world began reeling and spinning like you'd never believe. I felt myself a-reeling and spinning right along with it. But I didn't seem to be keeping up somehow—or else I was going faster. I tried to walk to the chair that Mrs. Smith had indicated, but my feet wouldn't work. Besides, the chair had moved. I didn't know what was happening to me.

I guess Uncle Nat caught me. I really don't remember. I came to my senses on Mrs. Smith's couch with Doc bending over me and a whole cluster of people hovering near. It took me awhile to realize what was going on, and then I felt like a real ninny. I mean, it was the girls who had been hurt in the accident and here I was doing the passing out.

I struggled to sit up, but Doc reached out a restraining hand.

"Take it easy, Josh," he cautioned. "You've been through quite a bit tonight."

Was it my imagination or was there a bit of a chuckle in Doc's voice? I remembered the scene that he had walked in on upstairs, and I felt my face flush. But no one else seemed to notice.

"Mrs. Smith is bringing some broth and crackers," Doc said. "You probably didn't have any supper."

I refused to be fed like a child, though I did obey Doc and sat up slowly. Then I carefully spooned the broth with its crumbled crackers to my mouth. My head soon began to clear and things came into focus again. With the return to awareness came the recollection of my recent discovery, and I could scarcely conceal my excitement.

As soon as I was able to convince Doc that I could walk a straight line, I stood to my feet.

"Can I see Mary—the girls—again?" I asked.

"Matilda is already sleeping—and Mary might be, too. I gave her a little medicine to help. You can peek in on her—but just for a moment. You hear?"

There was a twinkle in Doc's eyes and I caught a quick wink. I flushed and nodded, then headed for the stairs.

Mary was almost asleep when I crept quietly to her bedside.

"Doc says I can say good night," I whispered, "but I'm not to stay long."

Mary gave me a dreamy smile—brought on more by the sleeping powder than by my presence, I was sure.

"How are you feelin'?" I asked, taking her hand.

"Sleepy," she murmured.

I kissed her fingers.

"You're not backin' out on me, are you?" I teased. "Haven't changed your mind, now that you've had a little time to think on it?"

Mary tried a smile. It was weak and lopsided in her relaxed state. Fighting hard to keep her eyes open, she squeezed my hand. "You don't get off that easy, Josh," she teased back. "I'm holdin' you to your word."

I leaned over and kissed her. "I love you, Mary," I told her again. "That's never going to change."

She stirred and tried to smile again. Sleep had almost claimed her.

I knelt down by her bed, my arm around her blanketed form, my other hand still holding hers.

"Go to sleep," I whispered. "I'll stay with you until you do."

She moved her head so her cheek rested against mine and then she sighed contentedly. It was only moments until her even breathing told me she was sleeping soundly. I leaned to kiss her forehead before standing to my feet.

She slept so peacefully, so beautifully. *Even with bandages and bruises, she's the most—the most lovely girl in the world, my Mary,* I thought. I could hardly wait for the time when she would be well and whole again—for the real courting to begin.

"Good night, Mary," I whispered. And then after a quick look around to see if Doc was lurking in the doorway, I tried a new word I'd never used before, just to see how it sounded. "Good night, sweetheart."

It sounded just fine.

Matilda's folks hired a motor car to come and take her home where her mother could nurse her back to health again. Since school was nearly out for the summer anyway, they just let the kids go a little earlier than usual.

Mary went back home to her pa and sister Lilli. I missed her something awful at our house, but it did make things a bit easier for me in regards to courting. Like I said before, how does one go calling on someone who is right there in your own house? Mary said that her being home with her pa right now was working out good because it would help to keep tongues from wagging. I hadn't even thought on that, but if it made Mary feel more comfortable with the courting, then I was quite happy to put up with batching it for the summer months.

I was in for a great deal of good-natured teasing when family and friends learned that I was actually courting Mary. I didn't mind. In fact, I rather enjoyed it. I didn't see Mary objecting much to it either. It was rather nice to be known as a couple. Made us feel that we really belonged to each other in some way.

I took a hammer and mallet to the frame of the Ford and to the fender dents. It wasn't a good job, but when I was done she could at least stand on four wheels and make it slowly down the road again. I even bought some paint and touched up the scars, but she never did shine and sparkle the same. I will admit that I sure didn't like the way she looked, but to my surprise it really didn't matter as much as I had thought it would. *And*, I reminded myself, *the accident, dreadful as it was, had brought Mary an' me together.*

In the absence of Mary, Uncle Charlie took over the kitchen duties again. His cooking wasn't near as good as it used to be. I suppose there were times I might've even been tempted to complain a bit—but I wasn't noticing much what I was putting in my stomach anyway. I was far too busy thinking of Mary.

Every day that I was able to finish up my work early enough, I chugged over in my beat-up Ford to call on her. I brought her field flowers that I knew she admired. I kept finding little things in town to bring a shine to her eyes. I picked the produce from her garden and toted it over so that she and Lilli could can it for fall. I tucked a member of the new litter of kittens in my shirt as soon as its mama had weaned it and took it over to Mary as a surprise. I brought news of Grandpa and Uncle Charlie and shared bits of information about the farm and clippings on garden care from the farm paper. And we spent hours just talking—about our plans, our dreams, our goals, and getting to know each other better.

I was hoping for a fall wedding. Just as soon as the harvest was in and the fall work was done. But I hadn't yet mentioned that to Mary. I was waiting for just the right time. It seemed to me that the right time would be somewhere in the first part of August—after the haying was done and before I went full tilt into harvest. That would give me time to shop carefully for a ring—maybe even go into Crayton. It would also give Mary time to make her wedding plans after she had said yes.

But before all that could take place, I had to ask her pa for Mary's hand in marriage. I wasn't worried about the prospect. I was confident that Mr. Turley would not hesitate in giving us his blessing. He had already indicated as much on more than one occasion. Still, I planned to fit in with all of the social obligations and do my courting in the proper fashion.

I fervently hoped and prayed that all the farm work would move along properly so that as much of my time as possible could be spent with Mary and so that none of the fall work would delay our plans. Things did go along quite well until we hit mid-July. I had been sweating over the haying, hurrying it up so that I might pass on to the next stage of the work. Just getting from one task to the next seemed to somehow hurry the days along until I could be with Mary.

But rain stopped the scheduled progress. Gazing at the foreboding sky, I sensed it was going to be more than just a shower. I felt awfully agitated as I steered the tractor through the gate and headed for its shed. I cast another look at the sky. From one horizon to the other, dark, ominous clouds hung above me with no break in sight.

I thumped a fist against the steering wheel. *The dumb weather is going to go and throw everything off schedule!* I fumed.

I did the chores in a sullen mood and went in for supper. Uncle Charlie was serving up his tasteless stew—again. I couldn't help but think of Mary's cooking. The roasts, the biscuits, the gravy. Then my eyes noticed big pieces of peach pie sitting on the counter.

"Where'd the pie come from?" I asked, knowing without asking that it wasn't Uncle Charlie's doing.

"Mary brought it over. She came to pick the beets."

Mary had been here—and hadn't even waited to see me.

"She was goin' to take ya some lunch in the field, but thet dark cloud came up an' she knew she had ta beat it home," explained Grandpa.

I nodded then, simmering down some.

I ate the stew, all the time thinking ahead to that pie. It was just as good as I knew it would be. My longing for Mary increased with each mouthful, not because of the pie itself. It was just a reminder of how much I missed her.

After supper I sorta kicked around. I helped with the dishes, noticing how careless we were about keeping the big, black stove shined up. I made a hopeless botch of sewing a patch on my faded overalls. I tried reading the farm magazine, but the words wouldn't sink into my thick skull. Finally I gave up. Scooping up Pixie, I headed upstairs for bed. But I couldn't sleep. I just kept thinking about Mary. Pixie seemed to know that something was bothering me. She licked at my hand and whimpered softly.

"Sorry, Old Timer," I said, swallowing my frustration. "I just miss her. So much. I know that courtin' is s'posed to be a special time—yet I keep thinkin' that if it wasn't for courtin', she could be here now where she belongs—with us. I don't know how much longer I can stand this—this waiting."

It wasn't that Pixie was unsympathetic—but she was getting old. I guess she figured that she deserved a good sleep even if I couldn't manage one. She took one lick at my cheek and then excused herself, settling in at her customary spot at the foot of the bed.

I lay there in the darkness, hurt and lonely, angry with the rain that still relentlessly pounded the roof above my head. *It's slowin' down everything*, I reasoned unrationally. *I'll have to wait even longer for Mary.*

The next day it continued to rain. I wanted to go to see Mary, but I decided my mood was so sour that I'd better keep to myself.

In the evening I moped around again. I don't know how Grandpa and Uncle Charlie put up with me. Finally I motioned to Pixie and headed for bed.

She didn't spend much time sympathizing that night. She must have figured it was my problem. After one lick on the cheek she found her way slowly to the foot of the bed and settled herself in with a deep sigh.

I lay there listening to the wind and the rain and hating both of them along with my own feelings. I couldn't sleep. I tossed and turned and sweated and shivered by turn. Grandpa and Uncle Charlie finally went to bed. I saw the light pass by my door, and then I was in total darkness. At last I could stand it no longer. I crawled from bed and pulled my pants back on. I shrugged into my shirt and grabbed my socks and shoes. I knew I would be quieter going down the stairs barefoot.

I heard Pixie stir and whine a bit as though she was asking what in the world I was up to, but I didn't even stop to stroke her soft head. I couldn't stand it one minute longer. I was going to see Mary.

CHAPTER 13

Plans

I didn't even have the good sense to put on my slicker. Before I reached the barn I was soaked. The water ran down the brim of my hat and dripped down the back of my neck. The wind lashed against my body, sticking my pant legs to my limbs and whipping my chore coat tightly against me.

I didn't dare try to drive the car in this weather. Chester had been given the freedom of the pasture and rarely ever fed near the barn. But one of the work horses was humped up against the corral fence, back to the storm and head hanging down. I called to him and moved to open the barn door. The horse was only too glad to hurry in out of the wind and rain.

I felt almost like a traitor when, instead of producing a scoop of grain, I slipped a bridle over his unsuspecting head. He didn't fight it but he must have been disappointed.

I had to walk him every step of the way. As I had guessed, the road was already slippery and he wasn't nearly as sure of foot as Chester. Besides, the heavy clouds made the night so black one could scarcely see the trees by the side of the road.

"Why didn't I just walk?" I mumbled to myself as we trudged along, but even with my question I knew that the horse was better at picking his way through the mud than I would have been.

There was no light in the Turleys' windows when I turned old Barney down the lane. I knew they would have all retired long ago, and half my mind kept urging me to turn the horse around and go home in sensible fashion. But I couldn't. I just couldn't. The other part of me said I had to see Mary.

I slipped the reins over Barney's head and flipped them around a fence post. Even to get across the yard was a chore. I slipped and slid my way to the house. My teeth were chattering and my whole body drenched. I'd probably catch my death of cold—but now wasn't the time to be worrying about that.

Rather than pounding on the door and waking the whole household, I went directly to Mary's window. I tapped with my fingers on the glass, wondering if she would hear as she slept.

But the blind responded almost immediately and the curtain was lifted back from the pane.

"Who is it?" Mary called softly.

As should have been the case long before now, I felt like a complete fool. *What in the world am I doing? What on earth will Mary think?* My thoughts and emotions tumbled together. *And her pa?* If he had been willing to give his consent, he surely would change his mind now. I wanted to bolt and run for cover, but I didn't. I just couldn't. I had to see Mary.

"It's me. Josh," I said as clearly and quietly as I could, so Mary would hear me but her pa wouldn't.

"What is it? What's wrong?" Mary's voice faltered, and I realized for the first time that of course she would come to that conclusion.

"No. No, nothing," I quickly assured her. "I—I just had to see you— that's all."

Mary hesitated for just a moment. "Go to the door," she told me. "I'll be right there."

And she was, with a heavy housecoat wrapped firmly about her. She held the door for me and then gasped.

"Oh, Josh. You are soaked to the bone. You'll catch your death!"

I couldn't deny it, so I just shrugged.

"Get out of those shoes and socks," she ordered, just the right amount of authority in her voice. "An' that coat!" she added. "I'll be right back."

I laid aside my dripping hat and pulled myself free of the rain-heavy coat. I pulled off the soggy shoes and tugged away the sodden socks. Embarrassed, I noticed the terrible mess that I was making of the Turley entry.

Mary was back just as the last sock came off. In her arms were some dry clothes and a rough towel.

"Mitch left them," she explained. "Use his bedroom and get out of the rest of those wet things. I'll put on some coffee."

"But—but I'll leave a trail all across your floor," I said hesitantly.

"A trail I can wipe up. Now hurry," urged Mary.

I hurried. Actually it was rather fun to be bossed by Mary.

It didn't take me long to towel myself dry and slip into the borrowed clothes. But I was still shivering as I headed back to the kitchen.

"Your pa's gonna want my hide," I said through chattering teeth as I held my hands up to the newly fanned fire.

"My pa would sleep through a hurricane," answered Mary as she placed the coffeepot on the stove.

"He would?"

"He would."

Mary had returned to her room while I had been changing and was now fully dressed. She'd even taken the time to tie her apron carefully over her kitchen frock. I noticed, though of course I didn't comment, that Mary was not wearing one of her Sunday frocks as she normally did when I came calling and that her hair was not as neatly groomed as usual. She had simply tied it back from her face with a ribbon.

"If nothing is wrong—with anyone," she said carefully, not looking at me from her place at the stove, "do you mind telling me what brings you out on such a night as this?"

I held my breath. Was there just a trace of scolding in Mary's voice? Was she angry with me? She had good reason to be. I waited a moment. Mary waited also.

"I—I couldn't sleep," I answered lamely.

Mary swung around to get a look at me. She must have thought I'd taken leave of my senses. The scar across her forehead from the accident showed faintly in the lamplight. It reminded me of how close I had come to losing her.

"You—you couldn't *sleep*?" she echoed and turned back to put another stick in the fire and needlessly shift the coffeepot.

There was more silence. Mary broke it. "That seems—seems like a rather—rather poor reason to be out ridin' in a drenching rain, Josh," she said quietly.

"It—it is," I admitted. Then I hesitantly went on, "Except that I knew the reason I couldn't sleep was because—because I needed to see you."

Mary stirred slightly but she didn't turn around to face me.

"I—I missed you," I stammered to a conclusion.

I saw Mary's back stiffen slightly. "You could have told me that at a sensible hour, Josh," she reminded me.

She *was* angry with me. Mary, who never got angry with anyone—who always found some reasonable explanation for the dumb things I did—who fought for me, defended me. She was angry—and I had never had Mary angry at me before.

Rooted to the spot, I was unable to decide what to do next. I should never have come—not at such an unearthly hour, not in the rain that dripped muddy puddles all over her floors. I had been inconsiderate and stupid. I had been thinking only of my loneliness—not the feelings and rights of Mary.

But Mary was speaking again—and there was a tremor in her voice. "I waited for you all last evening—all this evening. I knew you weren't busy. There was nothin' you could do in the rain. But you didn't come. An' finally I—"

But I had stopped listening to the actual words and was hearing the meaning loud and clear. Mary wasn't angry with me because I had come. She was angry with me because I hadn't come *sooner*.

I looked at her straight, slim back with the neatly tied apron, the gently sloped shoulders set in a plucky line, the head stubbornly lifted. It was enough to propel me forward silently, swiftly. I slipped my arms around her and buried my face in her hair. Tears came to my eyes, though I don't really know why.

"Mary," I whispered, "I came because I couldn't stand being without you any longer. I was so upset about the weather I didn't want to come and burden you with it all. But I—I can't bear it without you. I—I want you to marry me—as soon as possible. I can't stand being apart like this. Please, please forgive me for coming so late but—"

Mary turned in my arms. She was looking directly at me when I opened my eyes.

"Oh, Josh!" she cried. "Yes. Yes," and her tears mingled with mine as she pressed her cheek against my face.

I don't know how long I might have gone on holding her, kissing her, had not the coffeepot boiled over. With a little cry Mary jerked away from me and rescued the pot.

"Sit down," she said, wiping her eyes with a corner of her apron and nodding toward a kitchen chair. She hurried to clean up the stove and pour the coffee.

She pulled her chair up next to mine and rested her chin in her hand. "Now, sir, you were saying—?" she teased.

I laughed right along with her. Then I sobered. "I—I guess I was asking you to marry me and not in the most orthodox way," I admitted. "Not at all like I had planned. I've just gone and ruined the whole thing. I—I mean— I had these great ideas. I spent hours thinking about it. Selecting just the right words. Not just—just blurting it out." I stopped and shook my head. "I'm—I'm sorry," I whispered.

Mary reached out a hand and touched my cheek. "Sorry? Sorry for missing me? For loving me?"

"For spoiling what should be one of your most treasured memories. For blundering into something that should be very special."

"Josh," said Mary softly, her eyes filling with tears and her voice soft with emotion, "I have just been told that I am loved. I have been asked if I will share your life—for always. Josh, it doesn't get any more special than that."

A tear slid unchecked down Mary's cheek. I reached out a finger and brushed it away.

"I don't even have the ring," I confessed.

"You'll get it soon enough," Mary defended me.

"I—I haven't even spoken to your pa."

"He'll give his blessing."

Then I took a deep breath. "That's not all," I admitted slowly as Mary waited. "I—I don't want to wait," I burst out. "Not till after harvest. Not a month. Not even a week if—"

Mary's eyes flew wide open.

"I know it's not fair. That it's terribly selfish. But you won't come home until we are married and I guess I couldn't bear it even if you did—but honestly, Mary, I don't want to wait any longer to get married. I know—I know it's not reasonable, that a girl needs lots of time to make her dress and sew her pillowcases and—and do whatever else it is that girls do, but—"

"Sunday?" said Mary.

"We really don't need a big fancy cake an' all the trimmings, and we've got pillowcases, an' you could wear that pretty blue—"

"Sunday?" said Mary again.

I frowned, not understanding.

"I think I could be ready by Sunday if you can," Mary said calmly.

"Sunday? Which Sunday?"

"Next Sunday."

"*Next* Sunday?"

"This is Tuesday," said Mary, laughter in her voice. "That leaves us Wednesday, Thursday, Friday and Saturday. Then comes Sunday. I can be ready by Sunday."

"By Sunday? Next Sunday?" I stammered.

"Are you trying to back out?" she teased.

"Of course not. I—I just supposed that you'd need—"

"You told me already that you planned to propose—remember? Well, there is no cake or dress ready—*yet*. But Lou said she would bake the cake, and I did find a piece of lovely material and I'm really quick with a sewing machine. Both Faye and Lilli will help. They promised. And as for the pillowcases, Josh—that is the *one* thing that *is* ready."

Neither of us had paid any attention to the cups of coffee that now sat cool and unwanted before us. I pushed my cup farther away so I wouldn't tip it over when I put my arms around Mary.

"Sunday," I grinned. "Sure. Sunday." Then my mind began to whirl. I had a few things that needed doing before Sunday, as well. How in the world would I get it all done in time? First thing in the morning I'd need to head out for that ring. Two rings, in fact. Then I'd—I'd—well, I'd talk to Uncle Nat and Aunt Lou, that's what I'd do. They'd have a whole list of things I needed to attend to. I had no idea.

Mary stirred. "Pa?" she said.

"You said he'd sleep through a hurricane," I reminded her.

"And so he would," Mary smiled, ruffling my still-wet hair, "but not through the marriage of one of his daughters. You'd best try to get a comb through that hair while I go wake him," and she kissed me on the nose and went off.

My head started working again. "Barney," I muttered. "I didn't care for Barney." I looked about the kitchen for a slicker, not wishing to get a soaking again. Mitch might not have left anything else behind.

I spotted a slicker belonging to Mr. Turley and took the liberty of borrowing it just long enough to lead the horse in out of the rain and toss a bit of hay in the manger.

When I returned to the kitchen I managed to comb my hair and smooth some of the wrinkles out of Mitch's worn shirt. There was nothing I could do about the short legs on my pants. Mitch wasn't quite as tall as I was.

Mary and Mr. Turley arrived in the kitchen together a few minutes later. He still looked sleepy and confused, but Mary was radiant. She had changed her dress to the pretty blue one I had referred to earlier. Her hair was carefully pinned up, too. She gave me an encouraging smile, and I took a deep breath and began my little speech.

"Sir, I realize that this is an untimely hour, and I apologize for that—but I would—would like to ask for your daughter Mary's hand in marriage, sir. I—I love Mary deeply and she has—has honored me by returning the love, sir, and—"

I guess Mr. Turley had heard enough or maybe he was just anxious to get back to bed. He reached out and shook my hand vigorously. "I'd be proud, Son," he said huskily. "I'd be proud." Then in a slightly choked voice, he added, "It woulda made her mama very happy."

Mary slipped an arm about me and gave me a squeeze and then she ran off to waken Lilli and tell her the good news.

No one went back to bed that night, not even Mr. Turley. We stayed up until the sky began to lighten. The sun never did come out because of the clouds, but I didn't mind them anymore. We talked the night away, making our plans for the coming wedding. Then with the daybreak I kissed Mary goodbye, borrowed Mr. Turley's slicker again and mounted Barney for the trip back home.

I got home before Grandpa or Uncle Charlie had left their beds. Pixie was waiting for me, though, sniffing at the door, a confused look in her eyes.

I picked her up and held her close. "Pixie," I told her, "I'm getting married. Not 'sometime,' but Sunday. *This* Sunday." Then I threw all caution to the wind and bellowed for the whole house to hear. "I'm getting married! Sunday! This *next* Sunday. You hear! *I'm getting married!*"

CHAPTER 14

Sunday's Comin'!

I sure was relieved when it stopped raining. I had lots of plans to make and traveling to do, and it would have been most miserable trying to do it all in the pouring rain.

As it was, the roads were rutted and muddy, so it was out of the question to use the motor car. Mostly I rode Chester, and the horse heard many declarations of love that week. Even if they weren't meant for him.

I don't know what I would ever have done without help from Uncle Nat and Aunt Lou. Even Grandpa and Uncle Charlie lent a hand—mostly doing up my chores while I ran about. They were 'most as excited as I was.

I asked Avery to be my best man. A lump came into my throat as I made my choice. I knew Willie would have been standing at my side had things turned out differently.

Mitch would have been my second choice—mostly for Mary's sake, but Mitch sent back word that he wouldn't be able to make it by Sunday, and he gave Mary and me his best wishes. So I went to call on Avery and he grinned from ear to ear as he accepted my invitation.

Mary picked Lilli to be her maid of honor, and she was pretty excited about it too.

True to her word, Aunt Lou made the cake. She also organized some of the church ladies who offered to serve a meal following the ceremony.

Everyone seemed anxious to help out, and I knew that some of the reason was because Mary had lost her mama.

Even Sarah got involved. "Mama says I can serve the punch, Uncle Josh," she informed me and I gave her a hug and told her I knew she'd do a great job.

On Thursday I made the long trip to get the rings since our little town did not have what I considered suitable for Mary. How I wished for better roads and the automobile, but Chester did the best he could. We were both tired when we got home that night; even so I cleaned up and headed for Mary's house. I figured Chester had used his legs enough for one day, so I walked. It wasn't that far to Mary's if you cut across the pasture.

She looked a bit surprised when she opened the door to my knock.

"Expectin' someone else?" I bantered.

"No, Josh," she laughed, drawing me in. "But I wasn't expectin' you either. I thought you'd be far too busy to come callin.'"

"I was," I teased. "I am—but I thought you might like to have this before Sunday." I held out the little box that held her ring.

Mary gave a little gasp and reached out her hand. I pulled the box back. "Not so fast," I told her. "You haven't yet told me what a wonderful guy you'll be marryin' come Sunday."

Mary glanced back at the table behind her. I could see bits and pieces of soft white material scattered over it.

"If you don't stop pesterin' me and be on your way, there won't be a wedding," she warned me. "No dress—no wedding."

I turned to look more closely at the table, but Mary put a hand over my eyes.

"No peeking," she commanded. "It's not fair to see the dress before the ceremony."

"Then come out to the veranda," I suggested.

"For only a short time," Mary insisted, pretending she wasn't interested in the little box, as she allowed herself to be led to the veranda bench.

I seated Mary, then dropped to one knee in front of her. I reached for her hand and spoke softly, "Mary Turley, would you do me the honor of becoming my wife—Sunday next?" I added with a hint of a smile.

Mary reached out to ruffle my hair, then changed her mind and let her hand fall to my cheek. "That would make me the happiest girl in the world," she said, her gentle smile saying even more than her words.

I caught her hand and kissed the palm—then opened the small box and removed the ring. Carefully I slipped it on Mary's slender finger. "Oh, Josh," she murmured, lifting the ring to study it and then brushing it against her lips, "it's beautiful."

She leaned forward to kiss me as I knelt before her.

"Now go finish that dress," I prompted. "I don't want any excuses come Sunday."

But we lingered for a while, just talking about our plans and comparing progress. It was dark before I headed back across the fields for home. I whistled as I walked in the light from the moon. I had never been happier. I had just placed my ring on Mary's finger, and Sunday promised to be the greatest day of my life.

We were to be married immediately following the Sunday morning service. Everything, as far as I knew, was in readiness. I would wear my wedding suit to church. Mary and Lilli would slip out and change at Lou's just as soon as the service ended. Lou had things well in hand for our reception dinner with the help of the parishioners. Mary's silver service had been polished to perfection and stood ready and waiting to serve the guests. I knew the silver pieces were far more than a teapot and coffeepot to Mary. They were a small symbol of her mother at our special occasion. I also knew that Mary would miss her mama even more intensely on her wedding day.

On Sunday I was up long before daylight, polishing and licking and patting for almost an hour. Something unheard of for me. Grandpa and Uncle Charlie didn't even tease me. They themselves were far too busy licking and polishing.

At last we were ready to go. We had decided the road was dry enough to take the motor car. I'd attempted to polish it up the day before, though it still bore the dents and scars of the accident.

We climbed in, I started up the Ford, and we headed down our long farm lane. I wouldn't be doing any speeding, even though I could hardly wait to get to town. Here and there along the road, mud holes waited for the unwary. And we sure didn't want mud stains on our carefully groomed Sunday suits and shoes.

We were there lots early, and I paced back and forth as I waited for Mary and her family to arrive.

Matilda came, though her leg was still in a walking cast. "I wouldn't have missed this day for the world!" she exclaimed and gave me one of her hurried, impulsive hugs. "I'm so happy for you, Josh," she bubbled. "Happy for both of you."

She welcomed Grandpa and Uncle Charlie with hugs as well. "Oh, I miss you," she cried. "All of you. The summer has seemed so long." There were tears in Matilda's eyes. "But I have good news," she hurried on. "I got the school I applied for near home."

"Ya mean yer not comin' back—?" began Grandpa.

"Oh, I couldn't," Matilda said softly. "I—I mean—I'm happy for Josh and Mary, but it wouldn't be the same now. I—mean—it wouldn't be fair to newlyweds to have someone—"

Grandpa nodded but I could see sadness in his eyes.

I had to admit that I hadn't even thought of Matilda's dilemma. But she was right. It would be better for Mary and me to get a good start on our own without an extra person around. It was going to be enough for us to share the house with Grandpa and Uncle Charlie. I would talk with Mary later about the new teacher, but as far as I was concerned it was just about time that one of the other neighbors took on boarding duty.

"But they've found a new teacher to replace me," Matilda's voice interrupted my thoughts, "and I've found a new school—so everything has turned out just fine."

At that point another interruption, and a welcome one—the Turleys arrived. Mary gave a squeal at the sight of Matilda and ran to meet her, her arms outstretched. They hugged and cried and hugged some more. I didn't mind. After all, Mary and I could look forward to a whole life together, beginning today. I just stood back and watched the goings-on.

Then I realized that I should be welcoming Mr. Turley. I had never seen him at church before, except of course for his wife's funeral. I shook his hand and smiled, not knowing exactly what to say. He gave a lopsided grin in return, looking a trifle uneasy. By then the girls had settled down, and Mary came over to me and slipped a warm little hand into mine. I whispered "Good morning, sweetheart," into her ear and made her blush prettily. It was time for the service, so we all moved inside the church doors and found places to sit.

The service seemed unusually long. It was probably a very good sermon— Uncle Nat's always were. But for some reason I had a hard time concentrating on it. When I took a peek at the pocket watch I had gotten from Uncle Nat and Aunt Lou, I was astounded to discover it was even earlier than usual when the service was dismissed! Then I again felt Mary slip her hand in mine for just a moment, and I squeezed it gently in return. It was our little message to each other that it wouldn't be long until we'd be standing before the minister pledging our vows of love and commitment—and also that we were anxious for that moment.

Mary slipped away to Aunt Lou's as soon as she could, and I paced about checking to see that everything was in readiness. There certainly was no need—a lovely bouquet from Aunt Lou's garden graced the altar, and candles had been lit on either side. I straightened my tie—again—and smoothed back a wayward lock of hair.

At last Sally Grayson took her place at the organ and Uncle Nat stepped to the front of the church. That was my cue to join him. I gave Avery a bit of elbow and wiped my hands again on a handkerchief Aunt Lou had provided. I moved awkwardly forward down the aisle that looked as long as our farm lane. Boy, was I nervous. I tried to swallow but there was nothing there. Eventually Uncle Nat's reassuring smile came into focus, and I turned beside him along with Avery, cleared my throat and waited, trying hard to avoid all those eyes looking right at me.

Lilli came down the aisle next. She looked just fine. I'm guessing Avery noticed, too, for even in my mental fog I thought he was watching her progress rather carefully.

And then there was Mary, poised at the door on the arm of her father, ready to take those few steps that would bring her down that aisle to me.

Her dress was simple but very appealing, and suited Mary perfectly. Her veil fell forward over her face, partly concealing her smile and her bright colored hair. But I could see her shining eyes, and they told me all I wanted to know.

"Dearly Beloved . . ." Uncle Nat's firm voice was an anchor for my whirling emotions. The ceremony was a short one—but I meant every word of the promises I made to Mary before God and many witnesses. From her expression and the directness of her answers, I knew she meant the promises to me as well.

"For richer, for poorer, in sickness and in health . . ." The words rang in my ears long after they were spoken.

But the words that really caught my attention were "to love and to cherish—till death us do part."

I had heard much about love. And I felt I understood it. I had no doubt in my mind about my love for Mary. But did I know what it meant to *cherish* her? Not much had been said in my presence about cherishing. I determined to do some looking into the meaning of that word at my first opportunity.

When the vows had been spoken, Uncle Nat indicated that I was to slip the wedding band on Mary's finger. And almost before I knew it he was pronouncing us man and wife. I lifted Mary's veil then to give her the expected kiss and could see fully the shine in her eyes and the flush to her cheeks. She was beautiful, my bride!

Uncle Nat presented us to the congregation. "Mr. and Mrs. Joshua Jones!" What a ring those words had! Mary and I looked at each other, and I felt an astonishment and excitement I'd never experienced before. I wished I could stop and kiss her again, but we had to go outside so folks could hug us and kiss us and give us their congratulations and throw rice and take pictures and all those usual things. I went through the whole thing in a daze. What a shame, too, because I wanted to always be able to look back with clear memories on this incredibly important day in my life.

We were finally ushered back into the church basement for the dinner. Guess folks were fairly hungry by then. For some reason I still hadn't felt hunger pangs. I went through all of the motions of eating, though, so Avery wouldn't rib me about being "lovesick."

Our friends gave little speeches and the Squire twins sang "Bless This House" and Matilda sang a lovely song based on a scripture text from the story of Ruth. Little Sarah played a piano piece. Lou said she'd worked hard on it all week. There were a few jokes here and there, and I guess they were funny—I mean, folks all laughed. All in all, the afternoon passed in fine style. Then we had gifts to open. In spite of the short wedding notice, the congregation did themselves proud. We got some real lovely things. Mary was thrilled over the linens, quilts, tea towels and such for our home, and that made me happy also.

At last people began to drift off to their homes, and finally it was just the family members who were left. I took off my suit coat and began to pack the gifts away in the car and help with the cleanup. Mary, still excited and happy, was also looking a bit tired.

We finally got everything cleared away or stacked in a corner. Then we slipped over to Aunt Lou's for a cup of hot tea and some slices of pumpkin bread. Mary took the opportunity to change from her wedding gown back into her Sunday dress, still looking like the pretty bride she was.

Mr. Turley excused himself as soon as Lilli and he had finished the light lunch. As he kissed Mary goodbye, he held her close. I saw tears in his eyes as he turned to go, and I wondered what it would be like to raise a daughter you loved so much only to give her over into the keeping of another man— particularly when her father had so recently lost his wife. I felt a pang of sympathy for Pa Turley. I followed him out to his team.

"Thank you, sir," I said sincerely, "for all you have done to make your daughter the beautiful person she is. I will love her always, I promise you."

Then we moved toward each other and I have never had such a bear hug. It suddenly hit me—*I have a pa! I mean, a real pa!* I hadn't had one of my own since I had been a small boy. I stepped back and looked at this man who now was a part of my life. I couldn't express all I was feeling. Instead I said, rather hoarsely, "How about comin' for supper—Wednesday night?"

He nodded his head and climbed into his wagon. "And Lilli, too, of course," I called after him. I watched him go until he turned the corner, and then I hurried in to tell Mary of my invitation to her pa—*our pa*—before I forgot.

It was late by the time we got home. We unpacked the car of the gifts and things Mary hadn't wanted to leave in town—things like her ma's silver tea service. We also had Mary's suitcases, although many of her belongings still waited in her downstairs bedroom, not having been moved back to her home after her accident.

There would be no honeymoon—at least not at the present. I was sorry about that. Mary and I had talked it over, and she had assured me she didn't mind. But still I felt she was a bit cheated out of what she rightfully deserved.

"After harvest," I'd promised her.

"Josh," she insisted, "the important thing is that we will be together, not *where* we will be together." I loved her even more for that.

As we carried Mary's personal things into the house, it became apparent that we menfolk, in all our hurrying and scurrying on short notice to prepare for the wedding, had given no thought to the room arrangements.

"Where should I put these?" Mary asked innocently.

"I—I—in—in my room, I guess," I began, but even as I said the words I knew that wouldn't work. I had the smallest room in the house. My tiny closet was already crowded with my few things. Mary's would never fit there too.

Grandpa cleared his throat. "The master bedroom," he said. "I'll git my things right outta there," and he moved to do just that.

"Oh, no," insisted Mary. "I wouldn't think of putting you out of your room, Grandpa."

A debate ensued, but Mary prevailed. It was finally decided that Mary and I would use Lou's old room. It was much roomier than mine and had a much larger closet. I carried Mary's things up to the room, and while she unpacked I busied myself making the evening coffee.

Mary was soon back down and took over in the kitchen. "Boy, is it ever good to have you back!" I teased.

"So you just wanted a cook!" she teased right back.

I looked around at Grandpa and Uncle Charlie. They both wore a very satisfied expression, and I figured that bringing Mary permanently into our family was about the smartest move I had ever made.

CHAPTER 15

Beginnings

With the weather turned for the better, our household back in order and my wife nearby, I got back to the haying again. Mary immediately took over her kitchen. My, how she did scrub and clean. I'm embarrassed to admit we menfolk had let things get even worse than I had realized.

She organized the rest of the house too—like moving the rest of my belongings from my old room to our new one, straightening the pantry, properly patching my worn overalls, sorting out the canning jars in the cellar and all sorts of other tasks. Every time I came in she was busy with something, though she often stopped to give me a hug and a kiss.

On Wednesday night the Turleys came for supper. Mary did herself proud, but then I guess her pa and Lilli were used to Mary's good cooking. I had to remind myself that Mary had likely cooked Pa Turley more meals than she had cooked for me.

Mary made life totally different for me when she was there. I could hardly wait to get in from the field at night—and I'd always enjoyed field work. I looked toward the house a dozen times a day just to see if I could catch a glimpse of her. And she often slipped out with a drink of cold water or fresh buttermilk. She even came to the barn when I was milking and laughed as I squirted milk to the farm cat, chatting about her day, her plans for the house or garden while I did my chores.

Of course Grandpa and Uncle Charlie were awfully glad to have her back as well. Uncle Charlie seemed to walk a little jauntier, and Grandpa took to chuckling a good deal more. Though I was quite willing to share Mary's return with them, I marveled at the fact that she was really mine—just mine—in a very unique and special way. Every day the word "marriage" took on a new meaning for me, and I thanked God over and over for her and that He had thought of such a wonderful plan.

Friday night after all the chores had been done, the supper dishes washed and back in the cupboard, and we were gathered around the kitchen table enjoying various activities, I suddenly remembered my resolve to look up the word *cherish*.

My dictionary was up in my old room, I thought. But when I climbed the stairs to get it, I found that Mary had moved my few books as well. I went to Lou's room—I had to get that change made in my mind, to stop thinking of that room as Lou's—it was mine now, mine and Mary's. After rummaging around for a bit I found the dictionary. I flipped through the pages and came to the word.

"Cherish—to hold dear, to treat with tenderness, to nurse, nourish, nurture, foster, support, cultivate."

Wow! I read it again—and again. *I had promised before God to do all that!* I marveled. It had seemed to me that my loving Mary was sort of beyond my control. I mean, who could help but love Mary? But "cherish"—that was different. Most of the words in the definition were words of choice, of action—not feeling.

I knelt beside our bed with the dictionary open before me, and I went over each word in the list one at a time, promising God in a new way that with His help I would fulfill my promise to Him and to Mary. I even did some thinking on just how I might keep the promises. I prayed that God would help me to be a sensitive and open husband for Mary.

When I had finished my rather lengthy prayer, I heard a stirring at the door. It was Mary.

"I—I'm sorry, Josh. I didn't mean to interrupt. I—I—"

But I held my hand out to her.

"I want to show you something," I said, indicating the open book before me.

I rose to my feet and sat down on our bed. Mary crossed the room and sat beside me.

"Do you know what 'cherish' means?"

"Cherish?"

"Yeah. What we promised to do for each other last Sunday."

"Oh!" Mary exclaimed, her eyebrows lifting.

I traced the dictionary meaning of cherish while Mary read the words for herself. When she finished, her eyes met mine. We just looked at each other for a few minutes and then Mary spoke.

"Rather scary."

She was so serious, so solemn, that I began to laugh. I laid the dictionary on the bed beside me and reached for her. She snuggled into my arms and put her head against my shoulder, but I gently turned her face so that I could look directly into her eyes.

"Mary Jones," I said, enjoying the sound of her new name, "before God and with you as my witness, I promise to love you, to hold you dear, to treat you with tenderness, to nurse you, nourish you, nurture you, foster you, support you and cultivate your individuality—till death us do part."

I had needed to refer to the dictionary beside me a few times during my little speech, but I meant each word in a new way. When I finished there were tears in Mary's eyes.

"Oh, Josh," she murmured softly, "I love you so much."

That was really all I needed to hear.

I kissed her again.

"When you left the kitchen and didn't come back, I was a little worried," she admitted. "I thought—well, I don't really know what I thought."

"It took me awhile to find the dictionary," I confessed, "and then when I did, I needed some time to think it through and to pray for God's help."

I shifted so I could gather Mary more closely to me. The dictionary fell unheeded to the braided rug. I was through with it for the moment anyway.

"I need to go make the coffee," Mary murmured, but she didn't sound too convincing.

"Uncle Charlie knows how to make coffee," I reminded her.

"Yes—" But I stopped her protest with another kiss.

"We don't get much time alone," I reminded her. "I want you to tell me all the ways you can think of for me to keep the promises I've just made."

It was some time later that the smell of fresh-perked coffee drifted up the stairs and into our room, and Mary and I smiled at each other. It seemed that Uncle Charlie had found the coffeepot.

I finally finished the harvest. It wasn't a great crop, but it would get us through. The fall had been a dry one. In fact, the last moisture we got was what had come in July to delay my haying. I smiled every time I thought of that rain. It had speeded up my marriage to Mary, and for that I owed the rain a great deal.

We decided to further postpone our honeymoon. Mary said it was silly to spend the money when it might be needed elsewhere.

Mary got all her garden taken care of, and we settled in for another winter—one totally different for us, for now we had each other.

Matilda and Mary kept in touch by way of letters. Matilda's leg had mended well and she was enjoying her new school. There were even hints that some young man she had met was becoming rather special to her.

In November Lou gave birth to another girl, Patricia Lynn, her coloring darker than Sarah's. This little mite demanded a bit more attention than Sarah had as an infant. I looked at Lou with her family of four and wondered what it must be like. Certainly it meant work and sacrifice—but I figured it would be more than worth it.

With Matilda gone we had decided to subscribe to our own paper. I guess we had all become intrigued with the reading material that kept us informed of the world's events. Many evenings were spent sharing the paper around the kitchen table.

We were saddened and horrified by the news reports of the stock market crash. It seemed to be of great significance to many people—even causing suicides and such things. I couldn't understand how that whole financial world worked, though I did feel sorry for those who were directly affected by it all.

It sure didn't have much affect on our life, however. I mean, no one in our small community ever had money to invest in any stocks or such. The results of that crash would have little, if any, repercussions in our town, I reasoned. We were a bit relieved when the newspaper stopped screaming horrid headlines about the crash and went on to something else.

Winter came—according to the calendar—though the look of things didn't change much. There was no snow to speak of. The weeks trailed on, following one right after the other, and the world outside was just the same—brown and bare. Mary kept talking longingly about snow, and I must admit I was wishing for a good snowfall, too.

Christmas was nearing, though it was hard to get in the holiday spirit without a white world outside. But family members began to sneak around on their way to hide something somewhere. Secret whisperings and plottings made life rather interesting and fun. Then the whole house began to smell like a bake shop as Mary turned out special cakes and cookies. I wondered if we'd finish eating all those things even by Easter time.

Mary talked about trimmings for the tree, and I hoisted the boxes down from the attic and she went through them. I'd never realized before what a sorry lot they were. Mary set to work making new ones and even spent some of her egg money in town to replace several items. I could see that she received a good deal of pleasure out of making Christmas something special for all of us.

I looked forward to Christmas—but it sure would be nice to have some snow.

CHAPTER 16

Christmas

One little skiff of snow dusted the ground a few days before Christmas, and Mary got all excited over it. But it sure didn't last long. Before it had even covered the ground it began to melt off again. Mary was disappointed and I was disappointed for her. There wasn't anything I could do about snow for her Christmas, though.

"Josh," Mary said on the Saturday before Christmas, "we need to get a tree."

That was no problem. We had lots of small trees down along the crick that would look good with Christmas decorations.

"I'll get one," I promised.

"I thought maybe we could go together," offered Mary, and I grinned in appreciation.

"Great! When would you like to go?"

"Right after dinner—if that's okay with you."

"Fine."

And so the two of us headed out for the crick bottom right after the noon dishes were done.

It was colder than it had looked. I wondered if Mary might not be bundled up warmly enough, but I guess the vigorous walking helped keep her warm. Anyway, each time I asked her, she assured me that she was just fine.

The farm dog went along with us. Truth was, any time one of us went out, we didn't get far without Fritz at our heels. We didn't mind. It would have been fun to have Pixie along too, but she couldn't run very well anymore. She seemed to have arthritis like Uncle Charlie. Anyway, she didn't do any more walking than absolutely necessary. I even carried her upstairs each night. Most of her day was spent curled up in her little box behind the stove.

The pond in the pasture was frozen, and we took some time to slide back and forth. Sorta like being a kid again.

"We should have a skating party," enthused Mary, but I really didn't know who would want to come. All our old friends were either married with youngsters to care for or else had moved away.

For some reason I thought of Willie—maybe because he had skated with me on this very pond. Boy, I missed the guy. It still didn't seem real to me that he was gone—actually in heaven. I could see his face so plainly, could hear his banter and laughter—could sense his feel of mission and commitment when he spoke intensely of the needs of African villages for the gospel. Boy, I missed Willie.

I thought of Camellia. She had gone across the ocean to Willie's people now. I put money for her support in the collection plate the first Sunday of each month, and Uncle Nat forwarded it on to the Mission Society. We got an occasional prayer letter from Camellia, too. She loved Willie's Africans. She was kept busy with her nursing, for they were a poor people and many of them, old and young alike, had physical needs. Camellia was glad God had called her to this work. I still had a hard time picturing Camellia, the golden girl, trudging through destitute villages, visiting dirty, unkempt huts with medicines and love. But God did wonderful things with those who obeyed Him. Used people in ways we would have never dared suggest. Mary and I prayed daily for Camellia.

Mary brought my thoughts back to the present with a jerk when she lost her balance and ended up on her back in the middle of the ice. I was afraid she might have hurt herself, but she was laughing as I bent to help her and soon we were both down on the ice rolling and laughing.

It was fun until old Fritz jumped right into the middle of the fracas. He was barking and prancing and taking quick licks at our faces. By now Mary and I both decided we'd had enough, so we scrambled to our feet and started off again on our Christmas tree quest.

I'd figured it would be a quick, easy task. But with every tree I pointed out, Mary was sure we could do just a bit better. So on we walked, checking out tree after tree.

I was beginning to worry about getting home to do the choring when Mary at last found the very one she was looking for. It was about my height, with full, even branches.

"It will fit just fine in the parlor," Mary exclaimed and then added matter-of-factly, "Of course I will need to trim it up a bit."

I smiled wryly. She could trim it all she pleased just as long as we could cut the thing and get on home.

It wasn't hard to cut it down. It was a bit harder to get it home. There was no snow, so we couldn't drag it because Mary was afraid of damage to some of the branches—*probably the ones she'll eventually trim off anyway,* I thought but didn't say. That meant we had to carry it. Mary insisted on sharing in the effort. I lifted the big end and she took the small one, but carrying a tree, particularly one that has large, full branches and sways in the middle, is not an easy task.

We tripped about as much as we walked. The dog didn't help matters. He kept running around the tree and our feet, constantly getting in our way and tripping us up even more.

"Why don't *I* carry it?" I finally suggested.

"Oh, Josh. It's too heavy for one person."

I could have told her that it was too heavy for *two* people—but I didn't.

"I think it would be easier," I dared insist.

Mary looked reluctant. "Do you want it on your back—or your shoulder?" she finally conceded.

"My shoulder," I decided.

"I'll help you lift it up."

It didn't work very well that way either. Possibly it would have if Mary had allowed me to trim off some of the bottom branches—but she wanted the branches to come right down to the parlor floor. It was prettier that way, she said. So I was trying to carry a tree on my shoulder with branches right down to the bottom of the trunk. They poked me in the face and knocked off my hat.

I finally dumped the thing to the ground, and Mary gave a little gasp, fearful that I had broken some of her precious branches—which there were far too many of anyway.

"Look," I said, a little out of patience, "why don't I just get the team and wagon and come and haul it home?"

"Can you drive back in here with the team and wagon?" Mary wisely asked. I would have had to cut my way in and out again. There were no trails except those the cattle had made, and they were too narrow for a wagon to travel.

"Then I'll hook Barney to the stoneboat," I threw out, keeping my voice even.

Mary tipped her head slightly to consider it.

"It should work," she nodded in agreement. "You can sorta snake your way in and out among the trees."

I didn't like her description. "Snaking" didn't seem like much of a way for a man to travel.

"We need to put it someplace so you can remember where to find it," Mary continued, and I got even more huffed at that.

"I'll remember," I said flatly. "You think I'm an old man or somethin'?"

Mary looked a bit hurt by my response. "Of course not," she assured me apologetically; "but the trees all look alike an' *anyone* can forget."

She stressed the anyone.

"You forget that I was raised on this land," I reminded her loftily. "I know this crick bottom like the back of my hand. Roamed through here all my life—fishin' and huntin' cows."

Mary nodded but said nothing more.

We stashed the tree up against two anchored ones and started off for home. I checked the sky. The sun was already low on the horizon. I would need to hurry to get back for the tree before dark.

Mary reached out and slipped her mittened hand into mine, and I gave hers a bit of a squeeze. I wanted her to know I really wasn't mad at her or anything. We walked in silence for a while and then Mary began to chat about how she was going to decorate the tree and how pretty it would look. I could sense how special it was to her, and I was glad I hadn't insisted on lopping off some of the lower branches. "Nourish and nurture her" flashed through my mind, and I gave her hand another squeeze.

At home Mary went right on to the kitchen to get busy with supper, and I went to the barn to get old Barney.

It didn't take me long to get down to the crick bottom with the stoneboat, and I figured out how I'd slip right in, pick up that bulky tree and get back to the farmhouse in a jiffy.

I drove directly to where we had left it—but it wasn't there. Nor were the two trees we had braced it against. I couldn't believe my eyes. I started looking around, this way, that way, and the more I looked the more confused I got. I had to use the axe a few times to untangle the stoneboat from the brush, and that didn't make me so happy either.

All the time that I was searching, it was getting darker and darker. And I was getting madder and madder. I don't know why. It was my own dumb fault, but I was mad at Mary. I don't really know what she had done. Just been right, I guess. Anyway, I kept right on looking, too mad and too proud to give up. At the moment I couldn't think of anything more humiliating than showing up at home without that tree.

But in the end I had to give up. I was so confused I didn't even know which direction to point old Barney to get him back to the barn again. That made me even madder. Not being any snow, I didn't even have tracks to follow—though I was glad for that in a way. I sure wouldn't have wanted anybody to have followed my tracks through that brush. They'd have laughed at me for sure.

I finally conceded defeat and just gave Barney his head. He weaved in and out—*snaked*, if you will—and finally came out into the open again. There across the field were the welcome lights of the farmhouse.

Mary ran to meet me as soon as I pulled into the yard. If she was disappointed about me not finding her tree, she didn't voice it.

"I was worried," she said instead.

"Too dark," I sorta growled. "I'll have to go pick it up later."

"Supper's ready," she told me. "Do you want to eat before you chore?"

I nodded—which she probably couldn't see considering how dark it was. Mary started back to the kitchen. "I've fed the pigs and chickens," she called over her shoulder, "and Grandpa carried the wood and water."

It should have made me feel great. Here I was coming in late without having accomplished my errand and chores still ahead of me, and I found them half done already. But it didn't make me feel great. It made me even madder. *Don't they think I can even do my own work?* I fumed.

I put Barney back in the barn and fed him. No soft words or appreciative pats for him tonight. I pushed a barn cat out of my way with a heavy-booted foot. He was lucky. I felt like kicking him.

On the way to the house it hit me. I was acting like a spoiled child, not a married man—and certainly not like a Christian husband who had promised to *love* and *cherish*, with all that it meant. Mary had done nothing to deserve my wrath. She was trying to make Christmas special. For me, for Grandpa, for Uncle Charlie. She had wanted a special tree. Had tried hard to help with the work of getting that tree. It wasn't her fault I couldn't find my way around my own woods.

But she had been right, she would likely—likely look at me with I-told-you-so in her eyes. *If she does*—

But I stopped right there beside the woodshed and prayed, reminding myself of all of my promises and asking God again to help me keep them. It didn't change my circumstances any, but it did make me a better supper companion.

The tree was not mentioned or the tree ornaments that sat waiting in the parlor either. Nor did Mary look at me as I had expected her to. She found something to busy herself with that Saturday evening and chatted away as if everything was just fine.

I loved her for it. It seemed that Mary was doing a much better job of keeping her promise to "cherish" than I was.

On Monday morning I hooked Barney up again. I still didn't know how I was ever going to find that tree, but I'd find it if I had to spend the whole day looking.

Then Mary complicated things. She came from the house, all bundled up, and smiled sweetly at me. "Thought I'd ride along," she stated in a matter-of-fact tone.

My head was spinning. *I'm going to be humiliated again.* I'd boasted of knowing my own crick bottom, of having a near-perfect memory. Both statements had proved to be false. I took a deep breath, gritted my teeth and directed Barney to head for the woods.

Halfway there I got this brilliant idea. I gave Mary a big grin and motioned for her to scoot up beside me.

"Wanna drive?" I asked her. Her face didn't brighten as I expected. For a moment I feared she might turn me down. Mary had her own little code of what rights belonged to the man of the family. But when I passed Barney's reins to her, she grinned and accepted them without further comment. I inwardly sighed with relief.

I was afraid as we neared the brush that she might pass the reins back to me. I had to do something to prevent that. I leaned over and lifted the axe to my lap.

"You drive," I said as casually as I could, "an' I'll cut any little shrubs that get in our way."

Mary just nodded.

We reached the woods, and she began to "snake" her way through with that stoneboat. Not once did she get hung up on anything, so I never got a chance to use that axe.

And would you believe it, she drove straight to that tree.

I made no comment as I loaded it. It filled up the stoneboat, so Mary and I had to walk back. She didn't seem to mind, and I sure didn't. On the way home she left the driving to me. I never even thought to share it. I was too busy wondering just how she had done what she had done. I mean, dead on! Right to where that tree stood waiting.

When we got back to the farmyard Mary went in to finish the washing. I put Barney away and went to do up a few odd jobs. I knew that in the evening we would be decorating the tree in the parlor. I looked forward to it now that we finally had the thing home.

We ran into another snag the next day. I didn't see it coming, though I should've been smart enough to sort it all out beforehand. You see, ever since Lou and Nat had married, we had always spent our Christmases with them. Lou had made the arrangements, cooked the dinner and everything. All we fellas ever did was show up.

Well, that's not quite true. We did our own shopping, wrapped our own gifts—in a manly sort of way—raised the turkey that we chopped the head off and plucked. But other than that, Lou took care of everything. I have no idea why I expected it to just remain that way.

Anyway, I should have been alerted when Mary said one morning as Christmas neared, "Do you mind if I invite Pa and Lilli for Christmas dinner?"

Of course I didn't mind. It sounded like a good idea to me, and Lou always cooked plenty of everything. We ate leftovers for days after Christmas was over.

So I heartily agreed to the arrangement. I even rode over to the Turleys and extended the invitation myself. I stayed awhile too. Just to chat with Pa Turley and to play a couple games of checkers. He didn't have much male companionship now that Mitch had left home, and I guess he missed it. Mary was happy when I returned with the news that they would be glad to come.

The next day Mary spoke about Christmas again. "I think you can bring in the gobbler now," she informed me. "I want to get it dressed and out of the way so everything won't need to be done at the last minute."

That made perfect sense to me. We men had always left it to the last minute simply because nothing else needed doing then for us. I had no idea what Mary's many tasks were going to be, but she was always powerful busy with something.

I killed the gobbler, plucked off the feathers and carried him to Mary's kitchen. She took over from there and soon he was ready to be hung outside in the shed where he would be kept frozen until needed further.

That night as we retired, Mary spoke again—and this time the truth of her Christmas plans finally got through to me. "Would you like to invite Nat and Lou?"

At first I couldn't understand the question at all.

"Invite—to what?" I asked innocently.

"For Christmas."

"We don't bother none with invitations," I said to Mary, tossing another sock in the corner. "We've done it so long now everybody just knows without invitations."

I figured in my ignorance that Mary had just reversed the order without meaning to.

But Mary hadn't reversed the order. She had known exactly what she said. "What do you mean?" she asked, stopping in the middle of pulling the pins from her hair.

"Well, I suppose the first few Christmases Lou invited us. After that— well, we just knew that every Christmas we would go there. Oh, not always 'there.' A few Christmases Lou's packed everything up and had the Christmas out here at the farm. But mostly, unless it's planned beforehand, we go on into town."

There was silence for a few minutes. Mary started to slowly unpin her hair again. "That was before you had a wife," she said softly.

I looked up then. Something in her voice was sending me funny messages.

"What do you mean?" I asked, wondering if I should have caught it already.

"That was before you had a wife," she repeated slowly as though I was dense or something.

"What does that have to do with it?" I dared ask.

Mary's voice raised a bit and she answered rather quickly, "It has a good deal to do with it, I should think."

"It hasn't changed the fact that we are still family—that Lou—"

But Mary swung to face me and I could see a stubborn set to her chin and a hurt look in her eyes. I didn't get any further. At least not just then.

The silence hung heavy again.

Finally Mary broke it. She fought to keep her voice controlled—even.

"Josh," she ventured, "what do you think has been goin' on around here for the past several days?"

I shrugged. I couldn't follow her.

"The bakin'? The plannin'? The tree? The turkey?" Mary went on.

I shrugged again. I had the feeling that no matter what I said I was going to be in trouble.

"Christmas, Josh. Christmas," Mary said with emphasis. "I have been gettin' ready for our first Christmas. Now, if I wasn't going to be allowed to *have* Christmas—why've I been allowed to *prepare* for it?"

"It's—it's not that you aren't allowed," I stammered.

Mary ran a brush through her hair. "Good," she said simply. "Then we will have Christmas as planned. Do you want to invite Nat and Lou?"

Oh, boy! Talk about not communicating. We were running full circle.

I stood to my feet and crossed to stand in front of her. Somehow I had to get things cleared up.

"Mary," I said in exasperation, "we always—Grandpa, Uncle Charlie and me—go to Aunt Lou's each Christmas. Every year. We—"

But Mary had turned her back on me. It made me angry. I wanted to reach out and turn her around again. Make her face me.

"That was before," she insisted.

"Before? What does that have to do with it? Before! It doesn't change Christmas. We are all *still* family. Families are to be together at Christmas. Not just—just little chunks of them. All of them. Can't you see? Don't you understand?"

Mary wheeled around then. There were tears spilling down her cheeks. "No," she stated with a sob, "*you* don't see. I've worked for days, Josh, no—*weeks*, to get ready for this first Christmas. Always before I've had to leave you at Christmas and go home to my family. Well, now *we* are family, Josh. You and me. I wanted this Christmas to be ours. To be special. I thought you wanted it, too," she sobbed. "But now—now you say that Christmas is to be a trip to town—to Lou's to have dinner together. Well, I care about the family as much as you do, Josh. I love Lou and Nat—and the kids—but that's—that's not the way I had planned our first Christmas."

Mary was crying hard by the time she finished her speech. I found myself wondering if Grandpa and Uncle Charlie were hearing every word. The walls certainly were not soundproof. Well, let them hear. This was our business.

I tried one more time.

"It's not that I don't want our Christmas to be special," I argued. "To me it is always special to be with Nat and Lou."

Mary reached for a corner of her nightgown and wiped away her tears. She didn't cry any further, and I thought I had won. That she had finally listened to reason.

She didn't say "very well," or "fine," or anything like that. In fact, she didn't say anything at all. She just laid her brush back down on the dresser and walked around the bed to slip into her side. She even allowed the customary good-night kiss after I had put out the light.

It was some time in the middle of the night that I awakened. I had the feeling that I'd heard something, but as I lay there in the darkness, straining to hear whatever it had been, there was total silence. And then it came again. Just a shaky little sob from Mary's side of the bed.

I rolled over then and reached out a hand to her.

"Mary?" I questioned in a whisper. "Mary, is something wrong?"

"Oh, Josh," she sobbed, slipping her arms about me. "I'm so sorry. I shouldn't have—shouldn't have been so insensitive. I—"

"What are you talking—?" I began, not understanding, completely forgetting our little tiff at bedtime.

"Of course you want to be with your family, like always. I'm sorry that I—"

So that was it.

I held Mary and let her cry. All the time I thought on what had transpired. For the first time I began to see and understand Mary's thinking. We were family now—Mary and I, and with the years we might be blessed enough to have other family members join us. We had the right and the responsibility to make our own traditions—our own Christmases. Sure, the rest of the family would always be dear to us—and we could share and be with them—but not *lean* on them. Not depend on their traditions anymore.

My hand patted Mary's shoulder, and I lay staring into the dark thinking and praying a bit, too.

I had slipped again. I had failed in cherishing Mary. I had not been sensitive to her needs, had not nurtured nor supported her. Would I ever learn?

"Mary," I whispered against her hair, "you were right and I was wrong. I'm sorry. Truly sorry."

There was silence again. I dared to continue.

"We should have our own Christmases. *We* are family. It's important to—to both of us."

Mary tipped her face in the blackness. "It's all right," she said. "I don't mind. Really."

But I wasn't turning back now. "I'll go see Aunt Lou tomorrow," I informed Mary. "Grandpa and Uncle Charlie can still go. We'll have Lillie and Pa here."

"No," said Mary. "We'd be splitting up family. That wouldn't be right."

"I'll talk to Lou," I insisted. "She'll understand."

"*I'll* talk to Lou," said Mary. "We'll work it out."

"But—" I began. Mary reached one finger out in the darkness and placed it on my lips.

"Trust me?" she asked simply and I nodded my head against her finger to assure her that I did.

CHAPTER 17

Adjustments

Grandpa drove Mary in to see Lou the next day. He was looking for an excuse to go into town anyway. I figured he had some more Christmas shopping to do.

Everything worked out just fine. It was decided that Christmas would be at our house with Uncle Nat, Aunt Lou and family, Pa Turley and Lilli, all around our table. Mary would take care of all the arrangements for the dinner. Grandpa confided to me that he felt Lou was a bit relieved. The new baby was still keeping her up nights a good deal.

Lou and Mary also agreed that in the future each would take turns having Christmas dinner. That sounded like a sensible arrangement to me. It gave both women a Christmas "off" and yet allowed each to have Christmas just her way on the Christmas when it was her turn.

I was proud of Mary. She had been sensitive and caring—and yet had shouldered her share of family responsibility.

That Christmas turned out to be the best I had celebrated up to that point in my life. Mary did a fine job with the dinner—just like I'd known she would. The turkey was cooked to perfection, the potatoes fluffy and the gravy as smooth as silk. All the good things she had been baking over the previous days appeared on the kitchen sideboard—right along with the honored silver tea set from which she served the tea and coffee.

The weather was fine—though we never did get our Christmas snow, nor any other snow, for that matter. The families arrived early and left late, and we all had a great time together.

Of course Lou's four little ones added a lot of spark to the occasion. Sarah was too grown-up now to be relegated to the children's status. Jonathan too had matured a lot over the summer months and wasn't nearly as hard to keep track of, but Timmy more than made up for him. Someone had to watch the boy every minute. I finally had to carry Pixie up to the bedroom and shut the door on her. Timmy insisted on petting her and holding her, and poor old Pixie's bones were too fragile for Timmy's kind of handling. He tried to be careful, but being a small boy he was pretty awkward at showing his affection.

Baby Patty slept a good share of the day. Aunt Lou ruefully commented that it might mean a long, wakeful night. I had no idea what that was like and wasn't particularly interested in finding out.

Pa Turley really seemed to enjoy being with the family. He watched the antics of the children with loud guffaws and slaps to his knees. I couldn't help but wonder, *What'll he think of having grandchildren of his own?*—though I felt I knew.

Lilli was quiet. She helped Mary in the kitchen, but her mind didn't seem to be on it much. I wasn't too surprised when along about midafternoon Avery appeared at our door. I invited him in but he declined. Said he'd come to take Lilli for a bit of a drive. We teased them some, but they just flushed and bundled up to get away from all of us.

When they returned Avery accepted our invitation to share leftover turkey and homemade buns. We formed a little foursome and played dominoes. Mary and I won, hands down, but I don't think our opponents were doing too much concentrating on the game. Avery and Lilli were the last to leave that evening.

We were all tired but happy when we retired. Mary and I cuddled close in Aunt Lou's old bed and talked over each of the day's happenings. It was fun to go over it all again.

"You know which gift I liked the very best?" Mary asked me.

"Which?"

"The mirror. The new mirror."

I wasn't really surprised. I'd noticed her stretching or stooping, trying to see herself in Lou's old mirror. The gilt was wearing off at just the wrong place.

"What was your favorite?" asked Mary.

"Oh, boy! That's tough. I liked them all."

But Mary wasn't to be put off so easily.

"Come on, Josh. Favorite."

I reviewed the gifts Mary had given to me. "I guess the pullover sweater," I said after much thought.

"The sweater?"

"And do you know why? Because you made it yourself. For me." I paused a moment and then went on with a chuckle, "And you know why else?"

"*Why* else?" teased Mary. "Is that proper English?"

"Of course it is. *Why* else would I say it?" I bantered back and Mary gave me a little jab in the ribs.

"Okay—so *why* else?" she asked me.

"Because it actually fits," I laughed. "It has two arms—and they are the same length. It has a hole up top for my head and one at the bottom for my waist."

By now Mary was chuckling too but she gave me another playful jab. "Are you saying you didn't think I could knit?" she accused me.

"No," I answered, dodging away from another jab, "but I have seen a few sweaters in my day that were made by girlfriends or new brides. You had to ask to be sure what the thing was."

Mary gave me one more jab. That one I figured I deserved.

On a cold, windy day near the middle of the month, I came in one morning to find Mary in tears. I couldn't think of anything I had done, and I was sure Grandpa or Uncle Charlie wouldn't do anything to make her weep. For a moment I feared Mary might be ill, and that scared me something awful.

I didn't ask questions. I didn't have time. Mary threw herself into my arms and sobbed against my shoulder. By now I was really worried. My eyes traveled to meet Grandpa's across the room, but he wouldn't look at me. He was busy staring out of the window at the bleak, sunless day. Uncle Charlie was nowhere to be seen.

In my mind I frantically reviewed family members, wondering if bad news had come in some way while I'd been out. But I hadn't heard a horse, and the farm dog had been with me all the time. His ears were sharper than mine, and he most certainly would have heard if someone had come.

"Sh-h-h. Sh-h-h," I tried to quiet Mary, brushing aside strands of fine hair from her tear-streaked face.

"Sh-h-h. Tell me. Tell me what's wrong."

Mary swallowed hard and tried to get control. "It's Pixie," she finally managed to gasp out. "I found her in her box behind the stove."

"Pixie?"

Mary burst into fresh tears and clutched me even more tightly.

I wanted to free myself and check on Pixie. The little dog might be in need of some attention. But I couldn't just leave Mary. Not the way she was feeling now. I held her more tightly and rubbed her shoulder and patted her back.

When her tears finally subsided, I put her gently from me and went to kneel beside the stove to check on Pixie. It was far worse than I had feared, and my whole being rushed to deny it. The little body was lifeless. There was nothing I could have done. She was already stiff and cold.

Tears came to my own eyes. I picked her up as gently as I could and ran my hands again over the silky sides and let my fingers toy with the floppy little ears. *She's been a good dog—a good friend,* I mourned. Pixie had been with me ever since my dearly loved Gramps had found her for me so many years ago. Boy, would I miss her. It reminded me of how much I missed Gramps.

I knew Pixie was old, that she had been stiff and arthritic and in pain much of the time. She was far better off having just slept her way out of life. But I still fought against the reality of it. If I'd had the power right then, I'd have brought her back.

I didn't have that power, so all I could do was hold her up against my chest. The small body sure didn't feel like it usually did. I was used to her little tail wagging gently as I petted. I was used to a little lick with a pink tongue every now and then. I was used to warmth and energy. And now there was only the quiet, stiff, lifeless little form. I felt almost repelled by it—but I couldn't put her down. I just kept running my hand over her, speaking to her as though I thought she should awaken.

Mary came to where I knelt and laid a hand on my head, running her fingers softly through my hair.

"I'll fix a box," she said quietly.

For a moment I wanted to protest. Pixie had been *my* dog. I would fix the box. And then I remembered how much Mary had loved her too and I nodded in agreement, the tears flowing again.

I pulled Pixie's small bed out from behind the stove and laid her gently back down. Without a backward glance I arose, pulled my heavy mittens back on and left the kitchen.

I found the shovel and a pick and chose a spot in the garden. I wanted her to be down under the trees beside the grave of my first little pup, the one I had named Patches. *Gramps brought me that puppy too,* I remembered as I raised the pick above the frozen ground. It was hard digging. Maybe that was good. I needed something difficult to concentrate on for the moment. I put my full strength behind each swing of the pick. Then I shoveled out the frozen clumps of dirt, making a hole big enough to hold a small box. A small box with an even smaller dog.

Tears froze on my cheeks as I worked. *She might've been small,* I thought, *but she was all heart.* All heart and love. I'd never known anyone who had loved me like my small dog had. She asked no questions, demanded no apologies. She just loved me—Josh Jones—just as I was.

I guess I got a little carried away on the size of the hole. I made it bigger than it needed to be, but perhaps I wasn't ready to go back to the house yet. I needed a little more time to be alone. With Pixie's death went my last visible memory of Gramps. Oh, I had lots of memories. Things that I treasured as I pulled them out and thought on them—which I did often. But with Pixie those memories had been different, more vivid. Each time I picked up the little dog I could see the age-softened hands of Gramps as he handed her to me for the first time.

I remembered Aunt Lou sharing with me how Gramps had walked into town after my first puppy was killed and searched the town streets until he had found me another puppy. I remembered too how small Pixie was, and how Gramps had told me that she would need special care and love.

Pixie had been my little love-gift, that's what she had been. It was Gramps special love for me that prompted the giving, and it was Pixie's and my special love for each other that had helped us share so many things over the years.

And now she's gone. I had known all along that one day it would happen, but I had just kept pretending in my heart that I could hold it off somehow.

I finally stopped my digging, wiped the frozen tears from my cheeks and went to put away the pick. I would still need the shovel.

Mary had the box all ready. She had lined it with some soft material that made Pixie look as though she were all cuddled in and snug as she liked to be. The lid was next to it, and I knew Mary expected me to put that in place after I'd told my little dog goodbye one last time.

I ran my hand over the silken fur and then placed the lid on the box. I pulled on my heavy mitts and looked at Mary.

She had wiped away all her tears, but I could still see the sadness in her face.

"I thought you might like to be alone," she said softly to explain why she didn't have her coat on. I nodded, surprised that she knew me so well so soon, and then I picked up the little box and went back to the garden.

After I had completed my sorrowful task, I stayed outside for a while finding little chores I could do. Mary didn't come looking for me. When I finally decided I was ready to face the family and go on with life, I went back to the kitchen. I could smell the coffee brewing even before I opened the door, and I realized just how chilled I was.

Mary's eyes met mine and we spoke to each other even without words. She smiled then, just a tiny little one, and I gave her a bit of a nod.

Uncle Charlie reappeared. We tried to talk normally at the table. Didn't seem much to talk about, save the weather. It worked for a time. By then I had thawed out a bit and was feeling some better, though I knew it would be a long, long time until I got over my hurt. Mary knew it too. I could feel her love and understanding even when a whole room separated us. It was a marvel, this being man and wife. I began to wonder how I had ever functioned before Mary had changed my whole life. I hoped and prayed I would never need to function without her again.

For the first time in my life I began to realize what Grandpa had suffered over the years without Grandma—and why Gramps had commented to me about being anxious to get to heaven. It gave me a new respect and sympathy. And I think it opened up a whole new understanding of the word *love* for me too.

Life Goes On

I came in from the morning chores expecting breakfast on the table as usual. It was—after a fashion. The pot of rolled oats still simmered on the stove, the coffee bubbled in the coffeepot. Thick-sliced bread was toasted, the table set, but it didn't take sharp eyes to know that something was amiss.

"Where's Mary?" I asked Uncle Charlie, who gave the lumpy porridge another stir while Grandpa poured the coffee.

"She's not feeling well," Uncle Charlie informed me and went on quickly when he saw the look in my eyes. "Nothin' serious. Jest a tummy upset, she said. Bit of the flu, I 'spect."

I didn't even wait to remove my outside wraps but headed for the stairs.

Mary was lying on the bed in her clothes, so I knew she had been up.

"I'll be fine," she assured me wanly. "Just—"

I'd already heard that little speech from Uncle Charlie. I sat on the bed and laid a hand on her forehead.

"I don't have a fever, Josh," Mary protested. "I already checked it myself."

"You feel hot to me," I argued.

"As cold as your hand is from chorin', anything that isn't freezing would feel hot," Mary reminded me. "Go on," she prompted. "Go have your breakfast."

"Aren't you going to eat?"

"It would be pointless," insisted Mary. "I'd just bring it right back up again."

"Could I bring—"

"Josh," said Mary with a bit of impatience, "I can't even stand the *smell* of it."

I tucked a blanket about her and left her then, though I was still worried even with her assurances that she'd be up soon.

True to her word, Mary came down later. She still looked pale, but she insisted that she felt just fine. She proved it by taking over her kitchen chores.

For the next three mornings the scene was repeated. I was getting kind of tired of Uncle Charlie's version of our breakfast porridge—even though I'd eaten it most of my life. I was also getting very concerned about Mary. One morning she didn't make an appearance until almost noon, and even then she looked as if she should be back in bed. I tried to talk her into staying in for the day so she could lick this thing, whatever it was. But who was I to argue with a woman who's made up her mind?

When it happened the fifth morning in a row, I decided something must be done. Without saying anything to Mary, I saddled Chester and headed off to town. I figured it was about time Doc was consulted about the matter.

Doc arrived at the farm soon after I had returned home again. By then Mary was up and about. She looked pale and often turned her face away when she lifted the lid to stir a pot, as though she couldn't bear the sight or smell of whatever she was cooking.

Mary looked surprised when I ushered Doc into the kitchen. Then she set about putting on the coffeepot, probably assuming that he had just popped in to warm up on his return from a neighborhood call. Doc was content to wait, visiting with Grandpa and Uncle Charlie, but I could see that he was watching Mary carefully out of the corner of his eye.

"Hear you haven't been feeling so well, young lady," Doc said as he stirred in some cream into his cup.

"A bit of a flu bug, I guess," Mary answered off-handedly as she passed him a plate of cookies.

"Maybe," agreed Doc. "It sure is making the rounds again. But Josh thought I should check it out, just in case."

All eyes turned to me. I was especially aware of Mary's.

"It's not always flu when the stomach acts up," Doc went on. "Josh is right," he said in answer to Mary's expression. "No harm in checking."

After we had finished our coffee, Doc sent Mary up to our room to prepare for the examination.

"Do—do you think it's serious?" I ventured before Doc went up to join her.

He put his hand on my shoulder as he rose. "No point in worrying about it till you have something to worry about, Josh," he said, while Grandpa and Uncle Charlie nodded solemnly in agreement.

He wasn't gone long. When he appeared in the doorway I was all ready for the explanation of Mary's illness. I started to ask but Doc stopped me. "Mary is waiting for you," he told me, and I felt my heart constrict with fear. I ran up the stairs two at a time and flung the door open.

Mary was propped up on two pillows. Instead of pale, now her cheeks were a trifle flushed and—I crossed quickly to her after swinging the door closed behind me. I wanted privacy if I had to hear the worst.

"Sit down, Josh," Mary said gently. I did so and took her hand in mine.

"Is it—? Are you really sick?" I managed.

"No," Mary answered and her eyes were shining. "I'm just fine."

"Then—then—?"

Mary began to smile, then giggle. Here I was about to die of worry and she sat there giggling like a silly schoolgirl.

"Josh," she began, and took a deep breath to try to calm herself. She seemed about to explode with excitement. "How would you like—like to be a father?"

"I'd like it," I stammered. "You know I would. We've talked about it—"

"Good," squealed Mary, "because you are going to be one!"

Her words didn't make much sense, but the way she was pulling on my arm and beaming made me realize that something good was happening—something extraordinary. I started sorting through the conversation again, looking for the answer and finally it got through to me.

"You mean—now?" I yelled back, grabbing her by both shoulders.

"Well—well—" she teased, but I had already jumped up from the bed. I ran down the hall and bounded down the stairs two or three at a time. "We're gonna have a baby!" I shouted to Grandpa and Uncle Charlie, who were both on their feet and hollering along with me before I could make full circle. Then I ran back up the stairs again and grabbed Mary. I held her close and we laughed and rejoiced together.

I finally stopped rocking her back and forth and held her at arms' length. "You didn't know—?" I questioned, gazing into her face. Somehow I thought that women automatically knew these things.

"I suspected," she admitted, "but I still wasn't sure."

"When?" was my next question.

Mary screwed up her face. "The timing's not great," she said slowly. "The baby will arrive right in the middle of harvest."

"We'll manage fine," I quickly assured her. "We'll find you some help."

"So this is why you've been feelin' sick?" I went on.

She nodded.

"I don't remember Lou being sick like that. It scared me," I admitted.

"Some women are. Some women aren't," Mary explained matter-of-factly. "Anyway, it shouldn't last for long, Doc said."

But Doc was wrong. Mary continued to feel sick for many weeks. Months, in fact. She lost weight and looked pale and fragile. It tore me apart to hear her in the mornings. I felt responsible for the way she was feeling and I sure would have gladly taken her place.

We menfolk took turns cooking breakfast. I even hung a blanket over Mary's door so the odors from the kitchen wouldn't bother her as much. Other than that, it seemed we simply had to wait it out.

In March we had a visit from Lilli and Pa Turley. They brought both good and bad news. Lilli brought the good news. Bubbling as she shared it, she told us that Avery had asked her to marry him and she had said yes. The wedding was set for June.

Pa's news brought sadness to Mary's eyes.

"I've decided to put the farm up for sale," he informed us.

I saw Mary start and wondered what thoughts were going through her mind. She didn't speak them then; she simply nodded.

"I've given it a lot of thought," went on Pa Turley. "Mitch isn't interested in farmin'. He has him a good job in the city now." Pa Turley sat twisting his coffee cup this way and that as he looked into the steaming interior. "Don't 'spect he'll ever return home to the land . . ." His voice trailed off.

"Never was no good at batchin'," he mused after a moment of silence.

"What will you do?" Mary finally found voice to ask. My thoughts had already jumped ahead, and I was about to call Mary aside to suggest that we offer Pa the downstairs bedroom.

"Emma—yer aunt Emma over to Concord—has been after me fer some time to move in with her. She'd like someone about the house to keep things in order like—an' she knows I don't wanna be alone. She thinks thet it would work best fer both of us."

"And what do you think?" Mary asked calmly.

"I've no objections," Pa Turley answered a bit quickly. "Always got along with Emma the best of any of my sisters."

Mary looked at me and I nodded. She took a big breath as though in relief, her eyes thanking me as she said, "You're welcome here, Pa."

Pa Turley pushed back his chair and waved the offer aside in one quick motion. "Oh, I couldn't," he protested.

"And why not?" questioned Mary. "We've got the room. We'd be glad to have you, wouldn't we, Josh?"

"Sure would," I assured him. "A room right there," I said, pointing to the downstairs bedroom, "or one right up there at the head of the stairs. Take your pick."

Pa Turley seemed to be having a mental debate. He finally sighed deeply and pulled his chair closer to the table and his cup.

"Much obliged," he said with feeling. "Guess it's always good to know thet yer wanted. But—I think thet we'd best leave things be. I—I would be welcome here. I know thet. But Emma—Emma needs me. There's a difference there, ya know? No, I think thet we'd best let things be as planned."

Mary and I looked at each other, and we knew that we had to let him decide the matter. "Well, as long as you know you're more than welcome, Pa," I told him.

"You'll visit?" asked Mary.

"Oh, why sure," he promised. "Got three girls all a'livin' here. 'Course I'll visit. 'Sides, I sure wanna keep up on the grandchildren."

Mary and her pa smiled fondly at each other.

That night Mary and I lay in our bed talking over the day's events. I decided to tell her what had been churning through my mind ever since the Turleys' visit.

"I've been thinkin'," I said softly into the dark, "I'd like to buy Pa's land."

I felt Mary move slightly in order to see my face. It was too dark in the room, so she settled back in her spot beside me.

"You need more land, Josh?" she asked.

"Not—not really. Not right now. But—but it was your home, your family's land for as long as I can remember—as long as *you* can remember. I thought— I thought it might be hard—that you might sorta like to keep it."

There was silence and then Mary said softly into the night, with a break in her voice, "Thank you, Josh."

I ran my hand over her soft hair and traced the scar over her eye with one finger. "Besides," I went on slowly, "who knows? Maybe we'll have a son and he'll need the land. I'd be pleased to give him his grandpa's farm to work."

Mary chuckled at the thought and put her head on my shoulder. "If you can—if you can work it out, Josh, I'd be most happy about it," she whispered, and a sob caught in her throat. "It would only seem right, wouldn't it—and it would make Papa so happy."

I decided on a trip to town the very next day to see what arrangements could be made.

The banker was agreeable, and Pa Turley sure was. It took some time to get all the paperwork sorted out and processed. But in the end the Turley farm belonged to the Joneses. Pa acted like a heavy burden had been lifted from his shoulders when I handed him the check for the farm. He couldn't say anything. He just reached out and gave me a big bear hug, and I knew he felt that he wasn't really giving up the land—just handing it on to his family.

He had a farm sale then and packed his few belongings for moving on to his sister's. Lilli went to live with Faye to await her wedding to Avery.

Mary and I drove Pa into town to catch the train for Concord. He'd already said goodbye to his other two daughters. He didn't have much to say on the way, but his eyes sure did study out every farm and field as we traveled along. *It's like he's closing the door on his past life,* I thought, *and getting ready to open a new one.*

When we got into town he excused himself and said he'd like to take a bit of a walk before the train pulled in. Mary had groceries to purchase and I had some harness parts to pick up, so we let him off and promised we'd be there at the station when the train arrived.

I wondered what the little walk was about. Figured he might have some old friends he wanted to say goodbye to or something—and then I saw him head off in the direction of the cemetery.

He was going to say his goodbye to Mrs. Turley. Guess he missed her far more than any of us knew. More than he'd ever miss the farm. Maybe sister Emma would be good for him—though of course I knew she'd never take the place of the one he had shared life with for so many years.

Like we'd said, Mary and I were both there when the train pulled in. 'Course the tears flowed some with the goodbyes. I knew it was hard for Mary, but she was brave about it. And then the train was pulling off and we were alone on the platform, the wind whipping Mary's coat about her small form. I took her hand and led her from the station. More than ever, she was mine to care for now. She had neither ma nor pa to lean on when she needed them. I was really all she had.

CHAPTER 19

Happiness

With the addition of the Turley farm, I had even more fields to plant that spring. I knew Pa Turley had been a good farmer in his day, but perhaps he'd sorta lost heart since the death of Mrs. Turley. Anyway, there was a lot of catching up to do in working up the land.

Mary was patient about my long, long days. Many times I saw her only at breakfast and for a few minutes at supper before I fell into bed exhausted. She didn't make many trips to the fields, either, with refreshments as she had usually done. Partly because it was more difficult for her with the baby coming, but mostly because some of the new fields I worked were so far away. Instead, she packed a lunch for me each morning.

We didn't get much rain at all that spring, so I wasn't slowed down any with the planting. In fact, it was so dry that neighboring farmers were all talking about it and wondering if the seed would have enough moisture to sprout.

The crash of the faraway stock market did affect us. I guess it affected the whole world. Everyone sorta held their breath, waiting to see just what calamity would strike next. I prayed that there wouldn't be one and that I would be able to take care of the family members who were my responsibility.

Lilli married in June as planned. Pa Turley came back for the wedding and spent a few nights with us before returning to Aunt Emma. Mary was so glad to see him. While he was there, he and Grandpa and Uncle Charlie all worked on a cradle together. They seemed to take great pleasure in the project, and Mary of course was thrilled.

The grain did start to grow. Here and there green shoots began to poke their heads through the soil, and I felt more relaxed. With a good rain I was sure we'd be well on our way. But the rains still didn't come, and pretty soon the small spears began to turn kind of yellow and wilt in the sun. I guess I should have faced the facts then, but I still kept hoping that with a good rain the grain could pick up again.

The summer was a hot one too. I felt sorry for Mary, being heavy with child as she was. The heat was especially hard on her. But she didn't complain. Just slowed down with the many jobs she had. Without rain her garden wasn't looking near as good as it normally did, and that bothered her. She and Grandpa carried pails of water to some of the plants, but it was too much work to try to water the whole garden.

When haying time came, the crop was thin and stunted. I worried about how we'd make it through the winter for feed as I put what hay we had up into stacks. Wasn't near as much as most years.

I guess the thing that kept me going that summer, the knowledge that brought excitement to both Mary and me, was the anticipation of the arrival of our child. The whole family was waiting for the baby, and now that Mary had gotten over her morning sickness and seemed to be feeling fine except for the heat, we were all sorta counting the days.

What harvest there was that year was so thin and runty, I wondered if it really merited cutting—but like all the farmers around me I went to work in the fields anyway. Lilli came to help Mary. It sure was decent of Avery to allow her to come, them being newlyweds and all. Mary was grateful for the help, and she and Lilli seemed to get along real good in the kitchen together. They didn't even need to talk about certain things—seemed to just understand what each one was supposed to do without saying so.

While Lilli was there, most of the canning was done. I had our little bit of grain ready for the threshing crew. Mary was hoping we'd get the crew out of the way before our little one decided to join the family. For her sake, I was hoping so too.

Mary and I talked a lot about our coming baby. Of course we talked "boy or girl." I told Mary I'd be happy with either one—but I think she knew I figured a son would be pretty nice. I mean, I had this extra farmland and all, and I sure did hope that someday a son would be farming it. *But a girl would be nice, too,* I decided as I thought of Sarah and little Patricia. Patty was walking now. She was over her fussiness and was a cuddly, lovable, contented little darling. I didn't mind the thought of a daughter one little bit.

The threshing crew had just moved in and set up, and the first load of bundles had been placed on the conveyer belt, when I glanced toward the house and saw Lilli standing in the yard waving her apron back and forth like the house was on fire. For a moment I couldn't understand her action, and then I realized the waving was meant to get my attention. Even so it took a while for me to understand what Lilli was trying to tell me.

"Go ahead, Josh. I'll take over here," said a voice beside me, and I turned to see Avery also watching the waving apron.

Then I understood what it was all about. It was Mary. *It must be time . . .* I dropped the pitchfork right where I was standing and took off for the farmyard on the run. Lilli saw me coming and turned to hurry back into the house.

Puffing from the run, my chest heaving and my lungs hurting, I just looked, wild-eyed, around the little circle in the kitchen, hoping that someone would give me information.

Lilli was stoking the fire and putting the kettle on. Her back was to me but she spoke anyway—evenly, controlled, just as though nothing out of the ordinary was happening.

"It's time to fetch Doc, Josh."

I headed for the stairs. I had to see Mary first.

She was lying in our bed, her face damp with perspiration, her hair scattered across the pillow. When she saw me she managed a weak smile, but I could see relief there too.

"It's time, Josh," she whispered.

I went to the bed, knelt beside it and took her hand. For a moment I couldn't speak. I pressed her fingers to my lips. She reached out and gently brushed at my cheek.

Before I could even tell her that I would hurry, her hand tightened on mine and she squeezed my fingers until they actually hurt. Her face drained of all color and her breath caught in a ragged little gasp.

It scared me half to death. I was sure something was dreadfully wrong. And then she began to relax again. I could feel the tension on my fingers lessening, and Mary let her head roll back on the pillow so that she could look at me again.

"Go, Josh," she whispered. "You'd best hurry."

I nodded and was gone.

I hadn't been using the Ford much, but I ran directly to it now. I prayed that it had enough fuel to get me to town and back. I also prayed that it would start right off after sitting for most of the summer.

It did start. I thanked God all of the way down the lane, and then I wheeled onto the road and headed for town just as fast as I could push that thing.

Doc wasn't home. I nearly panicked. Thanks to his wife, I found him in the barber shop getting his monthly haircut.

"It's Mary!" I gasped out. You would have thought I had run all the way to town. "Mary needs you. Now."

Doc didn't fool around any. He jerked the white cloth from around his neck.

"I'll be back, Charlie," he flung over his shoulder and left with only half a cut. Then we were off for his house to pick up his bag and whatever else he needed.

The trip home was a fast one. I turned once to look at Doc to see if I was scaring the living daylights out of him, but he was grinning just a bit as he held on to his hat, and I got the feeling he was actually enjoying the ride.

We wheeled into the yard and screeched to a stop right before the picket fence. Doc grabbed his bag and headed for the house. I wasn't far behind. Only Grandpa and Uncle Charlie were in the kitchen when I entered.

"How's Mary?" I asked, and Grandpa told me that Lilli was up with her and she seemed to be doing fine.

I started pacing. Back and forth across the kitchen. I knew Uncle Nat had been with Lou when some of their babies were born, but that was one detail Mary and I had forgotten to talk about.

I wasn't sure I'd be good company in the birthing room. I was afraid I'd go and pass out or something right when Mary needed me the most. Oh, if only—if only there was some way that I could help her!

Lilli came down, her face a mite pale. She spoke as she walked right on by me to poke at the stove again.

"Mary wants you."

For a minute my feet wouldn't even move. I stood there, staring blankly after Lilli, licking dry lips and trying hard to swallow. And then I suddenly found my legs and propelled myself forward and up the steps.

Doc was bending over Mary, talking to her, calming her. I didn't want to get in his way so I went around to the other side. Mary, her face damp from her exertions, turned to look at me. She didn't say anything, just reached for my hand. I leaned over and kissed her on the forehead—right on the scar from her accident. Mary sort of buried her face against me for a moment, and then another contraction made her stiffen and pull away.

I looked at Doc. How could he stand this? She was—she was—

"She's doing fine. Just fine. You're doing just fine, Mary. Won't be too long and it'll all be over," Doc was murmuring, his voice more a drone than speech.

According to Doc, things progressed quickly. For me it seemed to take forever. But it did eventually come to an end. Like a wondrous miracle—one minute we were in the throes of birthing agony, and the next minute we were parents. *Parents.* I could hardly believe the fact even though I'd been waiting for it for months. But there he was—*our little son*—mine and Mary's. Red and wrinkled and wailing his head off.

I heard Mary chuckle and I wondered if she was totally aware or under the influence of some of Doc's ether. But she looked at me, her eyes big with wonder and then tears began to form and run down her cheeks. "A boy, Josh," she whispered. "A boy." And at that moment I knew that Mary had wanted with all her heart to present me with a son.

I leaned over to kiss her and smoothed the tangled hair back from her face. Oh, how I loved her. How I loved that new little bundle she had just presented to me. A son. Our very own son.

"William Joshua," I whispered, for that was the name we had already chosen.

"William Joshua," echoed Mary, and her eyes shone, the hours of pain totally forgotten. Just then Doc placed the still-squalling little bundle in Mary's arms.

"Isn't he beautiful?" Mary was crooning and I had to admit that he was. *There's different kinds of beauty,* I thought with a smile as I looked into the little face all scrunched up with his efforts to cry.

Mary began to pat the baby and croon to him and the crying ceased. "I'll bet he's all tired out," she whispered. "It's hard work being born."

I hadn't thought of that. I had some idea now of how tough it was for Mary—for me—but for William Joshua? Maybe it was, I admitted.

I kissed Mary again—almost delirious in my happiness. Then I bent down to kiss the top of the head of our little child. He stirred a bit, and I pretended that he looked right at me and knew just who I was.

Mary pretended right along with me. "So, you are getting acquainted with your papa, William. You are one lucky boy. You have a wonderful papa. He'll take you fishin' an—"

Tears were on my cheeks. I hugged Mary and our son closer.

There was a tap at the door and I looked up, realizing then that Doc had quietly slipped from the room. It also dawned on me that there were some other anxious family members who were waiting down in the kitchen below.

Mary called, "Come in." And they were all there. Lilli and Grandpa and Uncle Charlie. The color was back in Lilli's cheeks and Grandpa was grinning like the world had just turned right side up and Uncle Charlie looked so relieved and proud at the same time that I wanted to chuckle.

They tiptoed in to peek at the small baby resting on Mary's arm.

"It's okay," said Mary. "He's awake."

Then they all started talking at once, saying what a fine baby he was and who he looked like and how alert he was and asked what we were going to name him and all that.

We had to slow them down and sort things out and finally were able to announce that his name was William Joshua. Grandpa looked across at me and nodded in understanding and agreement.

Doc returned and told us that Mary needed some rest. In spite of all the commotion, William Joshua had already fallen asleep. Lilli lifted him tenderly from Mary's arm and placed him in the nearby cradle. I went to look at him again, suddenly torn. I wanted to be near Mary, but I wanted to study my son. Doc settled it for me.

"Out with you, too, Josh," he informed me. "You can come back again when she's rested a bit."

I gave Mary one more kiss, took one last look at my son and reluctantly left the room. I didn't realize until I fell into one of the kitchen chairs how emotionally drained I was. I was glad for a cup of Lilli's coffee to sort of perk me up.

"How's the crop?" Grandpa asked, making conversation, and that brought the threshing sharply back to mind.

"I don't know," I admitted. "They were just starting to run some through."

I decided I'd best get back to the field and find out just what was happening.

CHAPTER 20

Tough Times

Unfortunately, the crop was even poorer than I expected. I should have known that it wouldn't be worth much, but I'd kept hoping that something might be in those near-empty heads. There wasn't much grain in the bins. It had me concerned, for a heavy farm payment was due at the bank. I knew it was going to be tough to cover it. We'd all have to tighten the belt. Considerably. But I hoped I wouldn't need to bother Mary with the worry of it.

Lilli stayed with us until Mary was back on her feet. Avery came whenever he could and spent the night. I knew he was anxious to get his wife home again.

William was an easy baby to have around. He scarcely cried at all, it seemed to me. But then I was in the fields or the barn a good deal of the time. Besides, William didn't have much need for fussin'. If Mary wasn't available, Grandpa or Uncle Charlie were. I figured as how they'd have that youngster spoiled long before he cut a tooth.

I put it off as long as I dared, and then one day I went out to make an honest assessment of the way things stood. I'd hated to face the truth, but the bank note was due the next Monday. I knew I had to figure out just how I was going to make the payment.

The picture wasn't a rosy one. There was barely enough seed grain to plant again come spring.

"If I can just make it through to another crop," I told myself, "then we'll be back on our feet again."

I reached a hand down into the bin and let the kernels of grain trickle through my fingers. Dwarfed and skimpy, they were nothing like the seed I had worked so hard to build up. But I was sure that with a couple years of good rains, I could be right back with good seed again.

I pulled a piece of paper from my hip pocket and a stub of a pencil from my shirt and started figuring. I had a little money laid aside, but it was nowhere near enough. There wasn't any grain to sell. I'd need every bit of it for seed come spring and to feed the cattle and hogs through the winter.

I jabbed at the paper with my pencil. Who was I trying to kid? There wasn't nearly enough grain to winter the stock. Some of the stock would have to go.

I had worked so hard to build up those bloodlines—some folks were saying I had the best breeding stock in the county. I sure didn't want to part with any of them.

But on the other hand, I reasoned, that would make them easier to sell—and at better prices.

I really got down to figuring then. After I had it all worked out on paper, I went back to the house.

Mary had dinner on the table. I crossed over to the cradle in the corner and looked down at my sleeping son. For once he wasn't being held by someone. He sure had changed already. His face was round and smooth and his nose and eyes were no longer red and swollen like they'd been when he was newborn. He had lost some of his dark hair too, but Mary didn't seem concerned about it. Babies did that, she said. Actually he was getting prettier and prettier—if boy babies don't mind being called "pretty." Lots of folks said he favored me, but every time I looked at him I saw glimpses of Mary.

"Been sleepin' like that most of the morning," boasted Mary. She had come to stand beside me. I slipped an arm around her waist and gave her a squeeze. The future didn't look nearly as bad with her beside me and our son to love and nourish.

"Your dinner's gettin' cold," Mary reminded me. I joined Grandpa and Uncle Charlie at the table, and we bowed our heads while I sincerely thanked God for His many blessings.

I could have discussed my plans over our noon meal, but I chose to wait until Mary and I were alone. William had awakened and insisted on being changed and fed immediately, and Mary cooed and smiled and went off to oblige. I went up to see them as soon as I had finished my bread pudding.

"He's been good, huh?" I asked, sitting beside Mary and lifting one of William's wee hands in mine. It looked rather lost there.

"Real good," said Mary, kissing his soft head.

We sat and admired William for a few minutes longer. He sure was growing fast.

"I'm going to be gone for most of the afternoon," I informed Mary.

She looked up, waiting.

"We'll need most of the crop for seed. I decided to sell off some of the stock so we don't need to worry none about winter feedin'."

"Couldn't we just buy us some more grain?" Mary asked innocently.

"I think it's better this way," I said without emotion. I didn't add that we didn't have money for more grain. Didn't even have enough money for the payment at the bank.

Mary nodded, quite willing that it would be my decision. She trusted me. That very fact made my stomach knot up.

"You going to ship?" she asked, knowing that market hogs and cattle were shipped from town by train.

"Think I'll give the local farmers a chance. They're always talkin' about my herds and wishin' they could add some of my stock to theirs."

Mary nodded again and I could see the pride in her eyes.

I kissed them both and went on down to saddle Chester.

I rode all afternoon—from farm to farm, and the story was always the same. No one had feed. No one had money. Over and over I heard the same words.

"Boy, I'd like to, Josh. Been wantin' to get some of yer stock fer a long time. But right now ain't a good time. Crop too poor. No feed. No money. Maybe next year after we git 'nother crop in the bins."

But next year wouldn't help my dilemma. I needed cash *now*.

By the end of the day I was about spent. It wasn't just that the ride had been tiring. It was the whole emotional drain of the process. And I'd been unsuccessful. I would need to resort to shipping the stock, and I knew the price I got for slaughter animals would not be nearly as good as that paid for breeding stock.

I hated to go home and face Mary. I was afraid she would read in my eyes the fear I felt inside.

I tried to shake off my foreboding. We'd make it. It would just be tough for a while and then the crops would get us on our feet again. All we had to do was make that bank payment and ease our way through the year until the crop was up again. We could make it. It would be good for us to have to cut back a bit. Make us even more appreciative of the good harvest—the bountiful times.

Before I went into the house I sat down on a milk stool and pulled out my paper and pencil again. It would take more critters than I had first counted on to make the payment. It was really going to cut into the herd to meet that bank commitment. And I'd have to go see the banker the first thing in the morning and ask for a few days' extension. There was no way I could get my payment in the mail in time for the original deadline. I hoisted myself off the stool and tucked away my figurings.

Mary gave me a smile when I entered the kitchen, but she didn't ask about my day. I was glad. I didn't have an answer quite ready yet.

It wasn't until we were retiring that night that the subject was discussed. Mary waited until William had been changed and fed and tucked in for the night. After we had finished our regular devotions together, I stretched out full length beneath the fresh-smelling sheets and was about to shut my eyes, hoping for early sleep and maybe postponement of a difficult discussion. But Mary slipped her hand into mine.

"How'd it go, Josh?" she asked me.

I hesitated for just a moment and then answered honestly, "Not good."

She was silent, giving me a chance to go on.

"Oh, everywhere I went folks were anxious enough to buy. They just don't have any feed either. I should've thought of that. Whole country was dry this year."

"Any way to get the stock to where folks *do* have feed?" asked Mary, and I wondered why I hadn't thought of that. I lay there thinking about it now—but came up empty.

"I wouldn't know how," I admitted. "From the reports in the paper and on the radio, the dryness has covered a large area. I have no idea where folks might have more feed than critters." I sighed deeply and Mary's hand tightened on mine. "Besides," I went on, "I would have no way of making contacts or of getting the animals beyond the county."

"What are you going to do?" asked Mary.

"Ship. Market them. There's another market day on Thursday. I'll get 'em in for that."

I had to round up a crew of neighbor boys to help me drive my stock to town. It seemed that every farmer in the whole area was like-minded. When I arrived with my cattle, the holding pens were already filled to near bursting. I knew without thinking on it that I needed to knock a few more dollars off the price I would get for the animals. It always happened that way when the market was flooded. I wished I'd brought along a few more yearlings.

The bank manager was decent enough. He admitted that it had been a tough year—that all the area farmers were having a hard time. He said the same thing that I had been saying to myself—over and over. Things would all straighten out next year when the crop was taken in.

There was nothing for me to do then but to wait for that stock payment to arrive in the mail. I thought of it constantly. Prayed that it would be enough. But it wasn't. Not quite. I took it to the banker and promised to sell a couple more cattle. He nodded solemnly and applied to the loan what I had brought.

Mary knew I was troubled. She left me alone for several days, and then I guess she decided we needed to talk about it.

"How bad is it, Josh?" she asked and I knew that she wanted, and deserved, an honest answer.

"Pretty bad," I admitted. "But it'll be all right. I made the loan payment. I was sorry to sell as much stock as it turned out I needed to, that's all. It was good stock. Too good for slaughtering. It should have been used to help other farmers build their herds. But it couldn't be helped. Everybody's having a tough time. No feed. Prices down. It just couldn't be helped. We get these cycles from time to time—and then things bounce back. We'll be all right with another crop."

"Anything I can do?"

I could have said, "Economize. Watch each dollar. Skimp all you can." But I didn't need to say those things. I knew Mary would do that without me asking.

"We'll make it," I said instead.

We lay in silence, each with our own thoughts.

"We have the egg money," Mary offered.

I drew her up against my side. I knew she'd stretch that egg money for all it was worth.

CHAPTER 21

Planting Again

Winter dragged by on reluctant feet. I guess I was just too anxious for spring to come so that I could get to the planting again. I was weary of trying to make each dollar stretch and of seeing Mary skimp and save. She never complained though. Nor did anyone else in the household.

The little snow that did fall was soon blown into small, dirty piles mixed with top soil from the parched fields. I'm sure if we'd had seven feet of snow that winter, none of the neighborhood farmers would have complained.

Our William gained weight steadily and became more interesting—more of a "real person"—with each day. He was our bit of sunshine over a bleak winter, and the hours of playing with him and hearing his squeals and giggles more than brightened our lives.

The whole household doted on him, but thankfully he didn't seem to get spoiled. He contentedly lay in his cradle and talked to himself as he tried to catch his chubby toes or the items that Mary dangled over his head.

At last the days began to warm into some kind of spring. I finally decided I could start work on the land. I didn't need to wait for the snow to melt—there was none. I didn't need to wait for the fields to dry either. The stubble was dry as tinder. I didn't use the tractor. There was simply no money for fuel, so I hitched up the farm horses and began to farm the way the land had been farmed for many years before me.

I'd forgotten how much slower going it was with horses. Often my eyes would wander to the shed where the tractor sat silent. The row of shiny, unused farm machinery I had bought over the past few years to pull behind it seemed to mournfully becken me. I longed to return it all to use. There was no use moaning. This spring it was not meant to be. As I planted I told myself that things would be better next spring.

I came in from the field each day dusty, tired and sometimes a bit out of sorts. The ground I turned with the plow was powdery or chunky hard; and as my eyes watched the clouds, I saw no sign of spring rains.

Mary tried to keep everyone's spirits up with talk of how well the chickens were laying and how perfect the new calves were and what a good litter the last sow had given us. I knew I should be thankful. I really was thankful, but in the back of my mind was the nagging doubt that all those things might not be enough.

I'd hoped for a rain before I actually did the spring planting, but when all of the land had been tilled and still dry as a bone, I decided to plant anyway. If I got the grain in the ground and the rains quickly followed, I'd be even further ahead. Yes, I decided, that was a good plan.

So I planted the seed—every last kernel I had. Placed it right there in the dry ground with the faith that every farmer must have each spring—the faith that at the proper time, within the structure that God has ordained for seed time and harvest, the rain would come, the seed would germinate and a harvest would result.

The grain lay for a week before a cloud even appeared in the sky. It didn't develop into much, but we did get a light sprinkle. I knew it had scarcely dampened the ground. Still, it brought hope. The whole town was buzzing with talk of it when I drove in to pick up groceries and the mail. Everyone was hopeful that there would be more clouds coming with spring rains in the normal fashion, and I came home in much better spirits. I guess all the jovial bantering and lighter chatter had helped.

Mary smiled as I placed the few staples on her kitchen table.

"Did we get a letter?" she asked hopefully. I was usually excited when we received one of our rather rare letters. I shook my head but grinned at Mary in my new-found cheer.

Grandpa wandered over to the table and listlessly turned over the two small sales pamphlets. He missed his daily paper—as we all did. The paper was just one of the things we needed to forego during our belt-tightening time.

"Farmers are pretty excited about the shower," I reported to Mary but including Grandpa and Uncle Charlie also.

"Say that it's most certain to stir up some more storms," I went on.

Grandpa nodded. "Gotta be rain up there somewhere," he agreed.

Uncle Charlie used his two canes to lift himself from his chair by the window and join the rest of us at the table.

"They reportin' how much they got?"

This was common talk when farmer met farmer. "Had three quarters of an inch over our way, but Fred says thet he got a full inch." Or, "That heavy shower dumped two an' a half inches at my place." Always the rains were measured, the amount that fell of utmost importance.

I shook my head. "No one seemed to get more'n we did—didn't measure much. But it's a good sign."

Grandpa and Uncle Charlie both nodded, relief in their eyes. Mary said nothing, but she went to the cupboard and got out the coffee. She put the pot on to brew, and the aroma of it was soon wafting out deliciously around us.

We all settled in around the table with pleased looks on our faces. It was the first time in months that we'd shared afternoon coffee. There hadn't even been before-bed coffee for Grandpa and Uncle Charlie anymore. It was another of the things we had learned to do without. Coffee—weak coffee— was reserved for breakfast, and each of us was allowed only one cup a day. Mary never touched it. She said that her nursing baby was better off without it, though Doc had said a cup of coffee wouldn't hurt young William. I figured Mary was just going without to save more for the rest of us.

It wasn't hard for me to go without—and I often did. Said I didn't feel like a cup, or it wouldn't sit quite right on my stomach, or something, and shared the cup with Grandpa and Uncle Charlie. Not a sacrifice for me. I could drink it or leave it. But Grandpa and Uncle Charlie were another matter. Especially that before-bed cup. They had done it all their lives as far back as I could remember.

So the coffee aroma that drifted to us was a celebration of sorts. And we all knew it. I guess that made it even more special.

Mary went even further. She sliced some bread and spread some of her carefully hoarded strawberry jam over it—thinly, I might point out. She set this on the table to go with the coffee.

Boy, what a feast! More than the coffee and jam was the promise. We'd had one rain—only a shower, really—but a rain. It meant that we'd probably be getting more, that things would soon be back to normal again. And what a relief that would be to us all.

But it didn't happen that way. A few more clouds rolled up, and we all hoped and prayed that they would bring us moisture. But the wind blew them right on by without so much as a sprinkle. Even the pasture land was beginning to look like barren ground. I knew I had too many cows feeding on it and that I should sell off a few more. But I just kept putting it off and putting it off, hoping and praying that rain would soon have things green again.

At last I remembered the good advice I'd received from Mr. Thomas, the farmer who years before had kindly showed me the proper way to farm. "A few good, healthy cattle are better than a bunch of skinny, sickly ones," he'd said, and I finally gave in and made arrangements to get half a dozen of them to town.

I didn't spend the money I got for them but tucked it away. Besides, it wasn't all that much anyway and wouldn't have made much difference in how we were living. The price of cattle had dropped something awful.

The hot, thirsty summer was a repeat of the previous one. As I walked about the farm trying to keep the barns and fences in order, my feet kicked up little puffs of dirt and sent them sifting up to stick to my overalls or drift away on the wind that was constantly blowing.

I'd never seen so much wind. The continual howling nearly got Mary down. She complained about few things—but the wind was one of them. I saw her unconsciously shudder when a gust rattled the windows or whipped grit against the panes.

All summer long she fought to save her garden. With our finances as they were, it was even more important that she have produce to can or store in the nearby root cellar. Day by day she carried water by the pail and dumped it on her plants, coaxing them, imploring them to bring her fruit.

Grandpa helped all he could, huffing and puffing under the heat of the sun and against the strength of the wind. Uncle Charlie was past the stage of being able to carry buckets, so he stationed himself beside William's cradle and watched over the sleeping baby in Mary's absence.

The garden did produce—but all of us knew that it wouldn't really be enough to see us through another winter with any kind of ease.

Toward the end of summer another calamity struck. The well that had served us faithfully for as many years as the farm had stood went dry. Grandpa himself had dug it and it had never failed before. I guess we'd always assumed that our water supply was unlimited. But now, no matter how hard I pumped, there was only a small trickle, and then we had to wait a few hours until we could produce a trickle again.

It was heartbreaking, especially for Mary. There was no way she could help her plants now. She left them to the elements, canning what she could as soon as it was ready.

I was thankful for the crick for the sake of the stock, but even the crick was lower than I'd ever seen it before.

There wasn't much to harvest that fall, but we went through the motions. I did manage to salvage a bit of grain that I hoarded away carefully for next spring's seed.

Surely next year would be different. We'd had dry spells before, but they'd never lasted for more than a year or two. We all set our jaws and readied ourselves for another slim winter.

William celebrated his first birthday. Or rather, we adults celebrated for him. He did seem to enjoy the occasion. We had a whole houseful over, almost like old times again. Nat and Lou and their family came along with Avery and Lilli. The house was alive and full of laughter and cheerful chatter, and William laughed and clapped and chattered right along with us.

No fuss was made, but each family brought simple food items with them. Lou had a big pot of rabbit stew and some pickled beets. Lilli brought deviled eggs and a crock of kraut. With the roast chicken Mary prepared in our kitchen, we had ourselves quite a feast. There was even a cake for the birthday boy—and some weak tea for the adults.

Sarah appointed herself William's guardian. She hardly let the rest get a chance to hold and cuddle him. But over her protests he did make the rounds. He was walking now, faltering baby steps that made everyone squeal with delight and William beam over his own brilliance. He seemed to know just how smart he was and spent his time toddling back and forth between eager, outstretched hands.

It was a great day for all of us, but when it was over and a thoroughly exhausted William had been tucked into bed, a sense of dejection seemed to settle over the house. It was as though we had been released from our prison for one short afternoon and had then been rounded up and locked up again. The day had been a reminder of how things had been, and maybe each of us secretly feared it would never really be that way again.

We didn't speak of it, but we all knew it was there—a fear hanging right over us, seeming about to consume us, to hold us under until we ran out of air or to squeeze us into a corner until we stopped our struggling.

I didn't like the feeling. I wanted to break loose and breathe freely again. I wanted my wife to sew new dresses and cook from a well-stocked cupboard. I wanted my son to have those first little shoes for his growing feet, toy trucks and balls to play with. I wanted Grandpa and Uncle Charlie to be able to sit around the kitchen table and sip slowly from big cups of strong coffee.

For the first time in my adult life, I wanted to sit down and weep in frustration. And then I looked across the table to where Mary sat mending work socks. They had more darning than original wool, and I saw the frustration in her eyes. By the stubborn set to her chin I knew she was feeling the same way I was. It put some starch in my backbone.

"Why don't you leave that for tonight?" I suggested to her. "It's been a busy day."

I went to the stove and shook the coffeepot. There was just a tiny bit remaining. I poured in more water from the teakettle that sang near the back of the stove and set the pot on to boil.

"Bit left there yet," I said to Grandpa. "Why don't you and Uncle Charlie finish it up?"

Grandpa nodded without much enthusiasm. He was feeling it too.

I took the sock from Mary's hands, laid it aside and then led her up the stairs to our room.

We didn't talk much as we prepared for bed. As soon as we were both ready, I lifted our family Bible down from the shelf. We always read together before retiring. There was nothing new about that. What was different was the way I was feeling deep down inside.

"Would you read tonight?" I asked Mary.

She took the Bible from me and turned to the book of Psalms. Given a choice, Mary always turned to the Psalms. She began with a praise chapter— one that was meant to lift my spirits and bring me comfort. It should have done that for me. I had much to praise God for. But tonight—tonight the praise seemed all locked up within me. Mary hadn't read far before I was weeping.

I would never be able to explain why. Maybe I had just been carrying the hurts and the worries for too long, I don't know. Maybe I'd been trying to be too brave to protect the rest of my family. Anyway, it all poured out in rasping sobs that shook my whole body. Mary joined me and we held each other and cried together.

After the tempest had passed and we were in control again, we lay for hours and talked. Just talked, until long into the night. I don't know that we solved anything, but we lifted a big burden from each other. We shared our feelings and our fears. We joined, strength with strength, to weather whatever lay before us.

"We'll make it, Josh," Mary dared to promise.

"I still have the loan payment to make," I confided. "I only have a small portion of it saved, and I've no idea how I'll get the rest."

"We have more livestock."

"I hate to sell—"

"But we'll build the herd again. After the rains come—"

Always. Always that was our answer. Things would be better. We'd be back on our feet—after the spring rains came.

CHAPTER 22

Hope Upon Hope

I never wept over our situation again. Not that I viewed tears as weakness. Maybe I hurt so deeply that I knew tears would not ease the pain. Or maybe I came to a higher level of faith. For whatever reason, I never came near to tears again.

I sold off more of the livestock. There really wasn't much choice, but it pained me to see the herd I'd worked so hard to build less than half its former size. With the sale of the stock, plus what I'd managed to tuck aside and a bit of Mary's hard-won egg and cream money, we somehow managed to make another loan payment.

But that meant there was little money to tide us over the winter months. I took my rifle and hunted grouse and rabbit and managed to add a bit to the stew pot. Mary talked of butchering a few chickens, but she hesitated. We'd already used all the old hens and all but two of the roosters.

"It's sort of like killing the goose that laid the golden egg," Mary commented to me. "We need those eggs—both for ourselves and to sell in town."

I knew Mary was right, so we held off dipping into the flock further.

Then I thought about the piece of treed crick bottom on the Turley land, and I decided there might be a bit of money in cord wood. Mary clutched at the idea right away, her eyes shining.

"What a wonderful idea, Josh!" she exclaimed. "But I do hope the work won't be too hard on you."

"It's not the work that worries me," I admitted. "We'll need to find a buyer before it means any money."

"Oh, I'm sure we'll find somebody," she enthused. "Everyone needs firewood—even in hard times."

It turned out that we were able to sell it. All I could cut, the buyer at the lumberyard said. It seemed that he had some kind of connection with city folk and shipped the wood out by rail car.

But the earnings were a mere pittance. Took me two or three days of back-breaking labor to make enough to buy flour and sugar. Rumors were that the man from the lumberyard made himself a pretty good profit just to act as go-between. It bothered me some, but I felt I had little to say in the matter. I kept at it. At least it might see us through another winter.

I used Barney and Bess for the skidding, alternating them day by day. I didn't have the feed or the chop I normally would have been feeding my horses, so I liked to rest them as much as I could. Chester was a bit too light for the hard work or he would have done his share, too.

Somehow we managed. It was tough, but we all were able to keep body and soul together. I was thankful for that much.

The second winter of scanty snow came to an end. When the patches of dirty drifts melted, I was back on the land again.

It didn't take as long as usual to do the spring work. I didn't have enough seed grain to plant all of the fields. There was no use working up those that couldn't be planted. The soil would just erode even more.

Mary planted her garden too. She had carefully kept every possible seed so she wouldn't need to buy. She even exchanged some with neighborhood women. All together, she managed to get a reasonable garden in the ground. She knew better than to even start drawing water from the well. There simply wasn't enough there. She saved every bit of dishwater and wash water that was used, though, and carefully doled it out to her plants.

I had never seen anything like the dust storms that came that year. They rolled up from the west, raising hopes that maybe a rain cloud was on the way, and then blew in with nothing but flying dirt and empty promises. Dust lay over everything. Whole fields seemed to be airborne, swirling madly about us. Mary came to hate the dust even worse than the wind.

Along with the dust came the grasshoppers. There wasn't much for them to eat, but they seemed to flourish anyway. I knew even without walking through the fields that there would be *no* crop this year. I went back to cutting cord wood.

Near the end of August Uncle Charlie took sick. It was a Sunday morning, and Mary had our breakfast on the table and William all ready to go to church. Uncle Charlie still hadn't made his appearance. It wasn't like him. He lingered in bed now and then, having spent a restless night, but never on a Sunday morning.

We sat down to the table, our eyes on the stairway, thinking surely he'd be showing up at any minute.

Mary turned to me. "Do you think you should check, Josh?" she asked.

William pounded his spoon impatiently on the table and called in his babyish lisp, "Eat time. Eat time, Unc'a Shar-ie."

Grandpa forgot his worry long enough to have a good chuckle at William. Mary stopped the boy from banging his spoon, and I looked toward the stairs again.

I went on up then, and there was Uncle Charlie on the floor beside his bed. He must have been trying to get out of bed when he took a fall.

It scared me, I'll tell you. It frightened all of us. We abandoned our plans for church. Grandpa and I lifted Uncle Charlie back onto his bed, and I saddled Chester and headed out for Doc.

By the time we got back, Uncle Charlie was conscious and rational. He still wanted to go to church, but Doc said he had a pretty nasty bump on the head and was to stay in bed for a few days. Besides, it was already too late for church anyway.

After Doc had done all he could to make Uncle Charlie comfortable and left a bit of medicine for him, Doc and I walked down to the kitchen. Mary had poured a cup of morning coffee and set it at the table for him. She'd fed William, but the rest of us still had not had our breakfast. The familiar morning oatmeal had not improved with age, but we ate it anyway. It did fill the void.

Doc sat down for a neighborly visit. He told Mary of new babies in the community—even shared the secret of a few on the way, and told of people in town moving in and those who were moving out. He even shared bits and pieces of world news—things that we would have been getting out of the newspaper had we still been receiving one.

And then he turned his attention to William.

"Your boy sure looks healthy," he said to Mary, and Mary beamed.

"Come here, fella," Doc called to the toddler and William trotted over to be lifted up on Doc's knee.

"You ever see one of these?" Doc asked and dangled his stethoscope before William. I don't suppose there was a kid in our whole area who hadn't played with Doc's stethoscope at one time or another. And it had fascinated every one of us, too. William was no exception. He turned it around and around in his hand, then tried to stick the smooth, round end into his ear.

We all laughed.

"So you're going to be a doctor someday," commented Doc. "But you've got it backward. This is what goes in your ears. Here, hold still."

He helped the little fella with the instrument, and William's eyes grew wide with wonder. I had a pretty good idea that he was hearing absolutely nothing, but the feeling of something holding his head from each side must have intrigued him. He sat perfectly still until Doc removed the ear pieces.

"Well, I'd best be running," Doc said at last. "Someone might be needing me."

He lifted William to the floor and reached for his hat. "Yes, sir," he said, his eyes still on William. "You're a nice, big boy for two years old. Almost two years old," he corrected himself. "Your mama has taken real good care of you."

I walked with Doc to get his team. It was an awkward moment for me. I hardly knew where or how to begin.

"Doc," I finally blurted, "in the past we've always paid you cash for your visits, but I'm afraid—"

Doc stopped me before I could even go on. "I know how things are right now, Josh," he returned confidentially. "We'll just put this here little visit on your account."

"But I don't have an account," I reminded him.

"You do now," said Doc, "and don't you go worrying none about it either. You can take care of it just as soon as you get another crop."

Doc came three more times to visit Uncle Charlie. On his last visit Mary had a little chat with him too. It seemed her suspicions were correct. She was expecting our second child.

I should have been happy—and I was. But this time I was worried too. How would we ever feed and clothe another child? William was already doing without things he should have had—and he was better off than most of the children in our area. Lou passed on to him many of the things Jonathan and Timothy had worn.

But in spite of morning sickness again, Mary was happy. It fell to Grandpa to entertain young William until Mary was able to be on her feet. I was still busy with cutting wood and unable to give much assistance in the house.

Uncle Charlie got steadily better, to our great relief. By the time William celebrated his second birthday, Uncle Charlie was again able to join us at the table. By then Mary was feeling much better, too.

There wasn't any crop to harvest, so I just kept right on working in the woodlot. Now and then the lumberyard owner would pop by and have the wood loaded onto a truck and hauled to the railway yards. He'd pay me each time he made a pickup, and I tried hard to put some of it aside. But there wasn't much of it in the drawer when I went to count up the money. I'd needed to spend most of it for necessities throughout the summer and fall. I would have to sell stock again. Even with the sale, I wondered if it would be enough to meet the payment. My heart sank at the thought.

I was heading for my room to do some more figuring when Grandpa's voice stopped me.

I turned to look at him. He and Uncle Charlie were at the kitchen table. There was no coffee to drink, but maybe it was hard to break an old habit. Anyway, they still pulled up their chairs each evening and sat there—chatting, even playing an occasional game of checkers. But often they just sat, waiting for the time to go to bed.

Mary had already gone up to tuck William in for the night, and I knew it wouldn't be long until she would be waiting for our devotional time together.

"Got a minute?"

I nodded.

"Charlie and I think it's time we talk."

I didn't have any idea what was coming but I felt my stomach began to tighten.

"You got another payment to make," Grandpa said as I pulled out a chair and lowered myself onto it. It was a statement—not a question.

I nodded again.

There was silence for a minute. Uncle Charlie sucked in air, much as he used to suck in coffee.

"You got it figured?" went on Grandpa.

I lowered my head for a moment and then brought it up to face the two men. "No-o," I admitted. "No—not yet."

"In thet case," said Grandpa, shoving a lidded tin toward me, "we want ya to have this."

I looked from Grandpa to Uncle Charlie.

"If we'd 'a knowed what straights you was in, we'd 'a given it long ago. Feel bad we've been lettin' ya sweat it out alone," said Uncle Charlie, an unusually long speech for him.

"It's the Turley farm," I admitted. "It probably was a mistake to take on more land, especially with the drought."

"I figured it a smart move," Grandpa hurried to say. "One ya couldn't pass up, really. Just a shame thet we been prayin' fer rain ever since. But thet'll change. Just need time, thet's all. Just time."

I appreciated Grandpa's vote of confidence and Uncle Charlie's nod of agreement. Then Grandpa pushed the can farther toward me and this time I reached out for it.

I pulled it to me and pried off the lid.

I stared in disbelief. It was full of bills.

"It ain't much," Grandpa was saying, "but it might help some."

I knew then what I was looking at. It was the total life's savings of Grandpa and Uncle Charlie. I pushed the can back toward them, fighting hard to swallow.

"I can't—I can't take that," I finally was able to say.

"What'll ya do then?" asked Grandpa without hesitation.

"I—I—" I swallowed. "I still have some stock. I can sell—"

"We been thinkin' on thet," said Grandpa. "It don't seem like a good move. I mean—ya sell it all off an' then where are ya? Soon as the rains start up agin, ya got no herd to build on."

I knew he was right. I'd thought that all through myself and come to the same conclusion.

"We don't know when the rains—" I began, but Grandpa cut in.

"They'll come," he said simply. "Always do."

But when, I wanted to cry out. *When? After it's too late—after we've lost everything?*

I didn't say it. Instead, I looked first at Grandpa and then at Uncle Charlie.

"It might not be enough," Grandpa was saying. "We don't know how big those payments be. But take it. Make it do fer ya what ya can."

"But you've worked all your life to save this money," I persisted. "I can't just take it and—"

Uncle Charlie waved an arthritic hand as though to brush aside all my arguments. "Josh," he said, "you've been boardin' an' beddin' us fer several years now. Ain't either of us worth a lick a salt. But ya ain't hinted at thet. Neither has Mary. Now, iffen the farm goes—then what, Josh? This is our home too, an' I reckon as how we'd be hard put adjustin' to 'nother one."

" 'Zactly," agreed Grandpa.

"But—" I tried again.

"No 'buts,' Josh. Just take it on in an' make thet there payment, iffen it'll do thet, an' get thet monkey off all our backs."

I had no further arguments. I thanked the two men before me as sincerely as I could and tucked the tin under my arm. I had no idea how much money was in the can. It wouldn't be much, I knew. Grandpa and Uncle Charlie had never had the opportunity to stash away large sums. But maybe—just maybe it would be enough to keep us afloat. Maybe—just maybe—it would help us make it to another spring.

CHAPTER 23

Sustained Effort

There was enough in the tin can to make the loan payment—with some left over to help us through the winter. I went to town the next morning with the money tied securely in my coat pocket.

I was getting to hate trips to town and avoided them whenever possible. It seemed whenever I went there was news of another foreclosure and another area farmer forced off his land.

It wasn't as hard for those who had been there for years and were well established. Some had no payments due at the bank and could manage to sort of slide by even though money was tight. But for those who had just invested in land or stock or new machinery, the matter was quite different. It was almost impossible to stay afloat, given the economics of the times along with the drought.

It saddened me. I guess it also frightened me. The thought kept nagging at me that my turn might be next.

I didn't know what I'd ever do if I lost the farm. It wasn't just the fact that I loved it—had always loved it. I figured I had about as much of that farm soil running through my veins as I had red blood. I couldn't imagine myself anywhere but on that farm.

Grandpa had settled the farm. He and Uncle Charlie had sweated and toiled and built it to what it had become. It belonged to us. To all of us. It belonged to my son some time down the road.

Farming was all I knew. I was not trained for anything else. I had no other home, no other possession, no other profession. If I lost the farm I would lose far more than a piece of property. I would lose my livelihood, my heritage, my family home, my very sense of personhood. I wouldn't fit any other place. I knew that without going through the experience.

And knowing all of that, and knowing also that Grandpa and Uncle Charlie shared my feelings, I took the gift of money they had given me and tried to buy the family a little more time. And I prayed that they were right. That the rains were soon due back again.

I felt better after I had made the payment. I didn't miss the surprised look on the banker's face when I drew out the small roll of bills, but he asked no questions and I volunteered no information. I was handed my receipt of payment and left the building.

I stopped long enough to buy a few groceries, among the parcels a pound of coffee for Grandpa and Uncle Charlie and some cheese for Mary. She had made several remarks over the last few days about how good cheese would taste. Then I bought a sack of grain to feed her chickens. It would do us all well if we could keep the hens laying.

I was about to head for home when I remembered to pick up the mail. There rarely was anything of importance, but I checked it out anyway. Later I wished I hadn't even gone to the post office.

Mr. Hiram Smith was ahead of me at the wicket. "Howdy, Josh," he hailed me and I returned his greeting.

"Another rough summer," he commented sociably and I agreed that it was.

"Hear more farmers are having a hard time."

I nodded to that too.

"Did you have any crop at all?" he asked.

"Not much," I admitted. "I turned the cows on it. Wasn't worth the time of trying to harvest it."

It was his turn to nod. "Too bad," he pondered. "Sure too bad. Farms're up for sale all over the place." He didn't even wait for a response from me. "Trouble is," he went on, "no buyers. Why, ya can't even give one away. Nobody's got money to buy. That's how it is. Too bad."

It was all the truth—but it was all old news by now. I was about to ask for my mail and move on.

"Ya hear 'bout Avery?" asked Mr. Smith.

I hadn't, and I stopped mid-stride. I wasn't sure I wanted to hear about Avery if it was going to be bad news—and from Mr. Smith's expression, it looked as if it would be. But Avery was my brother-in-law. If there was something wrong, I had to know.

"Lost his farm," said Mr. Smith, rather callously to my thinking. "Just gettin' started, too. An' him newly married an' all. Too bad." He shook his head one more time and moved toward the door, shuffling through advertising flyers as he did so.

I went all sick inside.

It was Mary that I thought of first. I knew how deeply the news would trouble her. *Poor Mary. And poor Lilli—and her expecting their first child, too,* I mourned.

Now the postmaster took up the tale of woe. "Sure too bad. Sure too bad," he repeated as he shook his head much as Mr. Smith had done. "Me, I can't even keep up with the comin' an' goin' anymore. Move in—move out. Jest like that. One after the other—"

"Where—where did Avery—?"

"Oh, he didn't move. Least not away from the area. He jest moved on home again with his folks. Same mailbox as always." The most important thing to the postmaster seemed to be keeping his mailboxes straight. I started to move away.

"Don'tcha want your mail?" he called after me, and I turned back. There was one letter addressed to Mrs. Joshua Jones and a few advertising pieces. I threw the flyers in the wastebasket as I walked past it, and stuck the letter for Mary in my pocket.

I couldn't get Avery and Lilli out of my mind as I headed the team for home. Most of all I dreaded telling the news to Mary. But I knew she had to be told.

I broke it to her as gently as I could and held her while she wept. Then we bundled up, left William in Grandpa and Uncle Charlie's care, and drove over to Avery's folks.

Just as I had been told in town, we heard directly from Avery that he had lost his farm. He was pretty down about it, but Lilli was keeping her chin up.

"We'll try again—later," she said confidently, "when the crops are growing again and the rains are back."

In the meantime she was sharing a house with five other people and her child would soon be number six.

"How are you?" Mary whispered to her.

"Fine. Fine," she insisted. "Just anxious to get it all over with. Only three more weeks now. That's not so long."

But the house was already crowded. Avery and Lilli had a very small bedroom off the kitchen. I couldn't help but wonder where they would squeeze in a small crib.

Times were tough. Really tough. But at least they had a roof over their heads.

In all the turmoil I had forgotten to give Mary her letter. I found it that night as I undressed for bed.

"Oh, I'm sorry," I apologized. "I forgot to give you this. I picked it up at the post office today."

I didn't add that I was more than a mite curious about the letter.

Mary tore the envelope open quickly and withdrew one formal looking page. She scanned it, then went back to read it more slowly. She looked pleased with the contents. I was relieved. I was afraid it might be more bad news.

"It's from the school-board chairman," she told me. "I wrote inquiring about boarding the teacher."

I was surprised. Mary had said nothing about it.

"He's happy to have him stay here," Mary continued. "The place where he's been boarding hasn't worked out well."

I knew that the present schoolteacher was a middle-aged, single man. He had been the butt of many community jokes, a rather strange, eccentric fellow.

I looked at Mary again.

"Are you sure you want to take him on?" I asked her.

"Can't you see?" said Mary. "This is a direct answer to my prayers. I asked God what I might do to ease our situation, and He brought this to my mind. So I wrote the letter and left it with God—and He has worked it out so that Mr. Butler is willing to stay here."

"But—" I began, but Mary wasn't finished.

"The money will help buy groceries for all of us, and I might even be able to help with the loan payment."

"But the work," I protested. "You have more than enough now, and with the new baby—"

Mary waved that argument aside too. "Grandpa helps in the kitchen and Uncle Charlie keeps William entertained. Mr. Butler will be gone most of the day and will be leavin' every weekend. Won't be much extra work at all."

She had it all figured. I couldn't help but chuckle.

"You're really somethin'," I said to Mary, gathering her into my arms. She just smiled and let the letter flutter to the floor.

Much to my dismay, Mr. Butler arrived with a spirited horse and a buggy. There had been no warning that I would be expected to stable a horse and provide feed. I couldn't even feed my own horses properly.

But even before I could raise the question Mr. Butler explained, "I've arranged for Lady Jane to be housed"—"housed," he said—"at the school barn. Todd Smith will be her groom."

I nodded, relieved. A "groom," no less.

"I needed the buggy to bring my things," he went on.

His "things" consisted of several trunks and suitcases and a couple of carpet bags. I wondered how he would fit it all in the small bedroom off the kitchen and still leave himself walking room. I never did find out, for I never entered the room after Mr. Butler took possession, and he always kept his door tightly closed.

Even Mary didn't go in that room. Mr. Butler preferred to do his own "keeping." Once a week Mary laid out fresh linens and towels and Mr. Butler replaced them with the soiled ones. It was a good arrangement for Mary.

He was a strange-looking little man, all right. A large nose dominated his small face, and his chin was almost nonexistent. Eyes, dark and piercing, hid behind thick, heavy-rimmed glasses. He was bald. At least I'm pretty sure he was, but he had this trick of combing his hair from deep down on the side and bringing it across the top to join the other side so you didn't really see the baldness. When he stepped out into the wind, he was very careful to pull his hat down securely until it almost included his ears. I couldn't help but wonder if he had nightmares about it suddenly blowing off, his hair flying straight up in the air, waving to all those who watched as his bald spot was exposed to the world.

He didn't have much to say to us grown-ups, but he took to William right away. With his love for children, I guess he made a good school teacher. Anyway, the time he spent in the kitchen with the rest of the family was whiled away with William and picture books. He would pull a chair near the warmth of the kitchen stove, lift William on his knee and spread out a book before them. They spent hours together, his quiet voice explaining to William the wonders of the Wall of China, the mysteries of the planet Mars, the secrets of the ancient Egyptians or the flight patterns of tiny hummingbirds. I'd look across at Mary and suppress a chuckle, or at Grandpa or Uncle Charlie with a wink. William might be a sharp little fella, but what could a child of two possibly understand of all that?

Still, William went right back for more—every time he had the opportunity. And he sat there on that teacher's knee and drank in every word, his eyes wide with wonder, his chubby finger pointing at the pictures, his baby voice trying to repeat some of the difficult words.

When Mary would announce that it was William's bedtime, the teacher always looked rather disappointed, but he lifted William carefully down, closed his book and retired to his room.

We made it through another winter and I began to scan the skies looking for rain clouds. Though clouds did form from time to time, they just didn't seem to have much moisture in them. But I scraped together enough money to buy a bit of seed grain and planted a couple of my fields.

The birth of William had interrupted the harvest. Now the arrival of our second child brought me in from the planting to ride off for Doc.

Everything went fine, and before I could scarcely draw a breath, our second son joined the family. As soon as I had breathed a prayer of thankfulness that Mary and the baby were both fine, the reality of another doctor's bill took some of the pleasure from the occasion.

"I'll just add it to your account, Josh," Doc said quietly as I went with him later to get his buggy. We were getting ourselves quite a sizable account with Doc.

Our new boy was another beautiful baby. Plump and healthy with lusty lungs. William studied him in awe. Not until the new baby finally closed his eyes and his loud little mouth and went to sleep could we get William close enough to actually reach out a hand and touch him on the cheek. From then on he seemed quite pleased with his baby brother.

We named him Daniel Charles after Grandpa and Uncle Charlie, and the two men beamed as we announced the name.

We found a neighbor girl to take over the kitchen duties until Mary was able to be up and about, and somehow we managed. Baby Daniel settled into the family unit just fine, and I finished my bit of planting and went back to the woodlot again.

More of my fields drifted away as spring gave way to summer. I could only hope that some of the soil from many miles away might stop at my land. If the wind didn't work out some kind of exchange, I feared there would soon be no more topsoil to farm.

Poor Mary struggled with her garden. It was hard, discouraging work. Not much grew and the grasshoppers relished the bit that was there.

School ended and the teacher moved out. Mr. Butler promised before he left that he would be back again in the fall, a relief to all of us. We had learned to rely on that little bit of income.

William missed him. He kept asking for "Mr. Buttle and 'is books." Mary tried to explain, but of course the time frame of "months" is difficult for a child to understand.

One midsummer afternoon I went for a long walk across my dreary-looking fields. The stalks were stunted and scarce. I plucked a head of grain here and there, chaffing it between my hands. There was nothing much there. I could feel the burden on my shoulders heavier with each step. There was nothing to harvest—again.

I crouched down in the field and dug at the ground with a stick, flipping back dry, dusty soil. Down, down I dug looking for moisture that was not there. Nothing. Why hadn't the rains come? What had happened to our world? *Seed time and harvest. Seed time and harvest* kept running through my head. God had promised it. Had He failed to deliver on His promise?

For a moment I was swept with anger. I was tempted to shake my fist at the heavens. What had I done to deserve this? What had Mary done? We had tried to be faithful. We—But I stopped myself. I knew it had nothing to do with that. Then the many years of trusting, of leaning on my Lord drained the anger from me.

"I need you, God," I whispered. "More than ever, I need you."

It was with heavy steps that I returned to the farmyard. I couldn't shake from me the feeling of impending doom. I had fought for about as long as I could fight. I didn't have much strength left.

After supper was over and the dishes returned to the cupboard, everyone settled in around the kitchen as usual. I tried to busy myself with figures and plans, but my mind wouldn't concentrate. I finally laid it all aside and climbed the stairs to the room where my two sons slept.

What a picture they made. William clutched the teddy bear that Sarah had made for his Christmas gift the year before. His dark lashes fell across unblemished cheeks and the thick brown hair lay damp across his forehead.

Baby Daniel slept in almost the same pose as his older brother—arms atop his blankets, his head held slightly to the side. But there was no teddy bear. Danny clutched only the hem of the blanket Mary had made. Now and then he pursed his little lips and took a few sucks as though he was dreaming of nursing.

I stood there looking at them both and the insides of me went cold and empty. *They're countin' on me. They're countin' on their pa and I'm goin' to let them down. Both of them. Both of them—and Mary. And Grandpa and Uncle Charlie . . .*

I'd never experienced such pain. Deep, dark, knifing pain that brought no tears of relief.

I turned from my two sons and pulled the curtain back from the window so I could look out over the land I had loved and worked for so many years. There was no escaping it. We were facing the end.

I didn't even know Mary was there until she slipped her arms about my waist and laid her head against my upper back. A shudder went all through me.

She stood there for several minutes, just holding me, and then she spoke. Her voice was strong and even, though her words came to me in a soft whisper. "What is it, Josh? What's the matter?"

I had to get it out. Had to put it into words.

"We're gonna lose the farm," I said frankly, a cold harshness to my words.

Mary said nothing but I felt her arms tighten around me.

William stirred in his sleep and his hand pulled the teddy more closely against him.

"It's the payments, isn't it? If you hadn't bought Pa's farm—"

Of course it was the payments. I stirred from one foot to the other in my impatience.

"I just made the wrong move—the wrong decision. I thought it was right—at the time—"

"No, Josh," Mary hastened to interrupt, "it wasn't wrong. Not the decision to buy. It was a wise thing to do. The *timin'* was just wrong, that's all. And no one—no one could have foreseen the future. Could have known how things would go. No rain—"

Grandpa had said the same thing, and in my head I knew they were right. But my heart? I had prayed. Had asked God about the purchase.

"Sell it, Josh," continued Mary. "Sell it."

"Can't sell it," I said, my voice now baring the impatience that my shifting feet had shown. "There's no one to buy."

"Then let it go. Just let it go. I know you sorta bought it for me—and our sons. But we'd be better—There will be other farms over the years. Maybe even Pa's again. We can buy later for the boys."

"I—I can't let it go," I protested hoarsely.

"Did you promise Pa? He'd understand, Josh. He'd not hold you to it."

"No, I didn't promise your pa. He didn't ask for a promise."

"Then let it go. Let the bank have it."

I turned then and took Mary by the shoulders, looking deeply into her eyes. There was no light on in the room, but the moon spilled through the window making her face light with a silvery glow. I could even see the faint scar across her forehead.

"You don't understand," I stated, with a great effort to keep my voice even. "If they take your pa's farm, they take this one too."

I felt Mary's body tremble.

"I signed them this, Mary. I signed it over to the bank when I took the loan. If I don't pay—"

But I'd said enough. Mary understood. She pressed herself into my arms and began to weep softly.

Maybe her crying helped us both. At least it brought some tenderness, some compassion back into the coldness of my heart. I stood holding her, caressing her, letting her cry.

It didn't last long and then Mary straightened her shoulders and lifted her chin.

"We've come too far to give up now," she said. "There *has* to be a way." I shrugged helplessly. Mary wiped her nose and went right on. "We still have stock to sell. The teacher will be back. I don't need all of his money for groceries. You can take out more cord wood, we'll—"

"Mary, we—"

"We'll make it," she repeated. "God has seen us through this far—He won't let us down now."

For a moment I found myself wondering just what God had done on our behalf. The rains still had not come. We hadn't had a crop in three years. But Mary soon reminded me.

"Folks all about have been losing their farms, but we still have ours. We been meetin' those payments year by year—somehow. We are all still here, all healthy. We've always had food on the table an' shoes on our feet. He's seen us through all of this, an' He'll keep right on providin.'"

I felt a wave of shame rush through me. God had been doing far more for my family than I'd been thanking Him for.

"We'll make that next payment," said Mary again, her chin set firmly. She looked around the room. At me. At our two sons as they slept. "There's too much ridin' on it not to make it," she murmured in a half whisper; then I heard her simple, fervent prayer, "Help us, Lord, please help us."

We did make the payment. It was always a miracle to me. But we had to drain ourselves down to practically nothing to do it. We sold off almost all my good stock. I would have gladly sold the tractor and the Ford, but there were no buyers. What hurt the deepest was watching Chester go. We kept only the work horses because we simply could not get along without them. Chester brought a good price, even with the economy like it was. I could do nothing else but sell him. Mary cried and I think I died a bit when the man came and led him away.

With all of that, I was still short for the bank payment. And then a letter came in the mail from Pa Turley. When Mary opened it, money fell to the kitchen table.

"This ain't much," he wrote, "but I hope that it helps in some way."

"Did you—?"

"No," Mary shook her head. "Really. I didn't say—"

The letter went on.

"Hear what a tough time everyone is having so I thought I'd send each of my girls a bit."

Mary laughed and cried at the same time. We added the bills to our little pile. It just met the bank payment.

CHAPTER 24

Striving to Make It

There was nothing more we owned that we could sell as far as I could see. We'd already spent all of Grandpa and Uncle Charlie's meager savings. The woodlot on the Turleys' farm was quickly being depleted. With so few vegetables and fruits canned or stored in the cellar, Mary's task of putting food before her family was very difficult and certainly would take a much larger portion of the teacher's board money. In fact, I didn't think she'd be able to make it stretch to do even that.

We had our backs against the wall, that was for sure. I began to make some inquiries in town about some kind of employment. As I feared, I could find nothing.

Then our whole community was shaken with a tragedy. We nearly lost Doc. Guess there wouldn't have been anyone in the whole neighborhood whose loss would have affected us more—unless it would have been my uncle Nat. Both men had been leaned on a lot during our hard times and looked up to a good deal during the better times we had experienced.

It was a heart attack. Doc was rushed off by motor car to the small hospital in Riverside. Mrs. Doc went right along with him and stayed by his bed to wait out the illness.

Doc had likely delivered everybody in the area, thirty-five and under. He'd sewed up cuts, taken out appendixes, nursed us through mumps and all sort of things. We'd miss him being there for us. Fact was, we didn't know how we'd ever get along without him. We all prayed daily that his life would be spared, even if his full health was not restored.

In the days following the heart attack, I kept thinking on the account I had with him. I owed Doc a considerable amount of money, and I had no way in the world to pay it. I was fearful that Mrs. Doc—we always called her that for some reason—I was afraid that she might be needing the money with the hospital bills and all, and I knew that the right thing to do was go and see her about it as soon as I had the chance, even if I didn't have the money. I could at least promise small payments just as soon as I could scrape something together.

In a few weeks' time news came that Mrs. Doc was back at the house in town, Doc having improved a good deal. I decided I'd best get on in and see her.

It was tough—but I made the call. Mrs. Doc looked a bit surprised to see me; then she welcomed me in like a long-lost son. I guess she felt that way about all the "babies" Doc had brought into the world.

After a bit of chitchat about Doc and how he was doing, I got right to the point.

"I came about my account," I said.

She seemed a bit bewildered.

"I was afraid that you might be needin' payment with Doc in the hospital an' all," I explained further.

She shook her head emphatically. "Oh, Doc would never leave me in need," she stated. "He made sure that he had everything cared for in case anything should happen. He's a good man, Doc is," and the tears started to form in her eyes.

Relieved to hear that they were not in dire straits, I told her, "I'll look after the account as soon as I'm able. Things are a bit tight right now, but I hope to get a job and then I can send some money month by month."

"There's nothing to pay, Josh," she told me softly.

"But there must be. I owe him a fair bit of money—Uncle Charlie, our baby. Just haven't been able to look after it yet."

Mrs. Doc went to a corner desk and withdrew a rather large ledger. "Come here," she said, and I went as bidden.

She leafed through the account book and I saw the names of our neighbors and friends listed there. They seemed to have fared better financially than the Joneses—I didn't spot a one of them who was owing Doc money. And then Mrs. Doc flipped another page and there was my name—Joshua Jones. Each entry was carefully made. Each sick call to our house and each of the deliveries, and the cost was clearly and carefully recorded in the column to the right. But it was the bottom of the page that made me gasp. There written beside the total was the distinct notation: "Paid in full."

"I—I don't understand," I stammered. "I didn't have money. Who—who—"

"Doc did," she said simply, the tears filling her eyes again. "The night of his attack. He must have known that something was wrong. He got up in the night. I found him here at his desk. Cancelled out every account in the ledger—every debt—Doc did."

"But—but—"

She closed the book softly and slipped it back into the desk drawer.

"He loves his people, Josh. His community. He never wanted to take—just to give. He likely would never have taken payment if he hadn't been looking out for me. I'm cared for now, and he doesn't need any more."

I couldn't speak. All I could do was embrace the elderly woman. Then I returned to the brisk, cool air of the autumn day. I had much to think about as I trudged the street, still inquiring about work.

I heard about a government work project that was hiring. Mary hated the thought of it, for it would take me miles away from home and the family. We talked about it until way into the night and finally decided that it was the only thing we could do. With most of the stock gone, there wasn't much choring; and with no feed to speak of, the few remaining farm animals mostly had to forage for themselves anyway. Even Mary's chickens had been turned loose to fend for themselves. There still was a cow to milk, but Grandpa insisted that he could manage that.

With great reluctance I packed a few things in a carpet bag and prepared to take my leave. I wouldn't be needed at home for the next spring's planting. There was no seed grain in the bins—nor any hope of getting the money to buy any. I would just simply work out until our world had returned to normal again. And who knew just when that might be?

It was heart-wrenching to have me leave. Mary wept as she stuffed worn and oft-mended socks into a corner of the bag.

"They'll never get you through another winter," she sniffed. "They're nothin' but patches now."

"Where ya goin', Papa?" William asked, but the lump in my throat was too big for me to be able to answer him. I pulled the young boy into my arms and buried my face against his hair. He thought it was some kind of a game and started messing up my hair and tugging on my ears, squealing with glee. I wondered just how long it would be before I heard the boyish voice again. The thought made my chest constrict and brought tears to my eyes.

I continued to wrestle with William until I had myself under control. It was hard enough for Mary. I was supposed to be her strength.

We did the rounds with hugs. I guess it was the hardest moment of my life. William cried when he couldn't go with me. As I looked at little Daniel sleeping peacefully in his cradle, I tried to picture how big he'd be by the time I returned. I would miss so much of his growing up.

"Don't forget to write," reminded Mary for the third or fourth time. "I've packed the paper and envelopes in the side pocket there."

I nodded. I'd write. That would be all I'd have of home.

"Don't worry about things here," repeated Grandpa. "We'll manage just fine."

Oh, God, I groaned inwardly, *why does it have to be this way?*

Mary stepped out onto the cold back veranda for one final goodbye. She clutched her sweater tightly around her and turned to me with tears streaming down her cheeks.

"Don't worry, Josh," she whispered encouragingly in spite of the tears. "We'll manage—somehow."

I held her for a long time, trying to shield her from the cold, from the pain of parting and the heavy task of assuming all the responsibilities that I should be there to shoulder. *Why? Why?* I kept wondering, but the wind that whipped across the yard and tore at the weather-worn shutters had no answer.

"You'd best get in. You're freezing," I said to Mary, and I kissed her one last time and stumbled my way down the steps to the wagon. Grandpa was waiting to drive me to town to catch the local train.

I'd never realized how far it was to town before—nor how quickly our farm faded from view as we topped hill after hill.

The work camp was filled with men like myself. Desperate men—trying hard to make it through another winter in the only way that seemed open to them. Decent men—forwarding every penny they could spare back home to wives and family.

We talked about home in the evenings, after the work of another chilling, grueling day that numbed our bodies and tortured our muscles. We lay on our hard bunks and told one another stories about our wives, our children. It was the only pleasure we had. Except for the times when we allowed ourselves to use one more of our carefully rationed pages—one more envelope—one more stamp—so we could write a letter home. We lingered over those letters, savoring every word, pouring our love and longing into each sentence.

No one ever bothered a man who was writing. A hush fell over the bunkhouse and each man took to his bunk in respect for the one who held the hallowed position at the single, crude desk. Writing home was a sacred rite. It was as close to the family as we could get.

Mail day was even more special. We each hoarded every speck of privacy as we pored over our letter. And then we did a strange thing—we went over and over every tiny item of news it held with everyone in the bunkhouse.

The work was difficult. I'd considered myself used to hard work, but this new thing—this swinging of a pick into hard-as-granite soil as we chopped to make way for a new canal across the arid, frozen prairie—was something quite new for me.

Many gave up and went home. Their backs simply could not endure the strain. It was never a problem for the job foreman when men quit. He had a long waiting list of men who yearned for a chance to put their bodies to the test and earn precious money for their families.

We had four days off for Christmas. Most of us walked the fifteen miles to town that night after putting in a full day's shift. We wanted to catch the train in the morning.

When the train pulled in to my familiar station, I stopped in town just long enough to buy a small trinket for each family member before I hoisted my bag and hurried home.

You should have heard the commotion. They hadn't known I was coming. We hugged and cried and hugged some more and everyone tried to talk at once, knowing full well that the time would pass too quickly for us to get everything said.

I couldn't believe how the boys had grown. I kept saying it to Mary over and over and she'd just smile.

We had a simple Christmas together with Lou's family. In spite of bare cupboard shelves, Lou and Mary managed to put together a tasty meal. The children didn't seem to miss the turkey and trimmings. They had fun just being together. That night Mary stayed up into the wee hours of the morning trying to darn my socks again. She patched my overalls and sewed buttons back on my coat, but there didn't seem to be much she could do about my worn-out mittens. The pick had been awfully hard on them.

"Josh," she said, "there's just no way to fix them."

I nodded. "They're fine," I assured her.

But the following morning when I joined the family at the breakfast table there was a new pair of mittens. She must have stayed up again most of the night in order to knit them. They were the same color as her chore sweater, which I noticed was no longer hanging on the peg by the door where she always kept it. I tried to swallow away the lump that grew large in my throat.

I left again right after breakfast. It was no easier than the first time. I had no idea when I'd be home again.

I guess it was my Bible and the time I was able to spend reading it and praying that got me through that long winter. Several other men in the bunkhouse turned to worn Bibles too. We talked about the things we were learning. It helped us to sorta put other things into proper perspective.

I told them about Willie one night. About how much he had loved God and how much I had loved him and how we had named our first son after him and all. They listened quietly.

"It's funny," I admitted. "He always went by 'Willie' even though his name was William. We named our boy in honor of him, and I think of Willie most every time I look at my son—and yet—yet—I've never been able to call him Willie. Never. Don't know why. Guess it still just hurts too much."

Heads nodded. I'd never been able to share that with anyone before. I guess I figured they wouldn't understand. But these men—there was a strange friendship between those of us who shared the simple, crude bunkhouse. Maybe because we were all so vulnerable. Maybe we had nothing to hide. We all knew just where the other one was coming from. None of us had reason or cause to boast. We were sorta laid bare, so to speak, before one another. And we needed one another.

I told them about Camellia too. Though I didn't bother to try to explain what Camellia had meant to me at one time. I just told them about Camellia and Willie and how she had gone out to Africa even after Willie had died there.

They were rightly impressed with Camellia.

And then I told them about the letter I'd had to write to the Mission Society, how it had been one of the hardest things I'd ever done in my life. How I'd told the Mission Society I just didn't have the money to support Camellia for the present and that just as soon as the rains came and I had another crop, I'd take up the support again.

A nice letter came back from them saying they understood and had managed to piece together Camellia's support from some other sources; but that hadn't taken the sting out of it for me.

"It's sure tough right now," mused a fella, Eb Penner. "Not just fer us, but fer the churches. I hear as how some missionaries have even been brought home. Jest no money."

"Hard fer the preachers, too," continued Paul Will. "Our parson hardly gits enough to git 'em by—an' he has 'im a family of seven. Grabs any job he can to make a dollar or two, an' so do his younguns—but ain't no work fer anybody."

"I stopped goin' to church," came from the corner bunk where Tom reclined, rubbing his hands as though he could work off some calluses. " 'Tweren't no comfort there, far as I could tell. Ever' Sunday, there was just more bad news of someone losin' their place or bein' outta food or some such. We was all asked to pray. I got tired of prayin'. Nothin' ever come of it anyway. Seemed I should be doin' more fer those in need than jest sayin' a prayer or two—an' I had nothin'—nothin' left to give."

No one in the room expressed shock. We'd all fought the same thoughts, the same feelings at one time or another.

"I kept on goin' anyway," admitted Eb. "I mighta felt a little helpless in the midst of my sufferin' brethren—but I'd a been downright lost without 'em."

"You see the collection plate?" Paul said. "Pittance. I don't know how any preacher's family can git by. Sure, a chicken here, a jug a milk there, but still I can't figure it. Tithe of nothin' is still nothin'."

The man was right of course. We'd always given our tithe. Even Mary's egg money was carefully counted and a tenth laid aside. But even at that we only dropped a few cents in on Sunday, and ofttimes there was nothing at all. We wondered, too, how Nat and Lou ever managed, but they made no complaints. God provided, Lou always said with a smile, but their clothes were threadbare and their table scantily served. It had been hard, all right, on those serving the churches.

"Well, one of these days it'll all get turned around again," said someone on a brighter note, and the conversation went in another direction. We all had great plans about what we'd do just as soon as the dry spell was over. For many it meant starting from the bottom again. They had already lost all they had. Businesses, farms, belongings. But still, to a man, we clung to that seemingly illusionary promise of the future.

I wrapped old rags around my hands to try to keep Mary's new mittens from developing holes. I wasn't worried about my bare hands on the cold pick handle. It was just that I couldn't stand the thought of ruining her gift to me—the mittens her love had kept her up all night to provide for me. The rags worked after a fashion, and then the weather finally began to warm up, and I tucked the mittens away and went barehanded. The frost left the ground, making the pick work a bit easier.

Being a farmer at heart, the melting of the ice and the warmth coming up from the soil sent my blood to racing. It was hard for me to keep my eyes off the skies. If only—if only the rains would come.

But even if they do, I reminded myself, *I'll still need to stay with my pick and shovel.* I had not been able to save even a few pennies. I sent all that I made back to Mary and the family so they could get by.

CHAPTER 25

Another Spring, Another Promise

That night I wrote another letter to Mary. I seemed to get more and more lonesome with each passing day. Would the ache in my heart never ease? I had thought that it would get easier with time. It hadn't. Not at all.

After I'd written my letter, I lay on my bunk for a long time just thinking. Then I took my Bible and began to leaf through it, looking for some kind of comfort in its pages. I read a number of Mary's Psalms and they helped, but I was still aching with the intensity of my loneliness.

I need my family, I kept saying over and over to myself. *I need Mary.*

But I was caught in a box. If I went home to Mary I would surely lose the farm. Even if I wasn't able to save anything for the bank loan, my being here away from my family would sow "good faith," I reasoned. Yet I wondered how much longer I could hold on here. If only—if only God would provide some way for me to make those payments—to hold the land. If only—if only the rains would come so the land could produce again.

I started praying. "God," I admitted, "I'm at the end of myself. There's nothin' that Josh Jones can do to provide for a future—any future for Mary, for my sons. I can hardly provide for the present. I don't know which way to turn, Lord. I just don't know how we can go on like this. I need them. They need me. But to lose the farm. What would we do then? Where would we go? We have nothin', Lord. Nothin.'"

The Bible slipped from my fingers and rested on the bunk beside me. I picked it up and held it to my chest for a moment, thinking and praying silently, then I shifted it back to read again. My eyes fell to the page that had opened before me. At some time in my growing years I must have read the passage, for it was underlined as though it had impressed me. I read it again now.

> Although the fig tree shall not blossom,
> neither shall fruit be in the vine;
> the labour of the olive shall fail,
> and the fields shall yield no meat;
> the flock shall be cut off from the fold,
> and there shall be no herd in the stalls.
> Yet I will rejoice in the Lord,
> I will joy in the God of my salvation.
> The Lord God is my strength.

I reread the passage again and again until the tears that filled my eyes prevented me from reading it further.

It was all coming clear to me. The welfare of my family didn't depend on my strength. If so, they would be utterly destitute. I had been totally inadequate. But even more astounding, it didn't depend upon my fields either, or the herds that I had so carefully built. It was God all the time—just like Mary had tried to tell me. It was God who had cared for my family—had met their needs. We didn't need anyone or anything else.

" 'I will rejoice in the Lord—the Lord God is my strength,' " I kept repeating over and over. Oh, what a freedom! I could finally let go. I could shift my heavy load onto another's shoulders. Somehow—somehow God would work it out. Somehow He would see us through. Maybe we *wouldn't* keep the farm—but if not—well, He'd help us to manage without it. Somehow!

By now soft snoring reached to me from the other bunks and I knew the men around me were getting much-needed rest. Yet I continued to inwardly pray and praise until late into the night. When I rose the next morning, it was with new strength.

When I picked up my pick and shovel and fell into line, the task had not changed—but my attitude had. God was in charge now—I would simply wait for Him. But for now—for now I was on the payroll of the government. They expected a full day's work. All through the morning the sound of rhythmic blows sounded on the gravelly banks around me. The work continued on the irrigation canal gradually worming its way across the barren and desolate prairie land. By this time in the season, the sun had climbed higher in the sky and beat on our backs with intensity, making us sweat heavily with each swing of the pick or scoop of the shovel. Men complained of the heat as ferociously as they had complained about the cold.

"Wish it would rain," grumbled a voice to my right. "Sure would be a relief from this dust." I wasn't the only one who often lifted his eyes to the sky, but still no clouds formed.

I lifted my pick again to let it strike the ground with a dull thud. My back ached, my shoulders ached, my arms ached. I was about to swing again when a voice stopped me. Someone was calling my name.

"Jones," I heard again. "You're wanted."

I hoisted my pick and shovel and followed the beckoning hand. One never dared leave tools behind. You were useless on the job without them, and there simply was no money to replace them should they disappear.

"The phone!" shouted the messenger. "Over in the foreman's shack."

I flipped my pick and shovel over my shoulder and started at a jog for the building, my insides churning. Who would be phoning me and what possible message could they have?

With a trembling hand I picked up the receiver. There was a crackling in my ear.

"Hello!" I hollered into the mouthpiece.

"He—lo," came back a broken response. It was Grandpa. My whole body froze. Something must be terribly wrong. He wouldn't squander money on a telephone call unless it was extremely important.

"That you, Boy?"

"It's—it's me. Josh," I managed.

"Hang on!" yelled Grandpa.

I was about mad with anxiety. Why would he call me and then say "hang on"? Then another voice came on the line.

"Josh?" It was Mary. I felt great relief. At least Mary was all right.

"Josh?" she said again.

"Mary! Mary, what's—"

"It's raining, Josh." Silence. "It's raining."

I looked out at the clear, hot afternoon sky. There wasn't a cloud in sight. No—wait! Way to the northwest I could see clouds against the distant horizon.

"It settled in right over us. It's been raining for three days now. I waited to call until I was sure it wasn't just a shower. I—" But then Mary began to weep.

There was a bit of a pause and next thing Grandpa was on the line again. "Rainin', Boy," he informed me. "Third day. Just comin' down like ya haven't seed in years." He chuckled. "Clouds still hangin' over us. We near got drowned comin' into town."

"Sun's still shining here," I managed to reply. I was trembling now, still hardly able to believe the report.

"Maybe it'll move yer way after it's finished with us," Grandpa chortled.

Then he spoke words that I will never forget. "Come home, Boy," he said.

"Come home?"

I heard him swallow. "We already got some crop in."

"Crop?"

"Yep."

"Who?"

"Mary an' me. Some of it's showin' already. This rain will really bring it."

"How'd you—? Where'd you get the seed?" I floundered.

"Bought it."

"Bought it *how*? Where'd you get the money?" I asked, unable to grasp what Grandpa was saying.

"Mary gathered it—somehow—she's been savin' pennies. Little bit each month from what you've sent. I don't know how she did it, but she managed to git herself quite a little pile."

"But surely that wasn't enough to—" I could imagine the small bit of seed those few dollars would buy.

"Well," confessed Grandpa, "she—she also sold the silver tea service."

"What? Where?"

"Some lady—out-of-towner. Seemed to want it real bad. Took a mighty fancy to it. Paid a good price, Mary said."

I was too stunned to speak. I knew how much that tea set had meant to Mary. For a moment I just stood there, thoughts whirling round and round as I tried to take in everything Grandpa was telling me. The silver tea set— gone. Mary saving, planting. A crop already in the ground and growing. It was all too much—too much for me.

The realization of the cost of the call finally got me talking again. "Is she still there? Mary?" I asked.

"Yep," and I heard Grandpa hand her the phone.

"Mary?"

"Yes." Her voice was no more than a whisper.

"Mary, I'm coming home."

There was only a little sob, caught somewhere in Mary's throat.

"I'm leavin'—I'm leavin' right now."

"Oh, Josh," sobbed Mary.

"Mary—I love you."

I hung up the receiver then and turned to the foreman at the desk. "I'm leavin'," I informed him. "I'm going to pack up my gear and will be right back to pick up my pay. Someone else can have my spot on the crew."

He nodded. It was done 'most every week. An exchange made.

I ran all the way to the bunkhouse. I was going home! *I'm goin' home!* I exulted. *Back to my wife—my Mary. Back to my family. Back to my farm.* We hadn't lost it. The rains had come. Sure, things were tough. Sure, we had a ways to go in order to rebuild, but we still had our home—our land. We were going to have another chance. God was giving us another chance for seedtime—and harvest!

EPILOGUE

Though the story of Josh and his family has been totally fictional, readers like to feel that they know a little about what happens to the characters in the future. So let's travel on and add a bit to the family story.

Though the years following the drought were difficult for the Jones family, Josh eventually became known as the best and most prosperous farmer in the area. But with the increase in crop production and the rebuilding of his herds, Josh never did flaunt or waste his wealth. Besides Camellia in Africa, he eventually shared in the support of nine other missionaries.

To the family were born six children. William and Daniel were joined by Andrew, Violet, Irene and Walter. Andrew was the one to farm the Turley home place. And like his father and mother before him, he too became actively supportive of missionaries, among whom were three members of his own family. William went to Sierra Leone, Violet to Japan, while Daniel pastored a small mission church among the Canadian Indians. Irene married Phillip Moresby, the son of the doctor who came to take Doc's place. Phillip too trained as a physician and joined his father in the family practice. Walter, Josh and Mary's youngest, eventually was lost in the Korean war.

All five of the remaining Jones children married. To Josh and Mary were born twenty-three grandchildren, and they saw the arrival of seventeen great-grandchildren to bless their old age.

Grandpa lived to be ninety-six, but Uncle Charlie left behind his arthritis-ridden body at the age of seventy-four.

The family has scattered now. With the passing of time and the mobility of our age, they no longer cluster about the home farm. Where do they live? Well—here and there. Perhaps—just perhaps—you share your neighborhood with some of them.

Looking for More Good Books to Read?

You can find out what is new and exciting with previews, descriptions, and reviews by signing up for Bethany House newsletters at

www.bethanynewsletters.com

We will send you updates for as many authors or categories as you desire so you get only the information you really want.

Sign up today!